THE
PIRATE CAPTAIN™
THE CHRONICLES OF A LEGEND

TREASURED
TREASURES

D1518970

KERRY LYNNE

CompassRose Books
By the Board Publishing

The Pirate Captain: Chronicles of Legend
Treasured Treasures
Copyright © 2018, Kerry Lynne second edition

ISBN 13: 978-0-578-44356-0
ISBN 10: 0-578-44356-2

Cover art and formatting by Streetlight Graphics

To Eleanor and Dr T:
You are still the wind and seas which drives
and keeps this fragile vessel afloat!!!

From one's fears springs hope that they might overcome.
That hope, however, delivers one to the threshold of fear, for
now they realize how much they have to lose...
And so spawns hope everlasting that they shan't.

1: THAT UPON WHICH
THE GULLS FEAST

MOTION WAS THOMAS' DEFENSE.
If he didn't stop moving, he was fine. The least moment of stillness, however, even so much as to make water over the side, and the grief beset him.

He went through the motions of speaking when spoken to, answering when questioned. To smile was painful, eating impossible. And sleep...?

What the hell was that?

He'd tried drink. Waste of good rum it was, like water off a whale. Besides, with the enemy lurking just over the rise, it was unwise to be caught in a drunken stupor. The enemy was bottled up... for now, thanks to the blundering captain who had run his ship so hard up on the reef it couldn't be cleared short of blowing her up.

That could change, however, so very, very quickly.

The *Lovely* and *Ciara Morganse* lay at anchor, two queens, their courtiers attending their wounds. With the *Lovely's* shrouds so compromised by the *Gosport's* explosion, longboats, sweat and blisters had been required to pull her away from the battle site. A limping *Morganse* led her to the north side of Ransom Passage, to Dead Goat Island. A fair anchorage there, smaller, the surrounding land far less hospitable — the island being as barren as death, the rocks looking far too much like tombstones — but protected from both the sea and vessels. The scouts had reported the reef at Ransom's west end was still blocked; no other vessels could pass, ones large enough to be of hazard, at any rate. Even at that, maneuvering through the reefs in order to take on two pirate ships, ailing or no, would not be for the faint of heart.

Lingering in the bay where the battle between the *Lovely*, *Morganse* and *Gosport* had taken place hadn't been an option.

They couldn't get the hell away from there fast enough: burning wreckage, debris... and the bodies, bobbing and jerking like they were doing some strange f'c'stle jig as the sharks and fishes fed. When those had eaten their fill, the crabs and scavengers would take over. By the sound of the gulls, their hoards blackening the sky, there was still a fair feast to be had. The wind blew the worst of the smell away, but the occasional whiff was enough to remind everyone of the carnage which remained there.

His arm stung like hell. The *Lovely's* loblolly boy—a man of forty, if he was a day— had hastily stitched it up, while the chirurgeon proper had been up to his elbows with the more seriously injured. For as vicious as the fighting had been, the Lovelies had fared well: a handful of deaths, a larger handful of wounded. He hadn't spoken to the *Morganse,* hence had no notion as to her butcher's bill. The *Lovely's* own dead laid in wait. No one had the heart to see anything over the side. The depths of the open sea were the only place for that.

At one point, he'd caught his reflection. Livid and blistered, the sweet oil and salve had him shining like a basted goose. One side of his head and eyebrow singed to a stubble, he was about as bare as that plucked goose, too, the smell of burnt hair meeting his nose at every turn. His left arm was bandaged to the fingertips, and he limped, his damned back having taken a notion to kick up again. His sleeve had been sliced off at the shoulder in order to attend his arm, and his shirt hung in ribbons, shredded by a combined force of battle and the *Gosport's* self-destruction.

Judging by the holes, he thought fingering the cloth, he came damned near to being shot or run through several times.

He still walked this earth, however. Nathan and Cate didn't.

The *Morganse's* beloved captain was gone.

During the battle, when the *Gosport* had broken into flames, the *Morganse* had sounded retreat. A good number of her people, however, had failed to be aboard before she broke off and had taken refuge on the *Lovely,* instead. They would have witnessed their captain's inglorious end. Thank the heavens, for they saved him the uncomfortable business of having to take the word to the *Morganse* himself.

There was an odd stillness in the air; it was common after massive death. Like a boat bobbing after its people had disembarked, the world always seemed to require time to adjust. This, however, felt like a balance might never be regained. The life was gone, if not out of the world, then out of him... and those around him. The sun shone considerably dimmer, everything more dull.

He was caught in irons, adrift. Decisions wanted to be

made... but just... not... today. He wasn't alone in that. There was a definite heaviness of foot and spirit aboard. There was no denying that the world was considerably duller with Cate and Nathan gone.

Running a hand down his face, for the hundredth time Thomas tried to make sense of it all. He had seen enough death to know that there was rarely any sense to be found. The bastard most deserving to die was often the one still standing, while the purest of heart laid still. The sight of Cate and Nathan going to their deaths, locked in each other's arms, flashed over and over in his head. Hell, it played out before him, if he but closed his eyes or allowed them to linger on anything. He should have stopped them, but how? There had been no warning, no notion Nathan was about to do something so harebrained. Oh, aye, seeing Cate lying there, pinned to the deck by Creswicke's sword, was a shock, but who the hell could have been else?

Guilt was Thomas' greatest burden. It ate at him like a festering gut wound.

If only... If only he hadn't tricked Creswicke out of his stronghold...

If only he hadn't talked Nathan... hell, shamed Nathan into meeting Creswicke...

If only Nathan had kept his promise to Cate and not gone after Creswicke...

If only he hadn't schemed up this "perfect" damned plan.

In calmer moments, he could find a fittingness to the whole thing, for Nathan, at any rate. Taken by his sea was the only way for him to go. As for Cate? With Nathan was her place.

Dammit to hell, Creswicke had not won. Nathan had the final word, spilling the bastard's guts on the deck. But why the hell did it feel like Creswicke walked away the victor?

The tears were gone. Hell, he'd shed enough to float the *Lovely*. Now he was given to staring off. Not lost in thought, just... lost, his crew obliged to tug on his sleeve to bring him back among the living.

Thomas had fallen into one of those stares, when two Lovelies—Coleman and Fassir, waisters, larboard watch—came up behind him and cleared their throats.

"Beg pardon, Cap'n," said Coleman, tugging his topknot. "Mr. Al-Nejem begs us to tell you there's something ashore you should see."

Thomas turned a baleful eye on the pair. "*Something*? What in the hell do you mean by *something*?"

Shying at his vehemence, the two exchanged strained looks. "A body, sir," Fassir finally ventured.

"A body?" Thomas shot back acidly. "Hell, there's a bay full of them just over—"

"Not over there," Coleman delicately interrupted. He angled his head in the opposite direction, toward the bay in which they sat. "It's... it's..."

"'Pears to be Captain Blackthorne, sir," Fassir put in.

Thomas followed their point and saw the gulls circling near shore.

Why the hell couldn't Jones or Calypso or the damned fish just taken him and have done with it?

Inwardly groaning, Thomas pushed away from the rail and trudged behind them.

"Pull over to the *Morganse* first and see if Mr. Pryce is in the way," he said once seated in the awaiting boat.

Thomas tiredly rubbed the back of his neck. He had no notion if Pryce was in command or not, but as First Mate the man would have been Nathan's nearest thing to a friend aboard. He'd wish to be there for this.

With her black hull, the *Morganse* looked like a panther lying in wait, currently licking her wounds, to be sure, but lethal all the same. With her elevated stern and f'c'stle, she was a throwback from another time. The red paint artfully dripped to look like the blood of her victims dripping from her decks had served to deter many an enemy. How the hell Nathan had ever come by her was a mystery; the world's taverns and pothouses were filled with stories, each one more outrageous than the next. Nathan had risen from the ashes of destruction and brutal abuse like the proverbial phoenix. He had appeared at the *Morganse's* helm, mumbling something about "gifts" and "mercies" to any and all questions, but offered nothing anyone could hang their hats on. Thomas had sailed with Nathan long enough to come to appreciate the connection between him and that ship. Granted, every captain felt things so simple as loyalty or possession with their vessels, but what was between Nathan and the *Morganse* went far past that.

As the bowsprit passed overhead, Thomas felt eyes on him and looked up, half-expecting to find a f'c'stleman or hand on the seat-of-ease peering down. The beak and forerigging, however, was empty. The sense of being watched persisted, strengthened, and he looked up again, directly into the figurehead's gaze.

A chill shot through him. Surely his imagination was gaming him. Blinking, he peered up again.

4

"Jesus and Mary!" he declared, with such vehemence two oarsmen missed their strokes.

He gulped and stared, for it was Cate, or rather her likeness, looking back.

One arm obscured by the folds of her gown, the other curving skyward, he would have recognized her among a hundred others. The hair streaming back to nearly the cheekplates wasn't the same color, but every detail — brow, cheek, nose, and mouth, right down to the bold line of the jaw — was Cate to perfection. His eye traced the line of her neck and downward...

His hand curled on his thigh with the memory of the fullness of her breast.

Yes, they were just that size.

The eyes weren't that neither-blue-nor-green, unnameable color of hers, but they stared down at him with that same ram-you-damn-you look of hers.

Jerking his head away, he rubbed his eyes. They had to be playing tricks. By then, the boat had progressed to the point he was obliged to look back over his shoulder. She was still there.

He glanced about in hopes someone else might have noticed the resemblance.

Nothing, the dim-witted louts were too lost in their own brown studies.

The *Morganse* must have already gotten the same word; Thomas' arrival caught Pryce halfway down her side. Pryce sat heavily on the thwart across from Thomas and they pushed away.

Other than the grunts of the oarsman, it was quiet in the boat, both men contemplating the boards at their feet. Pryce looked old beyond his years. Grizzled he might have been, Pryce still had the ramrod forbearance of a man accustomed to being in command, one not to be trifled with.

The boat retraced its path under the forepeak. Resolved as he was not to look up, Thomas wasn't master of his own eyes. He jerked and shied at finding Cate still staring down. Perhaps he had been hit on the head harder than he had thought. Or maybe he had just gone battle-happy, seeing and hearing things.

"Has the *Morganse* refitted her figurehead?" he heard himself ask. As protective as Nathan was over Cate, it seemed damned odd for him to have her likeness put out there in all her naked glory for all to see. He could see the men perhaps opting for such a thing in remembrance. But, still, an artisan with skills necessary for a likeness such as that were rare creatures, the work itself demanding months, not days.

It took Pryce a moment to stir from his glum reverie. He

straightened and swiveled a severe eye on Thomas. "Nay, sir. Hardly the time fer that," he said dryly in his West – Countryman rumble.

"I never realized it looked so much like—" Thomas murmured, still staring. Why the hell he hadn't noticed before was a grand part of the shock.

"Like Mr. Cate?" Pryce asked, looking back. "Aye, it gave many and many of us pause the day we pulled her from the water."

Thomas nodded a vague acknowledgment. Cate had come to the *Ciara Morganse* by way of kidnapping, a case of mistaken identity—Nathan had always been a navigational genius, but kidnapping hadn't been his forte. The strong-willed, crazy-woman had jumped and nearly drowned, before they finally got her aboard.

Pryce turned in his seat, his wry smile lopsided by virtue of a blade having taken the lower section of his face. "T'was what ye might call one o' those coincidences, altho' more than what seems fittin.' A gift or curse from Calypso and I've heard her call both, and not just by the men," he added, with a significant arch of his brow.

"How the hell—?" Thomas murmured, stopped, and then shook his head. When it came to Nathan and the *Morganse*, too much was beyond explanation.

Thomas tried to find solace in Cate being immortalized, that face which could stop men in their tracks never to be forgotten. But the loss was just too raw...

He tore his gaze away and fixed it on the boards at his feet once more. He shifted to ease his arm; the climb down the *Lovely's* side hadn't done it any favors. It was mortal quiet in the boat, the working of the oars and shriek of gulls the only sound. This wouldn't be the first time at finding a body, but the men were thoroughly spooked.

"How goes it?" Thomas finally said. It seemed a shabby thing to be sitting knee-to – knee with a man and not speak. The unasked question was "Who's captain aboard the *Morganse* now?"

The seat under Pryce creaked as he shifted his weight. "Me... fer now," he added, with a significant arch of his brows. "Could change directly."

No surprises there. It would be fitting for Pryce, as First Mate, to take command. One would have to be as green as hay not to expect a number of changes to come. Pirate ships could be troubled waters whilst settling on new leadership, especially after the abrupt departure of a captain as highly-regarded as Nathanael Blackthorne.

"Do you think to sail 'er?" Thomas asked.

Pryce squinted into the afternoon sun and eyed the *Morganse*. "She'll sail fer no one else." He slid an eye toward Thomas. "Perhaps t'would be best to put her out o' her misery and scuttle 'er now, afore she runs herself up on the rocks and takes all hands with her. She threw herself on the rocks afore, when the Cap'n wuz give up fer dead; nuthin' says she won't do the same agin."

Thomas nodded. That tale had made its way around the world a score of times and in as many versions. All agreed on one point: there had been a mutiny, led by the woman of Nathan's heart. The mutineers had sailed away, leaving Nathan for dead. Their hopes of grand fortunes, however, had been quickly dashed by the ship running aground and sinking. How she was resurrected, Nathan at her helm, was another subject of a good many more yarns, many of which were perpetuated by the man before him. Mariners were storytellers one and all, but Ezekiel Pryce was a king among them. He could weave a tale, enchant his audience better than a snake-charmer.

"The Cap'n always intended fer Mr. Cate to have 'er. 'Tis a wonder if the barky woulda floated even for her," Pryce added dubiously under his breath. "Mebbe them both bein' female n' all they might o' gotten on, but..." The sloped shoulders moved in a vague suggestion of a shrug.

"Between unfriendly waters and the ship aimin' to sink 'erself, every man-jack one o' them are afraid to trip the anchor lest she throw herself on them rocks straightaway. Best scuttle 'er where she lies,' specially with them company ships a-breathin' down our necks." Pryce finished by angling his head to the west and the reef beyond, where a virtual flotilla laid in wait.

Thomas nodded solemnly. It was only a matter of time before one of those ships broke through and came swooping down on them.

"True enough, the Cap'n wuz the only one what knew these waters," Pryce went on. "I'm fair reluctant to venture it. 'Tis what's a-keepin' anyone else from a-wantin' to try."

The *Morganse's* new captain dropped his graying head and shook it. He blew a sigh, long and weary. "The mood right now 'tis t' jest let 'em all go together."

Thomas wanted to argue, but couldn't. He'd come blessedly close to chucking it all and walking away. A ship and a crew relying on him were what kept him there.

Nathan had always been the charmed one. He had dared

the sea time and again to take him, and she'd always refused... until now. Glancing up at the circling gulls, Thomas considered perhaps the sea had repelled Nathan yet again.

"What with there bein' a fair selection o' vessels so ready to hand," Pryce went on, pointing with his chin toward the unseen reef and lurking flotilla. "Some fancy to take their pick and set up for business." He swiveled an eye on Thomas. "Others fancy shippin' with you, should ye be in need of extra hands."

"I'll be looking to take on a good number," Thomas said amiably. It was a rare thing for a pirate ship to carry a full company. He and Nathan had always been firm believers in the more hands the merrier. It cut into the shares, but also made the work a damned site easier. "Mark me, I don't desire to leave you short-handed."

Pryce gave a rueful chuckle. "Have to know yer aims afore ye know if'n ye've the men to do 'er."

"Nathan would be relieved to know the *Morganse* is in good hands," Thomas said earnestly.

The wrecked mouth drew back into what served as a smile. "Ye'll forgive me fer sayin', but 'tis grand news to these ol' ears. I feared resentment, what with you n' the Cap'n bein' so tight."

Thomas opened his mouth to argue. Vengeance could well have been in the heart of many, especially pirates. It wasn't as if Pryce had a hand in Nathan's demise or had contrived in some nefarious fashion to overthrow him. It was just... hell, the natural order of things, he guessed.

"I'll depend on you to keep the memory of the great Captain Nathanael Blackthorne alive."

Pryce beamed at that prospect. "That I will, sir!" Emotion caused the rumbling voice to break.

"Not 'sir,' now, Pryce," Thomas said, sobering. "We're equals."

The twisted smile fell as Pryce stiffened. "Not on Mother Clarey's life! Ye'll not live to see the day I set myself up as yer equal, *sir*."

⁓⌾⋯⌾⁓

As they neared shore, the coxun leaned to say "'Tis in the cove over there, sir," nodding, "But, what with them rocks and this wind, 'tis better to put in over here."

In the close confines of the cove, the waves agitated like a stirred pot, the rocks' ominous black heads poking their heads out promising certain destruction to any who ventured near.

Thomas grumbled an impatient "Carry on."

The boat's keel ground into the sandy shallows. Thomas and Pryce drew a deep breath, bracing for the gruesome business at hand. Stepping off the gun'l, they waded ashore to where a small contingency solemn as pallbearers stood waiting.

Al-Nejem stepped from among them. "The cove yonder, sir. The foragers happened over there and…" Usually as unflappable as a bollard, the man's English suddenly failed him.

Thomas glanced around to find them all as skittish as a bunch of haunted old maids. The least provocation and they would all bolt.

They struck off upshore, away from the camp, to an isolated corner of the bay. Few had ventured that direction and for good reason: nothing was there, until now. Around an outcropping of rocks they went to the foot of a small cove. There, more men huddled, peering anxiously toward the water, waiting for someone to tell them they didn't see what was before them.

The sight of a corpse was nothing new. Still, Thomas' gut flipped, as it always did, for it was never a pleasant sight, not even when it was the enemy's floating there. This, however, was far from an enemy. Turning to and fro like so much storm wrack, a body floated. Face down, tiny bits of silver flashed about the head as it rose and fell on a wave.

"Jesus Mary, Mother of God," murmured Pryce.

Thomas would bet his last farthing Pryce was no Papist, and yet he crossed himself, nonetheless; Thomas fought the urge to do the same. As they had pulled across, a part of him kept thinking, nay, praying that this would turn out to be a wild herring, a cast-off beef barrel or a sea cow sunning itself.

No such damned luck.

No one had ventured to wade out and retrieve Nathan's remains. None had the nerve. The sailor's life was a hazardous one; bodies, in the natural way of events — battle, wrecks, accidents — were day-to-day. But this wasn't a battleground; there had been no wreck, nor accident. This was none of that, and it had them thoroughly spooked.

The back of Thomas' neck crept. Bodies floated; no one would argue that. The elements of nature could account for a great number of occurrences, but it stretched credulity that any of those could have resulted in Nathan's body being clear over there. The Strait's current alone, strong enough to stagger a frigate, should have bore it away, out to the open sea.

Still, there it was… There *he* was.

The body was but a score of yards off-shore. With time, the tide would carry it in, but to wait didn't seem the decent thing. Thomas opened his mouth to bid the men to bear a hand, but clapped it shut. This wasn't a chore to be delegated; this was duty for a fellow captain, for a friend. He looked at Pryce, grim and staring next to him, to see if he was of the same mind.

A distracted nod was his answer.

"Get some canvas," Thomas said, throwing off his hat. Loutish bastards should have at least thought of that.

Throwing off their boots and weapons, he and Pryce waded out with a single thought: to see this through credibly. It wasn't just the water or loose sand underfoot which made his legs feel like they were made of lead. It was knowing all too well what lay ahead. The same wave revealing the silver bells also showed legs, splayed in the typical dead-man's way.

The arms weren't to be seen.

Thomas missed a step, and then pressed on, all the more determined.

Torn off by the *Gosport's* explosion, tangled in the wreckage or chewed off by the sharks: the how of how the limbs came to be missing made little difference. There was nothing to be gained in dwelling on the morbid details. The absence could explain the heavy, lumpish way the body rode the heaving surf, not free-floating, but encumbered.

Another wave passed; the corpse rose and fell. Thomas caught a glimpse of something light in the turbid water: a sleeve. The body bobbed and the point of an elbow broke the surface. His mind eased a bit. The arms were there, tight to the torso; Nathan was relatively whole.

The gulls circled, a few daring to land nearby and greedily eye their prospective banquet. There was no pulpy mess at the back or head from the beasts pecking. Still, the fishes would have been feasting these days since. Too often, he had seen the dead look fit as life, until they were rolled over, revealing something which could barely be identified. It was revolting enough when it was a fish or a turtle, but a man... a friend...

"Damn," Thomas muttered, batting at a diving gull. Godsend, he didn't puke.

A lifetime of friendship flashed before him. He and Nathan had known each other since the first hair sprouted on their chins. Their friendship sprang out of their mutual suffering as they learnt the ropes. Over the years, mischief and mayhem led them down many a path of destruction, while Nathan's natural leadership and navigational genius saved their arses. When that failed, his ability to charm the scales off a fish softened the hearts of master, bosun and captain alike. They had caroused, whored, bled and wept together. And now, Thomas resolved to remember that smile and the good times, and not this corrupted lump.

A sideways glance at Pryce revealed the man was struggling with much the same thoughts.

As they neared, the body bobbed again. In the swirling water, Thomas caught sight of mahogany-colored hair wisping about Nathan's shoulders. He stumbled; Pryce gasped and swore.

Suffer and burn him! Nathan still held Cate exactly as when they went over the *Gosport's* side: tight to his chest.

They were together, even in death.

Thomas swallowed down a surge of bile. Seeing Cate's face ravaged by bloat and rot...?

Why the hell hadn't his precious sea just taken Nathan? Thomas thought for the hundredth time.

Hell, he and Nathan had never discussed their last wishes. Every sailor had but one: over the side, into the sea, with two roundshot at their feet. Buried on land was naught but a mariner's banishment to eternal hell. A burial at sea now, however, would mean holding the body until they were actually at sea; putting Nathan over the side while anchored in the bay risked reliving this scene all over again.

As for Cate...?

Hell and furies!

A myriad of even more morbid details arose as they drew nearer. Death could render limbs as stiff and unyielding as wood. A good deal of force might be required to pry the pair apart, possibly to the point of breaking bones. A more practical voice wondered why not just leave them as they were, send them to their final reward as they were meant to be: together?

Nay, that would be the shabby thing. Just show some grit and see this damned nightmare through.

The water was nearly to Thomas and Pryce's chests by the time they reached the bodies. Thomas murmured a small thanks that Nathan's head and cloudy water obscured Cate's face. Her death grin looking up at him would have been more than he could bear. He jerked away the tangle of weeds, his nostrils pinching, prepared for the stench. This many days, in this heat and sun...

Thomas reached for Nathan, expecting the cold, flaccid flesh of a corpse. The arm under his hand, however, was as giving and alive as his own.

"God's my life, he's not dead!"

Sputtering in disbelief, Pryce reached out and jerked back with a startled curse.

11

They seized Nathan with one intent: get his face out of the water, but Cate's dead weight thwarted every attempt.

"Nathan! Nathan, let go!" Thomas tore at Nathan's arms, now not caring if bone snapped.

"Give over, Cap'n!" Pryce shouted, yanking with equal force.

As feared, Nathan's hold was as unyielding as bands on a barrel. No amount of tugging, twisting or heaving could get them apart, their desperation to do so often leading their rescuers to cross purposes.

A small inner voice cautioned that perhaps dying was Nathan's intent. If Cate were dead, he'd wish to go with her. Thomas could already see Nathan's acrimony, hear the berating he'd take for denying that wish. Every instinct, however, screamed to save his friend and damn the consequences.

As they struggled, they had worked their way toward shore, shouting "He's alive! He lives!" A good many on shore waded out to bear a hand. Their enthusiasm, however, only resulted in a well-meaning confusion of snatching and yelling. Farther in, more came to help drag the two bodies up onto land. There, Thomas and Pryce fell to their knees and began a grisly tug-of-war, pulling on one, and then the other.

"Let go. Nathan, let go. We've got her! Give over…!"

The frozen arms twitched, and then again. Another mechanical jerk and Nathan's grasp loosened, the two coming apart with a suddenness which sent Pryce tumbling backwards. Leaving Cate where she lay, they dragged Nathan up beyond the high-water line. Near chaos erupted, suggestions shouted, several racing off to fetch a barrel, the time – honored method of reviving the near-drowned.

Sprawled, fingers curling into the sand, Nathan raggedly drew the precious air into his starved lungs.

"Stand back, the lot o' ya's," Pryce bellowed. "Stand off, I say!"

Nathan wormed around and made a floundering attempt to crawl back toward the water, his mouth moving like a dying fish.

"Clap a stopper in your gobs! He's trying to say something," Thomas shouted.

Through the maze of legs surrounding him, Nathan extended a shaky hand toward where Cate lay and wheezed "Help her!"

Thomas glanced to Pryce. A minute shake of the head confirmed his very thought:

Cate had been hard and cold as a corpse.

"Help her!"

Nathan's desperation jolted Thomas into action, if for

no other reason than to satisfy Nathan — and himself, for that matter — that they had done everything for her.

Thomas knelt next to the body and laid a hand on her arm. He jerked back. She wasn't dead... but neither was she alive... yet.

"Help her!"

Nathan's hoarse plea broke Thomas' shocked stare. Many a sailor believed drowning was God's hand and wouldn't raise their own to interfere. Too many times, however, he had seen that hand easily batted aside. He reflexively did as he had for countless others: fling Cate over a bent knee, ball his fist and drive it hard into her back... once... twice...

Cate convulsed and retched, spewing out a blackish-green glob. Another blow and she inhaled with a noise like metal grinding.

"Cate! Kittie" Each of Nathan's hoarse cries brought her further into the land of the living.

Thomas flipped Cate over and choked a sob of disbelief seeing her full for the first time. She was surprisingly whole. He fumbled at her middle where Creswicke had run her through. The skirt's fabric was slit, but nothing more. No blood, no wound, nothing.

With a joyous cry, Thomas clutched Cate to his chest. Eyes still closed, she arched and screamed. With the fierceness of the possessed, she fought scratching, kicking, wild to be free. With a startling burst of strength, she broke away and made a staggering lurch across the sand.

"Not the water!" Nathan cried.

Thomas dove, snagging Cate by the ankles. She shrieked and clawed; it was like trying to confine a wild cat. He was twice her size, and still it required every bit of his strength and bulk to overpower her. In spite of her struggles, he scooped her up and carried her to near where Nathan lay. Thomas sat, forcing her into his lap, trying to ease her, but she would have none of it. She kicked and bucked in a combination of fury, torment and terror. At the same time, however, the pink of life bloomed in her, to the point Thomas began to question how he could have ever thought her dead.

Defeated, dejected or just plum worn out: whatever the reason, Cate finally slumped. In her depleted state, she was reduced to kittenish writhing and a sort of keening, like a damned funeral dirge, full of bewilderment, anguish, and a terror which prompted those standing near to cast furtive glances toward the water from whence the pair had just came.

Bluish and paler than the sand upon which he sprawled,

Nathan alternated between gagging and gulping air. All the while, however, his one eye was fixed on Cate, willing her to prevail. Finally, he stirred, floundering like a newborn calf trying to find its legs. He rolled up on all fours and puked up a pitch-like glob.

"We need to get you two aboard," Thomas said, in broken bursts over Cate's weeping. Dragging two bodies through the surf and now wrestling with a frantic woman was heavy going and had him thoroughly winded.

Head hanging between his arms, Nathan resolutely shook his head and croaked "Not the sea... Not... yet."

Thomas gaped at Nathan in puzzlement. Nathan and the sea were nigh inseparable; this sudden fear was a puzzle. He cast a wary eye toward the cove, the bay and the open sea beyond. With the day's last rays flaring on its glassing surface, it looked peaceful enough, but Nathan had always had a second sense about the sea.

"Very well, then," Thomas finally managed. "It looks to rain. Rig a dodger and set a damned fire!"

His bark broke the men's stunned stares. It was the excuse they needed to take their leave—Cate's wailing was setting everyone on edge—making horned signs or clutching their talismans, murmuring entreaties or incantations to whatever gods of protection as they went. Only Pryce lingered, hovering over his captain, the question on his face the same as everyone else's.

Let them gawk, Thomas thought moodily. There was nothing to be gained else. They were mariners; rational explanation or not, they would come up with their own, filled with half-truths and outrageous claims. The only truth would be the one indisputable fact: two people, given up for dead, were now alive. Thomas settled back; Cate quieted, a bit.

"How the hell...?" Thomas demanded.

Everything pointed to something more bizarre and unnatural than his old eyes had ever witnessed, and yet he couldn't fathom what. Haggard and as near death as he might seem, the rasp of Nathan's breathing and the writhing body in his arms were proof that, impossible or no, it was now fact.

Nathan had collapsed on the sand, an arm extended toward Cate. He lifted his head enough to roll a quelling eye and then dropped it back down.

A fire was built; a flint struck, and the flame grew. Lying on his side, Nathan leaned toward the fire, seeking its life-giving warmth. The light flickered on a face still pale as death. The shadows danced in his sockets, making him look like the Grim Reaper still sat on his shoulder.

Thomas tightened his arms around Cate and rested his cheek on her head. She was wet as a whale and smelled of the sea, but Lord, it felt so good to hold her, something he had thought to never do again! He closed his eyes, wetness spilling down his cheeks as he murmured a prayerful thanks. These last days, he had cursed himself for not having taken more notice of what it felt like to hold her. Now, Providence had provided him a second chance, and he wasn't about to miss the opportunity.

A lean-to was rigged over Nathan, a low, two-sided affair fashioned out of sailcloth lashed over spars. Another tall enough to accommodate a man standing was set up next to it.

Emitting a growl of effort, Nathan pushed up to sit on his haunches. "Give her to me," he gasped over Cate's lamentations. He gestured with a hand too heavy to lift. "She'll have no peace else."

Nathan squirmed around to lean against a derelict mast, tossed there by a storm. Cate's distress rose an octave when Thomas rose to his feet. As predicted, once in Nathan's arms, she quieted. Rootling her head into the crook of his shoulder, her wails were immediately reduced to whimpers. Thomas sat back, his suddenly empty and useless hands twitching on his thighs.

A bottle was delivered. Nathan cleaved onto it and took several large gulps, closing his eyes in glorious relief. Thomas took the bottle next. He had no notion of what was in it, nor did he care. It met the important requisites — wet and alcoholic — and took a hard pull. In the turmoil, he had forgotten his arm. Now it ached like a demon. It was a fair guess some of the stitches had torn, he thought vaguely looking down at the sodden bandage, now blooming red. His first thought was Cate would tend it. One glance at her quivering form, huddled against Nathan, struck that notion by the board.

The firelight caught on a raw line encircling Nathan's neck, another at his ankle. Not really a wound, or rather not the kind typical of blade, ball or splinter, he didn't recall Nathan having it on the *Gosport*, but then a great many details went unnoticed in the furor of battle.

Disquieted by what they had just witnessed, while at the same time anxious to spread the word, the men retreated. A nod set Al-Nejem and Pryce on their way, leaving the three of them alone. In the ensuing quiet, Nathan rocked Cate, murmuring things too low for Thomas' ears. The fire's merry crackle and the soft liquid sound of the waves lapping the shore filled the ensuing quiet. From up the beach came the sound of the camp, now kicking up bob's a-dying. A part of Thomas strained to do the same, to dance around the fire and hoot with glee. To do so, however, meant rising, and he lacked the strength for that. One look across the fire was quelling enough: Cate and Nathan might be breathing, but neither looked far enough removed from Death's door to celebrate yet.

"How the bloody hell...?" Thomas repeated, all the more determined.

Grey as the wood at his back, Nathan slid a sideways look. "Answer is obvious, I should think," he said in a thick rasp.

"Obvious," Thomas sputtered, incredulous. "Two people coming back from the dead?"

Nathan's eyes rolled slowly closed, declining to argue else.

"I've heard the stories," Thomas began cautiously. He had heard about Nathan on every waterfront on the Seven Seas: mutiny, death, and resurrection. He'd only believed a fraction, until he laid eyes on the man. Ten years was rarely kind to anyone, but Nathan... well, it was as if he had left himself behind somewhere and was walking about in someone else's skin.

"This has something to do with... before?" Thomas ventured cautiously.

The roots of this miracle ran deep, to over a decade ago, when Lord Breaston Creswicke, Nathan's employer and long-time rival, had accused him of thievery. The power in those waters, with every authority of every robe at his beck-and-call, Creswicke's tangled web of dupery left Nathan abused, whipped, branded, and beaten to the point his mum would struggle to recognize him.

As broad as the question was, Nathan smoked his meaning directly. He cut a minatory glare from the corner of his eye, but was otherwise silent.

"How we wound up there, I'll never know," Thomas said, shaking his head in wonderment. He and a friend had put the near-dead Nathan into a boat—a stolen boat, his first act of piracy—meaning to spirit him away. The boat, however, had proven to be possessed, or something like, for it had sailed like a compass to north, drawn toward an island few knew existed.

"You were at Death's threshold when that woman—or whatever the hell she was— made us leave you behind. I know what I saw, and I'm still not sure what it was."

Thomas eyed Nathan, waiting for him to argue or contradict. He didn't.

Jerking a satisfied nod, Thomas pressed on. "I saw things I never seen before, nor do I ever wish to see again, but that still doesn't mean she's nothing more than an old, half-daft witchy woman who convinced herself she's Calypso."

He paused to take another drink. "Never was so glad to put a place to my rudder in my life! When she sent us off, I said my goodbyes, because I figured you'd never live to see the dawn."

Thomas peered at Nathan through one eye, looking for answers sure to never come. Eyes closed, still laboring for every breath, Nathan only moved his head enough to concede.

In the growing twilight, the *Morganse* could still be seen sitting on her moorings. A month after leaving Nathan with that obeah, he had shown up revived and reborn, with a ship and willing crew. Any and all inquiries were always met with the same blithe dismissals and evasions. Only Nathan and whoever that devil-incarnate woman they had left him with knew the truth. In that twisted brain of his, Creswicke had imagined Nathan crawling back to him, to live like some pet on a leash. Creswicke had to have been sadly disappointed when Nathan rose like the proverbial phoenix.

"I always wondered how you came up with her," Thomas mused.

Nathan coughed, a certain amount of satisfaction expelled with the phlegm spat out.

"You came back from the dead before," Thomas pressed.

Two fingers moved, not in denial.

"Is that when you got those?" Thomas pointed with his chin at the silver bells in Nathan's hair. In every case, in conjunction with those stories, the name "Calypso", or whatever name befitted that particular nook of the world, was mentioned. What the hell one had to do with the other he had no notion, but there was too much coincidence to believe else.

Believing in a goddess wasn't a stretch. A man couldn't be at sea a fortnight, without seeing things which bore no other explanation other than the hand of God or the Devil, in whatever form one was inclined to call them. He had been raised to know "the only God." Once at sea, however, he had quickly come to learn there was little difference between that God and the next, one idol holding significance only to the one worshiping it. If there be a God above, then to believe in one of the sun wasn't a reach. And, if there be one of the sun, then one of the moon or seas was entirely reasonable.

Nathan's shoulder moved in equivocation. "Promises were made."

"Prom... I won't ask," Thomas sighed, wearily rubbing his face.

One eye cracked open and there was the glimmer of a smile. "Best not. T'wouldn't be the truth, anyway."

Thomas dropped his hands and glared. "I *will* have answers."

Nathan was quiet to the point Thomas thought perhaps he had finally succumbed to exhaustion and drifted off. Whimpering and twitching, like one locked in a bad dream, Cate seemed to have done so. Finally, his head moved the fraction necessary for his cheek to come to rest on the crown of Cate's head. His arms tightened about her.

"All you could wish," came in a hoarse whisper. "Just... not... now..."

❦⁕

Exhaustion settled in, Thomas' body feeling like it was filled with the very sand upon which he sat.

He shifted, wincing as he sought to ease the hot pain shooting down his leg. Cate was asleep, Nathan only pretending. He couldn't bring himself to take his leave, and so he hunched near the fire, instead, staring into the flames. The sounds of jubilation drifted in broken bits from down the beach. Two rising from the dead was grounds for high celebration.

The forecasted rain began to fall, the heavy misting kind, hissing on the fire's glowing coals. He sat unmoving and uncaring; he was already wet as Neptune's court.

He was no nearer to knowing the truth than when he had started. He was weary, but considerably lighter of heart than when the sun had raised the yardarm. The world was bright once more, the thought of facing tomorrow no longer filled with dread. Solitude was no longer something to be feared, his own company now tolerable.

Thomas threw his head back and looked up at the stars. "Thank you. Whoever in the hell you are, thank you."

2: REALITY'S COLD SHOULDER

C ATE DRIFTED IN A SWIRLING void, like a leaf caught in an eddy. A pervasive darkness surrounded her, mind-numbing, soul-soaking and eternal... and pressing, always pressing. It was a foreign world where her heart was still, her blood chilling in her veins. Air was water, and yet she breathed it, existed in it.

Above, a circle of light appeared, dull yet promising all she could ever wish. Crawling or swimming she couldn't tell, she struggled toward, toward that promise of anything and everything... if she could just reach it. The thing kept moving, evading her effort. Like some mythical tortured soul, she advanced, only to slide back down, all the while weakening... ever weakening.

A dark blot rose over her. Her searching hands found something solid and cleaved onto it. Arms came around her, ones she instantly knew: security, haven... respite.

Nathan!

Gasping, she clung to him, fearing if her grip was to loosen, she might sink back into that abyss, now yawing beneath her like the jaws of Jonah's whale.

There were voices, but deadened, as if heard through water. Weakening, her grasp loosened, and the blackness consumed her once more.

❦

Drifting still in the black void, the circle of light loomed before Cate once more. Tantalizingly within her grasp, eternal loneliness eminent if she failed, she lunged.

Arms flailing, she gasped and coughed, a long wracking bout. "Easy, darling. Easy now."

More ragged than usual, she still knew Nathan's voice. She blindly seized the arm that came around her and clung.

"S'all right, darling. Shh...." he chanted, rocking her as one might a child with night terrors.

Everything pitched and yawed, like a raft in a storm. Nathan was her anchor, her rock, and she hung on, weathering the storm. The quaking with fear gradually gave way to shivering with bone-deep cold. At length, Cate pried her eyes open to find a world resembling when she had been spun as a child: blurred images speeding past. Any move of any sort only made it worse. Head resting on Nathan's shoulder, she blinked owlishly. She felt like Jonah after his return, and yet couldn't explain why. Her heart thudded dully in her ears, her blood... life... began to stir.

Like that sparked tinder, it caught and grew. Gradually, she became aware of someone, several someone's standing near. She looked up into a number of men lined around, staring down like owlets on a branch.

Finally, her surroundings steadied, the raft became land. With effort, Cate focused on Nathan, kneeling next to her.

"Don't try to speak, darling." He straightened the blanket about her. Yes, a blanket, the quilt from their bunk on the *Morganse*. "Words will come easier in a day or so."

She stared, wondering how he knew what she was thinking or feeling? Dark smudges under his eyes and deep lines bracketing his mouth, he looked worn and so very weary.

"T'was the same for me," he said matter-of-factly, smoothing the quilt's folds. "Before, that is. 'Tis somewhat easier the second time around... somewhat."

A shifting of her weight revealed a pallet under them. The sound of rain hitting something drew her gaze up to a low canvas shelter overhead. It was surrounded by an encampment of sorts, made up of several larger ones gathered around a fire, the raindrops hissing as they struck.

"I'm gonna be sick." Cate barely had time to roll away, hitting the sand instead of their bed. Nathan held her, for it was the violent, belly-wrenching, throat-tearing variety, once and then again... and then again, making sounds like a distressed ox. At the end, she fell back against him, gasping.

"What...? Where...?" she stammered.

"Shh... shh..."

Breathing consuming most of her energy, she slumped against him.

She was keenly aware of water in any form, and its threat. It was everywhere, falling from the sky, shining on Nathan's face and spangling in his lashes. It lapped on shore like snapping jaws. Even the saliva pooling in her mouth threatened to drown her.

"Ah, something to drink!" Nathan twisting about revealed a man bearing a pewter cup. A face thrust before her. Round and beaming, it was so familiar, and yet no name would come. The nameless soul plunged a glowing loggerhead into the cup, making its contents hiss and bubble like a witch's cauldron.

More water.

Cate mussed her head against Nathan's shoulder, wrinkling her nose. "What is it?"

"Something from Mother Kirkland's larder, represented to cure everything from ague to vapors. Now drink."

He pressed the cup to her lips. Steam curled up, the moisture filling her nose, seeking to suffocate her. She jerked away, but was stopped by a strong arm about her. Any further resistance required more energy than existed, and so she drank under Nathan's watchful eye, alert for a repeat performance of being ill. The liquid was viscously hot, with a strong metallic taste, but it wasn't unpalatable. She closed her eyes and reveled in the glorious warmth and fortification. Apparently, Mother Kirkland held brandy in high esteem.

With each sip, Cate's reeling world steadied a bit more. She became increasingly aware of men gathered around, their chants of "Praise God, they're alive" and "Praise the heavens she lives" sounding like a rosary. Her gaze drifted across the surrounding faces, neither seeing nor recognizing. Finally, she fixed on the round one, now peering eagerly over Nathan's shoulder.

Kirkland.

Nathan calling the man's name made it easier to grasp. Puffed and reddened, the cook's face was contorted by the confusion of one having been deep in sorrow, and was now plunged into the unmitigated joy of seeing someone one thought dead now alive.

Dead.

The chaos of battle on the *Gosport,* the clash of weapons, and the smell of blood and death: she recalled all of that clearly. The rest, the finer details were lost. The cold and numbness was clear; it suffused her entire being. She could see herself lying on that deck in a pool of her own blood, staring as the life drained like sand in a glass... Time running out. Nathan appeared over her, his face twisted with anguish. And then, he faded like a snowflake on a hot griddle.

Trying to think was like trying to stir a half-baked pudding. The mental image made Cate queasy. The pallet under her tilted. Seized by the sense of falling backwards, she jerked.

Nathan made an adroit grab for the cup, saving them both from a scalding.

"What...?" she croaked. A fit of coughing seized her, bringing up a goodly amount of fluid and other hideous stuff. "What... happened?"

Nathan coughed, only slightly less congested. "We were... gone."

One voice rose from among the others. It had an odd, yet familiar ring, demanding her attention, like a fist thudding on a distant door. She looked up and found the face, creased with concern. She groped for a name through the swirling soup of her mind. It came some moments later:

Thomas.

Gradually, she came to trust her eyes enough to realize it wasn't just her blurred vision which rendered him so difficult to recognize. On the one side were the bronzed and fair features she knew so well; the other side was fiery red, the blond hair and eyebrow naught but a pale stubble. She remembered him on the *Gosport*, at Nathan's side, cutlass in his fist, his face contorted with battle. Thomas' graveness, his obvious concern and relief set off a flood of confusing emotions. Fear, sorrow and regret all welled up in a choking sob.

Overwhelmed, she threw her arms around Nathan and wept. Rocking and making little soothing noises, he held her, stroking the crown of her head.

Crying is an exhausting business. Cate soon tired and sat back, sniffing. Nathan pulled a handkerchief from among the tumbled bedding. The routine of having her face swabbed and nose blown helped to regain a sense of normalcy. She smiled, self-consciously.

Next they'll be burning feathers. She wasn't ordinarily some swooning woman inclined toward the vapors, but she was damn near it now.

With cryptic orders, Nathan had the cup refilled and helped her drink. His smile was indulgent, but his eyes were narrowed and searching. She sensed he wished nothing more than to lie next to her, and oh, that he would! She was close enough to see the greyish tinge under his tan and the smile never touching his eyes.

Words failing, she met his gaze with one of her own. He pensively fondled, the droplets of rain gleaming on his bent crown.

"Aye, I know," he sighed, resigned. "You've questions and justifiably so."

Her gaze swept their general surroundings and ended on him.

"We're on Dead Goat Island; Ransom Passage is just there," he said, pointing with his chin into the night.

She nodded, vaguely recalling the geography. Oddly, at that moment, their exact location was of minor importance.

Nathan threw his head back, draining the cup. "'Tis a grand shock; was for me the first time, at any rate," he added under his breath.

Cate glared. "Shock" was the damned understatement of the century. "But... I...? We...?"

"Don't try to make sense of it, darling, for most of it you can't." His gentle smile faded as he muttered "I'm not so sure of a lot of it meself."

She coughed and cleared her throat, a wholly unladylike sound. "How... long...?"

"I have no notion how long we were gone. Thomas represents it was only a couple days. I'm obliged to take his word for it."

The shift of a large body and disgruntled grunt drew her attention back up to Thomas. Looming over them, he glared down, and then stomped away.

The darkness from which she had just escaped threatened once more. The world pitched and yawed, like the capering deck of a ship.

Weaving where she sat, Cate pressed her fingers to the bridge of her nose. "I... I... was... dead?" she rasped.

"Aye... mostly."

She made a low growling noise, annoyed by Nathan's evasions and half-answers.

Thunder rumbled softly. The rain came down harder, virtually obliterating their surroundings, leaving Cate and Nathan afloat in their little shelter. The rhythmic patter had a palliative, lulling quality. No longer possessing the energy or wherewithal to resist, Cate's eyes rolled closed. If the void desired to take her, then so be it.

"Sleep, darling." Nathan's voice seemed to originate from a mile away.

Comforts were murmured; shushing sounds accompanied her being lowered. Fear, nay, terror of being alone seized her, and she groped for him, but with arms made of sand. A hand, his hand caught hers. She felt the soft warm press of his lips on the back, and then it was settled on the pillow next to her head.

"Rest easy; I'm right here. We're together now. 'Tis all what matters..." he said, stroking her head.

Her mind seized upon the thought, like a drowning soul to a raft, and floated away on it.

Nathan's first day back among the living was not all he could have wished.

Thankfully, the night was over, the darkness being too mindful of what they had just escaped. He'd fixed an eye on the fire, a bright steady reminder that he had succeeded in returning to this world.

He had lain next to Cate and watched the night give way to what should have been a grand and glorious display of sun. Day, with its light, warmth and glory, was what he needed, what they both needed. What they got, however, was something more befitting of the Channel: gray and grizzling, the sun skulking like a sodden ship's biscuit in the fog, making him wonder why he had struggled so hard to return to this world. The fog brought wafts of mist, sometimes dense enough to reduce to a thin drizzle. When not raining, the moisture condensed on every surface, leaving everything and everyone wet, rendering everyone's mood as foul and dull as the atmosphere.

His own wakefulness had been Cate's disruption, and so he had risen. He had reluctantly left the fireside next to their shelter, the need to move and feel land under his feet more compelling than the need for warmth. He walked woodenly among the work crews along the strand. The beach was a-flurry with activity: knotting and splicing, butchering, tearing junk, wood and watering. Mouths to feed, a ship to attend were perpetual demands. The heaviness of foot and dull eyes wasn't entirely attributable to the soup-like atmosphere: those were souvenirs of the night's celebrations.

The sulking day did nothing for the odd, disjointed feeling which clawed his chest. He'd been told he and Cate's absence had spanned but a few days. For all he knew, it could have been a few days; it could have been a fortnight—hell, perhaps two. It was like waking from a fever to discover days had passed, days which would forever be gaping blanks, like the pages in the ship's log, never to be filled in, except with hearsay and speculation.

Hunching his shoulders against the chill, Nathan cast a glance back toward where Cate lay. At that distance, the flames of the fire, licking hot and bright in the swirling grey, were the only means to find the spot. The canvas shelter beyond was but a darker blot, Cate a nondescript lump under the quilt. When he left, she had been still, so very, very still. After her restless night, it was a relief to see her peaceful, but the stillness—so bloody damned near lifelessness—was still a worry. It was best that she slept; this miserable inclemency would do her no good. He would have her to sleep a fortnight—hell, two fortnights, if it would allow her peace, allow her to wake healed. If what he had endured the first time could be taken as an indicator of what awaited her, then sleep would be a blessed oblivion.

Land and sky being so alike, to the point of not being able to tell up from down, only added to his disorientation, making his struggle for normalcy all the more difficult.

And that was the worry: normalcy, or rather, whether it might ever be regained?

So far, escaping death's grasp a second time came easier. The hopelessness, despair, and destitution of before were absent. He considered that the difference was purpose. Before, his purpose had been lost, dead at the bottom of the sea. Now, he had purpose, two purposes: his two ladies, one dark and the other so very, very fair laying under a dodger a cable's-length away. Perhaps forewarning was forearming. Unlike the first time, he had gone over the *Gosport*'s side with the luxury of knowing what awaited. Cate had no such luxury. But neither was she alone, and by all that was holy, she would be spared the ardors he had suffered.

Nathan drew up to stare at the slate-colored cove. Visibility was barely more than a toss of the aforementioned biscuit. Somewhere out there, his ship presumably lay. Not being able to see her was disquieting. Included in that bothersome gap of memory was her welfare. He knew the beating she had taken during the battle, for every strike to her was a blow to him. How she fared now weighed heavily on his mind, on his heart.

Fog was a tricky business. Every sailor knew its deceptive nature, its way of bouncing, enhancing and deadening sound, until the nearest could seem the farthest. Still, knowing that, the disembodied voices of those aboard her were so clear, seeming to originate so very near, he feared she might ground.

He closed his eyes and cleared his mind, reaching out with all his senses.

Aye, battered and licking her wounds, but she was well.

He swallowed down the urge to hail one of the boats plying between ship and shore, and go have a look.

Cate.

That, *she* was what kept him landed. He couldn't be so far from her, not for that long, not yet. After a restless, dream-churned night, she had been sleeping when he took his leave. She was surrounded by men bid to bear an eye, but to be at such a distance was unthinkable.

"Cap'n? Cap'n!"

KERRY LYNNE

Assuming the most normal countenance as could be managed, Nathan turned to meet Pryce striding toward him.

"Give you joy o' you 'n Mr. Cate's return!" Pryce declared heartily. Unfettered pleasure softened the gargoyle-like face. And, if Nathan wasn't mistaken, that wasn't mist collecting at the corner of his eye.

Words failing him, Nathan civilly angled his head.

"And Mr. Cate?" Pryce asked, with a hopeful glance in her direction. The "Mr." reference was a result of the old salt's and most of the hands' belief that women aboard were bad luck. Calling her "Mr." somehow confused the powers which controlled such things.

"She'll do," Nathan assured. "She has a spirit and fortitude which could put all of us to shame."

Pryce eyed him critically. "Beg pardon, sir, and if I may be so bold, ye look fit to topple over. Nuthin' to be gained in the people a-seein' ye as compromised," he added under his breath. "Come, sit."

God bless and seize his soul, how could they expect less after what he had just been through? Resurrection wasn't without its consequences, although benevolent looks from those around revealed many saw it as more miracle than tribulation. One didn't arise from the dead in shining spirits and in the pink. It left one dull, battered and drained, rejoicing being too much of an effort. Walking... thinking... hell, breathing consumed every shred of energy.

Conceding, Nathan moved as casually as one might on wobbling pins, Pryce's clandestine hand at his elbow seeing him safely seated atop a pile of stores.

"How bad was she?" Nathan asked.

Typical mariner, Pryce knew straightaway the inquiry was in reference to the *Morganse*, and sobered. "None so bad, considerin'. We'd made enough weigh a-fore the *Gosport* blew. The *Lovely* took the worst of that."

Nathan felt a pang of sympathy for Thomas. Any captain worth his salt suffered for any ship the same as if it were his own. "How goes the repairs?"

Pryce launched into a detailed account. Nathan nodded with great interest, in spite of most of it rolling off him like wet off a walrus. He was as muddled and queasy as after a fortnight of carousing. He had always known his First Mate to be a blessing, but now even more so. The man knew his ropes!

"I took the liberties to pass the word to the *Lovely* for Mr. Cate's dunnage be brought ashore."

Nathan offered thanks on her behalf; it seemed the fitting

26

and decent thing to do. All other considerations failed him, at the moment.

Gazing toward their fog-enshrouded ship, Pryce fell into an uncharacteristic contemplative silence. "Was a-thinkin' on scuttlin' her on her moorings, seein' as how she would sail for no other man."

"Believing your own stories are we, Pryce?" Nathan asked, dryly.

"T'was no denyin' after that mutiny, she foundered on a reef and sank."

"Aye," Nathan began agreeably, "but was that due to mutton-fisted seamanship or a charmed ship stricken with grief?"

"Either, or," Pryce said, with an equivocating gesture. "All I can say is, not a man-jack among them was willin' to weigh anchor without ye."

"She would have sailed for you."

Pryce twitched, whether from surprise or dismissal he couldn't tell. "Still, woulda been the none so small matter o' convincin' them o' that."

For the first time, Pryce turned to look fully at Nathan. His grizzled brows drew down to almost touching. "Forgive me for makin' so bold again, but ye be a-lookin' a mite too much like the last time. Do ye remember?"

Nathan winced. Those had been dark, dark days... nay, months following his first return to the living. Whether the man had sought him out or had just stumbled across him was anyone's guess, for he would never say.

"You were walkin' death," Pryce recalled affectionately. "A man what couldn't die who'd lost the will to live."

Nathan winced; Pryce's analysis wasn't far off the mark. At that point, immortality stared him in the face, or so he had been told, and his ship lying at the bottom of the sea. His daily hope had been for Providence, the gods, or whoever in the hell was in charge of such things to come take his wretched carcass and be done with it.

"Did I ever thank you?" Nathan asked.

"Time 'n agin," Pryce said ducking his head.

"Aye, well, thank you again." The food and shelter Pryce had provided had allowed him a few weeks' more existence, the few more weeks which had allowed him to contrive an answer to his dilemma. If Pryce hadn't come along...?

Shivering again, Nathan cast another worried glance over his shoulder toward where Cate lay.

Lord, just to lie down next to her and sleep for the next week... two weeks...

"Not bloody likely," he said aloud.

"Beg pardon, sir?"

A curt wave staved off further inquiries. His rejoicing would be reserved for Cate; seeing her thrive would be his grandest reward.

"Orders?" The shifting of Pryce's feet showed the voice of duty was calling.

Nathan tried to think. It was like the damned fog had seeped into his skull. "Nay, just... carry on," he finally landed on. "You've done me and the barky proud."

Beaming under the praise, Pryce made to take his leave, but turned back, flushed with elation. "Give you joy!"

At some point Nathan started walking again, for he found himself well down the strand, near the ropeworks, the spin yarns spitting out cordage like web out of a spider's arse. Rattling down shrouds, back and forestays, chafing gear: refitting and repairing required miles of the stuff.

"Nathan? Nathan!!"

"What?" he barked. Thomas' booming voice could try one on a good day. Why the hell the fog hadn't deadened that was a wonder. "Damn your sottish eyes, I'm right here!"

"Aye, but you weren't attending. I hailed you several times."

The words formed in his throat to argue, but Nathan also knew it would be in vain. Burn and blast his bones, Thomas was probably correct.

His gaze was drawn back to the fog where the two ships laid on their moorings. "Pryce represents the *Lovely* took the worst of it."

The corner of Thomas' mouth twitched grimly. "She did. Another day of knotting and splicing, however, and she'll be fit for whatever is thrown at her."

Nathan was keenly aware of a dull pounding aside from the one in his temples: the surf on the reef beyond the Passage. The unsettling part was it seemed to emanate right aft of his ship.

"How does it stand out there?" he asked. A vague nod incorporated the passage, the reef and the open sea beyond. It was damned disquieting to have no notion as to how things laid.

Thomas grinned. "Creswicke brought damned near a squadron on the promise of catching you."

The recollection brought a smile to both faces, for both had predicted as much. Thomas had lured Creswicke into the rendezvous by offering to deliver Nathan on the proverbial platter. Both men knew Creswicke well enough, however, to expect treachery, and the scheming bastard hadn't disappointed.

"The *Gosport* made the reef, but the *Stately* grounded directly behind her," Thomas went on.

"That would be Durham commanding, last I heard," Nathan said, one eye closing in recollection. "Always has been a clap-on-all-sails, damn-the-yards-and-knees, blundering cove."

Thomas grinned. "Well, God bless Captain Durham's blundering, for not another could pass."

"And now?"

Thomas glanced at him and then away, forming the simplest explanation, God rest his soul. "The lookouts report the bulk o' 'em hauled their wind. Probably heard Creswicke is dead, knew the likelihood of being paid went with him, and lost heart. A couple of cutters or schooners are sniffing about, but..."

Nathan nodded absent-mindedly. Mercenaries could be a bloody-minded lot, but when the money was gone, so were they, off to find the next open purse.

He lifted his face to the breeze, although to call it that was to flatter it, for there was barely enough to fill a pocket handkerchief. The other thing he knew about fog was that it was capricious stuff. In one place, it could hang so thick one could barely see to the end of their arm, whilst less than a half-league away, another might be squinting against the glare of the sun.

"Do you fancy they'll try us?" Lord, he hoped not! He barely possessed the wherewithal to put one foot before the other. A call-to-battle was unthinkable.

Thomas snorted. "They'd have to gain the courage to try the reef. And now, with this," he added, casting an eye skyward, or rather what seemed to be the sky. "'Tis no weather for trying reef, nor passage. I might venture a boat out there to have a keek," he added, in a cautionary afterthought.

Still, in the height of desperation, one might pull the ship through the reef and passage, laboring on the oars like an Algerine galley, but that would mean arriving with the men exhausted before the battle even began.

"Creswicke's death won't go unnoticed. Revenge, arrest and restitution would dwell in the hearts and minds of many," Thomas observed.

Nathan turned slowly to look up. "Aren't you sounding the learned cove?"

"Every man-jack what can sling a yard will cum a-huntin' fer yer arse," Thomas said, in a creditable imitation of a f'c'stlejack. He abandoned that for his natural deep rumble to say "We only need be forgotten long enough for us to make repairs and haul our wind."

Another uneasy silence fell, the air between them thick as the fog with unasked questions. Nathan waited. Thomas could be as tight-lipped as a virgin on her knees when he wished. Or, as just then, he could be as transparent as Cate's old shift when something was on his mind.

Nearby sat a cluster of men tearing junk. Judging by the bales of oakum stacked about, both vessels still required a fair amount of caulking. A stirring of air brought the smell of tar stoves from offshore, confirming that conclusion.

"You look like hell," Thomas observed.

"Save the flattery for the street trollops." Nathan rubbed his face hard with his hands. "Sleeping is no longer a natural thing."

He turned to look at Thomas fully for the first time. They had known each other since their voices had barely dropped. Never had he seen his friend so aged. Nearly a head taller than himself, square, bold and blond, a plundering Viking must have ravaged Thomas' three or four-time great-grandmother, for he looked like one. Much caressed by the ladies, Thomas was much the worse the wear, now.

"I might return the favor, by saying you look like a goose greased up and half-roasted. That arm looks to be in sad need of a sling," Nathan added, a bit more sympathetically.

"I'll do," Thomas huffed, cradling it nonetheless. "Yesterday's escapades didn't do it any favors."

Nathan opened his mouth to say he should bid Cate to tend it, but clapped it shut. She wouldn't be attending anyone for a good while.

Apparently, Thomas' mind ran in much the same direction. He cast a significant look in her general direction. "Cate doesn't appear to be faring much better."

"She'll do," Nathan muttered, hunching his shoulders.

"Like hell. After... everything she was barely holding her own. Now, with this..." Thomas dolefully shook his head. "She looks to sleep the day away."

Looking to his feet, Nathan winced. He didn't need a reminder of the last few weeks' events: Cate kidnapped, brutalized, used hard by untold numbers, and then branded. True enough, she had recovered, but barely. She put up a brave front, but she was still as fragile as a crystal goblet, fit to shatter at the least unsuspecting vibration.

And now, with all this...?

"When she deems the world is worth waking for, she will.

She's warm, dry and safe; the rest is but details." The last came with a dismissive flutter of Nathan's fingers.

He rounded on Thomas and stabbed a finger into his chest. "Goddamn you for dragging her into this!"

"*Me* dragging her?" Thomas gaped. "In a less charitable moment, I might point out you had a large hand in it, as well."

"How the fucking hell did she wind up on that ship?"

Thomas threw his arms up in frustration, wincing in pain. "Damned if I know. I did as you bid—"

"Pah!"

"You're not asking anything different than I've asked myself a hundred times over." Cradling his arm, Thomas set to stalking back and forth. A limp rendered him all the more aged-looking.

"I sent her ashore with four of my best men, just as *you* asked," Thomas added, cutting off Nathan's further expostulations. "They were to take her to the far side of the island, to the spring, just as you asked."

Nathan jerked a nod; he knew it well. Fresh water and forest had been the very reason he had begged Thomas to take Cate there. She should have been able to hold out there for days, safe, hidden, away from the battle. Instead, she wound up in the damned middle of it.

He pressed a hand to his gut, the churning sensation striking anew at the shock of seeing her on the *Gosport*. In the smoke and chaos, he had thought—nay, prayed it was just her fetch following him. His heart had swelled at seeing the fire of battle in her eyes. Fear took different people in different ways. Some shrank back, cowering, seeking a hole in which to hide; others soiled themselves, whilst others rose to the call. God rest and seize her soul, Cate was one of the latter. Terror or fury alike, full at a man was her response and damned the consequences, and damning those had been, this time.

"Creswicke had her for God knows how long," he heard himself say.

"It was only for part of a day... and the night. She looked well." Thomas spoke in the spirit of helpfulness, but then shied at realizing how lame that sounded. Untold horrors could be visited upon a soul—especially a woman—and never a mark made.

They both knew what time in Creswicke's hands meant; the cold-hearted bastard could make Satan blush. His own captivity had been roughly that same duration. Cate had required weeks to heal from Creswicke's handiwork wrought during roughly the same.

Nathan shivered and swallowed down the lump of illness which rose in his throat. "If he laid a hand on her, I'll—"

"You'll have to pursue him to the Gates of Hell to do so. I sent him well on his way, after you two... were... gone," Thomas finally managed, his voice tightening.

"I'd done for him already or so I thought," Nathan said in his own defense. Battle could be so damned confusing.

"You did," Thomas assured. "I was a bit... vexed, at the moment. Ol' Nick might have a hard time recognizing him, what with him carrying his head under his arm."

Both smiled at that image and with the satisfaction of their enemy having met final justice. Nathan had always fancied Creswicke's demise to have involved a great deal of time and infinite pain. After a decade and more of seeking his revenge, to have it end so quickly seemed a dull finish. It was all too quick; agony, long and eternal was what the foul-lived spawn o' the devil deserved.

Thomas' reasons for hating Creswicke were more vague, but then, no man ever shared everything. In the spirit of friendship, Nathan had never pressed for answers. Sharing meant heaving to dredge it up, like shingle from the ballast, foul with years of accumulated muck. 'Twas far less filth and stink to just let it lay.

Thomas jerked off his hat and ran a frustrated hand through his hair. "Suffering Christ, Nathan, what the fucking hell happened?"

It took a moment to smoke Thomas' meaning; he was no longer speaking of the battle. "I'd think it obvious," Nathan said mildly.

Thomas seized Nathan's left arm and jerked back the sleeve. "I saw you lay this open with your blade."

With a certain distance, Nathan regarded the pale forearm and the scar across it, pink and freshly healed. He had forgotten that bit. So much on the *Gosport's* deck was a blur, and yet so much was clear as crystal, as it was likely to remain for the rest of his days.

Thomas straightened, suddenly aware of the score of men nearby, eyes goggling, ears flapping. He seized Nathan with an iron grip and half-pushed, half-dragged him down shore, out of earshot.

"I see you go over the side into sharks and flames, and two days later, you pop up like a goddamned... sprite, without so much as a by-your-leave!" Thomas demanded in a strained but lowered voice.

"Difficult to explain," Nathan said to his feet.

"Try," came through clenched teeth. "Give me the honor of at least one grand, magnificent lie."

Nathan glanced up at the man now towering over him. The look was too familiar; there was no abating him when he was in that mood. Over the years, they had saved each other from peril and perdition more times than either could count. On that basis alone, an explanation was owed.

Closing his eyes once more, Nathan sought the all-precious few seconds of rest found behind his lids. When they popped open, he found Thomas' deep blue ones inches away. "It all stems from a family curse, going back generations on me mum's side."

Thomas stiffened, struck momentarily speechless by Nathan actually conceding to his demands. "Who? Cursed you or your family?"

"Calypso, ages ago. Whether me or me family is one-in-the-same."

Thomas propped his hands on his hips. "And why would the very one who cursed you save your life?"

"Because," Nathan began, glaring up into that half-cooked face, "she doesn't wish me dead, she wishes —" He stopped short. How the hell does one explain that bit? "Suffice to say, she wants me, or rather, what I can do for her."

Retreating a few steps, Thomas puzzled on that. "Your mum was some kind of auld one, wasn't she?"

"Nay, she only spoke to them." Nathan grimaced at that small lie. His boyhood had been filled with rumors of sorcery and witchcraft, and the persecutions which always accompanied those. There was no denying Mum knew many things, more than what was fitting, things which a soul had no business knowing. As for the how and the why of it, he had inquired, as all sons might. She had always claimed his own skill at evading a question was his father's trait. Alas, Mum wasn't without blame.

"You've come back from the death three times now," Thomas announced.

"Nay, only twice."

Thomas had the good graces to at least look chastened. "You were doing a damned good imitation of it when me 'n Garrick left you." He shuddered. "Never seen anyone nearer to dead and still breathe."

"After His High-Arsedness was done with me, I only wanted to die. No one would let me," Nathan said, cutting an accusing glare. "That one wasn't Calypso. She can't come ashore," he qualified at Thomas' apparent confusion. "Thank heavens for that, for there would be no peace else," he added under his breath. "She was a half-sister or some such nonsense. You know how those gods are."

"No, can't say as I do," came back coldly. "We couldn't tell if it was woman or beast."

Nathan smiled faintly. "A comely lass compared to Herself."

Thomas eyed him severely; Nathan kept his face carefully blank. Thomas was in one of his bullish moods. As when anyone found themselves face to face with said bull, backing one's sails and tiptoeing around was most often the best tack.

"Well, the least you could have done is warn a soul," Thomas huffed. "I was worried to distraction."

"There wasn't time, if you'll cool down enough to recall. Besides, what was I supposed to say? 'Meet me on shore in a couple days?'"

Nathan bit his lip. It wasn't just injury which had left Thomas in such a ragged, harried state. The hard lines of grief creased the blistered face. The few days of their absence had aged him years. "I didn't know, if it would answer."

"You believed enough to slash your arm and throw yourself to the sharks," Thomas pointed out, peevishly.

"I didn't do it for that," Nathan said, toying with the rent sleeve.

Nathan set to pacing. "You think it's such a blessing or some grand game, going about with some goddamned goddess sniffing in your wake? I didn't ask for this. It's not as if I went on some glorious quest, seeking blessings or charms. She's no benevolent angel; she's like a damned shark... but at least the shark you could shoot and be done. With this—"

Nathan blew a frustrated sigh and rubbed his hand roughly over his face, pretending not to see it shake. "God's my life, if only Mum were still here. She could sort this out. I have no notion of dealing with spirits or goddesses, or whatever in the hell you call them. Give me a stiff weatherly ship 'tis all I ask."

Extending his arms, Nathan looked down at his bandaged wrists, smiling faintly. He could still hear Mum, see her face, urging him to drink the tea meant to ease the pain. Tattooing pressed the tolerances of grown men. For a lad who'd yet to sprout hair on his chin, it had been agony to have those woad tattoos applied. Those at his waist and neck had been there since infancy. Lord, how he must have wailed then.

"They were meant to stop the witchy bitch, but as for the rest—" Dull-wittedness and frustration rendered him speechless.

Nathan looked up at Thomas, now towering over him. "I did what I had to, and would do it a hundred times more, if the circumstances were the same. So belay that caterwauling and go turn someone else into stone with that glare."

Thomas eyed him critically and then yielded. "You look like you're fit to keel over. Go take a caulk," he said, with a companionable clap on the shoulder.

"Nay," Nathan said, sliding out from under the big paw. "As good as it sounds, nay. I'll do."

"You'll fall over is what you'll *do*."

"Nay, I have to see her safe." Now he was the one being bullish, but there was naught to be done for it.

"She is," Thomas pointed out. "I have to see her—"

Thomas took Nathan by both shoulders and gently shook him until he blinked and looked up. "She. Is. Safe. You made it. You're back, both of you. Nothing can get her now."

Nathan slumped, leaning into the supporting hands. He closed his eyes for a precious few seconds of respite. Stiffening, he forced them open and smiled up feebly. "If only it were that simple."

A delicate cough broke them apart to find a pair of Lovelies waiting. "Mr. Rashid's compliments and duty, sir. He desires you to..."

Nathan seized upon the fortuitous opportunity and stepped away.

⌒⤳⫯⤶⌒

Nathan made his way up the strand, back toward their lean-to. He drew up short at seeing Cate's spot on their pallet empty. The blanket tossed aside, only a hollow in the oakum-stuffed pallet remained, like a damned ghost image of her body. The poles near the fire, where her clothes had been drying, were bare.

She was gone.

"Where's Mr. Cate?" he barked.

A sodden group of Lovelies and Morgansers huddled around the fire looked up.

"B'lieve I saw 'er a-headin' thataways, Cap'n," offered one, angling his head toward the mist enshrouded beach and rocks beyond.

"Aye, sir!" piped another. "A-goin' for a walk... like."

"'*A walk like*'?" Nathan echoed, coldly. "How long since?"

The cockle-headed louts looked at each other. One finally found the wherewithal to shrug, damn all their gallowsy eyes! "A bit."

Nathan reeled around. "A bit?!"

"Aye, a bit... and mebbe a wee bit more," the hapless cove added, with a furtive glance up the shore.

"Suffering Jesus on the cross, you bunch o' ill-begotten, cod-handed miscreants can't get your minds off your cocks long enough to mind one woman?" he demanded over his shoulder, already striding in that direction.

As he passed, he looked hopefully to Beatrice, roosted atop one of the support spars. In the past, the wretched beast had been of guidance in finding Cate. Now, the pile o' feathers only raised her sodden hackles and gave him a beady-eyed stare.

Cursing, he slapped Hermione, the ship's goat, on the rear, urging her the hell out of his way. All thoughts of rest going by the board, he gave an angry swipe and lengthened his gait up the shoreline, Beatrice squawking "Thrice-damned princock" in his wake.

"*A bit*," he grumbled. "The sun and the tides: everything a man could desire to keep track of the time, and the gobs can't pull their heads out o' their arses long enough to take notice."

He glanced at that same sun, not so much as to check the time as to judge how much light might remain should this become a prolonged search. He found no more than a brighter glow in the otherwise gloom. Damned untimely time for the weather to go sour. He lifted his faced into the breeze. It smelled of a change coming. Whether for good or worse was the question?

With two crews ashore, the beach was churned and trampled. Small and delicately boned, hers were easily picked out from amid the others. Eventually, those took him far enough for the sand to return to its pristine self. There he picked up her solitary trail. The dimples of her toes—Like little turtle heads, they were—and heel—His hand curved with the recollection of how its perfect roundness fit his palm—were connected by a thin, arched bridge. Her high arches were just one more of a series of elegant curves which led so pleasingly to her ankle and calf. They weren't, however, the prints of a soul with a purpose in mind. Halting, angling this way and that, they had the look of one without direction, as if being led off by some inexorable power.

He vehemently cursed the unthinking sods around the fire again when the prints veered toward the water and then disappeared. Whether they had been obliterated by the rising tide—He checked the sun again; aye, rising it was—or Cate had actually gone into the water set the blood pounding in his temples. He fought down the images of the waves reaching up like fingers, grasping her by those slim ankles and dragging her back into the sea, never to be seen again.

"Nay, I would see her," he vowed to the waves. "I'll come looking and it shan't be pleasant, you treacherous, swivel-tongued plague o' the deep!" he added, shouting by the end.

Those images, however, caused him to scan the gunmetal-colored water again and again, dreading the sight of a body floating.

Nothing...

His imagination would allow him no peace. The visions of Cate lying at the bottom, her hair wafting about her face like copper-colored kelp, weren't readily quelled. He forced his feet to keep moving, every step feeling like he was knee-deep in the surf. Finding Cate would be the only way to allay his fears.

"If I'm wrong, then show me where the hell she is," he yelled at the water.

A cold draft at his nape made him shiver. A downdraft, a natural phenomenon with fog, he told himself, not the breath of any unseen demon, but it bloody well felt like it.

The cunning harpy's breath had been like a blast at the high sixties...

"When she breathed at all," Nathan muttered moodily, jerking his shoulders.

More like exhaled, she had, in satisfaction of a goal achieved, a task well-done, a foe dominated.

The beads of moisture on his brow weren't a result of the fog. Heart hammering, his gut in a moil, he fought down the increasingly sick feeling, in spite of finally finding footprints leading away from the water's edge. Proof positive Cate still walked this earth.

"Hah!" Nathan barked victoriously over his shoulder, as he turned to follow her path.

Damnation and seize his soul, he hadn't wished Cate to have any part in this. And now, here she was, dead in the middle of it, and by his own hand!

Bartering to save her had been a mistake. He knew that, now. Hell, he had known it then, but it wasn't as if he had any choice in the matter. Now the calculating harridan knew what Cate meant to him. His hand had been tipped, his cards shown. She had a new weapon. He would have no peace, now.

It was an uneven, rocky stretch of shore, dotted with tide pools. Looking too much like bottomless pits, underworld lairs where the duplicitous malkin or one of her minions might lie in wait, Nathan carefully avoided them. Mysterious disappearances weren't always so mysterious. There was often a simple answer: taken. He was damned living proof of that as was Cate... now.

Victory came in spotting Cate, finally! She sat on a ledge

overhanging the water. Feet dangling inches above the waves, she stared down at her hands limp in her lap. Still as a figurehead, only her skirts and hair moving in the breeze, she looked not of this earth, but like one of those fabled sirens, calling the sailors to their demise in the rocks.

Nathan made to speak, but fear seized his throat. He coughed and tried anew. "Kittie."

Sink and burn him, she didn't move.

He called her name repeatedly, at the same time advancing cautiously. If he was to startle her, she might fall in, or leap off and swim away, like one of those cursed selkies his mother had told of: seals who came ashore as women. He was damn near in her line of sight; why the hell didn't she move or see him?

Finally, he was near enough to venture touching her.

Cate jerked and blinked, her face pinking with pleasure. "Nathan."

"You wandered off." He gleaned as much scold from his voice as could be managed with having the life scared out of him. Since Creswicke had taken her, she shied at a moth landing on a feather. In the meantime, he fought off the urge to grab her and give her a solid shaking.

Her eyes rounded with earnest innocence. "Did I?"

Hands twitching at his sides, Nathan waited, watching Cate's toes work the air, the mist shining on those delicately curved arches. The standoff broke when she swayed; he grabbed her and bodily turned her toward him, to a less precarious position. Pale as a jib, her features red and swollen with crying, the sight of her still touched his heart. His grip tightened when she weaved again, nearly toppling over backwards into the water below. The unsteadiness he understood for he suffered much the same: the damned world tilting like a deck in a double-reefed tops'l breeze.

It was a struggle for her eyes to meet his. He had seen men strengthened by trial and tribulation. He had no notion as to how it was with women. Never had he seen Cate shy from confrontation, and woe that she would have, at least once in a while, for it would make living with her a mite more bearable. But now...?

"Pinch me." Head hanging, her voice was so small, he wasn't sure he heard.

Looking up, Cate thrust out her arm. "Pinch me!" In his hesitation—Surely to hell she didn't mean...?—she started tearing at her bare arms, grabbing up bits of flesh between her fingers, and grunting in pain.

"Stop it! Stop it!" He wrestled with her. Ultimately, he caught her by the wrists and forced her arms down to her sides. Still, she struggled with surprising strength.

"Stop it! Avast, I say," he growled in her ear. "Belay! Stop it!"

Finally, Cate yielded. He stood back, chest heaving. "What the fucking hell do you think you are at?"

"Pinching myself, trying to prove I'm awake and not in some nightmare."

"A nightmare to be alive, or alive with me?" he asked carefully, his chest tightening to the point he couldn't breathe. Too many times, he had saved a number of others from death, only to be cursed for it after. Everyone had their personal definition of Hell; it gave him an ill feeling to think she might be living hers and cursing him for it.

Cate clutched her head, like someone suffering a megrim. "It's a nightmare, with all these things whirling around in my head."

She dashed at her face and stared down at the resulting wetness. "I don't know if these are for joy or for sorrow. I don't feel anything: cold, joy, hunger... nothing!"

Shaking her head in bewilderment, Cate twisted around toward the cove. "Someone, some*thing* keeps telling me I belong... out there. Land is no longer where I belong; the air is like trying to breathe water..."

Nathan opened his mouth to point out that she was babbling, but discretion prevailed.

Instead, he nodded, a weather-eye fixed on the offing behind her, lest it rise up and grab her.

"You're confused, darling. 'Tis normal after... everything," he finally landed on. "Time is all you need. You'll know soon enough that land and air are your friends, and with me as where you belong." The last was punctuated with a gentle, admonishing shake.

Nathan ducked his head several times, trying to catch her gaze. Before, he could often guess what she was thinking, those cursed eyes allowing him in. Now, they were blank and dull.

She swayed again, alarmingly, nearly toppling over again.

"I need to get you back—" he began, taking her by the arm.

"Dammit, Nathan! I need—" Twisting away from his grasp, she swallowed hard. "I deserve a straight answer," she said shakily. "So many, too many crazy things keep running through my head. Is it real or have I gone mad? Tell me straight what the hell happened?"

Nathan stood back and drew a breath to insist; the determined set of her jaw stopped him. His hands reflexively curled closed at the feel of her body. It was that of a corpse: cold and unyielding.

"Answer me!" she cried.

Head bent, Nathan blew a long, weary sigh. He had been dreading this. The bow would hit the waves now, but how the hell to go about explaining was the wonder? And it was nigh impossible to think with the sea lurking just behind her, threatening. "Very well, but let's at least get somewhere out of this wind."

Either out of weariness or confusion, Cate meekly nodded and stood.

He cast a loathsome glare toward the sea as he handed her down from the ledge.

Ha! Mine!

3: NOT THE DEVIL, BUT NEAR ENOUGH

CATE ALLOWED HERSELF TO BE guided inland. Around the fog-slickened rocks and tide pools they went, Nathan's hand at her elbow. The land being so foreign underfoot, his arm, often coming around to guide or steady her, was a blessing. His touch was the greater blessing; like a lodestone reminding a compass needle of its duty, it stirred her spirit, calling it back to where it belonged. She squeezed his hand time and again, a half-smile having to suffice where words failed.

She was led to a nook in the lee of the rocks. Away from the wind and water, the small space was markedly quieter and hence, far more abiding. He saw her seated atop a log tossed there by a storm. She sat, staring down at her hands in her lap. She experimentally moved each finger, acutely aware of the working of the muscles and tendons, trying to sort out if it belonged to her or someone else.

Silver flashed. A ring, its design she knew without seeing: roses, intertwined over a latticework. A face rose before her, ruddy and fair, bright with avidity as he had placed it on her finger. The recollections flashed like fireflies on a summer night—husband, home, family—all fading as quickly as they appeared.

Her gaze drifted to her wrists. Matching bracelets of knotted cord encircled them, with odd bits of shell, wood and coral at the dangling ends. The sight of those brought another face to mind, dark-eyed and bronzed by the sun.

Her brown study was shattered by a flask thrust before her.

"You're shivering. Drink."

Cate stared at the leather vessel. In point of fact, she was shivering, but whether from cold or fear, weariness or joy she had no notion. With an irritated grunt, Nathan sat next to her and tipped the flask to her lips, softly repeating "Drink. Drink" until she complied. Expecting rum, she sputtered and coughed. "It's arrack," he explained, half-apologetic. "Got it from that Mohamaden First Mate of Thomas'."

Several more sips reduced the shaking to frissons, shooting through her with the regularity of waves rolling ashore. Scowling, Nathan urged her to take several more, until the tremors lessened further yet. The spirits were fine, but his thigh pressing against hers had an even greater palliative effect. His intent seemed to prevent her from jumping up, but the warmth radiating through her skirt, the blood and bone of another living soul next to her, was the most gratifying of all. She yearned to press her entire length against his and just bask in it, soaking it up like a hearthstone.

Sitting there, she made a deliberate inventory of her body, seeking clues as to what exactly had happened to her, to them. What Nathan represented was too impossible, and yet, no other viable explanation presented itself. The wooden log under her had more feeling than she did. There was no pain of injury, no ache which came with being beaten, no nausea or rumbling gut. There was no headache common to fever; she was weak and woozy, but not the kind which came from illness.

Nathan sat next to her, so silent and patient, she suspected they might sit there 'til sundown, should she desire it. The problem was she had no notion of what she wished. Peace? Quiet? At the moment, the most intriguing was to return to the little cabin Nathan had built for her, where they could lie together in eternal and everlasting peace.

That pleasantry was shattered by more confused visions. They kept popping into her head, like a floating bottle, sinking into oblivion, and then periodically popping to the surface to allow disjointed glimpses of the conscious world, only to sink away once more, reality denied. She bent and clutched her head again, gouging her nails into her scalp, in the hopes the pain might ease the chaos there.

It didn't.

"All these things, visions keep wheeling about in my head. It has to be a dream, a nightmare. It can't possibly be real." She looked up, imploring.

Nathan's shoulder bumped hers as he took a drink. "Tell me," he said, hoarsely. "I'll guide you where I can, but I need to know what—" His throat caught, and he fell quiet.

"I was in Hell," she said, kneading her head. "I was burning, flames leaping up—"

Nathan smiled, tight and grim. "That wasn't Hell, darling. It was the *Gosport* burning."

Cate nodded vaguely, the recollection of the bang of great guns and rattle of muskets confirming his claim.

"I was running," she said haltingly, "through smoke. Something was chasing me... the Devil... I think—"

"Not the Devil, but near enough," he mused. "It was His High-Lordshipness Creswicke."

She nodded again, somewhat assured. The pieces were beginning to fall together; perhaps she wasn't entirely mad. The sounds and smells of battle were familiar. The sheer terror of being on that deck made her heart quicken; the acrid stench of burning tar and hair filled her nose, and she coughed. The terror faded at the joyous relief of seeing Nathan appear out of the smoke, cutlass in hand, Thomas at his side. The joy dissolved into terror once more, not for herself, but for Nathan, fearing he might do something wild and foolish.

"I fell... I think. I was lying there and... and—" She gasped and bent, clutching her side in pain. "I was laying there," she ground out through clenched teeth. The screams of the wounded and dying filled her ears, and she wondered if one was her own? "I couldn't move... The flames were coming closer and closer—"

The rest was lost in a flood of tears.

Nathan slipped his arm around her shoulders and rocked as she sobbed. "S'all right, darling. S'all right. You didn't burn; neither of us did."

The pain in Cate's side eased. She groped her side in search of the wound, a bandage, something should have been there.

Nothing.

Confusion and panic made the search grow more frantic; Nathan's hand stopped her. He goaded her into taking a few more sips of arrack, observing her closely, until she was sufficiently composed.

Head bent, he fondled the flask. "You were dying before me eyes. So I did the only thing I could: I took us over the side, to Calypso, or whatever in the hell name out of the half-dozen or so she might answer to."

He looked quickly for Cate's reaction, the flask poised should it be needed. Clutching the fabric of her skirts, she closed her eyes and stiffly nodded. Ages ago—or so it seemed— Nathan told her of a family curse, generations old.

"But, you were always trying to avoid her, Calypso, that is," Cate qualified, straining to follow.

Shifting self-consciously, Nathan's mouth quirked. "Aye, but now I needed her help."

Cate looked back toward where the camp laid, invisible beyond the rocks. "They keep staring like someone died."

"Many did, including us... for a while," he went on quickly at seeing her blench.

It was all so confusing. The submerged bottle bobbed to the surface, allowing visions to flash past. Many were crystalline, too clear to deny. And yet, others were vague, as if she had stumbled into someone else's nightmare.

"I remember... bits..." she began unsteadily. "Somewhere... wet and cold and black...? Is that what... was I... we... dead?" She shivered. The cold had been no flight of imagination; it had been of the bone-soaking sort. That and the mortal loneliness, the kind which scarred the soul.

It hadn't been the Netherworld as described by lore and scripture. It hadn't been fire and heat, but wet and cold, and eternal, pressing darkness. Nathan had once claimed the tortures of Hell weren't universal, but custom-tailored, plucked from one's own mind. She shuddered, not from cold, but from the thorough effectiveness of whoever created hers.

A sinking sensation hit Cate, of being dragged back down and down, back into the void from which she had just escaped, back into the pressing cold and penetrating emptiness —

With a startled shriek, she jerked to catch herself. Like the rock that he was, Nathan caught and steadied her. She thrust out a hand, and he shoved the flask into it. She took a drink, and then another.

"Where...?" she began and gulped. "Where did she take us?"

Nathan's lip curled in disgust. "I never knew what to call it: cave, grotto, lair, den..."

Cate nodded. The one conformity with the conventional version of Hell had been the sense of someone, not a person so much as a being, holding court.

"I'd considered it existed only in me mind, but if you've seen it..." His voice trailed off, resigned.

Cate leaned back and saw Nathan fully for the first time. He was a shadow of himself. Drawn and haggard, shoulders sagging, the several days' growth of beard matched the dark smudges under his eyes. Hatless, barefoot, shirttail hanging, he was no longer the pirate she knew. The lack of weapons was a shock, for rarely did he go about without at least a pistol and sword, a knife in his boot... something! She shifted uneasily and glanced about the small clearing, realizing with considerable disquiet how much she had come to depend on him and those weapons for her safety.

It wasn't just weariness which rimmed his eyes with red...

That imaginary bottle bobbed to the surface again, allowing a glimpse of the night before: the glow of the campfire's coals, the beach quiet, she lay on her side in the arms of someone who was silently weeping. Whether tears of joy or sorrow she'd never know, for the bottle sank and she was dragged back down into the sea of oblivion...

In those red-rimmed eyes, Cate caught her own reflection: wild-haired and haggish; gaunt and half-bent, a sight sure to scare small children. Raising a hand to smooth her hair, she noticed something else...

"A bell is gone!" She kept thinking there was something different, but couldn't put enough lucid thoughts together to figure out what. The two silver bits in his mustache, smaller versions of those in his hair, were as much a part of him as the gold in his teeth. Now, there was only one.

Nathan lurched to his feet. He retreated several steps, his jaw working in sudden fury. "The conniving shrew went back on her word."

"But I don't follow," she said, shivering in the sudden absence of his body heat.

He set to pacing, his bare feet pounding the sand. "After the mutiny and... everything," he began, with a generalizing wave of his hand, "I was in deep negotiations for me life and for me ship. I played Old Harry in the doing, but she finally agreed: she was to give two persons life, as she had done for me. Two lives, at my pleasure."

Cate closed her eyes, trying to recall what he had told her about the curse. So many of the finer points were lost, but the crux of it was Calypso had thought to have had Nathan in her possession, but he had wheedled his way out, exchanging the immortality she had bestowed upon him for the life of his ship. Nathan often claimed he'd given his soul for his ship, that she was a part of him, but Cate had dismissed it as merely his turn-of-the-tongue, another figurative reference, as people — sailors, most particularly — were wont to do.

Still, Cate kept her eyes closed for a while longer, not in weariness or befuddlement, but to revel in the glorious sound of Nathan's voice. It was a marvel at how anything so ragged — damaged by violence in his youth — could be such a comfort and touch her in so many ways. Wherever they had been in that mysterious interim, loneliness had been the greatest terror. She had searched that loneliness to find not just any living soul, but one in particular, her salvation depending on it.

Cate opened her eyes to find that salvation staring down at

her, concern crumpling his brow. "But how...? I mean, why did you think to... make her promise such a thing?"

Nathan looked away. "Seemed a good idea at the time, that there might be someone in me life worth saving. I had no notion of who or what or when. For the most part, at the time, I was just looking for ways to make her life miserable." The last was added with a helpless rise and fall of his shoulders.

He looked up, eyes brimming with wetness. "And thank the gods for it. You were dying before me, and not a damned thing to be done for it. I slashed me arm," he said, extending it to display the slit sleeve, "because she could always smell my blood like a damned shark. I knew she would reach us *long* before Davy Jones might."

Nathan slumped on the log next to her. The hand on his leg balled into a fist, the cords rigid under the skin. "The treacherous, two-faced, double-tongued dowdy went back on her word. She wouldn't raise a hand to you until I served her."

"But she couldn't touch you. The tattoos protected you." On that point, Cate was clear.

"More like I couldn't touch her," he amended, wryly. "But the effect was the same: the very thing which had protected me all these years was now me greatest curse."

His gaze settled on his hands on his thighs. Both wrists were bound by linen strips, similar ones at his ankles and neck. The bottle to bobbed to the surface again: the night before, she had awoken to see Nathan sitting under the neighboring dodger, as Millbridge bandaged his middle.

"Aye, she couldn't touch me," Nathan said. "The only way to do what needed done was to be rid of the damned things, and meself the only one to do it."

The sound of his voice jerked Cate back to the present. The arrack balled into a sickening lump in her stomach. Nathan sat very still as she ventured a trembling finger and lifted the linen at his wrist. Where the pattern had once laid was now a scabbed groove.

"You mean, you cut away —?" Her mouth moved, but words failed. "My god...

Nathan!" Tears welling, she threw her arms around him. "It had to have hurt... horribly!"

"None so bad. Well, aye, it stung a bit," Nathan amended at her disbelieving choke. "Shh... S'all right, darling," he cooed as she sobbed. "I did what I must to save you. T'was as simple as that. T'was none so bad: a flick of the knife and, Bob's your uncle, it was done. Saltwater cauterizes wonderfully."

Cate waved a hand for him to stop. Her imagination was

doing a very fine job of painting the self-mutilation picture: slicing at his body, peeling away his own skin, as if dressing a rabbit.

"I did it. There was naught else to be done, and I did it." His words were clearly meant to appease, but failed in every way.

Finally, Cate quieted. Smiling indulgently, Nathan found her hand and took it in his, fingering the dangling bits of her bracelet. "With these, she couldn't lay a finger, or fin, or whatever in the hell she had at the time," he finished, with an irritated grimace.

Realization building, Cate looked down at her bracelet in horror, her hand flying up to her necklace. "You mean you've been preparing for this, *all this* time!?"

"Always, darling. Not this specifically, but against whatever the hell might come to pass," he announced proudly.

Nathan sobered, earnestly searching her face. "When you first came, I fancied you were from her, a gift or treachery, or herself, for that matter. Then there came the point when I didn't care. I wanted you and damn the consequences; if I was to live in eternal servitude, at least it would be with you."

He fondled the necklace's decorative knot resting at the hollow of her throat. "When you allowed me to put this 'round your neck, I knew then it was you and only you. It would have burned like a cross on a witch, else."

"But then, how did...? You expect her to... save me... if she couldn't touch me?" Cate sniffed, dashing her face dry.

"Those kept her from taking you, and doing God knows what, using you against me.

Saving you was just a... a... favor."

Cate nodded, as if she understood. She didn't. The steadying effect of the arrack apparently had met its limits. What solid footing she had attained was dissolving fast. Again, visions tumbled through her mind, like an overturned barrel of cats. The most persistent was of a man and woman, deep in the throes of lovemaking.

She seized the flask from between them and took another drink, swallowing several times before it went down. "I remember seeing you... lying with me, but I was watching from a corner of the room — a cave or whatever —"

Stiffening, Nathan plucked absently at the bandage at his wrist. "She came to me as you," he said quietly. Clamping his lower lip between his teeth, he slowly shook his head. "God help me, I thought at first the cunning she-devil had relented and agreed to honor our bargain, and had allowed you to live. But then, I realized —"

Cursing, he rose and resumed his agitated path.

"She can imitate what can be seen, but she has no notion of what it is to feel, what makes you... you," he added, stopping to gaze affectionately down at Cate. "You're like a hot coal when I take you in me arms, quivering with want."

Nathan leaned, bringing his nose near Cate's neck. "She couldn't duplicate your sweet scent, nor the one when you've gone slick with want. And your skin ripples when I touch you." He ran his finger along her arm, smiling faintly at the response. "You make that little sound when I enter you and I know I'm pleasing you."

His hand dropped away. He stood back, head bent, droplets of moisture glistening on the dark crown. "Damnation and seize my soul, the vindictive jade made me do it before you."

Nathan made several more animated passes then drew to a halt and stared off. "It was damned odd, I'll say that," he said, more to himself. "You under me and then, at the same time, to look up and find you staring back with those dead eyes."

There was the odd question of how someone dead might be watching, but with everything so far beyond logic, it seemed a silly point.

"And don't go imagining grand raptures," he said narrowly, stabbing a finger at her.

"It was no lovemaking."

Cate ducked her head. He knew her too well. The mere thought of any woman so much as sharing his company caused her to see through a scarlet veil.

"Entering her was like swiving a cold fish. If I was compelled to name a passion at that moment, it would have been unmitigated fury and the desire to wring that miserable neck. The only thing stopping me was to do so would have been too much like strangling you," he added, looking thoroughly wretched.

Nathan ran a shaky hand down his face and sighed. "Plague and perish me, she's a crafty wench, I'll give her that. It was like I was pumping life into you: the harder I served her, the more alive you became."

He shook himself from the trance he had fallen into and declared flatly "I finished me business and it was done."

Cate pressed a hand to her stomach, ill with remorse, for she couldn't help but feel responsible.

If only —

She gouged her nails into her palms, chastising herself with the pain. The vision of him in the act was sharp enough that she could also see his body eloquent with loathing and disgust. The violence in every thrust was disquieting, for he had always been such a gentle lover. Seeing him being so brutish was a shock, for it was like watching him being that way with to her.

Still and all, jealousy prevailed. She was as green with it as the tuft of coarse grass growing at her feet. Her face heated with shame. She'd been abused by men, knew perfectly well the only emotion involved in rape was cold hatred... and yet, she couldn't help but wonder...?

Brightening, Nathan shook his head, making the bells in his hair jingle and declared victoriously "Only seventeen, now!"

Cate nodded and forced a smile, for that was what seemed expected.

"I cut one off and threw it at her, wishing she might choke on it," he said in sudden vehemence. "T'was all I could do to keep from shoving it down her slimy throat."

Exhaustion and bewilderment combined made Cate teary. Nathan crouched before her, found her hand and grasped it. "I vowed I would go with no other women, Kittie, and I haven't, I swear. She doesn't count as a woman, because she's not one, no matter what efforts. She's a calculating, false-tongued ogress —"

"Who's now quite probably carrying your child," she said bitterly. *The one I'll never have.*

Her dart found its target; Nathan sat back on his heels. "'Tis no offspring o' mine.

Any product of this joining won't be recognizable. It's not as if I have to worry about him popping up to sign on to ship with me," he added sourly.

Cate jerked her hands away and tucked them into her armpits. Being faced with the fruit of his joining with another was a nightmare she had already lived. The lad — his mother a whore, by all accounts and recollections — hadn't exactly "popped up," but he had wound up aboard the *Ciara Morganse.*

"I'm not immortal now, am I?" Cate asked warily.

Nathan jerked at both the sudden change of subject and the notion itself. "Nay, at least I don't think so." He considered, and then shook his head. "She didn't represent as much."

He looked up, the coffee-colored eyes softening with affection. "Don't I wish seeing you safe were that simple."

Cate considered she wasn't near so sanguine.

"Creswicke *is* dead... isn't he?" The condition of death suddenly seemed so very temporary. Hell, if she and Nathan could rise from the dead who was to say Creswicke mightn't do the same? Seeing his dead body would have served nicely, for she could have then spit on it.

Nathan seized the flask and raised it in a toast. "As dead as the proverbial doornail."

Sobering, he sought her hand and laced his fingers through hers, the soft calluses on his palms abrading hers. "His High-Arsedness is no worry to either of us. He's dead, his ship exploded, his parts scattered to all points of the compass. The only hazard he could offer now might be to the fishes choking on what bits remain." His mouth twitched with a smile at the thought.

Cate's disbelief must have shown, for Nathan rose and turned away. The fog surrendered, and the sun broke free, its rays streaming strong and hot down into their nook.

The whole thing was so confusing. A part of her insisted this was all some drink or fever-induced dream. Soon she would wake to Nathan lying next to her in bed, in that little shack. Of one thing she was sure: she needed him, now more than ever.

She rose unsteadily, her arms at her sides, too heavy to lift. "Hold me... please?"

Nathan turned, swallowed hard and said hoarsely. "I thought you'd never ask."

He slipped his arms about her, tentatively at first, as if fearing she might shatter or recoil. Seeing neither was to happen, his embrace tightened, and they clung to each other, his body quaking as hard as hers.

"Please don't leave me, please! I know it sounds childish and weak," she choked.

"Nothing weak about you, darling."

His grasp softened to one cradling a delicate egg. "Give yourself time, darling. I know it's a shock. T'was months before I could finally put it behind me. No worries," he said at feeling her slump at that daunting thought. "I'm here. You shan't do this alone."

There in his arms, she was acutely aware of beating hearts, his heart echoing in hers to the perfection of his blood flowing to nurture her.

"This is what I needed most of all," she sighed, molding herself to him.

She felt him smile against her neck. He stood back and touched a finger to her chin, bringing her face up. The coffee-colored eyes inches away found hers and held them as he smoothed her hair back from her face, tucking it behind an ear. "'Tis what I needed, too, more than 'tis decent to admit."

Nathan found Cate's hand between them and laced his fingers through hers. "Our lives are entwined; neither of us can exist apart again."

At length, Nathan held her back. "You smell like the bottom, and I can still smell her on me, most particularly in some areas as more than others," he sniffed, looking disdainfully down at himself.

In the back of her mind, she had been aware of an odd, noxious smell rising from both of them, a combination of mud, seaweed, carrion and filth. Her clothes were stiff and chafing with salt, and sand seemed to sift out at every step.

"This island doesn't boast much, but it does have something of an oasis at the stream's headwaters. Come," he said, putting out his hand.

"It's a bit of a climb," he added, angling his head inland. "Are you up to it?" The narrowing of one eye and the lilt in his voice suggested he was dubious on the point.

Cate took Nathan's hand. Muddle-headed she might be, but one thought was clear: with him, she could go anywhere.

As they walked, Cate got a firmer fix on her whereabouts. She recalled seeing the island proper from across Ransom Passage. Her impression of a pile of broken tombstones discarded by giants grew stronger as they moved among them. The tumbled slabs, most higher than a man's head, put her to mind of the Highlands: dark and ancient-looking, their surface mottled with lichens and bird droppings. The climb of which Nathan had warned wasn't so much a matter of slope, but navigating over and around those rocks. They picked their way along, Nathan often pausing to hand her over one, and then another. His slow advance was ostensibly for her benefit, but she had the impression he benefited as well, for there was none of his usual huffing or haranguing about her laggardliness. Patently patient he was, so very, very uncustomarily and disquietingly, patient.

Nathan led her between two stones, standing like solemn towering sentries, into a narrow canyon-like space. The shaded regions of the steep walls and floor were carpeted with moss, tiny ferns and orchids clinging to the ledges and fissures. They picked their way up a path, the rustling sound of water announcing the presence of a waterfall long before it was seen. The water sheeted over a domed rock like a veil over a maid's head, forming a pool at its foot.

"How do you keep finding these places?" she asked in awe. In the few months she had known him, Nathan had taken her to several such watery havens.

Already busy with undoing her laces, Nathan glanced to see if she were trying him on. Finding only honest curiosity, he shrugged. "Any captain worth his salt knows every drop of freshwater and splinter of wood within at least a hundred leagues, in any direction."

As he helped her slip off her stays, she suddenly felt like a blushing maid. There was no reason for such shyness. Granted, her shift was thin, but it still covered her. In spite of that, every bit of will was called upon to keep from crossing her arms over herself. Typical Nathan, he missed little. One brow arched at her struggle, but he said nothing... *again*.

So damnedably, insufferably patient.

A part of her reticence to undress was the nagging voice which, since her wakening, had pointed out the impossible: she was up and about, unharmed. So much was muddled, but the memory of lying on the *Gosport's* deck, Creswicke driving his sword into her gut, was crystalline clear. By rights, with such a wound, she should have been, if not dead, then bed-ridden. Instead, she was moving about, unscathed.

More which made no sense.

Closing her eyes, she steeled herself and searched her side, more determinedly. Her probing fingers followed the rent through the layers of fabric, her entire being twitching when she ultimately touched her own skin. No wound, nor scar, not even a lingering sore spot. Nothing but skin, smooth and perfect.

Nathan drew the searching hand away and kissed the knuckles. Mouth quirking, he took a half-step back and pulled his shirt off. His body was as familiar as her own, including the multitude of scars. Two glared out like strangers at a family dinner: one, athwart his forearm; the second on his side, exactly where Creswicke had speared her.

"Nathan!"

She lunged forward, but he artfully dodged her searching efforts, holding her away at arm's length. "'Tis fine."

"It's healed?" she asked, in disbelief. By his own word, it had only been a few days since the battle. It couldn't possibly be healed.

"Aye," he said casually, releasing her when she no longer resisted. "Not sure how, nor do I care. 'Tis done."

"But it must... it had to have hurt," she countered, straining to comprehend. "Some... for a bit."

So much of what happened on the *Gosport* was confused or just blank, and yet two things were starkly clear: lying skewered to its deck like a fish, and Nathan kneeling over her, his face contorted with grief. At the time, she had worried for him, wondering who so near and dear to him might be dying? That vision then dissolved into naught but cold and dark, drifting in an eternal emptiness.

Cate shivered, and not from the temperature of the day.

The act of twisting to fling his shirt atop her stays revealed a scar on Nathan's back, direct in line with the one in front, where Creswicke's sword made its exit.

First the tattoos, and now this. There seemed no end to his suffering on her account.

Nathan saw her distress and smiled encouragingly. "The opportunity presented itself and so I did," he said simply. "My reward was to see your pain gone. T'was no matter," he went on, at seeing her tear up.

He made a broad gesture at himself and the network of scars there. Lash, blade and splinter had made its mark. "I'll confess to being a vain man, but none so much as to mourn one more among the many."

He laid a hand on the back of her shoulder and the scar there, the remnants of a battle on a Scottish moor. "I would have taken them all for you, that I could. Especially that one," he added, nodding at her bandaged forearm, "but the practicing Xanthippe claimed it was too old and beyond her powers. She represented it was put there by an evil she couldn't undo."

He looked away and added quietly, "For once, I think the shrew was being honest."

Cate toyed with the linen binding on her arm. A thickened slab of a brand lay underneath, put there by Lord Creswicke. That bit of scarred skin was like a hundredweight on her arm. She could do that, now: feel it; acknowledge it. Looking at it directly, however, was quite another thing. Not yet. A slip of a knife and the thing could be gone, and she had considered doing that very thing. She and Nathan, however, were of much the same mind on that point: to cut the thing away somehow made Creswicke the victor. The malicious bastard's hand might still be on them, but their living in spite of him was their victory.

"I can't look at you without seeing the price you've paid for being with me." Tears thickened Cate's voice. The scar on Nathan's cheek, another on his shoulder blade, were all markers of the price he paid in rescuing her from Creswicke's clutches. Now, his arm, back and side showed more expense on her account. "It's a debt I can never—"

Nathan ducked his head to find her eyes. "Ah, but you can, darling. Live, and allow me to watch. 'Tis all I ask."

His smile, so warm with affection, caused her to attempt to do the same.

"You said... once... that..." Dashing the wetness from her cheeks, she faltered. The night he had told her of the curse so much had been said, there was a strong possibility she had confused, overlooked or mistaken some of the finer points.

"You said there were... consequences," she finally managed delicately.

According to the legend, giving Calypso a child meant the loss of one's virility. "I'd be no more use than a eunuch to you" Nathan had explained. He had given Calypso his seed; the question was what else the sea witch might have taken.

"I'm whole," Nathan announced. His breeches, already hanging low, were easily slipped down over his haunches. He straightened and held his arms out in display. He was, indeed, whole, his genitals dusky amid the black thicket of hair.

Realizing then than she had been holding her breath, Cate breathed a private sigh of relief.

"As for the consequences..." Nathan mused, rolling the word in his mouth. He looked down to regard himself and then shrugged. "I would do it all the same and ten times over, if it were to have the same result."

Nathan's outstretched hand cut short any further ponderings on her part. "Come, darling. Let us see what miracles the waters of Mother Earth might provide."

His warm solid grip and the feel of living flesh were like another brush of the lodestone on a compass' needle.

The pool at the foot of the falls was roughly half the size of the *Morganse's* afterdeck, small by many standards, but large enough to accommodate two. At its deepest, the water was but mid-thigh, but it was a vast improvement over the basin and bucket, to which her daily ablutions were usually confined. A slightly sulfurous smell rose as they waded in, but it was fresh not salt, warm enough not to be shocking, and cool enough to be refreshing, with enough sand underfoot to provide a solid footing. Nathan led her around to under the falls' arching spray and together they stood, allowing the water to pour over them.

It was glorious!

When they were as sodden as two sponges, they moved to the shallows. There, they scooped sand from the bottom and scrubbed, Nathan washing his privates with a vigor which bordered on self-abuse. Her body glowing, Cate lay back in the water and floated, her hair swirling about her shoulders like wisps of kelp. Treading water, she admired the curve of muscle and bone in Nathan's back and legs as he rinsed their clothes. High on his chest, like a bull's-eye, lay the circular divot of being shot, it twin on his back, the edges blackened with powder from the pistol being fired at very close range. His body was scarred, but the worst ones were those which didn't show, those inflicted by treachery and betrayal. Those of the heart ran far deeper and more permanent than those of the body.

Once the clothing was spread out to dry, Nathan dove back in. Skimming the pool's bottom, his head popped up next to Cate, sleek and dark as an otter. She rolled into his arms and they remained thus for a good while, basking in the glory of holding and being held. Resting her head against his, she closed her eyes as he rhythmically stroked her back and soaked in his nearness. She did so whenever the opportunity presented itself, like a squirrel collecting nuts for the winter, building up a storehouse of memories against the day when he was gone. Admittedly, that dark day didn't seem as imminent as before. Now, a stronger connection existed, like the silk thread of a spider's web: thin, strong, but not indestructible.

For now, they were together.

Nothing else mattered.

Wrinkled and covered in gooseflesh, Cate and Nathan emerged from the pool fresh and as renewed with life as nymphs. The moss might have been softer, but the sun's heat was more enticing, and so they lay out on a bare stone ledge and basked like old cats before a fire. Cate extended her arms and stretched until her joints popped, bringing as much of her body into contact with the sun-warmed rock as possible. At that point, she wondered why she had earlier questioned her rightful place: land was most definitely where she belonged.

Nathan lounged next to her as he often did in their bunk: ankles crossed, one hand behind his head. A mariner's life had provided him the ability to sleep anywhere, on any surface. Oak deck or granite, he laid as easy as if it were a feather tick. It couldn't go unnoticed that his lids were lowered, but not entirely closed, wishing to appear as though he slept, but not able to entirely surrender.

The waterfall was quiet, by most standards, but it made enough noise, to block out an entire world, including the nearly three hundred men just over the hill. The random shrill of a sea gull and the low thump of waves on a distant reef was the only other intrusions on their haven. Such seclusion was to be treasured. Living aboard meant having to share Nathan with the ship and his crew. Even in their bunk, they had to be ever-mindful of listening ears and prepared for the preemptive cough of word of an emergency which demanded the Cap'n's attention.

"They'll be worried for us." Even uttered in a half-whisper, her words seemed to shatter the quietude.

Lids still lowered, Nathan's shoulder jerked. "Aye, they might, as soon as they get their noses out o' their grog long enough to notice we're gone, the dung-souled, grass - combing louts."

Cate followed Nathan's example and closed her eyes. Figuratively and literally, they had sloughed off not just salt, rotting kelp and sea bottom in the pool, but everything which had happened.

It was time to heal.

Alas, if it were only that simple.

The greatest obstacle was one nagging thought: what if...? What if she couldn't put this behind her as Nathan clearly expected? Throughout life, she had suffered unspeakable damage at the hands of others and had recovered — barely — and put it all behind her — barely. What if this most recent event was the proverbial straw from which the camel might collapse?

Her prime worry rose from the fact that she didn't feel herself. Her surroundings, her own being, were foreign, as if she were residing in someone else's skin. She felt shattered, like a tattered stocking unraveling; the most well-intended handling — as in trying to reassemble it into something functional — threatening further damage. A looking glass was what she needed. That had been her means before: a shard scavenged from a rubbish heap into which she checked daily, to see if anyone looked back. Gaunt and haunted, a half - starved ghost had peered back then. What would she find now? There were no mirrors; the pool's water had been too disturbed to offer any solid impressions. Her only guide was those around her: Nathan, Pryce, Thomas, Kirkland, and the crew. All had claimed to recognize her, but there was no denying that many a face had been strained.

Cate brought her hand up, and probed the curves and planes of her face — cheek, nose, mouth, brow — in search of what might be familiar.

"You're fidgeting like a f'c'stlejack on the Sabbath," Nathan observed mildly.

She jerked her hand away, pressing her palm to the rock under her. "I don't know how to do this," she huffed. "How does one go about recovering from death?" There were no papers or books, no sermons at church, or advice from elders or mentors to consult. "Death isn't some stone in the road one trips over and then presses on. You managed before," she added at his silence. "How does one do it?"

More silence, to the point she thought he mightn't answer.

"Live," Nathan finally said. "Laugh, cry—a lot," he added, at opening his eyes to see the wetness on her cheeks.

His hand found hers between them, his fingers lacing and re-lacing through hers. Finally, he shrugged. "Put one foot before the other, darling," he said quietly. "And soon, before you know it, you're back among the living."

His grasp still firm on her hand, Nathan resumed his feigned rest, the lashes not quite touching his cheeks. Still, it was a not-so-subtle hint, and Cate composed herself to do the same.

"How the hell did you come to be on that ship?"

Cate jerked and turned her head, but found Nathan unmoved, eyes still closed.

"I went to great lengths to see you safe," he went on, conversationally, "and—"

"I'm sorry!" she cried. She curled into a defensive ball and burst into tears.

Nathan rolled to hook an arm over her, comforting as she sobbed.

"Sorry for what?" he prompted when she finally quieted.

Sniffing, she gaped at him. The village idiot would have known what she meant. "For everything!"

Grief and regret came pouring out. Ships damaged and sank, men injured and killed, all because of her stupidity. "It was my foolishness. When I saw the ships jammed up at the reef, I thought they were coming to attack and I panicked."

Nathan chuckled ruefully, his arm tightening around her. "They were 'jammed up' because the *Stately* was aground, blocking the passage. No one was getting through."

"I know that... *now*," she said bleakly. "But at the time, I could think of nothing but warning Thomas... and somehow, you, to stop you from sailing right into the middle of it." The words were coming faster and faster. "So I ran back or tried to. I got all turned around and ran into one of Creswicke's landing parties."

With no cloth handy, Nathan palmed the wetness from her cheek.

"If there was any blame, it's on me, darling. 'Twas my fault you were in the middle of all that. I dragged you into it, instead of seeing you safe."

She stared, his image distorted by tears, and wondered where he fancied that might be.

"*Anywhere!*" he blurted at her silent question. "Hell, the next continent, if need be," he went on with a frustrated swipe.

In a clatter of bells, Nathan sat back on his haunches, his fists working on his thighs. "I should have been more careful.

Instead, I exposed you to worse than Dante's inner circle. Never again," he said vehemently, his balled fists going white. "*Never again.*"

The chill of the depths returned, and Cate shivered. If the place he had taken her had been one of Dante's circles, then loneliness was, indeed, an element of Hell. Mortal and soul-soaking it had been; not the kind which came with loss, but the eternal kind, of never having known love or being loved.

Nathan twisted around, glaring. "Did His High-Arsedness lay hands on you? Say he did, and I swear—"

She looked away. "No" came out before she was sure it was the suitable answer. "What if he did?" bubbled up, but she bit it back. Nathan's vow was reassuring, but the bald truth rendered it an empty threat: the man was dead. Besides, no amount of revenge ever undid a wrong.

But had Creswicke touched her? Harmed her... the last time, that is?

Cate rubbed her brow furiously, trying to recall. Visions rose and fell with that bottle again, not in a seamless flow, but jerking forward and back, disjointed and nonsensical. A fogged image formed of sitting in the *Gosport's* Great Cabin materialized, Creswicke's slight figure before her, remarkably disheveled for one usually so impeccable. Emotions were the clearest memory: terror, shock, disgust and an ill-feeling in her gut. That all dissolved with the joy of seeing the *Morganse* through the stern window.

Suddenly, she was being shaken, Nathan shouting "Kittie!"

"What!?"

Clasping her head between his hands, he searched her face. "You drifted off."

Once assured that she was well, he sat back but still eyed her, his fingers drumming on his leg.

"You flatter yourself, darling, to think this all—*any* of it was your fault. Events were set into motion long, long ago. It would have come to pass even if you had been the obedient lamb and followed your keepers."

He cut another sideways glance, the corner of his mouth twitching with the need to smile. "Obedience, however, has never been your strength."

Running a hand along the curve of his mustache, he sighed, suddenly weary. "Aye, a few things might have gone slightly different in the end, but it was an inevitability brewing, since—" He caught himself and coughed.

Cate averted her gaze to allow him as much privacy as one might enjoy sitting naked on a rock.

Nathan rarely spoke of what happened between him and Creswicke. Thomas had allowed a little more, leaving her imagination to fill in the rest. Even with that, there were vast holes. She never pressed either man further; her personal struggle to keep ghosts at bay left her reluctant to stir up those of others. All versions, however, agreed that Nathan and Creswicke's animosity went back a pair of decades. The East India Trading Company had put them in the same circle: Nathan, on the up-and-coming captain's list; Creswicke Senior, a Company official. Handsome and brash, Nathan had to have been a competitor for all involved, including Creswicke, the Younger, seeking to shine in Creswicke, the Older's eye. A sequence of wrongs, misdeeds and comeuppances had culminated in making Nathan and young Creswicke prime enemies.

The ultimate wrong, however, had been when, Creswicke, the Younger, as the Governor of the newly chartered Royal West Indies Mercantile Company and Nathan's employer, had contrived to have Nathan arrested on a host of false charges, all intended to destroy him, both personally and professionally. The final blow was false testimony and a bill of sale which declared Nathan the son of one of Creswicke's slaves, which by law made him Creswicke's property. A brand on his palm sealed Nathan's fate and ultimately sent him into piracy.

"Having you with me only served to put you in the middle. It shan't happen again. Upon me honor, it shan't happen again."

Nathan's cold conviction made Cate shudder. He frowned at seeing it. "You're safe, darling. He's gone. No one can—"

Cate found his hand where it rested on his thigh and squeezed. Capable, solid, strong, softly callused, it was a sailor's hand. Scarred and weathered, by sea and battle, they were the hands which held her life, the hands which held her heart.

Nathan's kissed her knuckles. Clutching her hand, his dark head bent, he traced and retraced the shapes with his thumbs. "We're joined now, Kittie. I'll always know your sorrow; you'll always know me joy or pain."

His words would have been ever so much more assuring if his conviction hadn't been so diluted by trying to convince himself. She smiled, nonetheless. He had seen her through an inner circle of Hell. She could endure anything, so long as he was with her.

"You need your rest," he announced and laid back, making a great show of getting comfortable once more. "You need the sun at your face and the earth at your back."

It seemed an unusual sentiment for a man of the sea, but Cate lacked the wherewithal to point that out. Besides, it was a struggle to find anything "usual" about any of this.

"You're the one who needs to sleep," she observed.

Nathan cut his eyes sideways and then away. He smiled, one tightened by discovery. "I'm afraid to close me eyes. Afraid to stop moving, for that matter; afraid of where I'll wake up."

He brusqued his face with his hands, the several day growth of beard rasping on his palms. "T'was the same before."

Nathan had told her a bit about the tribulations he faced upon his return from death. He had bedded women by the score, in need of a warm body next to him, but even more to prove that he lived. She couldn't reproach him for any of it, for she was feeling much the same.

Rest. Reprieve. Peace. Those were what she needed, the man lying next to her necessarily involved in all three.

"I'll sleep when you do," he urged, concern softening his edge.

Cate wriggled sideways, until she lay next to him, her head pillowed on his shoulder. She pushed aside a braid and kissed the sun-burned throat above the bandage and then settled. Nathan rolled and fitted himself behind her, as he always did in their small bunk, the fronts of his thighs against the backs of her legs. He sighed contentedly once... twice... and then quieted.

4: STIRRING THE ASHES OF DESTRUCTION

IN SPITE OF NATHAN'S ARM growing heavy, Cate knew he didn't actually sleep. His breath slowed, but his body was still rigid, either unwilling or unable to relax. Alas, she was reluctant to close her eyes herself. It wasn't so much out of fear, but the lingering sensation of being inside a whirling top when she did. Like a drunk going to bed, she planted the flat of one foot on the rock to keep from being flung over.

A sound interrupted her thoughts. A pounding, similar to the surf on the distant reef, but different. This was deeper, more sporadic... and much, much more immediate.

While Cate was still trying to sort it out, Nathan was already on his feet. "Guns... Great guns."

She blinked at seeing him snatch on his clothes, tossing hers to her at the same time.

"Where?" she asked, stupidly.

"The bay," he said, fastening his breeches. "I'd know *Bone Shakr* and *Bloody Bess* anywhere."

Cate nodded vacantly. Knowing one gun from another was beyond her realm of expertise.

Nathan made a frustrated noise at seeing that, short of sitting up, Cate hadn't moved. In almost a single motion, he urged her to her feet and dropped her shift over her head. Her skirt was next, hastily fastening it.

Nathan was tugging on her stays when they heard sequential thump of a broadside. His head jerked, pleased. "Aye, Thomas is in the mix, now."

"I thought no one would move with that fog." At least, that had been the general conjecture overheard that morning. She remembered clearly, not so much because of the fog, but because it robbed the small armada lying nearby of all threat.

Urging Cate on her way with one hand and fumbling with her laces with the other, Nathan cast a seaman's eye skyward. "There's no explaining fog; rain can lift or drop it like a forecourse. I've seen the sun shine at the maintop and hang so thick you couldn't find the bitts on deck. It could have lifted out there long before here."

Nathan darted away, following the stream toward shore. Laces flapping, Cate ran behind, Nathan pausing now and again to help her over the rocks. At one point, he angled away from the waterway, cutting an overland path.

By then, the guns had settled into the more sporadic rhythm of full battle. With the salvos overlapping, it was difficult to be sure, but Cate thought she could make out two, three, perhaps four batteries hammering away, as if that armada had finally broken through and descended on them. Dread made her legs grow heavy, and she soon became short of breath to the point she had to stop or be ill. Bent, hand on a knee, the other braced at her stomach, she looked up through a tangle of hair into Nathan's impatient glare.

"Go," she wheezed, flailing a hand. "I'll catch up."

"Not bloody likely." He cocked an ear toward the invisible battle. "'Tis fine. I can hear those enterprising coves getting their arses handed back to them."

It was one of the worst attempts at nonchalance ever witnessed. Every fiber of his being twitched with the need to see what was happening.

Cate pushed upright. Nathan frequently claimed his most endearing memory of their first meeting was of her retching on his deck. There was a good chance he was about to be provided with another precious moment. At least this time, there wouldn't be an entire crew watching, she thought grimly. Gulping several draughts of air, she waved him on, heavy-footing it behind him.

With every stride, the rumble of the guns grew louder, the acrid smell of gunpowder sharpened. Rounding a tumble of rocks, the beach opened before them. Her imagination having run wild, Cate expected to see a fleet jamming the bay, a legion of Marines invading the beach. Bent and gasping, the vista was nothing like.

The fog had lifted, the Caribbean sun now brilliant. What might have been a glorious tropical scape of sky, sea and ships sitting peacefully on their anchors, however, was marred by another kind of fog: powder-smoke, enshrouding the ships, four of them, bashing away at each other. In a show of defiance, the *Morganse* and *Lovely* had unfurled their flags. Both with black fields, the *Morganse's* was a skull framed by angel wings and crowned by an askew halo, tears of blood streaming down its cheeks; the *Lovely's* bore a red heart pierced by a cutlass. Many a foe had been known to lose heart and drop their tops'ls, surrendering at the mere sight of those banners, but apparently these two invaders — one bright green, the other black — were made of stiffer stuff. Smaller than the *Morganse*, and even the *Lovely*, Nathan had referred to such vessels as "fore-and-afters:" low and sleek, they were the smaller, handier sort preferred by many a pirate and privateer.

On shore, instead of the imagined legions of Marines, only a small contingency stood on shore, presumably the camp guards. As Cate and Nathan approached, they came to meet them, the drifting smoke wafting about their knees. Their familiar faces were a comfort: Ben, the *Morganse's* child, Millbridge, the ship's ancient, and Kirkland. Two others, Millbridge contemporaries, were Lovelies. All were armed to the teeth.

"You had time to prepare for action?" Nathan shouted over the boom of guns.

"Oh, aye. The lookouts earned their salt today and gave us plenty o' warning," Millbridge said in his creaking voice.

"They looked to take the *Lovely* first," said Ben, leaning to be heard. "But we slipped our cable, and now the bilge-sucking scow is fighting both sides."

Nathan squinted into the smoke. "Who is it?"

"Someone that could read represented *Brazen* was on the sternplate of the one abaft the *Lovely*," Ben piped eagerly.

Nathan nodded vaguely, the name failing to ring a bell. "And the black one?"

Heads shook all around.

"Dunno, never seen 'er," Millbridge finally offered.

"'Tis no wonder," Nathan sighed. "With His High-Arsedness issuing letters-of - marque to every grass-combing lubber what can muster a cod barge, they are popping out like fleas off a drowning dog."

His conjecture no exaggeration. The virtual squadron gathered outside of the reef a few days ago, all drawn by the promise of capturing Captain Nathanael Blackthorne, was proof. Visions of a lurking armada still running strong, Cate craned her head to peer worriedly up and down the beach.

"No worries, the reefs assure no surprise landing parties." Nathan assured her. "As I said, darling, just a couple enterprising coves. They aimed to catch us napping, overwhelm us with their bravery. Rot and perish the infernal bastards, there goes the mizzen gaff!" he cried, more in acrimony than remorse.

She stared at him, uneasy with this sudden uncanny way of

reading her mind. Had she suddenly gone transparent, or had this brush with death left him a diviner or seer? Or were these new powers gifts from Calypso? Any and all explanations were quite disquieting.

"Blood thirsty lot, aren't they?" Nathan observed, mildly. He pointed with his chin toward the red "No Quarter" flags at the attackers' backstay. No man was to be shown mercy; it was to be a fight to the death.

A cackling chuckle broke from Millbridge. "Aye, t'will make slittin' their throats out – of-hand seem a favor."

So caught up with the desire to see, Nathan had inched his way out into the water until he now stood knee-deep, shattered wood, spent wadding and ash floating about his legs.

"Avast, not the water! Seize her up! Get her out of there!" Nathan roared at seeing Cate attempt to follow.

His vehemence startled Cate into immobility. Spurred by their captain's urgency, Millbridge and Kirkland, one to each side, physically lifted her by the elbows and carried her, not just out of the water, but beyond the reach of the most ambitious wave. There they set her down and took up posts like a brace of truculent watchdogs.

"Curse and damnation! They're using grapeshot," Millbridge muttered under his breath.

Low growls of indignation and curses came from all on shore. It meant the cannon balls had been replaced by canisters filled with pellets. The effect was like a gigantic shotgun blast, meant to kill and maim, and as many as possible.

"MacQuarrie's happy as a worm in mud on this one!" Nathan declared, at seeing the black hull take a hit. "Nothing sets up a gunmaster like bang-and-smoke."

Cate smiled at the mental picture of the ship's gunmaster, built much like his precious charges, with the same bellow and bark, pride lighting his face like slow-match as he stalked among his crews.

The thump of the guns reverberating in her chest, Cate's hands worked at her sides. Men would be injured, in need of help. Having lived among them for only a few weeks, the Lovelies she only knew in passing. The *Morganse*, however, was home, her people the closest thing to family. Impotence plagued them both. Nathan called out the damage wrought—forestay snapped, shroud sprung, martingale by the board—his body jerking and twitching, as if he were personally being struck.

"Go!" she finally shouted. "Go to her! I'll be fine," she urged louder, when he didn't move.

Nathan bit back several remarks before he finally uttered a

distracted "Nay. I'm not— It'll be fine. Ah, see! They're hauling their wind, with their tail between their legs and a dozen excuses on their lips."

The black hull had flashed out her jibs and tops'ls, and made for the offing, the *Lovely* giving her a few parting shots as she passed.

"Damn, she's grappled on. They're boarding!"

Nathan whirled around at Ben's cry. The *Brazen* was now tight up against the *Lovely's* side. The roar of great guns was replaced by the crackle of small arms—pistols, muskets and swivel-guns—and the clamor of hand-to-hand combat.

"She's dropped her tops'l!" came a cry from somewhere upshore shortly after. A victorious cheer went up. Finding herself now alone, the *Brazen's* topsail lowered. Whether the sign of surrender was on her own volition, or if some Lovelies had done it for her, was unknown, but the effect was the same: the fight was over.

The *Brazen's* "No Quarter" flag flapped silently in the breeze.

◈

The battle over, the guns silent, the smoke soon tore away, and the sun broke out in its usual Caribbean brilliance.

Silence could, indeed, be deafening... or deadly, or whatever the saying was.

But still no one, no word came ashore.

Cate paced, Nathan doing the same close behind. The assumption which begged to be made was that all was well on the ships. To her untrained eye, Cate judged the *Morganse* and *Lovely* were battered, but not beaten. There was no telltale lean indicating damage below the waterline. Neither was there the smoke of a sailor's greatest horror: fire. Still, the ship's people were her true worry. The waist of a ship wasn't called the "butcher shop" for no reason. It was there the human body could prove to be a shockingly frail thing, flying metal and wood reducing them something resembling slaughtered swine.

"I should be out there," she heard herself say.

"Why?"

She whirled to find an incredulous Nathan, hands on his hips, standing there. "Because... because... they need me," she finally blurted, and then added at his puzzlement "The wounded, they'll need—"

"They'll do," he said, with an irritated swipe. "They're none so bad. See, they're sluicing the decks already. Not enough injured to bother."

Cate wasn't convinced. The pink-tinge of the water jetting from the scuppers indicated someone's blood had been spilled. Who and how much was the worry?

"Wounded will be coming ashore," she pointed out to his apparent failure to comprehend. "We should at least make preparations."

The men standing about gaped as if she intended to lasso the moon. In spite of their reticence, a brusque wave from Nathan set them into action.

Still, no word came.

Worry and pacing wasn't without a toll. A sudden wave of light-headedness struck, Nathan catching Cate as she staggered. A puncheon was brought, she ensconced atop it, Nathan standing over her.

At long last, in almost simultaneous precision, a boat finally pushed off from the *Morganse* and *Lovely's* side. Nathan started up the beach to meet them. Within a few strides, however, he stopped and came back to where Cate still—unwittingly—sat and helped her to her feet.

"I'm not an invalid," she complained, as he ushered her by the arm.

"No, luv, you're as sprightly and fresh as a spring lamb," he said dryly, still urging her along.

Fair and head-and-shoulders above the rest, Thomas was readily spotted among the incoming Lovelies. Cate's concerns for him were appeased at seeing that he was—to some degree, at any rate—erect and mobile. Still, anxiousness unwittingly drew her forward, toward the water. A tightening of Nathan's grip stopped her.

Thomas stepped off the boat's gunwale and waded ashore. A breath Cate hadn't realized she was holding came out in a relieved *whoosh!* The sight of him, flushed with battle and beaming with its success, made her wish to throw her arms around him and give him a victor's welcome. The urge was curbed, not by the sweat and grime, blood spatters or smoke-blackened face, but the blood running down his arm.

Suffering none of her reserve, Thomas bent to sweep her up with his good arm and gave her a solid squeeze.

"Give you joy o' your victory!" Nathan declared. Once Cate was set down, he clapped Thomas on the back hard enough to make him wince.

"The mumping sods miscalculated the *Lovely's* willingness," Thomas announced to the growing audience. Men were pouring out of the boats and upshore.

"And our accuracy." Leaping from the *Morganse's* boat,

Pryce came up, grinning through a smoke-blackened face. The declaration brought a rousing cheer.

Thomas reached around behind himself and shoved a man out. "May I present John Pomphrey, captain of yon fair vessel *Brazen,* our brave enemy." A prompting cuff was delivered to the back of the man's head, knocking his hat off in the process. "Make your obedience, lad, to Captain Nathanael Blackthorne."

Pomphrey jerked at the name. Eyes rounding, he managed something which only the most generous might have called a bow.

"How old are you?" Nathan blurted. Roughly Nathan's height, the *Brazen's* commander was willowy with youth. The only softness was a pair of dull, moss green eyes peering out through the smoke and blood masking his face.

Pomphrey stiffened and raised his chin. "Two and twenty... sir."

"Two and twenty," Nathan grumbled under his breath. "And what the hell was all this foolishness about?" His demand was punctuated by an angry swipe at the bay and the general destruction.

Dashing the sweat from his face, Pomphrey shrugged. "Aimed to cut out the *Morganse.* We figured two against one—"

"And, where the hell did you fancy that brig out there had gone?" barked Nathan, pointing to the *Lovely.*

Pomphrey puzzled on that. "Dunno. Figured she was... gone."

Exasperated hisses broke from the still-growing crowd "And?" Nathan prompted.

The Brazen jerked at being expected to continue. "And... when we looked in and found two, we decided to take the brig, put a prize crew aboard, and all three cut out the *Morganse.* Most would give their right arms for those odds," he added, his thin chest puffing.

"And your mate—"

"Captain Downs."

"Ah, yes, the gallant *Captain* Downs chose to take the *Morganse* on his own?" Nathan pressed, mildly incredulous.

Pomphrey stared at the bay with the bewilderment of failed genius. "Dunno what happened. He was with me until... Perhaps wind or current—"

"Or outright ineptness," Thomas interjected.

Pomphrey nodded, conceding the point. "And then, the *Morganse* opened fire."

"Too bloody right," Pryce put in heatedly. The grey eyes— known to stop a hand dead in his tracks—swiveled on the hapless lad. "As soon as we seen the lay of it, we slipped our cable n' cum in range. We looked to entertain the one, whilst the *Lovely* did fer t'other."

Pryce threw a scornful glare toward the far point where the black hull was last seen. "She'll not be a-goin' far; we hulled 'er fer sure. She was pumpin' hard, forestays separated 'n her bowsprit gone by the board. Those fore-'n-afters can't get far without a heads'l."

"Spoken like a true square-rigger," Nathan mused.

Pryce shrugged, unabashed. "She's limpin' like a whipped pup a-runnin' fer its mama." "And may they rot in hell." Glittering hatred hardened Pomphrey's eyes. "The bastard lost heart and hauled his wind."

"Careful, lad," Nathan said, ominously. "You may come to envy them."

"So...?" Thomas prompted with a jab of the elbow.

"So, I... me and my men," Pomphrey went on, regaining his pride, "decided to stick with the plan: take the brig, and then take the *Morganse*."

"You cheeky, bloated upstart!" Nathan blurted. "You might have the heart, but I'll not hesitate to point out you lack either the brains or wherewithal to select a better consort. This has got to go down in the annals of maritime history as one of the most cod-handed, bungling efforts ever witnessed! Who the bloody hell—? How the hell—? Oh, never mind," he finally ended, throwing his hands up in surrender.

The *Brazen's* hull—green and bright as spring grass—and the name itself was almost more irony than one could bear.

"Very well," Thomas said, cutting Nathan's further expostulations short. "You know the way of it: join up or suffer the consequences. I've a full complement, as does Captain Blackthorne; we're in no dire straits for hands."

Thomas' hand came to rest on the pommel of his sword. "Are you prepared to take the oath and go before-the-mast, *Captain* Pomphrey?"

The image of life at sea brought notions of unfettered freedom. In truth, a sailor's life had more layers than an Austrian torte in the way of chain-of-command, traditions and customs, controlling everything from his duty, to when he ate, slept or was buried. A pirate lived under all of that, plus an added mantel of rules, rites, and etiquette. There was the Ship's Code, drafted by the men themselves and signed, which laid out a way of life specific to that ship. Overlying that was the Brethren Code, with its time-honored practices nearly two centuries old. It was that codex which addressed captured crews. Typical of a sailor's pragmatic approach to everything, the captives were offered two simple choices: join... or die. In all practicality, what other choices were there? A ship laden with prisoners, perhaps doubling its population, taking up space, food and attention was an unworkable prospect.

It seemed simple enough, but to a great many, becoming a pirate was a fate worse than death. During her time aboard the *Morganse*, Cate had witnessed several ships taken and had seen the new faces appear, but whether by design, compulsion or circumstance she had no notion. Intellectually, she knew the rest had been killed, but hadn't actually witnessed the deed. She shifted with the uneasy feeling she was about to do that very thing.

Nathan regarded the lad with a calculating eye. "Some claim let the captain live and find yourself a prime bosun." His countenance darkened. "Whilst others claim let him live and you've gained yourself a prime sea lawyer."

"I'd rather die!" Pomphrey hissed, paling.

"I like your way o' thinking," Nathan declared. Old habits dying hard, he reached for a weapon which wasn't there. Thomas' hand stopped him.

"That can be arranged," Thomas said. "The gods preserve us from compelling a man to go against his principles."

It couldn't have been timed any better: from the *Lovely's* direction came the death cries of several.

"Sounds like some have already made their decision," Thomas declared, fixing an eye on Pomphrey.

The lad was mute, indecision hunching his shoulders.

Thomas straightened, imposing himself. "I'll not doom a man who can't stand by his decision. You have your parole until the rest have chosen. I cannot, however, promise my men's forbearance beyond sundown. You and your men will be the evening entertainment."

Cate looked to see if Thomas was serious. He was... deadly so.

The savageness in his smile made Cate shudder. Blood-spattered, several days' stubble on his jaw, red-rimmed eyes, and bleeding: he looked the right Tartar.

A broad hand came down on Pomphrey's shoulder and squeezed hard enough to make him wince. "Sunset, m'lad, and your life either changes or ends. 'Tis your choice and on your head."

"Kill 'im," Pryce muttered, as Pomphrey was led away. "By that gait, I'd wager he's a weapon in that boot."

"Aye, well, that will just make the rope which hangs him

that mite longer, making the drop that mite sharper," Thomas said, coldly.

"God's my life," Nathan declared. "Someone was harebrained enough to actually hand that puppy a ship?"

Thomas turned slowly to eye him. "You weren't much older with your first command."

"Perhaps not older, but at least the wiser. I knew enough not to throw away meself, me men and me ship!"

Thomas made a skeptical noise. "His crew will be swabbing the blood and guts they spilled on my decks. Then they'll be brought ashore. Nothing to be gained in dirtying the decks again, or obliging everyone to look at their bodies bobbing about, if we put them over the side. You're senior here," he added, grinning at Nathan. "'Tis your venture, hence your right to put a finish to them."

"Ease off! This was *your* venture," Nathan shot back.

True enough. Thomas mightn't have had a hand in the most recent attack, but this grand gathering at Ransom Passage had been his handiwork. Cate pressed a finger to her temple, trying to sort out how long ago it had been since Nathan had told her of that plan and sent her off with Thomas.

A week...? A fortnight...? It could have been a month, for all she could tell.

"Your men won't appreciate being robbed of their justice," Nathan said.

A low clearing of a throat called Thomas a few steps away to confer with some of his men.

"The butcher's bill?" Nathan asked of Pryce.

"Fer them, they'll be hard pressed to man a watch." With a furtive glance toward Cate, the First Mate sobered slightly. "None so bad fer us. Some'll be confined to their hammocks fer a bit, but most is on their feet n' fit fer duty."

Cate wondered how much of this performance was for her benefit, looking to set her mind at ease. It failed miserably, since she was so very familiar with both a battle's aftermath and the sailor's flair for the understatement.

Pryce stepped aside and leaned to say "I've bid those what can bear it to be moved ashore." His booming voice was lowered to a whisper, more gentle and benevolent than she would have thought possible, to the point of scaring her.

With a preemptive cough, Nathan drew Pryce aside, leaving Cate and Thomas, now returned, alone. Seeing Thomas' blood pooling on the sand at his feet spurred her into action. A pluck at the binding on his arm revealed it was actually two, one hastily knotted over another.

"Hurting?" It was an awkward preamble, but she was suddenly tongue-tied. "'Tis nothing," he said, flicking the red from his fingertips.

Thomas moved and swore. By his movement—a mere twist of his torso—she judged it wasn't his arm which pained him: it was his back, an old injury.

"Your arm might be 'nothing', but it needs attending. Come, sit out of the sun," she added at catching sight of his glowing face, which looked to be throbbing.

Thomas allowed himself to be led under a dodger where a table—two puncheons and a couple of planks—had been set up. He sat atop a barrel beside it, putting his face roughly the same level as hers. Closer now, she could see the blotches of scorched skin shining bright through the powder soot.

"You look like a rabbit burned on a spit," she mused. It was difficult to think how close he came to being horribly scarred.

Hanging his head, he grinned. "I've been called several things of late."

Indecision froze Cate: his face was raw; his arm was bleeding.

Thomas ducked his head to break her gaze. "Mayhap it be best to stop the bleeding first, don't you think?" he suggested, delicately.

Face heating, to the point it must have resembled his, Cate set to removing the blood – sodden bandage. Much to her frustration, her fingers proved to be naught but useless clubs. Thomas took the knife from its shoulder scabbard and handed it to her. The blade alone was longer than her hand, and she almost dropped the thing. Under his stern eye, she gripped and re-gripped it. She had tended injury and wounds, swabbed blood and sewn torn flesh since time out of mind. There was no reason for her to be so giddy-headed and queasy now.

Cate closed her eyes and tried to summon her strength. What drove her was the need to be useful and, in a moment of pure honesty, in the hope doing so might bring her nearer to normal. But it was so damned difficult to remember what normal was.

She determinedly slipped the blade's tip under the cloth's edge, only to find her hand shook to the point of being a hazard to both of them. Thomas gently took it from her; a deft flick and the blood-soaked linen fell with a *splat!* at her feet. She looked at the gash running the length of his arm, and then up at him, hard and accusing.

"It's not from today," he said defensively.

"Yes, so I see," she said, probing through the blood. It was somewhat reassuring to see it had been hastily sewn and with sailmaker's thread. Most of the stitches now, however, had been torn, leaving the whole thing to resemble ground sausage meat. "You've been abusing this."

Jaw working, Thomas met her look with an unrepentant one of his own. "Several times, as events demanded."

Cate flinched at the word "events."

Like pulling bodies of his friends out of the water? Like defending his ship whilst those same, apparently ungrateful friends stood on the beach and watched?

"There's something odd about waking up with your arm damned near tore off and no notion of how the hell—Mmmph!" He clamped his lip between his teeth at her touching a particularly sore spot. "All I remember is being knocked out colder than a mackerel when the *Gosport* blew," he managed to squeeze out.

Her hand hovered over his glowing cheek. The fire's heat still seemed to reside there, radiating on her fingertips. "Was this from the explosion, too?"

The lake blue eyes held hers, searching and uncertain. "No," he said quietly. "That was from the fire—"

Cate blinked.

"Aye, the fire—you remember the fire on the *Gosport?*" he prompted gently.

She nodded vaguely. Perhaps... Maybe... A bit... Hadn't Nathan said something about that very thing a bit ago?

Cate drew a deep breath and focused on Thomas' arm. Where to start, was the question? At first glance, removing all the stitches and starting afresh seemed the most prudent. On the other hand, just replacing only the torn meant far less discomfort. Either way, the ragged skin needed to be trimmed; in its current state, it would be like trying to mend a raveling sock.

She clenched her fist into the fabric of her skirt. A far steadier hand would be needed.

The arrival of water, rags and a roll of bandages provided a momentary distraction. Cate mechanically talked her way through the process, wetting a cloth first to clean it. As she worked, she was aware of Nathan under the neighboring dodger, holding audience with Pryce and several others.

Thomas turned his head and bit back another hissing grunt.

"Sorry," she murmured.

Dammit! Why the hell was she so ill at ease around him? A head taller than most, his height and breadth might have put off many, but she was used to that, or rather, should have been. She had been around blood and violence for a large part of her life. Or was she just being faint-of-heart? Either way, it smacked of an inner weakness which was abhorrent.

A hand came down over Cate's, stopping her in mid-motion.

With a choked sob, Thomas' other arm swept her up tight against his chest. "Goddammit to fucking hell, I am glad you're back," he said, his voice thick with emotion.

At length, Thomas let go, roughly swiping his face on his sleeve. Head hanging, he looked sheepishly up from under what remained of his brows. "You must think me the blubbering oaf, gone entirely soft, but... dammit, I'm glad you're here." The last came framed with a broad grin.

Cate was aware of her mouth moving, but wasn't sure if anything actually came out. Apparently, grieving for the loss of friends was no less tribulation than coming back from the dead.

Thomas pressed her knuckles to his lips, ignoring the smeared blood, and fiercely kissed them. The blue eyes, now fluid, came up. "The world just didn't see worth occupying without you... and him on it."

"I never meant—" she began. Tears welled at the thought of the anguish he had been unnecessarily put through. But then, how did one go about apologizing for dying? It wasn't something done by choice, and yet, by Nathan's testimony—the only thing she had to go by—it had been exactly that.

Thomas swallowed hard. "I know."

"I mean, I never wished—"

"I know." His fingers tightening around hers, he turned her hand over to kiss the tender skin of her wrist. He smiled up through the stubbled lashes and said thickly "Dammit to hell, just don't let it happen again."

He straightened and withdrew his grasp. Following his gaze, Cate looked over her shoulder to find Nathan, stopped in mid-conversation, watching from the nearest dodger.

Sniffing—God! Was she crying again?!—Cate picked up the rag and set back to work. Her hands, however, were still like blocks of wood, causing her to drop the cloth. Saying "Sorry," for what had to have been the dozenth time, she curbed an oath and swished it yet again.

As she worked, she glanced up at several Brazen prisoners, looking hang-dog and sullen as they were herded past. "Isn't slaughtering them all a bit ruthless?"

Thomas shrugged impassively. "They meant to take our ship. We're only doing what they aimed to do to us."

A few swipes, and the cloth slipped from her hand again.

"This will have to be sewn again," she announced, toeing the rag aside.

"It's f—" Reality and her severe eye stopped him short. He sighed. Having anything stitched was never pleasant; the prospect of it being done to an already raw and throbbing arm was even less pleasant. He nodded shortly. "Very well, then. Just have done with it. I've a ship to attend."

At some point, Cate's blood box had been delivered. Wiping her hands on her skirts, she opened it and searched. Someone must have been in it, for nothing was where it should be. She shoved things about, bottles, tins and implementa clattering onto the table. At one point, feeling the stare of Nathan and every man on the beach, she paused to knock the hair from her face, for she had forgotten what she was searching for. Finally, with a small exclamation of success, she victoriously held up the tiny scissors for all to see.

It took several tries before Cate could settle her fingers into the handles with any amount of confidence. Thomas' jaw worked with the resolve of not to move, but his skin still twitched, blood welling anew. The scissors' end suddenly becoming two, and she looked off, blinking. A stifled groan drew her attention to the line of wounded filing past. Some half-carried, others leaning on another, a trail of blood in the sand marked their path. Some were familiar faces, some not, but all would need attending.

So much to do.... So much...

Her breath caught. The beach tipped and spun, a whirring buzz filling her ears. An arm caught her — Thomas', she thought dimly — and the rest was lost.

As many times as one might recall losing consciousness, there was often an equal number of instances when they did not.

Cate sputtered and coughed, jerking away from the sulfurous stink.

"Avast and allow her air! Bear a hand, there. Bear a hand, dammit!" came Nathan's voice inches from her ear.

The stink cleared a bit, and Cate felt herself being hauled upright into a circle of faces — it had to have been a score or more — all peering at her, grave and concerned, Millbridge with a smoldering feather in his fist. Her senses regained further to realize she was now in Nathan's lap, Thomas hovering over his shoulder.

"I don't know what happened," she said, in answer to the question on every face. Her vision sharpened, faces merged; the previously supposed score now only a handful. Nathan's brows drew down to the point of nearly touching. "You went pale."
"She should be bled —"
"She needs rum —"
"Pinch her ear —"

"Slap her wrists —"

The suggestions from the onlookers collided overhead; Cate melted under the din. The body under her heaved, and she was being carried. She found herself gazing over Nathan's shoulder at the small parade of worried faces following behind. The sun's glare gave way to the cool shade of a dodger and she was lowered onto what she recognized as their makeshift bed.

Seeing her settled, Nathan sat back on his heels. "When did you last eat?"

"When did you last eat?" she countered testily. How the hell could a grown man sound so much like her mother and at her most disapproving?

Looking like one confronted by an unwelcome truth, Nathan snatched a mug from a bystander's hand. A sloshing sound and the smell of broth rose from it. He cocked a challenging brow and threw back his head, the long muscles in his scarred throat moving as he emptied it.

With an emphatic gasp befitting of one who had just downed an entire firkin, he said "There! Now you."

A similar vessel was eagerly thrust forward by Kirkland; Nathan seized it and shoved it toward her.

"It's whipped egg and ale," he explained as she suspiciously sniffed. "Drink up like a good'n. It will set you up like a Christian." His voice held more hope than confidence.

A part of Cate wished she might guzzle the whole thing, just for the satisfaction of retching it back up all over him. At the moment, however, that exhibition required far more energy than she could muster. She looked down at the mug, her arms suddenly seeming to belong to someone else. Muttering under his breath, Nathan pried the handle from her unmoving fingers and pressed the rim to her mouth, his other hand at the back of her head, as one might guide an infant.

"You have to eat," he chanted as she sipped. "Be no more than a walking skeleton living on scraps, else."

Past haunts flashed through the dark eyes. Nathan rarely spoke of his previous return from Death, but Pryce had told of encountering him shortly thereafter, and described that very thing: a walking skeleton, living on handouts and scraps.

Nathan saw her worry and made a faltering attempt at a smile. "It shan't happen to you. I'm here, darling, to see to it that you are as indulged as the fatted calf."

Kirkland's face thrust forward, anxious with intent.

Cate mutely nodded, gratified, but at a loss as to how to express it. Instead, she dutifully drank. It could have been broth;

it could have been from the bilges, for it would have all tasted the same.

From behind her came Kirkland's sigh of a task achieved. "Soft diet... no beef or mutton... a bit of stewed fish, perhaps..." he muttered as he walked away.

"You're doomed now," Nathan said, with an indulgent roll of his eyes. "It'll be naught but pap for the next fortnight, until you tell him else." The last came with the hopeful air that she might do that very thing.

She didn't.

She couldn't...

Not with the world buzzing around her like a cloud of annoyed bees.

Still, no matter how much anyone wished, there was a limit as to how much her stomach would allow. She rolled away and curled into herself.

Sleep didn't come. Fear of closing her eyes, fear of where she might find herself next, made it impossible.

In its stead, Cate watched the world like a fish in a bowl: a part of the world and yet entirely separate.

Thomas sat under a dodger across the fire, the *Lovely's* lobolly boy now picking up where she had failed, failed miserably. With naught to do but witness her failure, her fists curled against her chest, useless. Thomas' eyes found hers and held them, putting on as encouraging face as one might with a needle being driven through their flesh. The task finally finished, his arm was bandaged, and a sling fashioned. He sat heavily on a log by the fire. A bottle was delivered, and he took several pulls.

The sun dipped, the air cooled and the fires dotting the shore glowed like a strand of amber jewels. The men gathered around, drinking, laughing and hooting, a haze of blue tobacco smoke curling above their heads. Strains of music—fiddle, fife, hornpipe and a drum—floated on the breeze, along with clapping and singing of a f'c'stle jig. A shadow swooped past; Artemis, the *Morganse's* resident barn owl, on her evening hunt. Beatrice roosted atop the ridgepole of a neighboring dodger, preening and settling in for the night. Hermione circled the fires, nosing her shipmates in hopes of her evening grog and tobacco. The giggling pair of Young Ben and Maram, the *Lovely's* de facto cabin boy, darted about in their own rough-housed version of tag.

The shock of she and Nathan's resurrection had given way

to a soaring jubilation of the day's victory. Usually, such a mood was contagious. Indeed, it fought to gain access in Cate, but it knocked at a door to which she had no key. The guilt of not partaking in the celebration found fertile ground, but even that wasn't sufficient to compel her to rise. She had endured hardship, sewn their bodies, eased their ills, listened to their dreams and written letters home. They were the closest thing to family in years, and yet now, these men were as much strangers as her first day aboard.

Nathan stepped into her view. Cate inwardly groaned at seeing a bowl in his hand. This never went well. He had appeared at her side with the regularity of the ship's bells, bearing various conveyances of everything from portable soup, to pap, to more egg-and-ale, heaven help her.

He knelt before her. "What is it?" she asked, peering down into the glutinous grey mass in the bowl.

"Stirabout... I think." Assuming a more positive attitude, he thrust it at her, grinning. "It'll set you up."

With a conspiratorial glance over his shoulder toward the none-so-distant Kirkland, Nathan leaned closer to whisper "Eat up like a good'n and fair commons shan't be far off."

Cate considered it a thin promise, at best. Besides, what was suddenly so damned grand about being "a good'n"?

Still, Nathan had proved to be a substantial opponent. In truth, had he wished, he could have pried her mouth open and poured it down, for she lacked the strength to resist. Cate obediently took a bite, rolling the mass of tepid oats in her mouth for a bit before her throat would allow it passage.

Nathan watched in sympathy. "It was months before I could keep anything down. It had to be that hag's doing; I swore I could feel her fist in me gut," he added, touching the spot.

The bite Cate was about to swallow rose back up and she prayed for no further mention of being ill.

"You're doing better already," he said brightly, falseness ringing like a ship's bell.

The sound of agitation up the beach saved her from a second bite. Her thankfulness for the timely distraction dissolved, however, at the sight of a cluster of torches bobbing on a half-trot toward them. Nathan rose to his feet at seeing one break from the group and head directly for them. It was Ben, hanger in his fist.

"Cap'n! Cap'n! Prisoners have escaped!"

"How the bloody — ?"

"Overwhelmed the guards — Took their weapons — Headed

inland..." Breathless, a jerk of the head behind him finished Ben's thought.

Being the one to deliver the bad news meant also being the one to face the results. Ben stood bravely in the face of his captain's outrage. A similar outburst came from Thomas' direction at learning the same from Al-Nejem. Rising, he strode around the fire, his First Mate and several Lovelies close behind.

"Bid Mr. Pryce to —" Nathan began.

A wave of Ben's hand cut him short. "Done and done, sir. A search party was set off directly. He sent me to warn —"

"Get 'em!"

Shouts befitting a boarding party broke from the darkness behind them, eliciting a startled yelp from Cate. The escaped Brazens leapt out and charged, weapons on high, some bearing no more than a rock in their fist.

Caught between protecting Cate and meeting the attack, Nathan froze. The indecision lasted no more than the time required for a few grains of sand to fall through a glass, but it was still costly. By the time he turned, the first was upon him. The firelight caught the assailant's face as they bowled over: Pomphrey.

At almost the same moment, Cate screamed at being leapt upon as well.

"No!" Nathan bellowed. Spinning to her rescue, he exposed his back and took a fist to the kidneys. Staggering, he dodged Pomphrey's blade, and then whipped an elbow into the man's ribs. Weaponless himself, Nathan had but one choice: dive inside the sword's arc and grapple hand-to-hand.

Cate rolled and thrashed, her fingers curled for the face of her assailant. He rose, snatched a handful of her hair and dragged her along. Cate aimed a foot at his crotch, but not with the intended effect. Kirkland appeared and flung a pot of steaming liquid, sending the Brazen screaming into the dark. Cate lay quivering, surrounded by heaving bodies and the smack of fists hitting soft flesh, the stink of pierced gut joining the blood and sweat. More Morgansers and Lovelies arrived from up the beach where more fighting could be heard. Through the tangle of legs, she caught a glimpse of Ben wielding his sword with murderous intent, Kirkland brandishing a cooking spit like a pike.

Weight and size should have been Nathan's advantage over Pomphrey; his compromised state and Pomphrey's element of surprise negated all of that. A cutlass at Nathan's throat, Pomphrey let out a victorious hoot, but it proved premature. Nathan kicked backwards, a move which would have been far more effective had he been shod. Still, it was sufficient distraction for Nathan to next drive an elbow up into Pomphrey's jaw. The reeling Pomphrey kicked out, catching Nathan in the chest. The wind knocked out of him, Nathan sagged on his hands and knees, head hanging between his arms.

Cate shrieked a warning as a Brazen charged from behind Nathan, a rock aimed at his head. He rolled away. But the move brought him squarely before Pomphrey again. The latter's sword arced up for the killing blow, when an arm came out of the darkness from behind and hooked him by the neck. Bellowing in fury, Thomas lifted Pomphrey from his feet and squeezed. His face going dusky purple, Pomphrey dropped his cutlass and tore at the arm. Nathan seized the dropped weapon and rose, poised to strike. At the last instant, Al-Nejem stepped in, and laid Pomphrey's gut open with one brutal swipe.

Nathan fell on his knees next to Cate, frantically patting her over to assure that she was well. The rest of the attacking Brazens dealt with, Thomas hunched anxiously over them, bloodied sword still in his fist. What little she had eaten surged up in her throat; she rolled away, Nathan holding her while she retched. When there was no more to come up, she sat back, gasping. Water was brought to rinse her mouth and Nathan swabbed her clammy face with his sleeve.

Once satisfied she was well, Nathan launched at Pomphrey's body. "Goddamned fucking little gutless bastard!" he seethed at the staring, lifeless eyes. "We gave you and the rest of your dung-souled, miscreant crew your parole, and this is our thanks!" With another stream of expletives, he kicked sand at the body.

Once more, the name "*Brazen*" seemed all the more fitting.

Torches bobbed toward them, more Morgansers and Lovelies running to lend a hand. They arrived to find the only thing left to do was give joy of the victory.

Nathan stood back, chest heaving, and swiped the sweat from his face. Pryce appeared, bloodied but bright with triumph. Up shore, the fighting continued, but soon died there, as well.

"Who the fucking hell was on guard?" Nathan bellowed.

Al-Nejem said something low in Arabic; Thomas gravely nodded. "Some yours, some mine, or rather, were."

"Three were killed directly," Pryce put in. "The rest won't have the opportunity to repeat their mistake."

"How the hell did they manage—?"

Pryce cocked an 'I-told-you-so' brow. "They had knives hidden; others just used a rock," he added, toeing one next to his foot.

The *Morganse's* First Mate heaved the resigned sigh of one

about to deliver more bad news. "They meant to take one or all of you hostage and gain back their ship."

"There has to be near a score o' fires on this beach. Damned bit o' luck to guess which was ours," Nathan said. "There's the high-stink of a rat about this. We need to sniff out the double-tongued —"

"Done 'n done, Cap'n. They will be served out directly." Pryce spoke with a coldness which made Cate shiver.

A flow of orders broke from the pair of commanders. The pair of first mates was set on their way, leaving the two captains and Cate alone.

"Should have killed them all straightaway," Thomas threw into the ensuing silence. He shook his head and made a wry noise. "Fancied there had been enough blood shed for one day."

"Had the parasitic bastards begged, we might have allowed them the privilege of seeing how long it might take to starve on this barren rock." Something in Nathan's voice said he would have considered that long, slow death quite fitting.

Shortly, Pryce reappeared at the firelight's edge; a jerk of his head beckoned Nathan. Thomas mouthed a curse and sat heavily on the fireside log. Cutlass still in his fist, he cradled his arm, the bandage blooming red once more. Cate rose to go attend him, but her legs wobbled and then buckled. She sank down, useless to him and the score of others who doubtlessly needed tending.

Thomas stared into the fire. Feeling Cate's gaze, he looked up and arched a brow. "A bit ruthless, am I?"

Cate sat hunched on the pallet, the full realization of the attack and how out - numbered they had been incrementally sinking in.

She felt dazed when there was no reason to be. Personally, she had taken no worse of a tumble than from rough-housing with her brothers. She had escaped relatively unscathed as had Nathan and Thomas —

Had she thanked him, yet, for saving Nathan's life?

She prodded through her murky mind, straining to recall, searching the wherewithal to do so.

The rush of battle fading, the men, torches in hand, moved among the bodies, toeing them, looking for any of their own, to those who weren't. Her eyes followed the blood - filled tracks of the dead being dragged off. Her gaze hung up on several more lifeless humps scattered down the shoreline. From the corner of her eye, she caught a sharp motion and heard the satisfied grunt of the *coups de grâce* being delivered. She turned her head, desperate to fix on something else. They fell upon a pool of blood squarely before her, dark and shining. Jerking away, her eyes landed on Pomphrey's foot, his toes poking out through the grey coils of his intestines. Another cut of the eyes, and she found the more comfortable sight of Kirkland's makeshift pike stuck in the ground, grey bits of brains dangling from its tip.

By whatever means or luck, a number of Brazens still lived and were gathered together. Amid threats and grumbles, the prisoners were herded away, looking so very much like sheep to a slaughter as they were taken out of sight. The dust of their footsteps had barely settled before Al-Nejem appeared from the darkness and beckoned his captain. Sighing, Thomas heaved himself up. He paused to cast an almost apologetic glance toward Cate and then disappeared in the same direction as the prisoners.

All of their mates accounted for, the wounded seen to — relatively few, by all reports — the men gathered about their fires, their torches stuck in the sand around them. Their spirits now soaring, they recounted their part in the victory and drank toast after toast. Nathan's voice could be heard now and again among them, accepting accolades, laughing. Soon, his outline, sharp against the flames, separated from the others as he strode toward her.

Nathan plopped down next to Cate. Wincing, he bent carefully to rest his head on his arms. "Goddammit! I should have never let —" He clamped his lower lip between his teeth.

Cate squeezed his arm in support. "It's fine... We're fine —"

He cut a cold look from the corner of his eye. "I was unarmed and useless."

Cursing under his breath, he straightened. A thin stream of blood trickled down his neck from Pomphrey's blade. He dabbed at it, rubbing the resulting red between his fingers. He sighed, suddenly sounding so very weary. "What a precious commodity this neck o' mine is. Seems everyone desires to slit it, wring it or just plain sever it."

The thought of how near he had come to being killed again — in defense of her, again — caused the gorge to rise in her throat. A split lip, puffed knuckles was the only damage... this time.

But the next... there would always be a next.

"Come lie with me," she said softly.

Nathan glanced toward the joyous men; his shoulders rose and fell, like someone resolving themselves to yet another unpleasant task. He crawled in behind her and sank down with the sigh of doing something long-anticipated and never thought to come. Molding his body to hers, his arm curved around and he found her hand. Cate pressed back against him, luxuriating in the warmth no fire or sun could ever supply.

Amid the sea of high celebration, they laid in their small island of seclusion, reacquainting and reaffirming, while at the same time reassuring. The flex of an arm or shift of a leg spoke what no words could express: their unmitigated joy and relief of being alive and, most of all, together.

At one point, the celebration around the fires suddenly stopped. The men rose, took up the torches and filed away in the same direction Thomas and Al-Nejem had gone. They disappeared around the rocks, the faggots' glow on the night sky marking their route.

A quietude befell the shore. The land breeze brought Artemis' whistle and fanned the fire's coals, which briefly brightened, and then collapsed.

"Did I ever say 'thank you?'" Cate asked.

The ensuing silence was long enough to make her think Nathan either hadn't heard or didn't mean to respond.

"For what?" finally came back, truly puzzled.

"For... everything," she said lamely. "For coming to rescue me on the *Gosport*; for saving me — "

Shifting restlessly, Nathan made a dismissive noise. "'Tis nothing."

"Hardly," she said, equally dismissive.

His arms tightened around her and he whispered "Dying 'tis no answer, darling. You shan't be rid of me that easily. We're joined now, in a way what — "

The rest was lost in a distant cry. High and so thin with agony as to be barely human, it came from the direction of the torches' glow. Its end was overlapped by another, and then another: pirate justice being served. Short work was made of most; others were not so lucky. Cate stiffened and sought to bury her head under the pillow, shout, do anything to block the sound. Nathan spread himself over her and clapped his hands over her ears. Rocking, he made shushing sounds and murmured nonsense, even hummed tunes, but to no avail. She could still hear it.

"You can't be surprised; you can't be shocked," Nathan chanted.

"I'm neither," she sobbed.

And that was the hell of it. A large part of her was glad to hear it, for those were the very ones who had sought to kill Nathan. That part of her wanted them dead, in the slowest more torturous way possible. The problem was the small remaining part which argued for Christian forgiveness: turn the other cheek and all that.

"They signed their death warrants when they chose to attack us, when they demanded no quarter. We still gave them a chance; the mumping louts made Thomas and I pay for our softness. And now, they are paying for theirs."

A part of her screamed that she should be surprised, that she should be shocked. But all she could think was "if the tables had been turned, it would have been Nathan and Thomas screaming at their throats being slashed."

The cries of the dying were joined by a louder chorus in her head, of those heard another night. Not so long ago, after being accosted on the *Morganse,* Cate had lain through the night praying for the groans and pleas to end, knowing that in doing so she was wishing the unfortunates dead. In the morning, there had been no trace of the accused, the mood aboard complacent, Nathan non-committal. She had never asked what had been done, had never wished to know. Her violators were dead, pirate justice served. That was enough... or so she had been told.

Finally, the night fell quiet, deadly quiet. Nathan held her tighter than ever, defensive and possessive.

From far up the beach, male voices broke the stillness, torches on high as the men returned to the beach, Thomas' unmistakable outline in the lead. They returned to their fires, laughing, their spirits as soaring as the sparks spiraling skyward. Beatrice resettled atop a nearby water butt and began to preen. Hermione laid, eyes half-closed in goatish pleasure, chewing her evening tobacco.

Cate and Nathan lay together, but by the rigidity of his body she knew he was awake.

"You should sleep," she said.

"So should you," came back mildly, hoarse with weariness.

Cate mussed her head on the sack-and-oakum pillow. "I'm afraid where I'll wake up next."

"As am I." Nathan shifted, bringing his entire length, from nose to toes, in contact with her. His hand found hers against her chest and clasped it, tracing and retracing the shapes of her knuckles. "You're here and I'm here. 'Tis all that matters."

A long quiet ensued. Thomas went to one of the nearby dodgers, threw off his weapons and boots, and with a weary groan, lay down.

Cate wriggled against Nathan, basking in his glorious warmth. "Thank you. I don't think I said that."

"Aye, you did," came back with tempered patience.

"Oh."

"S'all right, darling. I've lived to be cursed by many a man for saving their miserable lives. My greatest fear is you'll come to do the same."

She twisted around to kiss him on the cheek. "I would have never asked you to—"

"Allowed, nor thought to ask, yes, I know." Nathan settled her back into his embrace, and then fell into a pensive silence.

"'Tis why I never explained the two bells," he finally said. "I knew you'd corner me into some blood oath which I'd never be able to honor. Thank *you*." She felt him smile. "You saved me soul from that not so small dishonor."

Her hand found his where it rested on her thigh. "You're a noble man."

Nathan sighed, resigned. "God deliver me."

He pressed his lips to the back of her hair. "Sleep, Kittie." His breath blew warm on her neck. "You're safe."

5: WHO DO I THANK FOR THIS?

THE NEXT MORNING, SUN SHONE down with its usual, insufferable Caribbean brilliance.

Cate sat on the pallet, quilt hitched about her shoulders, blinking and lumpish. She would have loved to participate in the day, if only she could find the wherewithal to do so.

It had been a hellish night, but apparently only for one, she thought, dully.

Nathan was already up and about, seemingly loving this day as much as he loved every other one he met.

The camp was already alive, cook fires stoked, coppers steaming and the smell of grilling fish sharp. Youssef and Kirkland worked at neighboring fires, enjoying a companionable harmony never thought possible, the latter wearing a bandage on his head — How that had come to pass, she had no notion — like a medal of honor, being met with congratulations at every turn.

Gazing up the beach, one couldn't help but observe a lighter mood; one might almost call it buoyant, the kind which came with a grim task complete. In the fogged reaches of her mind, sometime in the night, she recalled hearing someone — perhaps Thomas — saying "Tossed the bodies inland. Let the gulls and crabs have the bastards." It was a grim pronouncement, for it meant the dead Brazens were denied the traditional seaman's burial, dooming them to the ignominy of sea gulls picking their bones for all eternity.

That lighter mood sought to lift her up, like helping hands, but in vain. She sank back down, the inert lump that she was.

Cate watched as a work party of six or so separated from the general activities, stiffening as they came toward her with the determined step of the duty-bound. She shied at them closing in around her. Instead of addressing her, however, they addressed each other in desultory remarks of "Clap on. Seize up. Lash on. Secure. Tally 'n' belay," as they set about stretching lengths of canvas over the supports of the shelter over her.

The last of the four walls was still being affixed when Nathan's head popped in through a gap.

"What is all this?" she cried, alarmed. "I don't need—"

"Privacy."

The word stopped her dead. It was a notion so foreign, it took her a moment to fathom his meaning.

Nathan's head withdrew like a turtle into its shell.

"We'll suffocate in here," she called after him.

Feeble as her protests might have been, they were in earnest. The canvas cut off the breeze with a suddenness which made it feel like a hand had been clapped over her nose and mouth. Combined with the darkness, it was like being entombed, which gave way to a rising panic.

The final touches to the canvas were barely finished when Nathan's disembodied voice called "Four paces and about face! If I catch any of you skulkers peeking that eye will be mine."

Preemptive coughs, a shuffling of feet, and an attentive silence befell the immediate surroundings.

A sliver of brilliant sunlight stabbed Cate's eyes as the canvas parted with someone coming in, Nathan, judging by the jingling of bells.

She gave an indignant yelp and batted him away at first her laces being grabbed and then her hem. "What are you at?" she demanded, evading further assaults.

Even in his most urgent, amorous moments, Nathan was never this rough and abrupt.

She had never refused him, never told him "No"—not in that way, at any rate. But neither had he ever come at her without so much as a kiss or announcing his intentions in some way. She was accustomed to lying with him with an entire crew just the other side of the bulkhead; doing so with nothing but a bit of canvas, and listening ears only a few feet away, was quite another thing!

"Will you stop that!" she insisted, pressing down her hem with the flat of both hands, dodging his attempts at her stays with a jab of her elbow. It was like wrestling an octopus!

With the exasperated huff of one whose best intentions were going unappreciated, he finally—finally offered an explanation. "These clothes," he said with an abrupt swipe. "They have to go."

"Clothes?" Cate sat back, thinking surely she had misheard. Her eyes were accustomed enough to the dim by then to see his dark outline kneeling next to her. "Since when do you worry about—?"

"I bid for your dunnage to be brought ashore, but those slab-sided villains-of-a-crew of his haven't seen fit."

Cate could only assume that "his" had to be Thomas. "I should think their time is a bit forsworn," she pointed out tartly.

One brow twitched at his opinion of that. "Orders is orders," he said censoriously. "Otherwise, you're nurturing naught but a festering brood of sea lawyers."

"But why this sudden fixation with what I'm wearing?" She relaxed a bit, but still alert for the next assault.

He glanced up and then away. "Appearances."

Now she was the one to cock a brow. Appearances were always the last thing on his mind, and they both knew it.

"You died in these," Nathan finally conceded, yielding to her severe stare.

She cocked a brow, unconvinced.

"Very well," he huffed. He drew several breaths, forming his reply. "I look at you in... in *that*," plucking at her skirt, "and all I can see is you lying there, dead, those vacant eyes looking back at me."

He bent his head and slowly shook it. "I can't bear it. I can't..." Now it was his voice which shook, much to her regret.

"Well, there's still a smell," she conceded, dipping her nose toward a sleeve.

Nathan shrugged, a hand rising and falling in apology. "I thought to have washed it out, but..."

"What about you? Those are the same clothes you died in."

"Do I smell?" he asked, plucking at himself.

Cate leaned and delicately sniffed, braced for whatever might meet her nose, the possibility of horrors of the underwater lair roiling like a bubbling pot. She sniffed and then, somewhat reassured, sniffed a little deeper at finding only Nathan: male musk and the faintest hint of cinnamon and oil of orange. The cinnamon she knew from brushing his teeth with a frayed root, a ritual performed with the long-suffering air of following parental instruction. The oil-of-orange she had never seen him apply as so many men did as a hair dressing. Sometime in his not so distant past, Nathan must have done so, for the not unpleasant scent still hung about him.

He reached beside him to display a bundle of what she thought at first to be just more canvas, but of an odd, darker color. "I contrived to have something made."

She pulled an item from the top and shook it out find the old sailcloth had been made into a skirt. "How did you manage all this?"

"Scripps and his mates can fashion anything. The shift was fashioned from that shirt you wore that first day aboard."

His nostalgia made them both smile. The shirt had been a very fine lawn which made for a very sheer shift, she thought holding it up to the shaft of light squeezing between the surrounding canvas.

"The skirt is from some old duck," Nathan said, fingering the hem, clearly proud of the accomplishment. "And the stays are jumps, just as you like."

She tried to keep track of all involved, so that she might thank each and every one, but was soon lost. The effort—and by so many—was touching, albeit that they were no doubt motivated by one driving captain.

"How did you know my measurements?" she asked, holding the stays up to her chest. They were surprisingly near to a fit.

Nathan waffled a bit at that. "Oh, I just—" He spread his hands. "Your waist is about thus," he said, almost more to himself. "And your sides are..."

He went off on his litany, Cate now the one with her mouth slightly agape.

"They've all seen; they all had a notion," he qualified.

It was a bit dismaying to think she had been so thoroughly observed by all, not just Nathan, but every man. In the midst of all these repairs, a bunch of men had hunched together, laying it all out. Knowing sailors, each one would have felt obliged to offer their hapennies' worth. Half-listening, she examined the seams—straight and even as a London mantua-makers—and the fine stitching.

"I desired something a bit more, eh, appealing in the way of color. We've cochineal somewhere on board, but that mumping master-o'-the-hold had no notion as to rousing it out."

Cate strained to think who that poor soul might have been. Come to think on it, as keeper-of-the-prize-book, it might have been herself.

It was difficult to tell in the lighting, but the clothing looked to be a soft buttery – brown color. "Then what did you use?" she asked.

Nathan shrugged. "Onion peels from Kirkland, I think. That hulking cook of Thomas' threw in something from that devil's kitchen of his, as well."

A tug at her laces called her back to his intentions. In a space barely high enough to sit up, shifting her clothes was easier said than done. The laces soon became hopelessly entangled. Huffing in frustration, Nathan drew out his knife.

"No, not that!" she shrieked.

A sputter mirth came from just outside.

The corner of Nathan's mouth tucked up. "Sorry. Forgot." She had a horror of the things, and he knew it.

Still, with such a hopeless tangle, there was but one choice, and she knew that, too. She plucked the knife away, wedged its tip where it would do the most good, and slit them herself.

Nathan's helpfulness wasn't always that, pushing when it wasn't necessary, pulling when not called for, but eventually — amid a lot of short remarks — the mutual end was achieved.

Nathan sat back on his heels to regard her. "That's better," he declared, with a satisfaction which made Cate glad for the effort.

A word from him and the surrounding canvas was jerked away with even more suddenness than it had been hung, exposing Cate to both the day's brilliance and a crowded beach. A good many looked on with eager scrutiny, their murmurs and grins suggesting they had a hand in the making.

Squinting against the sunlight, she could see her new outfit's the truer color: brown, but with a far more golden cast. Their haste in the dying process showed in the uneven streaks of lighter hues. It was not her best color, not by a far cry, but she would die before complaining.

She swallowed down a shriek of protest at seeing Nathan step to the nearest fire and pitch her old clothes into the flames. Dusting his hands in satisfaction, he drew up before her.

"I had a seat-of-ease rigged just there." A point of his chin directed her to a short distance away where a cubicle of canvas sat discretely behind some rocks.

Cate stared up wondering how, in the midst of everything, he could be thinking of something so trivial. "I don't need that. I can just go behind the rocks." At the same time, she was touched that he would be so thoughtful.

"With all these ogling louts skulking about? I think not!" he huffed primly and stalked off. Within a few strides, however, he spun back to shout "Use it!"

⁂

Whatever elation of spirit Cate had enjoyed soon sank away. Pulling the quilt up about her, she sat hunched on their pallet once more, feeling too much like a blade of grass some distance before her: broken, trampled and being buried alive a bit more by each passing tread. She could hear the rumble of Nathan's voice somewhere in the distance.

Sloth. It was represented as a mortal sin, indulgence dooming one's soul to damnation. She considered whatever Hell awaited for this weakness couldn't possibly be any worse than what she had just endured. Resist or succumb: that was the question. Surely something in between existed, something which didn't require effort or resolution.

She pressed her hand to her stomach. If only the nausea could be as far removed as the rest of her.

At one point, her gaze was interrupted by a cup shoved into her hands. She stared at it.

"It's coffee."

Cate looked up to find Nathan standing over her. She looked down at the cup and then back up.

He knelt next to her, urging the steaming brew up to her mouth. "You like it."

Feeling the looks of far too many, Cate obediently took a sip. Alas, one wouldn't please; Nathan sat next to her, obliging her to take another and then — damn his stubborn soul — another, intermittently taking a drink himself in some sort of misguided show of goodwill.

In the interim of waiting for the cup to be refilled, Cate's sideways glance found Nathan gazing at his ship, longing evident in every angle of his body. Cate's gaze followed his and settled there, as well. The promise of home laid in the *Morganse*, her single greatest wish, at one point. Her gaze drifted back to Nathan beside her. Now, all she desired was to be with him, which meant being on that ship, for there was the only place he would ever flourish. To take him ashore would be the same as putting a tropical flower in the Highlands and expecting it to flourish.

"Go to her," Cate urged softly.

Nathan blinked and looked to the sand between his feet. "Nay, I'll do."

"Go to her." Cate bumped him encouragingly with her shoulder. "She needs you as much as you need her, more perhaps."

Nathan's mouth worked with several responses. Finally, he straightened and closed his eyes, going very quiet for several moments.

"She's fine," he announced, opening his eyes. "Ship-shape, even-keeled and squared away. From clew to erring, to bosuns to palm-and-pickets, she's in good hands."

Something swooped past overhead. Yipping in alarm, Cate ducked, throwing up her arms.

Nathan curved a protective arm around her. "Easy, luv. 'Tis only the gulls fighting over their newfound feast." He angled his head inland. Cate smiled unsteadily, barely assured by the notion of the dead Brazens flung there.

"C'mon, a bit more, that's it. T'will rectify the humors and set you to rights," he said, urging the cup to her mouth.

They drank in amiable silence, Kirkland refilling the cup several times.

Her gaze drifted down to his bare toes wriggling in the sand. "Where are your boots?"

Nathan glanced disinterestedly down and then shrugged. "Gone, and good riddance. Insufferable contrivances they were, hot and heavy, and took an age to dry."

"If you didn't like them, then why were you wearing them?"

His eyes cut sideways as if the answer was obvious. "T'was all to be had at the time I lost me last ones. Should be something available now, however," he added, with a thoughtful look toward where the Brazens had been taken.

"You'd wear a dead man's shoes?" she asked uneasily.

"I'd be barefoot this last two decades and more if I didn't. It's not as if a shoe cobbler awaits at every port. Come to think on it, I can't recall the last place I saw one," he added, his jaw wrenching sideways in thought.

Seeing her continued disquiet, Nathan patted Cate on the leg. "We pirates — sailors in general, for that matter — come by shoes the same way we come by everything else: either sold at the mast or taken as prize."

Cate wriggled her own bare digits in the sand. In a world of men, women's shoes would be even more difficult to come by. On an occasion or two, he had provided shoes for her. Now, hers were gone too, presumably lying on the bottom of the sea next to his.

She dimly recalled seeing the *Brazen* prisoners being stripped of their effects as they were marched past. It wasn't the hangman's perquisites, but it was damned close.

Nathan reached around behind Cate. He drew a cord from under their pallet and she inwardly groaned. Surely, he didn't mean to resume her knot lessons, not now, not in the midst of everything else!

To her vast relief, however, he began knotting himself. She watched in idle fascination of his hands. She could lose herself in watching them do anything, from tearing off bits of soft tack, to cleaning his pistol, to just drumming on his belts. The things those clever hands could do when she lain with him made her womb flutter. Long-fingered and elegant, as expressive as the man himself, his were sailor's hands, sun-browned and calloused. The backs were a network of scars, new crisscrossing the old. Over those were the brighter, more recent cuts and scrapes gained during the night's conflict.

Nathan was a tenacious teacher; her knot lessons leading to hours of unspeakable frustration. Thank the heavens, she wasn't expected to learn something so intricate, a pattern so very similar to his tattoos…?

Her eye slid down from the long strip he worked on to his wrist, a bandage covering where one of those tattoos had once lain. A bracelet now hung there. She reflexively felt her own arm, wondering how he could have managed to remove hers, for it was too snug to slip off, and there was no closure. For that matter, ankles or wrists, all of hers were in place.

"You didn't have that yesterday, nor that," she added, noticing one about his neck. It was identical to hers, right down to the knot at the center.

Intent on his work, one shoulder rose and fell. "T'was a long night."

"You believe those will protect you?" There was a time when Cate had thought them strictly decorative. Now, alas, she fully understood and appreciated their purpose.

The shoulder moved more emphatically. "They did for you. 'Tis no guarantee where that scheming demon o' the deep is concerned, but 'tis me only hope," Nathan said, casually. "Now after… everything."

Everything, indeed, Cate thought moodily. Her world seemed to have been set on ends of recent, violence, mayhem and death lurking at every turn. She tried to remember the last moment of total peace she had enjoyed: in that little shack he on… whatever that island's name had been.

"Are those bothersome?" It was difficult to overlook the bindings about his limbs and neck, pale against his bronzed skin. Guilt gnawed at the sight of them: six additional scars, all because of saving her.

"Tis no more than an annoyance."

She made a skeptical noise. "I see you wincing every time you move."

The dark eyes flicked sideways, and then away. "Aye," he reluctantly conceded. "Me middle catches at every bend or breath. There's naught to be done for it," he said, catching her hand seeking his shirttail. "I've suffered far worse before."

Sighing at Cate's dubious stare, he extended his arm. "Very well, see with your own eyes that I'm not purulent, nor rotting."

Carefully lifting the linen's edge, she peeked. It was as he claimed, the stripped skin was scabbed but mending nicely, with no untoward redness or oozing.

Seeing her satisfied, Nathan set back to work, his fingers seeming to move of their own accord. She sat watching, the coffee in her stomach forming a sour ball with the question which burned to be asked.

"You're planning to set sail, aren't you?"

"Admittedly, darling, we can't remain here forever," he said, with his usual insufferable pragmatism.

Alas, at the moment, an eternity on an island — minus nearly three hundred men, of course — with him was a singularly appealing thought.

"Where are you — *we* off to?" Speaking freely of the future — a future with Nathan, didn't come naturally, yet.

"His High-Arsedness is gone," he declared with cold finality. "There is a grand peacefulness what comes with knowing the bastard is dead. I'll rest considerably easier."

"You don't sleep," she observed. By his own admissions, the necklace and bracelet were proof of that.

"Not now," he said, unabashed. "But I will... someday."

The corner of his mouth tightened. "Just two more souls need to be stricken from this earth, and I shall rest as peaceful as the proverbial lamb."

Cate looked away. She needn't inquire as to who he meant: Hattie and Maubrick, the two who had led a mutiny against him, shot and left him for dead. He carried the pistol balls in a small pouch, waiting for the day when he might return them in kind.

"I would have thought you would have had enough of killing." Guilt seized her chest, for a good deal of that recent violence had been on her behalf.

"Revenge is a fine thing." Nathan cocked a brow at her. "You should try it."

"It changes nothing," Cate said to her hands in her lap.

Creswicke was dead and gone, deeply immersed in the Seven Circles of Hell, if there were any justice. But the weight of his hand was still upon Nathan. There were no magic wands, nor incantations nor potions. *Nothing* changed. The "S" for slave, thick and brutish, of a size usually reserved for livestock, would still be on his palm, still robbing Nathan of his former life, still banishing him to piracy.

That same hand weighed heavily upon her, she thought looking down at the wrapping on her wrist. A "P" was now her mark. Still unable to look at it, she knew it was there, the image of the red-hot iron burned into her memory as deeply as the letter on her skin. Nothing could erase that, nor the horrors which accompanied getting it. She pressed her hand to her abdomen; in those scars laid more ghosts, of ravishment and violence. The burning gorge of hate rose in her throat, one which refused to be swallowed down.

Cate looked up into Nathan's face and an expectant silence. "What?"

"I said," he began, with measured patience. "You look fit to kill, darling,"

"No, it's... it's nothing. It'll pass," she said, industriously brushing at a non-existent spot on the quilt.

"Ah, but may I be so bold as to say that is where you are categorically wrong," he said sternly. "It won't go away."

He leaned closer and tapped her arm with an emphatic finger. "Revenge changes everything, darling. The Bible contains a great many verses on the subject."

Cate looked up through one eye. "Since when are you the Biblical scholar?"

Nathan thrust his hand before her. He wore the leather palm as did many swordsmen. This one, like most other, served as protection, but of a different sort: it covered the brand on his palm, the one which declared him, his children and his children's children all property of another.

"Since the day I decided I was going to live, instead of letting that pustulant bastard think himself the victor. I ran my blade through him and a thousand years were lifted from me shoulders."

Nathan's fingers closed, pressing the thickened scar of his brand onto hers, creating a new connection: marked and banished, and both by the same hand. "Allow it, darling, for it *will* answer."

Cate pulled free and thrust her arm out. "I can kill him a thousand times over and *that* will still be there. Yours, too!" Nothing could make it go away. He had killed Creswicke, and it was still there. Nathan had died and resurrected, and it was still there. No magic, nor potion, nothing short of self-mutilation would erase it.

Nathan dispassionately eyed the linen binding on her arm. "That is filthy." His expression brightening, he rose to his feet. "Stand by."

Stepping behind their shelter, Nathan threw back an old sail covering trunks, hampers, and boxes, the sum total of her worldly possessions. Opening one of the hampers Thomas had given her, he rummaged, burrowing ever deeper. With a small exclamation, he straightened, holding up a length of lace. Clamping it in his teeth, he knelt before her; a flick of his knife slit the old binding away, Cate—unable to look—resolutely fixing her gaze on Nathan's face, now inches from hers. He had shaved that morning, his skin taut and shining. The night's violence had left its mark: a small split on his lower lip and several dark blotches of welling bruises. Weathered, dark and wild, a pirate in every way, the bit of lace looked absurd fluttering from his mouth, tangling in his braids.

Feeling her watching, Nathan looked up. The cinnamon flecks in his eyes flashed to almost the color of amber when the sun caught them. They studied her intently, the vertical grooves between the brows deepening.

"What?" she asked, shifting self-consciously.

"Nothing," he mused, grinning. "I'm just looking at me lovely lady, thinking how lucky I am that she would have me. There!" he declared giving the strip ends a final tug. "What do you think?"

With some trepidation, Cate looked down. Her shoulders dropped at seeing the lace had been neatly wound around her forearm, effectively covering the brand.

"If you're given lemons, make lemonade," she observed, fingering it.

His grin broadened. "Can't say I'm familiar with that bit o' wisdom, but I can't argue with the logic."

Settling next to her once more, Nathan picked up the half-done bracelet, now working with a speed which made the cords seem to knot themselves.

"As I've said before, darling, there will be no peace until that grasping, mutinous wench and that drooling cohort of hers are sent back to the hell from which they were spawned." He grew more heated with every word. "I'll not abide her sitting in witness of your abuse. The thought of her and His High-Arsedness being in cahoots against—" The rest was lost in a vehement sputter.

She shifted nearer, uneasy. "You believe Hattie will try something again?"

He snorted, loud and emphatic. "Ambition is her altar and she worships with the regularity of a nun," he said, coldly. "I'll walk as tall as Thomas when I've finally done for her."

The very man arrived at the fireside just then, muffling a groan as he slumped on the log.

"There's a look what would turn cream to curds," Nathan observed under his breath.

Nathan knew his friend well, as many others apparently

did, one look prompting them to divert their path to down along the waterline, well out of the line-of-fire. The less alert regretted their blunder. Mr. Jamil soon appeared. The *Lovely's* chirurgeon was a pinched, saturnine creature even in his most genial moments. Now, he was all the more sour with concern. A low, sharp conversation between doctor and patient ensued in Arabic. Thomas resolutely shook his head and went through the motions of proving his well-being. Jamil retreated out of range, but lingered, his loblolly boy a few paces behind.

Some moments later, Thomas swayed where he sat. Cate was on the verge of calling out when he lurched to his feet and wove precariously. He would have toppled into the fire had it not been for Jamil's readiness. Batting the medico away, Thomas took a few faltering steps and was necessarily caught again by Jamil and Maram. Together they guided him to a dodger and laid him down.

Cate was up and at Thomas' side before Jamil straightened. He puffed and glared. During her time on the *Lovely*, she had worked next to him. He was a man who firmly believed a woman should know her place. Now, as then, only his captain's presence spared her a rebuke.

"Goddammit it, I'm fine," Thomas declared, dodging their questing hands.

"Yes, as we all can see," Cate said, tartly. She laid a hand on his forehead, confirming what she already knew. "How long has this fire been burning?"

Thomas turned his head and held up a shielding hand. "Someone rig a damned cloth."

"Sun bothering you?" Cate asked. The sensitivity was even further proof of his condition as if any was necessary.

"No!" The pinched corners of his eyes suggested the truth lay far from the claim.

A burst of Arabic from Jamil sent Maram and the loblolly scampering. From somewhere behind her, Nathan barked orders.

"Willow bark," she directed to the hovering Kirkland. "In the blood box —"

He was off before she finished.

In the interim of waiting, Cate set to removing the bandage, much to Jamil and Thomas' further displeasure.

"Stop snorting and huffing. You sound like a bull in a box," she said to Thomas.

"Then stop acting like I've one foot in the grave," Thomas grumbled.

"And so you well might. A man of your *experience* should know the risks involved here." Her compassion was tempered by her irritation at his damned stubbornness and, to a larger part, her own guilt. He would have never come so near to ruin if it hadn't been for her blundering.

She was self-aware enough to realize that the source of a large part of her blooming anxiety lay in another wound — not an arm, but a hand, Nathan's hand — going bad. It had been a nightmarish time, one day blurring into the next of sitting at his bedside, fighting the fever, knowing any faltering on her part might result in Nathan being reduced to a cripple. She shook her head, resolutely sending those memories back to where they belonged. Nathan had prevailed intact, with nothing more than a thin red line, one more small scar among the many. God's will and her determination, Thomas' fate would be the same.

Cate fumbled to undo the linen strips, sniffing delicately as she lifted them away. No stink; no ominous ooze. So far, so good. The flesh was hot, the wound livid, but they had caught it in time... hopefully. In the meantime, a piece of sail was rigged, blocking the sun and bringing a grunt of approval from the reclined patient.

Kirkland arrived with a steaming cup. "This should ease your headache," Cate said, handing it off to Thomas.

The minatory arch of her brow caused Thomas' protest to die before it was born. Grumbling, he sat up and drank it down, a grateful sigh accompanying his return to the prone position.

Maram returned with the makings of a poultice: a pannikin of hot milk, a yellowish, telltale skim of linseed oil shimmering on its surface. Cate's nose twitched — she had used the same on Nathan — and she shook off a wave of light-headedness. Soft tack, the traditional method of application being unavailable, moss was substituted. Cate dipped the waded moss in. The smell rose in a steamy fog and hit like a fist. The hot flesh, inflamed skin and stink of impending putrefaction all combined, and suddenly it was Nathan lying before her. She let out a pained cry and threw herself over the prone body, sobbing.

Hands lifted Cate away and gently shook her into sensibility. Peering through the distortion of tears, she found Nathan there, Thomas, as did all nearby, staring in bewilderment. Nathan held her until she no longer shook. Swabbing her dry with his sleeve, he guided her away to their dodger. There she sat, a little confused, and a lot embarrassed.

"I'm sorry! I don't know what — ?" She choked and gulped. "First, there was — And then, I thought — "

"Shh, shh," Nathan chanted, rubbing her back in small circles.

"But I — "

"Stand easy, darling. 'Tis all — "

"But I — " She stopped, realizing that she had no notion of what she meant to say next. No coherent thought was to be had. She looked around, searching for something, anything to cleave onto: a thought, a purpose... anything!

"I should be over there. Thomas is fevered. He needs — " she began, gathering her feet under her.

For all her determination to rise, Nathan's light hand on her shoulder was sufficient force to stop her.

"I can't just sit here." *I'm of little use to him, Thomas or myself,* she thought ruefully.

"Can and will," Nathan said, with parental preemption. "He has his personal physikan; he's in competent hands."

Cate looked up to gape. Never, in all the time she had known him, had Nathan ever uttered a nice word in regard to Jamil or any other medico.

"You can call out, if you so desire, although I wouldn't suggest it," he added, with a roll of his eye. "Never have I seen such an ill-lookit mannikin as that. Cross him and a pillar of salt you'll be. I know what will buoy you up!" he declared, at seeing her spirits sink even lower.

Nathan rose and went to rummage through the trunks again. Ducking back under the canvas roof, he returned bearing a hair brush. "Let us see if some order can be made of this maddening tangle. You're scaring the men and I saw two sea gulls veer off."

Cate raised a self-conscious hand.Bathing in the waterfall, and then teased by wind and humidity, her hair had bloomed into an even more rampant bramble than usual. There was no peering glass, so she could only imagine. Dark smudges under his eyes, face grey and haggard: if Nathan's appearance was any guide, resurrection did little for one's looks.

Not waiting for an answer, Nathan settled behind her and began to apply the brush. With her hair in such a state, the brush's first few passes met with considerable resistance. Still, he worked with the patience of one who had nothing else to do.

Cate closed her eyes, tilted her head back and sighed complacently. "There is nothing more glorious than having one's hair brushed."

It was a strain to recall the last time her hair had received such thorough attention. Such a luxury was usually reserved for one who had a lady's maid, or a large family with sisters, or girl-cousins galore.

"I used to do this for Mum," Nathan said, clearly pleased. "It was one of the few things I could do as a lad what would give her pleasure."

"It takes me back to Tiacita, my old nurse." She smiled faintly. "After five brothers, the woman proved patience wasn't infinite."

"Willful and wild, even then." Admiration softened his voice.

"I used to squirm and shriek, like a piglet under a fence."

"Like trying to free a kedge from a fouled bottom" had been Nathan's observation on getting her to talk about her past. She usually resisted, but she found it steadied her just then, like a storm-ravaged tree sending new roots into the ground. Seeming to realize the same, Nathan tilted his head, intently listening.

"Tiacita would have to do it when Father wasn't about or we'd all hear of it, so I was bribed with *turrón*. It's a sweet made with honey, dried fruits and nuts."

Nathan pointed with his chin toward the galley table nearby. "The honey jar 'tis just there."

His knowing the jar's location made her smile. Nathan had a prodigious sweet tooth, dipping a fingerful several times a day.

"Tiacita and Mama were determined to make a lady of me. They both claimed my willful ways would be the death of them. I guess they were," Cate added bleakly. Her mother had died when she had been a young girl, Tiacita a few months after. It seemed not all memories could lighten one's spirit.

"They had high aspirations for me. I'd be quite the disappointment now," she said, sinking further.

"I daresay I would be a mother's nightmare. Have been, come to think on it," Nathan added, privately musing.

The hurt in his voice made her turn around and grasp his arm. "No, not you or because of... here," she said earnestly.

Blithely waving off her apology, Nathan turned her back around and plied the brush once more.

"I meant I was a disappointment on every count," Cate went on. "I was too tall, my shoulders too wide, my jaw too square, my feet too big... She had such high aspirations for me, I could have married a duke and it should have been a prince."

"Not easy being the family embarrassment."

Cate twisted around, unsure if he was referring to himself or his mother, disowned by her family when she had a child — Nathan — out of wedlock. "You think your mother would be embarrassed to see you now?"

What smile he managed faltered. "Mum's are both our blessing and our curse, are they not?"

Nathan's thumb pensively stroked the brush's bristles with a soft ruffling sound. One shoulder moved self-consciously. "I am what I am. Life dealt her a hand, as I was dealt mine."

His smile stiffened with resolve. "She'd do as every mum: smile and declare her enduring love, all the while her heart breaking with it."

Cate turned back around, considering. "Mama seems to be with me a lot, just now," she heard herself say.

She lived with ghosts on a daily basis. The ghost of her mother was there at every glance into a glass. The ghost of her father was in the color of her hair. She secretly wriggled her wedding ring between her fingers; the ghost of Brian was there. Her womb twitched with the ghost of a child lost. The ghosts of men resided in the scars on her stomach and of a war in the one on her back. The brush with death, however, had stirred them up.

"It stands to reason," Nathan said easily. "You were on her side for a bit. It seems to agitate them, the deceased that is, like a ladle in a stewpot. They will settle back directly and she'll leave you be."

Cate hoped not, at least not right away. Granted, it was disquieting to have her mother's visage pop up with the clarity of the living, but she also found a grand comfort in having her near just then.

"You're the experienced one in all this," she observed, looking back over her shoulder. A cant of his head conceded. "Who came to you, the first time that is?"

He was silent for so long she thought he mightn't answer. "Several, Mum among them," he said at last. "One might conclude they thought me in dire need."

"And now? I mean, did the same ones come this time?"

"Aye, some." He frowned. "Come to think on it, I'm not altogether sure who the hell they were. Must be the others wouldn't be bothered."

"Or they were too far away?" she offered helpfully.

Nathan's smile tightened in appreciation of Cate's well-meant, although thoroughly inept, intentions. "Mebbe. It all depends on your version of the hereafter, I suppose. Perhaps we can beckon them, the ones we relied on most in life. Or perhaps they come of their own volition. Or they happened to be the bunch idling about. Your Mum hasn't come to you before?" he asked, surprised.

"No, only Brian—"

Seeing Nathan twitch at her blunder, Cate caught her lip between her teeth.

Damn, she was usually more careful.

Nathan never liked hearing of her dead husband. In truth,

if a visitor was expected from the hereafter, it would have been Brian, for he had done so many times before.

Come to think on it, he had been surprisingly absent for a good while.

Mama might have scared him off, she mused.

Brian had been nephew to the chieftain of Clan Mackenzie, one of the largest and most influential clans in Scotland, but her mother, a cousin to the Spanish throne, would have disapproved of him out-of-hand. Only a direct descendant of the Hapsburgs or Bourbons would have brought a smile.

"I never got to say goodbye to Mum. She fell ill," Cate went on, spurred by Nathan's attentive pause. "They told me I was too young, that I would upset her: they gave all sorts of excuses, and then she was gone." Her hand helplessly rose and fell in her lap.

At barely thirteen years, she had stood looking down into a hole in the ground, each hollow sound of dirt on the coffin lid taking her mother further and further away.

"I saw her laid out in her shroud..." Cate gulped and said in a thin voice "But it wasn't her. She was already gone. I never had the chance to say —" Her throat tightened and words were lost.

Nathan found her hand and grasped it, solid and encouraging. "Then say it now, whilst she's here. Do it, darling," he pressed at her reticence. "Whilst the gates between here-and-there are still ajar. It might be an eternity until you see her again."

He sat back and folded his hands as one might at a casket's side. Feeling rather foolish, Cate glanced about, wondering how one went about summoning the dead. Nathan's persistence — there was no denying him, when his mind was made up — prompted her to do as what seemed fitting: close her eyes and go very still.

The beach and men faded from her awareness, and she lost all sense of time. A warmth, a sense of belonging and being loved bloomed, suffusing her entire being, and her mother was there. Cate put out her hand and said what she had waited nearly two decades to say: confessions and declarations, dreams and disappointments, aspirations and aims.

It might have been a minute; it might have been a week, when Cate opened her eyes into Nathan's, grave and searching.

"Done," she said, a bit breathless.

Eyes brimming, Nathan found her hand and squeezed. "Good. And was she as ashamed as you expected?"

The warmth still glowed within. Not the one of belonging or being loved; it was the glow of a child absolved of a parent's scorn.

KERRY LYNNE

"No." Cate swallowed the lump wedged in her throat. "She said she understood."

It was some moments after he had begun brushing again before he asked "Was anyone else there? Father? Brothers?"

Still choked by emotions, Cate shook her head.

"Aye, well, that's good. Perhaps it means they still live."

She hadn't seen or heard from what remained of her family in a pair of decades. The thought of them still living was a comfort.

"What about you?" she asked finally. "Did your father or... anyone come?"

"No," came back with a shortness which made her turn and stare.

"Then that means he... they are alive." She was unsure if such hopefulness was fitting. Nathan spoke so rarely of his family, it was difficult to know.

"My sister found her peace," he said, almost in benediction. "As for the others, last time I saw or heard anything from them, they were waving good-by as I sailed away."

"What about your father?" Cate prompted after a prolonged silence.

"He's dead, dead to me, as I was to him."

⌒∾◯⦅∾⌒

Nathan set to brushing once more. The first several strokes were abrupt and rough, but slowly he eased back into his earlier gentleness. Cate fell quiet, sorely regretting having stirred the stewpot.

The worst of the snarls worked out, the brush now made long, smooth passes through her hair, the rasp of the bristles filling the silence between them. The hypnotic effect of the rhythm, Nathan's fingers following the curve of her skull, lightly touching nape, temple or ear provided a peacefulness not achieved in a very long time. For a while, she allowed herself to think that all might be well, after all. All she needed was Nathan; the rest would follow.

From out on the bay came the rap of chisels, adzes and hammers of the carpenters working on both ships. From up the beach the armorers' anvils banged away, hammering out nails, bolts and all the hardware a ship required. The shore between their small camp and the main one was a snowbank of canvas, either in repair, or being made over into tarpaulins, hammocks, sacks, bonnets and a myriad of other things, Billings and his mates stitching like furies. No one lounged about; everyone labored, but that hadn't dampened their spirits. If anything, the morning's high spirits had expanded, laughing and jesting, regaling one and all with their part in last night's fight.

Her eye wandered toward Thomas. A cloth on his head, a poultice on his arm, he lay with the rigidity of one wishing he was anywhere else but there.

Nathan reached to take Cate by the chin and hence, her attention back around to him. "I'm bearing an eye. He's being attended. That sot of a pill-roller of his just paid a visit and his cabin boy is sitting like a hound at its master's knee."

He shifted, ostensibly to be able to reach the hair at her shoulders, but in reality blocking her view. Lids lowered as he worked, his lashes fanned in black crescents on his cheeks.

"What are you smiling at?" she asked.

"Nothing."

He ran the brush down a lock, the corners of his mouth tugging up in pleasure at seeing it fall into a long coil. Feeling her gaze, he blushed as he arranged the tress at her shoulder. "Who knew oakum could be so fine?"

They smiled together at how many times he had compared her hair to frayed out old rope.

"So now that your nemesis is gone, what do you aim to do?" she asked. After wishing someone dead for so long, Nathan had to have felt a bit aimless.

"Nothing," he said, simply. "Precious little will be different. The law hasn't changed: I'm still his property, or rather a part of his estate, no different than the houses, horses and bird dogs," he added matter-of-factly.

"It's so unfair." She had seen Nathan take command of a room, just by the simple act of walking through the door. She had seen him step before an angry throng of two hundred and have them eating out of his hand directly. To see him reduced to such triviality made her half-ill.

"Hell is filled with people waiting for fair," he said philosophically, teasing out a snarl. "How often have you celebrated the benefit of it?"

"Not often. It does help to at least believe it exists," she said, defensively.

He made a wry noise. "The Company will continue. Perhaps not with the same drive for money and success as with His Lordliness at the helm, but there will be a successor. The investors, stockholders and board of directors would have insisted on that. Some poor whey-livered cully, who probably never saw the inside of the headquarters, is being informed this minute of his new station. As for the personal property and fortunes, there was no Lady Breaston—"

Cate stiffened. "Yes, there was."

"No—"

"Yes, there was," she said, with even more conviction, the ember of recollection glowing brighter. "He married—"

She stopped short. This next bit wasn't going to be well-received.

Nathan made a rude noise in the back of his throat. "Who the hell would be grasping enough to marry—?"

"Prudence," Cate blurted and braced for the eruption.

Prudence, a young girl by any description, had been kidnapped by Nathan for the sole reason that she had been Creswicke's fiancé. Pampered, guileless, ill-mannered through her heedless self-interest, in many ways, she and Creswicke deserved each other. Still, Cate had chafed at the girl—not a woman, by any stretch of the word—being forced into what amounted to no more than a business-arrangement marriage. At last, and only for Cate's sake, Nathan had risked arrest and helped to intervene. She had left thinking the marriage avoided, Prudence living comfortably with an aunt, and Nathan pleased only because Cate was.

And so Nathan's eruption came, not quite with the anticipated violence—in deference to Cate's reduced condition, no doubt—but as a low, subterranean rumble. With five brothers, a Highlander husband—one with a vivid imagination—and living among two hundred sailors, Cate's ears were hardly virginal, but the tirade which spewed from Nathan was impressive, in both vulgarity and vehemence. Launching to his feet, he would have thrown the brush had she not plucked it away at the last moment. Possessions weren't her obsession, but neither did she wish to see something so hard come by be flung into the bay.

Cursing, Nathan churned back and forth, sand spurting up at every step. Finally, he stopped, glaring down at her. "How the bloody hell do you—?"

"I saw her. She came to visit me while—" Cate stopped. This next admission would only throw brandy on the flames.

"Why the hell didn't you tell me?!"

"I forgot." She hung her head; it sounded so very lame, and yet it was the truth. With everything else which had happened of late, a few surreal moments in a cell had slipped her mind.

"She came while I was—" Cate clamped her lower lip between her teeth. "Been beaten to the point of insensibility" didn't roll readily off the tongue.

Still, Nathan deserved an explanation, and so she told him haltingly, wishing to get it right and, more importantly, not inadvertently exaggerate, hence making matters worse, all the while shrinking under his growing malevolence. She shivered at the cold, darkness and loneliness of the cell in which she had been locked crept in again. She swallowed, her throat seized once more, with the thirst then.

"It was all I could do to open my eyes," Cate said. "And there she was. I thought she was a dream." Bloodied and battered, she had lain rigid, afraid to move lest her body hurt even more. The metallic clatter of keys and creak of hinges had brought her into consciousness, the rustle of silk skirts and the smell of pomander cutting through the stink of dank stone and her own filth.

"More like a blessed nightmare," Nathan snorted.

"That, too," she sighed, shuddering. "She was the happy new wife."

"So I should imagine, with his position and fortune at her beckon," he said dryly.

Nathan stalked back and forth. "I thought you said you had it all arranged, so that she didn't have to—Pah!" he said, arcing an angry swipe. "'Tis all by the board now. No good deed ever goes unpunished."

He paced some more, grumbling darkly under his breath. Finally, he drew up, rigid with fury. "That ungrateful little seed o' Satan came, saw you beaten to—And didn't raise a hand to help you, after everything we, *you* did, risked life, limb, hell capture for her benefit and never did a thing to help—?"

"She might have tried." Cate rubbed her temple and the ache which had suddenly settled there. Spoiled, self-indulgent, naïve: many words could be used to describe the young girl, considerate or compassionate not being among them. God, if Prudence had possessed a fraction of just one of those traits! The beating, branding, being brutalized: all might have been prevented, if…

"If wishes were trees, there would be no seas," Cate heard herself say.

Nathan managed a smile, for it was one of his favorite axioms. "Well said, darling."

He stomped several strides toward the water and stared. Laughing bitterly, he turned back and spread his arms. "I now belong to her!"

Throwing back his head, Nathan let out a throat-tearing bellow, stopping many within hearing in mid-stride. Those who knew him best made themselves as inconspicuous as possible. Those who didn't know him gaped until the wiser elbowed them into safety.

Nathan sat heavily next to Cate and swore, beating his fist on his leg. He swore again, with even more vehemence and flourish.

"I'm sorry. I never should have—" Cate began.

Smiling weakly, Nathan patted her encouragingly on the leg. "Not to worry, luv. T'was something what needed knowing. Suffering Jesus on the cross, I never expected—" He stopped short, letting the thought die.

"She'll now have what was most important: position and money," Cate observed, and then shuddered. "Neither of them will keep one warm at night."

"Nothing could warm that cold corset."

It was no struggle for Cate to imagine what living alone felt like. The years of her own solitude and desolation settled over her. Her grip loosened, and she was dragged back down into the black pit; she hunched over and dissolved into silent tears. Nathan hooked an arm about her and rocked, murmuring nothings with the grim resolve of a man faced with a woman crying and with no notion of why. Swiping at her eyes, she looked over to see Thomas raised up on one elbow and looking over, stern with concern.

"I'm sorry," she sniffed, half-directed at him, half at Nathan. "I don't know what's wrong with me! What... what was it like for you... the first time?"

"I told—" Nathan stopped and exhaled, in search of patience.

His arm tightened about her. "Aye, it was hellish," he said, soft with understanding. "I was adrift and aimless, and bent on proving they were wrong to let me live. Me ship was dead, and I was—" He swallowed hard. "Alone."

His loneliness dragged her all the lower, weighing her all the more by not having been there for him. A part of her knew it was senseless, for she hadn't even known him then. And yet, a larger part of her burned to somehow intervene and make it all right now.

Cate leaned back into the shelter of his arms, his liveliness and solidness her solace and strength. "Will it... will we ever be like we were?"

Nathan turned her. Taking her face between his palms, he looked deep into it. "Of course, we will."

In spite of best intentions, doubt still pinched the corners of his eyes, desperate hope tightening his voice.

He kissed her, warm and giving, assuring her where words failed, with a hint of what awaited when they were in a condition to do something more.

At the end, Nathan turned Cate and settled her into his arms. Their hands found each other and held on.

He pressed his cheek against her crown and whispered "You're doing fine, darling. We're together. Nothing matters beyond that."

6: LEMONS, OR LEMONADE?

THOMAS STRODE UP THE BEACH. When questioned, some of the hands had represented Nathan and Cate had been seen coming this way... Sometime... Maybe...

The tracks before him might have been fresh or might have been days old. If they had merged, then he would have known the pair were together and would have wore about— He didn't wish to be a part of that scene!—but they hadn't. Running in the same direction, they were clearly on two different paths: the smaller weaving and wandering, the larger straight as an arrow, the heels dug deep at every step.

True enough, Nathan had always seemed to function on a level different from everyone else. Too much of the time, it was like he was trying to outrun Death himself. More than once, Thomas had thought him to have gone round the bend, most especially after he returned from... there, in the care of that mage: laughing into the silence, crying out in the night, staring off at nothing, carrying on a conversation with no one but himself.... And haunted, so very, very damned haunted. To call him half-crazed would have been a kindness, and yet, kindness was what they gave him, coddling him like a quail egg.

And yet, Nathan enjoyed uncanny luck, luck which could only be credited as a guardian angel, a very frazzled guardian angel, to be sure.

In his current search, Thomas had damned near circumnavigated the island. He would have had it not required sprouting fins. Had Nathan been the only object of this search, he would have swum it, for that would have been well within the realm of the man's asinine notions of where a man ought.

But Nathan wasn't alone. He was with Cate... the gods willing.

Thomas expelled a small sigh of relief upon finally spotting Nathan, his greater relief reserved for when he found Cate. Alas,

Nathan was alone, sitting atop a rock, sharpening a sword. He didn't look up at Thomas' approach.

"You're up and about?" Nathan observed, testing the blade's edge with his thumb.

"Aye, fever broke. Can't afford to be lying abed for two days—"

"More like three."

Thomas batted an annoyed hand. "Fire's gone out of it." He flexed his arm, meaning to prove his point, but stopped short.

"All I need do is get these damned stitches out and have done with it." He glared down at the offending limb. Jamil had him bound up in a sling so tight one would have thought it was broke.

"What the hell are you doing clear out here?" he demanded.

Nathan mutely looked up; a slow turn of the head directed Thomas' attention farther down the beach to a lone figure.

Cate.

Thomas' shoulders dropped and the reserved relief was released in an explosive exhale. He watched her, motionless except for the skirts billowing about her legs. "What is she doing out there?"

Stopping in mid-motion, Nathan looked up again. Resting his arms on his legs, he sighed, resigned. "That," he said, and ran the honestone in a long, even stroke down the metal's edge.

Thomas narrowed his eyes, thinking perhaps there was some aspect he was missing. Surely Cate was doing more than—

"Staring?" he asked.

Silence was Nathan's consent.

"Again?"

A slight cant of the head was Thomas' answer.

Thomas watched Cate for several moments more. Arms crossed, hair whipping about her head, she gazed at the water. Following her line of sight, he did the same, thinking perhaps there was something—a ship, a gull, a bit of sea wrack, a cloud shaped like a butterfly.

Nothing.

Sadly, it confirmed his suspicions: the only reason Cate stood there was because the rocks tumbling out into the water had stopped her. Thank the gods, or she'd be circling the island, wearing a trench in the shore, else.

Turning his head so very slightly, he covertly regarded Nathan. No alarm. No frustration. No concern. Just waiting.

Sighing, Thomas took the weapon from Nathan and examined it, turning it in his hand, testing its weight, balance and grip.

"Nice piece of craftsmanship," he said approvingly, handing it back.

"Aye, found it in the *Brazen's* swag. Mine... disappeared. You don't mind?" Nathan asked, cocking a brow.

Touching his heart, lips and forehead, Thomas ducked a bow. "By your leave. I'll enter it as part of my share. You owe me, now." He grinned; the prospect of a humble Nathan was a pleasant one.

"I owe you far more than a sword and a brace of pistols," Thomas said, sobering. The idea of a humble Nathan was also a disarming one. "You'd do the same for me."

"I have," Nathan said, mildly. "Tho' twasn't quite the same."

"I was nearer to death than life; it counted." The occasion hadn't been so grand as being rescued from the clutches of a sea goddess. Leave it to Nathan to trump everyone. But Death's door looms just as large, regardless of who poses as the doorman.

Thomas diverted his attention up the beach again.

No, she hadn't moved.

"How long —?"

"She's not touched," Nathan flared, defensively. "I never said —"

"I can hear you thinking clear over here." Jerking his shoulders, Nathan set the stone to the blade once more. "She's just... recovering."

"Recovering." Thomas rolled the word in his mouth. "Coming back from the dead has to be a shock, I should imagine," he said dryly.

He waited for the explanation; one anyone with the sense of a kevel would know was expected.

He waited in vain.

Over his lifetime, Thomas had sharpened more blades than shells in the sea, but the grate of the stone on metal suddenly set his teeth on edge. He grabbed Nathan's hand to stop him.

"How long did it take for you to recover the last time?" Thomas demanded when Nathan finally looked up.

Nathan stared off, grim as a parson. "Months." Freeing himself from the restraining grasp, he set back to honing once more.

"Hell's fury and damnation, she doesn't have months! None of us do. You know as well as I, we can't sit here much longer. The air is getting thicker by the day and only worse to come," Thomas added, rolling his eyes toward the island's interior. One would have thought, hoped the gulls and crabs might do their work a bit faster. Times before, it had seemed a carcass was stripped to the bone overnight. Wishful thinking did have a way of clouding one's judgment.

He waited for a reaction from Nathan: an acknowledgment... a temper fit...!

Nothing.

Very well, a full broadside it would have to be.

Thomas bent and thrust his face into Nathan's. "She needs her own kind. She needs women!"

Nathan sat back, open-mouthed.

Ha! A reaction at last!

"And where the hell do you fancy I'm to find those?"

"Hell, anywhere," Thomas declared, with an aggravated swipe. "It'll be a damned sight better than on an island, with a bunch of—"

"Pirates?" Nathan interjected, glaring.

"No," Thomas shot back, backing his sails a mite. "I was going to say 'men gawking at her.'"

Thomas set to pacing as best as his seized-up back would allow. Days of lying about had done it no favors. "None of this is answering and you know it better than I," he said, turning to stab an emphatic finger at Nathan. "She needs her own kind."

Nathan opened his mouth, but clapped it shut. "Later."

Curbing a curse, Thomas made several more short passes. Finally he drew up, propping his free hand on his hip. "Why no water? I've seen you stop her every time she threatens to wet her feet. What the hell is still out there?"

He shot a look of loathing and morbid curiosity toward the Straits and the offing beyond, and then eyed Nathan severely. "'Tis damned odd to see you afraid of the sea."

Nathan leaned with greater intent over his work. "It's not me, and not the sea."

"Dammit to hell, Nathan! Allow me a straight answer for once! I've two ships and crews depending on me not to send them out into God knows what. If there's some damned demon o' the deep out there, then tell me."

Nathan felt the jab. His failure to fulfill his responsibilities—perceived as much, at any rate—had obliged Thomas to worry for both ships. There was no malice, no malicious intent, just doing what a captain does.

The high, thin scrape of the stone filled the silence between them.

"Truth be told—" Nathan began.

"At last!" Thomas extolled to the sky.

"Truth be told," Nathan went on more determinedly. "It's... it's Cate. She's not... ready."

"She might never be ready," Thomas said, looming over him.

Thomas leaned closer. "She needs her kind," he hissed, lowering his voice, lest he might be overheard. He'd known women to have the ears of a hound at the damnedest times.

Nothing.

"Think, man! Think!" His fist curled with the desire to grab Nathan and give him a solid shake.

"I am!" Nathan shot back, bullishly.

It was time to break off the engagement, wear ship and strike on a different tack.

Sobering, Thomas turned toward Nathan. "Would you mind doing mine?" He touched his sword while at the same time lifted his incapacitated arm in example. It was nigh impossible to sharpen a blade one-handed.

Nathan stowed his own and obligingly put out his hand. "Just as well; any edge you've every touched was duller than when you started." He tested the weapon's edge with his thumb and shook his head in dismay. "Been cutting anvils down to size with this?"

Thomas stood mute; it wasn't a question meant to be answered. He stood over Nathan, watching him oil the stone and set to work.

"I've another favor to ask... as a friend," Thomas said, some moments later.

"Name it."

"Allow me to take Cate—"

Nathan sat back, glaring up. "Go get your own damned goddess or obeah, if you're looking for wishes granted."

Well, it was going well, he thought, better than expected: Nathan hadn't skewered him.

"You know damned good n' well Harte, or whoever the hell pokes his mast over that horizon, will be looking for you, not me."

"His High-Arsedness could well have told Harte this rendezvous was all your idea," Nathan declared, stabbing a finger at him.

Thomas smiled at recalling the audience in Creswicke's office. "The thought of my masterminding a betrayal like that, he damned near leapt over the desk to kiss me."

"Which means that over-powdered fop would not have been mum on the not-so-small victory of trapping me. His first move, after closing the door behind *you,* was to send a message to Harte."

"Which is all the more reason everyone will believe I'm *not* in consort with you," Thomas insisted. "Dammit man, think!

Harte, or whoever the hell else, is after you. The *Morganse* will take the fire, not the *Lovely,* and you know that."

He caught himself shaking a fist in Nathan's face and stowed it.

"Besides," Thomas said, seeking a calmer note. "Any fool can see Cate's not up to a battle. Hell, she jumps like she's been shot when someone strikes a flint."

Nathan hunched his shoulders and set his jaw. "She. Just. Needs. Time."

Thomas stood back, glaring. Anyone who knew Nathanael Blackthorne for more than a fortnight knew the look of stubbornness befitting of a barnacle. At the moment, on that rock, he was looking all the more like one.

Time to house the guns. His tops'l wasn't doused yet, however.

"You look like hell," Thomas observed mildly.

The corner of Nathan's mouth quirked. "Good, because I feel like it. Sleep is no longer a pleasure. At least, she sleeps," he added with a wistful look upshore.

"Sorta," Thomas scoffed. "What was all that commotion last night?"

Nathan rolled an eye up at him. "What do you suppose?"

So, yes, it had been what he supposed. Her screams had brought him up off his bed like a bosun's pipe. She sat on their bed, rocking and keening, clutching her side, the very side she had been run through. During the weeks she had lived with him, he had soothed her through many a nightmare, none of which she would remember in the morning. Those, however, had been nothing like this. The entire camp was looking the worse for wear, for there was no escaping those shrieks.

Thank the gods for rum! It had been his path to sleep. Nathan, on the other hand, hadn't taken a drink since he had been first dragged up on the beach. Alas, for he had to be in bad need o' one.

Moving closer, Thomas clapped Nathan companionably on the shoulder. "Go sleep. Take a caulk," he went on over Nathan's protests. "You'll be no good to her, nor anyone else, if you're half-dead."

"No, later. When she's safe and —"

"I'll stand watch," Thomas said, prying the barnacle from its rock. "I'll bid Pryce and Al-Nejem to join me, if you think me insufficient in the face of whatever the hell you find so worrisome," he added, throwing a cautious glare toward the water. "I have men who will give their lives at my word. They'll stand watch with me."

Whilst making his argument, he had gotten Nathan as far as

on his feet, but no further. Thomas gave the man a firm nudge. "Go. Make weigh and I'll fetch her."

Thomas started toward Cate. His stride slowed, and he looked back to find Nathan hadn't moved. "Go!"

"Not without her."

God's my life, the man is as haunted as she.

"Very well, stand-by and we'll rendezvous here," Thomas sighed.

Nathan stared in Cate's direction, his jaw working. "Might be best if we both have a go at this."

Thomas exhaled slowly through his nose. "Very well, then. Don't just stand there backing-and-filling. Spread some canvas."

Their approach was weighted by dread: not that of facing a storm, but something far less manageable. Cate's hair might have been darker than aged cherrywood, but it was red and a befitting color it was. She could be as volatile as a keg of fine-grain powder, with a temper and a tongue which could cause a f'c'stleman to blush.

"This never goes well." The remark was muttered so far under Nathan's breath, Thomas wondered if it had been meant for anyone to hear.

They stopped a few strides short of where Cate stood, hoping she might notice their presence.

She didn't.

Nathan stood mute as a figurehead. Finally, in the face of not knowing what else to do, Thomas cleared his throat loudly. He began to think the effort had been ignored, but she finally turned, not startled, but casually, as if they had been standing there the while.

"You're up and about." Her conversational remark none of her customary cluck or worry typical of when someone was ailing.

"Aye," Thomas said, ducking his head. "Nathan desires to take a caulk... me, too," he hastily added at Nathan's prodding.

It was an announcement which should have caused that same f'c'stleman to stretch his eyes.

"Very well, go," she said vaguely, turning back to the water.

"I'm not leaving without you." Nathan's declaration was uttered in a tone which made her stare and then shy.

"I'm fine," she said in a small voice. She pointedly fixed her attention on the Passage before her. "I'm not so foolish as to not be able to follow a shore back," she threw back over her shoulder, with a flash of the aforementioned volatility.

Nathan inched as near as possible without touching her. "I'll not rest without you at me side, and you know that well," he said lowly.

Shifting to put himself more in front of her, Nathan put out his hand. "Come lie with me. Allow me me peace."

Years of commanding men didn't prepare a man for dealing with a woman. He had seen Nathan wade into a riled mob and have them eating out of his hand in a matter of moments. Bless his soul, Nathan knew her, too.

Cate looked down at the offered hand and then up.

"Come, darling. Thomas tires; let's see him back to his cot."

She turned to peer at Thomas with interest. "You look pale. Perhaps you should lie down."

Ignoring the still outstretched hand, Cate turned and struck off back toward camp with the firm step of it having been her intention all along.

⁂

Nathan jerked upright on the pallet. He knew before he was awake that Cate wasn't next to him and looked frantically about. He slumped in relief at finally spotting her: by the fire, curled at Thomas' feet. The slow rise and fall of the coat covering her showed she was asleep, praise the heavens! Thomas sat on the log next to her, quietly chatting with Pryce and Al-Nejem. Several others, presumably the loyal Lovelies pledged for Cate's protection, stood by.

Blinking and stupid, Nathan rubbed his face hard in his hands. He hadn't slept; at least, he didn't think so. How the hell it came to be so dark, so fast defied all logic, however?

He pushed to his feet and went to share Thomas' log, Cate now between them. A plate sat at Thomas' side. Nathan nodded approvingly at the cheese and soft tack, the corners nibbled like a mouse had been at them. A cup sat in the sand next to Cate's head, the smell of broth rising from it.

The hand of Providence was everywhere.

Thomas grinned. A smug Thomas was a thoroughly annoying visage.

Looking down at Cate, Nathan leaned to ask quietly "How long...?"

"As long as you," Thomas said simply.

Still feeling wholly disoriented, Nathan glanced up at the night sky, taking note of clouds, wind and weather. Venus was still high; as suspected, it hadn't been dark long.

He looked down at Cate again and couldn't help but smile. There was an angelic, peaceful air about her, one long, too

114

long unseen. He couldn't take his eyes off her. It had been his affliction since the day she boarded, the very moment he saw her, dripping and puking on his deck. Just then, her hair was a-tumble about her face, allowing only a bit of one brow, cheek and tip of her nose, slightly turned up and bright from the sun, showing. By her own admission, she had her father's fair coloring, a Lowland Scot, as best he could recall, her mother being some second cousin or some such to the Rey of España. That fair skin would redden even if she was at sea a decade. It gave her a freshness, a perpetual youthfulness which would cause her to look like a maid when she was silver-headed.

Lord that we might both live long enough to see the day.

His fingers twitched with the desire to brush away the lock tickling the corner of her mouth. What stopped him was the fear of waking her; he desired her all the peace she had finally found.

He had lain with her in his arms, trembling and twitching, jerking and murmuring, her breath ragged, as if she were being chased. Sometimes she went as rigid as a bowsprit. Other times, her body gone cold and lifeless, her skin as flaccid as a corpse, he feared the worst and poked her, sometimes pinching to the point of nearly breaking the skin, in order to rouse her.

That was why he didn't sleep: fear of what he might wake up to.

Often he tried to picture her as a little girl, skirts hitched and frolicking in the waves, a time before dying mothers, cold fathers, predatory men, war, starvation, life in its entirety had changed her. Lord, the fire and spirit she must have had then! Hardship and tribulation aged one beyond their years; any fool knew she was but a shadow of her former self, a shadow rendered all the dimmer after being with him. Bullock, the other bastard skulking in the night, Creswicke: he should have stopped it, should have seen some of it, any of it... hell, all of it coming!

But he didn't, and she had paid the price.

Cate stirred, mussing her head on the arm under it. A hand came out from under the coat, groped about, found his foot and settled. She inhaled and let it out, slow and silent, as contented as he had witnessed in a long time. Or, did it only seem so? Hardship and tribulation also distorted time; years became days, seconds became months. It was little wonder one felt older, for the soul might well think itself decades older, when only a week had passed.

Nathan shook himself and stiffened his spine.

God's my life, I'm a maudlin cove tonight!

He plucked a bit of cheese from the plate and popped it into his mouth, chewing pensively as he stared into the flames.

The camp's merriment was considerably restrained, laughter lowered, the music reduced to a fife and fiddle twiddling repeated strains, as if one was teaching the other a new tune. He paused in mid-chew at realizing a silence had fallen around the fire and looked up to find expectant looks on every face, as if a direct question had been posed to him.

Swallowing, he slipped his foot from under Cate's fingers, rose and leaned toward to Thomas. "Walk with me."

The two captains looked significantly at the others. They nodded in full understanding.

Yes, they would watch her.

Thomas allowed Nathan to lead the way, down the shoreline, away from camp. The lights and voices faded, and the night closed in. Overhead was a dome of stars he'd known since he was a lad: the Pleiades, Capella, Aldebaran, Castor and Pollux. Thomas walked silently beside him. Nathan had hoped—a dim one, but a hope nonetheless—the quiet they found out there might provide him a bit of peacefulness. God's wounds, he was in desperate need of some. Thomas, knowing him well enough to know something was on his mind, walked in amiable silence, allowing him time to muddle it out.

Damnation and seize my soul, this isn't easy!

"I was thinking—" Nathan began.

One brow cocked, Thomas cut a sideways glance. "Always a positive sign."

"Pomphrey wasn't the last. There's more coming, and soon."

Thomas grunted with the satisfaction of having come to that conclusion long since.

"The men are getting restless. Sun, rock and sand is an abrasion to high spirits, and they are dulling quickly."

"You have a plan," Thomas observed mildly.

"An unprepared pirate is a dead pirate." Nathan sketched a bow in mid-stride. "Give them what they wish to see, right?"

Thomas drew to a sudden halt. "Are you saying we should—?"

"I am."

Grunting, this time with reserved displeasure, Thomas looked off, considering, measuring, evaluating: no differently than Nathan had done for a good while before giving it voice.

Finally, Thomas nodded shortly and grinned. "Very well."

Appeased, Nathan turned his attention to the *Brazen*. Resting on her moorings, the reflection of her lights danced on her hull. "That hulk fit to sail?"

"Nearly."

Nathan nodded in half-interest as necessities and repairs were listed; none were remarkable, none might keep a vessel at anchor. When the litany was complete, he reached up to clap a hand on Thomas' shoulder. "Well, make it so, *Captain.*"

It took Thomas a moment to realize what Nathan was saying. "I don't need any damned ship!" he sputtered, backing away from the accolades.

Thomas' reluctance came as no great surprise. He'd step to the line when it came to a crew in need of a steadying hand. This was different: this was assuming command of a prize, taking on a consort.

"Aye, well, 'tis a pity, because you've got one now," Nathan said, evenly.

"What the hell am I supposed to do with—?"

"Promote someone for starters," Nathan said, with a flick of his hand. It seemed bloody obvious, but captaining was known to disarm some. "Surely you have someone prime for command. What about that First Mate o' yours?"

"Mebbe," Thomas said, already deep in thought.

"Well, find someone. Roll the dice, draw straws, play blind-man's bluff if you must, but the ship is yours. Muster a crew, for we shan't tarry. Looks like you've the beginnings of a fleet, *Commodore*!"

Nathan blew a private sigh of relief. There had been the chance—a vague one, but a chance nonetheless—that the *Lovely's* good captain might have refused the *Brazen* out-of-hand. He would have, had the capstan been turned. Double the ships, double the headaches, to his mind. T'would have been a pity, for she looked too fine o' vessel to just scuttle, or cast adrift and a hazard to every unsuspecting cove afloat.

He turned, meaning to head back to camp, when a hand came down on his arm to stop him.

"As I have your attention, there's another matter," Thomas said.

Bloody hell, this didn't sound good, Thomas looking as solemn as Solomon himself.

Solomon drew a deep breath and looked to his feet.

God's my life, this is serious.

"I fancy it will come as no great surprise that there's mixed moods among the men— all of them, including mine—regarding shipping with you. Some think you the luckiest thing walking, whilst others think you're the right hand of Old Nick himself." The end came with an explosion of air and a peek from under Thomas' brows.

"Half are scared witless and the other half are immobilized

in awe, think you're some damned god incarnate, while others think you're the Devil himself," Thomas went on.

Nathan looked to his feet, too. No, 'twas no great surprise a'tall. He'd have to be half – blind and a total buffoon to not see them either pass close enough to touch Cate's skirts or his sleeve, whilst even more gave them both a wide berth, making horned signs and groping for charms, or spitting and mumbling incantations. While some avoided him like the Egyptian pox, others glowed in his presence, as if whatever blessing had brought him back from the dead might somehow befall upon them, immortality by association. They could call him anything they wished — already had over the years — but he hated like hell to see Cate reviled and cast in the same gutter as he.

Thomas waited for a reaction or comment. With none in the offing, he pressed on, now more captain than friend. "What with those from the *Brazen* who signed on, we've enough to man all three vessels creditably. We mightn't be able to fight both sides," he added, with not a little regret, "but we can sting anyone who crosses us hard enough to wish they hadn't."

Nathan braced his head in his hands, suddenly too weary to think on any of it. He had but one sole purpose: Cate. Beyond that —

"I was thinking it might be best if Pryce and Al-Nejem were to see to it. Away from the Captain's eye might be the best place for such decisions to be made," Thomas suggested.

Nathan mutely nodded, the weight-of-the-world off his shoulders. Manipulating, bullying and cajoling a crew just wasn't in him. Let the men ship as they might; the undecided could jolly well sit on this rock and let starvation be their pleasure.

"Very well, muster your meeting. Give me warning so my shadow mightn't accidentally fall on it. Once the dust has settled, let me know if you're short-handed in any way: coopers, armorers, topsmen..." A wave of Nathan's hand completed the thought. A ship might have a full complement in terms of numbers, but the likelihood of every position and skill level being an able hand was slim.

"We'll make all preparations to weigh anchor," Nathan said, turning upshore again. Thomas cocked a severe brow. "And if a mast nicks the horizon before?"

"Then win your anchors and haul your wind out o' here. Cut the cables if you must and let the stragglers learn how to swim."

The blood pulsed in his veins. Snoggers, he felt alive again... finally! With His High – Lordliness dead, the world promised a new order, the chance to lead something akin to a normal life, whatever in the hell that was. It was an odd sensation:

the hatred had buttressed him for so long, he nearly toppled over in it sudden absence. It was like a nagging pain, not fully appreciating its extent until it was gone.

The prospect of "normal" was a worry. It had been so many years, he couldn't recall what that meant, what that had been. He looked up at Thomas next to him, stern and commodorely in the rising moonlight, and wondered if perhaps his friend might recall what he had been like before... everything.

He slapped the thought away like an annoying gnat.

Christ, he was grass-combing dolt! Too much water had gone over the decks for such maudlin stuff as that.

Just one thing remained.

Even if they managed to slip the Straits unnoticed, the waters would be alive with vessels searching, the Royal Navy — Commodore Roger Harte presiding — most predominate. He'd be a mutton-headed lubber to expect else and Cate right in the damned middle of it.

"Damn your miserable, dung-hearted soul, you're correct," Nathan blurted. "Cate needs... something more, more than what can be managed here."

Thomas free hand lifted to the heavens. "Where's the logbook! This one needs entering: Nathan Blackthorne conceding he was wrong!"

"I don't dare take her to any town, but there is somewhere, someplace... safe." Suffering Jesus, it felt like an eighteen-pound great gun was sitting on his chest.

They took several more strides before Thomas finally said "Where?"

"Near."

Straining to think, Thomas stopped, looking without seeing at the cove. "Where?"

"Near," came back with a significant lilt. Heaven help him, has the man gone that dense?

"Wh—? I'll be a...! It's still there!?" Thomas asked, gaping like a beached fish.

"Still."

Thomas looked off into the night in astonishment. "Damn! I'd forgotten—"

"Tell that one to the parrot. You've been gone from these waters for nigh on to a decade, but you haven't gone feeble. There's her own kind there: women. It's decent and, of prime importance, 'tis safe."

Deep in his own recollections, Thomas nodded distractedly. "Been a long time since— " The sentence was left unfinished, the rising moon catching his reddened face.

"Hopefully, long enough for them to forget."

"I'd venture to guess the same might be said for you."

Nathan looked up to find Thomas grinning down at him. Grimacing, he looked to his feet. Had Thomas posed the question, he would have said he didn't know exactly how long it had been since his last visit. Truth be told that would have been a bald-faced lie. He knew right down to date, day and the watch bells when he had tripped his anchor and hauled his wind out of there.

"Eh... Let's just say it might be best if you were to arrive ahead of me, offer a bit of warning—" Nathan said slowly.

"And take a little of the heat."

Nathan sighed and ran a hand down the curve of his mustache. "That, too. I vowed to never step foot there again—"

Thomas chuckled with untoward pleasure. "They sent you packing, eh?"

"—But for her—"

"For her you'll risk decapitation, dismemberment and gelding."

The ensuing silence was filled with unfulfilled expectancy. "I won't ask," Thomas finally said.

"Best you don't." Damn him, he can hoot and roar with laughter on his own time.

"Very well," Thomas sighed. "If there's a red flag at my jack-staff, stand off."

"You're a true friend."

Thomas shrugged off the half-complement. "You'd do the same for me."

"As I recall, I have," Nathan grinned up.

Thank heavens, neither one of them asked for a listing, for neither had the wherewithal nor the time to go through them all. Suffice to say, the years they had known each other hadn't been spent sitting in the shade at their ease.

"What about her?" Thomas asked, with a significant look back toward camp.

Nathan sighed wearily. That eighteen-pounder on his chest just became a thirty-two. "I'll tell her."

"You damned right," Thomas declared, ramming a finger into Nathan's chest. "And make damned sure you actually do it this time."

"I will, I will," Nathan said, ruefully rubbing the sore spot.

Thomas was, of course, referring to the most recent time he had sent Cate off with him. It hadn't been his most stellar moment. He had meant to tell Cate in advance, but matters—careening a ship, managing men—had gotten in the way.

Oh, hell, very well, he had been a thoroughgoing coward. Telling her would have only led to harsh words, her screeching like a fishwife and then tears, bodily harm not being out of the realm of possibilities. Alas, all the aforementioned had come true. He was already considering ways for this time to go differently, to be better.

There were none.

Squabbling, screeching, crying, and yes, bodily harm were all in the offing. Death was beginning to look like something just this side of Fiddler's Green.

"Can you mind her *this* time?"

Thomas flinched at the barb finding home. His chin took that all too familiar bullish jut. "On my life, and you know it," he hissed vehemently.

Thomas turned to take his leave, but stopped. "You mean it?"

"Damn your black heart, yes!" Nathan said, glaring up. It was like a knife to the gut to admit he couldn't provide for her. Even worse was the prospect of what was to come next.

"And you're going to tell her," Thomas insisted.

"Yes, I'll tell her!" He would have looked forward to the gallows more than this.

Nathan rubbed his face in his hands. "This is going to destroy her. She can't manage—"

"It's the right thing, Nathan," Thomas said, leaning over him. "Don't let any damned demons tell you different."

"Tell you what different?"

The pair spun around to find Cate standing there.

❧

Thomas touched his forehead in salute and scurried away into the night. "Coward," Nathan called.

"Nay, survivor!" came back from the darkness.

In the ensuing silence—a long and unhealthy one—Nathan gazed longingly in Thomas' path. There would be no witnesses to his death. Cate could well throw his body amid the dead Brazens, the crabs eat his face off by the morrow, and no one the wiser.

Wrapped in Thomas' coat, the tails hanging nearly to her ankles, Cate watched his departure, as well. When he could no longer be seen, she turned to Nathan, stiff with suspicion.

"Would you care to take a walk?" He grimaced. That sounded as lame as a one-legged parson.

"Walk?" echoed back, sharp with incredulity.

Nathan sighed internally; it wasn't a thing he wished to do, either. What he wished was for this nastiness to be over, so he might be at liberty to lie with her with a clear mind.

A clear mind! And where the bloody hell do you fancy finding something you haven't had since you were twelve?

He debated between nonchalance and histrionics. The former won, for it required less effort.

Murmuring a small prayer befitting of commending a soul to the deep, he drew a breath and said conversationally "We were just discussing our… situation… in general."

Christ, that came out like a mumbling mump.

Cate glanced around, as if fearing something jumping out of the night, and inched closer. "Situation?"

"We're sitting ducks here," Nathan explained, in a slightly stronger tone. "Harte, or more skulking privateers like that last pair, might show up, and we mightn't be so lucky next time."

There was no prevarication in that; the danger was an honest one.

The warning wasn't lost on Cate, and she moved nearer still. "You said it was safe here."

"It is."

She spun around, the jade eyes fixed on him. "Except? There's an 'except' in there, I can hear it."

He gulped. This would be where the prow hits the wave. "Except 'tis not a place I'd wish to be blockaded, with the Royal Navy polishing the coast, and us obliged to slip out under the cover of darkness. Yon reefs are treacherous enough under full daylight."

"You did it before. You slipped in and no one —"

"Not with you aboard," he shot back, vehemently.

It took Cate a moment, but she was no fool. The green eyes narrowed. "You're sending me with Thomas." For many women, it might have been considered a strident outburst, but for her, it was a meek, disbelieving whisper.

She went pale, paler than she already was. He braced for her to fly at him as she had countless times before.

But she only stood there, eyes, which could have cut like a blade, going dull. "Damn you and your 'joined and always'!" Her voice went hoarse with hurt and betrayal. "You promised never again! You said— You promised—"

"I promised to never again to put you in harm's way, *never* again!" He'd swabbed her blood from the deck once. Drown and sink him, he had neither the stomach, nor the heart to do so again! Better her screaming in fury than screaming in agony.

His vehemence sent her stumbling backwards, withdrawing into the coat like a dormouse into its hole.

Chest heaving, Nathan regained himself. He had dreaded this confrontation, dreaded her fury; now he found himself wishing for it. She was a ghost of herself. He worried, for he still wasn't sure he had gotten all of her back. Parts seemed to have gone missing: her essence, her spirit. He wouldn't put it past that scheming witch-o'-the-deep to do something of the sort, some trickery to force his return. The only thing which stopped him from going and having it out with the witch was the worry he mightn't return.

"Thomas will be taking you where you'll have a decent place to sleep and food, and your own kind."

Cate choked a harsh laugh. "You say that like I'm some kind of a two-headed calf."

"You're not ready for—"

"Go ahead, say it!" she said bitterly, backing away. "I'm infirmed... ill... daft... touched."

"You're not—"

She hunched the coat higher about her. "It's like before: you and everyone keep staring, like you expect me to fall into some kind of fit."

His jaw worked with the urge to say "No, this was nothing like before."

Hell and furies, had that only been a month ago?

Before, she had been beaten, tortured and used hard. Sad to say, in too many cursed ways, her condition now was much the same: empty-eyed and addled. She jumped like she'd been shot when a plover took flight. Asking as to what she wished to drink could result in either a blank stare or tears, or both. And heaven help the unsuspecting bugger who inquired as to how she did.

If it was a fever, he could cool her with cloths. If it was a gash, he could salve and bind it. If she was screaming or seeking to unman him, he could have fended her off.

But, this... This...!

All in all, he was all the more convinced that she was in no condition to endure the bang-and-crash of battle.

With the coat double wrapped about her, the tails nearly dragging the ground, she looked like a little girl in her father's clothes.

"Must you wear that thing?" he asked, tugging the sleeve.

"I couldn't find yours," she said, with an edge of resentment. She pulled the garment tighter about her. "I'm cold; I can't warm up."

"I know, darling." He ran a weary hand down his face. "Believe me, I know."

It was the very thing which had driven him to bedding scores of women... very well, whores: the desperation for warmth. Were he to be completely honest, there had been another element: the even more driving need for physical contact, the press of flesh, moving, warm and alive, next to his. He eyed her, wondering if that had been a reaction unique to himself; Cate had shown none of that particular inclination... yet. Neither had he, come to think on it.

Odd, very, very odd.

Even in the dimness, he could see the coattails quake with her shaking.

"Allow me to warm you." He put out his arms, but she only retreated farther.

"I just need a little more time," she said, meekly.

"Time is the one thing we don't have. It's the one thing I can't give you. Goddammit to bloody hell!"

Nathan whirled and struck a rock with his fist. Letting out a small yip, Cate shied like a startled deer and quaked all the harder. He hadn't seen her cower from him since another unfortunate outburst, some months ago.

Still in dire need to hit something, he churned up and down the high-water line, instead. "I can't give you what you need. I'm useless. I can't—"

He turned and drew up short, nearly running into Cate, having stepped into his path.

She looked up at him so beseeching it struck the wind from him.

"I only need you," she said, small and pleading. The hand on his arm shook as hard as her voice.

His shoulders slumped. "If only it were that easy."

Squeezing her hand—a cold, hard thing like ice—he canted his head toward the cove and the sea beyond. "There's the not so small matter of *her*."

"*Her*?" Backing away, Cate looked out at the water in horror. "She's waiting?"

"Aye, well, that's the thing of it; I have no notion. She has no use of me—the... thing is done," he said, with a dismissive flap of his hand. "But, after that last tomfoolery, I can't trust the skulking, devious harridan to not go back on her word and do God-knows-what."

It was a tragic state of affairs when one couldn't depend on a god to keep their word. One would have thought a bit more honesty could be expected from such a superior being.

Apparently, lofty position didn't necessarily go hand-in-hand with lofty ideals.

"She can't touch you, darling," he added quickly at seeing Cate shrink and shy. He touched the necklace's knot at her throat. "You're protected; that much we *do* know."

"And you?" she asked, fixing her eye on the one he now wore.

Nathan withdrew his hand and sobered. "All I can hope is whatever capers she decides to cut up, they will be targeted at me."

He thanked the heavens when Cate didn't press further on the issue, for he had nothing more than that: a hope, hanging by a spider's thread.

"Please, don't do this," she pleaded in a tight whisper. "I can't survive another loss, when I've yet to survive the last one."

He closed his eyes. Heaven help him, he couldn't look at her. This whole scene was too much like brow-beating a child.

"I have to, darling. This could get rough, *very* rough. My failure could put you directly into Harte's hands. I *will not* risk that."

On that he was firm. Nothing, no one could compel him to do that. Summoning every ounce of guts and willpower he possessed, he opened his eyes.

She was gone.

⌖

Silence closed in around him like a shroud, pressing over his face, seeking to smother the life from him. He cursed the stones, the damned things looking too much like a giants' tossed graveyard.

"Jesus, no! Cate? Cate!? Cate!!" He peered into the night, trying to think which way she might have gone.

Inland was negated straightaway: too stone-jammed, too malodorous, too forbidding. He looked to the sea next—he had dragged her back from it a couple times—ready to rip the stuff from his neck and limbs, and jump in. All he found, however, was a flat, undisturbed surface heaving gently with the swell. He cocked his head and listened hard for the sound of splashing, crying out, struggle... anything! There was nothing more than the rattle of crabs in the rocks, the churr of a night insect, the distant camp laughter.

The shore, she had to have taken the shore, but which way? He took several strides toward camp, but skidded to a halt. If she had gone that way, he should have seen her silhouette against the firelight. Squinting hard, searching the beach, there was no sign of her. Spinning around, he raced in the opposite direction, sick with terror that she'd vanished or been taken, plucked away. Running, praying to whatever powers which might be to let him be swift enough, he called for her until his lungs and throat burned.

Finally, he spotted Cate on the shore, her way blocked by a tumble of rocks. With her back to him, in the gunmetal moonlight, she looked ethereal, not of this world. Caught between the urge to sweep her up and hug her, and giving her a solid shake and a tongue lashing, he stopped a few paces away. His breath came in rasping gasps from running; he made a concerted effort to curb it, lest even that small thing might disturb her.

Dashing the sweat from his face, he started to speak, swallowed hard and tried again. "Cate?"

Nearer now, he could see the coat skirts quivering like a moth's wing. Head hanging, arms clutched about her middle, she jerked her head away at the sound of his voice, refusing to look at him. He inched closer, still careful not to touch her, for fear she might vanish like that very ghost.

"Kittie." He extended his hand; no other words came, for there was nothing left to say.

Still she didn't move, as if she were dead, yet still standing.

The need to touch her brought his hand over her shoulder, fear of scaring her out of her wits making it hover. She whirled around, tear-filled eyes searching his. He put his arms out. She was near enough, now, all she need do was lean forward and her head came to rest on his chest. Shoulders shaking, she silently sobbed, beating his chest with her fist to a faint chant of "Damn you... Damn you... Damn you."

The breeze blew, cooling the wetness on his own cheeks.

He held her, until she slumped, exhausted and senseless. His bones shook with weariness, and yet he found the wherewithal to pick her up and carry her back to their bed.

The camp was quiet, inordinately so, in anticipation and deference to their return, he thought. No one wished to witness, nor be any part of the inevitable scene. Even Thomas, the whey-livered coward, had made himself scarce. By the glow of the fire's embers, he lowered Cate onto their pallet and, with a long, silent expulsion of air, lay next to her.

She rolled to him, and they lay as they did in their bunk: one half atop the other, her leg over his, his chest her pillow. It was the first time since their resurrection she had done so. His greatest hope was that small gesture meant he was forgiven, or at least that forgiveness was in the offing. That hope sparked second thoughts. Perhaps all she did need was time.

But time was the thing he, no one had.

Shaking with exhaustion and relief, he held her. When the tremors finally stopped, he traced and memorized her every shape, texture and smell, as he did whenever the opportunity presented. He'd learned the value of this exercise when he had thought to have lost her before. It was how he kept her alive in his heart and, in all likelihood, kept her with him in Death. The tangle of hair of a color no one could name and eyes much the same; that elegant sweep of collarbone and the sweet, tender notch where neck and jaw met, which had been a fascination since the first time laying eyes on her; fine skin, so flawless as to make a man forget what he was about. Something new was always found, as he did then: a small scar at the underside of her arm, a tiny bump at the backside of her ear.

At length, he settled her into his arms and reveled in the sheer joy of holding her, her warm, heavy weight dragging him down into his own drowsy world.

A sailor's life was doomed to be one of countless goodbyes and separations.

Somehow, someway, this had to stop. He had to find a better life, end the danger, end the stalking.

⁓꙳⁓

Deep in swirling realms of slumber, Cate still knew Nathan was next to her. His measured movements, tinkle of bells and the slope of the mattress were all combined to indicate that he was awake, sitting up and not wishing to be discovered. It was early. The heaviness of the air and lazy lap of the waves all pointed toward the day was still in repose, neither man nor beast stirring.

All conclusions were confirmed when she opened her eyes to Nathan. Head bent, the quilt rumpled over his crossed legs, the purple and coral of impending dawn outlined his bare shoulders. At one point, by some means, he had acquired a replacement pair of boots. Heavy-soled and silver-buckled, more like half-boots, they sat in the sand at his knee.

"What are you doing?" she asked groggily.

Nathan looked up as if caught at something he preferred to have gone unseen. He guiltily raised his hands, allowing the growing light to catch on a bundle of hairs stretched between his fingers. Rubbing the sleep from her eyes and peering closer, Cate finally recognized them as being from her own head. She leaned back, patiently waiting for an explanation. Indecision etched his features, to the point she thought she might wait in vain. He glanced in hopes dispensation might be found. She cocked a brow. It was her hair, and therefore, an accounting wasn't unreasonable.

Finally, obligation prevailed. He ran his fingers along the hairs, straightening and aligning. "I wanted, *needed* something of you." His voice was lowered, in deference to the hour. Still, a whisper seemed a shout.

"I'll get my bag," she said, pushing up. "You can have anything you wish."

Among her dunnage was a bag. To the unknowing eye, it was a hodgepodge of useless junk. In truth, it was the sum total of her worldly possessions, each paltry bit a token or remembrance of a former life. It was hard to believe a man who had a shipload of swag, a virtual treasure chest at his fingertips, would be interested in such sentimental bits, but she'd give any or all of it without equivocation or exception. Nathan was her life, now.

"Nay," he said, gently stopping her. "Those are but things; I desire something of *you.*"

Cate rubbed one eye in both sleepiness and confusion. A month and more ago, Nathan had discovered that bag. Always over-sensitive to the merest allusion to her long – dead husband, he had been sorely put off by finding the mementos. In the spirit of allaying his concerns, she had secured a few strands of her hair about one of his braids. The exchange had been a small, small token, a feeble gesture, but at the time, nothing more seemed fitting.

"But, we already —"

An abrupt wave cut her short. "It proved more temporary than I could have wished. Mine was lost somewhere on the *Gosport.*" He tugged ruefully on his own hair. The loose lock, wavy with years of being braided, bore the blunt end of having been sliced off.

"As for yours...?" Catching his lip between his teeth, he touched the knot of her necklace, where he had affixed his own hair. "It wasn't near enough."

Cate settled comfortably back down on the pillow. "Then tell me what you wish of me? Blessings? Blood?"

"God's my life, I've seen far too much of your blood already! 'Tis a wonder you've any left."

"Very well, then, what?" she asked, earnestly. "You said —

just the other day, as I recall—that we were connected." Much was confusing, but on that point, she was certain.

Nathan ducked his head, suddenly shy. "Aye, I know what I said. And I also know what I feel," he added, now firm with conviction. "I needed something I can touch, can look at and see you. I wish something large enough to find you in a swirling tempest with me eyes closed; something which I shall tally on with a knot known to endure a full gale, in the roaring sixties."

As a young girl, Cate had several suitors, their young, smooth-faces shining with earnestness as they had begged a token and breathlessly made pledges. Neither she, nor Nathan were young or naïve. Both were wise and scarred, and still staggering from the last blow Fate had dealt them. Tokens of affection seemed so trivial, and yet recent events had confirmed an already hard-learned lesson: things could take a drastic change and without so much warning as a snap of one's fingers, a tattered piece of tartan suddenly becoming all which remained of a life.

Cate ran her hand up to fan her hair out about her head. "Then take all you wish. Snatch me bald, if you must."

Nathan hesitated, thinking she might be making game of him. Seeing her sincerity, he leaned closer. From the extreme corner of her eye, she watched as he sorted through the hair spread out on the pillow, selectively plucking.

"It's all different: copper, red, russet, ginger... even gold," he said, with the quiet delight of discovery. Feeling her watching, he flushed. "I wish to have every color, so I might recall how it looks when you lie next to me."

Once satisfied with his selection, for a man who knew how to knot and splice in the foulest of weather and in the dark of night, it was a small thing for him to twist the hairs together into something resembling a thread. He found the severed lock and deftly twirled one about the other.

Watching as Nathan worked, Cate lay with a hand beside her head. It had landed there casually enough, but there were those of the philosophical sort who claimed nothing happened purely by accident. Nathan's speech had put her in mind of something. Her gaze fixed on him, she inched her hand to the nape of her neck. Searching there, her eyes rolled closed in silent thanks at finding what she sought: the tiny braid, his hair entwined into hers, was still there.

When Nathan had started brushing yesterday, she had feared discovery. Barely more than a few hairs thick, it had been either too small or too deep to be detected. And thank the heavens! Nathan missed precious little, but he missed that, just as he had missed when she had done it.

The sober part of her urged that she tell him, honesty always being the better policy. Knowing of its existence might give him a bit of ease, perhaps enhancing the connection he so desperately sought. When she had done it, she had felt underhanded, conniving, and so very daring to presume such a familiarity. Even now, she felt covert and conspiratorial, but not enough to put it into words.

A large truth was that preservation of dignity wasn't what kept her from unveiling the lie then. It was the glory of the secret itself. It was hers and hers alone, precious if for no other reason than it existed. Nathan, nor anyone else, knew.

She pressed her fingers a bit tighter, feeling the braid's grooves and planes, a small bit of roughness amid the silken. Being at the nape of her neck, and no peering glass about, she'd never see it. But now she did, a reverse image before her, at any rate, the mahogany, copper, and russet, one or two nearly golden, interwoven with the ebony, the contrast giving it an almost checkered look.

As Nathan secured the braid with a final hitch, Cate briefly closed her eyes in a departing benediction, and then withdrew. Her hand came to rest on her stomach, and she worked her fingers together, preserving the sensation.

"Do you ever undo all of... that?" she asked, eyeing the mixed-up mass of braids snaking about his shoulders. Her fingers itched to get into the multi-colored bits of rag and thread binding it, put it into some kind of order. She had only known Nathan a few months, but never had she seen him raise a hand to those locks. Logic dictated it would require some kind of maintenance if for no other reason than to re-secure what had been worked free by wind and wear.

"Once, every twelve-month or so. What are you looking at?" he asked, warily leaning away.

"I'm trying to visualize you without it." She narrowed one eye. It was blessedly difficult to imagine that raven head plain, smoothed back into a tail and tied. Or, perhaps he might wear it in a single braid, in the seaman's fashion, one which, by all appearances, might reach past the middle of his back.

"I think not," Nathan said, moving his head beyond her questing hands. "We're still recovering from the removal of one. Rot and perish us, if we were to remove them all!"

"Sometimes I try to see you without all of this," she mused. Unlike the fashion of the day, Nathan wore a mustache and beard in the Spanish-style. When first met, he wore a full beard, a ferocious great thing, which made him look more bear than human. Completely shaven she'd never seen.

He drew back at that. "You object? Smooth as a baby's bottom is more to your taste?"

"No, I mean—" she began quickly, regretting having broached the subject. Nathan had been the first man with facial hair she had ever kissed. Bristling, yet at the same time soft, it had felt odd and tickled, their more arduous moments leaving the lower part of her face and lips bright red. Those sensations, however, where quite scintillating in some of her more tender parts.

"No, I'd miss it," she said, her face heating.

Mouth quirking, Nathan took her arm from among the bed clothing and kissed her wrist, applying that mustache with great deliberation to the tender underside.

"Yes, definitely miss it," she said, a bit breathless.

In times past that gesture would have been an overture to something far more impassioned. Now, Nathan only sat back, pleased.

Nathan was a full-blooded man. He might have been picky at table, but he had a healthy appetite in bed... or anywhere else the opportunity might present itself. Living among two hundred others, and Nathan desiring her to be regarded as something more than the one warming the captain's bed, had brought their public life to appear more like brother and sister. Out of the crew's sight, however, they came together with a force which verged on mutual destruction, being apart from morning until night often posing an intolerable strain.

His current forbearance was the question now. Rarely had they gone a few hours, let alone days without joining. Was it in deference to her condition? During her recent recovery, he had come to her bed only through her insistent invitation and even then, he had been more gentle and giving in his love-making than ever. He was much the same now, and yet different: even more reserved, almost withdrawn.

Or was he still as dazed and disoriented as she? Or, was it the aftereffects of joining with Calypso?

Dislike? Disinterest...? Or disability?

"I'll be no more than a eunuch" he had said, in the process of explaining the curse.

"Cate? Kittie?"

"What?" she said, irritated by Nathan's insistent nudging.

"You wouldn't answer," he said, peering worriedly. "You went... vague, somehow or another. You're shivering," he said, laying a hand on her arm. "Come here."

Nathan lay down. Guiding Cate's head into the crook of his neck, he pulled the quilt high about them. Between the cover and

Nathan radiating heat like a small stove, she was truly warm for the first time since their return. Basking in it, she molded herself to him, wishing they were both naked, so she might soak up every possible bit.

It was very early, but the camp was coming to life, Kirkland and Youssef stirring about the galleys, poking the fires, Ben and Maram fetching water and wood. The canvas overhead and pallet underneath provided as much of a private nook as could be managed on a beach populated by several hundred. Entwined, Cate and Nathan idly traced the other's curves and planes, not in lust, but in the need of constant reassurance that the other lived.

"How long?" she asked, her voice thin with dread. The impending separation hung like a storm cloud.

"Soon."

Cate closed her eyes and woodenly nodded, a tear squeezing from between her lids.

"S'all right, darling. Within the day we finally haul anchor from here, you'll be lying in a bed—" Nathan began.

"I have a bed," she said, rocking her hips.

"Something off the ground and far more fitting," he said, glaring censoriously down the long line of his nose. "You'll have a decent meal in your belly—"

"Don't let Mr. Kirkland hear you say that. He'll be devastated."

Nathan's shoulder moved, conceding. "The man is a genius with what he has to work with."

His arms tightened encouragingly about her. "And most of all, you'll have your own kind."

"You keep saying that like I'm a five-legged calf."

"Well, then a place where not everyone has hair sprouting from every crevice," he said, unperturbed.

Cate ducked her head to press her nose into the hair on his chest, thick and springy. She inhaled, dreamily. "I'd rather have you." Softer than his mustache, it was another one of his fascinating textures.

"And so you shall." Nathan shifted under her. "After all, who's to say? We mightn't encounter a single vessel; we'll arrive together and all this conflagration will have been for naught."

Cate rose up to look him in the eye. "Then, see? I don't need to—"

He lifted his head to meet her look with a gimlet one of his own. "Thomas concurs.

Hell, it was his idea, so you'll find no solace there."

Cate lowered her head next to his, silence filing her complaint.

For some while, Nathan's hand had repeatedly followed the grove of her spine, making her want to purr like a kitten. Her pleasure was interrupted by the sudden awareness of an expectant pause, suggesting he had just said something.

"What? I'm sorry... I didn't...?"

"I said," he repeated, with strained patience. "Perhaps you'll make a friend."

Cate sat up, gaping. "Friend?"

"Aye, when was the last time you had one of those?"

She wanted to say "When was the last time you had one?" but curbed it.

"Recently, *very* recently," she said, instead. "You, and then Thomas," she added at his interrogatory grunt.

That was met with even more derision.

Nathan worked his head, discontented. "I meant women friends, ones you might chat with, tell your innermost secrets, swap receipts, whatever the hell it 'tis women do."

Cate eyed him, bemused. "All of the women you've been with, and you have no notion what we *do*?"

He started to demur, but then narrowed his eye. "I know whatever they are doing, they change when there's a man about, so you'll allow me pardon for me ignorance, for I'm disqualified as an inconspicuous observer."

Cate wondered if, at any moment in his life, Nathan had ever been inconspicuous.

Smiling, she laid her head and twirled her fingers the hair on his chest. "And it drives you men crazy, doesn't it?"

"It is a wonder," he sighed.

They lay listening to the camp continue to wake. It seemed no one could greet the day without a certain amount of noise: yawning, coughing, hawking, spitting, farting and urinating. With the large numbers of men, even with the bulk of them well upshore, it was certainly no chorus-of-angels.

"Am I that much of a burden?" Cate asked, the chill returning.

The body next to hers stiffened; the roving hands stopped. "I should think I should be the one to ask that."

"What?" she blurted, jerking up.

The hand at her back balled into a fist, the brown eyes struggling to meet hers. "The day you came into me life, I was damn near the death of you. Aye, it was my men what boarded that hulk," he went on over her sputtering. "But it was the same as my hand sending you into the water."

Nathan looked away, his mouth working. "I put you in his High Arsedness' hands and was damned near the death of you then," he went on, shifting irritably. "And then, on the *Gosport*, I *was* the death of you."

It took a moment for him to find the courage to meet her gaze. Eyes shimmering, his throat moved as he swallowed. "If you wished to be shut of me, I shouldn't blame you."

Cate stared. A stirring of air at her mouth suggested that it hung open, and she clapped it shut. A number of remarks rose, but then slipped away. "You've already died because of me. I'd call our accounts square. As you said just the other day," she went on, dropping her voice into a feeble imitation of his, "You'll not be shut of me that easily."

He smiled, the single bell in his mustache sparking in the growing light, rendered all the brighter by its solitary state. The sight broke her heart: deprived of its partner and all because of her.

She ventured to delicately flick the tiny silver bit with her fingertip. "You were wise not telling me what those were for. I would have never let you—" Regret tightened her throat to the point of being unable to finish.

"Aye, well, call me a spoilt, unobliging cove, for I did it for me own selfish reasons." Nathan bent his head and kissed a spot over her heart. "I wanted to live and the only way to achieve that was to have you with me."

He pressed his forehead against hers, the walnut-colored eyes now only inches away looking deep into hers. "So, there you have it, and not another word of it to be heard."

Nathan meditatively toyed with the knot of her necklace. "There's to be no further guilt, other than what I've put upon meself. Any misery you might suffer for the rest of your days shall now be on my head."

Cate took his head between her hands and buried her lips into the silken crown. "I absolve you of all sins."

Settling his head on the pillow once more, Nathan waggled his brows. "All sins?"

"All."

The gold and ivory of his smile flashed in the blooming light and he settled her into his arms anew. "I knew you were a woman of character the moment I saw you."

7: BLESSED NAPE!

NATHAN SAT ATOP A STACK of firewood, near enough to watch Cate, yet far enough so as not to vex her. She flared like a shrew with its tail afire at the least hint of being shepherded. He went through the motions of cleaning his pistols—worming the old charge, dismantling, reaming and oiling—years of practice making it as routine as swallowing or breathing. The task occupied his hands, whilst freeing his mind and, more importantly, providing a prime excuse for his being there where he could bear an eye. Alas, sitting there, busy yet idle, also rendered him approachable, and so his attentions were repeatedly prevailed upon on. The interruptions were annoying as a rash, but they also added to the credulity of him being there.

Cate sat by Kirkland at a cook fire with the air of not being quite sure how she had come to be there and with no notion as to how to go about doing aught about it. The hand of Providence was in her landing with Kirkland; the man had the patience of a saint when it came to her. Thank the heavens, she hadn't wound up amid the bosun's mates—squabbling like a flock of ill-tempered geese further up the strand—or with the equally strident Hoops and his mates, the bucket assembly apparently not progressing to his specifications.

She sat with her hands folded in her lap. A damned disquieting sight. Idleness was never her nature, not before all this, at any rate.

As for now...?

Nathan ran a weary hand down his face. Sink and burn him, how the bloody hell was anyone to know what her nature might be now?

The glare of daylight made the bruises on her arms stand out like tar blots on a deck. He had caught her several times, mostly in the night, tearing at herself. She did it with a violence which prompted him to offer to do it for her, so the damage might at least be mitigated. The marks brought hard looks from the men, damn their scrofulous eyes!

Peace was what she needed, and lo that she might find it, for seeing hers would allow him his.

A prickle, like worms crawling at the nape of his neck, prompted Nathan to check the sky, and then the offing. It wasn't a sense of impending doom, but of something lurking, and had been with him since first light. The cove was as busy as shore. The watering was still in progress; boats pulled to the *Morganse*, trailing butts like a mother duck and her ducklings. Another floated a spare yard to the *Brazen*. Still much to do there.

The *Lovely* and *Morganse's* guns had been accurate; the battle might have been brief, but the damage to the *Brazen's* sails and rigging had been near-mortal. Whoever outfitted her had been a close-fisted cove: twice-laid cordage and canvas which made one envy a pocket kerchief. By all accounts, her sail locker contained more mold than cloth. She took on a foot of water per watch just sitting at anchor. She was no Pharaoh's gift, but she would be squared-away and set up like a Christian vessel, directly.

The foragers' boats made for shore piled to the gun'ls with full nets. Oysters for supper. He glanced about for Hermione— dozing and munching her cud in the shade—and wondered if she was of a giving mood, the possibility of Kirkland's chowder hanging in the balance. It was Cate's favorite... usually. He smiled wistfully at the prospect of seeing her eat to the point of bursting. Nothing would please him more than to see her round and soft as she had been, albeit briefly. Ribs and bones on a woman were like a ship without its rigging: you knew what it was, but it was a damned strain to think what was to be done with it.

Nathan stifled a groan at the thought of the inevitable confrontation which would arise over the galley kettles between Kirkland and Youssef, the *Lovely's* self-important cook, whenever chowder was in the making. The Mohammedan had convoluted notions as to what constituted a good dish. Thomas seemed to thrive on his vile concoctions, but—

Nathan stiffened at seeing Cate suddenly rise and take her leave. Kirkland turned toward his commander's roost, and raised his arms in a dramatic and thoroughly puzzled shrug of apology. Nathan waved him off. In all likelihood the man was innocent. He strongly suspected the cook incapable of forming a cross word, let alone uttering it.

Lowering the barrel he was reaming, Nathan followed Cate with his eyes. She passed within a biscuit-toss and yet failed to acknowledge him. Not out of anger—that mood he would have recognized straightaway — but more like she just didn't see him. He looked down in order to confirm he hadn't gone invisible. He wouldn't have put it past that scheming harridan-of-the-deep to have added that to her revenge.

He watched Cate's path closely. God help him, if she took the notion to wander off again. She had led him on one merry, heart-in-his-throat chase after another. It was a shock and a worry how difficult it was to spot one woman among fifteen score of men, to the point of questioning his own manhood. Age? Eyesight? Or just plain slipping? Thank the gods, she had opted not to go inland — the corrupting Brazens flung there a likely deterrent — for it would have been like searching a rabbit warren to find her.

They were connected now in many ways more. The simple fact was he wasn't complete without her. Dying together did that apparently, mingling of souls, unity in suffering: whatever the hell it was. He had put his mark on her — a stronger one — yesterday morn. God help him, he had been inferior when they had gone over the side, allowing her to be ripped from his arms. The earlier token had been small and weak, dangerously so, but enough for him to find her in that swirling nothingness. Never again! Her token was a solid presence at his shoulder, now. Now, he could find her through any tempest, through a hundred hells.

Grumbling an oath under his breath, Nathan rose to his feet, but sank back down at seeing Cate stop at Billings and his palm-pick-its. Whiter than the sand upon which it laid, the canvas spread out in varying stages of creation and repair. Awls and needles flashing, thread reeling out by the league, the canvasmen worked at a feverish pitch. An exchange of words, nods and becks from the men, awkward, nervous twitching from Cate, they made room and set her to work.

Billings and his crew soon resumed their conversation. Low-voiced and self-conscious at first, as usual, they soon forgot Cate was there and fell back into their comfortable chatter. He had always admired her ability to walk among men as if she belonged. Most women grew faint-of-heart at being one-among-the-many, sailors in particular, being such a coarse and ill-lookit lot. God knew, she had taken her hard knocks at the hands of men. Many a woman would shy, but she met sailors with the same boldness as she met everyone and everything. Second to her spark and fire, of all her traits — and he could fill a logbook with them — that one he admired most.

In fascination he was of the graceful angle of those gloriously wide shoulders, the curve of her neck when she bent her head, that maddening tangle blocking her face. Her hands were another fascination, fine-boned and delicate, and oh, what they could do! He winced and shifted to ease the ache just at the thought. One look at Billings' gnarled and roughed hands showed sailmaking was heavy work. There were no worries for Cate's, however. They had given her light work, fashioning fodder bags out of Number 8 canvas, worn and soft as her old shift. What joy he took in seeing her was dampened by what he didn't see. A part of her presence was still missing: her bubble, her spark, her ram-you – damn-you spirit. She worked distant and within herself, speaking only when the work required, and silent else.

Finding the pistol gone forgotten in his hands, Nathan resumed cleaning.

A short way up the beach, Rowett and Scripps bickered over mixing the grog. Suffering Christ! He was on the verge of shouting the *Morganse,* any ship of his, had always been and always would be a three-water ship, he thought, holding up the pistol barrel up and peering through it.

Clean as a cook's coppers!

Four-water was for wastrels and the Royal Navy.

This lounging about seemed to have left their minds as empty as the bottles at their feet. Hodder's voice rose over the quarreling, berating one of Petrov's mates for rendering the block pins too short. Sailors weren't land creatures; this sitting about was beginning to wear on everyone. They were all feeling that same prickle, growing as testy and quarrelsome as fishwives.

A shadow fell over him; Nathan looked up to find Thomas standing there.

He angled his head toward Thomas' arm, now free of its sling. "Don't let Cate or that drunken sawbones o' yours see that."

A part of him wished Cate just might spot it and rise to fly at Thomas like a harpy, and bring him up all-standing. Any kind of fire, at any provocation, would be considered a blessing, for it would be a glimpse of her old self, proof that it still existed, giving hope that it might flourish again.

"You're looking brighter, too," Nathan added approvingly.

In the spirit of proving his wellness, Thomas lifted the arm but stopped short, looking more like a fledgling crane flapping its wing. "I pitched Jamil's bolus when he wasn't looking," he said, wincing and clutching the wing now. "Damned nostrums are designed to keep a man down, I swear."

"Aye, well, if you're cured, he's out o' business. 'Tis why I never let those drunken, slab-handed sods near me. Damned few are ever the better for their attentions."

"I seem to recall you benefiting greatly from one digging a ball out of you," Thomas said, severely.

Nathan snorted. "I swear he used a dull spoon."

"Nay, he sharpened it first," Thomas said, grinning.

"He dug around like he was searching for gold." The memory was an unpleasant one: sprawled on a pair of lockers lashed together, writhing in the blood of those before him, grinding out curses around a rum bottle jammed into his mouth, the bastard's sweat dripping on his face.

"Lead was all he sought and found it, I might point out," Thomas said, dryly.

"A blind five-year-old could have done as well. Woulda been more sober, at any rate." Thomas cocked a brow. "You lived."

"In spite of him and a week of fever, aye," Nathan shot back without malice.

A heated discussion over whether another length should be stretched on the *Brazen's* new forestays'l between Billings and company filled the ensuing silence between them.

"You got something against that tooling?" Thomas asked mildly, eyeing the oiled rag and pistol in Nathan's hand. "You're rubbing it like you wish it gone. We can go check the armorer's locker; there's bound to be something less fancy."

"Away w' ya," Nathan said, with a short wave.

Something was clearly on Thomas' mind; an idle-minded Thomas was as rare as a meek bosun.

"I sense a purpose to this visit?" Nathan finally prompted.

Thomas opened his mouth, but the pop of a pistol — two pops from far down the beach interrupted him. Both heads swiveled in that direction, the Pass and Tumbedown Island beyond. An interminable few moments later, two men appeared around the point crying "Cap'n! Cap'n!"

Thomas was already several strides toward them. Nathan started directly behind, but drew up. He reached out and grabbed a man passing — Moore, quarter-gunner, larboard watch — with a suddenness that spun Moore in his tracks.

"On your life, watch her!" Nathan jabbed a thumb toward Cate, and then rammed a finger into Moore's chest. "Make sure she's still there when I return. On your life, stand-by or die!"

Nathan's vehemence brought Moore to retreat several steps in the general direction of his new duty station. Puzzled as to what was to be done with a woman just sitting there, Moore solemnly nodded and made a grand show of turning to fix his gaze on her.

Once again, Nathan rued the deaths of Hughes and Cameron, two Highland crewman who had been as dedicated to Cate as two shepherds, and had been as stolid and trustworthy, too. More importantly, Cate had trusted them implicitly, had always been at her ease when they were about. Of all the men he'd lost over the years, those two had been a sad, sad loss.

Nathan raced up the beach toward the growing turmoil gathering around Thomas and the messengers. One look at Thomas' stern scowl confirmed his own annoying suspicions. This wasn't good news, but then lookouts rarely delivered glad tidings.

"Signal from the lookouts report a ship," Thomas said at Nathan's arrival.

To press the messengers further would be of little use. They had fulfilled their duty: reporting a signal from Tumbledown's heights, where the lookouts were posted. Waiting was their only option, now.

Thankfully, a boat soon appeared at the mouth of the bay: a gig, sail taut, and her men still pulling for all they were worth. They could have been propelled by the wings of Pegasus and it wouldn't have been fast enough for those waiting on shore, a few resorting to jeering shouts to compel them faster. Finally, the boat came near enough for several to wade out and drag it in. One man leapt from the gun'l, crying "Sail, sir!" as he waded ashore.

"Where away?" the captains demanded in unison.

The messenger bent to brace his hands on his knees, winded. "Hull... down... but..."

"She's big, sir," put in the second coming up. "Bloody, damned big."

"The *Resolute*." Nathan would have bet his last tuppence on that one.

"Royal Navy," said Thomas, grimly.

"Aye, their largest, Commodore Roger Harte, commanding. 'Tis fitting she would make her appearance," Nathan said dryly. "Reports of the demise of his ladder-to-success would bring him sniffing about. He would have found himself a pilot by now, one who fancies he knows these waters enough to at least navigate that reef without foundering."

"Eighty guns is not something I'd wish to engage, had I a choice." Thomas' tone wasn't lost on Nathan, but his warning failed to take root.

He cocked a wry brow at Thomas. "Aye, well, you mightn't be so obliged."

Nathan looked toward the offing. Bless the nape of his neck! Rarely had it failed him. The feeling of worms crawling under his skin hadn't been misguided: the King-of-Worms loomed just over the horizon. He didn't need to see the ship; he could see her in his mind's eye, as clearly as if she had dropped anchor in the cove. From the lookouts' vantage point, "hull down" would put the *Resolute* a good ten or eleven miles from the reef's opening.

Damnation and seize his soul, he would have preferred to meet her on his ground, at his choosing. Alas, there was naught to be done for it now. A part of him was pleased, nay relieved. Enough of all this lounging about.

Breaking from his brown study, Nathan looked skyward. "In this, she won't be making more than five or six knots. We've time, but not much. Pass the word for Mr. Pryce and Mr. Hodder. We're to win the anchor with all haste."

The last was broadly directed toward any Morgansers about them. Thomas did the same in rapid-fire Arabic. The two captains turned and headed stride-for-stride back toward camp, occasionally bumping shoulders as they ducked and dodged their way through the men and stores already on the wing. There was no panic, only making haste. An eighty-gun, fourth-rate bearing down would hasten the step of even the dullest witted.

"Are we to haul our wind the same way you came in?" Thomas asked. Both minds were running far beyond the shore they strode.

Nathan snorted. "Not with this wind. Have you seen a glass of late?"

"No."

"Aye, neither have I," Nathan reluctantly conceded. "But I'd bet me last farthing something is brewing." A horde of sea gulls roosted on the point, fluffing their feathers and looking to settle in was a sure sign of a blow.

"Nay, our best bet is to bear north," Nathan went on. "The reef will keep any vessel in pursuit out of range, until we've cleared it. Then it will be an outright race. You know the plan?"

"I do," came back shortly, ruffled by the inference that he mightn't. "Dammit to hell, I don't like it. It's a damned foul business leaving you alone to face eighty guns. It's foolhardy and a damned inflated view of yourself."

"It will answer and you know it," Nathan said, evenly. "My, aren't you the inflated devil, thinking the world can't turn without your protective hand?"

Thomas was the one to snort, then. "That hand saved your sorry arse more times than you care to count."

"Then let it save an arse once more, but not mine."

"And Cate...?"

The thought brought Nathan up all-standing. He looked

back toward where she had been last seen. "I'll fetch her," he said with more confidence that he felt.

It wasn't difficult to imagine what it would be to have her aboard. He had witnessed it, agonized through it, lived gut-wrenching day, after gut-wrenching day of it. He'd seen her killed, braved Hell for her—and glad to do it—but never again, not if there was a fraction of a chance to do else. It was better to endure her screams of rage than screams of pain, or even worse, dead silence.

"I can't do this, can't think, unless I know she's safe."

Thomas drew himself up to his full, imposing height, his hand coming to rest on his sword. "They'll have to go through me and a good portion of my crew to get to her."

Nathan smiled, gratified. The idle observer might have thought that declaration naught but high-talk, smacking of foolhardiness. That cock wasn't all crow, however. One – armed, a face like a half-cooked squab, Thomas looked all the more the bloody-minded Tartar.

Leaning closer, Nathan said under the blare of bosun's pipes "Check the lockers on both vessels. There should be a green-and-white flag of some sort."

"Aye, I mind it," Thomas said, after brief consideration. "Found it when we took the *Lovely*. Had no notion what the hell it was for."

"'Tis the Company's private signal, or so I'm told. At the foremast top, I believe," Nathan said, closing one eye with the effort of recalling. He probed his mind's eye for the thousandth time, seeking to verify what that traitorous Hyde had revealed. Granted, a man being beaten would say anything to appease his inquisitor. Everything else the mumping sod had uttered had proved to be true. In a corner of his mind laid a vague recollection, or had he flagellated himself for not noticing the damned thing flying, to the point he actually believed he had seen it on display in Tortuga harbor?

Thomas looked to his feet pensively, then allowed Nathan a sly grin. "I see where you're going with this."

"Good." The single word came wrapped in equal amounts of earnestness and relief. It was both fitting and reassuring that both minds would work as one. The grander assurance was the man before him, looking more the pillager than his Viking ancestors. There was no one Nathan would prefer to have on his quarter.

Pryce and the *Lovely's* First Mate converged on their captains at the same time. Orders, one set in English, another in Arabic, overlapped each other. More were directed toward the duty and watch captains, who also descended upon them, all strident with their queries, complaints and concerns.

At last, the men were sent scrambling on their way. Duty called Thomas elsewhere, leaving Nathan alone. He turned to find a round-eyed and pale Cate standing there, tears streaming down her face. He glanced about for Moore; he'd have that powder-brained, parasitic excuse of a whoreson's balls for breakfast for abandoning her.

"Now? Already?" she said in a hoarse whisper, barely audible over the commotion. "No, not yet... not now... not..."

His chest feeling like a hawse wrapped around it, Nathan could only nod.

"How...?" She swallowed hard, her chin wobbling. "How long... before...?"

Nathan bit back the impulse to point out the answer was obvious. Hermione's startled bleat as she was being toted past seemed to say it all. The shore swarmed like a kicked up anthill. Dodgers struck, fires doused, coppers dumped and stores streaming toward the boats: it was amazing how much a couple hundred men could bear away, striking camp with the efficiency of desert nomads. "'Tis only a matter of the boats loading."

Cate lunged forward and clutched his shirt, her words coming faster and faster.

"Please, don't—Please, don't make me—I'll be good—"

"I can't—"

"I'll... I know I've been a bother, but I'll mind every word. I'll stay in the hold," she added, unable to hide her loathing.

"With you aboard—"

With a frustrated growl, Cate retreated. Head hanging, she refused to look at him. They started a jerking dance: Nathan trying to make her look, Cate turning away. Around and 'round they went, until he finally grabbed and shook her.

Gently, man! Gently, lest she fall apart before your eyes.

"Listen to me. Look at me!" He took her by the chin and brought her face round. "Three days." He thrust the fingers before her. "Three days and I'll be back."

She jerked away and stepped back, hurt sharpening her eyes. "So you say."

Nathan exhaled through his nose, seeking patience. "Might I point out 'tis not my word in question here," he said with all due delicacy, in spite of the urge to grab her again and give her a more solid shaking. "I've kept me word every time we've parted. You are the one who is never where you ought."

Cate sniffed, a dismissive wave ending with a dash at her eyes. "None of that was my fault, most of it, anyway."

"And you'll accept that line were I to say the same?" he asked knowingly.

Nathan shifted his stance to avoid being plowed into by someone rushing past, blinded by their arms being full. He and Cate were an obstruction in the rushing tide of men and stores. Hands working at his sides, Nathan spared a brief look toward the bay's mouth and the unseen offing beyond. There wasn't time for this.

"Darling, this isn't a debate, nor even a discussion. The decision is made. 'Tis done."

He looked down at the crown of Cate's bent head. He expected the jaguar—And sweet, merciful heavens, what a blessed sight it would be!—but found something ready to shrink rather than attack, withdrawing like a crab into its shell. Once more, as he did as regularly as the glass, he worried that two-faced mage-of-the-deep had played some cruel trick, that he hadn't gotten her all back, there was some part of her being kept. He closed his eyes and hardened his heart, chanting to himself all the reasons why this had to be.

"For once, go and do as you are asked." Nathan's mouth twitched with the need to smile. "I know 'tis contrary to your nature, but please, do as you are bid, just this once."

"And if I do it this once, will you stop sending me off?" she asked coldly, looking up.

The answer came without hesitation, for on that he was firm. "I'll never make a pledge that risks not seeing you safe."

It wasn't what she wanted to hear, and he knew it.

"One crisis at a time, eh?" he said lightly. There was nothing to be gained in bashing her with his victory. His last wish was to relive their last parting: shrieking at each other like a couple of harpies. "Let's not look for trouble what hasn't found us yet."

Nathan ventured nearer again and dipped his head, seeking to catch her eyes. "Please, darling. Promise?"

"If you promise to come back," she shot back, sharp and accusing.

He smiled benevolently. "I've told you, darling. There is but one place for me. Be it live or be it dead is beyond my control, but I will never leave you. I might be gone, but I will never leave. You have me word on that."

Cate finally looked up and smiled, faltering and so very, very brief. "I would prefer alive."

He smiled, in spite of himself. "Then we are of the same mind, at last."

Nathan cupped her cheek in his palm and said urgently "Be there. Promise... now."

Shimmering with wetness, her eyes found his and lingered. A fine tremor coursed through her, the muscles of her jaw tight as cords under his hand.

"Three," he said, holding up the fingers again. "Three days and I'll be back. All I seek are open arms if you find you can't open your heart."

Cate stood, mute and staring.

"I need to know you'll be there, or I can't do what's to be done else." He ventured closer, his mouth hovering over hers. "Kiss me. Send this sailor off with the memory of you on his lips, something soft in his arms and with a reason to live."

She brought her face up to his, more out of reflex than desire. He had expected, nay hoped for her familiar fire, the fire which had scared him the first time, but had come to relish. He hoped in vain. Her kiss was cold, her lips flaccid and lifeless. All the more proof of her diminished condition, more proof that this was the right thing to do. He would rather lose her trust, possibly lose her altogether, than lose her life.

Nathan kissed her as thoroughly as was allowed through stiff, unyielding lips, finding the assurance and solace he needed and allowing her the same. Alas, she would have none of it, denying him in every way.

One or the other or both of them shook so hard he could barely hold on. He pressed his forehead against hers, breathing in her scent, committing it to memory — as if he could ever forget! "I'll see you out to the —"

Cate broke free and growled "Damn you, don't bother!"

As big as he was, at times Thomas could move like a damned cat. There he was, in time for Cate to slip back into the protective crook of his arm. "Don't worry. As you say, I'll be exactly where I belong."

Nathan flinched, her well-aimed dart finding its target. She knew him too well to miss.

With concentrated effort, Nathan dragged his attention from Cate up to Thomas. The two men stared at each other with the sudden realization that the moment was nigh. Both knew Providence's capriciousness; life had taught them it wasn't being over-dramatic to think this might well be the last time one might lay eyes on the other. Words suddenly failing, a handshake didn't seem near enough and they clutched each other in a bear hug, Thomas' one-armed version nearly popping Nathan's ribs.

"On the next horizon."

"On the next horizon."

Eyes fixed straight ahead, Nathan stiffly swung into the waiting boat and it pushed away. Sitting heavily on the sternsheet, he twisted around to look back at the shrinking image of Cate and Thomas, together.

"Goddammit, Nathan, take care—" Thomas' shout was cut short by Cate crumpling in a heap at his feet. She sat staring, hands limp in her lap.

Nathan's hand tightened on the gun'l. God send the men didn't see him wet-eyed and shaking as a lass!

He coiled, ready to leap out and swim back for her. A hand on his arm stopped him.

"Cap'n... Nathan...?!"

He tore his attention around into his First Mate's severe look.

"'Tisn't time," Pryce hissed.

Sagging, Nathan watched Thomas scoop Cate up, limp as a sodden hammock, and wade out to the *Brazen's* boat. Thomas settled on a thwart, Cate on his lap, head lolling on his shoulder.

Soon, too damned soon, the boat bearing Thomas and Cate disappeared among the throngs of others pouring from shore. Nathan leaned far out, straining to hear. Was she crying? Hysterical? Hell and furies, if he could only see!

Pryce leaned and said under his breath "'Tis well, Nathan. She be where she need be."

Nathan sank back onto the thwart and stared resolutely ahead.

8: A PLOVER'S GAMBIT

NATHAN CLAPPED ONTO A ROPE and hand-over-handed up the *Morganse's* side. His foot touched the deck, and he sagged, catching a shroud. Feeling a number of gazes on him, Pryce among them, he straightened and turned.

He smiled self-consciously. "There was a time I never thought to do this again."

Pryce's destroyed mouth drew back into a grin. "Beggin' yer pardon, sir, but may I be so bold as to say 'twas a time we never thought to see it."

A small cheer went up, some venturing to clap the Cap'n on the back, giving him joy of his return.

They filed away to their duties, leaving Nathan and Pryce relatively alone. The latter sobered. "She's been a-waitin' for ye, as always. Yer aboard now, Cap'n; she'll sail fer us, now. Go take a caulk," he added, with a flash of uncustomary familiarity and warmth.

"Everyone keeps saying that. I'll do."

With a dismissive flutter of fingers, Nathan strolled aft through the throngs of men, if for no other reason than to prove his point. In some apparent fit of fatherly forbearance, Pryce followed close behind. Nathan stopped to find the man puffed and grinning like a parish cat. He glanced about, in search of the grand secret or accomplishment which might be the source of this mirth.

"Such equanimity isn't usually your nature," Nathan said narrowly. He waited, showing Pryce he wasn't going anywhere, until the pease were spilt.

Deflating somewhat at being pressed, Pryce acquiesced. "'Tis you, or rather the sight o' ye. Yer yerself, or the nearest to, than what's been seed in many and many a week."

Nathan opened his mouth to object, but sighed, resigned. "That bad?"

"And more," came back emphatically. "Not as the men wuz aggrieved."

Nathan glanced cautiously around. Most of the men's attentions were inordinately fixed on their duties, flaking sheets what didn't need flaking with the intentness of the ship's welfare depending on it. His eye caught a Brazen near the foremast, his malevolence stark amid the prevailing glowing spirits.

"Aye, the barky can set up a man as nothin', almost nuthin'," Pryce added, with an embarrassed cough. "A-beggin' Mr. Cate's acceptance and pardon," he mumbled into his chest.

"She'd be pleased to hear such high praise. I fancy she would understand the difference between herself and a ship."

"'Tis a rare woman what appreciates that, Mr. Cate bein' one o' the rarest."

Nathan flushed with pride at hearing her so appreciated, and by this curmudgeonly old salt. "Get on with you, then."

The hands were hard about their duties, the duty captains barking orders, prodding the laggardly. Nathan felt as unnecessary as the third eye on a cat; anything he might do would only add to the confusion. He nodded in acknowledgment as the joy of his return was given, joy of being under way, joy of whatever victories might lie ahead. The superstitious mariner in him caused him to touch wood. He sought but one single victory: seeing Cate safe.

Nathan stepped into his cabin long enough to check the glass. As suspected: dropping. Weather was nigh. Once more on the quarterdeck, he slipped into the narrow space between binnacle and helm. There, he appeared commanding, whilst at the same time, was out of the way and, more significantly, at leisure to gather his wits. With his back against the wheel, he grasped the binnacle's edge and drew several deep breaths, inhaling the smell of the sea — Yes, it was purer there than when smelt from land — tar and canvas. Being aboard fed his soul as nothing else could.

From there, he answered whatever queries were cast his way, most of which could have been sorted out by a prime greenhorn. The people's efforts were as transparent as the binnacle glass: it was their way of welcoming him back into the fold, for — bless their thieving souls — they knew the value of routine and authority. He was back at last, back to normal, whatever in the hell that meant. And yet, a part of him was missing, a hole as gaping as the sea. He had the odd, disquieting sensation of being back where he belonged, and yet wholly out of his element.

He glanced south again. As anticipated, the island blocked the *Resolute's* view... for now. If Providence was of an amenable mood, it would remain so, until the three vessels were safe away. The plan was a fairly simple one: whilst the *Resolute* picked her way in from the south, they would be weaving their way out to the north, Dead Goat Island blocking the view. The *Resolute* would look into the bay; Nathan grinned, imagining the look on Harte's face at finding the anchorage empty. Then, the lookouts would give the hail of three ships, hopefully hull down, if that same Providence continued to be abiding. The *Resolute* would give chase; that was a given. The worry was if she should set her sights on the wrong vessel.

This was between him and Harte. And, if the options were made clear, Harte would realize his duty, and leave the *Lovely* and *Brazen* to go on their merry way.

Small challenge, easily achieved. Now, for the doing.

It wasn't the heavy trod of those at the capstan or the twiddle of the fife playing "Stamp and go!" — signals of impending departure, which had excited him for over a decade — which set his blood stirring then. It was the *Morganse's* liveliness, a quickening of spirit, her eagerness to be rid of her earthen tether and spread her wings reverberating up through his soles, which brought him to life. They needed to make weigh with all haste, and she knew it. He felt the instant the anchor freed the bottom, his ship bringing her nose about, sniffing for the wind, before the thing broke the surface.

Squidge, the ship's steadiest hand, took the helm, leaving Nathan free to con the ship through the treacherous hazards which lay between them and the reef opening to the north. The secret to their success would be to look sharp, move smart and haul hearty. The gods were generous, the wind fair. There would be no tacking, no worries of missing stays, no risk of having to wear. Disaster, however, could lie in one grass-combing, cod-handed lout caught sleeping at his sheet.

The three vessels rounded the bay's northernmost point and fell into line, the *Brazen* bringing up the rear. They ran near enough to track the *Morganse's* exact path, and yet far enough so as not to be a hazard to themselves or each other. Still, were the *Morganse* to go aground, it would mean the demise of all, for there was no room to veer off.

Nathan watched the *Brazen* with particular interest. Fore-'n-afters were, in many respects, like most ships, but they were also creatures unto themselves. A practice cruise would have been far more preferable, in deep waters and no land in the lee, plenty of room for her people to learn her temperament and whims. As it was, Thomas would be obliged to rely on the remaining Brazens and whatever experience which nested under his hat. Still, the pressure of imminent doom at the least miscalculation was known to strike a man dense.

The *Brazen* set a jib the size of which gave Nathan pause.

Damn your eyes, Thomas, this is no time to play the flash!

Speed was a delicate balance between making all haste, maintaining sufficient speed for steerage, and preserving their keels. Only the foolhardy would allow haste to be their master, for it could also be their undoing. Even at Nathan's height at the maintop, the tension on deck was palpable, only the most dull-witted immune. It revealed itself in different ways: some set to their duties with double intensity, whilst others forgot theirs entirely. Some went silent and sober, whilst others' tongues flapped like loose boluns.

"Silence fore and aft!" Pryce bellowed.

"Or, become a right Tartar, savaging every poor cove what blunders into his path," Nathan observed under his breath, as he moved higher.

Settling comfortably on the crosstrees, his back against the mast, Nathan fixed his eye forward under the foret'gallant, to the water's shifting patterns ahead. Light and dark, brilliant and dull were calling cards of what lay submerged. A false channel would present itself directly; there was no room, nor time for dead ends. He looked skyward, and then the offing, alert for the first sign of a change in wind or weather; the glass said it would do both. If the wind was to die — A rare thing that time of day, but the signs couldn't be ignored — their only hope would be hours of sweating on the oars. If the wind stiffened, it could mean a lot of bursted bellies from hauling on the sails.

The heaving roll of the offing agreed with the glass: weather, soon, but not immediate.

They had time.

The familiar, dare he say homey, feel of the elements working with and against his ship, the wind seeking to push one way, the sea working her another, strengthening by the moment. All combined, the barky took on a slow, pitch-and-roll motion. Through the wood at his back, Nathan could feel her, alert and keen.

"Two... Two and a fathom... Two and a half... Three..." Smalley, heaving the logline in the mainchains, was obliged to shout over the increasing roar of the surf breaking on the reef.

The sheetmen spit on their palms and hitched their trousers.

No one need be told; any tar worth his salt could look over the side to his watery grave awaiting. The air was thick with tension, not the kind which came with the eminent threat of ball and splinter, but knowing there was no room for error.

A blur of hyacinth-blue and rustle of feathers marked Beatrice's arrival. Alighting well to leeward, outside the mainyard lifts, she ruffled and smoothed. She cocked her head and fixed him with a beady eye.

"*Grease me stick.*"

"I thought I told you to stay with her." God knew Cate needed every watchful eye what could be managed, and the beast was a better alarm than a mastiff.

"*Damn you.*"

The bird's higher-pitched timbre—hauntingly like Cate—made Nathan turn and stare.

"One sharp-tongued woman aboard 'tis enough. Avast that jabbering or I'll feed you to the sharks, and not a tear shall be shed." The displeased bark of a passing gull added credit to his threat.

"Ready on the helm," Nathan called down, some moments later. "Three points to larboard, on me word. Ease off the mizzen. Thus, thus." A mite more pressure on the rudder was needed; all the jibs flying had her heavy on the head.

"Helm about."

The *Morganse* curved; the t'gallants swung, their blocks and yards creaking overhead. Shouts and curses from the bow: Mr. Fox and his f'c'stlejacks doing what they did best.

Nathan swiveled his attention aft. The *Lovely* made her turn with the precision of a close-order drill. Looking ahead once more, his eye caught a ripple in the water, just forward of the *Morganse's* bow. Contrary to all wind and wave, it was circular, an unnatural smooth patch at its center. A shadow under the water showed itself, briefly but enough to see the spire of rock. Had the breeze been a mite stronger, neither ripple, nor shadow would have been seen.

"Starboard your helm point and a half!" Sucking in, as if it was his own flanks being threatened, he leaned out to watch the dagger-like projection slip past.

Bringing up the read, the *Brazen* was now making her turn with the same exactitude. There was no missing Thomas in her tops. How in the hell he managed up there with only one arm was a wonder? Nathan glanced beyond the *Brazen* to the bay's far side.

The *Resolute* was not to be seen.

So far, so good.

"Touch up that foret'gallant brace, you ill-conditioned sluggards!"

The flogging canvas was restored to its rightful taut curve.

Nathan squinted at the span of variegated blue ahead, not against the glare, but with the effort of recalling. A lot of water had been over the decks since he had last threaded this, and he was nowhere near as crisp as he could have wished. Even with a memory sharp as an awl, there were no guarantees. The ever-changing aftermath of storm, coral, sand and wind all added to the uncertainty. Soft curves of coral lay to windward; to leeward fingers of black rock curved out, looking to claw the hull.

"Steady, lass," he said, patting the wood under him.

A metallic flash alongside marked a school of fish rising from the depths. The arching curves of a troupe of sea hogs frolicked in the bow wave. The sight brought murmurs of approval, some saying the hand of Calypso was with them.

"God's my life, I hope not!" Nathan's exclamation elicited a squawk of protest from Beatrice. He dashed at the cold sweat which suddenly popped out on his brow.

The fish were a good sign, one more among the many observed whilst winning the anchor. It wasn't Friday, nor the thirteenth; no overturned buckets, allowing the ship's luck to run out; no Mother Clarey's chickens spotted and Millbridge's ague was in remission: it was a good day to sail.

"Ready on the helm. Look alive on those sheets or we'll all be fish bait!"

Hodder and his mate's voices echoed up, augmented by the *thwack!* of their starts hitting wood.

"Hard over!"

The yard overhead swung, Nathan reflexively ducking his head. "Hold! Stand on."

Their goal was now directly off the bow: a strip of relatively calm water bracketed by surf breaking high on both sides. Damn, it looked narrow. The first captain to put his vessel through there had to have had balls the size of a 24-pounder and solid brass, at that. He wasn't ashamed to admit his own were feeling a mite shrunken, just then.

Heart in his throat, Nathan watched the *Brazen*, until she made her last turn. Brisk and handy she was, although hauling that jib about had to be a gut-grinder. Now squinting against the glare of the sun, he fixed his attention back on the task to hand.

Smalley's chant hadn't ceased. "Three... Three and a fathom... Three and a half...."

The bottom was dropping, but the bottom wasn't the worry.

The water might be deeper, but the cursed rocks could be all the taller, the keel in all the more peril.

"Ease off the boluns. No more than three, Mr. Pryce. Easy, lass, easy," Nathan said under his breath, patting the wood at his back. "You've plenty of chance to kick up your heels. Come up a fraction. That's good," was directed below.

Another glance behind.

No *Resolute,* yet.

"Ready! Stand-by and look alive. This is going to be a wicked dog leg."

It was going to be a sheetman's nightmare, with barely time to tally-and-belay before having to let-go-and-haul again. He fixed his eye on the shifting patterns ahead and around. Surely, the opening was still there; surely, wind and storm hadn't filled it in.

"Hard to larboard... now! Hard over. Goddamned your festering eyes, clap onto those sheets and haul!"

Nathan leaned and craned his head to watch the submerged dark shapes slip past. Heart in his throat, he mentally counted the seconds, calculating depths and distance. His gut lurched at feeling the *Morganse* shudder at hitting something.

"Helm?!" Damnation and seize his soul, if they sheered a rudder—!

"She answers, sir." Squidge gave the wheel an exemplary working.

Nathan barely had time to recover and give thanks before the next turn was upon them.

"Ready...!" He checked the wind and surrounding waters once more, for any sign of an untoward puff or lull. "Hard to starboard!" he shouted, grabbing the t'gallant shroud as the *Morganse* swung.

He whipped his head around at hearing a hollow grinding sound, one every mariner knew and dreaded, coming from aft: hull meeting rock. He looked back just in time to see the *Lovely* stagger. Sails luffing, her people scurrying about and shouting, she hesitated, and then steadied and filled. He watched carefully, but there was no sign of manning the pumps; she wasn't hulled. A shrewd knock, but not lethal.

"Do you see the opening, Mr. Squidge?"

"Aye, sir," came back with a wry edge. He would have to be a cross-eyed scrub to miss that calm amid the turbid.

"Very well, then nothing to do but head for it."

The *Morganse* took on a heavier rocking motion at meeting the stronger seas. A touch-up of the boluns and she leveled, now throwing an even finer bow wave.

A long list of things which could still go wrong running through his mind, Nathan remained aloft until the *Lovely* and *Brazen* were clear. With the *Lovely* on the far part of the dog leg, the *Brazen* was in direct sight. Still he waited, seeing the *Lovely* through. The *Brazen* flashed out her foretops'l and she was through.

A final look up the coast.

Nothing.

The *Resolute* still hadn't cleared the point.

God bless that skulking hulk!

This was answering better than he dared hope.

Nathan automatically reached for a backstay, but hesitated. There would be nothing more embarrassing than a captain plummeting to the deck. He clapped onto a shroud instead and slid down, walking the rail aft.

"How's she handle, helm?" he asked, mounting the quarterdeck, still worried for their rudder.

"Bless her, sir. She's tight as a virgin!"

"Very well." Still, a functioning rudder didn't necessarily mean one unscathed. "Rig a line over the side and take a look, anyway."

He could have saved his breath. It was already being rigged, Sombers stripping down in preparation for a dunking. One more glance aft, assuring all was well, and then he looked about to take his bearings.

"West by a half nor'west, Mr. Squidge."

The breeze was steady, making all plain-sail possible. Packing on all she could wear, the *Morganse* opened up and stood out to the open sea.

The mood aboard lightened. The Watch was stood down and sent to their rest. Few slept; most milled about the decks. All eyes were fixed aft, not on the *Lovely* or *Brazen*, but beyond on the sinking Dead Goat Island, where the *Resolute* should make her appearance directly, *if* she had taken the bait.

The bells rang. Nathan glanced at the sky again, and then again as the sun made its inexorable path.

Allowing the time for the plan—the *Resolute* to arrive at the empty bay, backtrack from whence she had just came, and then sail like smoke-and-oakum to catch up—to come to fruition didn't come easily. Granted, he had been cutting such capers for years, but so much, *too* much rode on this. There was the hope—a thin, but so very delicious one—that the wind had either turned contrary, or better yet, had died altogether back there, obliging the *Resolute's* people to sweat at club-hauling her out. Better yet, perhaps the challenge might prove too daunting, and she would opt to just lie in wait for a foe that was never to come. That would be too, too perfect, and too ironic, a sweet justice allowed only the Fates' most favored.

In the lull, Nathan was drawn to the leeward rail and the view of the *Brazen* there. He'd bid Thomas to keep close, so the *Morganse* might fall off quickly, if the *Resolute* was to smoke their ruse and open fire. Leaning on the rail, he smiled. Those fore-'n-afters cut a fine line in the water. Weatherly and stiff—a bit heavy at the stern, aye, but a day's sweat in the hold could fix that—the *Brazen* looked willing to give far more than she was currently being asked.

The green-and-white flag at her topmast, the *Lovely* simultaneously unfurling hers, declared them sailing for the Company. Nathan touched wood again with the prayer that traitorous Hyde in Tortuga Harbor had been truthful. So damned much hinged on that not-so-small point. Hell-fire and death, if that blubbering cove proved false on this! He wasn't so gullible as to put all his blind faith in that mumping villain's word; logic also rode on Hyde's side. The existence of some sort of private signal was fitting. There were a great number of privateers hired by Creswicke; the skulking rats needed some means to find each other. Besides, he only needed the *Resolute* to believe the lie long enough for the two vessels to sink the horizon, unhindered and unharmed.

Nathan reached for the glass, but then drew back. It wouldn't be fitting to be seen gawking like a moonstruck calf. He liked to think he could see Cate, at the rail, looking back. He curled his arm against his chest, savoring the feel of her body there. He'd held spars which had been warmer and less unyielding.

He shook himself. This mooning about was exactly why she was over there. The dread on her face, her body eloquent with loathing, every time he sent her to the hold was like a pike to the heart. No man with half o' brain would allow her on deck, exposing her to splinters, balls, grape, falling tackle... They didn't call amidships "the butcher shop" for nothing. No matter the hard feelings, if it was the cold shoulder the rest of his days, it would be better than seeing her sheered in half by a ball, or holding her down and listening to her scream as they dug a shiver out of her.

The shout of "Sail ho!" from the maintop was barely heard among the hoots and jeering cheers at the *Resolute* popping into view. Nathan glanced up at the red-trimmed sails overhead and prayed they might do their part.

Have to be a grass-combing scrub, not to know. But then, the wise never under, nor over-estimate their foe.

His hope was that those sails would be like a red flag before a bull. There was no doubting the *Morganse,* but there was also no doubting Harte's vagaries of mind, either. One never knew when the glare off those gold epaulets might blind him. Staring aft, Nathan considered giving him a leeward gun, should His Ramrod-Up-His-Arse prove shy or inattentive.

Instead, the *Resolute* came about, paid off, and threw on more sail.

Even without a glass, Nathan could make out the pennant at the frigate's peak. God forbid one might consider saving that bit o' bunting from wind or weather. The Commodore was aboard, of course. He'd have bet his captaincy that His High-Nosedness would be there. Harte did love his pomp and flourish: brass gleaming like gold; uniform buttons like diamonds; white hammocks rolled to hoop-perfection along the bulwarks; decks as white as sand, and the hell to pay for the first tar drip to mar them...

God's my life, he must have made those poor sods serving him lives a living hell.

He'd served on such floating hells, with captains convinced of their only-one-under – God status. He'd felt their lash, carried the scars to this day, as did far too many others. Such tyrants were the birth of piracy, why ship's articles and the Brethren's Code existed.

A grand part of Harte's rocket-like climb up the ladder-of-success had been through the patronage and good graces of His Lord-High-Arsedness Creswicke. No unholier alliance ever existed. Harte was also convinced his ascent up said ladder would have reached even more towering pinnacles had it not been for one person: Nathan Blackthorne. His history with Harte was many years long and filled with escapades, none ending the way Harte had intended: Nathanael Blackthorne's head skewered on his bowsprit.

The bells rang, the Watches mustered, and onward they sailed, the *Morganse* doing everything she could to stay with the *Lovely* and *Brazen's* slow pace, whilst at the same time look to be running for her salvation. The wait for the *Resolute* to fetch their wake was interminable. Common knowledge dictated a vessel which outweighed the others by a hundred tons or more would also out-sail them. It had been months since their last encounter; Nathan wished he knew more about the frigate. Just because she was Royal Navy didn't necessarily mean she was in prime condition. Admirals could be ill-disposed, captains fell out of favor, stores in yards run short. Was her bottom as sweet as the *Morganse's*, or was she carrying a great skirt of weed? Had she been recently refitted, her spars and cordage fresh, or was she held together with tow and tar, a wink and a prayer?

Closer now, Nathan found the *Resolute* had changed little, since last seen. As pompous and grand as her commander, she was gilded and painted up like an expensive harlot, the brass bowchasers polished to the point of nearly outshining the gilt. Housed and bowsed, her ports closed, Nathan couldn't see her armament, but knew them as well as his own: long guns, 18-pounders above, 24's below, with bow and stern chasers, swivel guns and tops large enough to hold a couple score of Marines. She could throw a broadside in the range of eight hundred and forty weight-of-metal. Compared to the *Morganse's* three hundred and sixty, it was a substantial difference, especially when those balls were tearing down the decks at you.

The secret was to just avoid that short-coming altogether.

Amid the low hum of the crew's conversation, observations and speculations on the approaching frigate, Nathan watched with keen interest, alert for any indications of either her physical state or the state of her crew. Putting into port for a badly needed careening could mean being stripped of her prime officers and hands. She could wind up hauling anchor with a crew of green pressmen or sorely under-complement. He watched how she went about setting on more sail. Brisk, but still slavish to traditions and Navy ways.

"Very well."

He smiled in appreciation at seeing the *Lovely* and *Brazen*, by means of a long outcropping of coral, form a loose sort of wedge, not overt enough to appear obvious, but definitive enough to funnel the *Resolute* to leeward, and hence, giving the *Morganse* the weather gauge.

"Sly dog, Thomas. Sly dog."

Nathan watched with keen anticipation as the *Resolute* neared and ultimately overtook the *Lovely*. Was it hopefulness or true evidence that she looked to have no intention of engaging the brig? Flags ran up, a gun to leeward — a half-charge — in protest to the brig's failure to yield to the frigate's grandeur and get into her lee.

The prudent commodore, looking to take on a ship known for its gunnery, known for its fighting spirit, known to have already bested him several times over, might value having another ship to strengthen his numbers and, hence, guarantee success. That, however, would mean the prudent commodore would have to share that success. Commodore Vainglorious tipped his hand when he popped over the horizon alone, without the fleet which lay at his fingertips. And now, he passed the opportunity to take a prize, gain a consort with which to sail.

Still, with the frigate bearing down, the *Brazen* pressed on with every scrape of canvas she could in good conscious wear. Nathan couldn't see it, but he'd bet his hat she had an old jib set to leeward, as did the *Morganse*, allowing all the appearance of sailing her best, but alas, falling short.

Just give them what they want to see.

In time, the *Lovely* steadily receding in her wake, the *Resolute* overtook the *Brazen*. Another gun to leeward, another jerk on the signal flags, pointing out the schooner's impertinence. Nathan crossed his fingers, hoping Thomas had the good sense — and bullheadedness, in the face of her refusals — to keep Cate out of sight. One woman among all those men would stick out like a bowsprit.

He grinned at seeing — Right on cue! Thomas had the timing of a stage performer! — the clew on the *Brazen's* headsail gave way, a critical loss for a fore-n'-after. The foredeck crew scrambled about the flapping sail, arms waving, a bosun starting all within reach. It was a grand bit of acting, worthy of Haymarket Theater. Soon, the entire complement of foresails was all a-hoo, the entire foredeck looking like Mother Clarey's laundry. The *Brazen's* bow swung to the wind, and she was dead in the water.

Nathan waited to see if there was anything in that performance which might cause the *Resolute* to smoke their ruse, fall off and take a closer look. Second thoughts, self-doubt or wearing wasn't Harte's style: straight ahead, full-and-by, like a charging bull and damn the consequences. With his benefactor now dead, Commodore Vanglorious would be all the more desperate to show his worth. Fleets could be disbanded, commodore flags revoked and, in a blink, the unhung sod could well find himself back down to post captain, ashore and on half-pay, all that gilt and glory rotting in some locker in the tropical heat.

The moments ticked, the white line of the *Resolute's* bow wave streaming down her sides. Movement at her waist, and then aft, word of the *Brazen's* hardship being delivered to the quarterdeck. Pointing. Discussion. No orders to the helm. No further signals raised.

The *Resolute* sailed on.

Blindness had always been the man's virtue.

"Ah, yes, give them what they wish to see, and they see it every time."

"Beg pardon, sir?" said a startled mizzen hand.

"Nothing. Nothing."

Nathan bid the helm to ease up another fraction, the boluns loosed a bit, more importantly, the *Morganse* slowing a mite, all in the spirit of giving the *Resolute* that bit more confidence, her people fixing their attention on her, rather than the *Brazen*. He shifted to the windward rail, in order to see around the *Resolute* to the *Brazen*. The performance was still on, her foredeck still swarming. With each rise and fall of the swell, the schooner's hull incrementally sank out of sight, until only her masts showed. Those shrank, as well, until they were no more than a black prick against the clouds... And then they were gone, taking Cate with them.

Nathan shivered, in spite of the Caribbean sun.

Lifting his head, he closed his eyes; Cate came to him, as clear as if she were standing next to him at the taffrail.

Goodbye, darling. A few days, no more, I promise.

He opened his eyes and glared down the depths slipping past.

You gave her life, now keep it for her.

9: BLESSED HUBRIS AND HER SISTER, DOOM

N OW, IT WAS DOWN TO just two ships.
Now, the games might begin!

If luck held, it looked to be a long, long day, two or three, if luck didn't smile.

The topsmen laid aloft, the f'c'stlemen forward to touch up the sails, an exercise more for appearance than function. A semblance of a Watch was resumed as many as could be spared standing down.

"Why not just leaver 'er in our wake?" Pryce's question was posed not out of malice, but idle interest. "The barky can manage easy enough."

"I don't wish to just vanish and leave the wolf loose to roam. I wish to pen that skulking predator for a while. There might be the entire West India fleet out there, but that one," Nathan said with a meaningful stab of his finger toward the *Resolute*, "shan't annoy us, nor any other fair vessel and for a good while. I mean to dangle the carrot in front of that ass's nose, until the *Lovely* and *Brazen* are but distant memories."

Nathan walked the decks, encouraging those who needed it, praising those who deserved it. MacQuarrie, looking as thoroughly downtrodden as an abandoned puppy at his guns being left cold, brightened at the orders for more shot and canister filled. With no hot meals possible after the galley fires were doused—mandatory, before the powder-room could be opened—Kirkland served up broth with biscuit and cheese, many men eating at their posts lest they miss a moment of the chase.

Kirkland furrowed his brow and clucked worried words as he delivered a cup of the same. One sniff, however, and Nathan's stomach closed. Hot coffee, however, answered very well. An entire pot soon sat hot and steaming in a fiddle on the binnacle.

Years of being pursued had provided Nathan with a strong sense of when he was being watched. Feeling the *Resolute's* eyes on him, he idly strolled to the rail, propped one hip and sipped, staring across the water as if it were a Sunday cruise. Still, from the corner of his eye, he watched the frigate, taking in every minute detail. Something caught his eye, and he set down the cup with a clatter and scampered to the maintop, and then the t'gallant trestletrees. Swinging a leg over a yard, he fixed his attention aft.

"Pass the word for Mr. Pryce," he called to a descending topsman.

Shortly, the First Mate's grizzled head popped up next to him, the questioning lift of his brows typical of one with much to do and little tolerance for the trivial.

"When was the last time we met that hulk?" Nathan asked, his gaze unwavering from the frigate. "As a chase, that is?"

Easing himself on the opposite trestletree, Pryce considered. "As a chase? Ehh...? Never, that I recollect. Squared off. Yard-to-yard... A-chasin'... A-crossin' 'er hawse... Lyin' off... A-rakin' 'er stern... Never chased," he finished, surprised by the discovery.

Nathan nodded, his suspicions confirmed. "Observe, if you please, the wake of yon gallant vessel."

A few moments, and then a few more passed.

"Blessed Mother, Mary and Joseph! She's a-saggin' like an old whore's tit!"

Nathan curbed a smile, gratified it hadn't been his imagination. Wakes were never as straight as a furrow. Every ship slipped sideways, the stronger the wind, the more the slippage. A large part of navigation involved allowing for it, a four-to-one ratio not beyond the realm of reasonable. In point of fact, they curved like a maincourse in a gentle breeze. The *Resolute's,* however, curved like an archer's bow.

"For every league she makes, she has to be slipping five, mebbe six —" Pryce observed.

"Or seven." Nathan clucked his tongue in disapproval. "Judging by those jogs in her wake, she's a helmsman who doesn't mind his duty. She's passed over two shallows, and never so much as a sheet touched, nor lead flung. Her Master is either oblivious or values speed more than his keel."

"And, God's blood and wounds, look at her packing on the sail! T'will press her down by the bow. There! See, she's a-luggin' already."

"Aye, as that martyr-of-a-Master is undoubtedly well aware. But Commodore Ramrod-Up-His-Arse has always been a firm believer in the more the better," Nathan said, complacently.

"Like the dutiful and, dare I say, masterful tactician that he is, the good Commodore is doing everything he can to gain the all-precious weather-gauge. Very well, then..."

Grasping a lift at a violent lee lurch, Nathan looked skyward, taking in the elements, and then scanned the sea. They were running a larboard reach, the wind nearly square on the beam.

"You've a plan, Cap'n?" Pryce asked, with the same eagerness as a hunting dog seeing its master pick up a fowling piece.

"I do, indeed." Nathan grinned, in spite of himself. It was a touchy business, sailing hard whilst staying close. "A little panic on our part 'tis needed. We'll swing the logline like our lives depended on it. Wave your arms. Shout! Bid Hodder and his mates to make like they are starting a man, now and again."

"Ain't never no startin' on a—!"

"I know that and, in all likelihood, they do too, on an intellectual level. Starting, however, is commonplace over there, and they will be best-pleased to see us do the same."

Pryce conceded, but didn't bother to hide his disgust at the notion of any member of the Brethren suffering such abuse.

"Tantalize, Master Pryce. Entice. Lure," Nathan said with an emphatic roll of his eyes. "We wish to stay out of range, but near enough to be a temptation. Ease off on the boluns, until we've lost a half o' knot; a mite more won't go unappreciated. Make it known I'll have the arse of the first mutton-fisted lubber what allows a sail to luff," he added, ominously. "Touch up the drogue over the side. Hell, drag our feet over the side, if we must. Just stay close, but beyond those guns."

"Has to be a'drivin' 'im mad, a-wonderin' why you haven't blocked his wind and brought this to a head."

"Or, he just fancies us to be in too much awe of his superiority to try him. Very well, we'll give him what he wishes to see."

"Cross-seas is cuttin' up rough," Pryce said, grabbing for a lift. Pitch and yaw combined, the mast had to have been carving a hundred-foot arc. "Don't like the looks o' that either."

Nathan followed his First Mate's gaze to windward, and the dark and churning sky there. "That, dear sir, you'll come to bless in a few hours."

They sat swaying with the swell, intent on the vessel aft, her white mustache stark against the sea's deep blue.

"Is it you or Mr. Cate what the Commodore is a-desirin' so bad?"

"Intriguing question, isn't it, Pryce?" Nathan mused. He waved a dismissive hand. "Make it so, Master Pryce. Make it so."

Pryce stood. Instead of descending, however, he leaned

around the mast to peer gravely. "Are ye up to this, Nathan? Ye look quite fagged in."

He attempted to feign no notion as to what the man was talking about, but to no avail. Intuition and wisdom was what made a capital first mate, and Pryce was among the best.

"Last time, ye—"

"Aye, that was then," Nathan said, abruptly. He was all too familiar with his past failings and shortcomings. "This is different," he said with as much conviction as could be managed whilst balanced on a t'gallant yard, nearly a hundred feet above a heaving sea. "I'm fagged, aye, but not finished."

Touched by Pryce's genuine concern, Nathan smiled encouragingly. "Go. I'll do."

The severe eyes critically scanned him like he was a freshly-trimmed sail. Then Pryce jerked a nod and clambered down the rigging like a gigantic ape.

"And bid the helm to come up another point," Nathan called after him.

❧

Nathan leaned back to revel in the ensuing quiet. High in the rigging was the closest to privacy one might achieve on a ship. It was one of the perquisites of being a topsman and why he always relished that duty.

Pryce's query regarding Harte's motivations was a fair one, one which had been churning in his own head since the *Resolute* appeared. Harte had pursued him for so long, it was a foregone conclusion or, that was to say, had been. Now, with Cate in the mix, whether the target was himself or her was the ever-pressing question. During their last meeting, Harte had expressed interest in her, and few men could pass the woman without pause. But he wasn't so naïve as to think it had been entirely a matter of chivalry, worry for the fair lady in the hands of scurrilous pirates. There was the not so small matter of the warrants for her arrest, and Harte was a grasping cove. With Creswicke—his proverbial golden goose—dead, his paths to fortune and glory would be all the more desperate. Nathanael Blackthorne's head swinging from the *Resolute's* bowsprit would bring far more glory, than a traitor from among a ragged bunch in kilts aiming to overthrow the Crown.

And damn that cursed lout of a husband of hers, for allowing her to get caught up in that feckless disaster! And praised the gods for seeing her through it.

Harte's pipe dream would no doubt involve taking them

both, or worse yet, arresting Cate, if for no other reason than to spite his prime nemesis.

Whatever the Commodore Ramrod's motivation, it was of little consequence. The plan and the outcome remained the same. A certain part of Nathan would have loved nothing more than to sink the bastard, return with the Commodore's head swinging from the *Morganse's* bowsprit and that wretched pennant flying upside down at her topmast.

Nathan took the opportunity to close his eyes; years of being aloft had taught him how to take a caulk aloft, without it being his death.

God, for just a little peace!

The bell clanging—five bells—jerked him alert. He sat up and rubbed his face hard. "Later, mate," he said to a startled petrel—another harbinger of the coming storm—dipping past.

The difference in his ship was tangible. The boluns eased, the sea anchor dragging all the more: with less speed, the ship had less drive, which made her all the more victim to the waves, causing the topmast at his back to carve an even more erratic arc. She strained under him, growing cross with the need to be on her way, to show what she was made of.

He reached around and patted the mast at his back. "Patience, me luv. Patience."

The call of duty prevailed and Nathan made ready to swing out of his roost. Out of habit, he reached for the backstay, but then withdrew his hand. Pryce's shrewd observations hadn't been far off the mark. He was fagged. He felt like a ripped out jib. He didn't trust himself, physically, at any rate. Not yet. There would be no advantage in falling from the tops like a sack of meal.

Feeling quite the lubber, he clapped onto a shroud and clambered down.

"Clear for action and batten down!" he shouted from the futtock shrouds. "Mr. Hodder!"

Hodder was there by the time Nathan's feet touched the deck.

"By the looks o' that out there," Nathan said, angling his head toward the looming weather, "hawses for preventer backstays mightn't be an excess, don't you think?"

"Gonna be wet as Neptune's court on this one," Hodder observed, mildly. "Do you desire storm canvas set, sir?"

"Nay, we'll stand off, for now. Nothing to be gained in saving the number-one for show. If we don't prevail today, there will be no ship to worry for her looks. Splinter netting, if you—"

"Done and done, sir!"

"Good man. Rig relieving tackle on the rudder as well."

"Anticipating it to blow that bad, sir?" Hodder's head came up in a clatter of rings. Clearly, his consultation with the glass had suggested else.

"Nay, not the wind. If Providence sails with us today, yon frigate will only have our stern for a target. Bid Mr. MacQuarrie to keep the port-lids closed for now," Nathan called as Hodder took his leave. "We don't wish to look too eager for a fight."

His mocking mirth brought a rousing cheer which echoed fore-and-aft as the Captain's words were passed along.

Nathan worked his way forward, acknowledging one after another well-wisher. The scurrying about was more out of formality than function. Clearing for action: the order had been long anticipated and only what couldn't in good conscience be done in advance remained. Conversation and orders were done over the bang of mallets hammering home the battens; the boats were double-bowsed on their booms, in readiness for the looming storm. He stopped to lay a testing hand on a bolun and murmured a word or two of approval to the captain-o'-the-sheets. By rights, it should have been taut enough for a giant to pluck a tune. As it was, it would have produced a dull, flat *thung!*

The bell rang.

The Watch changed, although little difference could be seen with all hands 'round. Nathan met Chips topping the forward companionway.

"Six inches in the well, sir."

Nathan nodded. As tight as the day she rolled off the stocks.

Smoke from the slowmatch tubs curled about his knees, its acridness sharp in his nose. The wet sand was abrasive underfoot. His heart beat like a call-to-arms drum and he wiped his palms on his breeches. Not out of fear—Lord, he'd last suffered that at ten-and-six!— but out of anxiousness, the need to get on with it. Under his feet, and through every span of rigging and thrum of canvas, he could feel his ship straining, like a coursing hound eager to be freed from its leash, vibrating to be rid of the drag and kick up spray in the chase's face.

"Cap'n! She's going for the wind."

The urgent hail from the mizzen made Nathan look to the *Resolute*.

Damn, he was slipping; he should have seen it coming. "Hands to the braces! Let fly that goddamned drogue!"

The *Resolute's* bowchasers fired as she veered and dove across the *Morganse's* wake, seeking the windward side, and the all-precious weather-gauge. No one could claim surprise. The true surprise would have been if Harte hadn't attempted to gain the ability to rob the *Morganse* of her wind at his whim. Now free of the drag, the *Morganse* leapt forward, the spars groaning under the sudden load.

"Double grog to the first gun to fell a mast!" Nathan shouted over the rumble of the gun trucks. "Fire as they bear! Bar and chain as will answer."

There was nothing to be gained in rendering the *Resolute's* decks a butcher shop. Damage to her rigging is what would put her by the board. Victory in a sea battle wasn't always about overwhelming odds. Too often, the difference between captivity and victory teetered on the one lucky shot, a fortuitous parting of a stay or block.

Nathan worked his way aft, the sharpshooters darkening the ratlines as they laid aloft. The *Resolute's* side disappeared in a cloud of smoke as she fired. Over-zealousness and ill – timing sent most of her shots too low. Nathan felt his ship shudder, a few finding her hull. A ball skipped on the waves and arched high overhead. A couple holes appeared in the tops'ls and the *twang!* of a shroud parting, but little more.

The frigate's sharpshooters now jamming her foretop and bows peppered the *Morganse's* decks, musketballs whining all around. The *Morganse* answered in rolling sequence. Smoke swirled the deck, the wind tearing it away. The forward crews worked feverishly, hauling on pikes to bring the muzzles around. MacQuarrie's men were methodical, virtually every shot finding a target, but vital hits were easier said than done. On the *Resolute*, rigging swung free, a few holes in her headsails, but nothing mortal.

Now with the roll, the *Resolute's* second volley was startlingly accurate, bar-shot whirring heavily through the air. There was the loud clang of a ball hitting metal, followed by the alarmed shouts of a gun crew, their gun dismounted. Curse and burn him, the frigate was crank, and thank the gods for it! She was heeled over so far, her lower tier of guns was more threat to the fishes. Her upper guns, however, were now finding their range. A spent ball landed at Nathan's feet and trundled past, followed by the sharp cry of it hitting someone's leg, breaking it.

Nathan was working his way aft one moment and was down on one knee the next. Pain struck, and he grabbed his leg, dimly thinking that, if it hurt, then it was still there. His hand came away bloody, but — praise the gods — he was whole. As he stood, testing the limb, a ball whizzed overhead, sending a shower of shattered rigging down through the splinter-netting. From the corner of his eye, he saw a block hit a man in the head, killing him instantly.

Another gust and the *Resolute* shot forward. The *Morganse* sagged, her mizzen and maintops'l shivering from the frigate stealing her wind.

Enough o' this! he thought, kicking aside the tangled rigging. "Helm! Veer away!"

The bosun's mates' shouts of "Ready about!" echoed down the deck. It was one of the few times he envied those fore-and-afters. They could come about with only a fraction of the to-do. Here, every sail abroad called for attending and virtually all at the same time.

Amid the flying balls and musket fire, the sail-tenders raced to the braces. As he mounted the quarter deck, the order rising to his lips was cut off by the sensation of tumbling. The next thing Nathan knew, he was face down on the deck, with a vice-like pain in his chest and the shouts of "Cap'n's down!" coming from all around.

The deck under Nathan's cheek vibrated with men running toward him. Still floundering like a dying fish, they seized him up and flipped him over. He blinked, looking up into anxious faces, Pryce among them. He was dimly aware of them speaking — their mouths moved, at any rate. Whether the dull thuds in his ears were words or the guns firing, he couldn't tell? The sensation of having the wind knocked out was an all too familiar one, and yet he still suffered the fear of having drawn his last breath. The fine numbness which filled him was even more alarming, for that sensation was categorically reported by every cove who lost a limb. His first thought was how furious Cate would be for allowing such injuries to happen when she wasn't about. The next thought was if she would have him if he were only half a man?

The spasms finally in his chest let go, like the seizing on a fished mast suddenly giving way, and he inhaled in a ragged gasp. Awareness returned enough for Nathan to realize where he was: now across the quarterdeck and up against the rail.

"I'm…! What… the… hell…?" he wheezed.

"Piece o' rail," declared Odgen. "Someone was a-watchin' ye, Cap'n!"

"Had it come at ye straight on, ye woulda been skewered like a sucking pig," added Squidge from the helm.

Nathan grimaced with the next breath, his chest threatening to seize up again. With that breath, the numbness faded and life flooded back with all its agonizing glories. Like a bunch o' mother hens, those around plucked at him, assuring themselves and him of his well-being. Not believing a word of it, he flailed, groped at himself. The gravely injured were routinely lied to; he couldn't name the number of times he'd seen men brutally maimed and be sitting up unaware, carrying on a conversation as if it were Sunday-church rigged.

His pounding heart finally slowed, and he realized the guns were silent. He blinked, working his eyes, and gasped "What's to do?"

"The slut tacked —"

"But she's falling away!" boasted Squidge.

"Then fall off, goddammit. Avast this pampering! I'm fine," Nathan shouted, batting the lingerers away. "Just bear a hand and get me up."

They protested, but finally yielded, allowing him to lurch to his feet, the deck seeming to pitch independently of the sea. He staggered half-bent to the rail and peered to see how the frigate laid: aft, deep in their wake. He didn't need to look; he could feel how his own ship fared. The slow, heaving rise and fall said she was in a following sea; the drop in the song of the rigging confirmed it.

Decisions begged to be made, but his head still swam. A bottle of brandy was offered. Nathan took a long, fortifying pull. Dashing his mouth with the back of his hand, thought began to flow a bit more freely.

"Get the wounded below," Nathan said, looking down at the ruin in the waist. "Any notion of a butcher's bill?"

"So far, one: Clifford copped it."

Nathan nodded; he'd seen it happen.

"The rest is the usual," Pryce offered.

It had been a short exchange, but he'd seen the decks reduced to a butcher's shop in less. They had taken a bit of a roughing-up, but walked away relatively intact.

Then, and only then, did he wish Cate might be there. He had closed his heart and mind to her, not thinking of her, for it was too painful. She rose before him then, nonetheless, compassionate and capable, those hands so very, very... *very* capable. She would have been in her glory pulling splinters and binding wounds; she could stitch flesh as handily as she could cloth.

He shook his head, clearing the thought of her away.

Nathan moved stiffly to the binnacle and leaned against it, taking several more long pulls from a flask. It was difficult to sort out which hurt more, his chest, his back or his leg.

The men were already cutting away the damaged rigging, and knotting-and-splicing like gigantic spiders spinning webs. MacQuarrie and his crews hunched around *Jumpin' Jehovah's* now wheelless truck. This was why one worked long and hard to gain able-hands, nurtured fine, seaman-like officers, and then do everything within their power to keep them. This was where their mettle showed. They knew their tasks and went about them with a fervor. Here, on a pirate ship, they worked for the love of the barky and the good of all, not out of fear of the next beating, or grog or rations cut.

His thoughts were broken by a row setting up forward, voices sharp and confrontational rising above the din of setting the ship to rights.

"What the f—?" Nathan muttered under his breath.

As he eased his way down the steps—he still couldn't wholly trust his leg—Hodder and Hallchurch wove aft through the debris and men, each propelling a man by the scruff. Several more bosun's mates followed close behind; Mute Maori and Chin materializing proved whatever this was about, no one was surprised. A progressive hush closed in behind the contingency coming toward him, all work coming to a curious halt. Sailors, for the most part, were a ghoulish lot, and took great pleasure in seeing another get their comeuppance.

Nathan inwardly groaned and cursed. He knew the obstinate look on those being compelled forward, and what they were about, before they opened their mouths.

"Got a couple o' sea lawyers here what are a-lookin' to be our undoing," said Hodder. One look at his stony countenance said it all: Yes, this had to be addressed, and *now.*

"Conspiring and talking mayhem," put in Hallchurch. "And as how things might be better over there." He pointed with his chin toward the *Resolute,* sailing hard, yet just out – of-range.

Like unruly pups, the accused were given a quelling shake and shoved forward. Nathan grimly nodded. 'Twas his own damned fault. He'd noticed these two skulking villains at the foremast—trouble brewing like a pot of porridge—and had meant to have a word with the duty captain.

"What's your name?" Nathan demanded of one, a squat, lumpish piece. It was a damned awkward thing for a captain not to know the name of every man he was about to lead to his death. They hadn't been sailors for long; they still had that sour landsman stench about them. They couldn't be Lovelies; Thomas never would have suffered such capers. They had to be Brazens; having just joined the Brethren.

"Gavin," the lump said adding "Sir" only as an afterthought.

Nathan arched a questioning brow, waiting for the other to find his tongue. "Curtis... sir."

"Well, Mr. Gavin, Mr. Curtis, I don't have time for this goddamned foolishness. Conspiring, eh? Is that the way of it?"

A glance at Hodder told him this wasn't the usual run-of-the-mill, idle griping or complaining as sailors were wont to do. Fists clenched and shoulders stiff, neither was in a state-of-contrition common to those brought before him. These were hard-horses, bloody noses and split lips indicated there had already been harsh words.

"We've grievances and desire t' be heard," Curtis said.

"We've got our right to speak!" put in Gavin pugnaciously.

"Suffering Christ, now!?" Nathan exclaimed eyeing the approaching storm and the ruin all around. "With the blood of your mates still running the decks?"

"'Tis our right to be heard. The rules say as the captain —"

" — is as next-to-God as yon Commodore during an engagement," Nathan finished for them. "More so, in fact, for he has an Admiralty to answer to." Having a good inch or so on both of them, he imposed himself over them, glaring. "I, on the other hand, answer to *no* one."

In a distant corner of his mind, Nathan conceded that, by rights, they had a point. He hadn't sought the people's approval of this venture, as was his obligation. The common threat looming over the horizon had answered for all, all except these pismire scrubs. As earlier suspected, they were Brazens, fresh off a Company ship, fresh out from under the fist-of-power. Many were led to run amok by these new-gained freedoms, until they discovered — often the hard way — that the responsibility of self-rule was far more unyielding than being ruled by another.

Gavin cowered, making horned signs. "Yer devil-possessed. Yer titched," he added, tapping his temple.

"Aye, sir," Curtis said eagerly. "Devil-possessed and a-lookin' to take this ship down to see Ol' Nick."

An impassioned "Aye" was muttered by several around, the popish crossing themselves.

"Ol' Nick, is it?" Nathan echoed. He was caught between laughing and punching the ignorant lout.

Caught up in their own fervor, the pair was growing a spine by the moment. "You a - comin' back from the dead, thumbin' your nose at the Devil. And now, there's a storm, a – comin' out o' nowhere – "

"It came over the horizon, just as every storm – " Nathan sputtered.

"Nossir!" came back with the conviction of the saved-on-Sunday pious. Gavin lowered his voice as if fearing that very demon might overhear. "'Tis the hand o' the Devil hisself!"

There was no faulting the man for lack of conviction; eyes rounded with fear, he shook with it in both body and voice.

"We had nothing but good omens." Nathan raised his voice for the benefit of those nearby. Those who couldn't hear directly would hear through their mates; word could pass faster than a man could walk. "It wasn't Friday, nor the thirteenth; no buckets were overturned and Millbridge's ague was tolerable. Hell, even the sea hogs escorted us out," Nathan finished, with an aggravated swipe.

The entire complement jerked at what they thought to be the sound of great guns, only to realize it was thunder.

Hopefully, they'll think it's the voice of God, Nathan thought moodily.

"Since I so handily managed to escape Lucifer's grasp, as you so cleverly point out, then explain to me, *if* you please, why in God's bleeding wounds do you think I would be so damned anxious to return?" Nathan growled through his teeth.

"Bewitched ye," Gavin said, appealing to the rest of the crew, as if it were obvious.

"Bewitched," Nathan repeated dully. He'd expected a lot of things, but Caesar's ghost, not this! "It's been my impression Ol' Scratch left spell-casting to the hags."

"These pimplish, sniveling excuses for men were a-talkin' up of sending you back to where you come from," said Hodder. "They represented they might sail this ship better themselves."

"Is that so?" Nathan mused, dryly.

He had to give the coves credit for a set o' brass balls: they actually nodded to Hodder's accusation, confessing to their own crimes. A glance aloft showed several more looking on with great interest. He scanned the surrounding faces, alert for any signs of affront or brewing malevolence. He'd seen it earlier that day and had ignored it, regretfully. He mightn't survive the next boil-over. This needed to be nipped and quickly. Superstitious fear was more contagious and deadly than the wharf fever or the yellow jack, and more difficult to eradicate than the Spanish pox.

"If you're so aggrieved, believe your souls to be in such dire peril, surely you're not alone. Surely," Nathan went on, with a grand gesture, "there are more of your mates much of the same mind. Anyone?" he demanded of the crowd. "Any one person willing to step forward on your behalf? Watch captain? Messmates? Tie-mates? Anyone?"

If anything, the people retreated, visibly shrinking back. Nathan exhaled a private sigh, his suspicions confirmed.

Nathan swiveled his full attention on the now somewhat disconsolate pair. "Yes, I saw the Devil and his lair, and it is *nothing* I ever wish to see again." The fist he waved was white enough to have belonged to the dead.

He was in a murderous passion. A significant cough from Pryce, now somewhere behind him, called him to something nearer his senses. Venting that black fury might make him seem demonic or crazed, proving the scrubs' point. Those who knew him best retreated farther, urging the unsuspecting ignorant with them. The duller-witted gaped, waiting to see what was to come next.

Nathan snatched Gavin by the shirtfront and shook him, his arms flopping like a ragdoll. "I am your judge and jury, now," he said, aloud enough to be heard over the rigging's rising moan. "The hell you fear is not below, but right here."

They were under fire, which—according to the Code—made the captain Jehovah. The decision of guilt was a foregone conclusion. Hodder could be a hard-horse, but he was a fair one, as was Pryce, now at his elbow, stiff with outrage. The fact that they were brought forward was proof in and of itself that the infraction was a grave one, too grave to be kept under-hatches.

Amid another rumble of thunder, the *Resolute's* bowchaser barked. She was in range, *again*. An uneven exchange had broken out between the *Resolute's* bowchaser, and *Merdering Mary* and *Bloody Bess*. The *Resolute's* was naught but a nine-pounder, but it was still capable of delivering a lucky shot. As predicted, the frigate's focus was the *Morganse's* stern, primarily the rudder, sending a ball through the gallery windows and down the length of her hull her greatest dream. A black veil of impending rain loomed just over the rail; the tempest's wind wouldn't be far behind.

Nathan stood back, the first droplets of rain pattering on his face. He entertained visions of long, slow torturous deaths.

Oh, for a little time!

Both of these unsuspecting half-wits should drop on their knees and give thanks for that storm, and the agony they were spared.

"Guilty of conspiring and endangering the vessel during an engagement," Nathan proclaimed, instead. "Any questions?"

The latter was directed to the on-looking crowd. Silence was their consent, many openly smiling and making agreeable gestures. The matter already settled so far as they were concerned, many were already laying aloft, in anticipation of the orders sure to come.

"Good!" Nathan barked. "I've no intention of taking the whole ship down, but I'm not above sending an offering. Over the side!"

His fist curled at the pleasurable prospect of personally helping these two lumps of wasted flesh off his ship. It wasn't fitting for a captain to do so, however. Chin seized one by the collar, Maori the other by the belt, and hurled them in a curving arch over the rail. With the *Morganse* tearing along as she was, the condemneds' cries faded quickly.

Nathan whirled around to the crew. "Carry on!"

He waited to make sure the men dispersed, the fire sufficiently quenched, before he rounded on Pryce. "I thought you and that hulking first mate o' Thomas' settled all this," he said in a low growl.

Pryce was looking remarkably miserable, at the moment. "We did, or thought as much."

"Weak minds and quaking hearts, eh?" Both Pryce and Hodder were fair judges of men, able to head off any quirk of character, but he didn't wish to come down too hard on them, because it was precious difficult to foresee the effect of smoke and blood on each and every one.

Chin and Maori got the benefit of Nathan's glare next. "Bear an eye for any more of this skullduggery. One hesitation, one false move, or even the suggestion of one, and we'll use them for sea anchors," he added loudly enough for the ears sure to be still listening.

The timid mutely bent their heads over their tasks; the scheming solemnly nodded and hitched their trousers.

Reefing and all final preparations was nigh complete when the storm hit. Luckily, it was already all-hands, for every soul was required. The first gust kicked the *Morganse* square in the stern, forcing her bow to dip. The second hit nearly square on the bow and she bucked like a spring colt, setting all sails aback with yard-threatening force. The wind backed, wafted, and then struck harder, yet.

"Close-haul 'er!" Nathan shouted. "Fall off!"

The yards swung, the canvas snapped taut, and the shrouds groaned with the load, the next wave arching over the f'c'stle.

KERRY LYNNE

The rain struck with equal fury, heeling the *Morganse* over, making it nigh impossible to see the next man. Hearing was impossible; speaking risked drowning. The sudden wind change set the waves crashing into each other. In the confused seas, the ship took an odd lee lurch, sending the more lubberly — probably Brazens — staggering. Nathan grabbed one by the belt to keep him from tumbling headlong into the bitts.

Everyone scrambled, but there was no panic, aside from a select few. One or two of the newest draft might have been at sea long enough to know fore-from-aft, and how to clap on to a sheet, but they had seen nothing like this. They had to be dragged by the collar from their cowering and solidly shook back to their senses.

Rain pounding the deck so hard it hung in a fog about their knees, Nathan was too busy for the next while attending his own vessel to spare a thought for any other. With her bow already to the wind, they hauled tacks and sheets.

Tacking was just as well, he thought, as the barky settled on a larboard one. Running with the wind was far too much to the *Resolute's* liking. Given a choice, he would have preferred to run with this, saving ship and crew a beating. Alas, the powers rendered such preferences naught but idle dreams.

His ship finally squared away, Nathan squinted into the sheeting rain to see how the *Resolute* was faring. Judging by the blown out sprits'l and flapping jib, she had been caught with far too much canvas abroad. She still had far too much canvas flying, by his notion. Knowing the Commodore's single-minded nature, there had to have been quite the argument going on, the Master pleading for her rigging, the Commodore demanding ahead full.

The Master must have prevailed. Sails were reefed or doused altogether, but not handily. The f'c'stle jacks knew their business, but the foremast...

"God's blood and wounds, she's a lugging slut," Nathan murmured under his breath. His heart was in his throat for the *Resolute's* Master as she struggled to settle on a course, sagging and veering, making her sheetsmen's lives a living hell.

His greatest worry was what to do if the slut actually missed stays. He'd tip his hand by having to back-and-fill, waiting for the *Resolute* to catch them up. He might ease off a bit more, he considered, looking up.

He almost cheered at seeing the frigate's masts steady and her bow come about. Her yards swung, headsails filled, and she fell onto the *Morganse's* wake, like a hound on a scent.

The chase was on, again.

After the storm's initial blast, the wind settled into something a damned site more than a tops'l breeze, but considerably less than a full gale. The *Morganse* heeled over, burying her chains. The boluns now taut as fiddle strings, the waves broke high over her bow and curled back, the waist awash in foam. She did what she was made for: shook it off, rose and looked for the next wave.

This was sailing!

Now, it was down to a tacking duel, running a zigzagging course as near into the wind as the ship could lie. Unless the *Morganse* chose to yaw and fight yardarm-to – yardarm, it was a contest of seamanship, rather than tactics: which crew was the ablest; which captain knew his ship best? Success now balanced on something as simple as a block or boltrope giving way, a stay parting. Those hawser preventer stays were worth their weight in gold now, preserving the *Morganse's* rigging and, hence, her people.

The rain eased from a deluge to driving sheets. On a philosophical note, one need only tilt back his head and open his mouth for a fresh drink. Between gusts, the rooftop-like pitch of the decks righted, allowing several inches of water to collect at their feet. With the scuppers flooded, when she heeled again, the water sheeted over the gun'l.

Wet as Neptune's court, indeed! The glass hadn't lied.

The bell clanged. The Watch changed. The *Morganse* tacked.

Once all was tallied-and-belayed, as many hands as could be spared were sent to their hammocks, sodden and weary. The galley fires still out, broth and whatever could be eaten out-of-hand was the day's fare. Grog was served out to warm the bones and heighten spirits, and as a none-so-genteel reminder of what they were fighting for.

Heads craned skyward, Hodder and his mates stalked the decks, worried for their precious rigging. Chafing gear was called for with a regularity which made Nathan consider rousing all hands to tear junk. MacQuarrie checked and re-checked his double-bowsed guns and their rings. No one wished a half-ton of certain-death careening about, plunging down a hatchway, and thence through the bottom of the ship.

Standing on the quarterdeck point, Nathan glanced over his shoulder. The stern pulpit blocked his view, but he couldn't shake the feeling of being watched. Leaning out over the rail, in a flash of lightning he caught the flare of metal near the *Resolute's* forechains. A brass glass; someone peering at them.

Snatching a glass from the binnacle, Nathan scrambled up on

the taffrail and then the stern. Braced against the sternlamp, he straddled the rail and peered back. In another lighting flash and he caught the glint of gold near the frigate's forechains. Saints preserve him, the pompous poof even had gold epaulets on his rain tarpaulin!

A wave broke over the *Resolute's* bow, dousing His Pompousness thoroughly;

Nathan openly laughed, a maniacal cackle.

The weather thickened and day became night. The frigate's sails often no more than a ghostly glow, she popped in and out of the gloom like a phantom, to the point of several men spitting and making horned signs. Not wishing to disappear in the night, Nathan ordered the masthead and stern lamps lit, and the cabin lights set ablaze. He wanted the *Morganse* to show like a fireship. It was an obvious fling or taunt but, by his judgment, the hook in this fish had long been set.

The watch bell rang; the *Morganse* and *Resolute* tacked.

"Ye've a plan." Pryce's speculation broke Nathan's thoughts. "Ye've tacked on the glass this last Watch n' more."

"I have, indeed. My only hope is that *they* are as observant as you."

"The barky can come up another point, mebbe two," Pryce offered, looking thoughtfully up.

"Aye, she can, but that slut can't," Nathan observed, nodding toward the *Resolute*. "I don't wish to lose her... not *yet*."

⋘⋙

Nathan hauled on the cabin door, slipped in and allowed the wind to slam it shut against the roar of the tempest. The resulting silence was almost deafening.

He stood there dripping, reveling in the glorious reprieve. He didn't mind the weather — that would be tantamount to a fish complaining of being wet — but a respite didn't go unappreciated, as did the chance to stand without clapping-on, of water not lashing one's knees, to open one's eyes entirely and draw a dry breath, or speaking without screaming. In that sudden quiet, he now could feel his ship's liveliness through the soles of his feet.

Aye, me lovely, doing what you do best.

Nathan shook off, adding to the several inches of water already sloshing about. In the blaze of the chandelier, a bright dash of color at the companionway rail caught his eye. Feathers streaked with dark lines of wetness, Beatrice withdrew her head from under a wing. Leaning with the yaw of the ship, she eyed him coldly, yawned and tucked her head back.

The cabin was his personal quarters, but it felt foreign. It wasn't so much to do with being cleared for action, everything which could possibly be moved stowed below. It was a matter of what had been cleared away: everything of Cate was gone. Her chair, her little stool, her blood box: everything. He closed his eyes and inhaled. Even her sweet smell, which usually met him at the mizzen, was missing, the acrid stink of hot iron from *Merdering Mary* and *Widwr,* and powder-smoke replacing it.

It was as if someone meant to erase her from his life, from existence.

Nathan muttered a curse. It was ridiculous, aye. He was being as overly sensitive as a young lass, but the feeling was as persistent and nagging as a bad tooth.

"She'll be there. She'll be there," he chanted under his breath.

He felt a certain reproachfulness from his ship. He leaned his head back, putting nearly his entire length in contact with the bulkhead. "You know damned good n' well why she couldn't be here. Not through this."

The *Morganse* took a crank lee lurch and then settled.

The glass was visible from where he stood. Steady. It hadn't dropped, but neither had it risen.

First bell of the First Watch rang.

"Eight-thirty." He spoke automatically, as he always did for Cate's benefit. The woman was the quickest-of-mind ever met, but could not learn the bells. Baffling. Incomprehensible.

He ran a hand down his face. *Where the hell did the day get to?*

They had just tacked... again, and likely would for some hours, days, hell, weeks, unless he could come up with a way of clapping a stopper on this escapade.

Nathan's lurched his first few steps, as if something he had been leaning against was suddenly gone. He rummaged through the rolled charts stored in an urn now lashed to the mizzen. Disappointed, he went through those between the beams overhead. Victorious at last, he spread the parchment out on the table, securing its corners with the honey crock, and tools scattered about.

Millbridge appeared bearing a towel. Nathan swiped his face and wrung out his sleeves.

"How bad is it?" Nathan asked. After shouting for so long over the storm, his "normal" voice sounded odd.

Millbridge, the ship's venerable, was purported to be old enough to have shook Noah's hand; other's claimed him Methuselah's grandfather. Whatever the vessel, the ship's eldest was always revered, and looked to as the ultimate judge on any and everything.

Millbridge's caved mouth worked, considering. "Not the worst, not by a long shot."

"Then damn the waves, full n' by!" Nathan declared good-naturedly, squeezing the water from his braids.

As Nathan handed back the towel, he noticed the dried blood on the elder's hand. "How do the wounded do?"

"Tolerable, tolerable. Restin' n' wishin' they was elsewhere. Had to tie Smalley into his hammock, insisting as he was to report, and a rib stove in."

"A tot for those who can bear it."

Millbridge angled his head, his version of making his obedience, and took his leave. He passed Kirkland on the steps, bearing a pot and cup. The powderroom had been long since secured, but it was still too rough to light the galley fires. A spirit stove had been employed to brew the coffee, thin but hot. A cup holding *charqui*, the dried meat strips standing in it like pencils. Nathan plucked out two, swirling one into the honey jar and tucking it into the corner of his mouth; the second was stowed inside his shirt, allowing the rain-soaked fabric to soften it for later.

Idly gnawing on the meat, he leant stiffly over the chart — his back had tightened up; it felt like he'd been bludgeoned with a capstan bar. His charts were his pride, a meticulously crafted accumulation of knowledge gained through a couple of decades at sea. Some of it came from personal experience, but a larger part had been gleaned from the experiences of others. Every shallow, shoal, reef, rock, port, jetty, point, headland or landmark were laid out in great detail. He flipped open the log book and rifled back through the pages, trying to recall when he had last been through those waters, hoping something might trigger his memory, something he could use...

The most pressing problem was that he had no notion where the hell they were. Aye, Ransom Passage lay aft, south and east. These waters were, for the most part, open with few obstacles. Sadly, that meant no land to fix. With the sun obliterated, and visibility slightly beyond the end of one's fingertips, they could be anywhere in a hundred-mile circle.

Nathan was still staring at the chart when Pryce came in.

"Potts and Furia busted a gut on that last tack"

Nathan nodded without looking up. "Not the first time for either." Nor for anyone else who had been to sea for long. "Millbridge is serving out tots as we speak. Find them some soft duty, so they might feel they are doing their part."

Pryce swiped the water from his streaming face and dashed

it on his sodden sleeve. "Masthead reports Desolation Rock. Just a glimpse—"

"Where away?" Nathan asked, looking up. A glimpse was all one needed.

"A mile or so, about three points off to starboard quarter."

"Hmm...." Nathan looked down at the chart again. "'Tis far more aft, than I would have guessed, but it's a bearing. One mustn't complain of small favors," he observed pragmatically. "It's a fix."

Pryce moved closer to study the chart as well. "Nothin' else within a two-day sail o' here."

"Except, this." Nathan tapped the northwest corner.

Pryce bent and squinted. "Eden Island?" He straightened, puzzled. "Nuthin' but coral n' gull shite there. T'would be hard pressed to fit all hands on it. 'Tis more hazard than convenience."

Nathan couldn't argue. Whoever had named the thing had a convoluted sense of humor. Barely higher than a man stood, it was naught but a jagged coralhead.

"Convenience is in the eye of the beholder. It has an elegant shoal—"

Pryce made a hawking noise. "Not what I've heard it called."

"An elegant hook," Nathan continued implacably. His finger traced the parallel dashes contiguous to Eden, curving like a one-sided anchor. "It must run a mile—"

"'N more," Pryce said, dubiously. The severe grey eyes swiveled up. "Ye've a plan, Cap'n?"

"I do, indeed. That, my friend," his finger tapping the parchment, "is the hook upon which we shall catch our fish."

"'N how d' ye figger that?"

Two slightly parted fingers tracked their current course. "We," Nathan began, lifting his index finger, "come in on this easternmost tip. At the last minute, we come hard about." The finger flicked off, as if glancing off the markings, "and sail off."

"And, the *Resolute*?"

Nathan's remaining finger continued on its track, slightly beyond the anchor's fluke. "She'll tack, but alas, as she has *every* time, she'll sag wide. She comes about like a bull in a privy."

Pryce nodded. No one could argue that.

"She comes about," Nathan went on, pivoting his fingertip, "His High Nobleness now threatening to flay their backs for their slowness. She'll fill with all haste, heave down hard and—" The finger stopped inside fluke's curve. "The fish is hooked, hard aground. Only hours of sweat and club-hauling will claw her out, and even then, not until this lays." A general wave indicated the dirty weather.

"Her Master will know it's out there, same as you n' me."

"Maybe," Nathan said, straightening. He considered the *Resolute,* her glowing mastlight visible through the rain-streaked stern panes. "He's crossed two shallows and never a lead was flung. He's either too green or too afraid of the Commodore's wrath to tell him else. As for the rest of her people, they could all be seasoned salts, or they could all be a draft so fresh the pale of Ol' England is still on their cheeks."

Pryce nodded through the litany, conceding most points. "They'll see it kicking up."

"It's black as inside a parson's hat out there. Between that and the heavy seas, it'll barely look any different than the other twenty square leagues of sea, assuming they can see beyond their bowsprit."

Pryce silently considered. Nathan thought the momentary pause a blessing; he was still figuring this out himself.

"If he smokes it and falls off early, then we tack and sail on," Nathan conceded.

Nathan glanced at the glass again, hoping it might give some indication of its intentions. Damned uncommunicative thing! He'd seen it blow like this for days; he'd also seen it die dead within a glass.

"If it comes to that, we'll pull out our pocket handkerchiefs," Nathan said.

"Beg pardon, sir?" Pryce said, distracted.

"Nothing, nothing," Nathan said, and bent back over the chart.

So much of the plan hinged on elements beyond his control. The wind had to hold, the dirty night persist. If the wind veered, or the weather lifted, he'd be back staring at the damned chart, in desperate search for another option.

Other than wet or death, nothing was for certain at sea. In these seas, an untimely gust or a cross-seas could outweigh the willingness of crew and vessel, and be their undoing. As always, they were at the whim of whatever powers controlled such things. Was the *Resolute* or *Morganse,* he or Harte in better favor? There was the chance it wasn't vessel or commander which vexed the powers, but some sin-ridden, blaspheming cove aboard. Or, were they all pure enough to get a pass to see another day?

"Tis a thin hope," Pryce finally said.

Nathan shrugged, for the decision was made, whether his First Mate agreed or no. It wouldn't be the first time they had crossed hawses. Having the old shellback on his side, however, would be a great comfort. "But one only a fool would pass up.

Providence has seen fit to provide us with an opportunity. I'd be an ungrateful, off-scouring scrub to deny that helpful hand."

With a bent knuckle, Nathan measured off the distances on the chart. "In four or five hours we'll know."

Eight bells.

The Watch changed; the *Morganse* tacked. The *Resolute* tacked, sagging and slewing wide.

Nathan smiled.

"Two foot and a half in the well, sir."

Nathan nodded a vague acknowledgment. She was working hard, wind and sea opening her seams. 'Twas a natural thing; a less weatherly ship would have double or triple that, her people pumping hard already.

He swiped the water from his eyes and tucked his chin into his chest in order to breathe. He smiled again when, during a break in the rain, his glass found the *Resolute's* officers clustered under a dodger rigged at the windward shrouds, looking half-drowned and miserable.

Nathan set to pacing the quarterdeck. The "how" of it was unclear — a prickling at the back of his neck, a knotting in his gut, perhaps the *Morganse* shying — but the "what" was eloquently clear: land, or a hazard of some sort, was near.

"Mr. Wareham, jump below and rouse Mr. Damerrel. Give him my compliments, and tell him he's required in the maintop," Nathan said.

The best eyes aboard in the maintop didn't ease his uneasiness. Nathan made several more agitated passes, the afterguard scrambling out of his way. Realizing he was making everyone's life miserable, he left. Forward was where he needed to be, where a clearer view and a better sense of the lay of things might be found. And so, forward he went. Scaling the foremast shrouds, he settled on the crosstree once more and fixed his attention ahead. Sadly, at the moment, he was lucky to see the tip of his fingers, let alone beyond the bow.

The present squall lifted and, at the top of the swell there it was: land, barely more than a coralhead sticking up, but land, nonetheless. Its jagged outline often merging with the waves, he wasn't sure if he was actually seeing it, or he had stared so long, his imagination finally chose to oblige him.

Damerrel hailed. Coming from downwind, Nathan barely heard the wind-torn cry, but didn't need to.

The rain lessened a bit more. Now, he could make out a

white line of surf churning slightly more than the rest. It might have been obscure then, but he could see the curving sand bar clear in his mind. The last time he had seen it the day had been clear and bright, the tide low, the sea flat. The ship becalmed, he had nothing but time to watch the pelicans doze and gulls preen. Like the drawing on his chart, the gleaming sand curved like a half – anchor, the shank to the west, to larboard, the hook running off to starboard, to the east.

Ben's head popped up beside him. "Mr. Pryce's compliments and duty, sir. He begs me to report Eden Reef dead ahead." The import of that furrowed the young brow.

"So, I see. My compliments and thanks to Mr. Pryce. And bid the helm steady ahead."

"But—" The prospect of displeasing Pryce scared Ben more than crossing his captain.

"Steady ahead," Nathan repeated evenly.

"Yessir," came back glumly and the lad disappeared.

Nathan settled back to his observations. The reef was now all the nearer. Location was the key; they were coming in too high, too much west. Perfection would be the *Morganse* making her turn at the most extreme point, putting the *Resolute* in the trap before it was ever sprung. Back at the helm was where he needed to be.

As Nathan descended by way of a forestay, he felt dissatisfaction radiating up from the deck like heat off a griddle. He landed on the f'c'stle and amid the jacks' grave faces. They were now close enough by then for this pig-tail-swinging group to know exactly what they saw, knew what a lee-shore meant. They also knew what would be asked of them, and the disaster which awaited should they fail. But still, good words and goodwill never went amiss.

"It's gonna be a hard tack, coming about at our peril." Nathan shouted over the elevated noise of that exposed deck.

Fox, captain-of-the-jacks, stepped forward. "She'll do 'er, sir! Cap'n wouldn't ask more than what the barky can give," he directed to his men.

The group, Nathan included, instinctively turned a shoulder into a wave a fraction before it broke out of the darkness and doused them all.

"Just let fly and haul like your lives depended upon it. She'll do the rest," Nathan called back, giving a kevel a loving pat.

Leaving the f'c'stle, Nathan waded—literally—along the waist, calling the hands together.

"I know we've been tacking all night," he shouted from amid them. In this weather, only the most immediate could hear, but word would spread faster than he could deliver it himself. "But we've one more and a grand one it will be."

"It'll be a gut-tearing, hellish few minutes," he went on. "We need to look sharp, heave hearty and we will be at our leisure, with double grog and our hammocks waiting. Make the barky proud!" He was obliged to raise his voice to throat-tearing level at the end, just to be heard over the cheers.

"All hands! Clear the braces and make ready. And make ready the kedge."

The last came somewhat grudgingly. Foolhardiness wasn't his burden; preparation was the best defense against failure, or at least a means to mitigate it. Even if this proved to be a vast misjudgment, the worst case would be the deeper-drafted frigate would run aground sooner, her momentum driving her in all the harder. All hands which could be spared were set to the tacks, to make sure they didn't miss stays.

Nathan pushed his way through the growing throng of men as they tumbled up and took up a position next to Squidge to con the ship. From there, he took the lay of things again and came to the same conclusion.

They were coming in too high.

"Starboard a half point. Dyce," he said, squinting forward through the flying spray.

All the while, he checked the *Resolute*: astern, to starboard and, more significantly, nearer the hook's end.

While on the f'c'stle, he thought to have felt a shift in the motion of the *Morganse*, the waves changing with the nearness of land. He could feel it now, his ship giving him warning. They were close, so very, very close.

Feeling eyes on him, Nathan looked up to find Pryce staring at him. "Care to put a name to what's on your mind, Pryce?"

Pryce jerked his head around and made a great point of fixing his attention elsewhere. "Nay, sir."

"Odd, because you've been staring for a great while." Nathan leaned closer to add under the wind's furor "I'm not titched." Winking, he tapped the side of his head.

"Never said —"

"No, and you never would," Nathan mused. "But, you're thinking it. You're watching me like Artemis on a mouse. I know what I'm doing; I've no intention of taking us down to see Old Hob."

The West Country voice, able to reach from keelson to kites in a full gale, lowered to a rumbling whisper. "Well, d'ye see, I've got this itch..."

"You're sure it's naught but a rash from that harlot you laid with last?"

"It's answered a'fore," came back doggedly.

"Aye, I know it well," Nathan finally surrendered. "It's the land-in-your-lee itch. Rest assured, you don't suffer alone."

Nathan wormed his shoulders inside of his shirt. No one in his right mind liked land in his lee, especially in this murk. The beaches were littered with hulks, and many a dirge was sung of ships that found themselves in that very position.

"This will answer, Pryce. That slab-sided tub is not expecting us to tack for another hour and more. It's the middle of the Middle Watch. Her men are thinking about nothing but their beds."

The mariner in Pryce liked it; the caution which his position demanded dampened it. "'Tis a-cuttin' it a mite fine, on a night such as this. Gonna be a hard tack."

"A real gut-tearer. Larboard another half point, Mr. Squidge. Thus."

The whites of Pryce's eyes flashed as he rolled them up toward the rigging. "She'll do it?"

"You know she will," Nathan said, evenly. He nodded forward toward the crew. "And so can they. At worst, we'll grind some weed off the bottom."

"Yer daft," Pryce observed admiringly. "Mebbe not titched, but damned daft—"

"You can engrave that on me headstone."

They both shuddered at the thought of being buried on land.

Pryce made a horned sign and spit over the rail. "Ye be in need o' either the hand o' God, or the hand o' Satan on this one. Or mebbe Calypso's hand," he added as an afterthought.

"God willing, not the latter!" Nathan declared heartily. "Just tell me which of the other pair I should pray to and I'll do it. On with you, then. Make it so."

"Land in his lee" wasn't the only sensitivity years at sea had provided Nathan. That same second sense was warning him of weather: it was up to something; a change was nigh. Whether it meant to go dirtier or lift, he had no notion, but at the bow was where he needed to be. T'would be far easier to thread this needle up there, and so he worked his way forward. Hand signals and speaking trumpets were usually relied upon, but either of those would be too vulnerable to an inopportune worsening of the weather. Instead, he posted sober, reliable hands along the deck to pass his orders aft. Ben was grabbed by the collar and taken along as a messenger ready-to-hand.

Near the forechains, Nathan shouted "Stand by!"

From the f'c'stle, the reef seemed as evident as a headland. The air was alive, like bees humming, with the reverberation of the pounding surf. How the hell the Resolutes weren't seeing it was anyone's guess? Craning his head, Nathan checked her lookout, once more: hunkered deep in his tarpaulin, miserable and wishing he were anywhere else than up there. No one over there seemed to be watching for anything, other than the next wave in the face.

He had amused his foe enough. The *Lovely* and *Brazen* were well away. It was time to scrape this dog shite off his shoe and be on his merry way.

Wiping the spray from his face, Nathan ran an eye to windward, watching the swell and wind tearing the crests. His ship was poised and ready, willing, as always. Never had she failed him. All she asked was a steady hand and a fair chance. Timing was the key: timing the wind, timing their momentum, timing the waves, timing the hands to their tasks...

Providence smiled. Another squall hit, the perfect curtain.

"Ready about! Let fly and haul!!"

Nathan's eyes were fixed aft, where the frigate was last seen. The tacks were freed. The braces swung. The headsails were brought around and the sheets were hauled home. The sheetmen's chant of "Heave! Heave! Haul with a will! Heave!" came from aft. The *Morganse* pirouetted as elegantly as a dancer, coming 'round, her own wake brushing her sides. The jib overhead "whumped!" as it caught, and the deck pitched. She lurched at a wave setting her down, her keel brushing the bottom. Like the champion that she was, she shook it off, filled, set her shoulder into the next wave and tore away, leaving the tumultuous reef to her stern.

Hodder's pipe of "Belay!" was lost in a rousing cheer.

Nathan raced aft, intent on where the *Resolute* should be. As quickly as the downpour closed in, it lifted, revealing the frigate standing on, ever deeper inside the hook. Finally, she came alive. Nathan couldn't hear, but he could jolly well imagine the furor on those decks: shouts, curses, starting and caning men like they were beasts-of-burden. Her loose headsails flapped. The yards came round — He'd have that foremast captain's hide, if it had been his vessel — her headsails swung — hung up on a stay, but swung, nonetheless. Her prow found the wind and...

The slab-sided slut didn't disappoint. She stayed true to her nature and hung.

Nathan's heart hung-fire for her Master. One errant wave, one untoward gust, and she would miss stays and fall off. That would present its own set of complications to his plan, a part of his mind already racing to work them out. He had sailed many a buttertub like her, opting to wear just to save the anguish. Wearing was always easier on man and machine, but turning all the way around on one's stern was awkward business.

Finally, the frigate answered her helm and her people's prayers. Her bow came around and she paid off. Sails filling, she heeled over and settled on her new course, like a hound on a hare.

At the mainchains, by then, Nathan swung out onto the chainplate, grasping a deadeye as he leaned out for a better view. "That's it, haul on those bolins. Harden her down. Heave with a will," Nathan coached under his breath, seeing the bow wave grow.

And then the frigate stopped with a force which set her yards bending like coachwhips.

"She struck!" came from somewhere on deck, the waisters capering about like gleeful children.

The next swell lifted the *Resolute* from her frozen stance and dropped her with a violence which made everyone wince. There she hung, the surf pounding as if she were a part of the sandbar.

She might claw off before daylight, but it was doubtful. The wise would wait for the seas to lay before trying to clubhaul out. Even after she clawed off, there was still the reef itself to clear. Given the way she sagged, it would be a long, long... long pull.

Pryce met Nathan as he came back over the rail. "Standing-by, so as to make sure she don't break up, would be the civil thing."

"As I recall, Mum was the last to expect something civil of me, and she did so in vain." Nathan said, grinning. "Has that rum finally rotted your brain, or has age made you senile? Do you fancy they would do the same for us?"

"Not in life, unless t'were you adrift. Harte would brave hell itself to see you hang."

"They've land in their lee—" Nathan observed.

"Barely refuge for the gulls," Pryce snorted.

"And boats still on their booms," Nathan went on blithely. "After all, nothing is impossible for the Royal Navy."

An icy down draft was the precursor of another squall rolling in. "The gods have just provided! We'll vanish in plain sight. Prepare to come about! Bear away east-by-south, helm!"

In the first drops of rain, the *Morganse* pivoted, putting the wind to her stern. The decks leveled and the song in the rigging dropped.

"Douse the lamps," Nathan shouted from amidships. "I'll hock 'n heave the first sodomite what strikes a light."

The *Morganse* rode away with the rain.

⌒⌒⦿⌒⌒

Nathan stepped into his cabin, with one singular intent: sleep, and all its glory!

The last squall had blown through to reveal the pink of dawn glowing on the line where sea and sky. He had waited to see his ship away safe. The ten-mile disk of sea visible from the t'gallant mast was clear.

He made the mistake of closing his eyes. The world pitched like the heaving f'c'stle he had just left.

The spot between his shoulder blades where he had been hit felt like a mule had kicked him, and his chest still tended to catch if he inhaled too sharply. He'd forgotten about his leg — Judging by the clean rent in his breeches, whatever hit him had been metal — but it ached like a demon now. In point of fact, it was difficult to find three things on his body which didn't hurt.

"Getting too old for this," he said aloud and winced at the rawness of his throat.

As a lad of one and twenty, he had bound about the decks with no more than a few winks snatched on the stays'ls to sustain him for days.

Aye, but you're not one and twenty.... And far from it.

Once again, his appreciation of Millbridge, and how the hell he survived for so long, raised another notch. His spryness was another wonder, Nathan thought, flexing his shoulder.

A virtual lifetime at sea had made sleeping more than a four hours running nigh impossible. He scowled at trying to recall when he had last slept even that: Goat Island, lying next to Cate, in the little cabin he'd built for her. It seemed an age, two ages ago, before... everything.

Long ago, too long ago.

He was sharp-set, his stomach feeling as if it were permanently attached to his backbone, and yet the time required to eat stood like an intolerable barrier between where he stood and his bed. As he crossed to the table, a vague wave toward the galley steps dismissed Kirkland and Millbridge, sure to be lurking there. No, he required neither of them. He swirled his finger in the honey jar and popped a glob in his mouth. He'd held body and soul together with less before.

Ignoring his captain's wishes—another perquisite of his age—Millbridge followed him into the sleeping quarters. "By your leave, Cap'n. Give over those clothes and I'll put them before the fires, whilst you take a caulk."

There seemed something altogether unfitting to have someone who had two, perhaps three decades on him to be pampering and fussing over him. If the "respect your elders" admonishments he'd received as a child held any water, it should have been the other way around. And yet, one look at the stern, seamed face and all notion of coddling went straight by the board.

True enough, Nathan was still wet as Jonah. He jerked his shirttail free of his breeches and heard a *splat!* at his feet. He looked down to find the *charqui,* stowed inside his shirt untold hours ago, lying on the planks, now softened to the point of near softtack. He shucked off his breeches and dropped the entirety into Millbridge's arms. A flick of a knife did away with the bandages at his limbs, waist and throat, all being too wet to be anything but a hazard and nuisance. As Millbridge took his leave, sodden bandages trailing behind, Nathan bent to pick up the *charqui* and took a bite. Idly chewing, he stretched out on the bunk in glorious pleasure.

The scuttle stood open. Cate preferred air and lots of it, so the standing orders were for it and stern windows to be opened when at all possible, an order still being honored in deference to her. The sun glared through the scuttle like a signal lamp, but he couldn't, however, bring himself to close it. To do so was like one more bit of her being cut away. Having learned long ago to sleep through anything short of a hail of "Sail ho!" or an untoward change in the wind, he flung one arm over his face and closed his eyes.

His worries of Cate's absence were for naught. She was there, her scent—sweet and heady—rose from the mattress like her arms, embraced him and drew him to her. His head nestled on her breast, her fingers traced the curves of his skull and shoulders. The knots of weariness melted. His body grew languid and loose—

The scuffle of feet and a preemptive clearing of a throat shattered the vision.

"Yes, Mr. Pryce?" he asked from under his forearm.

"Beggin' yer leave, Cap'n. Logline reports eleven knots and a fathom."

Nathan mutely nodded. He knew as much just by the feel of his ship.

"Orders?" the First Mate finally prompted.

Damn, I thought I'd seen to that.

"Dyce, Mr. Pryce. Steady as she goes. Fetch me if there's aught to be attended."

Nathan sighed, sinking deeper. He couldn't have opened his eyelids just then had the ship been foundering. "Just get me to her, Pryce. I can't be long without her. Just..."

Cate's scent rose up like arms once more and drew him down...

Cate came to him. She lay before him, that maddening tangle of mahogany tumbling about her head and those deliciously wide shoulders. Her nipples dusky as blushing roses with wanting to be suckled, her eyes the color of jade, were limpid pools, begging him to dive in. Those enchanting fingers beckoned him, and oh, the pleasures those fingers could provide!

He woke with his cock in his fist and his balls flaming. So far gone—Everyone knew it was bad for his health to hang fire—his only choice was to finish and damned quick! A man spent his life in the glory of the last time and in terror that it might have been his last. Every hair on his body as erect as the organ he held, he gritted his teeth, caught between the heavenly promise of finishing and the hellish agony that he mightn't. A pain struck like he'd been kicked in the groin, erupting in a tortured bellow.

Millbridge burst in, Pryce close on his heels. "Cap'n!?"

Nathan rolled quickly to put his back to them. "Go!" he gasped, rocking in pain.

"But, it sounded like ye—"

"Goddammit to fucking hell, go!"

The two left, colliding with each other in their haste. Chest heaving, bathed in a cold sweat, Nathan listened to their footsteps fade. He gingerly rose, went to the ewer and dumped its contents over his head. Hands braced on the washstand, he stood with his head hanging, dripping and sputtering. He was soft as an old sock, and yet he still ached, much like when he ached for Cate, but worse, deeper... and different.

He threw himself back down on the bunk and stared into the darkness. Sleep once hung about his neck like a 24-pound cannonball; now it eluded him. Tossing and turning, he considered perhaps he should go ahead and finish the undone—he still ached with need—but the prospect of being broken in on again cooled any and all thoughts. Besides, Cate was gone. He realized now more than ever that nothing was a substitute for her.

The light caught his wrist and the scab encircling it, cracked and oozing; being wet for hours had done it no favors. He fondled the bracelet he now wore. The clatter of the dangling bits reminded him of Cate... and a line of thinking he didn't wish to follow. He dropped his arm and drummed his fingers on the bunk's raised edge.

Finally, he lurched to his feet and half-limped out into the salon in search of something which, if not to ease his torment, would at least render him insensible. The cabin had been returned to its usual state, everything exactly as it had been before. A squat rum bottle sat waiting on the table. Someone had anticipated his need. He seized it—his hand closing around the neck much like it had his cock—and took a large gulp. Closing his eyes, he waited for the blessed effect. When none came, he took another. As he swallowed, a polite clearing of a throat came from somewhere forward of the mizzenmast.

"What is it, Master Pryce?"

"The wind's backed."

As Pryce approached, he seemed to take no notice of his captain's nakedness. Living forty-to-the-dozen, bare arses were a common sight. It had become a far less common sight with Cate about, although the men sometimes forgot themselves.

"Yes, so I see," Nathan said, looking up through the skylight. The mariner part of his mind had noticed, felt the t'gallants back and the driver shiver when the maincourse starved it.

"Do ye desire to tack or fall off?"

Nathan stared out the aft gallery, automatically checking the horizon—Clear; nothing nor no one following—as he considered. One meant returning to the arduous labors they had just endured; tacking was hard on men and the ship. The other was hard on one's nerves, his at any rate, for it meant going a hundred miles and more, out and around, in order reach their destination. The gods seemed to have abandoned them, now.

"Will tacking answer?" he asked finally. Decisions were as hard to come by as virgins.

Pryce folded his hands behind his back. "B'lieve so, dependin' on how close she's a - willin' to lie," he added with an arched look.

"I'll have a word with her." Nathan's half-smile was cut short by another twinge in the groin.

"Cap'n... Nathan...?"

Ah, now we're getting round to the true reason for his visit.

"Apologies fer a'comin' up on ye when—" He gulped. "When ye were... Well... But it sounded as if someone was a-slittin' yer throat, Millbridge a-thinkin' the same." A nod toward the companionway indicated the elder peering cautiously over the edge.

"T'was no such thing," Nathan said with a dismissive wave. They were men and not fresh off the stocks. They knew what men did in the dark, alone. Living elbow-to-elbow, it was as common as snoring; to deny it only made it all the more evident. Still, no man liked being caught in the middle of making love to a woman that wasn't there. "But I will admit, it damned near felt like that there for a moment."

Nathan drew a hand down his face. He held it there, watching it shake. "Just do what you will, Pryce. Just... get me — us there."

Pryce stepped over the coaming and looked back into the cabin. "Aye, Cap'n, ye need her and far more than ye need this ship."

END OF PART ONE

10: IN THE COMPANY
OF GABRIEL

S LUMPED IN THOMAS' LAP, HEAD lolling on his chest, Cate stared
dully over the boat's gun'l at the *Morganse*. She was vaguely
aware of their boat bumping against the others clustered at the
Brazen's hull, hands lifting her out and up the side like a sack
of meal, and setting her gently down on the deck. She wobbled,
obliging more hands to catch her.

"I'll take you forward, so you can see —" Thomas' voice came
from somewhere next to her.

Head hanging, Cate resolutely shook it. So rudely jerked
from her island Eden, she felt as exposed as a worm on a rock.
If they wished to fling her into one of those nets and lower her
into the hold with the rest of the cargo, it would have been fine
with her.

"I'll see you to the cabin, then," Thomas said, his frustration
barely shaded.

Had it been the *Lovely,* Cate would have known where to
find the retreat she sought, where she could withdraw like that
worm into the dirt. On the *Brazen*, however, she had no idea.
Instincts told her "aft"; that's where the captain's quarters — in
whatever form they might be — would be found. Surely there, or
near it, she might find a niche to crawl into.

Aft they went, Thomas' steering her on a weaving path
through the tumult of men and stores. The *Brazen's* smaller size
was reflected in her companionway: no more than a ladder and
nearly vertical at that. Cate looked down on Thomas' descending
head — the opening barely accommodating his breadth of
shoulder — with trepidation. No amount of skirt tucking would
allow for this.

"Bear a hand there!"

Their captain's shout stirred the nearby Brazens and Cate

was once more reduced to that sack of meal again as she was handed down to Thomas.

In the low-ceilinged dim below, Cate shied at the chaos of men jostling to get stores and gear squared away. Thomas might have said something, but his voice failed to penetrate the bedlam. Half-bent, he led her farther aft. At the end of short gangway, they stepped out of the gloom into a space ablaze with light. A curved bank of windows announced that they were at the Great Cabin, or rather, the *Brazen's* version of one. Had Thomas spread his arms, he could have easily reached from bulkhead to window.

Thomas nodded toward the built-in bunk. "I'll have a curtain rigged —"

"Save yourself the bother." Cate squeezed around the table and chairs occupying the center, and crawled up onto it. Rolling to face the wall, she curled into herself.

Thomas inhaled several times as if in preparation to say something. "I haven't forgotten you prefer the windows opened," he finally said. "Once we're squared-away, I'll pass the word."

Her back was his answer.

"I've a ship to attend. If you desire anything, hail Maram."

A large part of her wasn't sorry to hear him go. There might have been cross words had he lingered.

Crosser than on the beach?

The scene with Nathan still haunted her. Parting with harsh words was never wise and she knew it. She pounded her fist on the white-washed boards inches from her face. Dammit, she knew it! She might never see him again. But, if that did prove to be the case, then damn him all the more!

Too exhausted and resigned to do else, Cate lay staring at the bulkhead. A part of her was remotely aware of the ship coming to life: shouts, running feet, the stomp-and-chant at the capstan. Thomas' footsteps were distinctive, surprisingly light for such a large man. His voice drifted down through the skylight, now and again, sometimes in English, oftener in Arabic.

Damn him. Damn all men!

The idea of an island of nothing but women suddenly seemed just the thing. The acknowledgment, however, meant conceding Nathan and his insight, conceding that he knew her better than she knew herself.

There were no tears; this desolation and betrayal was far beyond that. All his high talk of "joined" and "belonging" and "being one;" sweet words from a man who relied on his wits and charms. Her anger, however, was more with herself, for having believed him, allowed herself to get caught up by those charms, the manipulating bastard...

A small, *very* small voice pointed out that, in spite of him representing else, Nathan wasn't in fighting trim. He, like herself, was still suffering the aftereffects. The charitable thing would have been to cut him some slack. And yet, when called upon, she found that she was as fresh out of charity, as she was a great number of other things. He had declared everything. And yet, when viewed in an objective, cold light, he had declared nothing. Affections, loyalties, fidelities: the list was long, but there was one glaring omission. Love.

Inadvertent oversight? Or, overtly overt?

"It's not so much what he says, but what he doesn't say." Pryce's words rang loud, and yet hollow.

"Yes, well, some things can't be assumed," she told the wall. "Some things need spelling out for the duller-witted."

The day matured, mellowed and then died. The cabin had been dark for a good while when Cate heard footsteps in the gangway and Thomas came in. He moved about with the exaggerated care of one wishing not to disturb, a feat nearly impossible for one so large in a space so confined. He uttered a muffled grunt, heavy with weariness and discomfort as he lay down somewhere. Cate rolled to find him stretched out on the stern seat, or rather as much as the confined space would allow. Still, his long legs were crossed at the ankles with the ease of one having slept there this last decade and more. With another grunt, he cradled his arm on his chest.

"Is your arm bothering you?" Unused for so long, her voice sounded strange in her own ears.

"I'll do," came back, eyes still closed.

"It should be—"

A sterner "I'll do" cut her short.

"I shouldn't wish to disturb your rest," he added a few moments later, slightly less edgy. "Do you wish anything?" he asked over her apology. "Food? Wine? Water...?"

"Thank you, no."

Another pause.

"You're angry with me," she observed.

His shoulder moved in a conceding shrug. One eye popped open and fixed on her. "You don't do yourself credit, I'll give you that. You should hang-fire on those seeking to help, Nathan most of all."

The admonishment, low-voiced though it was, struck like a slap in the face. "I'm sorry. I—"

"No, you're not," he mused, evenly.

He closed his eyes and made a great show of going to sleep. Cate rolled onto her back and stared at the beams.

"In case you're interested," came out of the darkness. "The plan went to perfection. Harte disappeared over the horizon, hard on Nathan's stern, leaving us to sail off unnoticed."

Thomas shifted restlessly. "I would have thought you might have come up to take a last, farewell look, but then you being seen on deck might have been all of our undoing," he conceded.

He turned his head to look out the window. Amid the blot of clouds low on the horizon, lighting flickered and danced. "They're getting weather out there, now. Knowing Nathan, he'll somehow turn that into his benefit."

Thomas swiveled around and said severely "The man died for you."

"I know," she said, miserable.

"And could well wind up doing so again, if all this goes south."

"I know," she said, her spirits sinking deeper. "It's just—"

"Just what?"

Cate's mouth moved, but no words would come. In order to explain oneself, one first had to know what they were feeling. She couldn't begin to identify what roiled and churned insider her, let alone put a name to it.

"I'm not myself," she offered into the expectant void. She shivered, wondering if she would ever be warm again.

"Ah," Thomas said dispassionately and turned away.

"Neither is Nathan," he said, some moments later. "But then, he has no choice. None of us do, not on this count, at any rate."

The wood under him creaked as he shifted. "Sleep, then."

"Your arm. I should look—"

"It'll do until the 'morrow. Lay your head," Thomas said, a bit more gently. "Lots will look better with the sun over the yardarm."

Like Nathan, years at sea had taught Thomas to go to sleep instantly, and he did so then, mouth slightly agape. Head turned slightly toward the window, the light of the distant storm played along the strong lines of his profile.

In the ensuing quiet, Cate propped herself in the corner, arms about her knees. She toyed with the oddments of her bracelet. Fondling the bits of stone, shell and wood brought Nathan before her. She smiled in the night, seeing him as clearly as if he were there just then, fastening the necklace about her neck. The walnut-colored eyes swiveled up, hard and accusing, and her smile faded. She had sent him away, cold and uncaring.

Cate clutched the oddments tighter and closed her eyes, conjuring Nathan again. He came reluctant and hesitant, like a scolded lad. She learned in the darkness that he was as he had promised: together... one... always...

"Damned well better be," she grumbled under her breath and laid her head, taking his vision with her.

༺ঙঙঙ༻

The bells, the running feet, the nautical calls, the creak of blocks and thrum of sails: the daily rhythms of the ship closed in around Cate. If she were to close her eyes, she could almost imagine she were on the *Morganse,* home again... almost. A smaller ship meant less souls, and considerably less space. Now, more than ever, no move could be made—going to the head, sneezing, snorting or sniffing—which wasn't known to all. The confined space also brought the hold and cable tier nearer, the stink of bilges and mud on the hawses rendering the air nearly too thick to breathe.

Desolation and devastation weighed Cate down like the *Brazen's* Number One anchor. And so, she lay pressed into the bunk's corner, staring out the stern window at the line where sky and sea met. The *Brazen's* schooner design included a flush quarterdeck, which put the Great Cabin down near the level of the sea... so very near. One might slip out the stern window without a splash, and no one the wiser. Nathan had implored her time and again against such inclinations. After their audience with Calypso, she now knew his fears, which had seemed random and baseless, were neither. But still, it was tempting, so very, very... *very* tempting.

Grasping the braid Nathan had knotted in her hair, she wished upon hope that the *Morganse's* masts might prick the horizon, bringing Nathan with her. It was a vain hope— everything was in vain—but one she clung to, for it was the only way she might be delivered from this torturous cycle of abandonment.

Futility was her greatest burden. Was it destiny, or was it Nathan's determination to keep them apart? He used all the right words to warm her heart and build her hopes. In one breath, he pledged and promised, fulfilled so many wishes. In the next breath, he sent her off, with all the affections of an unwanted child. He spoke of fidelity and forever, whatever in the hell that meant. Apparently, "forever" was but a few weeks in his world.

Damned his blackguardly soul!

196

The notion of "seeing her safe" was thin comfort. All she wished was to be with him. So simple, and yet even that small request was doomed to be denied. She'd been foolish and gullible, and had been repulsed. Her fist curled with the urge to cut the plait off and fling it through the window. And yet—pitiful, sniveling wretch that she was—she couldn't bring herself to lose what might prove to be her last connection with him.

The bell clanged. Cate started at the pound of feet which vibrated the wood at her back, the clash of mess kids seeming to originate in the cabin in which she laid. Some moments later, she jerked again, this time at the clatter of dishes coming her way. Maram stepped over the coaming, bearing a tray, Thomas close behind.

Throughout the day, Thomas had come in, ostensibly on ship's business: checking the glass, consulting a chart or making log entries. Several times he had opened his mouth, preparing to speak, but then left, grumbling moodily. Now, he stood, head bent under the beams as the tray was set on the table. Maram lingered long enough to light the swinging lamp, and then bowed, knuckling his forehead as he backed out.

Thomas gaze traveled about the cabin, finally landing on Cate. He cleared his throat, and then again. "You've not eaten the day."

"I'm not hungry," she mumbled into her chest.

In two strides, he was at the bunk's side. He bent, shoving his face into hers. "Do you find my company so distasteful as to drive you to mortal deprivation? Every time you're with me, you act as though you've been sentenced to Purgatory," he went on at her wide - eyed gape.

"You stare at me like you wished me dead. I don't fancy myself such a bad sort," he said over her sputtering objections. "Many, most women find my company agreeable, hell, even seek it! I don't curse—much—and I don't fart or belch. I take care to keep the cabin decent, and I shave... most days," he added, running a hand over his stubbled jaw.

Looking to his feet, Thomas drew a deep breath and squared his shoulders. "I swear this won't be like the last time," he said, looking up. "If I had been any kind of a man, I would have seen you up that hill myself, seen you safe. Hell and damnation, the whole damned thing might have been different. You and Nathan wouldn't have had to go through God-knows-what—"

He audibly gulped and turned to look out the stern window. His eyelids fluttered. "The thought of two of you lying dead at the bottom of the sea—" He clamped his lower lip between his teeth and slowly shook his head. "Every time I looked out, all

I could see was your faces looking up at me from those watery depths. I couldn't bear it, not again... *never* again."

Shaking with vehemence, his voice had gone so low she could barely hear.

Given the height of the bunk and Thomas' stooped posture, it was an easy reach to press her fingers to his lips. "Shhh," she said softly. "I never meant—"

Thomas smiled against her fingertips. "Well, then you gave a prime imitation of it."

He took her hand and worked it gently, his warm grasp revealing what he couldn't say, else: the hurt, the worry, the need for reassurance.

"I'm not blaming you," she said, sincerely. "It was my foolishness which was nearly everyone's undoing. I don't blame you. Neither does Nathan."

Thomas sheepishly looked up, the corner of his mouth quirking. "Aye, but he does. Granted, he's mute as a figurehead, but it's rarely a matter of what he says."

Cate turned her head to smile. Pryce had once told her much the same about Nathan.

"God knows Nathan can't keep from crossing his own hawse. How the hell he managed on his own all those years is anyone's guess." Thomas shook his head, mystified.

Considering all which had happened during those years of his absence, Nathan could have truly benefited from a guardian angel. Fair, chiseled-features, broad of body: Thomas made a creditable version of Gabriel personified.

Wallowing so deeply in her own self-pity, Cate hadn't paused to consider the effect of her moodiness on Thomas, on everyone aboard for that matter, right down to poor little Maram, tension pinching his small face when he entered.

"It's not you—" she began, her throat tightening.

Dropping her hand, Thomas stood back. "Very well, then prove it: eat... something... anything. God knows, I'd never hear the end of it, if I were to give you back thinner than when you shipped."

Cate eyed him suspiciously, wondering if she had just been duped.

"No, that was no act," he said, grinning. He found her hand and pressed the knuckles to his lips. "I meant every word, *every word.*"

Creaking with stiffness, Cate rose. Thomas saw her seated, the tray before her. It was a simple meal: cold fried fish and a few slices of meat. Youssef's, the *Lovely's* Moorish cook, hand was evident in the unleavened bread and honey, and a bowl of rice, bright with saffron and vegetables.

"I could probably weather all this far better, if you two would allow me to be a part of your plans," she said, nibbling on a spoonful of rice.

Slathering honey on a half-round of bread, Thomas smiled tolerantly. "No, you wouldn't. There's but one reason why we don't, and you know it well."

Cate nodded, conceding. Deep down, she knew why; Nathan had said as much. There would have been many more ugly scenes, acrimony and a lot of unfortunate things being said.

"You and Nathan obviously had some sort of plan. Conspiracy is difficult to hide," she observed.

"You're a perceptive woman." He chuckled with malicious glee. "That's gotta drive Nathan near mad."

Cate inclined her head in acknowledgment of the left-handed compliment.

"Aye, a plan it was. He's leading off the Royal Navy with the one thing he has: himself and his ship, whilst I—we," Thomas amended, glancing at the *Lovely*, visible through the scupper at the moment, "see you safe away, *and* it is working."

Thomas took up a cup on the table between them and filled it—wine, by the smell of it—and drank it down in a single gulp. Refilling it, he reached to set it before Cate.

"Where are you taking me?" she asked, sipping. Nathan had made a vague mention; if any further explanation had been offered, she hadn't attended.

Thomas sat back, folding his hands on his stomach. "If I told you, I'd be obliged to kill you."

Cate flinched, the knife clattering on the plate. Thomas lurched forward, seizing her hand.

"Apologies, lovely. That was a cod-handed jest. Sometimes, I can be as much of a slab – sided brute as Nathan." Peering intently at her, his grasp tightened, seeking assurances of her forgiveness. A flex of hers granted it.

Appeased, he sat back. Extending his long legs, the swinging lamplight playing across his features, he considered his next words. "I can't be sayin', because I've been sworn to secrecy."

She regarded him narrowly over her meal. "Sworn to Nathan, or sworn to someone else?"

Thomas threw back his head and laughed. "'Sworn to Nathan!' Now that would be a good one! Nay," he went on, still fizzing. "'Tis a pledge kept by a site more than just him n' me. None but a pirate is to know of it."

Cate set down her spoon and extended her arm. She had yet

to actually see it, but the P-shape of the iron used to brand her was as clearly etched in her memory as it was on her skin. "Do I qualify?"

Thomas' mouth tightened grimly. "Aye, I suppose you do. It's an island, a pirate island."

"Mateolage." Cate nodded. Nathan had told her of the pirate haven.

Thomas made a rude, negating noise. "I wouldn't wish my dead cat in that hell-hole."

Cate smiled. Nathans analysis of the place of his boyhood had been much along those same lines.

Thomas sobered, all levity vanishing. "We—pirates, that is—do all we might to keep this one secret. We swear an oath, vow to serve out—without exception or hesitation— anyone who has it on their charts, or cut the tongue out of anyone heard speaking of it."

Cate swallowed, pressing her tongue against her teeth to assure its presence. "Is that part of the Code I keep hearing about?" Nathan, Pryce and many others had spoken of it with a reverence and solemnity which invoked visions of an ancient tome sequestered in some remote sanctum.

"Nay," he said off-handedly. "Just pirate law."

"What's the island called?"

He looked up in round-eyed innocence. "An island that doesn't exist sure as hell can't have a name. If you don't name it, it isn't there."

She dropped her head in her hands and groaned "You're sounding more like Nathan all the time."

Jaws chomping, utensils scraping wood, the *clunk!* of the bread barges being passed: the sounds of a crew eating just a few feet distant filled the ensuing silence. The diners were a jovial lot, the prospect of grog in the near future elevating their spirits.

"How far?" Cate asked finally. Nathan had alluded to "a day."

"If the wind holds—and the glass says it should," Thomas said, angling his head toward the inconspicuous instrument on the wall. On the *Morganse*, it had been an elegant instrument of brass and rosewood; this one was no more than a glass tube suspended on a board. "We should raise it by sun-up 'morrow."

Cate set down her fork and leaned back. Thomas craned his head to peer at the plate. The sandy brows drew down. "You didn't eat much."

Her stomach was so closed the mere thought of another morsel caused it to take a threatening flip. The spices in the rice had set off a cozy little fire in her middle, however, and she was thoroughly sated.

Thomas reached to poke at the food on her plate, making an example of how much remained. The act brought his wounded arm directly before her.

"That needs tending," she observed.

"Nay, it'll do," he said, evading her questing grasp. "It itches like the devil, a sure sign of healing, aye?"

The bell clanged. The planks under her feet vibrated with benches pushing back, the crew rising and moving *en masse* toward the companionway.

Thomas rose to his feet as well. "I've the Watch." He drew up at the cabin door. A gracious bow was punctuated by a charming smile. "I leave you to your solitude. Rest... Dream... Do whatever you must to endure another night, lovely."

"If only it were that simple," she sighed to his receding back as he strode down the gangway.

❦

It was a brutal night.

The mattress stunk of mold and old sweat, its rough canvas like sandpaper as Cate tossed and turned. Her limbs twitched and jerked, refusing to remain still. Her mind rambled, thoughts overlapping and colliding to the point she couldn't say what vexed her, for none lingered long enough to be identified. Footsteps mere inches over her head were like water dripping. The voices were lowered to a night watch level, too low for the exact words to be made out, but they still added to her annoyance. The bells tolled, marking off the hours.

Cate had no notion of actually sleeping until she opened her eyes to a room flooded with the soft light of a day just born and pistol butts a few inches from her nose. A shift of her eyes found Thomas leaned over her, reaching overhead for the charts stowed there.

He looked down from under his arm. "Give you joy o' the morning." He was caught between whispering so as not to disturb her and yet be heard over the backdrop of sailing.

Cate withdrew further to allow him more room, a move made easier by the ship's heel. It was a small difference, but in such a confined space, every inch counted. Continuing his search, Thomas directed "Maram!" down the gangway. The cabin boy appeared, more immediately than one might have thought humanly possible, bearing a brass pot and cups. The latter were filled, the pot secured in a fiddle. Bowing, touching his fingertips to his heart, lips and forehead, he retreated.

Blinking, feeling thick-headed and stupid, Cate seized a cup and took a sip. From the mess area came the sound of the crew breakfasting, the smell of fried fish and porridge mixing with the fug of compacted, unwashed male bodies.

Thomas made a small, victorious sound, his search finally bearing fruit. He turned, ducking under the beams.

"You were meant for a larger ship," Cate observed.

"I more ways than one," he said, grinning.

Thomas spread the chart on the table, employing whatever was to hand to weight the corners. "It's been a decade, since I've plied these waters. I recall a—"

He stopped with an abruptness which made her look. Straightening, he swore, black and vehement, and slammed the table with his fist.

"Mr. Warren!" he shouted, with a fury which silenced the messing men.

Footfalls hurried up the gangway, with an "Aye, sir?" when someone, presumably Mr.

Warren, was near enough for respectability.

"Old Brazens: who do we have?" Thomas barked.

"Ehh... a bosun's second and third mate, a quartermaster's third mate, three carpenter's—"

"No master? First mate? Someone nearer to command, someone who might know what the bloody hell—?" Fury cut Thomas short.

"None, sir," came back with the measured banality of a subordinate facing an enraged superior.

A jerk of the hand dismissed Warren. Swearing again, Thomas set to pacing like a bear in a closet. The men resumed their meal, their conversation taking on that strained air of listening whilst appearing not. Maram came up the gangway, saw his captain steaming about, pivoted in mid-step and disappeared. Drawing her legs up, Cate shrunk further into her corner, lest she inadvertently come in line of fire. She had always suspected Thomas had a temper, but had never witnessed it, not to this extent, and a scary sight it was.

Cate clutched her cup tighter and took a sip, taking great care not to make any noise. The smell of toasting soft-tack drifted up from the galley and her stomach growled in anticipation. A cannon going off couldn't have seemed any louder.

Thomas cast a brief glance her way and batted a hand. "It's not you."

"I didn't think as much," she said, barely appeased.

"It's..." He gulped, trying to master himself. "It's... Dammit to hell, the fucking sod has it on here!" He ended with swinging a fist toward the chart.

One could only assume the "fucking sod" was John Pomphrey, the *Brazen's* captain, now deceased, and may he bless his lucky stars on that!

Cate cautiously craned her head toward the table. Ready-made charts were both costly and difficult to come by, obliging many a captain to draft their own. She was no navigator, but she had spent many an hour watching Nathan working on his. They were a thing of pride to him, artistically embellished and as exacting as was humanly possible. In comparison, this one was child's work, naught but inelegant scrawlings. Pressing the point, however, at that moment, didn't seem wise.

Thomas seized up the chart and shook it in her face. "There it is. Bold as the nose on your face, as if he doesn't care who or what—" He stopped abruptly, lest he violate his own Code.

"What does it mean?" was the obvious question, one which she didn't venture to ask. Obviously, Pomphrey knew about the island. The implications, however, the "what" and "why" of it were anyone's guess.

Growling, Thomas ripped the parchment into shreds which a vehemence that suggested what he might have done to Pomphrey had he been there. He flung the bits out the window, bellowing "Goddammit!", the glass in the skylight rattling. He turned and stormed out, men scattering before him, leaving Cate round-eyed and grateful for having weathered the storm unscathed.

The hail of "On deck there. Land off the starboard bow" was audible over the clamor of the crew breaking their fast. The cry and the men swarming up the companionway brought Cate racing out of the cabin.

She made her way up the gangway only to find the mess area empty, nothing but dust motes swirling in the hatches' checkered light. The companionway's steps, steep as a barn – loft's, stopped her. Impatient, she shouted up "Bear a hand below!" The padding of bare feet; hands came down, seized her by the wrists and she was delivered.

Blinking in the sun's glare, Cate found herself in both the familiar and the strange. The shouts, hum of the wind in the rigging, the slanted deck and water boiling down the sides like a mill race were all familiar, and yet—due to the *Brazen's* reduced size—everything was different. There were masts, but much smaller and farther forward, the mizzen being the only one seeming to know its place. The only familiar square sails were high up on the main and foremast; the rest were triangular and ran the length of the ship, like two great dorsal fins.

Cate wove across a deck as crowded as Covent Garden to the windward rail. There she rose on her toes, craning her head. Sure enough, on the rise, where the bright morning sky met the sea, laid a low, dark hump.

Land.

One would have thought months had passed, not barely a day since she had seen it. Between Thomas' earlier explanation and more recent outburst — It hadn't gone unnoticed that he had successfully avoided revealing the island's name — Cate was wildly curious to see this mysterious, and yes, mythical-sounding place. In her time on the *Morganse*, she had approached many an island, but none with such anxious expectation. The combination of excitement, anticipation and dread was like the first sight of land during her Atlantic crossing. The Brazen's weren't immune to those feelings either. They milled about the rail and rigging, all abuzz.

The bells rang. Time passed. The dark hump of land rose like a sleeping turtle. Cate remained at the rail, impatience not allowing her to do else. A sun-dodger was rigged out of an old jib sail and a seat brought. The *Brazen* might have been moving at a tearing pace — eight knots, according to the logline swinging in the chains — but it felt more like she crept at two.

Finally, the *Brazen* slipped through the reef, the dark hump now near enough to have transformed into a verdant and lush green. With the *Lovely* close in her wake, she wove through a disconcerting series of channels, shoals, and sandbars. Cate prided herself on her sense of direction, but even with the sun as a reference, she was soon lost, large islands proving to be clusters of smaller, individual ones proving to be one larger.

After one more of the countless turns, Thomas stepped up beside her and announced "There it is!"

Cate glanced cautiously up. His earlier fury had long since faded into lingering churlishness which only those compelled by duty braved. Now, his smile was there, although a bit forced.

"Where do we anchor?" she asked.

"Down shore a bit. We have to weather that point."

Duty called him away, leaving Cate to anxiously watch the shore slip by. She soon grew impatient. Lush, bright with flowering vines and sunset-colored birds, there was naught but jungle. Nathan had been so determined for her to be there, surely, there was more to it than this! The mood on deck suggested there was definitely more: the crew's anticipation was palpable, their conversation heightening at every turn. One couldn't overlook freshly-shaved cheeks, tie-mates busily brushing out and re-plaiting pigtails, festive scarves adorning necks, some even donning shoes.

The jungle ran unchanged for so long, Cate began to imagine — yes, it tended to run both wild and vivid, of late — the place was inhabited by naught but natives, dressed in skins and living in trees. Finally, signs of human occupation appeared: wisps of smoke, rising above the trees. Thatched roofs poked their heads from among the trees. Gaps in the sea holly and palmetto allowed clearer views of dwellings: small simple, shacks, but definitely European. People, dressed not in skins but European clothes, streamed down to the shore, waving and calling out.

Cate blinked and leaned to look closer.

Tall, short, wide, narrow, light or dark; white, yellow, brown or black; young and old, they were all women. They came in every size, shape and origin, but they were, by and large, but by a vast, vast majority women! Above the cry of gulls rose the high-pitched shriek of children, a small horde of them tumbling down and into the water.

Nathan had said he thought she might be in need of a little female company, but —

Make friends, indeed! Nathan, the Duplicitous had a hand in this.

"Who...?" she asked at Thomas' return. Surprise rendered her a bit breathless.

He leaned on the rail and cocked a hip. "Pirate folk," he said, waving back to the islanders. "Wives, mothers, sweethearts, sons, daughters, along with those too old or infirmed to be at sea, or with nowhere else to go." A point with his chin indicated a handful of men hobbling on crutches or wooden pegs.

"It's sort of a safe haven," Thomas went on. "Any and all are welcome, and can remain, so long as all conflicts stay out there." His head canted toward the open sea to their stern. "We figure, sooner or later — if we're so lucky as to live that long — any of us might be in need of such a place."

"Do you come here often?" Cate asked. All morning, Thomas had been as anxious as his crew. His restiveness, however, had been of a different sort: apprehension, like a lad about to be called up before the headmaster.

"The rule is if you're about and able, you look in and provide as you can. Most times, they're just pleased to see an able-bodied soul that's willing to bear a hand."

"Or, if you're sent here," she observed tartly.

"That, too," Thomas conceded. His hat cast a sharp shadow across his features as he squinted into the sun, looking a bit strained and preoccupied.

"When was the last time you were here?"

Her question caught him far afield. "Huh...? Oh, ehh... Eleven years."

Cate gave a low whistle. Since he and Nathan had parted ways, she mused privately.

Looking up, Cate noticed that, like his men, Thomas' cheeks gleamed with being freshly scraped, his hair smoothed and tightly bound. A clean shirt had been donned, hat and boots brushed. A twinge of jealousy struck and she looked ashore, and the women there, with new interest. Someone, somewhere he wished to impress.

The commotion of sailing increased with preparations to anchor: hawses laid, anchor a-cockbill on the cathead and buoys at the ready. Topsmen were sent aloft, sails doused and stowed, while others shifted nearer their sheet.

"On deck there!" hailed the masthead. "Ship—schooner at anchor."

All conversation stopped, all heads craned forward, several scampering aloft to have a look.

Thomas stiffened and swore. "Can you make her?" was directed toward the rigging.

"She's the *Revenge*," called the foremast.

"Report!"

One from up there slid down a backstay, landing light as a cat just a few strides away.

"What's your name?" Thomas asked with the awkward air of not having learned everyone's name yet.

"Beg pardon, sir, Jaggers," came back, knuckling his forehead.

Thomas angled his head toward the unknown ship. "And you know her, Mr. Jaggers?"

"Aye, sir. She's the *Revenge*," Jaggers announced, grinning.

"Hell, there has to be a score of ship's with that name."

"Would know that stern anywhere, sir," Jaggers went on, his confidence gaining. "She was moored at Bridge Town when we wuz there under Cap'n Pomphrey." He closed one eye, recalling. "Ten eight-pounders, with six-pounder chasers and two swivel guns aft, Pengelly commanding."

Thomas jerked around. "Bertold Pengelly?"

"Only heard tell; never laid eyes on 'im."

A few more questions proved the bottom of Jaggers' knowledge had been reached and he was dismissed.

Thomas emitted a puzzled *humph!* "Good ol' Bertold. We used to call him Vinegar Bert; he always looked like he had just eaten a bad pickle," he said in answer to her questioning look. "Bone-idle, shiftless lout he was, too. Looks like he captains the same way."

A disdainful glare directed Cate toward the *Revenge*. The bay had opened enough for the vessel in question to be visible. To Cate's eyes, she was more like the *Brazen* than the *Lovely*: a small schooner, a size and design preferred by sea marauders. Disarray and lack of care showed even to Cate's untrained eye. Dull and brown, as dried up looking as a piece of driftwood, her sails dingy and much-patched, the vessel was an example of one which had enjoyed none of the loving attention Nathan and Thomas bestowed upon their vessels.

"Is he... friendly?" It hardly seemed the fitting word, but Cate could think of none other.

Thomas shrugged, neither pleased, nor concerned. "Never knew the man to be a hazard to anything other than a bottle. It's two against one: we best her in guns, metal and men. Those eight-pounders are more for show than damage. If well-aimed and, with a bit of luck, she might sheer a spar. Overall, it's like flinging a dried pea at a boulder."

"Besides," he said, some moments later. "This is neutral ground. No grievances are to be brought past the mouth of the bay here. Start a fight, and you'll have a hundred infuriated women out for your head, their queen-and-master in the lead."

No grievances Cate repeated privately, wondering how they managed that. By her experience, a pirate's notion of grudge-bearing was rivaled only by Highlanders.

"At least, they haven't opened the guns on us," Thomas observed under his breath.

Cate followed his line of sight to the emplacements bracketing the bay's opening. Women stood about them, but most were only waving, not ramming wads. "You were worried they might?"

"Off-chance," he muttered, suddenly going vague. "And a fair hand they are at them, too," he warned at her skepticism. "I've seen them nick a bobbing barrel first try."

Cate looked at the island with new respect. Pirate wives, indeed! Rest assured, this visit was not going to be just some pleasant ladies' social. In truth, she hadn't had time to develop any expectation beyond some reflexive, mental images, and those were changing by the moment.

Thomas brushed past and wove his way aft. He snatched a glass from the binnacle and studied the *Revenge*.

"She looks to have no more than a harbor watch aboard, and a spare one, at that," Thomas announced. He lowered the glass. "One is compelled to assume it's safe."

"You don't sound convinced," Cate said, coming up beside him.

He shrugged. "This is where we are to meet Nathan. If we have to back-and-fill and stand on-and-off until he arrives, then that's what we do. Hail the *Lovely* and bid her to anchor athwart the *Revenge's* stern," he directed to Warren, at his elbow. "Bid her to stand ready to rake that scow, if the need arise. Rouse out the boarding axes and cutlasses; load them into the boats before they are lowered."

"I thought you said it was safe," Cate said uneasily as Thomas turned away.

He stopped and turned back. The corner of his mouth quirked. "We might get caught, but we won't get caught napping."

"You're sounding more like Nathan every day," she sighed, shaking her head.

With a malicious chuckling, Thomas leaned down. Waggling his brows, his voice dropped to a rough imitation of Nathan's. "Aye, an unprepared pirate is a dead pirate."

The *Brazen* glided in, the *Lovely* in her wake. A splash of the anchor, tops'ls aback, and she took on the stilted motion of no longer being a free-roaming creature of the sea, but anchored to land. With all apparent casual, the *Lovely* moved to the bay's opposite side and settled, the *Revenge's* stern directly abeam.

The deck was filled with a new kind of commotion: the shouts and calls of a ship squaring away, hatches being flung open and boats being roused over the side. Thomas moved about, pausing for a number of conversations and consultations. At one point, he briefly disappeared below, reappearing with an additional pistol holstered at his back.

He eyed Cate, considering, and, for a heart-stopping moment, she thought he might leave her aboard.

Finally, Thomas nodded, decision made. "You're coming with me. I don't aim to let you out of my sight, short of death."

He took her by the arm and pushed a path through the crowd, the bosun-like bellow of "Make a lane! Make a lane there, I say!" At the top of the accommodation ladder, Cate looked down the side, into the bobbing boat. This never went well. The gun'l was considerably lower than the *Morganse* or *Lovely's*, but it was still a daunting distance. She bent to tuck her skirts into her waistband, literally and figuratively girding her loins.

Thomas swung down, landing lightly on the boat's gun'l. "Bear a hand there!" prompted a man on each side of Cate, with arms like barrel staves, to seize her up and hand her down into their captain's waiting grasp. The crowd on the sternsheet parted like the Red Sea and she was seated next to Thomas. Seeking space, she wriggled her feet under the canvas heaped in the bottom, only to come up against the cold metal. Further questing with her toes found a number of musket barrels.

"Give way!" Thomas called.

The balance of the *Brazen's* boats filled and pushed off, forming an irregular parade behind them. As they dropped anchor, a number of small craft — dinghies, rafts or just a board — had pushed off from shore. Now, that flotilla of makeshift vessels, manned mostly by children, converged upon them. A number of the youths dove in and swam alongside, wriggling like tadpoles beyond the sweep of the oars. Some dared to grab hold of the gun'l and allow the boat to tow them, squealing and giggling.

Thomas sat hunched forward. Head bent, arms on his thighs, his body was rigid, except for one hand mechanically opening and closing, and a heel tapping the floorplanks. Many preferred not to be crowded when they were of such a mood, and Cate tucked her skirts, making to shift aside. A firm hand on her leg and a stiff smile stopped her. Their captain's mood served to dampened the men's spirits, their earlier eagerness having spiraled downward into something more like watchful alert.

Looking ahead toward shore, a welcoming party could be seen forming, a sizeable proportion of it men. During her crossing from England, Cate had been told one always knew a pirate when they saw one. Here the beach was lined with them. One, standing front and center, stood out, not so much because of his weaponry — the usual bristling of blades and firearms — but more in the way of his presence.

"Is that Pengelly?" asked Cate.

Thomas looked up, his affirmation drying in his throat. He stiffened, let out a low growl and swore with a vehemence which made several in the boat stare.

"Gascon Lesauvage," he announced, grimly. "We used to call him Little Sausage, but never to his face. It's been years... *years*, since I've seen the cross-grained, spineless bastard. He begrudged me the air I breathed, and I didn't give a fig if he breathed or no."

Thomas' fingers tightened in warning about her arm. "Stay close, lovely. This could get very interesting, very quickly. Stand ready," he directed toward his men, low but firm.

The Brazen's solemnly nodded. Coiled and ready, their eyes fixed ahead while their bare toes wormed under the canvas. A hand over the side sent the same warning to the following boats.

The boat's keel ground into the sand and Thomas handed Cate out, the welcoming party moving to greet them. With some shuffling and elbowing, the Brazens and Lovelies formed up around their captain. Squaring off and bristling like territorial wolves, the two factions sized each other up. Pirates considered themselves all part of the Brethren, all ruled by the same Code, and yet, Cate had yet to see one group approach another with anything less than the suspicion and animosity of rival Highland clans.

Lesauvage stepped forward. Up close, he was all the more the pirate, with the quick eyes of the hunted. The smudge of several days' growth of beard blackened the lower half of his narrow face. A scar ran from his low brow, through an eyelid and down to his lip. Whatever blade which had left the scar had also taken a corner of his nostril, leaving the hair to bristle out like a black caterpillar. Gold—an amulet or cross of some sort— flashed deep in his chest hair.

A raw-boned and square-jawed woman pushed her way forward. With pales eyes crinkled at the corners and strawberry-blond hair peppered with silver, she could have been either in her forties or in her sixties.

"No quarrels come ashore, *gentleman.*" The woman missed her calling as a bosun. What she lacked in volume was made up for in force, the pewter-colored eyes going from warm to cold in a blink.

Lesauvage spread his arms in the Gallic way and declared in a broad Burgundian accent "Thomas, *mon ami!*"

Thomas' glare stopped the Frenchman short of his intended embrace.

"Bella, how the bloody hell are you!" Thomas declared, pointedly pivoting his attention. "Still making the world miserable with your presence?"

"No more than you," she shot back, good-naturedly.

Adroitly seizing Cate's hand, Lesauvage swept off his slouch hat and bowed. "And who might this enchantress be?" A smile split the beard, revealing a mouthful of teeth filed to a point.

"The lady is under my protection," Thomas said, imposing himself. "She's the property of a friend."

A retort bubbled up at being called "property", but Cate

swallowed it down at observing the effect: Lesauvage mastered his leering smile, dropped her hand and retreated a half-step.

"Bella, allow me to name Cate Harper. Bella's the queen of the island," Thomas explained to Cate, with an expansive sweep of his hand.

Bella snorted. "Hardly call it 'queen'."

"Aye, well," Thomas went on, unperturbed, "you'd be wise to remember that she'll be both your judge *and* jury should the need arise."

He craned his head to see over the crowd. "Where's Pengelly?"

Lesauvage flicked his fingers as one might rid himself of a flea. "Gone. No longer with us," he said, over the derisive laughter of the surrounding Revenges. He beat his thumb into his chest. "Now, *I* am captain."

Cate had been around pirates long enough to know that there was no such word as "ex-captain." One was either in command or dead, mutiny being the common means to that end.

The ferret-like eyes settled on the *Lovely.* "And who is your consort?"

"Mine," Thomas declared in, a sudden flood pride.

Lesauvage regarded Thomas, the dark eyes all the more calculating. "Two ships! You have come up in the world."

Thomas shrugged. "Providence provides."

The Frenchman's hand shot out, seizing Cate's once more. He bent to kiss it, his tongue flicking between her fingers. "Ah, well, *mademoiselle* is far too fair to be left standing in the sun. Come!" he said, tucking her hand deep into the crook of his arm. "Join our *soirée, mon petit bouche de miel.*"

Cate's French wasn't perfection—not like her Spanish or Catalan—but it was passable enough to recognize being called "honey mouth." A low, threatening rumble came from deep in Thomas' chest and Cate's cheeks flared.

A flutter of the lashes seemed to be expected, and so she did. "*Jemti ne suis pas si doux,*" she said, sweet yet with a warning edge.

"*Vous parlez Français!*" The Frenchman gave her a familiar squeeze. "I find I must guard my tongue, as well as my heart."

"*Irons-nous?*" Lesauvage smoothly hooked his arm into Cate's, bringing her close enough to see the remains of his most recent meal hanging on his chin and chest hair. "Come! A feast and drink for all!"

Lesauvage struck off. From the corner of her eye, Cate saw Bella take up Thomas' arm and follow.

Thomas tried to disengage himself, but Bella's grasp was as firm as a grapnel. Still, he lengthened his gait, wishing to keep close to Cate and Lesauvage. He didn't like the way the bastard clutched Cate, leering, damned near drooling down her bosom. He obviously meant to charm and then board her in his smoke. The feckless lout had met his match there!

"What's he doing here?" Thomas asked, under the merriment of the men jostling around them. The Frenchman was currently too enchanted with his own drivel to hear what anyone else said.

"Might ask you the same." Bella swiveled a severe eye up at him. "You know the rule."

"I do. I'll behave." He'd have to be an oafish clod to have forgotten.

His gaze fixed on Lesauvage's back, Thomas leaned down, lowering his voice further. "Now, what about him?"

"Back your sails, you big lout," she said, affectionately patting his arm. "He looked in a day or so ago, like you and a score of others over the years."

Thomas smiled, in spite of himself. He was genuinely pleased to see Bella and, more importantly, to find her still in looks and health. Reunions after long separations often meant finding too many ill, too many passed on, and always the wrong ones. Time had made its mark: the ramrod back was a bit bent, the hair more silver, the voice a bit rougher, but the eyes still held the keenness of a shepherd-dog over its flock.

"Two ships?" Bella announced, looking out at the bay. "You've come up in the world.

And now, a comely lass at your side. You haven't changed."

Thomas rolled his eyes. "It's not like you think, Bella."

Once more, he pressed to catch Cate up, but Bella pulled him back. He glared down, but she only smiled in overt innocence.

"She's under my protection," he insisted.

"So you keep saying. You hover over her like she was your intended."

"Would it make any difference if I said she was?" He'd pose any lie, if it would be to his or, more importantly, Cate's benefit.

Bella's hoot of laughter caused several to take pause. "You?! Tie the anchor?! If you said you meant to limit yourself to two women a day, I'd call you a double-tongued liar. But one...!?"

"Then, what if I said I was watching her for a friend?" he asked over her cackling.

Bella made a half-hearted attempt to compose herself. "I'd wonder what blundering fool would be so fond-and-feckless as

to do that! It's like leaving a bear in charge of the honey jar—"
The rest was lost in another wave of laughter.

"She's Nathan's."

Ha! That brought her up all-standing.

"Blackthorne!?"

Cate looked back over her shoulder at the mention of Nathan's name. She didn't look distressed, but neither did she look pleased.

"Have to be," Bella concluded under her breath. "Only one you'd be so bold as to call 'friend.'"

Bella arched an eyebrow. "How is Nathan? Haven't seen him for a couple o' years."

"Oh, you know Nathan."

"Yes, don't we all!" declared Bella, with a roll of her eyes. "And he's coming here?"

"Directly. He's leading the Royal Navy off on a merry chase as we speak." Hopefully, that bit might get her to back her sails a bit.

The grey eyes sharpened. "I heard you two crossed hawsers, went your separate ways."

"Aye, well, a bit of knotting and splicing, and those hawsers are good as new."

"Indeed." She looked away thoughtfully. "I didn't think we'd see him again, after—" A cough finished the thought.

Bella tilted her head to regard Cate anew. "Nathan's aiming high these days, eh? Even in tatters, you can see she's quality. She has the speech and grace of a lady. That won't win her any prizes here," she warned. "Still, she looks too smart to be tied up with the likes o' him."

"Nathan has his assets."

Bella grinned, in spite of herself. "He does." She sighed wistfully. "Nathan knows how to make a woman forget what she is about."

Even at her age, Bella was still a fine figure of a woman. The thought of her in her prime made Thomas' loins tighten; she would have been a handsome woman. He was in awe of the man who had curbed her into matrimony, not unlike how he marveled at Cate's husband: able to manage her willfulness, without breaking her spirit. In point of fact, looking at her was like seeing Cate in her older years. Not necessarily the hair or eyes, although either could freeze a man in his tracks. Both had that go-to-blazes air, and a tongue quicker and sharper than a cat-o-nines. Like Cate, Bella had her tender side, but he wasn't so foolish as to think time had softened her.

"One look says it's not her conversation he admires so," Bella observed coolly. "Lord, those eyes? Is she a sorceress?"

"No," he shot back emphatically. And woe that she wasn't. He staggered a bit at the thought of the suffering she could have saved herself if she had.

"What's her gain? Come now, everyone has one," Bella insisted over Thomas' sputtering objections. "Granted, Nathan has his ways, but that one could have her choice. Why him?"

"Do not underestimate her."

Bella grinned up knowingly. "It would appear she has two conquests."

Thomas ducked his head at Bella's powers of observation.

He quickened his pace again, meaning to gain lost ground, but Bella refused to be rushed.

"She's making no secret that she's someone's wife," Bella said at seeing the flash of Cate's wedding ring. "Nathan get her with child? There's plenty of angel-makers elsewhere."

Cate's back stiffened and her step faltered at overhearing that.

"It's nothing of the sort," Thomas said loud enough for Cate's benefit. "Then you got one on her."

Thomas rolled his eyes again. "No! Good god, woman, quit firing off accusations like grapeshot."

By necessity, Bella was a hard woman, but he'd never known her to be so cold and judgmental. No one on that island was a paragon of virtue; expecting it of someone else smacked of high-handedness.

"Do not underestimate her," Thomas said, firmly. "She's been through war."

Bella burst out in a hearty laugh, shaking her head in disbelief. "A few weeks with Nathan could certainly make one feel like that."

At length, Bella sobered. "I'll admit, Nathan's the last one I expected to beat a woman."

"He didn't—"

"I may be old, but I'm not blind," Bella said, sternly. "She's been beaten and recent.

It's in the eyes, mostly; you can always see it there."

Thomas winced at the weariness in Bella's voice. Dammit, women suffered too damned much at the hands of men.

"That was Creswicke's handiwork." Thomas prided himself on never having raised a hand to a woman and had little use for any who did. Be damned if he'd idly listen to Nathan being accused of it.

Bella stopped in mid-step. "Creswicke!"

Ha! Caught her by the lee on that one.

"So, those two are still going at it, eh? And that poor thing got caught up in the middle." Bella made a disgusted noise. "Nathan doesn't mind who chokes on his smoke. Would have thought by now he would have learned he's never going to win that fight."

"That's where you're wrong, Bella," Thomas grinned. "He won. Creswicke is with Davy Jones, now."

"Dead?"

He jerked a nod. "As the proverbial doornail."

The pale eyes brightened. "Well I'll be...! Long live the King," she extolled to the sky.

Not wishing to fall too far behind Lesauvage, Thomas urged Bella to move along. They walked for a bit, Bella falling off into her own thoughts.

"Nathan always seemed to be looking for more than what any woman had to give," she finally said, almost to herself.

"He finally met one," Thomas said, his gaze unwavering from Cate's back. Bella looked up in disbelief. "Her?"

"Her."

Bella chuckled, dry and derisive. "And I'm to believe he values her so much he's left her to you?"

"Cuckoldry is *not* in her nature." On that one Thomas would bet his ship, both ships.

Bella made a skeptical noise. "Any woman—"

"Not her."

Leaning close, Bella inhaled sharply through her nose. "Is that disappointment I smell?" She laughed, waving off his objections. "Allow us time to shift lodgings; we'll make sure you two can be alone."

"Dammit, Bella—" The words died in his throat at seeing a woman striding down a path through the trees. She stepped out of the shade into the glare of light and he winced, the stab in his chest feeling like a broken rib.

Staring, Thomas gulped and rasped "She's still here."

No longer a master of his legs, he had stopped, at some point. Bella turned to follow his line of sight. She swiveled back to squint up at him. "Where else?"

Her fingernails gouging his arm broke his stare. "You know the rule," she hissed.

Thomas jerked away, ruefully rubbing the sore spot. "Dammit, aye, I know the fucking rule."

Lesauvage's grasp tightened on Cate as a wave of women and mariners lifted them from the waterline and swept them inland. Tucking her arm deep into his, he made a remark in French, too guttural for Cate to catch, and his men laughed. His hip familiarly bumping hers, he walked with the casual ease of strolling a park. The nearness allowed Cate several discoveries. Grease, presumably from his most recent meal, shone in his beard, his grasp slick with it. She turned her face away to breathe; he smelled like a boar and had the breath of a dead one. Nearer now, she could see the scar down his face was lined with a double row of pox-like divots, the footprints of something near sailmaker's thread used to stitch it.

The sound of Thomas' heavy tread close behind was her reassurance. His watchful eye was an even greater consolation. He had her back, in the most literal sense of the word. She had survived Bailey, a treacherous pirate friend of Nathan's; Lesauvage had none of Bailey's menace, but only a giddy-headed girl would think him innocent.

"One is rarely prepared to be met by such charming company, *Mademoiselle... Oh! Pardon moi! Madam* Harper!" he declared, catching sight of her ring, as she pushed the hair back from her face.

The man misses nothing, she thought, burying the offending hand into the folds of her skirt.

Caution was going to be the mandatory route. As in Bailey's company, every word and gesture would require careful measurement. While representing Brian's uncle at the French and Spanish Courts, she had learned the trick of noncommittal smiling and nodding.

Cate jerked and stumbled at hearing Nathan's name uttered in Bella's incredulous voice.

"Ah, so you know Blackthorne," Lesauvage said, observing her reaction.

He has the hearing of a ferret, too.

"Who doesn't?" Cate said airily and then grimaced. Something more clever would have been preferred.

"His name does go before him," Lesauvage said with grudging envy. "He'll be arriving directly?" he asked, his ear still canted behind them.

Well, if Thomas openly said Nathan was coming, then it was clearly no great secret.

Cate vaguely nodded. "So I am given to understand."

"You are his... *particular* of late hmm...?"

Thomas had already declared her as "property" and, in not

quite the same breath, announced Nathan's impending arrival, and so she would play along with whatever Thomas was at.

The Frenchman bent his head in admiration of the swell of her bosom, his fetid breath hot on her skin. "You are so fresh and sweet, not dried up like these sticks." A wave indicated the island's inhabitants.

Cate touched a self-conscious hand to her neck. Months in the tropics had done her skin no favors.

"My men and I come here for the... menu," he went on with a suggestive lilt. He sighed blissfully. "So many, many lovely, lovely dishes. Which one to pick?"

"The one least likely to give you indigestion, I should think."

"Ho, ho!" he chortled, in his Burgundian rumble. "A quick mind, as well. *Fascinat!* Nathan's tastes usually run to the more... *Como se qua? Lent d'esprit.* Slow-minded."

A measured smile pasted in place, Cate rose up as she walked to peer over the throng, trying to take in the island itself. Under the palm trees, the settlement clustered along the waterfront like chicks under a hen's wing. It was a hodgepodge collection of shack-like dwellings, no two alike in size, shape or construction. Any matériel, from wood and canvas, to hogsheads and crates, had been employed, including hatches, bulkheads, and spars. The smaller were barely more than lean-tos; others were more substantial, the largest an entire stern cabin set on land, a ship's bow poking out further down. Greenery — ferns, bushes and flower-laden ramblers — had grown up and over it all, softening the ungainly edges, blending it into something which resembled a village.

A great number of children scampered about, proof the island's fertility wasn't restricted to the lushness of its vegetation. By their looks, the island didn't suffer from poverty. There were none of the hollow-eyed waifs or beggars, so often seen elsewhere. They were slim and ragged, but with the sort which came with youth and healthy activity, not starvation.

The flow of people brought Cate and Lesauvage up over the high waterline to a pavilion-like, open-walled structure of old spars supporting a thatched-roof. Brick hearths, cook fires with steaming pots, and long wooden worktables, dusty with flour, marked it the communal kitchen area. To the other side ran long rows of tables and seating. The balance of the Revenges were there, either too drunk or too disinterested to go meet the newly arrived ships.

"I beg pardon?" Cate said.

His teeth, through a combination of broken, rotting or filed, gave Lesauvage's smile a jagged, animal quality. "You are

Nathan's *particular*, of late." He mouthed the word as if he might have said "whore."

He cocked his head, regarding her with avid interest. "A woman who can hold his interest for more than a day must possess some very special... talents."

His tongue flicked out as if probing for the bits of food caught in his beard. "Nathan and I are both sworn to the Brethren, both sworn to abide by pirate law, you know." The greasy fingers insinuated themselves between hers, working in and out in a suggestive rhythm. "It demands we share *everything*."

Cate jerked away, wiping away the grease and his touch. Swallowing down several retorts, she allowed "Alas, you aren't a member of —"

The rest died in her throat at seeing Lesauvage eyes round at something seen over her shoulder. Stumbling backwards, he murmured *"Très Sainte Vierge préserver et nous protéger!"* repeatedly crossing himself. His men fell back at the same time, mouthing oaths and making horned signs.

Cate turned to see the object of their horror: a woman, coming down a path leading from the far trees. Even at that distance, the clatter of charms and talismans, hanging from every aspect of her person, could be heard at every step.

Tall, head high, shoulders square, she had a queenly poise. The West Indies were the crossroads of the cultures of the world, and they seemed to have all come together in this one person. African was evident in her creamed cafe skin, the European showing in fine features. The high cheekbones and slanted eyes might have been an Oriental influence or perhaps indigenous people. The muted earthen colors of her loose clothing made her look like she had sprung from the jungle. The brightest part of her was a mosaic-patterned scarf which bound her head like a turban; a second one of a different pattern wound lower over her brows. She clutched a branch, adorned with streamers of feathers, dried weeds in her fist.

The creature-of-the-woods pushed her way through the crowd, her dusky gold eyes fixed on Cate. She didn't stop until she was barely an arm's length away, causing Cate to fall back, coming up against Thomas.

"You!" The woman leaned toward Cate and sniffed, sounding too much like a hog seeking truffles. Lip curled in disgust, she reared back and swatted the branch, Cate ducking to keep from being hit.

She leaned and sniffed again, as if confirming what she already knew, and brandished the branch again, obliging Cate to dodge.

"Why did you cum!?" The demand came in a clipped patois of French and Arabic, similar to one often heard on the *Lovely*.

"I beg pardon? I—" Cate stammered.

"Cate's—" Thomas began.

A swipe of the wand silenced him.

"I know who you are," she said narrowly. "You have the stink of Hades!"

Thomas moved to interpose between Cate and her interlocutor, but another slap of the wand and a severe look stopped him in his tracks.

"Away! This is between us."

The woman turned and started back in the direction from which she had come. After several steps, she stopped to bark "Cum!" over her shoulder.

As if some spell had already been cast, Cate meekly followed.

11: SAGE SMOKE AND TEA LEAVES

A S CATE WAS LED AWAY, she cocked an ear behind her, for the reassuring sound of Thomas following. That failing, her step slowed as she looked back to find nothing more than the dust settling. A sharp hiss from up ahead urged her onward.

It was a wonder, Cate thought ruefully as she walked. After all of Thomas' high talk of guarding and watching, he had suddenly gone remiss, leaving her to deal with whatever lay ahead all by herself.

On a well-trodden path, she was led inland. Beyond a line of trees, lay the working heart of the island. With its kitchen and herb gardens, wattled and well-tended, and provision gardens, now deserted, the barrows, baskets and carts abandoned in the haste of meeting the arriving ships, she was reminded of both her homeland and the Highlands. The pastures and outbuildings — milking sheds, farrowing pens and fodder barns — made the place all the more like a small estate as opposed to just a random collection of people and shacks. The sight of it all tugged at her heart and made her appreciate — albeit briefly — Nathan's thoughtfulness of sending her there.

The winding path narrowed, the trees closed in. They left behind the sun-saturated world and stepped into one of shade, the tree limbs like cathedral arches overhead. The path's dust was replaced by a carpet of vegetation in varying stages of decomposition. Here, the hum of life was all the stronger, where droves of sunset-colored parrots gabbled about, iridescent butterflies darted and flower-laden vines ran rampant.

Onward they went, the forest closing in until the sun's searching fingers could no longer reach. It was a world not of day but of a half-lit gloom, where light was perceived only by the relative depth of the shadows. The ground grew damp, their footsteps muffled by moss and leaf mold, the smell of rotting vegetation rising with each step. A stillness enshrouded it all, the cathedral becoming more like a tomb.

A tomb somewhere near the inner circles of a watery Hell, where the sultry air hung like an oppressive cloak, Cate thought, lifting the dank hair from her neck.

No bird called, no insect buzzed or stirred, no tiny feet scampered; no leaf stirred, the Spanish moss swaying only at their passing.

Forests weren't a foreign place; Cate had grown up in the wilds of the New World and had often traversed the Highland's forests, where the stuff of legends lived. The shadows gathered in the hollows and crept out in searching fingers. They put her to mind of the childhood horrors of ogres existing under her bed, to the point she danced from one side of the path to the other, hitching her skirts to avoid them. All in all, it wasn't a place she wished to be left alone, and she strove to keep close to her guide, her skirts now the brightest spot in the murk. Swaying with her step, the fabric's geometric pattern had a hypnotic effect.

They might have walked a mile; they might have walked a league. Water could be heard, not the roll of the ocean, but the rustle of a waterway, too distorted by the dense growth to tell if it came from a stone's toss or a rifle shot away. A sharp turn, Cate ducked under the nodding fronds of a fiddle-head fern, the forest opened, and the flat gleam of a river stretched out before them. No waterfowl, no birds, nor insects, nor frogs, not even a fish rising, it was as lifeless as its surroundings.

The path veered, and they followed the bank for a while. Finally, the stream widened into a lagoon-like area. A small cabin sat at its edge, so overgrown with lianas and moss it might have grown out of the forest floor. Glassless windows and stoop were festooned with hexes and charms bearing geometric symbols reminiscent of ones seen in the Highlands.

The complaining bleat of a goat came from somewhere near. They passed through several garden plots, herbs occupying most of them. Cate's wonderment at how any plant managed to grow in the gloom was cut short by looking up to find the woman had disappeared inside the cabin. The door stood open in apparent invitation.

In the stillness, the porch creaking was like a trumpet blare. Cate slowed at seeing rooster head nailed to the door, its dead eyes staring into hers. Stepping inside, she let out a small yelp at something brushing the top of her head. Looking up, she found a bundle of dried pods swung from the lentil.

Inside, the smell of herbs and things long dead met Cate's

nose. The woman struck a flint and the infant light revealed a single room, a table and stools occupying its center, and a workbench running the length of one wall. Rows of shelving, crammed to overflowing with jars, bags, bottles, cages and tins lined the walls. Books with archaic lettering on the spines stood on the shelves and spilled out onto the worktable, some bulging with bookmarks of string or ribbon. Coals glowed cherry bright from under a blanket of ash in the hearth, a cot next to it.

Cate stood while a few more dips were lit. As the light grew, she found the sense of being watched wasn't entirely imagined. Eyes stared at her from every direction, including the beams overhead: dead ones, of creatures furred, feathered and scaled. A raven sat so still in the window she thought it stuffed until it turned its head to regard her. Uttering a disgruntled "Caw!" it turned its attentions outside.

The woman spun around, the charm branch still poised in her fist. "Why did you cum?"

Already miserable and weary, Cate rolled her eyes. Her hopes had been time and distance might mollify the stranger's mood.

"I didn't 'cum'. I was brought, or rather sent. I don't know," Cate finally surrendered. Either scenario seemed to apply; the significant point was that she had no say in the matter.

The growing light sent shadows leaping and dancing on the walls, the inanimate seeming to come alive. Waving the branch, the woman circled Cate as if the measured space was her preservation. "Cum out! Show yourself. Appear as you are."

"I'm nobody. Just Cate... Catherine Harper."

"Lies!" came with another swat of the wand.

Cate jumped, startled. "Very well, I'm Catherine Maureen Harper."

"Lies!"

"Any additional name might get me drawn-and-quartered." Cate bit her lip, wondering where that confession came from.

Her inquisitor stopped, surprised. "You fear fire," she said, with the air of a grand secret discovered.

"Only in so much as they throw your innards into it in the process of that execution."

Cate rubbed her temples; a dull ache had suddenly settled there. The room was insufferably warm, the air barely breathable. "What's your name?" she shot back peevishly.

Good manners prevailed. The woman straightened and bobbed a stiff curtsy. "They call me Celia."

A flash of even white teeth marked a genuine smile which transformed her into quite the beauty, in an exotic way. "I am a *medsen fey*, a leaf doctor. The spirits come to me— sometimes in dreams—and tell me what leaves or cures is necessary for what ails a person. The health of every soul on this island is in my hands."

Cate glanced dubiously around. The charms at the windows and hexes, etched on the floor and walls, all pointed toward Celia's description being a bit of an understatement. An herb woman didn't need dead bats, nor bits of other creatures, nor jars of eyeballs, preserved in spirits. The gourd and pottery dishes brimming with stones, shells, crystals and bits of bone all pointed toward the darker arts. A crystal ball wouldn't have been a surprise. To press the point, however, would mean calling the woman what: a seer? Enchantress? Witch? None of those titles would be welcomed and might get her cast out into the forest, or worse.

"Why are you here? *She* sent you? Do not lie! I can smell her on you." Celia punctuated her point with another swat of the branch. Cate threw her arm up in self - defense only to have it grabbed. The semi-transparent eyes, seeming to glow in the dim, fixed on the bracelet, and then moved up to her necklace.

"Someone knows what they are doing," the *medsen fey* said, in grudging approval.

"They know the great powers and how to bind them. Earth and sea, wind and fire all eternally bound," she added, fingering the oddments at the bracelet ends.

"They supposedly protected me from Calypso," Cate said, pulling free.

Celia glanced up. "Calypso," she mused. "Is that what she is calling herself these days?"

Cate shrugged; Nathan used a number of names in reference to his watery nemesis; that one seemed his favorite.

"And how did you cum to know of these?"

"I didn't," Cate said simply. "They were a gift... of sorts." She dabbed the beads of sweat on her upper lip and glanced wistfully at the windows and the fresher air beyond.

Hands on her hips, Celia stood back, eyeing the knotted cords. "You can't be *her*, if you are wearing those."

A hand shot out; Cate yelped at several hairs being yanked from her head. Mumbling and clutching a charm at her throat, Celia held the hairs at arm's length as she moved to the hearth. There, she tossed them into the coals and bent to study the resulting tiny flames. The stench of burning hair thickened the already noxious atmosphere.

Celia turned back from the hearth with a more abiding air. "You were dead."

"Yes." The admission didn't come easily, but then they seemed to be pouring out like wine from a bottle.

An arched look said further explanation was expected.

No secrets here, either, Cate sighed.

The thought of the black void and penetrating cold made Cate shiver. She shifted a bit nearer to glowing coals, suddenly appreciative of the room's warmth. "I'm sorry, I don't remember much."

"Hmm, all the more curious," Celia said, pensively looking off.

Moving closer, Celia took Cate by the chin and peered into her face, the dusty gold eyes as sharp and searching as a falcon's. "You are Nathan Blackthorne's woman," she observed, standing back.

Cate brightened. "Do you know him?"

The stern countenance softened into almost a smile, faint yet wistful. "Oh, yes, for a very long time. He has a way of getting inside a woman. He is in you, strong and fierce."

The herb woman sank into her own reveries. Finally, she gestured to a chair. "Sit. Sit. A dish of tea?"

Cate's first instinct was to say "No", but suddenly found she was in dire need of something to drink. "Err... if you please." Something far stronger would have been preferable, but if tea was all which was offered, then tea she would take.

Celia bent over the cauldron on the fire and ladled hot water into a china pot. "Nathan gave you those—the necklace and such—did he not? His mother was a Great One," she added with reverence. "The powers would have been greatest in a sister, but a son can inherit much."

"You know of the Celts?" It was a bit of a surprise for someone residing in the West Indies to be familiar with a group limited to the British Isles.

Celia smiled indulgently as she reached for tins and herbs, taking pinches of this and that, and dropping them into the brew. "'Tis no great thing. No matter the language spoken in this world, the other world speaks the same."

The clink of china, the sound of tea pouring, the silver strainer, the queries of "Milk?

Sugar?" struck Cate with a sense of the civilized world inserting itself into this bizarre room with a force which almost made her chuckle aloud. She wouldn't have been surprised if a tin of Naples biscuits were offered next. She cautiously sniffed the cup set before her, poured a bit into the saucer and sipped. It wasn't the traditional gunpowder variety, but neither was it the bitter witch's brew she had feared. She detected bergamot—

minty and sharp— chamomile—earthy and floral—and a few others she couldn't name.

They sipped in an uneasy companionship. The hot brew did a fine job of beating down the chill which had beset Cate. In her increasing ease, she took the opportunity to look around over the edge of her drink. She had once visited an apothecary's shop in Barcelona, one known for its collection of oddities. This was that and more: a three - thumbed human hand floated in a jar of red-tinted spirits; an albino toad floated in the next; the skin of a two-headed lizard hung overhead; a bird's skin—perfectly divided with half male, half female plumage—hung from a peg.

"Your spirit is agitated."

Cate looked up to find Celia staring pointedly at Cate's hand as she unwittingly fiddled with the lace at her wrist. Cate forced her hand down to her side, but it was too late.

Setting down her dish, Celia leaned across the table. "Let me see" came with the authority of a healer.

With considerable trepidation, Cate obeyed and extended her arm.

Celia undid the strip with the well-practiced ease, her fingers cool against the tender underside of Cate's wrist. "You have not seen," she observed at seeing Cate turn her head.

"No, I can't—"

Celia's grip tightened. "You must," she said, low and urgent. "It is you, now. Deny it and your spirit will perish."

"How do you know?" Cate shot back testily and jerked away.

Celia straightened. The translucent eyes held Cate's, defying her to look away, as she unwound the turban. Free of its confinement, her hair tumbled about her shoulders. It wasn't the expected African kink, but a silken nut-brown, the ends going to gold, as if touched by the sun. More striking, however, was the image of a cross, burned into the high, round forehead.

"They thought me a witch, and so they gave me the Christian symbol to save my soul." The *medsen fey* made a skeptical noise. "I was supposed to be pleased they did not kill me."

Thoroughly chastened, Cate allowed her arm to be taken, her head still resolutely turned away. Her hand hovering over it, Celia closed her eyes and fell quiet, her brow furrowing slightly. Then she jerked away as if she held a hot coal.

"I can do nothing for this," she announced, and set to re-securing the lace.

"I never expected—" Cate stammered.

"This is the work of an evil man. Some operate as the hand of Satan, or Balor, or Eblis, or whatever you wish to call him, but not this one. Gods can be commanded; man cannot," she added, wryly.

When finished, Celia pensively drummed her fingers on the table. "This is Lord Creswicke's handiwork." It came more announcement than question.

"He's dead," Cate said, mechanically. She had to keep repeating that, until the reality sank in.

"How?"

Cate shifted at feeling the pain of Creswicke's blade once more, pinning her to the deck like a bug on a board. "Stabbed, beheaded, blown up, or so I have been told."

Celia sat back, pleased. "So, that evil is gone. I thought I felt a shift."

Head cocked to one side, Celia sipped her tea, the falcon still keen on Cate. "Something else vexes you."

Cate squirmed, feeling as transparent as that missing crystal ball. "I'm worried about... about Nathan." She looked down into her cup, wondering what might have been in the tea to prompt such a confession. She had felt under some kind of spell since Celia's appearance.

A china-on-china clatter marked Celia setting her cup down. "Worried? Why should you be so?"

Cate gaped at the woman's failure to grasp. "He's out there... somewhere," she said, gesturing toward the sea, wherever in the hell it was. "And I have no way of knowing if he's alive, or dead, or maimed, or —?"

One brow took a censorious arch. "You know. You know," she urged at Cate's denial.

Celia reached across the table and pressed her palm over Cate's heart. "Sit quiet and look here."

The pressure on Cate's chest increased, Celia's will radiating like prickles in a sleeping limb. Cate meekly nodded, acquiescing. Feeling quit silly, and having no idea what else to do, Cate folded her hands in her lap and closed her eyes. Barely to the count of three, she opened them into Celia's disapproval.

"No, seek him, as you know how."

Cate shot a peevish glance. Having someone poking about in her mind was disquieting, to say the least. "Very well."

Yes, she had reached for Nathan — once — as she had when Brian lived. In the Highlands, the ability had been called "taibhsearachd" — having a second sight — and had put her under a great deal of suspicion. It meant doing it only in the direst of conditions and in utmost privacy, which made it doubly difficult to do with someone staring. Her faith in her ability didn't extend to her accuracy, the ability to summon one without calling the other? Did lying at one's eternal rest render one deaf, or would she be faced with the awkward situation of Nathan and Brian appearing together?

Ugh! That would be a tangled mess.

She glanced up, hopeful Celia might suffer second thoughts or lost interest.

Finding neither was the case, Cate loosened her shoulders, arranged her hands in her lap, and closed her eyes. She slowed her breathing and focused on Nathan. The oppressive heat of the cabin and the weight of the woman's gaze slipped away like a loose cloak, and she stood on a sunlit deck. Nathan stepped out of the days' glare, bold and determined, as he always was on his ship. He stopped, the gold of his smile rivaling the sun's brilliance. She opened her mouth to speak, but then he was gone.

When Cate opened her eyes, Celia asked "What did you see?" with the tone of one already in possession of the answer.

The concession didn't come easily. "He was on his ship... and well." Cate's mouth twitched at recollecting his smile.

He was well...

So far, warned an inner voice.

Seemingly satisfied, Celia rewound the scarf about her head and resumed sipping tea. She stared into her cup for some moments, and then the gold eyes swiveled up, sharp and accusing.

"You carry his heart, as you carried his child, and yet you killed it."

"What?!"

The raven barked, startled by Cate's shriek.

"You misguided charlatan! You don't know what you are talking about—!" Cate lurched to her feet and steamed back and forth, batting at the pelts and herbs hanging overhead.

"You smell of violence," Celia went on over Cate's indignant sputtering.

"Violence!" Cate cried, mouth hanging half-open. She shook her head and repeated in an incredulous whisper "Violence."

"You smell of blood—"

"Of course, there was blood!" Cate shot back. "I was—"

"The angelmaker you went to was a butcher."

"Angelmaker!" Cate stopped short and glared down. "How dare you accuse me—!

Damn your misguided insights. There was no anglemaker, because there was no—"

"There was a child—" Celia went on, determinedly.

"No, there wasn't," Cate shot back, pacing again. The confined space only added to her agitation. "I would never—"

Cate stopped, rigid. Hands balled at her sides, she dug her nails into her palms, hoping the pain might wake her from this nightmare. It couldn't be. The hag was wrong, dead wrong! How the bloody hell could one who supposedly saw everything, couldn't see to the door on this?

"There was a child," Celia said, slow and emphatic. "Very small, its spirit yet to flower. It was a boy, with his mother's eyes and his father's smile."

Cate heard the truth in Celia's voice, saw it flooding the translucent eyes, and it struck like a fist to the gut, driving the air from her lungs.

"No! Oh, God! No...!" Cate's knees gave out from under her, and she crumpled to the floor. Braced on one hand, she clutched her middle, holding the child that never was, and sobbed. Celia was next to her, seeking to console, but failing miserably. Cate had heard all the platitudes; heard all the sympathy and hollow, automatic words too many times.

With a growling sound, Cate sat back on her haunches, shoving her hair back from her face. "You can see my entire life, but you can't see your so-called violence was me being brutalized? The blood wasn't from an anglemaker. It was because—"

Cate bent, collapsing under another wave of grief and loss.

At Celia's persistent urging, Cate eventually quieted and rose to a chair. There she sat, shattered and dazed, an empty, hollow vessel. She was vaguely aware of Celia moving, making the domestic sounds of replenishing the tea.

At length, Celia drew up a stool and sat, their knees touching. "Drink." She pressed a tin cup to Cate's lips. "Drink."

Lacking the will to resist, Cate did so. The steam coiled up into her head, the bergamot's sharpness cutting through the thickness of crying, the chamomile pacifying raw nerves. A tight nod gave thanks. Thanking the one who had just torn out her heart didn't come easily. A part of Cate loathed the woman for forcing the truth on her, for making her suffer it all over again. Living in ignorance had been ever so much more pleasant.

Cate groaned and buried her head into her hands. "You did not know of the child."

Cate couldn't see Celia's face, but her voice was gentle with apology and regret.

"No." Her fingers digging into her scalp, Cate tried to recall, tried to work out the math of the days and weeks between lying with Nathan for the first time and being taken by Creswicke. "I... I couldn't have been that far gone," she offered weakly.

Cate choked an embarrassed laugh. "Nathan knew...

somehow. I wouldn't believe him. I couldn't believe, not after... everything before. An angelmaker was the last thing I would ever seek; my problem was keeping them," she added bleakly.

"There were more?" Celia asked, delicately, and then in a more professional tone "How many?"

"Umm, I lost two, just in the natural course of things," she added, with a helpless wave. "And then another one, two," she corrected, swallowing hard, "were taken."

There was no other word for it. Both infants might have lived had they not been torn away by brutality.

Cate clamped her eyes shut, silently praying the woman mightn't ask her to explain, obliging her to relive it.

She couldn't. She wouldn't.

God's my life! She can see everything else. Surely to hell, she can see that!

"They were animals which used you; animals which took your child," Celia said. "You hate Creswicke, hate them all for what they did, for what they took."

Cate resolutely shook her head. "No, hating does no good."

"It vexes you and eats at your soul." Celia leaned closer. "Let it out. Have your vengeance."

Cate slid a sideways look between her fingers at Celia's forehead, now inches away. "Did you have yours?"

"Yes," came back fiercely.

"And yet, the brand is still there," Cate said, dully. She sat back, arms limp in her lap. "It changed nothing."

Celia took Cate by the chin and brought her face around. "It changed *everything*. I was free of their hand. His hand still rests on you, burdens you, squeezes your heart."

Sniffing hugely, Cate palmed her face dry. "My husband and his men killed the first ones. I was told to celebrate, but..." Her voice quavered, threateningly near another breakdown. She set her jaw, sheer willpower seeing her through. "But dancing on their graves didn't erase the consequences of their acts."

...the consequences of their acts.

Carved, beaten, used hard, and a child lost: God, how simple that made it sound.

Cate thrust her lace-bound arm in Celia's face. "The man who did this is dead, and yet I still wear this." Her voice shook, willpower giving way to fury. "I still have to live every damned, blessed day of my life with what those bastards did to me, what they took from me. Nothing... *nothing* I could do, that anyone can do would *ever* erase this brand or bring back my child."

The outstretched hand trembled; Cate balled it and buried it deep into the folds of her skirt. She drew a long quivering breath and said, a bit more composed "You said not five minutes past that Man's evil cannot be undone."

"Not the deed, nor the physical scars," Celia countered, evenly. "But the scars of the heart, those can be undone. They must, or they will squeeze everything from it." "No, you're wasting your time. I... I just don't think about it."

Celia found Cate's hand and clasped it. "Ah, but you do," Celia countered, kind yet insistent. "You think about it *always*."

"No... no." Cate shook her head mechanically. "I can't," came out in a thin rasp.

The grasp tightened. "You must," Celia hissed in her ear.

It was all just too much to bear. It was all proof positive that God and Providence were in partnership against her. All hopes or prayers would either be denied, or granted, only to be torn away. She'd inquired of many a priest as to what gross wrong she might have committed to deserve it. No answers were given. She had asked God directly, but even those prayers had gone ignored.

"All right, yes!" Cate leapt up and stalked the room again. "Yes! I hate them, the ones before, and the ones now... *all* of them! I hate them all with every fiber of my being."

She brought her fists down on the table with a force that rattled the cups and shot liquid from the pot's spout.

"Every time I close my eyes, I see them dying a slow, horrible death, suffering like they made me suffer. I want to kill every one of them—but I can't. I can't!" She was shrieking at the end, vibrating with impotent fury.

Cate put her back to the room and the woman, desperate for a scrap of privacy. With all her defenses suddenly ripped away, she felt as exposed and squirming as a grub on a rock.

She bent, clutching her arms tight about herself. "Yes, I want my child back. I want to hold it, and look down and see Brian's eyes, and know his life wasn't in vain. I wanted Nathan's child, so I might have something of him. He wanted it so badly and I—" Her voice caught at seeing the hope in those coffee-brown eyes, hearing it in his voice. The yearning to fulfill his wishes, to give him something so precious and unique, proof of her love, and yes, create a bond which might bind him to her, had verged on all-consuming.

She whirled back toward the table, glaring. "Damn you, is that what you wished to hear?"

Celia's mouth quirked, an unpleasant goal achieved. "Come. Sit."

Still agitated, Cate made several more circuits around the

room. Celia sat quietly, like the patient parent waiting for a child's tantrum to run its course.

"Your womb will bear no fruit, until it is drained of the poison."

Celia's threat struck a cord, and she knew it.

"What am I supposed to do?" Cate fumed. She rubbed her hands, now aching from hitting the table. "Just forget it, like everyone keeps telling me?"

"Your hatred burns too hot for anything else to grow," Celia insisted, tapping a finger on the wood before her. "You must be rid of it."

"How?" Cate demanded testily. She batted the hair from her face; the room's heat and humidity had made it bloom into a frowsy cloud.

Celia plucked a leaf from the end of her wand. Moving to the work table, she dropped it into a dish, blackened with use, and held it over a lamp flame. It smoldered and then flashed into flames; Celia spun and blew the smoke into Cate's face.

"Patience," she said over Cate coughing and fanning the air. "A way will present itself."

Celia turned and canted her head outside. "He waits."

Cate was ushered to the door before she could ask "Who?"

At the threshold, Celia took Cate's hands in a bone-grinding clasp. The sleeping-limb prickle, felt at their first contact, was now an electrical jolt shooting up her arms and into her chest.

"Release the hate, if not for your own sake, then for him," Celia said, low and insistent. "You hold his heart. Do not allow your hate to consume it."

Cate was half-pushed out onto the sloping stoop.

Semi-dazed and disoriented, she blinked. The shadows in the hollows had deepened and elongated with impending night. She inhaled, filling her lungs with the air—previously thought oppressive, now as refreshing as a mountain top—and expelled the noxious remnants of the shack's interior.

In the garden, a shadow moved. It separated from the others and came up the path toward her, a light bobbing next to it like a gigantic firefly. Only one person could be of that size and bulk.

"You've been waiting," she said as Thomas neared. She meant to be furious with him for having left her to that witchy woman—Knowing he was there might have provided a great deal more ease during the interview—but found her wrath was no longer to be had.

In fact, the moment she stepped over the threshold, she discovered a number of emotions, so alive just moments ago, were now gone. She dabbed the sweat from her temples and swiped at the lingering dampness on her cheeks. Those were both real enough as was the sting at the back of her throat from the smoke blown in her face. Every detail of what had been said or done was vivid, but the visceral emotions were gone. She was drained, yet strangely buoyant.

Thomas stopped a few paces away and lifted the lamp to peer into her face. "Better?"

"In regard to—?" Her response died in her throat at finding Thomas was no longer listening. He stood as still as the gatepost beside him, staring toward the cabin. The hand on the lamp stirred, two fingers lifting in a tentative wave. Cate turned to find Celia, just inside the door, returning much the same.

Thomas snapped out of his distraction, raised the lamp to peer at Cate again. "Better?"

Without waiting for an answer, he took Cate by the arm and propelled her up the path. "C'mon, show a leg or we'll miss supper. Been around Nathan too much; you've forgotten the rest of mankind prefers to eat, a couple times a day, if at all possible. Getting as bony as him, too," he observed, scowling down at her.

"You know her," Cate observed, nodding toward the shack, already no more than a dark lump behind them.

Lamp on high, he nodded. "Oh, aye, she's attended and mended all of us, at some point or another."

Cate walked next to Thomas, trying to match his stride. He was distracted and remote, answering her small talk with monosyllables and grunts. His mood allowed her to fall off into her own reverie.

A child! She could conceive! It was the miracle which she had been afraid to pray for. She giggled aloud.

"What?"

Thomas' impatient bark prompted her to look up. Apparently, she had slowed at some point, for he was several strides ahead, looking back.

"Nothing, nothing," she said waving him on, trying to master a huge grin.

"C'mon, will you spread some canvas. I'm sharp set as a boarding ax."

Cate obligingly followed, almost skipping. She pressed her hand to her belly. The scars were still there, but they no longer meant the same. A new hope bloomed and burned within.

She could conceive!

The urge to shout and caper with joy was almost more than

she could resist. The weight of a decade of barrenness was gone, her womanhood regained. She couldn't wait to tell Nathan—

Nathan!

Cate inwardly groaned. She was going to have to tell him, which meant conceding that he had been correct all along.

"Ugh! He's going to be insufferable to live with!"

"What?" came from ahead.

"Nothing, nothing."

The thought of him strutting around proud as a stud wasn't a pleasant one.

She wanted him... now! She ran the same math through her head as she had in the cabin, coming to the same conclusion: conception had to have happened straightaway. It happened once. Dare she hope it would happen again? The means to success would be a simple formula: all she needed was Nathan, eager and full-blooded, as he always was.

"Dammit, Nathan. Where the hell are you?" she said to the night.

"What?"

"Nothing. Nothing."

12: FRIENDLY FACES IN THE SNAKE PIT

THE SOUND OF RAUCOUS LAUGHTER, music and the smell of wood and tobacco smoke met Cate and Thomas long before they returned to the settlement. In their absence, the festivities had bloomed into something resembling Bartholomew Fair, pirate-style. Fires, large and small, including fagots and torches, dotted the shore, glowing like gobs of molten amber.

Lesauvage strode to meet Cate and Thomas at the pavilion, his arms spread in greeting. *"Bienvenue, mes chers amis!* I worried for your safety, running off together, eh... eh?" His brows waggled in lewd suggestion. "You must have worked up a great appetite, Thomas. Come, take part in our feast. *Bon apetit.* After, you can bless us with your presence, with full bellies and open hearts."

He found Cate's hand and pressed it to his lips. She tightened her fingers against his tongue's invasion as he pressed it to his lips. He swept a bow and returned to the merriment.

Thomas led Cate to the pavilion. It was the settlement's version of a Great Hall, with tables fashioned from everything from rough-hewn planks, hatch covers, to rosewood with the curved legs. Porcelain tureens sat amid crockery bowls, silver platters amid battered wooden plates. Two dogs fighting over a bone—a cloven hoof—summarized Lesauvage's "feast." From all appearances, it had been that very thing, yesterday. The skewer, head, hooves and scattered bits of bone were now all which remained. Flies buzzed lazily about empty baskets, bowls, bread barges and greasy trenchers scattered around.

Grumbling darkly, Thomas poked through the wreckage. With an exclamation of wry delight, he found an overlooked platter of fried fish and bowl of rice. Rummaging about further, he located a pair of relatively clean trenchers, and they sat.

In between shoveling rice into his mouth with a knife, Thomas grinned at seeing Cate staring at a multi-armed silver candelabra amid the pottery. "Not what you expected?"

Looking about, it looked as if the *Morganse's* swag pile had been belched up and spewed out: brocade settees sat next to rough-hewn benches; damask elbowchairs sat next to upturned buckets. Leathery men in pigtails, their faces and beards shining with pork grease and sweat, sported cocked and plumed hats, weskits of goldwork. Ropes of pearls hung on sun-browned bosom's; work-roughened hands protruding from lace sleeves, held delicate feather fans, bare feet poking out from under silk skirts.

"Not quite sure what I expected," she admitted. "But no, not exactly."

There had been precious little time to form an opinion. For that matter, what would an island of pirate wives look like: a tropical paradise, with women living in idyllic splendor; or a female version of Tortuga, with the women dressed in trousers, sporting pigtails and a Jolly Roger flying overhead? The word "wives" had brought several expectations to mind.

Pillars-of-the-earth hadn't come to mind, but neither had this, she thought, with a sideways glance.

Hard, rough, coarse-speaking as their mates, the wives' former lives appeared to have run in the way of whores, laundresses, pitcher bawds, fishwives and hawkers, with every corner of the world represented.

"How long has it been here?" she asked, plucking bones from her fish. Still a-roil with emotions, she went from ravenous to her stomach closed, sometimes within the time it took to fork the next bite.

Knife poised, one sandy brow cocked, considering. "A couple score o' years, as soon as the Brethren was formed, I should imagine. Never heard the exact when or how of it.

Where there's men, there's women they desire to see safe." He ended with an acknowledging bow toward her.

She smiled, conceding his point. Since her first hours of meeting, "safe" had seemed to be Nathan's favorite word.

"It's not grand, but compared to where most hailed from, it's damned near Fiddler's Green. What with no men—active or able, that is," Thomas amended, with a nod toward one passing on a crutch. "They are spared the depredations that men bring: thugs, skulkers, pickpockets, sneakthieves, brawling, pothouses, alehouses, whorehouses..." A swirl of his knife tip finished the thought.

"Odd observation coming from a man," Cate said, dryly.

One shoulder rose and fell as he industriously munched. "Men's vices and weaknesses inevitably drag the women down with them."

"So, in your version, Adam offered Eve the apple."

Thomas smiled, his blue eyes sparking mirth. "'Tis no secret the Devil is a man." He sat back, frowning, as if seeing her for the first time. "You need a drink!"

Dashing the knife clean on his sleeve, Thomas shoved it into its shoulder scabbard and rose, bringing Cate with him. "C'mon, I've just the thing."

Snagging a lonely wedge of bread from amid the ruin and popping it into his mouth, Thomas steered her to a nearby phalanx of casks.

"I know! Stop caterwauling, lovely. I know you don't like rum," he said leading her through the crowd gathered. He stopped at a tub at the far end, his face lit with eager anticipation as he filled a battered, silver cup. "I'm thinking you might be liking this one, however. A local brew, with a hint of something extra."

"Not bad!" She smacked her lips. The rum's burnt-sugar taste was masked by a citrusy tartness and several spices. "What's in it?"

The light of the torches caught the malicious gleam in his eyes. "If I told you, I'd have to kill you."

"Another part of that Pirate Code?" she asked, teasing.

"Nah!" He paused, thoughtfully rolling his eyes and scratching under his hat. "At least, I don't think so."

"I thought you meant to be alert," she said, watching him drain his tankard in one draught, and then refill it.

He swiped his mouth on his arm and winked. "Alert, aye, but not dull company."

In the spirit of self-preservation, Cate and Thomas left the crush of people around the casks and strolled about the fires. Slumped sideways in a chair of a proportion befitting royalty, Lesauvage was holding court at the nearest and largest. He must have been a bosun at some point in his nautical career, for he had the lungs of one when he hailed them.

Thomas' fingers dug deeper into Cate's arm, propelling her forward. "You don't hear him. Be damned, if I'm going to spend the entire goddamned night listening to that arse – wipe prating away."

Thomas navigated a determined course, weaving deep

among the smaller fires, but apparently not deep enough. A runner, roughly the size and age of Maram, appeared directly, plucking anxiously at Thomas' sleeve at being ignored.

"Captain Lesauvage's compliments and duty, sir, and the lady," he hastily added. "He begs —"

"Compliments to your Captain, but the lady and I are not at leisure." "But—?"

Thomas stabbed a finger into the lad's chest hard enough to slosh the liquid out of his tankard. "We are *not* at leisure."

Turning a sickly puce, the lad knuckled his forehead and sped away.

Stomachs sated, the pirate wives strove to satisfy a different sort of appetite, their husband's influence revealing itself in the singularity of purpose: they knew what they wanted and, with a ratio of two to every man, pursued it with the verve of a boarding party. Women might have been a sizeable portion, but Cate noticed the sailor's ways hadn't changed. They collected at one fire or the other by reasons apparent only to them, shipmates, language, religion or heritage seeming to have no bearing. Mariners, being by nature a loud lot, were even more strident when in drink. Their conversation, often twelve – to-the-dozen around any given fire and speaking shoulder-to-shoulder as if on a gale-swept deck, added to the cacophony of music, whooping and dancing.

Thomas and Cate strolled from one circle to another, pausing now and again to chat. Cate was met with a mixed reception. The Lovelies and, to a degree, Brazens knew her, and so were somewhat indifferent; the Revenge's, however, met her with lusty appreciation.

The islander's receptions varied widely from openly welcoming—a precious few—to reserve, to unveiled hostility.

At one point, Thomas slid an eye down at her. "I should have thought to allow you to shift your clothes into something more—" He stopped, at a loss for a fitting word.

Cate appreciated the concern but, at the same time, dismissed him out-of-hand. "I was hardly disposed toward worrying about what I had on my back."

She paused at hearing a passing islander—one of several, of recent—declare "La, aren't we topping the knob?" at hearing her high-born speech, one she hadn't thought to hide until it was too late. The irony of that coming from someone going about looking like a child playing dress-up in their parent's clothes was almost too much to bear.

"Besides," Cate sighed. "Any attempt at putting on appearances mightn't be the advantage one hopes for."

They were interrupted by yet another runner popping up at Thomas' elbow, bearing the same message from the *Revenge's* captain. The hapless soul was again driven to pleading, only to be brushed aside.

As they moved about, an increasing sensation of being followed prickled up Cate's spine and settled between her shoulder blades. Pretending to sip her drink, she looked around to find her suspicions weren't unfounded: a small group of men—remarkable in that they were entirely devoid of female company—hung in the shadows, moving when she and Thomas moved, stopping when they stopped. They posed as participating in the gaiety, but never drank from their vessels. She touched Thomas' arm, directing his attention with a cut of her eyes.

He leaned to whisper "Mine." An almost imperceptible nod assured she hadn't misunderstood. "If anything happens, seek them or Al-Nejem and *stay*."

She shivered at the prospect while at the same time strove to memorize their faces. Given they were pirates and seamen, unified by sun and weather, the task wasn't as easy as one might wish.

As they moved from fire to fire, the topic first on everyone's lips was Creswicke and, more significantly, his death. The Revenges sought information like gold coins on a beach, and the Lovelies were more than happy to play the High-Lords-of-the-Treasury. Like any significant event, the truth was the frequent victim to the fervor for entertainment, the product then passed on to the next and then the next, until the events aboard the *Gosport* became fantastic and beyond recognition.

Being captain and Creswicke's executioner, Thomas was sought for the ultimate word, and so he was often stopped. With the solemnity of delivering the Gospel, he answered any and all questions. Conceding Cate's injury, eliciting exclamations of shock and repugnance at a woman's blood being shed, he baldly omitted her and Nathan's death, flat denying it, no matter how hard he was pressed. Whether by previous arrangement or tacit respect, his own men, mutely watched the truth be slaughtered without so much as an eyebrow twitch. Cate watched Thomas in fascination, seeing a side of him heretofore unrevealed.

Nathan was a master at manipulating men; Thomas ran a *very* close second. He had the Revenges' rapt attention, their eyes rounding with appreciation. He was telling them what they had wished to hear, but above and beyond that, he was showing himself for what he was: a fighting captain, not afraid to "board them in the smoke;" one who, through guile, skill or luck, was a winning one. Judging by their reactions, such was not currently the case on the *Revenge*.

Luckily, a woman's view, in spite of also being first-hand, carried little water, and so Cate was left mute at Thomas' elbow. The role of idle-onlooker, however, obliged her to listen to the grisly details of the conflict over and over, watch time and again as his arm carved down with the finishing blow. Each telling was like her flesh being torn, each swipe another strike. The flickering firelight became the flames on the *Gosport*. A random flash of metal caught in the corner of her eye became Creswicke's sword; the men clustered about suddenly clad in green coats...

Emitting a small startled cry, Cate spun and scurried away, away from the pursuing faces and voices. She shrieked at being grabbed and spun around, a fist balling, ready to strike. She drew up at the last moment at realizing it was Thomas. Wetness made her look down to find she shook so hard she had spilled her drink. For that matter, her entire body was wracked with mild tremors. Thomas plucked the cup away and hailed for it to be refilled.

"All this... this talk of Creswicke..." she stammered. "It... It..."

"Aye," he said, solemnly. "It can't be easy reliving one's... demise," he finished, swallowing hard. "There's a good deal about the day I'd prefer forgotten, but none of it will I be sharing with those bunch o' ghouls."

"You enjoyed it," she sputtered, glaring up. "Telling them about... everything."

"Aye," he finally conceded, unable to meet her eye. "Speaking of it helps... somehow."

Cate stiffened; she had yet to find that to be the case. "They come to you for the truth and you're lying to their faces."

On that point, Thomas grew more determined. "I would look more the liar reporting your death, with you standing there next to me, big as life. Is that what you would prefer: me trying to explain what can't be explained? Bear in mind that hearing Nathan died might imply he's compromised, which might somehow emboldened that smirking slug to do God knows what," he added, with an irritated swipe in Lesauvage's direction.

He bent, thrusting his face into hers. "But, don't muddy the waters. That's not what's grinding your keel."

Cate turned away, hunching her shoulders defensively.

"Look, lovely, not everyone steps off Celia's porch smiling," he said with measured patience. "She has a way of telling too many what they don't need to know."

Looking at his feet, he cautiously peered up at her from under his brows. "Since you left there, you go from looking like the cove what just found the key to the spirits room, to looking like you wish to gut someone."

Feeling once more as transparent as a crystal ball, Cate couldn't argue. She had been edgy since leaving the cabin. It was like two people were living inside the same skin.

"There was a child!" She spread her arms and spun. She had been bursting to shout it at the top of her lungs since leaving Celia's. Her gaiety died at seeing Thomas gape as if she had just announced the sky was blue.

"Aye," he said, cautiously. His eyes rounded with realization and then dropped to her middle. "You mean there's another?"

Her hand reflexively rose to her middle. "No, not now."

Alas, if only!

"You sound like you're afraid someone might blame you, if there were," she teased. There was only one "someone:" Nathan.

Thomas snorted peevishly. "Wouldn't put it past him. Logic always hangs fire with Nathan when it comes to you."

Cate waved him off. "Stand easy, or off, or by... or whatever you sailors do. Nathan and I haven't—" She stopped short of revealing far more than was fitting. She mightn't mind, but Nathan could well have some very strong objections. On the other hand, she and Nathan lived and slept in full view of several score of men. What they had or had not done was quite probably common knowledge.

"How the hell could you not have known—?" Thomas stopped short and stared in wonderment.

"It's more complicated than you might think," she finally offered. She had lived in intimate proximity with him, lain next to him, offered herself to him, but none of that made it agreeable to discuss the irregular intricacies of her body.

"You knew back then?" she asked instead, looking up. "I did—Nathan said as much—and you had the look." "The look?"

"Aye, the look. Hark ye, I've been around enough women to know when they are..." His shoulder wormed under his shirt. She narrowed an eye, threatening. If he said "breeding"—Brian's favorite term—she was going to punch him. "In the family way," he finally managed.

Now it was her turn to flush and fluster. "If you've been around that many, then surely you realize each one is different."

How in heaven's name she had missed the changes in her own body was the pressing question? Her only excuse was that, for so very long, she had been so convinced it would never happen, all signs going ignored...

... if there had been any at all, she qualified, striving to think back, as she had since Celia's announcement.

The sequence of events dictated that she couldn't have been more than a month or so gone. With no regular monthlies, the times she had conceived before, it had taken a few months to realize that a new life was growing. Nathan, however, had known her body better than she and, damn his blackguardly soul, he'd been correct.

"I, *we* had hoped you'd fare better here," Thomas said glaring about. "Instead, hell, you're strung tighter than a bolun in a gale."

"I'll be —" She bit off the word "fine" dangling on the tip of her tongue. The word annoyed him and Nathan both. In truth, she felt the best she had in days, nay weeks. At the same time, however, emotions jangled just under the surface, like sunburned skin, ready to flare at the least touch.

"Do you need a moment to collect yourself? Need another drink?" Thomas suggested helpfully.

She looked down to find the freshly-filled cup was already empty.

Cate smiled up, appreciative of his earnest concern. "A few quiet moments," she almost said. The bare-faced fact was she had no notion what would give her ease.

"Look, have a care," Thomas said circumspectly from the corner of his mouth. He cast a warning glance in the general direction of the celebrants. "You're fit-to-kill looks won't go unnoticed. These women are not your run-of-the-mill skullerymaids and baker's wives."

"I know that," she huffed. "I was one of them for a good many years."

Thomas' mouth quirked. "Aye, I daresay you were," he said, ducking his head. "You'll know, then, the bloody row one wrong look can trigger. I'd bet on you to best the lot of them in a scrap, but t'would be better for all concerned, if we might avoid it altogether."

Words failing, she found his hand and gave it a promising squeeze.

"C'mon," he said, extending his arm. "Let's see if we might find a reprieve for both of us. And you have my word: no more talk of battles."

⌒◦⌒∾⌒

Cate and Thomas walked about, hanging to the edges of the gathering, avoiding any Revenges and hence, all battle-talk.

Eventually, the music and antics of a pair of identical twins performing all manner of acrobatics — tumbling from each other's shoulders, walking on their hands, and contorting their bodies to inhuman extents — made them pause, and then eventually sit. In between the performers' feats, dancers spun about, stomping the sand and hooting in drunken glee.

It was during one of those interims that, tapping her foot and sipping her drink, Cate began to notice a different kind of dance being performed, one much more subtle than the jigs and reels. It was a dance of the eyes, filled with longing when aimed toward Thomas, and enshrouded in a particular shade of green when aimed toward her. She had suspected something of the sort whenever she had been introduced, many of the women seeming to wish her not just off the island, but off the face of the earth. Her civil side wished to stand up and announce, at the top of her lungs, that she had no claim on him. The devious side, however, the one ramming inside like a bee in a bottle, made her shift closer to Thomas, pressing her thigh against his. She leaned a bit closer when he spoke, her hand resting on his arm, tossing her head and laughing just that bit gayer, begging her drink to be filled whenever his attention wandered. With smug satisfaction, she watched her efforts fan the fires of dislike like a bellows, until their glares were hot enough to forge iron.

Thomas occasionally cocked a severe brow, wondering what she was at. A bat of her eyelashes was his answer; he rolled his eyes, looking away. She felt the tart and manipulative wench, but damn them all!

One particularly lingering gaze from a black-haired beauty caught Cate's eye.

Following it as easily as a ship's anchor line, she found Thomas staring back. The sight made Cate see her own shade of green.

"You've an admirer," she observed, magnanimity winning out.

Looking like a lad with his hand in the biscuit jar, Thomas broke his stare and buried his nose into his drink. "I've duties."

His intent might have been resolute, but it couldn't command his eyes, which all too soon strayed back across the flames and lingered.

Cate shifted discontentedly and buried her nose into her own drink. Truth be told, Thomas owed her nothing in the way of excuses or explanations. Tall, broad-built and well - favored, he had his pick of the women, and he knew it.

At one point, Thomas abruptly rose and said "I shall return, directly."

Cate watched over her shoulder as he pushed through the crowd and disappeared into the night. A quick glance across the fire found the black-haired beauty gone, as well. Only a fool would think that a coincidence.

She squirmed in mild discomfort. Her cup was empty... again, and the call-of-nature was strong. She glanced around. Everyone was occupied by gaiety, partners and drink. A constant parade of people led to and from the bushes; the single ones were answering the call-of-nature; the pairs being called by a different nature's voice. Either way, the numbers made the possibility of stumbling over them in the dark too high to be agreeable. A safer realm was the privies, near to hand. She didn't wish to dwell on what Thomas was at just then, and logic dictated that he'd be at it a bit longer. There was plenty of time.

The privy door handle, identical to the rope fancy-work seen on board, made Cate smile. The mark of the Island-Which-Shall-Not-Be-Named being an island of sailors was inside, as well: a bucket of tow at the ready. She had barely hitched her skirts and sat, however, before hearing footsteps—heavy, and most definitely male—approach. She stiffened at hearing whoever it was stop just outside, near enough to block the light shafting through the dried wood's cracks. Sitting very still, she leaned and listened. The creak of leather and breathing confirmed her suspicions: a man, waiting.

"Have you forgotten what you went in there for?" "Thomas!" Cate yelped.

He wasn't smiling when she finally came out.

"You were gone," she said, in her own defense.

"I only stepped away to have a word with my men. I saw you skulk off like a sneakthief. Why the hell didn't you just go off like everyone else?" he growled, with a curt swipe toward the bushes.

"Because I still remember what happened another time I *just went off*. Surely, you recall it too." The incident had involved her being accosted and Nathan killing one of Thomas' crewmen.

Thomas' eye narrowed as a number of retorts rose and then were swallowed down. Exhaling heavily through his nose, a firm hand at her waist guided her back toward the fires. Within a few steps, however, he slowed at the prospect of rejoining the ribaldry. Cate wasn't sorry for it. The dark and relative quiet was a glorious reprieve, the nearest thing to privacy enjoyed in many a day.

Stopping, Thomas leaned against a palm and crossed his arms, the firelight gilding his profile. He fell into a pensive silence, leaving Cate to watch the vying and maneuvering for a man's attention. Flashes of pale thighs were proof of the extents to which far too man were willing to go.

"These women shouldn't be flinging themselves about. I mean, these are married women... with husbands... somewhere," she blurted at yet another couple darting off into the trees.

It took a moment for Thomas to return from wherever his thoughts had taken him.

He turned slightly to regard her. "You never struck me as the iron-laced type."

Cate bit her lip at sounding far more judgmental than intended. She didn't like herself for it, but there it was, as bold as the scores of men and women coupling in plain view. It wasn't the act which she found so irksome. Lord knew that was nothing new! It was Nathan's remarks of "doing it before a cheering crowd" ringing in her head; it was far too easy to imagine him there just then, doing that very thing, with one of these all-too-willing partners.

"Some of these women haven't seen their husbands or particulars, or whatever the hell you wish to call them, in years, with no notion if they ever will. It wouldn't be out of line to say these women are probably maintaining the same fidelity as their men," he added, with a wry snort.

Cate winced. What sailors did ashore was no secret.

"Don't look so shocked," Thomas chuckled, nudging her with his elbow. "I fancy you women get just as lonely as we men. Seems an amicable solution all around. Hell, Nathan's kept many a wife warm and many a night."

Cate turned her back, not wishing to hear that painful truth.

"It's sort of a part of our code to offer warmth and comfort to a wife in need," Thomas added, in a lame attempt to rectify his blunder.

"Just doing his part to help the cause, I suppose," she shot coldly over her shoulder. "Brotherly duty?"

"Something like that. Lots of us men-o'-the-sea have wives, and it's bothersome to leave them knowing they'll be alone mebbe for years."

"So, bedding them is some kind of fair exchange? I'll bed yours, if you'll bed mine?"

"Aye," he declared, cheered by his point finally prevailing. Then he frowned, rubbing his chin. "Although it don't quite sound the same coming from a woman."

Cate snorted. "Sorry to disillusion."

An uncomfortable silence fell between them. Cate sidled sideways out of his reach. Between an inner voice screaming *"Get off your high-horse, missy! You only lasted five years, before you flung yourself at the first man to come along,"* and the mental pictures of Nathan, who would never go wanting on an island of lonesome women, the entire discussion was too unsettling. She sought for a change of subject, and yet Nathan was still firm in her mind.

"I'm sensing a certain amount of, ahem, ill-will regarding Nathan," she observed.

"Half can barely contain their joy at the thought of his arrival, while the other half seem ready to gut him on sight."

If Creswicke had been the prime topic of discussion, Nathan had been the second. Her analysis was no exaggeration. How he managed to peeve so many, so thoroughly was the wonder? Knowing Nathan, it had to have been something to do with the bedroom, affairs of the heart.

"When was the last time you two were here together?" Cate asked, delicately.

"Oh... ehh... twelve, mebbe fifteen years ago. And no, I have no notion what the hell Nathan did to warrant this reception. God only knows," Thomas intoned with a roll of his eyes.

He peered back toward the fires over the edge of his cup. "Damned difficult to overlook daggers being thrown, in the figurative sense, so far, that is. Have to be a grass – combing dolt not to see they have us in their sights."

"Those daggers are for me," she corrected.

"You?" he said, lowering his drink. "You haven't been here long enough to gain that many enemies."

"Because of you." Now, Cate was the one to roll her eyes. Surely, he couldn't be that dense!

"Me?!"

Cate ticked off her points on her fingers. "I came with you. You haven't left my side. You are with me, ergo, you aren't with them." She angled her head toward a log being thrown on a nearby fire. "Those are the fires of jealousy being stoked."

Thomas considered, and then his shoulders dropped. "Ahh, the mysteries of the womanly mind."

"Not so mysterious, not really," she said tartly, smiling at his naiveté. "Just very alert to competition, rendering you all the sweeter prize."

"Is that what the hell that was out there?" A sweep of his hand indicated the fireside which they had so recently vacated. "And avast those cow-eyes; you know exactly of which I speak."

Cate ducked her head and nodded.

Tall, fair, comely... so very comely, she thought, looking up. Another surge of jealousy rose, along with some alarmingly dark thoughts.

"Make your choice very carefully, m'lad," she sighed, conceding to the inevitable.

Thomas crossed his arms, hunching his shoulders. "You make it sound like I'm shopping for a horse."

"Yes, well, something to ride, at any rate."

They stood in strained silence, making a point of watching the crowd.

She viewed the islanders with a resigned disappointment. Nathan's proposition of her making friends there had been a startling, although not unpleasant one. Living among two hundred men, she couldn't deny the sound of a feminine voice had been appealing. In retrospect, it was probably why she had so readily overlooked Prudence's shortcomings, much to everyone's dismay: the girl had been another female with which to laugh, share thoughts and just muse on the day-to-day.

Making friends was a long-lost talent, a skill which had never been polished to perfection. Her early girlhood had been isolated, what few possible friendships narrowed by her parents' concerns of associations with those below her station. When sent off to Charles Town, she had been too wild and willful for the genteel citizens to make any friends. It was at school that she found her first real, true friend: Mairi. It was that friendship which had delivered her to Scotland and, shortly after, Mairi to her death. After marriage, Brian's sister was the nearest thing to a friend. At the same time, however, it had been very clear that she would always be Brian's sister first, which made a great many confidences unsharable. After the war, and with Brian gone, survival had occupied every energy. For a while, Nathan had been her friend, but he was now her love, which put him in an entirely different category.

Thomas filled that role now, she thought looking up. Thank the gods, he had refused her advances months ago, for lying with him would have rendered that status impossible, and it would have been a pity to lose his friendship, for she had become so very dependent on him.

"I wish to hell I knew what that smirking worm was up to." Thomas' voice jerked Cate from her machinations.

She blinked to find him staring at Lesauvage through the milling crowd, a woman now astraddle his lap.

"You don't trust your fellow member of the Brethren?" Cate asked, lightly.

He made a rude noise in the back of his throat. "I trust him like I trust a sleeping scorpion: it doesn't have to wake to kill you. He's begrudged me the air I breathe since the day we crossed hawses. Slitting my throat in the night and taking my ship he'd do out-of – hand."

"He speaks as if he and Nathan were long lost brothers," Cate said, recalling their brief conversation.

Thomas made another hawking noise. "If you call going at each other with swords— which is what they were doing the last time I laid eyes on them—brotherly affection, then aye. It was something about a wench, as I recall. Sorry," he was quick to add, at seeing her flinch.

"There's no ignoring what Nathan is," Cate mumbled into her drink. "What he *was*."

"That remains to be seen."

He looked down at her, long and significant. "And then, again, perhaps not."

Seeing his cryptic message being ignored, Thomas swung his attentions to Lesauvage once more.

"'Tis always the chance the Little Sausage and Nathan mended fences, whilst I was away." Thomas spoke with the conviction of one thinking the moon might suddenly turn purple.

Cate closed one eye, trying to recall earlier that day—Gads, it seemed days, not hours ago!—when the *Brazen* had first opened the bay. "Your man said Pengelly and Pomphrey had been in the same port. That implies pirates and privateers working together?"

It sounded akin to the lion lying down with the lamb.

Thomas smiled faintly. "There's none so much of a difference as you might think. Pirate today, privateer tomorrow, pirate the next: it's merely a matter of which side you ship your oars, who is whoring for whose coin."

Cate nodded vaguely. Nathan's analysis had run much in the same line: privateers were wolves for hire, the lowest-of-low, willing to do someone else's dirty work for a price.

"For the men, it's often no more than a matter of who's buying their rum. For the captain, it's more a matter of whose coin presents the greater promise. In these waters, that was Creswicke's," Thomas added grimly.

Thomas fixed his gaze on the *Revenge's* captain once more. "Aye, he's up to something, or was," he added, considering. "Us showing up might have put his sails aback for a bit, but he won't be all-standing for long."

He fell into another distance silence. "Damned near an entire fleet were all at the Pass. The *Brazen*, her comrade-in-destruction, and now the *Revenge*: that's quite the rogue's gallery."

"I thought they came with Creswicke." A shoulder twitched. "Mebbe."

Cate shifted closer, the darkness and forest looming behind them suddenly threatening. "What does it all mean?"

Thomas sighed, growing even more grim. "Nothing I wish to think about. Finding this place on the Pomphrey's chart was more than just a coincidence, that's for bloody sure. Ah, there's Bella. C'mon, I require a word with her."

Assuming the appearance of replenishing their drinks, Thomas steered a course to intersect Bella among the rum casks.

The island's matron eyed him and then fixed on Cate. "You haven't found a way to wipe that scowl off his face yet?"

"A word." Thomas' seriousness wiped the smile from Bella's face.

A subtle gesture led her aside. Casting an eye back toward Lesauvage's fire, he lifted his mug. "Smile and make like we're talking about the weather."

Behind the facade, Thomas related finding the island on the *Brazen's* chart, Bella nodding intently.

"It's not good, but it's not surprising," she sighed when he finished. "Men come and go from the Brethren all the time. That our secret might be kept is a feeble hope."

"Couple that with this rogue's gallery of ships popping up, our King-of-Rogues here included," he added, nodding toward Lesauvage, "and it smells like something is up."

"Another attack, you're thinking?"

"Another?" Thomas blurted, surprised. "Smile, remember?" Bella cautioned.

His lips writhed back as he said "You've been attacked before?"

"Now and again. Nathan and his capers have caused us many a woe; he doesn't care who chokes on his smoke. I've asked, pleaded with him to let this thing with Creswicke go, but he only thinks of himself."

Cate stiffened at hearing Nathan being so abused.

"Is that why everyone looks fit to spit when they hear his name?" Cate asked. Her cheeks were beginning to hurt from wearing the same smile for so long.

"Some of it," Bella said stiffly.

A number of remarks bubbled up, but Thomas beat Cate to it.

"You might back your sails a mite on him. He's leading Harte on a merry chase, as we speak."

Bella lifted her drink, as if in a toast, but her expression didn't soften. "It was the Company who visited the last time or two." She smiled, broad and genuine. "They made the mistake of forgetting we have homes and children here."

She winked. "We stung 'em hard. They learned we aren't just a bunch of innocent women."

"And hell hath no fury like a woman defending that," Thomas mused through an artificial laugh.

The conversation shifted to the weather as a group passed within hearing.

"So, Creswicke is dead," Bella said, once it was safe. She sighed, a little resigned and a lot perturbed. "The waters will be stirred up for sure, now."

"Nathan wasn't alone in it," Cate interjected, cutting a significant look at Thomas.

"No, he most certainly had help." Idly kicking at the sand, Thomas had the good graces to look guilty.

A faint smile crinkled the corners of Bella's eyes, making her look the benevolent mother. "You two always were like a hand-in-a-glove. I've heard a good bit; I'm not so fceble-minded as to not be able to fill in the rest."

Cate wondered who would be so foolish as to think Bella feeble. "What are you thinking?" the very person prompted.

Thomas turned and pointed at a nonexistent item of interest. "Gaston has always been a grasping cove. No telling what he's stooped to, now, but he's like a cat at the kitchen door waiting for its cream. There's always the hope he'd just haul anchor. What brought him to do so the last time?"

"Boredom and no rum," Bella said grimly.

"Damn! Little hope of that now. Very well, then, forewarned will be forearmed," Thomas declared finally. "We'll start rousing powder and shot ashore tomorrow. Are those still French 12's out there on the point?"

Bella nodded.

"Very well, I've just the thing. I've an extra watch aboard and gun crews with orders to open fire, if the *Revenge* even so much as looks like she means to open her ports," he said.

Thomas turned to leave, but Bella stopped him with a hand on his arm. She checked to assure no one was within hearing before saying "Have a care. Gaston's cornered, and he knows it. He—"

Thomas looked up over Bella's shoulder and swore. Cate rose on her toes to see Lesauvage striding toward them, arms spread in a grand welcome.

"Now, isn't this the conspiring little group?" The ferret-quick eyes darted from one to the other. "One might think you are planning to take the Golden Fleet. Come!" he went on, ignoring their declamations. "Conspiracies are always better made with the brilliance of the sun on our heads. Tonight we celebrate, eh, *mon ami?*"

The latter was aimed at Thomas while an arm was hooked around Cate and steered her away.

Lesauvage guided Cate toward his fireside throne. With a quickness surprising for such a large man, Thomas inserted himself between them just as Cate poised to sit. Then, exclaiming, as if spotting a long lost friend, the latter curved an arm about her, and steered her away. Across the fire, after a certain amount of jostling and shuffling of a bench's occupants, they sat, Lesauvage glaring sourly through the flames.

Cate craned her head, looking expectantly around, and then regarded Thomas next to her, hunched and in a sulking brown study. "Wasn't there a long-lost friend you —?"

Thomas blinked and jerked back to the present. "Hell no!" He shot a withering glare across the fire. "I might have to look at the verminous weevil, but damned if I'm going to rub elbows with him or oblige you to do the same."

The art of conversation and pleasantry abandoning him, Thomas fell silent, leaving Cate to her own devices. Looking around, she found that, in the short time since she and Thomas had stepped away, the general scene had degenerated, the jubilation now resembling debauchery. The silken finery had suffered a host of indignities: laces flapped, bodices hung open, skirts sullied and torn. At her elbow was a man with a woman astride him, her bare breasts jouncing like she was riding a stiff-legged cob at a hard trot some inches from Cate's face. A short distance further down, another was being served by a woman on her knees. Cate touched a finger to her ear — the man next to her was a talker, keeping all within earshot abreast of his increasing ecstasy — and looked away, not out of embarrassment or consideration — the pair were beyond noticing or caring — but because she just didn't wish to witness. Turning her head brought the black-haired woman, the one who had been eye-locked with Thomas earlier, into view, now standing expectantly beside him.

Thomas obligingly moved over, making room, pushing Cate all the closer to her active neighbors.

Gripping her drink hard enough to make her knuckles burn, Cate fixed on the sand at her feet, annoyed at seeing her own act — a hand on Thomas' thigh, leaning, pressing her shoulder against his, laughing brightly — albeit a heavy-handed version, being played out by Raven-head. With the two heads bent together, one light, the other dark, it wasn't necessary to overhear what Raven-head was about. Cate chanted to herself that Thomas' only obligation to her was friendship, and he had given that without reservation. She had made her choice, and now he had to be allowed to make his.

To Cate's other side, the female half of the copulating pair now joined her partner's vocalizations. At length, with a long querulous groan—and a gasp of relief, on Cate's part— the pair reached their glorious end. They rose and staggered away, codpiece swinging in the breeze.

The sight of Lesauvage pushing his way toward them caused Thomas to break off his intimate conversation and swear.

The Frenchman struck a stance before them, swaying slightly, the flamelight dancing on his face. "They tell me Creswicke is dead."

Thomas glanced at Cate, shifted and looked to his feet. "He is."

"*Bon*! I am not saddened to hear it. They say you were there." Eyes slightly unfocused, speech was slurred, gestures a bit grand suggested he was drunk. On the other hand, as he came around the fire, his step had been as steady as a preacher's.

"In a manner o' speakin'."

Awaiting further elaboration, Lesauvage's jaw worked. Thomas stared, mute. "They say you had a hand in it," the Frenchman finally prompted.

Thomas leaned back and casually crossed his arms. "I did. Nathan gutted him; I just finished the job. He'll be looking for his head for all of eternity." The last came loud enough for the benefit of all.

Lesauvage's dark eyes cut to one side, and then the other at the resulting toasts and cheers. Murder flared in the black depths, but then was mastered. "One would think Blackthorne would have been overjoyed," he said, when the crowd had sufficiently quieted.

"He was."

The dark eyes sharpened. "Some claim Blackthorne was killed." "They were mistaken," Thomas said, coldly.

The musicians struck up a new jig. With a squeal of elation, Raven-head leapt up, begging Thomas to dance with her. Finally she prevailed and he rose.

With a cry of "*Danser tout le monde! Venez! Rejoignez nous !*" Lesauvage swept Cate up. As he whirled her around the fire, he whooped and beckoned for more to join in, until there was barely room to move.

Cate leaned as far from Lesauvage as his arms would allow. The evening's activities hadn't improved his pungency, drink, vomit and urine rendering him all the more ripe. They bumped and jostled, his hand driving her hip into his crotch at every turn. On the second or third pass, however, he slid off into the night, taking her with him. She dug in her heels, a scream at the ready.

"Shh! Calling out could go very badly for all concerned" hissed into her ear cut her off.

An iron arm at her back propelled her through the bushes, a vise-like grip on her arm grinding the bones of her arm whenever she faltered.

"Fear not, *mon cher*," he crooned. "All I desire is a walk in the moonlight and to enjoy this second treasure."

The light and music faded behind them, leaving only the sound of her escort's heavy breathing and the crash of several men on a parallel path nearby. Ducking to keep the branches from slapping her in the face, Cate kept a sharp eye, striving to keep her bearings. Judging by the glimpses of water twinkling through the greenery, they were roughly following the shore.

At last, they drew to a halt. Lesauvage's unfocused eyes settled hungrily on the edge of her bodice, and the rapid rise and fall of her bosom. "Nathan has an eye for beauty, to be sure, but his tastes usually run toward those with other... eh, shall we say, talents?"

Cate writhed against his grasp. The bushes moved with his men closing in, hopes of escape fading with it. She had a knife, but it was deep in her pocket. Still, she worked her free hand through the layers of fabric, searching.

"I beg pardon?" Her ignorance wasn't entirely a ploy. Her heart hammering like a beat-to-quarters drum made it difficult to hear.

Lesauvage took her failure to hear as an excuse to press himself all the tighter against her. She turned her head, his fetid breath now hot on her face. He grabbed her chin and brought her back, his fingers gouging the flesh. "Allow me the benefit of some of these talents, and it could go very well for you."

He gave her arm another vicious twist. Cate clamped her lower lip between her teeth.

Be damned if she would cry out as he seemed to wish!

Long ago, the lesson of an opportunity missed was often an opportunity lost had been learned. Not calling out the moment Lesauvage had pulled her off into the darkness was the first one missed. Screaming now would probably mean getting slapped.

Strains of music were reaching them; hopefully a good scream would reach back.

Bracing for the blow sure to come, Cate filled her lungs, and opened her mouth to scream. Lesauvage, however, took it as an invitation and clapped his mouth over it, kissing her. It was a choking attack, his tongue plunging deep down her throat. His eye caught a movement, and he jerked away, leaving her gasping and spitting out the rancid taste of him. Men, as silent as the shadows from which they appeared, encircled them, and her heart sank: Revenges, come to either cheer their captain on or join in the fun.

One look at Lesauvage's face, waxen as the moon, however, revealed that they were not his men.

Thomas stepped out from among the newcomers into a band of moonlight, Al-Nejem appearing nearby. Lesauvage spun Cate around, holding her before him like a shield, a knife at her middle. Thomas advanced a step; the blade pressed harder.

"The lady is with me." Thomas said impassively.

"She desired — "

"Then, she was mistaken."

Knife poised, the Frenchman darted a furtive look in several directions.

"If you're looking for those coves back there," Thomas said, angling his head behind him. "They were too fascinated with their own cocks to take notice of us. We should have slit their throats, but, alas, it's only their heads bashed."

Thomas moved a step closer. "You've one decision, mate. Make it a smart one."

The Lovelies were armed to the gills, but Thomas had drawn none. That condition, however, made him no less lethal. There was a murderous stillness about him. Only a lock of hair, silver in the moonlight, stirred at his ear, and his hands worked at his sides. It was easy to imagine those big hands seizing her captor and snapping him like a twig.

Apparently, Lesauvage's imagination ran in much the same lines. "Do you aim to kill me with your bare hands?"

"Would anyone mourn if I did?"

As it had since Lesauvage dragged her off, Cate's mind had raced, trying to think what to do. Being barefooted made stomping her captor's boot ineffective; long skirts rendered going for his knees or crotch a dubious proposition. Her most promising ploy was her favorite: pretending to faint, slumping forward, and then arching backwards, whipping her head back into his face.

Focused on Lesauvage he might have been, Thomas still

saw her thinking and cut her a quelling look. In two strides, he
closed in, the two men now virtually nose-to-nose, Cate wedged
between them.

"Give her over, and we'll settle this like—" Thomas began.

The crash of someone pushing through the bushes cut him
short. The sound grew louder, the branches trembled, and Bella
broke out. Elbowing her way through the surrounding men,
she assessed the situation with one sharp glance. She stepped
around, wedging her shoulder between the two, thrusting her
face into Thomas'.

"Your quarters are ready." The announcement was directed
at Thomas, but the authority with which she delivered it made
everyone twitch.

Her shoulder wormed a little deeper between the two men.
"Allow me to show you the way."

Not a soul present took it as a mere request. The body at
Cate's back vibrated with the desire to draw blood and to save
face. Bella felt Lesauvage's hesitation and slid him a severe eye
over her shoulder. The grasp on Cate loosened, and the knife
lowered. Amid the sound of pistols uncocking and blades
sheathing, Cate sidled out of his reach. Thomas put out his hand,
and she grabbed on. Before she took a step, however, Lesauvage
lunged to seize her by the wrist. Thomas hissed a warning, hand
poised over his cutlass.

"We'll speak again," the Frenchman growled, and then
retreated.

In a sweep of skirts, Bella turned and led off, back from
whence they had all came, Thomas and Cate close on her heels.
Cate felt more than heard Al-Nejem and his men, following as
silent as the shadows. Lesauvage struck a similar route, but
angled away, his lumbering crash marking his progress. As they
pushed through the undergrowth, Bella in the lead, Cate looked
at that ramrod straight back and wondered again who would
either be foolish or brazen enough to cross her? If their reception
upon arrival was any indication, Thomas had transgressed
sufficiently to earn an admonishment. Nathan had definitely
drawn similar displeasure, who knew how or why?

They broke out onto a well-trodden path, and Bella drew to
a halt.

"You probably would have done everyone a great service by
just killing him and be done with it," she said to Thomas, in a
voice lowered.

Thomas cocked a brow at the elder, and then Cate. "I would
have had others not been in the middle of it. I've a notion it will
come to that soon enough."

Bella looked off in the direction Lesauvage had gone. She sighed as one does when faced with an unpleasant, yet necessary task. "Well, best go defuse the situation. There's but one way to cool hot heads, isn't there?"

The pewter-colored eyes swiveled with significance on Cate, who mechanically nodded. Yes, she knew exactly what Bella referred to, what was expected of her. She also wasn't of a mood to stand there in the dark and quibble over whether it would or wouldn't happen.

Bella stepped aside and motioned them up the path. "You're in Number One. You know it?"

Thomas scowled, but then nodded, resigned.

"'Hot heads easily cooled?" he echoed, watching Bella disappear. "We men are so much clay in you women's hands?"

Still a bit shaken, Cate smiled unsteadily. "For the more dull-witted and gullible, I'm afraid so. C'mon, before your male pride is bruised any further."

The path they followed soon intersected a broader one. Wide, busy and lined with dwellings, this path had to be the settlement's version of "main street." Thomas turned with the resolution of one knowing his destination and turned, Cate striving to keep pace with his long stride. The shacks they passed might have been varied in the materiel in the way of constructed, but they were unified in having only one room, sailcloth doors and palm frond roofs. At the foot of a much smaller path, Thomas veered, going up it with the determined step of the doomed. A flower-laden bush being pushed aside revealed a somewhat larger shack.

Cate stepped onto the hatchcover serving as the shack's stoop, but then hesitated at the threshold. The night was too glorious to be abandoned. Suddenly, the confines of walls were a choking prospect.

"Might we just sit for a bit? It's been a hellish day; I just need time to unwind."

Seeming to be much of the same mind, Thomas motioned her to a stool. He sat at her feet and leaned back.

Much to her pleasure, Cate found that from where they sat provided a view of both the street and bay. A fat moon, hanging in a lopsided smile, reflected on its placid surface. Leaning back her head, she closed her eyes and focused on the distant, sound of the water lapping on the beach.

Cate opened her eyes to look down at the blond head at

her knee. A few minutes ago, Thomas had been coiled, ready to kill. Now he sat at her feet, bent and remote, deep in his own thoughts. He and Nathan knew each other to the point of knowing each other's minds; she envied that friendship, and the ease and comfort which came with it.

"Might I ask what you did to prompt Bella to scold you like you were seven?" she asked.

Thomas' head came up, taking a moment to smoke her meaning. She cocked a brow: yes, she had overhead his conversation earlier that day.

"T'was... nothing. A little..." He cleared his throat and finally managed "Malingering. It wasn't my fault, not really, not entirely, at any rate," he muttered at the end, more to himself.

"Careful, m'lad," Cate chuckled. "You're beginning to sound more like Nathan by the minute."

The bit of his neck, visible between collar and hairline, reddened. "It wasn't me charged with it."

Cate considered, and then, recalled the little wave and meaningful looks exchanged in the evening's twilight. "Celia?!"

Thomas jerked and glared up. "Perceptive wench, aren't you? That's gotta drive Nathan mad."

Silence was consent, however. Her surprise didn't come so much at Celia—she was a handsome woman—but the notion that a herbwoman might have any life beyond healing. Women of her calling were usually old and twisted, something more akin to a fish hag, living a solitary life.

It explained a lot as to why he hadn't been concerned when Celia had led her away. "Malingering," Cate mused. "I've heard it called a lot of things, but rarely that."

Thomas cut a sideways look and saw nothing less than a complete explanation would be accepted. A jug sat in the doorstep like a waiting gift. He pulled the wooden plug, sniffed and took a drink. Wiping the mouth, he held it up in offering, supporting it as she sipped.

He extended his hand to display one of the many scars. "I had a shiver in my hand. It kept festering, wouldn't heal... at least, I think that was the case," he said, twisting his jaw thoughtfully. Shaking his head, he went on. "It was odd having to go out there. Whenever someone was ailing, she usually found them. But somehow, that particular time, I found myself out there."

Thomas gulped, flexing the hand where it rested on his leg. Going distant, he pensively stroked a scar. "I know it sounds lame, but the next thing I knew—" He coughed, blushing. "Well, anyway, it was 'the next thing I knew' several times that day, and the next... and the next."

Cate looked off, a bit discomfited by the visions invoked.

His eye drifted in the general direction of Celia's shack and he smiled, wistful. "She's an incredible woman, much like you," he added, with a self-conscious glance. "Intelligent, willful and, God help me, can make a man forget what he is about."

"She's incredible," he sighed dreamily. "She knows things about a man that—" The blush deepening, he coughed again. "We had nothing but time to explore it all..."

He clamped his lower lip between his teeth and shook his head. "The welfare of the entire island is in her hands: men, women, children... infants—"

"But, a bit of passion doesn't—" Cate began.

His cold eye stopped her. "Apparently, it does for her, at least."

Thomas spread his hands to barely his shoulder's width. "A small lad, barely this long, fell to a fever. Like I said, she knows when someone is in need... except that day."

Cate mutely nodded. Yes, she knew exactly what he meant. She had seen and been told things in that cabin which could only be explained by powers far beyond normal.

"When they finally came looking, it was too late. By the end of the day, the poor thing was dead." The last came in a tight whisper. "But, you didn't—"

Thomas looked up, eyes shimmering with wetness. "Aye, but I did," he said heatedly. He drew a long breath and blew it out. "She represented lying with me robbed her of her sight."

"Robbed?"

"Well, not exactly robbed. Damnation, I'm making a hash of this!" He grabbed the jug and took another drink. "I distracted her, lessened her powers: take your pick," he said, with a frustrated swipe.

Thomas shifted on his haunches, his shoulders jerking. "Hell, you know how women can be when it comes to their children. They swarmed me like a horde of enraged bees, looking for anyone and everyone to blame."

Looking once more in the direction of the unseen shack, he gulped. "There was something there, something I hadn't found anywhere... not back then, at any rate," he added quickly, with a self-conscious glance at Cate. "It wasn't love, just two bodies coming together—"

He balled his fist, shaking with resolve. "I meant to never come back, except—" "Except for me," Cate said, dully. "But Nathan said coming here was your idea."

"Aye, for him to bring you here, not me," Thomas finished, even more miserable. "I tried to tell him, but you know how he is when he takes a notion about you. Hell and fury won't sway him."

Cate nodded, distractedly. Nathan's single-mindedness about coming there was all too clear. Heaven only knew the amount of wrangling Thomas must have endured before finally surrendering.

"Thomas, I'm so sorry."

His hand found hers on his shoulder and squeezed. "S'all right, lovely. The measure of a man is in how he faces disappointments."

Cate considered that it might be said of a woman as well. "Perhaps you could secretly —" she began helpfully.

Thomas smiled, as one did in the face of good, although misguided intentions. "Nay, she won't risk it. Those healing powers are her life. To ask her to give it up would be like asking Nathan to give up the sea." He blew a long resigned sigh, working one hand hard into another. "Now, I just have to do the same."

Cate didn't press the point. A one-night tryst was an inane notion. The ache she suffered for Nathan would never be satisfied by a stolen night. One bite of food to a starving man is often more torturous than hunger itself.

Her hand found his shoulder again. He covered it with his, warm and solid, acknowledging what neither could put to words. They sat that way for a long time. Surrounded by bushes, the shack sat slightly apart from the rest of the dwellings. Whether the bushes or the shack came first was difficult to tell, but it gave the impression of ducking behind them, like so many amorous pairs seen that night, seeking that hard-found bit of privacy. It led one to wonder why she and Thomas had been put there? She had expected to be put up in some dormitory-like situation or just sleeping under the stars. A roof overhead was an unexpected luxury.

From where they sat, the campfires were no more than a molten glow low on the night sky, the music now drifting in broken strains. If this place was like any other pirates ashore, the carousing was sure to continue until dawn broke. A group of merrymakers staggered down the street, hanging onto each other, breaking into song from time to time. Presumably, in their rum-soaked minds, they thought to be singing together, but the lyrics and tunes were as broken and uneven as their steps. Their passing made the ensuing quiet in their wakes all the more remarkable, allowing the solitude to settle in.

Thomas' loneliness was infectious. She missed Nathan, badly. A warm breeze brushed her face, soft as the moth's wing, stirring the palms overhead. Caribbean nights were wondrous, but she had become accustomed to Nathan sharing them with her. To look at it now only drove the loneliness deeper.

Cate propped her chin in her hand, gazing at the bay and the unseen sea beyond. "Is he out there?" she heard herself say.

Thomas' head came up to follow her gaze. "Oh, aye, he's there." "How can you tell?" she asked, looking down at him.

Grinning up, he bumped her leg with his shoulder. "Because, whilst you two were gone, the world went considerably dull. He's back and coming for you. Nothing would stop him from that."

Thomas went quiet, meditatively flexing his hand. "I envy you two, what you have.

What Nathan has, at any rate."

"Has he... said *anything*?" she asked cautiously. "As to what or how he feels about... me?" The last came in an incoherent mumble.

"You mean that he loves you?" Thomas laughed, loud enough to elicit a startled shriek from a bird in a nearby bush. "He says it all the time."

"I haven't heard it," Cate said, industriously brushing at a non-existent spot on her skirt. It was foolish and silly to put so much credence into one, prized, hard-sought and so very treasured word, but it would have made so very much difference. Assuming was one thing; knowing, hearing it was quite another.

A big hand closed over hers to stop it. She looked up into blue eyes, solemn and intent. "Listen to him. With Nathan Blackthorne, isn't what he says, but what he doesn't say."

"Now, you're sounding like Pryce."

"Good!" Releasing her, Thomas sat back. "He's probably the only other soul—aside from you—that knows him as well as I. Like I said, lovely, the man died for you. You can't ask much more than that."

A movement at the end of the doorpath caught her eye. Half in the shadows stood a woman, swaying her hips, ducking her head in invitation, her blonde hair flaring nearly white in the moonlight.

"Like bees to honey," Cate mused. "It looks like your next chance to be magnanimous is waiting."

Thomas' body was eloquent with temptation. Finally, he slumped, decision made. A regret-laden wave sent the lass on her way, disappointment enough to go all around.

"As I've said, I've... duties," he said, the last word barely audible.

Looking up at her, he scowled and laid a testing hand on her arm. "You're cold."

"A bit," she reluctantly conceded, wrapping her arms about herself. It seemed to have become a permanent condition these days.

Thomas rose to his feet and put out a hand. "C'mon, then, to your bed and your rest. You're falling asleep where you sit. I'll never hear the end of it, if you were to tumble off and break something."

He went inside and rustled about, eventually striking a light. Cate stepped in and stopped.

Given the primitive surroundings, she had expected to sleep relatively rough: a cot or hammock or perhaps just a pallet on the dirt floor. True enough, there was a bed, but not the common, wooden-framed one. This was a real, full-fledged bed, as might be found in a manor house, with carved spiral posts, and cherubs and garlands carved at the head and foot. Hard use, tropical heat and humidity taken their toll on the Berlin-blue damask curtains and woodwork, but it was a glorious bed, so vast it took up nearly half the room.

"That conniving—" Thomas stopped short and only shrugged at Cate's questioning look. "Bella's notion of a jest."

He offered no further explanation, leaving Cate to find the humor on her own. Perhaps it was in the bed itself, something so grand and elegant now sitting on a dirt floor. The chipped cherubs' noses and chins gave it all an odd, comical look. A hammock rigged in the corner, the dented basin on the rough-hewn washstand, and the chamberpot's chipped handle poking out from under it all seemed to mock it. Still, if the island's matron had intended to be funny, it escaped her.

"How...? I mean... where...?" Cate stammered, still in awe.

"Pirate," Thomas said simply.

A rustling sound in the corner made Thomas whirl around, hand hovering at his sword. A small mouse-like creature rose from the floor.

"Announce yourself, lass," he barked, lowering his hand. "Or get yourself skewered."

A sharp gesture on Thomas' part beckoned the girl in. A strip of cloth was wound about her head in lieu of a proper cap, but a number of pale wisps hung about her narrow face. Her many times too-large frock looked like it was wearing her. She stood worrying her apron, turned up several times at the waist, her small, round eyes, which only enhanced the mouse impression, never leaving Thomas.

"Is there something...?" Cate prompted.

Remembering herself, the child bobbed a curtsy, her bare toes working into the dirt. "I'm Abigail — Tabby, for short — mum," she said in a voice so small Cate had to lean to hear. Her eyes widened further at recalling herself once more, and she quickly added "Yer servant, mum."

"Servant?"

"Aye, mum," Tabby said, with the measured patience of the young explaining the obvious. "To fetch and carry, and help you dress and brush your hair," she added, with a reproachful glance at Cate's head.

Cate inwardly sighed. The last thing she needed was a servant but, looking down into those doleful eyes, she suspected rejection might well be Tabby's undoing. Just then, she had neither the will, nor strength to deal with any of it.

"'Pears as though you are in fine hands!" Thomas declared. He frowned at the child, quailing at the sound of his voice, nearly darting back into her corner.

"Rest, lovely," he directed to Cate, instead. "It's been a long day."

"Where will you — ?" she asked, as he turned for the door. "I'm sure you would rest better in here."

Thomas touched his hat. "I bid you good e'en, fair ladies."

There is such a thing as being too exhausted to sleep.

In Thomas' absence, Tabby had stopped shaking enough to undo Cate's laces, before she laid down in her shift, groaning and stretching until her joints popped in glorious relief. The bed smelled mildly of mildew and old sweat, but the sheets were clean. After the last couple days, it was all that mattered.

Untold hours later, however, and Cate was still awake, her temples damp with sweat, the day's heat seeming to radiate from the walls. From the stoop came the periodic sound of Thomas shifting; from the hammock came soft whoofing sounds of Tabby, periodically whimpering in her slumber.

Cate ran a hand over the cold and empty space next to her, rendered all the more so by the vastness of the bed. Compared to the bunks and pallets upon which she had slept on of late, the bed was sublime, positively decadent. Such exuberant grandeur, however, wasn't meant to be occupied alone.

With a slight turn of the head, she could see through the window. The moon had set, leaving the stars to shine in their full glory. She and Nathan had spent many a night sitting on the f'c'stle on just such a night. The thought of him looking at those same stars just then brought him a bit closer. She closed her eyes and tried to imagine the *Morganse* under way: the Watch voices hushed, the mast shadows striping the starlit deck. Would she be reefed for the night or all sails aboard, like giant moth wings? If Nathan were pushing hard, he might be at the helm, the binnacle light glowing on his face. Or, would he be sitting in his chair in the cabin, making entries in his log? Or, hunched over a chart, his brow furrowed in thought?

It was late, Nathan's favorite time: the small hours between one day and the next.

When his watch was over, he would clomp down the companionway steps, just above their bunk. Going through the salon, he would scuff to a halt at the bunkside to undress. He'd come to her smelling of canvas, salt and his own spiciness, his skin chilled by the night. The muscles of her abdomen tightened at seeing his eyes gone dark with need. His skin, golden in the candlelight, rippled at her touch, his fingers twining in her hair as he lowered himself over her, blocking out the light... and the world, for the next while.

Cate closed her eyes and wrapped her arms about herself, imagining they were his, holding her, pressing his lips at that little place at the base of her throat, his hand sliding down her back, cupping her buttocks, pressing her against his hardness.

Thomas moved, his boots scraping the wood, and the spell was broken.

Just to assure that it wasn't all a dream, Cate touched the braid in her hair and closed her eyes again.

I'm here, luv.

She felt more than heard his voice, its raggedness vibrating in her chest. Squirming, Cate heaved a sigh, and finally succumbed to exhaustion.

13: BEAUTIFUL SISTERHOOD

T HE CLANG OF METAL-ON-METAL JERKED Cate upright, leaving her blinking and confused as to her whereabouts.

Some waif of a girl—Tabby, stood with the offending ewer in hand. Making her bob, she offered an unapologetic "G' morn', mum" and continued to fill the basin.

Groaning, Cate rubbed her face.

Island... Pirate wives... chambermaids... It all came back quickly, too quickly by her measure.

The night had not been kind. Cate recalled wistfully of when sleep had been something to look forward too, restorative and peaceful. That, alas, was now a distant memory. The restlessness which had haunted her since leaving Celia's cabin had produced dark dreams, unknown faces and hands coming at her, and Nathan floating face down amid a number of other bodies, his braids fanned out about his head.

She shuddered.

Cate's gaze drifted to the threshold and the stoop visible through it, now empty. "Where's Thomas? Thomas?" she repeated at Tabby's blank look. A gesture toward where he had slept brought a glimmer of recognition.

"Oh, him," the girl said, with a disinterested sniff. "He went off with Miguela. She had him by the balls and her tongue down his throat."

Cate regarded Tabby, wondering if, at that age, she had any notion of what that meant.

Miguela.

She mulled over the name, trying to recall being introduced to anyone bearing it, in hopes a face might come with it.

Nothing.

Upon reflection, perhaps it was just as well. Faces brought familiarity and, worst of all, clarity. A faceless partner kept visions of what Thomas was at—and there were no doubts there—

pleasingly muddled. A question formed, several questions, actually, but Cate resisted. Questions would only bring answers, ones she didn't wish to hear.

Her gaze drifted further around the room. Sometime or another, her dunnage had been delivered—Lord, had she been sleeping that hard? The lockers and small trunk, her blood box among them, lined the wall. A sense of invasion caused a tart remark to bubble up at seeing their contents—her sole possessions—arranged atop, meaning to check the girl for taking such liberties, but the wherewithal to do so failed to materialize.

Tabby stood fingering some of the items, a disappointed scowl contorting her face. "They represented you were a great lady." She fixed Cate with an accusing look as if she had a hand in that deception.

Ah, her speech coming back to haunt her again.

"They are mistaken," Cate said through a jaw-cracking yawn. "I *was*... once, but that's long since gone. I'm sorry," she added at seeing the slim shoulders sink.

"I never seen a great lady," the child said, in the small voice of one whose dreams had been bashed.

Laden with inexplicable guilt and hoping for atonement, Cate offered "I have. Many." The offer appeared to have fallen on deaf ears.

"I mean to be a great lady's maid one day. I mean to work in a fine house, so very far from here," Tabby added, with a loathing glare out the window. Her stomach growled loudly, and she sobered. "You'll miss your breakfast, mum, if you don't step along."

The thinly veiled threat was if Cate missed hers, Tabby would suffer, too.

Subjection didn't come easily, but it seemed to be expected, and so Cate did, using the time to allow the fog and lethargy to dissipate. She sat quietly as Tabby went about the imagined duties of a lady's maid. The girl proved to be an odd mix of being shy as a fawn, and yet as demanding and insistent as a Mother Hen, clucking disapprovingly at any misstep or shortcoming on her mistress' part. As she went through the motions of dressing Cate—a grand total of two pieces to her wardrobe—Tabby began a sing-song monologue of "A lady must never appear without a fichu. A lady must never appear without her stockings. A lady must never..." Cate started to respond, but discovered straightaway that the interruption was unappreciated.

And so, Cate was reduced to sitting like a doll, being washed and dressed. Still, even if Cate moved to stifle a yawn, Tabby flinched and shrank in anticipation of being cuffed. Seeing as much, Cate tempered her annoyance, to the point of clamping her lip between her teeth against the pain of the hairbrush being jerked through snarl after snarl.

At long last, Cate was declared presentable.

Tabby balked at seeing her head for the door. "He... him... he..." "Thomas. His name is Thomas."

The girl nodded impatiently. "He bid you to remain, until—"

"Yes, well, I could bloody well starve waiting for him, couldn't I?" Cate shot back peevishly and stepped out.

❦

At the threshold, Cate sagged at the impact of the day. She glared up at the sun, wondering how it came to be so high already.

Moody and jaded, Cate stepped off the stoop and struck off for the pavilion, Tabby a few paces behind, calling out at anyone who threatened to impede their way, shooing chickens and kicking at the dogs that playfully tugged at her mistress' skirts.

Many of the island's inhabitants were still caught up in the previous night's celebration. A good many more, however, were as out cold as the fires around which they sprawled. One was obliged to assume the prone figures were Revenges, for, while their ship sat looking positively abandoned, the *Lovely* and *Brazen* were a bee's nest of activity, with boats and barges bobbing alongside, whips lowering net load after net load. On the beach, barrels, bales, crates, boxes of stores were piled high as a man's head.

It would seem pirates chose wives with particular fortitude, for only a few looked the worse for wear after a night of carousing. Cate's earlier observations of the island being more like a working estate—minus a manor house, of course—was proved all the more valid. In the glare of a new day, the earlier visions of an idyllic haven mightn't be as far off the mark. Not quite Eden before the fall, she thought, dodging a troupe of pigs fighting over a scrap, but a place where violence, vice and poverty didn't dominate their lives. There was no pallor of starvation, no aimless wandering of the displaced, no confused stares of the demented.

Deep in those thoughts, Cate paid little heed to the dwellings she passed, until movement inside one caught her eye. Slowing, she squinted into the dim recesses, and then froze.

Two people laid on a pallet, the small slim legs of one wrapped about the long muscular columns of another, fuzzed with golden hair.

Tabby came up beside Cate and sighed, disinterested. "Miguela. They'll be awhile."

She skipped on. Cate spun and followed, her feet pounding the dirt at every step.

Coffee, hot and black, lots of it... now! her consuming thought.

Cate arrived at the pavilion even more fractious and miserable. The wreckage of the previous night's feast had been cleared away, the pig carcass gone, praise the heavens! Now the tables and benches were occupied by a scattering of people. A coffee pot was spotted on the hearth and she dove for it. Cup in hand, she turned to find the long-suffering look of a handmaid burdened with an unthinking and, by all evidence, untrainable mistress.

Cate allowed herself to be led to one and seated. Tabby left and Cate huddled over her coffee. Hot and black is what she needed. Tepid and bitter from being on the fire for so long is what she got.

Since her youngest years, Cate couldn't love a morning without several draughts, much to her mother's displeasure. It had been the cause of her being banished from the family breakfast table and sent to the kitchens. It had been just as well, for the conversation there had been far more interesting. It was there she learned her guttural Spanish.

"It's not Thomas' fault," broke into her brown study.

Cate looked up from her cup and down the table toward the source of the smirking remark: a woman, among several others, red-faced with contained mirth.

"Fault?" Cate echoed dully.

"Everyone knows you threw him out last night," said another, much to the amusement of all.

Cate sighed. Apparently, there were no secrets on an island, either.

Civility seemed to demand conversation, and so Cate groped for a subject. Meals seemed a good neutral ground. "Has he... eaten?"

"Ate enough for four, and he'll need it," said the first, with a dreamy roll of her eyes.

"Poor Miguela," sighed another.

"Lucky Miguela," snickered a third. "She won't be good for anything else for the rest of the day."

Their mirth could no longer be contained, and it burst out

in girlish peals. Eventually, they quieted and went back to their conversation. Tabby set a bowl before Cate filled with a local version of porridge. A plate clattered down next to it bearing fruit and fried fish, limp, greasy and cold. The homey scent of fresh bread hung in the air, but she was informed it had already been consumed by those who joined the day at a more seemly hour.

"Cook said elevenses aren't in her realm," Tabby announced, with a severe pitch of her brow. She sat next to Cate and set about her bowl of gruel.

Women at the end of the table chatted and laughed. Cate poked at her food, feeling entirely isolated, the space between them yawing like a chasm. There had been a time when, as wife of the laird, she had been the social hub. Those sitting down there would have sought her company, strove for her insights and counsel. Aside from losing Brian, the loss of that sense of belonging and purpose had been the most devastating. Now, they belonged, and she didn't.

"... *three days...*" Nathan's voice echoed back, his fingers thrust before her.

And quite possibly the longest three days of her life. The notion of striking up a friendship seemed less probable by the hour.

Cate shoved a bit of fish between her lips. The coffee's lingering bitterness rendered the fish palatable, at least for the first few bites. She started to push the plate away when she noticed Tabby's eyes following it with the avidity of youthful hunger. An inviting nod on Cate's part, and the girl fell upon it like one of Egypt's locust. At one point, Tabby stopped. Cate glanced, expecting to see the plate empty. Instead, she found Tabby frozen in mid – motion, a bit of fish hanging inches from her slightly agape mouth. She followed the girl's arrow-straight gaze to find Maram, standing among the stores coming ashore.

In the few months since she had first met him, Maram was growing in to a comely lad. Cate wasn't without sympathy for Tabby's gobsmacked gape. She'd suffered much the same in her youth. One wondered if there was such a thing as charm by association, for the *Lovely's* cabin boy was becoming a dark version of his captain's golden one and much – caressed, if the surrounded circle of females of all ages was any indication.

Those machinations brought Cate to another discovery about the island. Setting down her cup, she looked around to confirm her suspicions: for the remarkable number of children, there were precious few lads of Maram's age. There was the possibility of a plague of some sort had wiped them out. A scourge of another sort seemed more likely: boredom, known to mortally strike many a young man. Upon reflection, it didn't come as any great surprise. Given the general restlessness of boys at that age, and pirate blood running in their veins... well, apples rarely tumbled far from the tree.

"I don't believe I will have any need for—" Cate began, meaning to dismiss Tabby and ease her misery. She stopped, however, saving her breath. There was little to be gained in speaking to someone's back.

As Cate continued to sip, a gathering of children tumbled in the dirt before her, tagging one another and performing all manner of antics in hopes of drawing her attention. Cate watched, or rather tried to. Shoulders burning, neck aching, it was nigh impossible to keep from looking in the direction of Miguela's shack, cursing herself every time she did.

The urge was like holding one's breath; when the need to look was undeniable, she cut the briefest of glances—entirely futile—and then fixed once more on her cup, her knuckles white around it.

The rational part of her pointed out that Thomas was a full-blooded man and needed an outlet, as any one might...

You mean like Nathan?

Begrudging Thomas exercising his baser needs was being shrewish and ill-natured. "Well, call me shrew, then," she muttered into her cup.

Noting only then that her cup was empty, Cate rose and went to the hearth to refill it.

Turning, she found herself face-to-face with several of the women from the end of the table. Two or three stood apart, their arms crossed in displeasure.

Civility demanded introductions, and so Cate made the attempt. "Perhaps I should introduce—"

"Yes, everyone knows your name," said the nearest. "I'm Simona." Approximately Cate's age, she had a pug nose and intense gray eyes. Her black hair was secured by a strip of checked fabric about her head. Her accent was an odd mix of French and something else, perhaps Portuguese. "Do you aim to wait for him or would you prefer to come with us?"

Not looking toward Miguela's shack came with great difficulty; the decision came with ease. The women could have been on their way to scrub night jars and it would have been preferable to this waiting.

"I'm with you!"

Leaving the pavilion, they fell in straightaway with another group and headed up the path together. Cursory introductions were made—Aggie, Hope, Lygia, Banu among others—some being familiar from last night. The bulk, however, kept their distance, regarding Cate with the all too familiar coolness.

Initially, their route was the same as Celia's: inland, away from shore. Soon, however, they turned onto one of the numerous paths. The women fell into small conversations, pausing to call out greetings or wave as they passed sheds, barns, pastures and gardens.

"They say you're Nathan's?" asked an olive-complected, square-built one named Lygia.

Before Cate could respond, Banu, an almond-eyed beauty with blue black hair, multiple rings on her wrists and a reddish tattoo running from lower lip to chin, asked "How is Nathan?" with more than passing interest.

Compared to what? Cate thought moodily, but discretion preserved her. "Well, I suppose."

"'Well, I suppose,'" echoed from ahead. "I'd heard Nathan was aiming high, but he must have snuck into the manor this time!"

"Slumming are we, dearie?" hooted another amid the jeering laughter.

Banu turned enough to eye Cate critically. "You're waiting for Nathan, and yet you're bedding Thomas?"

"Cuckolding Nathan Blackthorne and with his best friend. Blimey, I like the sound o' that!" cried a Cockney voice from behind. She slapped Cate on the back. "Well done, dearie! Well done!"

"He's coming for her," announced Simona defensively.

"Oh, aye," snorted Lygia. Still fizzing with mirth, she dropped her voice to a rough imitation of Nathan. "'I'll be back, luv, as sure as the tides and the sun.'"

"Aye, just like me Charles was to return in a month," chuckled another. "That were six year ago."

Amid a chorus of laughter, several more claimed similar stories of false promises.

"Settle your bonnet, Cate," Banu assured. "We'll all be as grey as Aggie here, a'fore Nathan Blackthorne has the nerve to show his face here again."

"He'll come and you'll all have a crow for dinner," Simona called out loud enough for all.

Banu turned again, scowling. "Since when are you his defender? Marthanna was never of any notice to you."

A motherly pat on the arm drew Cate's attention to Aggie

next to her. "Don't let them devil you, lass," she said under the women's chatter.

A Dubliner, by her accent, and the eldest, if the silver hair escaping from her cap was any guide. Aggie's square face was as creased as a crumpled shirt, the deeper lines of good humor framing her eyes and mouth. The spring-green eyes held the spark of youth, but she walked with the hitching gait of a martyr to bad joints.

"Nathan has his assets, to be sure," Aggie assured.

"Do you know him?" Cate asked, both surprised and curious.

"Oh, aye, or used to, at any rate. 'Tis better to say I knew his mum, Sarah; like a sister she was to me, God rest her soul," she added, quickly crossing herself.

"In England?" Cate asked. She didn't recall Nathan ever mentioning living on the Green Isle.

"Oh, bless the saints, no!" Aggie laughed, a sound like crinkling paper. "Matelotage.

My Horace and I lived there for a time. D'ye know it?"

Cate shook her head. "I've only heard of it. Nathan mentioned it... briefly," she added, with a grimace. What she didn't say was the black loathing that mention wrought.

"I shouldn't be surprised." Aggie's bosom heaved with a sigh. "The puir lad was miserable. 'Twas a pirate's haven, to be sure, and not a place for the meek of heart." She wagging a warning finger, knobby and rough with age and work.

"What was Nathan like as a boy?" Cate asked anxiously.

"Wild as a spring hare, he was. He had her spirit, he did." Aggie's eyes went distant at the recollection. "He would play outside down by the water from sunup to sundown. Sarah would drag him in, kicking and screaming. Willful, he was. And how he loved to read! She was always casting about for books. The other lads would chivvy him, until he'd run off, and his blessed mum aged before her time with worry before he returned."

Sobering, Aggie fell quiet, smiling faintly.

"Nathan was devoted to Sarah. He'd collect little shells and trinkets and bits, and make her wee pictures of birds, and flowers and such, and then make up grand stories about them; I think the lad just desired to see her smile."

Aggie paused to wave to someone at the cooper's shed as they passed.

"He was a good lad," she went on, with a heavy-hearted sigh. "But he hated it so; Sarah was his only joy. He drove Ol' Beecher mad."

Cate turned her head to hide a smile. Like Matelotage,

Nathan rarely mentioned Beecher, calling him everything from "a buggering old spawn-o'-the-devil" to a "bile-laden blighter."

"He didn't care for Nathan, did he?" Cate asked, delicately.

"Oh, I think Beecher loved him, but he would have loved Ol' Nick himself, if he was Sarah's," Aggie said, considering. "Beecher loved Sarah above all else. It was the talk of Matelotage when the crusty scalawag came back with her. 'Twas a shock to see the likes o' him go so soft over a woman, but the harder the shell, the more tender the crab," she added, with a philosophical shrug.

"Sarah was a beauty, and Beecher... well, you know," the elder said, with a knowing wrinkling of her nose.

"No, I don't. I've never met him." A not so small part of Cate was grateful for that.

"The Lord saw fit to give Beecher many gifts," Aggie intoned to the heavens, "but beauty wasn't one. 'Tis probably why he resented the lad so: he was too pretty, just like his mum," she whispered, with a conspiratorial wink. "Sarah was a devoted mum, but Nathan was her favorite and everyone knew it, including Beecher. It had been quite a gesture for him to take those children in the way he did and raise them as his own, and Heaven help any puir unsuspecting soul what suggested else," she finished with another palm to the sky.

Whatever Beecher's motivations might have been — desire for a family, love of a woman or, by Nathan's estimation, a need to control everyone and everything — taking in a brood of bastards — which, in cold evaluation, was exactly what Sarah's children were — and raise them as his own was a touching gesture. It was easy to harbor romantic notions of a man capable of that.

"Nathan said his mother died," Cate said.

Aggie fell quiet. "Aye. She got with child; the Lord saw fit to take the both of them.

Beecher was beside himself with grief."

The old eyes filled with tears and her chin wobbled. Aggie's voice cracked as she went on. "He found Nathan in a corner, holding the dead babe. There was a terrible scene, with carryin' on and cryin'. He wouldn't come out; he wouldn't let go. It was enough to turn a soul's heart to stone."

Cate swallowed down the large lump which rose at the vision of a dark-headed boy cowering in a corner, clutching a lifeless bundle to his chest.

"You remind me of her."

Startled, Cate nearly stumbled. "I beg pardon?" she asked, swiping her cheek.

Aggie tipped her head, thoughtfully regarding her, wisps of silver hair stuck to the wetness on her cheeks. "Blessed Michael and Mary," she said, crossing herself again. "you remind me of her, Sarah. None so much to look at, but something, a spirit, mayhap."

The group drew to a halt at the edge of a field and prepared to take their leave, the interview coming to a far too early end.

"What about Beecher?" Cate asked urgently. There was so much she wished to know.

"Is he still alive?" At last mention, Nathan had no notion if the man still breathed and would readily curse him, if he did.

"Oh, I suppose so." Aggie sighed, disinterested. "He's too ornery for the Devil to have him, so I expect he has nay choice but to stay on this earth."

Aggie touched a hand on Cate's arm and leaned closer to say under the chatter. "If and when ye are to ever see the lad, give him a kiss and tell him his mum would be proud."

The hand tightened warmly. "God and Mary go between ye both and evil."

Reluctantly Cate waved good-by to Aggie, privately vowing to seek her out again. Perhaps, a friendship mightn't be impossible, but a longer visit was definitely something to look forward to. It felt a bit like sneaking behind Nathan's back, but the opportunity to learn about his past was too delicious to pass up. With a departing look over her shoulder, Cate followed Simona and the others into a field. There they joined those already working, and she soon found herself literally up to her knees in harvesting melons.

Cate fell easily into the rhythm of slicing the stems with her knife and pitching them into baskets. It felt good to tuck her skirts up into her waistband and work, good honest pure labor, productive and useful, enhanced by the instant gratification of seeing basket after basket filled, hurdle after hurdle being wheeled away. Toes in the dirt, living things under her hands, sweat streaming in her eyes, smells of vegetation and damp earth, her fingers going green with plant juice: it was heavenly!

A setting breeze blew; Cate periodically turned, lifting her face and her hair. This field, as was many of the others, was surrounded by wild roses, to keep trampling beasts and larger varmints away. At the center was a raised platform where boys roosted armed with slingshots. Boredom, however, led them pretending the platform was a maintop, and they battled imaginary boarders until a hiss and cuff called them back to their duties. Other children moved up and down the rows, bearing water buckets and a gourd, or plucking beetles from the plants, the more precocious shooting them at one another.

As Cate worked, she was aware of the chatty buzz of conversation about her. She exchanged words with a few, but only as perfunctory, work-related remarks. Still, she took pleasure in listening, even if she had no notion of who or what they spoke. After living among men for months, the sound of a female voice was a true pleasure. She was keenly aware of word making its way around as to who she was, several shifting further away as a result.

The conversation suddenly broke off. She straightened to find Thomas coming straight up the row toward her, with a determination which made several retreat.

"There you are," he shouted when within hailing distance. "Where the bloody hell have you been? Looked all over, nobody seemed to know where you were."

Thomas drew up before her, hand on his hips. "What the hell are you doing clear out here? I bid you to wait."

"No, you told Tabby, not me." Cate flared being reprimanded, like she was a six-year – old, especially within view of so many who had just mocked her. "I wasn't about to stand about and watch, while you—"

"While I what?" he demanded. "You were still abed, playing the mistress-of-the – manor, so I—" He stopped and reddened. "Well, hell, when two people have the same goal, it doesn't take long."

"No matter how brief the performance, I prefer not to watch," Cate shot back coldly.

So far as she was concerned, the discussion was closed, and she bent back to work. An arm across her chest stopped her. She was obliged to look up, his face inches from hers.

"Rumors are flying. Something's up," Thomas said in a concerted effort toward civil.

"I need to speak to Bella directly—"

"So directly you had time to go shine the sheets?"

Dropping his arm, he stood back. "You are in a mood, aren't you? You're bristlier than a bosun's mate without his grog. How in the hell does Nathan manage you?"

"By realizing I'm not to be 'managed," she retorted tartly. A few murmurs of support and approval came from the onlookers.

One eye narrowed and Thomas exhaled slowly through his nose. "Can you at least stay where you're bid?"

"You're beginning to sound more like Nathan all the time," Cate smirked.

Thomas' face darkened. He glanced from the corner of his eye, also conscious of what now constituted an audience. Cate wasn't entirely without remorse. He had clearly been worried on her account; that had not been her intention.

"I supposed your men who are always skulking about would have had some notion as to 'where the hell' I was," she offered as a half-excuse. It wasn't entirely a fabrication; she had become so accustomed to Nathan assigning watchdogs, she had assumed Thomas would have done something similar. She glanced about, half-expecting to see them lurking behind the brambles.

Thomas sobered. "I had to send them off. Little Sausage and every one of his men— those not too drunk to stand, that is— have disappeared."

"Their ship is still—" she began, recalling the sight of the deserted *Revenge* just before breaking her fast.

"Aye, I know. Which calls into even greater question where the foundering blazes they've gotten off to. Rumors are flying, but—" He stopped short, aware once more of an audience.

"C'mon." Making an obvious effort not to grab her with the violence he would have liked, he seized Cate by the arm and bodily turned her around. "We need to speak Bella."

His grasp was light and, hence, easily writhed out of. "You don't need me. I'll be right here."

"I'll watch her," Simona offered from a short distance up the row.

Thomas glanced at her, and then regarded her a second time, as if trying to sort out if he knew her. He eyed Cate critically, measuring his chances of winning the argument. Finally, he jerked a conceding nod.

"I'm just going over there," he announced, angling his head toward the pavilion, invisible behind a row of trees. "You stay put!"

"Nathan has said that many a time." It was painful not to smile. "Tach!" Thomas spun on his heel and headed back up the path.

"Nathan said that, too!" Cate called after him.

A jerk of his shoulders and a backward bat of his hand was Thomas' answer.

"If a man were to look at me like that, deviling him would be the last thing I on my mind."

Cate turned toward the source of the remark. "What look?"

Banu rolled her almond-shaped eyes. "If you don't know, there's no help for you." Several nearby guffawed in agreement.

Banu's gaze fixed—with a certain amount of longing, Cate observed—on Thomas' receding back. "It seems a shame to waste something so grand. With that chest, those thighs and chest, he'd have the endurance of—"

"He's not a bull up for inspection," Cate huffed.

"Ah, but he's hung like one," declared several in unison. Cate opened her mouth, but clapped it shut.

Banu chuckled, as she bent back to work. "All I can say is, you'd be wise to warm up that bed o' yours, because no others will be cold."

"C'mon," Simona sniffed, taking Cate by the arm. "Let's move over here, where the air is fresher."

The move was more symbolic since Cate and Simona were limited to being near the baskets to be filled. As an extension of that symbolism, Cate put her back to the others as much as possible. The sting of being mocked was worsened by the sting of believing in what everyone recognized as a grand lie. She wasn't usually one to fall prey to such things, but for some reason she was particularly over-sensitive and vulnerable.

He's coming. He's coming, she chanted to herself.

Thomas believed as much. Either that or he was putting on a grand act, being the good friend that he was...

Nathan's friend, not yours, cautioned an inner voice.

By his own admission, Thomas' loyalty to Nathan knew no bounds. If that meant a bit of misleading and lying in her face, then so be it. The thought of such a betrayal stung all the more.

She shook her head, brushing the thought aside.

Since leaving Celia's, something else had annoyed her, like a deer fly buzzing around her head. She tried to ignore it, but it could be no longer. Learning of the existence of a child had been elating but, as her grandmother had always said, no sun rose without casting a shadow. The sun of knowing she was no longer barren cast the black shadow of another child had been lost, gone, taken. Another dream had been granted, a decade of prayers answered, only to be snatched away. And worst of all, in her determination to avoid disappointment, she had denied her prayers answered, and hence, been ignorant of the life which had bloomed within her.

Now it was gone, torn away. A child going unknown, uncelebrated, and worse, unmourned.

A dismayed cry made her look up to discover she had been pitching melons with such force a basket was knocked over, scattering its contents. Huffing, she scrambled to help the boys retrieving them.

A child.

It seemed such a simple request. Everyone else popped babies out, often in excess, and yet she was denied. She castigated herself, questioning why she was so needful to be fruitful. It wasn't like food or air, necessary to one's existence. It was more than just the Church bidding her to go forth, or other wives eyeing her middle critically and offering their well-meant suggestions involving raspberry leaves and waning moons, thinly veiled allusions to her not "doing her duty" or even going to far as to question Brian's manhood.

"Lord knows there was no lack of that," she muttered aloud.

"What?" asked Simona, straightening.

"Nothing. Nothing," Cate muttered into her chest, blushing at the recollections.

The less kindly had arched a brow and whispered of "punishments" behind their hands. She had prayed, seeking what sin she might have committed so she might atone, but no answer came. Apparently, contrary to all popular belief, babies aren't in the Lord's purview.

Wet with more than just sweat, Cate swiped her cheek on her sleeve.

She was caught in a swirling eddy of dark thoughts from which there was no pulling away. God, if only she could return to the peace of being barren! But apparently, in the eyes of whoever or whatever power which controlled such things, she wasn't deserving of that either.

She had been brutalized, beaten, used by God knew how many, and had survived, but her child, Nathan's child hadn't. The worry now was if she was so damaged she was barren again, that she might have to wait another decade. Or was her condition now permanent?

For the first time, she felt her impending mortality, her life being gobbled up in ten-year increments, until she was old and dried up, unfulfilled, a life wasted.

And all because of Creswicke.

"Dammit to bloody hell!" She collapsed to her knees and beat the ground with her fist.

She looked down at the lace on her arm. "'P' for pawn" Creswicke had said. He had destroyed Nathan's life and now hers. Dead as the proverbial doornail he might be, but his hand was still on them, pushing them around like pieces on a chess board, just as the bastard had intended.

Head hanging between her arms, Cate struggled to collect

herself, determined that these women wouldn't see her tears, ones which flowed far too readily. She was becoming a moody, sodden mess, but there was nothing to be done for it.

A distant rumble set her back onto her heels. She looked up to find everyone had stopped at having heard it as well.

"Thunder?" Simona asked, looking to the brilliant sky.

Cate shook her head. It was commonplace in the Caribbean to have the sun beating your crown whilst rain blotted it out just over there. That wasn't thunder, however. It was cannons — guns, on a ship — several of them, a rolling barrage.

Her first hope was that it was Nathan, announcing his arrival — He loved bang-and - smoke — but she dismissed the notion out-of-hand. That sort of ostentation wasn't his style. Looking across the field, the pure sky was marred by clouds, but not those of a storm.

It was smoke, rising in a billowing column rising above the trees. Judging by the puzzlement which surrounded her, it wasn't a dwelling afire, or anything else of the sort. A signal fire then, but to who and for what?

The growing buzz of voices worked its way across the field at seeing several lads, running like Death was chasing them.

"Ship! Company!" they called, racing past.

From the direction of shore came the rattle of musket fire and male whoops, sounding disquietingly like a boarding party. Female screams, sharp with panic and pain, was the final straw.

Harvest forgotten, the women hitched their skirts and ran.

Cate fell in behind the racing Simona and several others, the sound of fighting growing louder with each stride. They broke through the line of trees to find the peaceful shore had erupted into a fight. It wasn't a skirmish as might break out between rival crews or when drunken gaiety degenerates into a brawl. This was people setting about each other with weapons with battlefield seriousness.

Who? Why? There were no green-coats, as represented by the runners, only sailors, pirates.

Cate spotted a couple Revenges fighting with women. The telltale clue was the black strip of cloth tied to each of their persons.

The Revenges were attacking!

She mouthed an oath which sounded so much like Nathan it made her smile. He was with her, even in this.

Simona and the rest of Cate's co-workers had come out

downshore, away from the pavilion. From near it, a ship's bell pealed the alarm, its metallic clang pierced the chaos.

"Stations!" cried Lygia. The fieldworkers set off in all directions with the determination of one with a duty to perform. The thought of "duty" brought Thomas to mind. *Thomas! He'd be worried sick.* Cate rose on her toes to look up and down the shore for either him or Al-Nejem. With their height, they should have stuck out like masts. Neither was in sight.

Neither was Lesauvage. She reflexively ducked at the whir of heavy metal passing over head. She followed what seemed to be its path-of-origin. It led back to a ship, now visible at the island's far end. The dull, regular *thump!* wasn't her heart, as thought, but the guns going off with remarkable regularity.

"Admirable work" Nathan would have said.

Her throat clutched and her stomach took a threatening lurch at seeing the massive flag flying from the backstay: the blue-and-white of the Company. They were in league with the Revenges. It was too much coincidence to be else. Now the signal fires made sense!

Cate ducked at another ball hurtling past. Palm fronds rained down, sparkling with glowing embers. A fraction of a moment later, a whooshing sound marked fire breaking out, the heat buffeting the side of her face. Fanned by the wind, the combustion raced across the treetops, inexplicably passing some dwellings, whilst others burst into flames. The smoke, thick with the smell of burning wood, joined the more acrid one of gunpowder, choking and blinding everyone. The roar of the flames added to the chaos.

Simona whirled around to Cate and shouted "The children! There's a shelter... Gather as many as you can!"

A gust of wind tore away the smoke, and Cate saw a stream of women and children flowing in the general direction of inland, away from the fighting. Another waft of the smoke and they disappeared, visibility reduced to barely beyond the end of her fingertips. She'd seen enough to know that Bella had been correct: the islanders were prepared; there was a plan. Indecision tore at Cate. Her hand twitched for a weapon; she could fight, lend an effective hand. The children, however, had to be the prime importance.

A woman ran past screaming, spinning in circles, her wits completely gone. Simona snatched the infant from her arms and thrust it into Cate's. "Go!"

Cate set off, Simona close behind, blindly following the stream of humanity inland, the occasional glimpses of the skirts of others her affirmation that she was going in the right direction. Her urge to run was checked by the short legs of the very ones she sought to help. She scooped up several more children along the way. It meant slowing their progress all the more, but there was no choice about it. She herded them before her as she ran, urging the older to help the younger.

Sparks carried by the wind set off small fires in the dry grass. The wind fanned some into full blazes, driving them inland, devouring everything in their path. Another break in the smoke revealed the ship again. It was nearer yet, the Company flag looming all the larger. The sight of it set Cate's heart pounding all the harder, her feet digging deeper into the sand as she ran.

The bark of the guns, powder-smoke, confusion, the screams— God, the screams! It was the Rising, again.

A chill shot down her back and gooseflesh rippled down her arms, not from fear, but from the cold. The sand became half-frozen mud, her feet aching from slogging in it, the wind an icy blast, peppering her face with sleet.

Another ball landed, the force nearly knocking Cate off her feet. Bent protectively over the small bundle in her arms, she pressed on, but it was like a nightmare: needing to run, but couldn't. Eyes streaming from the smoke, Cate spotted another roaming child and snatched it up.

Coughing, clasping the hand of another, Cate shouted encouragements over her shoulder to those trailing behind. She dove to the ground, gathering them all together and flinging her body over them as another ball whizzed past. Gasping, she crouched there, shushing the now stiff-and-wailing infant, dreading the shriek of a child being hit. When propelled by an explosion, even the smallest bit or fragment of flying debris could become a hazardous missile. She heard an agonized shriek, but too far away to be any in her charge. Dirt and branches still raining down, she was up and running again, dragging, pushing and carrying the children. Her arms and lungs burned, her feet seeming to find no traction, and yet the chaos of the fighting faded. The cannonballs no longer whizzed past, and the air grew a bit more breathable. She could only hope it meant she was still in the right direction.

"Here!" Simona's shout from behind stopped Cate.

So intent on running, she had missed the shelter. Its creators had taken remarkable advantage of the natural landscape. Half-dug in, half-built up of walls ballast shale and a log roof made for an impressive bastion. More to the point was its strategic location: well out of range of guns, land or sea.

Cate didn't know whether to laugh or cry at seeing the pair of aged and bent men posing as guards. Pirates they were, in spirit at any rate, bearing their weapons, one a blunderbuss, with deadly intent.

She ushered her charges inside. It was a different sort of chaos there. Burrowed in like rabbits in a bolt hole, the press of bodies in the confined space, the smells of dank earth mingled with feces and urine of many having soiled themselves made the air almost a living element. Putting on brave faces, the older strove to console the younger, but too many had crossed over into hysterics and were beyond all help. A vast number huddled together sobbing and hiccoughing while others were reduced to rocking mute terror.

With a groan of relief, Cate handed off the infant into the waiting arms of someone who seemed to be in charge and stood rubbing feeling back into her own. The bewildered faces were like looking into those seen during the Rising. She'd seen them in the camp followers, in villages caught in the crossfire, and the displaced families. It was heartbreaking to think that such a short time ago, she had watched them tumbling and playing. No child should have to suffer this.

Cate stepped outside and leaned against a post to catch her breath. The guns still boomed with the regularity of a case clock. The smoke now hung like a fog, reducing the day to a semi-twilight. The wood at her back was a solid protection for those lucky enough to find their way there, but many, too many weren't so fortunate...

Save all you can.

"There's more, too many more still out there," Cate said, pushing upright. "I'll go—" As Cate turned, she saw Simona's foot dart out, but too late to avoid being tripped, and she went sprawling onto the ground.

Surprised and furious, Cate scrambled to get to her feet. Hands seized her and lifted her up.

"What the bloody hell—!" Any further expostulations died in her throat at seeing Lesauvage standing there. Several of his men appeared around him, virtually surrounding the entrance, weapons poised.

"You back-stabbing snake!" growled one of the guards, raising the blunderbuss. A pistol fired, and he doubled over, gut-shot. There was movement to one side; the other was skewered from behind. The one who had fired calmly reloaded his pistol and then aimed it.

Cate moved, meaning to shield the entrance, but Simona's grip stopped her.

"Don't you dare fire that with children about!" Cate cried. It was a ludicrous thing to say. Her only hope was the authority in her voice might cause some hesitation.

Lesauvage stepped forward just as a lad, blind with fear, ran past for the shelter. The Frenchman backhanded the boy, sending him tumbling out of sight.

"It doesn't take much of a man to—" Cate began.

The hand cocked back and slapped her. "Mouthy bitch, *n'est pas*?"

Lesauvage seized Cate by the jaw and brought her face up to his. "Unfinished business we have, do we not, *mon cher*?"

Cate's head reeled and her eyes watered from the blow, but be damned if she would let him see either her fear or pain.

Fingers digging into her flesh, he turned her face from side to side, inspecting, as if seeing her for the first time. "It is providential that you are so lovely, but you would be just as valuable if you were a hag. What I think is not important. It is what Nathan thinks, *non*? He puts a great store in you and will pay handsomely, *very* handsomely to get you back."

Through her watering eyes, Cate could see his unfocused ones. He was drunk or, better said, still drunk from the night before, the reek of it rising from him like rot from a corpse.

"I brought her, just like I promised," piped Simona, beaming.

Lesauvage's gaze never left Cate. "Indeed. *Bon*! A task well done."

His hand struck out, slitting Simona's throat with his knife. Round-eyed with shock, she sank to the ground.

"Annoying bitch with an unforgiving mouth," he said over Simona's final gasps. He gave Cate a quelling shake. "Scream and I will do the same to you. We'll use those snot – nosed brats inside for target practice."

More commotion from inside; Cate momentarily closed her eyes, willing them quiet.

"Blackthorne won't care," Cate pleaded, more as a distraction than ploy. "You know him, you've said it yourself: what's one woman among the many?"

"Pah! You have lorded yourself about like a queen. He will pay and pay *very* well. A grand and unexpected addition to the riches already to be had."

His gaze unwavering on Cate, her only warning was a twitch of one eye before he drove a fist into her middle. She doubled over and sank to her knees, sucking for the precious air driven from her lungs. Lesauvage grabbed a handful of her hair and jerked her face up.

"Open that mouth again, and your gallant Blackthorne will have to pay extra to get your tongue back."

Two Revenges led off, Lesauvage a bit behind. Cate, suspended between two more, followed closely, another pair bringing up the rear.

Still reeling from being hit, Cate stumbled along, sometimes being half-dragged in their haste. She cocked an ear behind her, listening for any indications of violence at the shelter. She counted the Revenges, and then again, assuring herself that none had lingered behind to do the children mischief.

Cate had held the thin hope that the attacking Revenges had just been a rogue group. Those hopes were dashed now, she thought grimly. The skulking worm had gone privateer, in league with the Company. The signal fire, the attack, the ship, landing parties: it all made sense, now, and Lesauvage was up to his armpits in it, just as Thomas had foreseen.

Thomas!

He would be wild with worry by now. From his perspective, she would have disappeared without a trace. With his men fighting for their lives, he would have little time to search for her, which meant little help would be coming her way.

It was heavy going, a roaming path rarely taken leading in the general direction of the remote side of the island where the signal fire still plumed in the sky. They moved with the air of those who had no enemy and yet were foreign to their surroundings. They were sailors, not woodsmen. Grumbling and cursing, calling out their frustrations, they crashed through the infringing overgrowth, hacking with more fury than effect at branches, moving with the same grace and caution as a herd of bullocks. Given the narrowness of the path, and the reluctance of her captors to let go, they were forced to crab sideways down the path, her arms soon becoming sore from being pulled.

Cate made every effort to keep her bearings. Escape was of the essence, but how?

Her hands hadn't been bound; that was a good start. Lesauvage was drunk, which made him blundering, and yet even more unpredictable. Still, if she was as valuable as he said, then his threat on her person would be an empty one. The forest's density would make for difficult going, especially in a skirt, but it would also provide easy cover in which to hide.

So, the embryonic beginnings of a plan. Opportunity was the next issue. Her escorts' grip made breaking free dubious, the dirk in one's fist and a pistol in the others' rendering it a dangerous proposition. The odds of success at making a break for it were lessened further by the pair just behind her. The key was to stay alert. Opportunity would present itself. It had to!

With a clear head came a fuller realization of Simona's betrayal. The extent of her cunning and deceit grew with every step Cate took. Clearly, she hadn't worked alone;

Lesauvage had been her accomplice, but who else had been involved? How inclusive had that circle of duplicity been? Tabby? The lovely Miguela, perhaps? Banu and Lygia?

Make friends, indeed! She'd give Nathan a large opinion of that notion next time she saw him. Dwelling on that thought kept alive her hopes of seeing him... sometime.

Cate's machinations were interrupted by the group's abrupt stop. She craned her head to see ahead and reeled back.

A group of men, a patrol was coming up the same path. Vines, leaves, trees, bushes: they were surrounded by green, and yet the particular shade of their coats stood out like blood on snow.

The Company.

Cate writhed and twisted against the hands holding her, wild with the need to flee.

Run! Hide! Let them shoot her. Anything to be away!

A rustle in the bushes and several more Company men stepped out, effectively surrounding them. The lack of alarm on anyone's part suggested that the meeting was somewhat expected. One of the newly-arrived shoved to the forefront, differences in dress and bearing marking him as the one in command. Lesauvage elbowed his way forward, and the pair squared off.

"I am Captain Gascon Lesauvage, commander of the fair vessel *Revenge*."

"Lieutenant John Blake." Civility prevailed, and he added "Your servant, sir" through stiff lips. The curl of his lip suggested he would have preferred speaking to a dead toad. "What the blazes are you doing skulking about in the bushes? You and your men are supposed to be attacking the settlement."

"And so my men are, valiantly, I might add. Success is but a matter of time."

Cate flared at hearing Thomas and his men being dismissed so out-of-hand, but fear had suddenly glued her tongue to the roof of her mouth.

Blake jerked at noticing Cate for the first time and glared at Lesauvage. "Orders were clear: no quarter."

"This one is worth more alive than dead," the Frenchman replied blithely. Cate was brought forward and held there. "This is Blackthorne's whore, his current whore, that is. He might pay for a corpse, but he will pay an even greater sum for her alive. Blackthorne is due to drop anchor in a day or two. We can lie in wait and collect the reward for him as well."

Blake eyed her, taking in her hair, eyes, age and general description. With a glimmer of recognition, he seized her arm and tugged back the lace at her wrist. Turning her head, not wishing to see, Cate watched from the corner of her eye as his face lit with discovery. He stood back and regarded her as if he had just found the treasure of the Golden Fleet.

Finally, he mastered his pleasure and sobered. "Standing orders for her to be taken at all cost."

"Blackthorne will pay more, guaranteed," Lesauvage insisted.

"Perhaps," Blake sniffed. "But His Lordship is gold in the pot."

"His Lordship is dead. His head lopped off and kicked into the sea," Cate blurted.

Both commanders glared and Cate had the sinking sensation she had just signed her own death warrant with that announcement. Still, Lesauvage might be unpredictable, but the prospect of being handed over to these green-coats made her queasy. Anything to strengthen his position would be to her benefit.

"The slattern speaks the truth," Lesauvage said at seeing Blake's doubt. "It's been the talk since they arrived."

Blake stiffened. "They?"

Lesauvage grinned at having wiped the smugness from the lieutenant's face. "A brig and a schooner put in yesterday. They are of little consequence," he added with a dismissive flick of his fingers. "A few score and no more."

To Lesauvage's dismay, Blake's smugness returned, heightened by a large dose of irony.

"Apparently you are unaware that the no-quarter directive included you. It would seem the snake has stuck out its head far enough to chop it off. Kill 'em." The order was given as dispassionately as if he had said "Pass the salt."

In a single motion, Blake seized Cate, drew his pistol and fired. Drink hadn't dulled Lesauvage's wits; he twisted, avoiding the shot, while at the same time dove to grab Cate. The maneuver saved the Frenchman's life, but was the death of one of his men. Amid the grunts and bellows of the fight which erupted, a brief tug-of-war ensued, Cate in the middle. With a scream like a skewered rabbit, another Revenge went down. A third speared kept Cate from being split like a wishbone. Valuing his life more than money, the gallant Lesauvage cut-and-run, disappearing into the thick foliage. Cate coiled to follow but was stopped by Blake's iron grasp.

"Sergeant Monroe," Blake said, passing Cate off to his men. "You, Parker, Quinn and Brown take this bit of treasure back to the landing, *with care*," he added, stabbing a warning finger at them. "Remember, she is of *great* value to His Lordship."

"Aye, sir," came back in a marble-mouthed version of a Lowland brogue. Cate dug in her heels as Monroe took possession, but to little avail.

"Stay alert," Blake called as Monroe's party moved off, back in the direction from which they had just come, Cate with them. "I wouldn't put it past those thieving scoundrels to try to circle back."

14: NO QUARTER

THOMAS STEPPED OUT FROM UNDER the pavilion. Scanning the settlement, he took off his hat and ran a frustrated hand through his hair.

"Where the hell are you, woman?" His remark was meant only for his own purposes, but was apparently loud enough for several passing by to hear, and then pretend they hadn't.

Finding Bella was like chasing a bilge rat. It had been represented to him earlier that she was here, at the pavilion.

"At the smithy, they said," he muttered, glaring back toward the cook fires. "Seeing to new roasting tongs."

He stood undecided. The smithy was at the far end, in the opposite direction of the field where Cate—damn her contrariness—was waiting.

"She damned well better be waiting."

"Beg pardon, sir?" asked a lad, drawing attentively up before him.

"Nothing, nothing," Thomas said irritably, waving him away.

I'll shackle her to my leg, if she wasn't.

Cate was a frazzled mess. She was on the verge of flying apart like a boltrope in a high gale. When this business was over, he meant to find a quiet corner and calm her, somehow. To achieve that could well mean putting a funnel down her throat and pouring rum down it, but by damn, he'd do it! Of course, there was Celia. Amid all those potions of hers, she would be bound to have something which would answer. After all, it was the visit to her place which had set Cate off, so it was only fitting that she'd set the woman to rights. But damnation, he couldn't go marching out there himself. He could pass the word... No, send something written would be more discreet...

He nipped off the thought. Bigger fish waited to be fried. He ran another hand through his hair, tweaked himself into respectability and jerked on his hat. There was no choice for it. Passing the word for Bella wouldn't answer. Never had before, at any rate. The smithy it is.

Thomas struck off in that direction. Wishing to be civil, he nodded distractedly to the women he passed, while at the same time was well aware of their gazes following him. Why women were so fascinated with his backside was beyond his comprehension?

The back of his neck felt like snakes caught under his skin and his gut roiled. Neither had ever failed him before: something was amiss. Whether it had anything to do with the Revenges disappearing or Lesauvage in particular was anyone's guess. One way or the other, it was too strong to be ignored, and he wouldn't rest until he had spoken Bella.

His thoughts were interrupted by seeing people going about their day-to-day suddenly stop, look up and point. He craned his head to follow their point, and then stopped dead, as well. A column of smoke rose above the trees at the island's western end.

"Anything out there?" he asked of those around him. Low, sandy and inclined to flood at the full or new moon, so far as he knew that end was as deserted as the day it was discovered.

Heads shaking and mutterings confirmed what he already suspected.

Shouting, like a town crier, coming from the island's interior, made him turn. The runner broke through the trees and skidded to a halt, scanning the settlement with wild - eyed desperation. Spotting Thomas at last, he sped forward. He drew up and bent, bracing his hands on his knees. "Bella?"

"Damned if I know. What is it, man?"

A shaky arm rose to point, but in the opposite direction of the fire. "Ship... Company... Landing — " the runner panted.

A barrage of musketfire from the trees onto the shore cut off the rest. A roar akin to the screech of boiled cats leapt out. They weren't green-coats, but men... sailors —

Goddammit, they were Lesauvage's men!

As if waiting for the cue, every Revenge in sight stopped, drew their swords and attacked without heed as to whether male or female. The women and his own men were caught by surprise and unarmed. Thomas felt more than heard someone coming up behind him and turned in time to block a blade with his own. He parried, blocked high, and then drove his dirk into the sod's gut.

Amid the erupting mayhem, one thought prevailed: Cate!

He raced back to where he had left her, serving out any

traitorous bastard in his path. He drew up well short of the melon field, however, and cursed at seeing it deserted.

"Cate!" he bellowed to the heavens. "Where the bloody hell are you?"

He spun around, listening, but—of course—the vexing wench didn't answer.

Goddamn the insufferable woman!

Muttering oaths of what he would do when he found her, Thomas spun and raced back toward shore. The screams of women came from all directions. There was a vast difference between a scream of pain and one of terror as in being molested. He stopped at seeing one being dragged off into the bushes. He served out the cove, begging for forgiveness with his breeches still down about his knees.

"Beg your maker instead," Thomas said coldly and slit him from neck to navel.

He helped the victim to her feet. Head bleeding, she hung onto him, hysterical. At last, at his urging, she took one unsteady step and then collapsed. He scooped her up and carried her, craning his head and shouting for Cate as he ran.

Back on the shore, the scene was worse than a deck raid. Granted, it wasn't the elbow – to-elbow conditions, but the brutality was worse. Women and children shouting and wailing, bodies strewn, limbs hacked, smoke so thick it was difficult to see more than a few yards. Cannonballs ripped the length, bowling down anyone in their path, the flying shivers adding to the carnage. Two fools were running with torches setting fire to everything in their path. With his arms already occupied, there was nothing Thomas could do but curse them to damnation, the smell of burning grass and wood joining that of gunpowder. A few strides more, and he spotted one of his own, hailed and sent him after the cursed firebrands.

Thomas deposited his burden at the pavilion where the injured would be collected until a sick bay could be rigged. Mumbling a hasty apology to the hysterics, he returned to the fight, shouting for Cate the while. He tried to convince himself that she was no innocent; she was as capable as any man in a fight. But that didn't stop his heart from his chest at spotting any woman down and stopping to see if it was her.

He'd seen a man go at a woman with a blade before, but never so many at once! Now and again, he caught sight of Bella, barking orders like a field marshal. He hated like hell to see women attacked, but it did his heart good to see them rally, then. Heaven help any many who was fool enough to attack a woman protecting child and home! Bella had represented not a dwelling was unarmed, and now they set about anyone who posed a threat, shrieking and clawing with the same deadliness as any man.

He gave over to the red fury and hacked, stomped, shot, stabbed, punched and bludgeoned one after another. He shot a Revenge point-blank attempting to take a woman right before his eyes. A few strides later, he crushed the skull of another with the empty butt. He focused his fury on the Revenges. Damn their traitorous, treacherous souls! At the same time, he kept a weather eye for Lesauvage, that double-tongued snake. He'd squeeze his head, until those eyes popped out like the little beads they were, and then feed them to him.

A barrage of musket fire went off with the unified sound of a military unit. It came from behind him, however, opposite of the first smoke. Damnation, they had been dropping landing parties all around the island all night, lying in wait.

The wind tore a hole in the smoke enough for him to make out a brig—20-guns or so, light enough to be able to clear these waters, and yet heavy enough to transport a sizeable number of troops and wreak a great deal of havoc—coming around the western end and was making for the bay. The gun emplacement at the point was being manned, but it was set up to protect the bay, not the approaches. With time and sweat, the guns might be moved and brought to bear, but it could well be too late, by then.

The ship came round enough to show the banner on her backstay. Just as the runner had represented: the Company.

The red flag at the main sent a cold chill down his back.

"No quarter."

That point was emphasized with the next round. The self-preservation gained with years at sea sent him ducking behind a tree just before hundreds of pellets tore past.

Canister. The mumping villain was using canister!

Several hundred iron pellets in one shot was meant but for one thing: mutilate or kill. This wasn't to conquer or to capture. This was to obliterate.

Broadside after broadside—full ones, not the rolling kind with a mind toward sparing the ship from tearing herself apart—the horror rained down, the cries of the wounded going up an octave with each. Thomas counted off the seconds between rounds—two minutes and thirty seconds, perhaps a little more; not the fastest ever witnessed, but neither were they the slowest—as he fought, ready to hit the deck, taking anyone with him as he did, a fraction before the next round. It became a version of a child's game: run, fight, dive, leap up, fight, dive...

His fear for Cate's welfare grew with every round.

Where the hell was she?

Hell and furies, there had to be a way to silence those guns! He hoped to hell they weren't asleep on the *Lovely* or *Brazen*, but there was nothing to be done for it. From their moorings, there was precious little they could do about the brig, until it opened the bay. But when it did, they'd best be prepared for a boarding. If all this didn't wake them, there was no hope. If they weren't murdered in their sleep, he'd murder them himself.

After yet another barrage, Thomas pushed up and glared at the brig. God send the magazine might spark and blow. His prayers stopped, and he stiffened at seeing she hadn't moved; she stood roughly in the same spot as before. He glanced at the sky and the wind. Blessed saints, she couldn't weather the point! That, or two ships' presence had changed her plans. Whatever the case, she was backing-and-filling, content with raking the settlement.

He laid flat to the ground at one point and watched a Revenge a few yards away be turned into something akin to a squirrel hit with birdshot. Damnation! If the Revenges were in league with the Company, then why were they firing canister on their own? Either this was a poorly organized endeavor—not entirely unlikely—or the Revenges were expendable.

Two minutes and thirty seconds later and on his belly again, the burst of musketfire made Thomas worm around to look. Another Company landing party somewhere—God's blood and wounds, it was like they were coming down out of the trees—but definitely upshore, presumably out of gun range. Still, it was a bloody-minded commander who would send his men into their own fire.

Up and running again, a scorched pig got tangled in Thomas' legs and he was sent sprawling. As he pushed up, he caught a glimpse of Cate—no mistaking that hair—herding a group of children, an infant in her arms. Of course! The woman wouldn't do else! Pushing to his feet, he shouted, but to no avail. Running toward her, his inner clock went off again, and he dove to the ground. Shards of wood still peppering his legs, he looked up, but she was gone, naught but a swirl of smoke marking the spot.

The fires were finding their own life, the heat making it difficult to breathe. The side of his face stung like it was burned anew. A bellow collected a half-score of his men, Al – Nejem among them. With one final glance to make sure Cate hadn't worn about, he set off in a dog-trot in her last heading. Within a few strides, the sound of different guns made them all stop. A cheer went up from his men, and from up and down the shore: the *Lovely* and *Brazen* had opened fire. The vessels' position allowed for no more than lobbing blind shots over land — it would be like shooting pigeons with your eyes closed — but it gave the brig something to think about. Success or futility depended on whose side Lady Luck chose. A stride later, and another joyous hail, Luck proved she wasn't blind: the brig's fores'l went by the board, taking a good number of spars and rigging with it.

Was it too much to hope that the tide of the fight had just turned?

Thomas pushed on, putting his blind faith in what was no more than a track of churned sand. He had no notion of where the gathering point for the children might be, but the scattering of dolls, toys and keepsakes dropped along the way gave him heart that they were on the right heading. Whether or not Cate would be at the other end of it was a matter he'd solve later. Inland, away from shore they went, the roar of battle fading behind them. He cursed the ambling shuffle at which they moved, but no man among them, including him, had the heart to bypass the confused and cowering children encountered along the way. At one point, he looked back and almost laughed aloud at the sight of Al – Nejem with a youth in each arm and half-strangled by another clinging to his back like a small monkey. With their arms so occupied, heaven help them if they encountered one of those damned patrols.

The collective howl of terrified youth led them to the shelter. Around a stand of bushes they went and there several women milled about what looked to be an entrance. His gut lurched, and he nearly stumbled at seeing bodies, one wearing a skirt, lying at the doorway. A few strides closer, heart in this throat, Thomas let out an explosive sigh of relief at realizing it wasn't Cate.

Thomas shouldered his way inside the shelter and stopped, unable to move any further. They were packed in like firewood. Howling, wailing, sobbing, screeching: every sound the human frame could produce combined in an ungodly din. Still too sun-dazzled to see, he shouted "Cate! Goddammit, Cate, answer me!" into the murk.

With their wits already shattered, the children's shrieks hit a higher pitch, cowering and scrambling to get away from him. One of the attending matrons took him firmly by the arm, shouting "She's not here" as she pushed him out.

"Where the bloody hell is she?" he demanded at the door, only to discover he was addressing the matron's skirt tail as she swept back inside.

Wiping the smoke from his streaming eyes, Thomas scanned the forest, and then back toward shore and the fighting there, all the while trying to put himself in Cate's shoes. Knowing her, her first worry, her primary concern would be for the helpless. She'd go back into the thick of things, she'd wade into Hell itself, if she thought someone, anyone was in need.

Someone tugged at his sleeve and he whirled around, hand at his sword. He pulled up at seeing it was naught but a lad, his crown barely reaching the level of his belts. The side of his face bright red, one eye swollen shut, the boy sagged under the weight of the blunderbuss he carried.

"The woman who was here? Where is she?" Thomas demanded.

"Break his neck and he won't tell you anything."

The female voice sharp in his ear made Thomas realize he had seized the boy and was shaking him. Letting go, Thomas wheeled about on the woman and shook her instead.

"The woman what was here, Blackthorne's woman. Where the hell—?"

"I bloody hell don't know!" she shouted back, red-faced.

Thomas checked himself and stood back, fists balled at his sides. "I need to—." His voice shook with desperation and he closed his eyes in an effort to collect himself. "I need— "

"The Revenges took her." Thomas spun back around.

"The Captain," the boy said, not puffed with import. "Lewis...? Lois...?"

"Lesauvage?"

The boy nodded. "Him and some o' his men."

Thomas looked down into the dead woman's eyes, her throat slashed and the churned ground. That alone told him she hadn't gone willingly. God's death and wounds, the woman had spirit. She'd fight, but at what price? He didn't wish to think how much of that blood might be hers.

"What direction—?"

Seeing Thomas' fist tightened, the lad dodged back a step. Shifting the blunderbuss, he pointed unsteadily toward the trees. "That way."

A single look set Al-Nejem to gathering his men.

Thomas reached for the blunderbuss, but the boy retreated further. "Go help your mother, son." He meant it kindly, but his blood was up, and it must have come out gruffer than intended, for tears suddenly spilt down the dirt-smudged cheeks.

"Ain't got no mum, sir. She's dead."

Two left as guards, the rest of Thomas' men formed up. He hesitated and then beckoned Al-Nejem aside.

"If anything—" he began, in low-voiced Arabic.

There had always been an understanding, but he needed to know, be assured that Cate would be seen to, so there would be no hesitation when it came to doing what needed to be done. Lesauvage, Revenges, Company: it mattered not who had her, they were all dead, in his eyes.

His First Mate solemnly nodded. Understood.

Afzal and Khalid led off. Having Afzal with them was a fluke of luck. A hunter in a previous life, the man could track a fish through water. The two led off, barely more than a biscuit-toss ahead, and yet out of sight in this heavy growth. Thomas, Al-Nejem and the rest followed, two assuming the position of rear guards.

They followed a wandering path, often no more than a stretch of trampled grass, but its general direction was toward the backside of the island where those damned patrols all seemed to originate. "Straight at 'em" might be a fitting tactic at sea, but on land, charging like a bull into the bushes was a fool's mission. In spite of every shred of his being screaming else, Thomas bided at this creeping pace, stopping every step or so to listen. The Revenges and Company were no landsmen, but circling around for an ambush wasn't unthinkable.

At the same time, one question burned in his mind: How long does it take to rape a woman?

Time was everything, and yet it might be the one thing Cate didn't have. Every lagging step, every pause, every hesitation was all the more opportunity for harm to be inflicted. So help him, if those skulking bastards laid hands on her, there wouldn't be enough left for either the Devil or their Maker to take when he was done with them.

From up ahead came a surprised inhalation and then sounds of a struggle, hand-to–hand and brutal. By the time he reached the scene, it was over. Afzal and Khalid stood over several dead Companymen. Thomas drew up beside one, an officer judging by his vestments, that by whatever happenstance was still breathing.

The man's eyes opened, and he glared up.

"The woman. Where is she?" Thomas demanded.

The lips drew back in a blood-stained grin. "Not here."

Growling a low curse, Thomas lifted his boot and drove the heel down. Amid the crush of bone and gristle, that grin was wiped away, his only regret being that the sod's misery was ended far too quickly.

Afzal crouched a short distance away, studying the ground like a mariner might study a chart. He pointed up the path. "They came from this way." He rolled his eyes at the surroundings. "The forest silent; many have passed."

Thomas nodded. The dead officer obviously knew of Cate, which meant wherever he had just been would be a prime place to find her. There was a blessing to this dense forest, he thought, flicking the sweat from his eyes. Any path, no matter how narrow, would be preferable to hacking a new one.

Afzal and Khalid struck off, Thomas and the rest assuming their positions. They crept along at the same insufferable pace. Thomas gripped and re-gripped his sword in impotent fury. His blood was up, and he knew it. And goddammit to bloody hell, he didn't care. He'd had women leave, chose another, dupe and even cuckold him. But never had one been snatched out from under his very nose. He felt a renewed and deeper compassion for what Nathan had suffered when Creswicke had taken Cate, a man of blood and action being reduced to a pewling milksop. He'd spent many a year in regions of the globe where they had a deep and abiding understanding of how to make a man suffer. He wouldn't scruple to employ any number of those tortures, now.

Under the rustle of the breeze in the treetops came a low whistle, something between a caution and a beck. A few cautious steps further, and he came upon Afzal and Khalid in a small clearing, kneeling over a trio of bodies, Revenges, by their looks. The pair of trackers were already going through the economic motions of ridding the dead of anything useful: shot, powder, weapons and the like. A flick of his knife and Khalid severed a finger, slipped off the ring and flung the rest aside.

The ground was plowed up, clods of sod, broken twigs and grass all signs of a struggle. The blood on the ground and clothing was still bright and glistening. It was recent, very recent.

"The Company came in from up there, met the Revenges here," Afzal added, looking dispassionately down at the bodies.

Thomas nodded impatiently. That much seemed damned obvious.

The tracker angled his head toward the bushes. "Three went off there. Four or so more went that way," he finished, gesturing toward the path.

"Any way of knowing who went where?"

Afzal indicated the tracks leading into the bushes. "Old boots and traveling light. Those up the path were probably Company: all new boots and walk heavy, like landsmen carrying shot and arms."

Following the tracks up the path, Afzal knelt to trace the curved impression of a barefoot among the boot prints. "*Memsaab* went this way. One, mebbe two wounded," he added, pointing to the droplets of blood, bright in a shaft of sunlight.

Thomas' gut lurched yet again at the possibility of the blood being Cate's. Damn the woman, hadn't she the sense as to when not to raise hell?

In the bare-faced truth of it, there was little decision to be made. Regardless of what might lay ahead, he couldn't leave the Revenges — Lesauvage, no doubt, among them — at their leisure, possibly free to circle back and ambush them. It meant dividing his forces and having to forego the pleasure of skewering that back-stabbing worm, but there were larger matters to attend.

"You and you." Thomas indicated two of his men and swiped in the direction the Revenges had gone. "Get 'em, and don't hesitate to make them suffer," he called in their wake.

Stepping over the bodies, they pressed on, Afzal and Khalid in the lead still. Reducing their numbers made Thomas all the more anxious to see this done. The blood and scuffle they just left showed Lesauvage and his men hadn't given Cate up readily. The notion of her in the middle of it only added to his apprehension. As they went now, it didn't require a tracking genius to see where their prey had stopped, branches broken, the ground stirred. Was it Cate putting up a resistance?

Dammit, woman, just go quietly along!

Or, were they stopping, stirring about because she was weakened, unable to keep up?

Every sense screamed that they were hard on the bastards' heels, to the point that, at times, Thomas swore he saw the branches still moving from their passing.

Thomas' head jerked up at the sound of a cry — female, but hoarse and garbled, more like a rook caw — from up ahead. Distorted as it might have been, he knew it was Cate. That she could make any noise at all proved that she was at least semi-alert. He briefly closed his eyes at that small blessing. Oaths and agitated voices indicated a struggle of some sort, and for the hundredth time he thought of what he would do if those sodding louts laid hands on her!

A low whistle signaled what he already concluded. Afzal and Khalid were desiring instructions. A motion sent Al-Nejem and several others to the flank. Sword in his fist, knife from its scabbard in the other, Thomas pushed forward.

Jerked and cursed by those holding her, Cate trudged on legs gone wooden and uncooperative.

"Orders is orders..."

She hung onto Blake's parting words like a talisman, for in those lay her salvation.

The moment Blake and his party were out of sight, there had been a stark and disconcerting change in her escorts. The Highlanders had often derided the Brits for their straight-laced, stiff-upper-lip, by-the-book mentality. Now, her preservation pivoted on them being all that and more. The least loosening of those laces, the least softening of that lip could spell her doom.

Whose orders, was the wonder?

On the one hand, it made little difference. On the other, however, there was a certain comfort in knowing whose signature was on one's death warrant.

Blake's surprise at hearing of Creswicke's death had been honest. That meant the all – precious orders had to have been issued before Creswicke's departure for his ill-fated and final rendezvous with Thomas and Nathan. That also meant the attack on the island wasn't retribution for that, but a standalone. But, why? The thumping the island had given the Company earlier? Or was it, as Bella accused, a payback for Nathan's capers? Or, was it just because the island was within Creswicke's sphere-of-influence and not under his thumb?

The latter seemed the most fitting if for no other reason than it was more befitting of the man's character and—even more importantly—it took the burden of responsibility from Nathan's shoulders.

Cate cut a sideways glance at her captors' middle and the weapon there: short, stout affair, larger than a dirk, yet smaller than a cutlass, designed for slashing. She'd seen enough Companymen to know it wasn't standard issue, and yet now one hung at every middle.

Take no quarter.

The island's death warrant had been signed days, possibly weeks ago.

She hated Creswicke all the more if that was at all possible. The philosophical would say it was a waste and the height of futility to hate one already dead, but there was no help for it. The venom built with every step she now took, a loathing and contempt for anyone who would unleash such violence on a bunch of women and children. Granted, they might be pirate wives and offspring, not innocents in the purest sense, but it was still a vile act.

Her step faltered; the one at Cate's elbow growled and gave

her a shove. The more they pushed, the more she balked, not out of stubbornness, but morbid fear. She meant to fight—put on a brave face, spit in their eye—and yet all she could do was quiver like half - steamed pudding to the point her teeth clattered against each other.

Cate fixed her gaze on Monroe's back, afraid to look any in the face, lest she might recognize one. The Company was large, the odds vast that she might encounter the same ones as at Creswicke's headquarters. Or, at least that's what she chanted to herself. Logic, however, rolled off like rain off a tarpaulin jacket.

Creswicke is dead. Creswicke is dead.

She choked a bitter laugh. First Nathan—twice—and then her: death in the Caribbean seemed to be a temporary condition. There was no reason to believe someone like Creswicke, already in league with the Devil, wouldn't manage the same. Darker thoughts began to wedge their way in: that Nathan and Thomas—hell, everyone had joined in a great lie, representing Creswicke's demise, when he was actually alive and well, and sitting in his office awaiting for her delivery.

Her breath came in ragged pants; the gorge of sickness worsened, its bitter taste of filling the back of her throat. She entertained herself with the satisfying prospect of spewing it down those green fronts or on their shoes.

Just like you imagined spewing another time, on your way to Creswicke's office...

Not again! Not again!

The brand on her arm burned anew as fresh as the day it was done. She pressed it against her side to quell the sting. The bile surged, and she gulped several times. Sweat prickled her temples, and her vision began to swim.

Get hold, Mackenzie. Get hold!

She would be no good to herself if she were naught but a puking, blubbering mess. There had been no one to save her from Creswicke's clutches then. There would be no one to save her now. Thomas, Nathan... no one would know where she was. She was alone, again, with nothing but her own devices to survive.

Still, like trying to curb enraged bees, the more she strove to check her emotions, the more agitated they became. The green coats to each side jostled and jammed against her, jerking and dragging her forward, so much like that day in Creswicke's headquarters...

The forest became the corridor walls, the hall way to the ante room where she had been dragged after...

The memory struck so hard she doubled over, would have crumpled to the ground had she not been held.

Burning with the need for revenge, Nathan had demanded numbers and names of those who had used her. She had claimed to remember nothing. It had been a lie, one of the greatest ever told, constructed to protect him and, more importantly, to protect herself from having to face what wasn't to be faced. The lie was then repeated, to the point of it becoming the truth, and she had reveled in the glorious peace which came with that ignorance.

Like a scab from a great wound, the truth tore away that peace, revealing the open rawness underneath. The truth was she knew every man who had used her, not by face—her swollen eyes had spared her of that—but by the smell of their breath and sweat, and the noise each one made as he reached his finish. Her eye fixed on the gold button of the coat beside her, and she flinched, feeling it gouge her chest, as they had as they writhed and grunted on top of her. Creswicke's face shoved near hers, leaned close, eyes bright and avid, cheering them on as if it were a sporting event.

The group stopped. Cate blinked stupidly, looking to find they were in a small clearing. Sergeant Monroe was facing her, the rest circling around. The stomach which had been up in her throat dropped and her blood turned to ice.

Monroe's face was fully visible for the first time: a florid, pudding-like visage, thin – lipped and gap-toothed. Sweat ringed his jacket and made a slow track down one cheek.

Tugging at his crotch, Monroe eyed her with unveiled appreciation. "You heard the orders, lads. We're to plunder all we can and teach these pirate bitches a lesson."

"His Lordship desired her untouched," said one nervously.

Monroe shrugged. "Then, we shan't leave a mark."

He stepped closer; Cate retreated, coming up hard against her guards, their breath hot on the back of her neck.

"Be abidin', lass," Monroe crooned. "An' we can all be friendly-like. We're just lookin' for a bit o' what you've been puttin' around to those pirates."

Heart hammering, Cate saw his mouth moving, but could barely hear. The exact words weren't necessary; his intentions were obvious. Dark spots started to dance at the edges of her vision and she concentrated on breathing. She needed a clear head, a clear mind. In Creswicke's office, she had been rendered senseless...

Never again!

Cate launched to get away. Failing that, she screamed, scratched, bit and kicked, until it required three to restrain her.

"We've a vixen here." Monroe slapped her once, and then

again, with a force which set her head reeling, insensibility looming all the nearer. "Not in the face," hissed one in warning.

Through watering eyes, she saw Monroe's countenance twitch with regret. Then he drove a fist into her middle, driving the air from her lungs.

"Hold her," Monroe said, fumbling with his flies.

A kick to the back of Cate's legs and her already sagging knees buckled, a foot planted on her calves assuring that she couldn't rise. Her arms viciously twisted behind her back and fists twined into her hair held her immobile. Monroe advanced, flies sagging open, his cock stretched out, quivering and dripping with eagerness. Those not otherwise occupied formed a line behind him. Lungs still spasming for air from being punched, Cate clamped her mouth shut and turned her head, only to have it wrenched back with a neck-cracking force. Iron-like fingers dug into her jaws, prying them open. The muscles burned, cramped, and then gave way. The fingers dug deeper, holding her mouth open like a cod on a plank.

Cate closed her eyes, but she could smell Monroe, musky and sharp with urine. She writhed and twisted, ignoring the tearing in her shoulders and scalp. With a curse hot in her ear, the fingers dug deeper into her cheeks, the tang of blood filling her mouth from the insides grinding against her teeth. Frustration and fury surged, and she screamed, a half – choked ragged thing.

A bellow filled the air, hoarse with fury. Like a puppet on a string, Monroe was yanked sideways, out of sight, one of the pair holding her disappearing much the same way. Suddenly free of restraint, Cate sagged onto her hands and knees, gasping, dimly aware of men going at each other all around. No doubt, the louts fighting among themselves over who would have a go at her next. Head hanging between her arms, from the corner of her eye she saw Monroe lying there, arms flung wide, the pudding face now frozen and still.

Damn him! Damn them all! Damn every man who thought he could have his way.

Damn them for thinking of her as nothing but a receptacle to stick their cock!

Monroe's very organ stood up like a rude gesture, mocking and taunting. His sword — that short, stout one noticed earlier — still hung at his belt, within arm's reach. Rage surging, Cate lurched to her feet, snatched it from his belt and swiped. She scooped up the severed bit of flesh and kicked it aside. Taking a double-fisted grasp on the sword, she stabbed, hacked and chopped at the body. The sword suddenly seeming inadequate, she snatched up a musket lying nearby and swung it like an ax at his head, again and again... and again... and again...

"*You must let go of the hate. You must let go...*"

Something, like a great festering boil, popped inside her and hate flowed like pus. Growling, Cate swung again and again, the meaty thuds and crack of bone bringing unspeakable joy.

"*Let go. Let go...*"

Sweat or tears, she couldn't tell which, stung her eyes and blurred her vision. The mass at her feet was no longer Monroe, but a parade of men, each and every one which had done her violence. Each blow dispatched one, beaten to oblivion as they had beaten her. Each one had taken a piece of her—her dignity, her pride, her future, her hope—and she took it back, one, by one, by one.

An arm swept around from behind and lifted her up and away by the waist. She kicked and squealed, wild to finish what she had started. The instant her feet touched the ground she whirled around, musket on high, and swung. A hand caught it in mid-air, wrenched from her grasp with maddening ease and flung it aside. Shrieking, she lunged for it, but was bodily blocked. She balled a fist and swung, connecting with a face, but the grasp didn't weaken. She kicked and clawed, bit and pummeled, but couldn't break the iron grasp. Somewhere, in the midst of it all, like a rap on a distant door, she became aware of being shaken, her name being called.

Huge hands engulfed her face. "Cate! It's me! Cate!"

Cate blinked and Thomas' face materialized inches away, the lake blue eyes wild with fear. She made an inarticulate noise, something between a sob and a gasp. She swayed, her knees buckled, and she collapsed into the safety of his arms.

❧

Thomas knelt clutching Cate, shielding her body with his against the fighting around them. His blood pulsed, the rampaging Viking awakened. A large part of him wanted to throw her down and feel the glory of his blade swiping the life from another of these Company boot-licks. Instead, all he could do was curve over her, protecting her.

A strangled cough and the last blow was delivered; his men had prevailed. One cove clung to life in a gurgling gasp; a final thrust put him out of his misery.

It was over... for now.

"*Memsaab?*" Al-Nejem asked from Thomas' elbow.

"She'll do. She might need help," Thomas added, peering

worriedly down at the quaking mass in his arms. He pushed away the hair, in hopes of seeing her face, but she only burrowed deeper into his chest.

Al-Nejem and the rest were already scavenging weapons, cartridge belts, powder and anything else of value from the bodies. Thomas rose, lifting Cate. Thank god, his legs held! Shifting her weight in his arms, they set off, back toward shore, his men forming a defensive barrier.

Dazed and bewildered, Cate made little mewling sounds. Fear of running into another patrol kept him from stopping to check her more thoroughly. Her body convulsed and shook, but she seemed sound and whole; she had certainly looked it, going at that Companymen like a demented Fury. She was blood from head to foot, but didn't cry out in pain. Hopefully, it was a good sign.

The forest opened into a small, park-like grove. Thomas swore under his breath at their ill-luck: a Company patrol was crossing it. Retreating from shore, he noted dryly. Running like the gutless scum they were.

The patrol made a ragtag effort to form up and fire, but — apparently in their panicked haste — all but two had forgotten to reload. The Lovelies weren't near so short-sighted. Thomas knelt, shielding Cate once more, until the sods were dealt with out-of-hand. His own body shook, torn between the desire to serve the bastards out and to see Cate safe.

Then they were up and moving again, the threat of encountering more patrols spurring them into all the haste as good conscience would allow. As they neared shore, Thomas became more and more aware of an uncanny silence there. Muskets still popped, now and then, but the great guns were strangely, and blessedly, silent. When they broke through the trees and into the settlement and found the brig hadn't moved. Even more significantly, she was quiet. The Company flag was gone, the no-quarter flag with it.

They had struck. Taken by what means he had no notion, nor did he care.

For all intents and purposes, it was over.

They pressed upshore through the turmoil of mopping up, putting out the fires and helping the wounded, his men falling away to bear a hand. Thomas fell in with the flow of casualties. He hadn't gone far before he came upon a cluster of islanders gathered before a trio. With their smoke-blackened making them look like a troupe of raccoons, Thomas had to be right on top of them before he recognized them as part of the *Lovely's* crew left as harbor watch.

"Mr. Felton, Mr. Kamal, Mr. Mostafa," Thomas said, nodding to each, the question of why the hell they were there, and not manning the ship, hanging like a bludgeon.

The three moved to reveal a pair of men hunched on the sand at their feet. Wearing green jackets and bloodied, one rocked in his place, holding an arm—probably broken—the other looking unlikely to live the day.

"What have we here?" Thomas demanded.

Mostafa toed the nearest. "Captain Griffin, of the fair brig *Mirabel*." A cant of his head indicated the now silent brig.

"This one is the first mate," Felton said, kicking the other.

"We took 'er, sir!" the three Lovelies announced in unison.

"We entertained 'em with the guns—Had to unship the rear wheels on the trucks and ream the ports for elevation—and then pulled around, and boarded 'er in 'er own smoke," Felton explained.

"Aye, they were too busy a-pattin' theyselves on the back to notice us a-comin' up the side," beamed Kamal.

"We demanded this one's sword in surrender, but he pitched it overboard," added Mostafa, scowling down.

"Indeed," Thomas mused, looking at the down-turned head. "Grace in defeat isn't your strength, *Captain* Griffin?"

"Fuck off."

"Filled with Christian charity, too." Thomas observed, dryly.

"Well done! Well done, indeed," Thomas directed to his men. "You turned the tide, that's for damned sure." He would have pounded them on the back and danced a jig had his arms not been occupied. "What do you have to say for yourself, *Captain*?"

"We were a-followin' orders: stand-off-and-on over the horizon, just in case that wily bastard Blackthorne gave His Lordship the slip," Griffin said to the sand before him. "After that escapade in Bridgetown, the reward for him was doubled. Every anchorage within two days' sail is being watched. He's trapped, still is, regardless of what happens to us." The last came with a combination of bullishness and pride.

"So, instead of him, you slaughtered women and children?"

Griffin twisted to glare up at Thomas. "We were to teach theses pirate whores a lesson, regardless."

A threatening growl resembling the animal sound of a mother protecting her young emitted from the gathering women. Thomas' fist at Cate's back closed, wishing for his weapon. It wouldn't change a damned thing, but damn it would feel good to cleave that smirking bastard's face, split that head like one of those melons the women were harvesting that morning.

God's wounds, it would feel good!

Cate stirred and moaned in his arms, calling him back to his duty. The red no-quarter flag was dropped in Griffin's lap.

"Give him to us."

Thomas looked up to find Bella, surrounded by an ever-increasing number of her constituents.

Griffin had reeled back at the flag. He looked up and shied at seeing the women closing in. One woman, armed or no, mightn't give a man pause, but a score, armed and furied, bloodied and battle-frazzled, gave all but the hopelessly simple pause.

"That blur you see is your life flashing," Thomas directed to the doomed souls at his feet. "Breathe deep, men, for it shall be your last,"

"They're yours," he announced to the women and turned to leave.

"What of the *Mirabel*, Cap'n?" asked Felton. "She's is taking on water faster than we can pump."

"Those broadsides took their toll, eh?" A glance at the brig proved Fenton's claim: she was sitting low and heavy, the bottom her inevitable destiny. A dry dock and several months' labor might save her, but there was little possibility of either. It came as no surprise: in the Company's eyes, vessels were expendable. Using a ship to the point of her self-destruction was a contemptuous thing, however, to his mind. He glared down at Griffin, his opinion of the scrub dropping another notch, if that was at all possible.

"Very well," Thomas sighed. "Man the pumps long enough to strip her." Lumber, cordage, canvas, stores, powder, hammocks: supplies which would be desperately needed to set all this mess to rights. There was a certain justice in cannibalizing the ship to repair the damages she had wrought. "Then let Jones have her."

"What about her crew?" Fenton asked.

Thomas eyed him, coldly. "You need ask?"

15: STARING TRUTH IN THE FACE

L IKE A COCKLE INTO ITS shell, Cate burrowed deep into the protection of the arms offered. Sunk in shock and misery, she was barely aware of being jostled as they ran. Voices, raised in anger and alarm, the clash and bellows of fighting, the air thickening with smoke and death only drove her deeper into her shelter.

The chest against her cheek vibrated; the words were lost, the arms around her tightening. She cowered deeper in morbid fear of being ripped from her haven.

More running; more shouts, but now not in anger, but hails. The running stopped. Sounds went from generalized and widespread to condensed, as if under a roof. The arms went away as she was laid down; she moaned in protest, scrabbling to regain her refuge, but was pushed back and shushed quiet. Feeling naked and exposed, she curled into a ball and rolled away. A voice calling her name, so throaty and rasping it had to be Nathan's, sent her hopes soaring. She opened her eyes to a face inches from hers, too obscured by soot to recognize. The blue eyes and the blond hair, hanging in sweat-dampened snakes, was enough, however.

Thomas. It was only Thomas.

She sank in disappointment.

Wracked with convulsive shivers, Cate laid, staring and blinking. The canvas and spars overhead, the seaman's knots securing them, the mariners' hails, hammocks, and the smell of salt and tar were all indications of being on board. But, that would mean these last few days had been all a dream, a very bad one.

Aching jaws, scalp and shoulders dashed that illusion out-of-hand. Unyielding solidness and rattle of palm fronds, combined with—most revealing of all—a predominance of female voices and children crying all pointed to her being on land. Her disorientation was further complicated by having to dodge Thomas' searching hands, which were far from gentle as he checked her over for injury.

"Did one of those louts—?" Thomas choked, his cracked voice failing.

Cate smiled weakly. "They tried" came in a voice she didn't recognize.

Did I scream that much?

Time was of little difference, but knowing her location seemed key. She was no longer in the forest, but as for the rest...? The noise of battles might vary from one to the next, but the sounds of the aftermath—the collective moans and screams, cries for help, cries of grief, agony and anguish—were identical. One inhalation dispelled any lingering doubt; there was no mistaking the smell of bodies, bloodied, shattered and ruined, in such close proximity.

A field hospital, she thought, looking up at the canvas roof once more: wounded tent, sick bay, or whatever they called it in these parts.

Cate was torn from her machinations by an explosive gasp of relief from Thomas. He said something under his breath, sounding much like "Praise the gods!" in whatever the language was. She looked up to find him beaming. Following his straight-as-a-spar line of sight, she found Celia making her way toward them, bearing a smile nearly as brilliant as his.

"You're well," he announced, pride replacing relief. "I kept telling myself only an imbecilic numbskull would trifle with you."

They struck up an odd stance: Thomas to one side, Celia the other, Cate lying between like Hadrian's Wall. In that island of silence, amid the surrounding sea of havoc, the pair carried on a silent conversation, an arched brow, a canted head, a faint lift of a shoulder speaking volumes.

Finally, Celia broke away and bent to lay a cool hand on Cate's cheek. "What happened?"

"She was—" Thomas' voice caught. He coughed and began anew. "There was trouble. Four or five... men, mebbe..."

Celia nodded, half-listening, knowing the answer before she even asked. "Let us clean off this blood and see what we have."

Glancing down at herself, Cate found the reason for Thomas' concern: from the chest down, she looked like she might have been butchering a bullock.

A basin was produced by the troupe of young assistants

following Celia. She wetted a cloth and began to bathe Cate's face.

"It is seawater, calendula and pepper," Celia said at Cate's sharp intake. "The pepper stings at first, but it slows the bleeding and eases the pain."

The dusky eyes held Cate's as she worked, learning there what she needed to know. At length, Celia's brow smoothed, and she stopped. "They didn't hurt you, did they?"

A cock of the brow emphasized the word "hurt" while, at the same time, indicated the question was posed for only one person's benefit: Thomas.

"No." The cleansing and examination had allowed Cate the opportunity to confirm what she already knew. A thickness and coppery taste at the back of her throat meant her nose had been bleeding, as had her split lip, but the bulk of the blood down her front belonged to someone else. She was bruised, contused and scraped, but overall unscathed.

"She's well," Celia directed to Thomas, and then to Cate, "Perhaps something to calm you a bit?"

Cate made to protest, but realized her convulsive shaking betrayed her.

"My work here is finished," Celia declared, rising. "Too many await to linger." The last came as a simple announcement, without either accusation or reproach.

Celia took her leave, a lingering farewell glance cast back over her shoulder at Thomas.

"Told you I was fine," Cate huffed, in her wake.

"It would be a mite more convincing if you could say that without your teeth chattering," Thomas observed dryly. "I'd feel better if you'd scream, scratch, curse, bite... *something*."

Cate frowned. She remembered some—Lesauvage, captivity, Companymen—but only in incomplete flashes, some making her start and jerk, none of which went unnoticed by Thomas. In light of everything which had happened, it was a wonder why she wasn't an emotional wreck.

"I did all that out there," she finally said with a vague gesture.

Her frown deepened with the effort of trying to sort it all out. "How did you know where to—?" Finishing the thought demanded more strength of mind than she possessed.

The corner of Thomas' mouth quirked as he considered. "You leave a wide trail."

The strong false note in his response suggested that it was far from the case. Still, she lacked both fortitude and will necessary to point that out.

As Cate lay there, she took in her surroundings more fully. As suspected, it was a sickbay, still in the process of being constructed, judging by the *thunk!* of mauls and shouting. The sailmaker and his mates' needles flashed with fashioning hammocks, but not quickly enough. Hammocks, cots, chairs with a board between them, lockers or crates lashed together, anything which might serve as a bed being put to use.

A man, bent with age, approached bearing a cup with concentrated intent. "Miz Celia bid you should drink this directly," was announced with the officious tone of one refused too often and weary of being reprimanded for it.

Struck with an overwhelming thirst, Cate reached for the cup, but her hand shook too hard to manage. His hand closing over hers and the cup, Thomas knelt on the bunk, lifted her up and guided it to her mouth. It was an herbal tea of some sort — although she would have drank it if it was the water from the bottom of the *Morganse's* gig — and she drained it in a few lusty gulps.

Thomas lowered her back down with eloquent care. In dribs and drabs, the sequence of events, first with Lesauvage, and then Monroe became clearer. With that came the conviction that Thomas would have seen her hacking at Monroe. Only a blind fool could have missed it, and Thomas was neither. She stared, waited for him to say something about the damned whale lying between them. But, he only hovered, plucking and tweaking at her.

Shame rendered her silent.

The tea answered admirably. The shivering diminished to no more than sporadic tremors. And then, with a long sigh, they were gone.

It was over. It had been close, too close, but it was over.

Thomas stood, shifting on his feet. "By all appearances, those cursed sods have surrendered, but there's a grand bit of mopping up to be done," he added at the sporadic pop of gunfire.

"Go," she urged with all the earnestness she could muster.

He found her hand and held it. Dark and searching, the lake blue eyes found hers. "Rest easy, lovely. A watch will be posted. None of those lurking bastards will get to you."

He fervently pressed her knuckles to his lips. "You're safe."

Cate smiled faintly. It seemed expected.

"I know. Go," she insisted at hearing him hailed.

A parting kiss on her forehead, and he was gone.

She settled deeper into the cot, watching Thomas weave through the crowd, feeling a pang of regret when he could no longer be seen. In spite of lying amidst a tumultuous press of people, she was in essence, alone. In the ensuing solitude, exhaustion of both mind and body laid like sandbags on her chest, her eyes refusing to remain open. And so, she closed them. She lay listening, knowing without seeing what was transpiring around her, for she had lived this horror far too many times. The smells of blood, misery ad death struck with diamond-like clarity:

It was the Rising. She was in a farmhouse, one among of scores of injured Highlanders. She lay face down, her shoulder laid open by a blade, one which should have cleaved her in half had the Lobster not turned it at the last instant. Men held her down and sewed her up. Inside, she was broken, but there was naught to be done for it. With no notion of what to expect from a wounded woman, they moved her to the attic. "Privacy" they called it, where she might scream and cry, and not disturb the men. Scream she did not. She couldn't allow it, for there were far too many, far more injured than she.

The tears did flow, however, in an unstoppable stream.

Alone, face down in the dark—not even a dip lamp had been spared—she had sobbed and shivered. Her tongue flicked out, feeling the parched and peeling lips once more. Water became her fixation. A cup of it sat at her head but, with every breath a torture, any movement risked crying out, the precious liquid was rendered as unreachable as if it had been on the moon.

She might have lain there an hour; she might have lain there a week. A flickering light on the wall marked someone coming, the joy of human company was quashed by the mortification of having soiled herself. Faces poked up from the stairway, somewhat dismayed to find she still lived. She begged for word of Brian. Did he live? How badly was he wounded? Anything...!

But they said nothing. The light receded, and she was in the dark, alone again.

Cate jerked from her reverie. The recollection had a diamond-like sharpness to it. No one should ever endure the desperate misery for want of a drink of water or a kind word, not if she drew breath.

Every nook of her body protesting, she pushed up, swung her feet onto the ground and set to work.

War had taught Cate many things. The most joyous day of one's life was when they realized they had survived it. Then came the fervent prayers that they never be obliged to endure that hell again.

The worst day was to find oneself reliving the horror, mired once more in that same gore and misery.

The flurry and chaos of battle was rivaled only by the fervor of the aftermath. The entire island was in high gear. As Bella had mentioned, the island had been attacked before. From every tribulation comes a benefit: now, they were prepared. Everyone, right down to the barely-breeched trotting behind their mothers, had a duty and knew it. Piles of medicinal supplies, butts of water—fresh and salt—wood for fires, food, blankets, beds: the preparations were executed with a precision befitting of a campaigning army.

The cannonballs might have destroyed much but, to her dismay, Cate discovered the island's prejudices were still intact. Her inquiries as to what she might do to help were met with everything from annoyance to cold glares. Finally, a bucket and rag was shoved at her, with instructions that she should go attend the casualties' sordid needs. The human body could produce a vast number of noxious substances and she did her best to clean them off. She bore no ill-will at being relegated to such low tasks, however. She was helping, and there was so very, *very* much to do. Still, when no one was looking—which was most of the time—she took up a water bucket and dipper, and made sure no one was without a drink.

Land and sea, Cate had seen many a man settle a leather strap between his teeth in preparation for a limb to be sawn off. That was distasteful enough. Seeing a woman do the same was thoroughly unsettling. She'd heard many and many a woman in the throes of childbed, but the screams heard now were unmatched. And a child's...!

No matter how many dead one might see, a child's shattered, lifeless corpse was a gruesome sight, and was nearly Cate's undoing.

Two died in her arms.

Cate straightened, wiping her mouth after vomiting—more like dry wretch, for her last meal was naught but a distant memory.

Damn, I fancied I was made of stronger stuff!

Amid the shouts of caregivers—necessary, if one was to be heard by the one at their elbow—the high-pitched chorus of agony and wailing infants rose over the lower-pitched keening of grief and despair. All that was against a repetitive backdrop of one soul, tied to a post, cackling in hysterical laughter, and the chant-like pleas for help and water. It was the latter which tore at Cate the most, and she often found herself washing with one hand, whilst serving water with the other.

"I left you in your cot; you weren't there."

Cate straightened from washing a man who had just vomited all over himself to find Thomas standing there.

"You expected me to be?" she asked, matching his testiness with her own.

"Nay," he said absently, scanning the general gore and misery. "Nathan said to look for the blood; you'd be there."

"He's here?" Hopes soaring, Cate lunged in the direction of shore. Thomas darted to block her.

"No," he said, apologetically. "It was just... something he said... once."

As Thomas turned away, the side of his shirt came into view, bright with blood.

"You're bleeding!" she cried.

"'Tis nothing," he said, twisting away from her searching hands. "Most of it belongs to someone else. I'll do."

He eyed her. At some point, an apron made of Number One canvas had been dropped over her head. So stiff it could have stood on its own, it was already covered with blood and an assortment of filth.

He smiled wryly. "I see what Nathan meant. You are in your glory. I give you joy of it."

Thomas tapped his brow in salute, leaving two bloody fingerprints amid the soot, and took his leave.

Shattered by musket or cannonball, hacked, sliced, slashed, splintered, shattered or burned: the islanders suffered every violence which could be visited upon the human frame. By way of doors, hatchcovers, planks or chairs, the bearers, Thomas often among them, delivered the wounded in a bewildering stream. Many more limped in under their own power and slumped wherever room might be found. Chairs, settees, ottomans: all the furniture which had provided seating around the fires the night before did the same there, causing the sickbay to bear an odd resemblance to a sitting room. Initially, the women and more critical were given the beds but, with the sheer number of arrivals, that effort was soon abandoned. When the beds, hammocks, cots and everything else ran out, the wounded were left on the ground, often with no more than a bit of old sailcloth under them.

Muskets and canister are indiscriminate. Man, woman, and child — some barely more than babes-in-arms — were struck with equality. Overwhelmed by shock and grief, many youths sobbed inconsolably; a pair huddled together between the cots, mute and round - eyed as owlets. With the flow of casualties came reports of rapes and barbarities. Such rumors were always rampant in war. A woman with her belly slashed open and clutching her fetus, however, made them all too true.

Sweat trickling between her shoulder blades, Cate hitched her skirts and picked her way through the wounded. Compassion could paralyze a soul: to attend one meant denying another; to tighten the bootlace tourniquet on one, meant leaving another shivering with cold; to prop up one choking on her own blood was to ignore another lying in her own filth. Cate hardened herself to the sights, while at the same time, provided what she could, praying all the while that someone to help her might soon arrive.

The heat of the day increased and the chant for water rose to a gut-wrenching drone. While administering to one, three more would be tugging at her skirts. Time became Cate's enemy, as she scrambled from one to the next, refilling bucket after bucket from the scuttlebutts. She worked down the rows, the victims becoming faceless in her hurry.

"Thank you... sir," said one in earnest appreciation.

Cate started, the dipper hanging forgotten in mid-air. Calling her "sir" meant he was from either the *Morganse* or *Lovely*. She peered closely at the soot-blackened face.

"Mr... Daniels." The name popped into her head a fraction before the moment became an embarrassing one.

"Aye, mum, John Daniels, foresheets, starbolin," he gasped through a jaw set against pain.

A Lovelie.

In truth, Daniels was likely beyond noticing or caring about any social blunder on her part: his middle was bright red and the stink of pierced gut hung about him. The loss of blood killed most straightaway, but not all were so lucky. In this case, the only thing the victim could look forward to as his gut festered and went foul was hours, perhaps days of unspeakable agony, a prolonged agony which would cause anyone within hearing to pray for a quick end.

Grey and sheened with sweat, Daniels' was the first truly familiar face; Cate couldn't in good conscience leave him alone to his misery. She bathed his brow and gave him more water. Still, as much as she wished it, she couldn't ignore the plaintive calls of the others and was forced to leave him.

Prayers were finally answered: help arrived in the way of three girls, the buckets they toted almost larger than the bearers. Their presence freed Cate to shift her attentions to bathing the incoming casualties. The directive was that every wound was to be washed with a solution of Celia's making, the same which had been used on Cate. When first applied, it stung like the blazes—for which she was frequently cursed—but within a short time, the overall pain eased and, more significantly, the bleeding slowed. In that process, however, Cate was brought face-to-face with many in need of nothing more than simple stitching, binding, or salving. She couldn't in good conscience leave them to suffer. Her blood box was sent for, and she set to work.

Cate had just finished stitching a leg and was preparing to bind it, when she noticed Celia standing over Mr. Daniels' cot.

"Can you help him?" Cate asked. The inquiry was dubious, and yet hopeful. There was the remote, very remote chance the herbwoman might have one miracle up her sleeve.

Celia's expression tightened. "Not him. Do you not see the black pall over him?" The translucent eyes met Cate's as she came up beside her.

Cate considered Celia over-estimated her capabilities. Looking down at poor Daniels, she wasn't quite sure what she saw. There was no black pall, but she knew what she smelled: the festering gut was making its grisly progress.

Celia knelt next to the cot. Secretively turning her body, she took something out of a small bag tucked at her cleavage, and then slipped it into the corner of Daniels' mouth. Laying a hand on his forehead, she closed her eyes, her lips moving silently. She rose into Cate's curious look.

"It is a bean," she explained in a low voice. "It allows them their peace and the ultimate mercy, the one their God will not allow," she added, with a resentful sniff.

"Some might say you're interfering with God's will, on that one," Cate countered, lower yet.

"He is not my god; I do not fear him." Celia jerked her shoulders. "It is the same mercy they allow an animal. It escapes me why they will not allow a fellow human the same?"

"I suppose we'll never know whose God is the right one," Cate sighed. Nathan had often referred to the number of gods represented on a ship, each man believing his to be superior to all others. "The Afterlife alone is probably the only place we'll really know."

"Perhaps we are there already," Celia said with a knowing smile. "Perhaps the answer is before you, but you are just not attending."

Cate stared, trying to smoke Celia's meaning. This, however, was neither the time nor the place for the philosophic, and so she returned to the half-bound leg she had been working on. She soon became aware of the intent gold-eyed look and lifted the binding so that her handiwork might be seen. With a mixture of surprise and approval, Celia nodded.

Cate angled her head toward the woman in the next bed. "I cleaned the burn, trimmed the charred skin, mixed a little oil of rose and lime water, and then dressed it with a feather." She spoke with the tone of expecting to be reproved and not caring if she were.

"Violence has formed you in many ways," Celia observed, approvingly. "You know wounds."

Cate sighed wearily. "I've seen my share." From girlhood, her life seemed so filled with injury and the suffering of others, she could only guess at what a life without it might have been. Fiddler's Green, to be sure.

"Your talents are being wasted." Celia directed the remark toward Polly, one of Cate's co-workers. The woman opened her mouth to object, but thought better.

"Can you work with Joe?" Celia asked with a hopeful lilt.

Cate inwardly groaned. Once a ship's barber and, hence, its surgeon, Joe Cornwall had a chest filled with implements which looked more like something from the Inquisition. Being reduced to one leg and one eye hadn't reduced Cornwall's verve for applying his instruments, which he did with the abandon of the Grand Inquisitor himself. Through the day, she had been called to assist in his butchery. She had turned her head and swallowed down the bile as his saws ground through bone, gagging on the smell of cooked flesh when the hot iron was whipped across the stump.

He and Celia had gone at each other at twenty-to-the-dozen in professional disagreements. Cornwall's work table—several lockers lashed together and covered with canvas—looked like a hog-butcher's shop. Everything, including him, dripped red, flies buzzing lazily about a basket of discarded limbs at his feet. The stink of rum oozed from him like he was sweating the stuff.

Now, Cornwall's single eye swiveled up from the blood spattered face of his current victim and fixed on Cate. Set in a permanent scowl, his countenance was nearly as gargoylish as Pryce's. His toothless mouth munching on a cud of tobacco, a stream of brown juice shot out, falling just short of her feet. "Ain't gonna have no wimmen fallin' out."

"I didn't before, did I?" Cate retorted. She would have preferred going back to hauling slops jars than this.

Years at sea, the habit of deferring to authority deeply ingrained, however, prevailed. Celia was in command and so her orders stood. Joe jerked a nod and set back to work. Celia's umbrella-of-authority provided Cate with a newfound credibility. Cornwall swore as he worked, but neither his venom, nor tobacco was directed at her again.

At one point, finishing his latest victim, Cornwall stepped away, presumably in search of his next victim. Cate groaned as she straightened. Dabbing the sweat from her temples with her forearm, she caught sight of a familiar face coming toward her: Thomas, bearing a casualty, one more in a long line. This particular one was female, judging by the pinafore and long hair swaying with his stride. At such a distance, the age was difficult to determine; a full grown woman could look like a child in his arms.

Finally spotting Cate, Thomas altered course. He laid the child before her. The moment her body touched the table, the little thing arched her body, screaming "Mama! Mama! Mama!" Her frenzied state gave her surprising strength, requiring both adults to hold her down. Her chant joined the shrieks of someone on the next table having a splinter dug from a burned leg.

"Where is Mama?" Cate asked over the combined din.

"Not to be found," Thomas replied grimly.

Cate rolled her eyes. Separated, like so many others. The sickbay was becoming the central gathering point where the lost or word of them might be had. Their calling out, desperation taking it to ear-splitting pitch, as they scrambled among the dead and dying only added to the mayhem.

An urgent hail prompted Thomas to step away, leaving Cate to hold down the frantic child alone. The returning Cornwall, now smelling even stronger of rum, poked a finger at the child's arm.

"Broke," he announced, with the same compassion as a judge passing a sentence.

The wrist looked out of joint, as well, Cate observed, as she wrestled to keep the child from flinging herself to the ground.

"Hold 'er," Cornwall said, snatching up a saw still dripping with the blood and bone fragments of his last victim.

"No!" The arm was shattered, but the bone hadn't broken the skin. There was hope, real hope of recovery and doing so intact.

The single eye fixed on Cate and narrowed. "It's broke. It'll take months to heal; might never use it again. Less suffering this way, quick and painless."

"Painless!" Cate shrieked, incredulous. "Which would you have preferred when *you* were the one lying there: a gimpy leg or a stump?"

Cornwall's answer was to seize the arm and poise the saw. Cate was now caught between covering the child and pulling her away. Brandishing the saw in Cate's face, Cornwall uttered a stream of curses which might well have made Nathan blush. Another burst was offered with opinions on a woman's place. Cate's counter of reminding him of where he was—or more to the point, where he wasn't—only to receive another scathing burst. A tug-of-war ensued, the child now shrieking in both agony and terror.

Suddenly, Cate was lifted away, the child going with her. Imposing himself, Thomas glared at Cornwall. He started to say something but, thinking better, plucked the girl from Cate and turned away. Cate followed close on his heels, Cornwall sputtering insults in their wake.

It was a short distance, only a matter of a few of Thomas' long strides, to Celia's table, but after Cornwall's butcher shop, it was as if they had stepped into another world. Neat, tidy, scrubbed, smelling of vinegar and sage, calm, confidence and compassion ruled there as they laid the child down.

"Do you know her? What's her name?" Cate pleaded.

Celia smoothed the black hair back from the child's face, and Cate's heart both leapt and sank.

Red, swollen with crying, contorted with fear and pain, failed to obscure her parentage. A cautionary voice warned Cate to not jump to conclusions, but how could she not? She had seen John; softened by femininity and youth, this one was but a mirror image—the same jet hair, the same high cheekbones and straight nose, the same shape of the mouth—stamped by the same father.

She looked to Thomas for confirmation that she wasn't by some wild fluke mistaken, and then Celia. A darting glance from the latter seemed to say "Yes" but it was too brief to be sure.

Celia took the small face between her hands and tipped it up, gently shaking her in supplication. "Dorrie! Dorrie, look at me!"

The eyes opened, and it was like looking into another's: the color of burned walnuts, with cinnamon and gold flecks, and—as if that wasn't enough—framed by double lashes.

Looking straight into those walnut-colored eyes, now locked with the gold ones, Celia said something too low for Cate to hear. Still murmuring, she ran a hand several times over the ebony crown, each time a bit slower and firmer. With each pass, Dorrie quieted, ultimately going nearly limp.

Celia passed a hand over Dorrie's forearm, a nod confirming Cate's earlier observation.

"We must work quickly; the sleep will not last long," Celia said, straightening.

"The wrist...?" Cate asked, indicating the hand hanging at an odd angle.

Celia stopped in her preparations. "Yes, it should be done, the sooner the better. Do you know…?"

Cate nodded without fully realizing what she was committing herself to. With so many in such urgent need, many of them children, a broken arm and dislocated wrist were so very minor. And yet, good conscious wouldn't allow her to leave this one to suffer.

"Yes." Already shifting her position, Cate spoke a bit more authoritatively than might have been fitting. She had executed the maneuver once and out of desperation: her brother had fallen from a horse — their father's favorite and one they shouldn't have been riding — and, in her panic, her brother screaming, their father sure to arrive any minute, she had grabbed and jerked.

Her brother, however, had been both older and larger. Dorrie's bones looked as fine and fragile as a quail's leg. If Cate was to jerk too hard, she might do damage to either the wrist or fracture; not hard enough meant having to do it again. Still, whatever she was about to do, it needed to be done soon, whilst "the sleep" was still upon the child.

Celia returned to her preparations, silence being her consent.

"Hold here, below the break," Cate instructed Thomas.

She clenched her fists, willing herself to stop shaking. This next bit was known to make a grown man blench and bellow. With a broken arm, in the bargain…

Cate shuddered and swallowed down a large lump. Resetting her grasp, she took a deep breath and, with an eye on the joint, jerked. There was the satisfying crackling *pop!* of tiny bones falling back into order.

Dorrie stirred, moaned, and then stilled. Celia gave a quick approving look. "Set the arm, if you please."

As Cate splinted and bound her arm, Dorrie's head turned, allowing the lamp light to fall full on her face. It was all she could do to keep from stopping to stare.

"*Hundreds.*"

The word had haunted Cate since the day Nathan uttered it. She had inquired as to how many women he had lain with. Many would have considered it a stupid question, one best left unasked. Many, most women would prefer to live in ignorance, but her character demanded to know its enemy. His response had set her world spinning while she accepted the number with as much grace as she could muster. After all, if Nathan was to accept her past, she was obliged to accept his, although one husband against hundreds of women hardly seemed equitable.

It required no great penetration to know that, in the natural order of things, there would be products of those hundreds of unions. Nathan had conceded as much, "three or four" that he knew of. John, however, had not been included in that sum; he had been a complete surprise to Nathan as much as she. Cate looked down at the ebony head and wondered to which category this one belonged?

Cate blinked from her brown study to find Celia looking on with great interest. "We will need boneset," she announced and left with purpose.

While Celia made her preparations, Cate bathed Dorrie and searched for further injury. She realized then the blessing of being a stranger, of being detached from the casualties. This face made it all personal, too personal —

A big hand came down over hers. "Cate, get hold of yourself."

Cate looked up into Thomas' grave face. "Don't you see...?" she hissed. "Can't you see who she is? Who her — ?" She choked, unable to finish.

"Aye, I noticed... something."

"Coy doesn't flatter you," she said coldly.

"Very well, yes. I'd have to have been a cock-eyed cod's-head not to see it. What the hell do you expect me to say? And no," he added hastily, holding up a desisting hand. "I have no notion who the mother is. Just wish to hell I could have found her, I'll grant you that," he huffed under his breath. "Could have saved us both a great deal of grief."

Thomas hunched his shoulders at another agonized howl and grumbled "Too damned many dead and those who would be better off if they were."

With no further injuries found, other than some superficial bruises and scrapes, Cate bid Thomas to move the still-placid body to a swinging cot. Hailed with urgency again, Thomas took his leave. In his wake, Celia arrived bearing a cup of medicinal tea and several slightly pounded leaves. Dorrie moaned and turned her head, refusing to drink — She had her father's stubbornness, to be sure, that scowl and wrinkled brow being all too familiar —

Celia produced a vial from her bulging pockets and dabbed a bit of its contents at the child's temples and behind each ear. In the meantime, Cate packed the leaves atop the point of the fracture.

In the same methodical way as before, Celia stroked Dorrie's head. "Let the deep sleep come, my sweet one."

And so it did. The eyelids grew heavy, closing over the luminous eyes, and the face fell lax.

Frowning, Celia's hand lingered on the smooth head. "I wish I had something for the terrors to come."

Celia straightened into Cate's curious look, realizing then

what she had been seeing all day. Like a ship's wake in a storm-tossed sea, an abiding calm followed Celia. Every person she attended still suffered agony, anguish and bleeding, but it was all considerably less than when she started.

She smiled self-consciously. "The 'sleep' is something I could do as a child; as I grew older, I improved. I have to be careful; some, many are inclined toward suspicion and—" She stopped short, unwilling to utter the rest.

Sleep-healing, temple sleep, incubation: Cate had heard of those in the Far East who could heal through such means. Not a miracle, in the Biblical sense, but the laying-on-of – the-hands of any description had a miraculous aura, especially to the afflicted.

Sorceress, spell-caster, witch: all carried a stigma and the threat of ruin, the brand under Celia's gaily-patterned headscarf physical proof, as if any were needed. Cate would have bet her shift Celia was none of those, but she also understood the burden of a born talent, valued by some, but misunderstood and distrusted by most. Cate's own small gift of connecting with those near and dear had earned her a lifetime of suspicion.

On that thought, Cate briefly closed her eyes and reached out, as she so often could.

No, Nathan wasn't there. Whether he had abandoned her or just wasn't attending she couldn't tell.

"I can only help the open-minded. Those with hearts closed by ignorance and suspicion," Celia added bitterly, "I can only offer potions and teas."

She patted Cate on the arm. "Cum, too many are waiting."

Cate reluctantly left Dorrie's cot to work more closely with Celia. She washed what she was told to wash, sewed what she was told to sew, set what needed set, binding it all when she was done. In between, she fetched buckets of hot water and hauled away buckets of filth.

She witnessed miracles, for it was something just short of that at seeing a gaping wound be pinched closed and the skin glued like paper. In most settlements or villages, such magic would have gotten Celia either pricked or drowned. But apparently, pirates were a more worldly lot and not an eye was batted.

Celia looked on with approval as Cate closed a scalp. "The needle is your friend."

Cate demurred. "Well, I know which end to grab."

Given a choice, Cate would have far preferred embroidering a busk than flesh, but if wishes were wings, everyone would be an angel. She was handed a book of needles of even finer quality than the finest London-made. She was struggling with a particularly difficult case, matters not being made any easier with the victim writhing and screaming — often before the needle was even applied — one leg flung over to hold them down, when Celia thrust an implement before her.

"It is a canula," Celia explained at Cate's puzzlement. A brief demonstration showed how the carved-ivory tool worked like an extension of one's fingers, only smaller and far, far more precise. Its miracle was in the tidy work and — glory of glories — saved time, which meant discomfort saved.

Caregiving, however, wasn't without its own hazards. Pain and terror robbing many of their wits, Cate was punched, kicked, kneed, slapped, clawed and bitten, scalded, stabbed, jabbed, elbowed, tromped and cut by her fellow workers. She took the blows as a sort of penance for all her failures and shortcomings, for all those past and present she had failed and all those she couldn't help now.

As Cate held down one screaming child, barely the size of a shoat — old enough to have teeth, however, she observed, when they clamped into her arm — as a splinter was dug from its side, her own tears welled, over-whelmed by the grief of having failed this one, as she had failed so many. She should have moved faster, gotten more children to safety. Once again, she cursed Lesauvage and his men, not only for attacking the island, but for having stopped her from achieving that goal.

There were no tears of grief, however. Her gaze drifted to the line of corpses outside the tent, the smallest looking like sacks of meal in their makeshift shrouds. If one couldn't cry for them all, then they should cry for none.

Ironically, the other miracle, amid all the death and dying, was the one of life being brought forth. It was a damned awkward time to be in child-bed, but Mother Nature rarely paid heed to convenience, when it came to that. Those deep in the throes of miscarriage, however, were the ones who gave Cate pause. Their groans — so very different in timbre from the physically injured — so strongly echoed the ones she had once made, she sometimes worked half-bent, as if the child were being ripped from her own womb. Demands on everyone's attention being what they were, miscarry or in child-bed, the sufferers were left to their own devices. After all was said and done, no mortal hand could change Nature's course. They weren't ignored, however. Clean cloths were brought, an eye kept, and an ear cocked for when matters grew nearer to the ultimate end.

Cate stood at the feet of a woman lying on the ground as

Celia examined her, the poor thing twitching and crying out, not in pain, but in terror at merely being touched. The bit of cloth discretely draped over her fell away to reveal her clothing split from chest to knees. Her abdomen and torso were slashed, one breast nearly severed. The realization that she had been brutalized struck Cate like a bludgeon and she stumbled back.

"No, I... can't...!" she wheezed in horror at Celia's expectant look. With the numbers of women being attacked — God help her, she couldn't use the word "rape" — Cate knew — intellectually, at any rate — that encountering the victims was inevitable. She worked with Celia, every step weighted by the daunting prospect.

Celia rose to catch Cate, her fingers digging into her arm. "You must —"

"I can't. Not her, not this! She's been —"

"You must!"

The exchange was conducted in a low-voiced hiss.

"The final step in healing is to help others do the same," Celia insisted.

"I know nothing," Cate flared, jerking free.

Celia slowly knelt once more, her gaze unwavering from Cate. "You know everything. You know their pain and, more importantly, you know their fears."

Yes, so much, too much, Cate thought, reeling back.

"Help her survive and overcome, as you did." Celia spoke without anger, and yet every word penetrated to the bone. "Turn from her now, and you turn your back on everything you have gained."

Cate swayed, dread freezing her in place.

Celia reached up and pressed Cate to her knees beside her. "She needs your help, not your sympathy, nor disgust. Can you give her that much? Or, am I to beckon someone else?"

Cate woodenly nodded in acknowledgment. Closer now, her gut roiled at the smell, not of blood, but the stink of a man: his sweat, his seed. Garnering her courage, Cate reached toward the prone woman. Seeing her hand shake, she snatched it back and buried it in the folds of her skirt. Fine tremors coursed through her in uneven waves and her bowels rumbled threateningly.

She gulped and rasped "I can do it" through a rigid jaw. She drew a deep, shuddering breath. "I'll need —"

"It shall be brought," Celia cut in as she rose.

Cate peered at the victim, thinking there was something vaguely familiar about her. The face, however, was too bloodied, the features too distorted to make it out. "Do you know her name?" she called to Celia.

"Lygia."

Cate looked down and gaped. That morning, she had walked to the fields with Lygia. She could still hear Lygia's girlish, bubbling laugh, see her snapping Mediterranean eyes as she had made them all giggle with her mimic of Nathan.

The knife cuts, the battered face, the blood, the abuse: it was too much like looking down at herself. Cate desperately sought to find the differences — the hair black and straight, the body shorter and thicker, the skin more olive — anything to help separate herself, but in vain. Lygia made a noise, something between a groan and a sob...

So much like the one I made.

Cate closed her eyes, straining to recall when it had been her lying there, what had been her greatest need, what had given her the greatest ease.

"Lygia, you're safe. You're among friends." The words were spoken in a strange voice. Cate opened her eyes to discover it had come from her lips.

"Lygia, it's me — " she began, more firmly.

Lygia emitted a shriek and rose up, scratching and clawing, fighting an invisible foe. Cate wrestled to quiet her, being punched and bitten for her efforts. Finally, Cate's strength prevailed and Lygia collapsed in a keening sob. Polly, a co-worker, arrived with hot water and cloths. They washed the now insensible woman; it was a state Cate recognized: shock, mortification and despondency overriding everything, including pain.

Just as it had for me.

Wishing to take advantage of this preoccupied respite, Cate took up a needle began sewing up one gaping length of flesh after another, the power of sheer will keeping her hand steady. She worked in quick economical motions, the element of time disallowing her to make more tidy work of it.

Just as they had to do for me.

Cate's own belly and sides twitched at every the pluck and pull of the needle. She remembered every stitch taken, screaming and fighting, Brian's strength and bulk the only thing which could restrain her.

Blood and other noxious liquids soaking up through her skirts, Cate murmured "I'm sorry" and a host of other apologies, whether in reference to the violence wrought or the pain she inflicted in the spirit of helping she wasn't sure. Just then, the poor soul was unaware, but Cate knew the words would find root, rising like an inner voice in the solitary hours to come, when the ghosts would run rampant. As she worked, several stab wounds were encountered and closed, the lack of spurting blood or stink of pierced gut giving her hope they wouldn't prove mortal. Lesser wounds were salved with honey or packed with sugar. The latter would have been prohibitive anywhere else, just by virtue of both scarcity and cost. But this was a pirate island, where sugar was as ubiquitous as rum, and it answered surprisingly well. Compresses, sent by Celia, were slipped between Lygia's legs and a shawl was draped over her for decency's sake.

Once finished, Cate twisted aside, fell on all fours and vomited, the dry-retching of a long-empty stomach. She sat back on her heels, gasping. A water bucket sat within reach; she took a dipperful, rinsed her mouth, spat, and then took a long drink. She threw her head back and closed her eyes. More victims of violation arrived in a steady flow. If she could help one, then she was compelled to help them all.

Before rising, Cate found Lygia's hand and clasped it. "Listen to me, Lygia. Spit in that bastard's eye," she said, low and insistent. "Prove you're the better one by surviving this."

Lygia moaned and turned her head away.

A departing pat on her arm, Cate rose. Moving to the next, she found the poor soul lying in a pool of her own blood. Knife still in her fist, she had ended her misery. With nothing else to hand, Cate drew up the sodden apron to cover the now-still face and moved on to the next. Whether by kismet, guiding hand, unwitting preferences or just blind luck, Cate worked for the next while among the abuse victims. Sometimes crawling from one to the next, knowing all the while that these were only the most critical. Being brought to the sickbay was a public declaration of what had been done to them, something most would avoid, if at all possible. They were a pitiful sight, lying or hunched together, shameful, bewildered, sobbing, bereft, sunken. She smiled tolerantly in the face of being cursed and told to "Get the bloody hell away!" She had uttered much the same words; Brian had taken many a tongue-lashing. And, as for poor Nathan...

Clamping her lower lip between her teeth, Cate shook her head. Bless his soul, Nathan was the only reason she still walked this earth. Had she been left to her own—as she had so vehemently demanded—she would have surely withered and perished.

She did what she could for the victims in the physical way. As for the rest, there was precious little: the deed was done, the damage wrought. Nothing, nothing could undo that, no matter how desperately one wished it. As much as they didn't wish to hear it—she certainly hadn't when it had been her lying there—

time was what these women needed. It was the ultimate balm, no potion, nostrum, counsel or advice would serve any better.

The greatest significance, however, was the secondary reward. Whether by insight, crystal-gazing or reading the bloody tea dregs, Celia had been correct, there was something to be gained through helping these women. Blood and grime weren't the only things being washed away by Celia's special solution: anger, frustration, remorse and, yes, guilt—for surely there was something she could have done to prevent it from happening—fell away, a latent sourness of spirit sweetening. She felt a special kinship with these women: they were all now members of an odd sisterhood. Unlike the Brethren, with their Codes of Conduct and signing of company books, this was not a membership of choice. They had been press – ganged, initiated by violence. Alas, unlike many, it was a secretive society, to the point one might sit among a score of fellow members in ignorance.

Cate's shame of her crimes against Monroe was brushed aside by a surge of pride: she had struck a blow, not only for herself, but for every woman ever violated. She had done to him what every one of these women wished to do: cut their attacker's cock off and fling it. Disgrace, however, prevented her from announcing her deed to one and all. She could, however, allow them a knowing nod and smile, conveying the silent message that justice *had* been served.

Cate was thinking, nay hoping she had seen to the last one, when she saw yet another arrival, curled into herself and moaning that all-too-familiar moan. The bloodied face and sodden skirts told the rest: she had been beaten, probably abused.

"It was as if those damned Revenges are like hounds sniffing out a hare," Cate muttered.

It was a bit of a surprise to see the bearers take the new arrival to a bed. Preferential regard, to be sure. Cate pushed up from the ground, stretched her back, and then bent to gather up the necessaries. She was but a few strides from the bed, however, when Polly blocked her path.

"I can help," Cate said, trying to get around.

Polly shifted, stopping her again. "With what? She's in no need of you queening yourself around, giving yourself airs."

Cate rocked back as if she had been punched. "Airs?"

"She doesn't need your kind," came with an ugly curl of the lip.

"My 'kind'!" Cate cried, indignant. "I've been helping, working with—" Her frustration and anger rose at another co-worker joining in to herd her back.

"We, *she* doesn't need *you*," said the newcomer, with an emphatic jab of a finger.

With a glare intended to glue Cate in place, the pair of shepherd-dogs spun away.

"Cum."

A low voice and a tug on the arm made Cate blink to find Celia standing there. "What do they have against me?" Cate asked, thoroughly wounded.

"You read? You write?"

"Well, yes, but —" Cate stammered. What the hell did that have to do with anything?

Celia's mouth quirked at Cate's failure to follow. "You are obviously from a higher station."

"But, that doesn't mean... I mean, I can still —" Checking herself, Cate drew a breath and tried to assume a less-educated voice, knowing her mother would be rolling in her grave at hearing it. "I can still —"

"It does not matter." The herbwoman flapped a dismissive hand. "Besides, it is not you, so much as —"

Their argument was lost in the siren-like howl of "Mama! Mama!" coming from Dorrie's cot. Cate lunged just in time to catch the child who, in her desperation, had half – climbed out and now teetered precariously on the cot's edge. Mindful of her broken arm, she gathered Dorrie up, thinking it a nightmare. The child's eyes, however, were wide open and fixed over Cate's shoulder. Cate stumbled and sagged at realizing "Mama" was the new arrival. She was the mother of Nathan's —

A face thrust into hers interrupted all further thought. "Get away, slattern!" Dorrie, still struggling with the single-minded doggedness of the young, was snatched away. Cate watched as the child was delivered and found herself looking into the mother's cold stare.

"First, they accuse me of putting on airs, and then they call me low names. Which is it?" Cate muttered, watching the tearful reunion.

"Cum. There is no helping those who do not wish to be helped. Cum," Celia urged, steering Cate away. "You are needed over here."

Cate stiffly resumed work, watching the while from the corner of her eye. At length, Dorrie was returned to her bed, and the mother's friends closed in around her. In yet another show of preferential regard for her mother, a piece of canvas was rigged around the bed, not large enough to entirely encompass the space, but sufficient provided a modicum of privacy.

It might as well have been made of stone, for it was just as impenetrable.

Her name was Marthanna.

Straining ears picked up that bit of information straightaway, but other details were much harder come by.

Curiosity, however, gnawed like a starving cur on a bone. Her nature being to know her enemy — yes, the woman was instantly elevated to that lofty status — Cate made one excuse after another, risking sharp hisses and glares, to sidle near. Her mind running in the way of dazzling beauties, the sight of which stopped Nathan in his tracks, she sought to get a look. The privacy curtain, tousled hair, shadows, people clustered about: all combined in a grand conspiracy against her. Through a combination of persistence and obsession, however, Cate gathered precious bits. Marthanna had been beaten, but not badly enough to entirely obscure her features. Underneath the bruises and swelling laid a pretty round face, upturned nose, vivid grey eyes and hair the color of aged oak.

Cate found herself standing a short distance from the curtain, staring, with a half - complacent smile. She took a certain morbid satisfaction in hearing the moans and suffering coming from behind it. It was unflattering and unchristian, but there it was!

She shifted under the feel of eyes on her. They knew. Damn them, they all knew. Now, the knowing glances and smirking smiles encountered since landing made sense.

Swallowing down a number of retorts, determined not to give them the satisfaction of seeing her mortification, she made a conscious effort to go be useful.

The most burning question, of course, was did Nathan know Marthanna was there?

"Stupid question! Of course, he did," she muttered, hurling a bucket.

If she had learned anything about Nathanael Blackthorne, it was that he did nothing without forethought; *nothing* was ever random, nor innocent. Nathan had manipulated her, played her like an instrument. Everyone, the entire damned island, every man, woman, boy and babe had been playing along in this little game. The only innocent in this seemed to be Thomas, and yet she was suspicious of his ulterior motives, as well.

And what of Dorrie? Did Nathan know about her? Had he willingly and knowingly sent Cate there, to encounter yet another of his natural children? It had taken something akin to a bat upside a mule's head to get him to realize, and then finally acknowledge John. Did that same scene await, again? Or, was he fully aware and accepting, the skulking cur?

Damn Nathan, the least he could have done was warn me! she thought, looking down at a linen strip unwittingly torn into shreds.

A mollifying voice pointed out that the opportunity to warn her hadn't presented itself; the departure from Dead Goat Island had been hasty, to say the least. And, what sane man would say "Oh, by the way, you'll probably meet my old... my old—"

What? Fling? Liaison? Bed-warmer?

A yelp of protest from the one Cate was currently attending brought her back to the present. With an apologetic nod, she stood back, hands working helplessly at her sides.

And that was the hell of it: she was helpless; helpless to change Nathan or the past; helpless at another woman giving him what she couldn't. Any revelations or hopes spawned in Celia's cabin suddenly seemed nothing more than silly, idle daydreams.

Cate drew a deep breath and swung about in search of something to do which might be less hazardous to all involved.

She swallowed hard as she passed Dorrie, now angelically peaceful as only a sleeping child could be in her cot. It was difficult to believe something so precious could be the product of a one-night tryst, a quick toss in the bushes. But then, to think that, she had to accept that there was something more between... *them*—God help her, she couldn't even bring herself to utter the two names in the same breath!—something more, as in an infatuation... a love?

Cate shook her head free of the images which rose with that.

What if Nathan had sent you here, knowing full well you would meet up, with the hope you would have all this settled before he arrived?

Cate straightened at the impact of that thought.

"Not bloody likely!" she said to the pile of dirty bandages before her. Be damned if she would be a pawn in another of his convoluted games, the scheming bastard!

If he were entertaining notions of some *menage d'tois*, he was coming to the wrong shop. She was as open-handed as could be, willing to give or share any part of herself or possessions. Food out of her mouth or shirt off her back, she would give tirelessly and willingly of anything to anyone...

Except for two things, she thought, working her wedding ring between her fingers.

That ring... and her man.

No, she was most certainly *not* Sharing's child.

"If that's shellfish and unyielding, then call me a bollard."

"What?" asked the startled patient before her.

With an irritated snort, Cate moved away.

She was a one-man woman, and expected, nay demanded the same. No negotiations. No grey areas. No equivocating.

Any confidence gained in Nathan's regard or affections — or whatever the hell one might call them — for her crumbled like an old crust of bread. Every step forward with him seemed instantly succeeded by two steps back. A part of her wanted to stand in the middle of the sickbay and shout "Yes, but Nathan is with me, now," except, as Lygia and a host of others had so freely and accurately pointed out, that wasn't exactly true. He wasn't there; he wasn't with her. He had slunk off and left her to stumble into this like a blind person into a beehive.

She and Marthanna would have it out — Oh, yes, rest assured, they would most certainly have it out, scratching and clawing like two she-cats! — but there would be an even more strident reckoning with him. She would have her pound of flesh, starting with his arse!

That reckoning was rendered impossible by one not so small detail: Marthanna was in the throes of miscarrying, losing a child. Among Cate's glimpses had been those of Marthanna's hands curved protectively over the bulge under her skirts, one which resembled one of the melons harvested that morning. Six, perhaps seven or eight months gone...Conceived, more or less, just a few months before Cate came aboard the *Morganse*.

Cate ground the heels of her hands into her eye sockets. "I have to stop this! I'm making myself crazy!"

If her demands, simple as they were, meant driving Nathan away, losing him entirely, then so be it. Living solitary once more was far more preferable to living in the rancorous misery of knowing his eye and heart were occupied by another. Proof of that lay in this dyspeptic shrewishness in her which grew by the day. It wouldn't be long before she wouldn't even be fit company for herself.

The hell of it was Cate bore a compassion for Marthanna and her current travails. Marthanna's cries had merged with two others, currently going through the same thing. Marthanna's, however, stood out, carrying a particular poignancy, rousing a begrudging benevolence in Cate. She hated the woman with every fiber of her being but, at the same time, every cry from behind the curtain tore reached into her own womb and wrenched it. She was so damned tender-hearted for the woman she wanted to throw her arms around her, so they might weep for her loss together.

In time, the two fell quiet, their ordeal over. Marthanna's continued for a bit more, and then faded, as well. The worst was over, of the body, at any rate. Cate knew the depletion which would fill her now, reduced to a hollow useless shell. Perhaps, Providence willing, that mightn't be the case for Marthanna. Many, so very many, could rise from this loss and go on to bear at will. Perhaps she was the only one the gods chose not to smile upon. The hope spawned at Celia's faded, melting like a snowflake on a griddle.

The damned irony of it all was that it made she and Marthanna sisters in yet another sisterhood, joined by the commonality of —

"Are you going to fill that or not?"

The perturbed voice jerked Cate from her reverie. "Sorry," she mumbled, dropping the ladle and stepping aside from the steaming kettle.

Hitching her skirts over the muck and mire, Cate returned to the injured, allowing their pain to replace hers.

Cate realized night had fallen when a lantern was set next to her as she packed yet another gash with lint.

She looked east for the sun, only to find it in the west and nothing more than a dull glow low on an indigo sky. Working her stiff fingers, she sagged against a post and closed her eyes. The day's din of human suffering—screams, cries, wails, shrieks, sobs, chokes, gasps: every sound short of laughter and hoots of joy a person might produce—was now reduced to low moans and coughs of the injured seeking their rest. Compared to the day's din, it was a blessed relief. Where Celia's "deep sleep" failed to answer, oil of the poppy for the women and rum for the men had been liberally applied. In the lull, most of her co - workers had slipped off in search of their well-deserved and long-denied food and rest.

All the will and genius of the island couldn't provide enough beds, leaving many to lie on the ground. It meant a day of bending, squatting, kneeling, crouching, stooping, and all their back-breaking, leg-aching variations. Cate took the opportunity to fulfill a day-long's dream and sat in a soft chair. The gilt was worn away, and the velvet was blood-streaked, the stuffing bursting out, but it was as glorious as a throne. She hazarded to lean her head back and closed her eyes. The land breeze had set in by then. It brushed her sweat - dampened temples. Sitting still, she could now smell herself, an odd combination of blood, vomit, urine, sweat and pot marigold.

She was filled with the odd sensation of being both numb and aching, the kind which came with pushing oneself beyond all limits. Her back felt on the verge of breaking in half, and her arms and legs were like clubs. And yet, at the same time, she was buoyant with the heady elation of having been useful.

At the tent's far end, someone screamed. Cate twitched, but didn't move. It wasn't a cry of agony, but of nightmares. The horrors of that day would haunt many for a lifetime. The flesh healed within a fortnight or so; wounds of the mind lingered. One woman still sat on the ground, staring and rocking, clutching a dead child, the swaddling clothes stiff with dried blood. No one had the will nor stomach to disturb her. Hopefully, God's hand would return her to her senses.

Another shriek, high-pitched and shrill, brought Cate's eyes open. Dorrie, having terrors, again. Alas, Celia's forecast had proved regrettably accurate. Nothing soothed the child other than being held.

Cate raised up enough to look in the direction of where Marthanna laid. Deep in a lavender-and-Valerian induced sleep, she was unlikely to attend the child. None of her protective cohorts were about either. Muffling a groan, Cate pushed up and shuffled over to the child's cot. As she gathered Dorrie up, she cast one eye over her shoulder, half-expecting to be reprimanded, "given a round turn" as Nathan liked to call it. No one stirred; no one came near.

Returning to her soft seat, Cate sat, rocking and singing whatever came to mind: long-forgotten tunes from her youth or little sing-song Highland chants. The half-sleeping Dorrie squirmed, making fussy, infantile sounds. Finally, she quieted, whether by virtue of Cate's presence or the terrors just running their course. Still, Cate gently swayed, reveling in the warm, heavy weight in her arms.

So deep in her slumber now, Dorrie's head lolled back, her face falling into the lantern light. Snot-nosed and tear-swollen, she was perfection, a delicate beauty, the sight of which made Cate's throat tighten. She bent nearer, trying to take in every detail. Upon closer inspection, unlike John—who had inherited nothing in the way of maternal traits—Dorrie bore much of her mother: a rounded forehead, the upward curl at the corners of the mouth, dimples, and a cleft chin. It was Nathan's long nose, but the end had a small ball, giving it a snubbed, pixie-like appearance. The sweep of brows, neck, skin and hands, however, were his, right down to the double-lashes curving on her cheeks.

A part of Cate wanted to hate the child, not just for her sheer existence, but for the joining between two people which she symbolized. Once again, she found herself wondering if Dorrie was the product of some passing, one-time tryst, or something deeper, more enduring? Nathan's "hundreds" implied he never tarried with any one for long, and yet—again, by his own admission—there had been those in which he had harbored an enduring interest.

Cate looked over her shoulder toward the half-hidden Marthanna, wondering for the thousandth time "Why her?" Why, with all the women on the island, had Nathan chosen her? Marthanna was comely, but she was no stop-a-man-in-his-tracks beauty. So, why her? What innate charms, beauty, graces or qualities had singled her out from the scores of others, all willing and all so very, very available?

"I fall can fall in love a dozen times a day," he had said. His was certainly a different definition of love than hers, but Nathan was Nathan.

And yet, by his own admission, beauty wasn't the sole deciding factor. Nathan had proclaimed he would have fancied Cate even if she had been hag-ugly. His heart-felt sincerity at the time had brought her to believe him.

Fool, for believing him? Perhaps.

She fingered the holes in Dorrie's pinafore. The smooth, round of canister shot or musket balls; the more ragged tears of flying splinters; clean slits from blades: each represented a potential disaster. Tears of gratitude welled at how close she had come to peril, snatched from Death's groping claws.

The tears of gratitude melded into the less appealing ones of resentment and hurt. Only a self-centered, unfeeling bitch would begrudge someone who could give Nathan what she couldn't.

"Then call me begrudging bitch," Cate murmured, sniffing.

Cate felt herself slipping further and further into the cold, shoved aside by hair the color of aged oak and a pair of doe-like eyes. Marthanna enjoyed what she could not: bearing Nathan's child; holding and nurturing it, watching it thrive, loving it, as she loved nothing else.

Her arms tightened as if in some desperate way holding Nathan's child might somehow strengthen her hold on him. Her joy of the anticipation of his return was dampened by the inevitable choice which now loomed dark and ominous on the horizon. If only she could bring herself to be more forgiving, more sharing, more willing to settle for just a part of him. Her inability to do any of that would force him to choose: the one who bore his child, and the other who couldn't. One needn't ponder long to foresee that outcome.

Dammit, she was being unreasonable! Nathan had several children and suffered no compulsion toward any of them!

Except, his heart isn't made of stone, Cate thought, looking down at Dorrie. He could never turn his back on something so precious.

Holding Dorrie was like holding the ghosts of all those which never lived. Cate's hand curved over the smooth head, imagining those first joyous moments of seeing her draw her first breath, wrinkled and pink with new life, loud in her protest at being so abruptly brought into the world. The ache in her breast and twinge in her womb were none so gentle reminders of the lie with which she was torturing herself.

"Very well, then, the lie I shall live... just for this little bit."

Desperate, silly and shallow, and—just for a few moments—Cate didn't care. There was no harm in pretending. One without dreams was already dead. If she had been resurrected, it had to have been someone's grand plan, some grand purpose for her. Calypso or some other higher power: it was the only way to make sense out of it. It was all beyond her comprehension, but for Nathan, for this—looking down at Dorrie—she would bear it and wait.

Dorrie whimpered, stirred. Cate rested her head on her crown, dark and silken, so much like another she had cradled on her chest. Moving gently from side to side, Cate hummed a different tune, one she had heard Nathan hum when he thought to be alone. She had barely gone through a verse before Dorrie emitted a contented sigh and settled.

Still rocking, Cate looked out at the night. The moon timidly poked its waxen head above the trees, its shadows pooling like an oil stain on the ground. The fires of destruction were now out, the lingering embers winking like fireflies on the dwellings and trees. Other fires had been set for warmth and light, but more importantly, a gathering place for the survivors, where they could share their stories and celebrate their victory.

The night echoed with the sounds of agony, grief, desolation and loss, some shared, some alone. Young and old, the faces of the passing bore looks as haunted as the cries. Sobs of grief came from where the dead lay in a row. People milled about, occasionally stooping to lift the cloths from the bloating faces to peer into them. Cate's arms reflexively tightened around Dorrie, treasuring her all the more.

Thomas appeared at the far side of the tent. Hair tumbling about his shoulders, shirt ringed with sweat and dried blood, he looked as worn as she felt. He set down whatever he carried, threw off his weapons and plunged his head into a water butt.

Remaining for longer than one would think possible, he finally straightened, sputtering and whipping his hair back with a jerk of his head.

Picking up his belongings, he came toward Cate, dashing the water from his face on his shoulder. "You look like hell."

"A fair assessment," Cate mused. "Because I feel like it." Her escapades of earlier in the day were coming back to haunt her: a sore jaw, a split lip, and a mouth's insides which resembled sausage meat. If she looked a quarter as bad as she felt, it was little wonder some children shrieked at her approach.

Thomas sighed and smiled wryly. "We'd better hope all that heals before Nathan sees you or there will be hell to pay, and *I'll* be the one doing the paying."

Touching the tip of her tongue to the opening on her lip, Cate had to agree. As desperately as she missed him, if Nathan was to see her then acrimony wouldn't be in it.

"When did you eat last?" Thomas didn't bother to glean the scold from his voice. "Nay, don't answer that. Here, I brought something."

He set a steaming mug atop the locker at her knee and a chunk of bread next to it. "I knew you wouldn't have the forethought for yourself." The scold came in the soft wrappings of concern.

Amid all the other aches, it was only then that she noticed a dull gnawing which radiated from her middle. That morning, Tabby playing the lady's maid and serene breakfasting seemed from another life. Still, the thought of food was wholly unappetizing. She leaned to sniff the mug experimentally. Her stomach growled in anticipation; Thomas arched a reproachful brow.

"You're as bad as Nathan," she said leaning back. "You love it when you're right."

A small shrug was her answer.

Thomas put his arms out. "Here, give her to me. C'mon, give over." He spoke with the tone of a man accustomed to being obeyed.

Reluctantly, Cate surrendered Dorrie, trading child for cup. She took a cautious first sip from the mug. Broth. It was hot, but nowhere near as perilous as Kirkland's coffee—

Kirkland's coffee. She smiled inwardly at the scene that brought to mind: in the *Morganse's* cabin, sitting at the morning table, Nathan across from her, drinking her first cup, waiting for it to bring her to love the day as much as he. It was her considered opinion Nathan never had a bad morning, just ones occasionally met with a little less verve than the rest.

Cate stopped halfway through the first bite. "Have you eaten?"

Thomas' haggardness, augmented by the residual soot in the creases of his face, answered the question without him. "Nothing that would stay down."

He made slow jigging circles as Cate tore off bits of breads — yesterday's, judging by the dryness — and dunked them in the broth. Her stomach cleaved onto each bit, growling and demanding more.

Nodding toward the darkness and the island beyond she asked "How goes it out there?" between bites.

"It's over, for the most part." He turned, bringing the burned side of his face into the light, as livid as his eyes. "Revenges and Companymen have scattered into the bushes like the vermin they are. Some even tried to take the boats; found several capsized on shore. Either way, we'll put them out of their misery by the morrow. I've men who can track a bird through the air. We'll get 'em."

The distant pop of a musket punctuated his point.

"Not to worry," he went on at seeing Cate cast a worried look. "I've doubled the guards for the night. You can rest in peace."

He made another hitch-stepped pass. "The fools took these women for being helpless," he said, in glowing admiration. "Their black-hearted souls are rotting in hell for that mistake."

Cate drained the mug and sat back as replete as if it had been a feast at Court. There was an off chance she now might have the strength to put one foot before the other; all she lacked was the wherewithal to stand.

Swaying in one spot, Thomas regarded her critically. "You should take off that apron.

It looks like it's wearing you."

Cate looked down at herself. The cumbersome thing had become so much a part of her, she had forgotten it. A delicate sniff revealed it was responsible for a fair amount of the previously-noted stink. Luckily, the strings could be reached from where she sat; she lifted it off and dropped it, the weight suddenly unbearable. As suspected, it was so stiff with grime and blood, it nearly stood on its own.

Her head resting against the back of the chair, Cate watched Thomas sway and pat Dorrie's back, cooing nonsensical verses.

"You've quite the touch," she observed, duly impressed. It hadn't gone unnoticed that he had plucked the child from her with the ease of having handled small ones before.

One shoulder noncommittally lifted and fell. Watching him,

Cate realized that, as open and genial as Thomas was, she knew precious little about him. Nathan had related a few anecdotes, and Thomas had given the briefest of dissertations about his sisters and to how he came to be at sea, allusions to a few intrigues included. But, as for siblings, cousins, family, nothing.

Nathan had represented that inquiring into a pirate's past was considered an impertinence, one which might well get one killed. Everyone had a past; if they were members of the Brethren, it was likely to be one best forgotten. If proof of that theory was necessary, she need to only look to her own case.

Exhaustion, however, rendered her reckless. "Do you...? I mean, have you ever had—?"

Thomas slowed to give her a hard look over his shoulder. "You mean, with all my debauching, surely there has to be a bastard or two?"

"Not quite what I meant," she mumbled into her chest.

Thomas snorted in disbelief. He looked down at Dorrie, but seemed to be seeing something, someone else. "No—well, aye, there was—" His voice tightened, and he swallowed hard.

"It... he..." His mouth moved wordlessly. "Didn't live," he finally managed in a rasp.

Cate winced, damning herself for having ignored Nathan's sage advice. A myriad of questions begged to be asked, but she denied them all.

Thomas inched his way to Dorrie's cot. He laid her down with eloquent care, shushing and gently swinging it by its strings. There was no missing the grunt he emitted as he straightened and turned away.

"You're hurt," Cate said, launching to her feet.

"I'll do," he said seeking to avoid her searching hands.

"As I recall, that's exactly what you said earlier," she said tartly.

First glance had allowed seeing only a shirt stiff with drying blood. Upon closer inspection, new blood showed bright in the dim light. Investigating fingers found a hole. She shot an accusing glare up at him and sternly pointed him to a stool near one of the surgery tables. He opened his mouth to protest, but saw the folly in that. He sat, pulling off his shirt without being asked.

Cate brought a pair of lanterns nearer and gave a low whistle at seeing the gash. Following the curve of a rib, it ran nearly the width of his side. It wasn't the worst she had seen that day; what was impressive was how he had managed to be so active all day.

"This should have been seen to hours ago," she said severely.

His carefully arranged innocence took on a bullish set. "The bastard saw this," he said, holding up his wounded arm, "and kept coming at my left, thinking it the weaker."

"He did a good job. I believe I can see all the way to your rib," Cate observed, probing.

Thomas shrugged. "He caught me, but I gutted him. I did that once, already," he said, shying when she picked up a bottle and poised it over his side.

"Good, because it will have to be done again, unless you wish your whole side to fester. This is Celia's," she added, hesitant. She knew how badly the solution stung; it had produced rafter-rattling bellows from many. On a raw, irritated wound as this one...

The name struck all objections from him. "I'll need something...?" Thomas asked, looking hopefully about.

Cate reached for a nearby bottle. He snatched it away and took a drink, screwing his mouth in disgust at the end.

"It's three-times-watered brandy and dubious stuff at that. It's all that's left, and we had to water that down to make it last." she said half-apologetically. She had never known brandy to go to vinegar before, but this had come close to it, the mere fumes burning her nose as she had mixed it.

"I've some aboard —" Thomas sighed and slumped, the prospect of passing the word for it to be fetched suddenly being more than he could manage.

Cate trickled a stream of Celia's mixture along the gaping flesh. Thomas inhaled sharply, paled, and swore, some of it sounding very similar to some of Nathan's more colorful oaths. He shook it off, beads of sweat now dotting the bridge of his nose.

Thomas' flesh shivered and twitched as Cate sorted out how to go about this. Ribs were particularly sensitive; this wasn't going to be easy on either of them. Judging by the scars lacing his side, this particular slash dissecting several, he'd endured this many a time before. Adjusting the light again, she twisted his torso, guiding one arm up over his head, the other atop his thigh.

"I've seen finer thread used on a Number Eight canvas," he said, eyeing the needle.

"Sorry, beauty won't be in this one."

The first stab brought a low grunt and a curse. By the third or fourth, Thomas fell silent, only his jaw working.

Cate worked as quickly, gentle being her intention. One would have thought, with all the wounds she had closed by then — it had to have been miles, all tolled — she should have been able to perform this blindfolded. Weariness, however, left her clumsy, hurting Thomas far more than was necessary. At one point, she flung aside the canula, the thing suddenly being more impediment than help. With it when all hope of small, pretty work faded; her only hope now was to not leave him looking like a laced-up bag of grain.

"How bad was it? The butcher's bill?" Cate asked at one point. The row of corpses had grown steadily through the day, a cloud of flies buzzing about it.

"All tolled so far, none so bad as it might have been. A score and more, so far."

Thomas stared distantly off. "Freebarn, gunner's mate, larbolin; Haddad, topsman, larbolin—"

"Daniels, foresheets, starbolin," she put in. "I was with him."

Thomas angled his head in appreciation; no captain wished for one of his to die alone. "Mahmood, master's second mate, starbolin..."

And so the litany went on, his voice shaking with more than just weariness. It was a grim list, but he seemed to find solace in naming each one, assuring none died forgotten.

"It's odd no Revenges or Companymen brought in," Cate said. Given the sheer numbers, it was reasonable to expect some to be injured. Only one had appeared in the sickbay; one of the women had let out a screech at recognizing him, and he'd been dragged off with the same care one might offer a rabid cur.

"Not bloody likely to, either," Thomas said, peering at her from under his arm pit. "Nothing to be gained in bringing in what's already dead." He leaned closer and whispered hoarsely "No quarter, no survivors."

"You'll not see their bodies among ours, either," he said with cold conviction. He aimed a short nod at the row of corpses. Some were now being sewn up in the seaman fashion, stones or bricks replacing the traditional roundshot at their feet. "They are getting the burial they deserve: right off the point. Let the current and the sharks carry them to their final resting place," he added with a sudden flush of vehemence.

"What about Lesauvage?" She couldn't curb the smile which the thought of his soul wandering eternally through the Seven Circles of Hell brought.

Thomas' shoulders wormed discontentedly.

"Hold still."

"Sorry."

"No sign of the two-faced worm," Thomas huffed. "He might have escaped in the boats. He might have been disfigured beyond recognition and is out there swimming with the fishes, as we speak," he added, pleased by the prospect.

"It was quite the fight." He managed a smile between the grimaces. "All I can say is, never go up against a horde of women fighting for home and children. They can be more bloody-minded than men. When their blood is up, there's no stopping—"

He stopped at seeing Cate flinch, his apt description of what had happened with Monroe causing her to drop the needle. He had seen Monroe's body; he knew... *everything*.

A finger on her chin brought her face up to his, and Thomas said solemnly "And sometimes, when that happens, it's entirely fitting."

Cate pulled away and ducked her head. "He was already dead, and—and—I don't know what happened. One minute he was lying there and the next minute—" She clamped her lower lip between her teeth. There was no describing what had transpired next.

Needle and thread dangling from his side, Thomas took her by the shoulders. His mouth quirked self-consciously. "You weren't there to see me on the *Gosport*. After you and Nathan were..." He swallowed hard, allowing her a glimpse of the grief he had suffered.

"Creswicke was dead, dead as any man might be," he went on determinedly. "It... It was barbaric and not a thing a civilized soul would brag about, but..."

His grip tightened as if willing his own conviction into her.

"You'll say it didn't change a damned thing," he went on, ramming a blunt finger into her chest. "And aye, that's so. You and Nathan were dead, but I'd do it again, so help me!"

Cate jerked away and pounded a fist on the table. "It wasn't right! It solved nothing."

"Really?" He hooked a finger under her chin and lifted her face. "You can look me in the eye, now. A day ago, you couldn't." His hand closed over hers where it rested on the table. "You're not trembling anymore, either. I'd say it solved several things."

He prodded her gently with an elbow. "Admit it. C'mon, admit it..."

"Alright, yes! Dammit, yes!" she burst out, glaring up. "Dammit, yes!"

She vibrated with fury. From childhood, her first instincts had been to hit back, to retaliate and with double the force, to the point of her brothers taunting her into it, knowing she would be reprimanded. The rod hadn't stopped her; if anything, it made her all the more determined. When she had been taken and brutalized, Brian had insisted that revenge for it was his rite, leaving her trapped in an eternal fight against that basic nature, like some epic mythical character.

God help her, it had been a glory to strike back, to see that face cleaved in half, to return the pain for just once! It hadn't been just Monroe, but Creswicke, and Bullock and the deserters in Scotland, all and anyone who had abused or wronged her. She had hacked them away, removed them like an unwanted growth. In the bald-faced truth of it, whatever she inflicted had only been a fraction of what been inflicted on her. It didn't bring back the child; it didn't erase the scars, but they were now considerably less.

Cate straightened, feeling several inches taller. "And damn anyone who tries me, again!"

"That's my girl. You've finally given yourself permission to be angry and do something about it." Grinning, Thomas applauded in dumb show. "Well done, lovely! Well done!"

Cate knotted and cut the thread on the final stitch.

Her attention shifted to Thomas' arm, slashed so horribly on the *Gosport*, resting on his leg. She frowned, fraught with indecision. The wound and its surrounding flesh were livid. The day's exertions had ripped several loose *again*, but it was at that awkward, half – healed stage now. Re-stitching would no longer answer. Her gaze followed the red blotches which peppered his arms and face from the fires' cinders. It was then that she noticed similar marks on her arms; painless before, now they stung like the dickens.

"I'll do," Thomas said, pulling away from her scrutiny.

Cate looked up into a face drawn with weariness. "You're sure?"

He made to shrug, but was too weary for even that small move as she busied with readying to bind his side. "You're alive and I'm alive. I won't have to answer to Nathan for either. As for the rest…" His gaze drifted to the destruction beyond the tent and fell quiet.

He sat, moody and distant, eyes hooded. As she wrapped the linen strip around him, his jaw worked and his hands flexed. Bones and tendons moving under the skin, they were warrior's hands: scraped, cut, bruised, knuckles ragged, nails torn, some to the point of bleeding. They were also the hands of a survivor, the old scars lacing them matching the ones on his sides. This hadn't been the first battle, nor would it be his last.

"I can't help but think—" Thomas began, quietly. "I can't help but think, if I had found Bella this morning, if I hadn't stood around like a lumbering lout—" Contained fury choked him. "I should have killed the bastard when I had the chance."

There was little doubt as to who he meant: Lesauvage.

"You couldn't have just killed him outright," she chided softly.

The blue eyes took on a predatory gleam. "Oh, aye, I could. One whip of the blade and it would have been done, that damned smirk his death mask. Everyone would have called me a brute, but at least they would have been alive to do so. Instead, my hesitancy—"

"Your scruples—"

"My hesitancy," Thomas repeated coldly, "cost everyone... everything," he finished with a frustrated swipe.

Cate stared in disbelief, a stirring of air at her mouth indicating that it hung open. "You think you could have prevented this. Of course," she muttered. "What else would a damned noble man think?" she added, rolling her eyes. "You're as bad as Nathan, thinking the entire world hinges solely on your act or failure to."

She stood back to glare up at him. "You, hell, we *all* know, you said yourself that this die was cast long ago."

A gash in his side was the only thing which kept her from giving him a solid shake. Instead, she shook a blood-smeared finger his face. "Instead of beating yourself for what you couldn't do, why not celebrate the glaring fact that you were here to stop it? Can you answer me that? If you're looking for Fate's hand in all this, there it is, staring you square in that lumpish face."

It took no great penetration to see her pleas rolled off like water off a deck. At the same time, it was difficult to berate him for the same regrets and guilt which had plagued her all day.

The blue eyes came up, all too briefly, to convey his appreciation of her intent, and then fell back to his lap. His shoulders slumped. It was a good thing they were so broad, for he carried the responsibility of the world on them.

So much like Nathan.

Was it pride, the habit of being captain or innate nature which compelled them? Drawn together in friendship by more than just circumstance, they were opposites in a number of ways, and yet they were alike in many more. Whatever the case, expecting them to do any different would be like asking a fish to take to the air.

The binding complete, Cate stood quietly. Through the hand resting lightly on his shoulder, hard and tense.

"Not as bad as a sea battle, but seeing women and children—"
Thomas gulped.

Looking down at the hands on his legs, he clamped his lower
lip between his teeth and dolefully shook his head. "I've served
in the butcher shop, seen men blown apart, heads busted like
melons, limbs reduced to shredded stumps since I was a lad.
But that had been men. Seeing women and children, some just
babes—" He ran a shaky hand down his face and swallowed
hard. "I picked up one that barely weighed as much as my
sword."

Thomas turned his head toward the row of corpses, ghostly
in their white canvas shrouds. A youth had been posted as a
nightwatch, torch on high to keep the questing rats, crabs and
dogs at bay. The flame's undulating light seemed to make the
bodies move.

"And to think, we won," Thomas said in wonderment.

Dorrie cried out again. Cate went to pick her up, but she
quieted before reaching her. Cate lingered at the cotside, gazing
down. Tucked deeply into the raised side, her face was obscured
by the shadows, making Cate wish for a lamp.

Gingerly donning his shirt, Thomas came up beside her.

"Night terrors," Cate whispered. "Except the poor thing has
been having them all day."

"Damn Lesauvage and the Company for it all," he said in
a low menacing, rumble. A big hand, roughened and grimed,
reached down to curve tenderly over the small head. "No child
should have to endure such a thing."

Cate smiled faintly, hearing the wet rattle of a sleeping child.
Her smile, however, quickly faded at another thought.

"When was Nathan here last?" she asked with effort.

Far afield with his own thoughts, Thomas frowned. "Umm...
damned if I know. Long about five years ago, I expect. Might be
what I heard him say."

"Not since?" she asked, looking up with dread.

"Nay, I don't think so," he said slowly. "I think I heard him
say five; Bella said as much; several others attested to the same."

Cate shakily nodded.

Thomas ducked to see her face. "Why, lovely? What's amiss?"

"Her, Dorrie's mother, is over there," Cate said, lowering
her voice. "Marthanna: do you know her?" Just uttering the
name required great effort.

Thomas considered briefly and shrugged. "I might have had a word with her sometime or another, but no, I can't go so far as to call her an acquaintance."

"She... she... she had a miscarriage today."

"One among the many, too many," he added. "Damnation, is there no end to the destruction."

He straightened at finally smoking Cate's direction. "Ah, and you worry if that one was Nathan's, too?" In spite of himself, the corner of his mouth twitched with the need to laugh.

"Shouldn't I be?" she sniffed. Tears were suddenly so very near the surface. "Tell me I'm being unreasonable. Tell me there is no earthly reason for me to think that." It had been a hellish day and her imagination was running as wild as the grass fires.

Thomas considered — briefly, all too briefly — and shook his head. "No, I'll not do that. I will say, in his defense, that he was adamant on having not set foot here for years. Judging by the reception around here, I can see why, " he muttered, with a rueful roll of his eyes. "But, no, I'll not swear to anything Nathan might or mightn't have done."

He eyed Cate, not bothering to hide his displeasure at what he saw. "You need your rest."

She looked longingly toward her cot, or rather, a place where she had lain at some point in time. Suddenly, sleep sounded more enticing than breathing. She worked her jaw, stopping when the ache brought back visions of Monroe. Every joint ached, right down to her scalp, the muscles in her stomach knotting, as if she had just been punched again.

"I know, lovely," Thomas said with gentle indulgence. "Someone else needed your cot, and I know I'd have to physically drag you all the way to your bed, so I had another rigged. I couldn't trust you not to fall out of a hammock and break your neck — I would have to answer to Nathan for that, and that's not a pleasant prospect — so there's a cot there, of sorts."

As he spoke, he guided her to a construction of branches lashed together and a bit of canvas stretched over, all suspended by ropes from the spars overhead.

Thomas stepped aside, his sweeping bow abbreviated by a catch in his side. "M'lady."

Lacking the strength to argue or resist, Cate climbed in. She hesitated at the wood creaking threateningly under her weight as she lay down. Muscles, over-taxed for hours on end, were reluctant to let go. Finally, her entire body loosened and, with an expulsion of air like a bursting bladder, she stretched out.

The mere act of lying down had long been relegated to that of an impossible dream; one might as well have wished to be the Queen of Sheba. It was exhaustion of not just the body, but mind and spirit, as well, every aspect of her being entirely drained. Only once before had she been driven to such depletion: the Rising.

That thought brought another recollection, of an entirely different after-effect of battle. Whether it was the need to plunder and conquer yet one more, venting surplus energy, the simpler celebration of having survived, a means toward regaining normalcy or setting the grosser humors back to rights, the effect was so very often the same: after a battle, many men sought a woman's bed. One need only look through an army's camp to see none of the females — from laundresses, to mistresses, to wives, to whores — laid alone the night after. At one time or another, Brian and Nathan both had come to her after engaging in a fight, urgent and needing, hard as the grip of their swords. She cocked a considering eye; it was reasonable to assume Thomas would be the same.

"Find yourself a warm bed and warm arms," she said as he turned to leave.

Thomas stopped abruptly and gaped, the fair features reddening. "You flatter me. I don't think I have the strength—"

"Find a warm bed anyway," she said drowsily. "A man like you shouldn't sleep alone, not tonight."

"You certainly did a hard-about on that count," he observed dryly.

"I know," she sighed. "Yesterday, I was speaking from moral high ground, to which I didn't belong." The thought of warm arms brought thoughts of being held, something she was so very much in need of just then. Loneliness settled over her like an icy downdraft before a storm. She curled tighter into herself.

"I appreciate the sentiment, but—" He gulped and smiled crookedly. "I'll do."

Her eyelids grew heavy and pulled closed. She felt the radiant warmth of his hand hovering over her head. Finally, it settled, as lightly as on Dorrie's.

"Rest heals a lot of wounds, lovely."

Bone-weariness has an odd way of distorting time. Cate had no notion of how long she had lain in her bed if she had actually slept or not.

She heard something so contrary to the screams, wails and shouts heard through the day, curiosity made her open her eyes. By some fluke of circumstance, from her comfortable repose, through beds, cots, tables and stores, she could see Celia's surgery table. In the golden halo of a watch lamp, turned so as not to be a disruption to those sleeping, Thomas sat atop it, Celia standing between his legs.

It took Cate a moment to realize what had roused her. A giggle, followed by something never heard before: Thomas' voice, soft with tenderness.

Lest any movement on her part prove to be an intrusion, only Cate cut her eyes from side-to-side for possible witnesses. Most in the sick bay were sleeping, the few that were awake too immersed in their misery to take notice. Secure in the solitude of the hour, Thomas and Celia were alone in the midst of a crowd.

A low chuckle from Thomas — it was odd to hear his deep voice so reduced — and then a softer one, more girlish than she would have thought Celia capable. They spoke too low to be heard, but words weren't necessary. So near, and yet a careful distance was kept between them, restraint eloquent in every move. His hand resting lightly at her waist, he leaned and canted his head. Would his eyes be teasing, as they so often were, or would they be soft with need, as seen only once and so very briefly?

Celia scooped salve from a jar and smoothed it on the burned side of his face. From babe to elder, the suffering and dying, Celia had been seen administering to all, and yet such gentleness was unwitnessed. Their faces partially obscured, Cate couldn't see their expressions, but the deep affection between them was so evident Cate was ashamed to be watching.

She turned her head and closed her eyes once more.

Again, Cate had no sense of how long her eyes had been closed. It seemed only a minute, but it could have been far longer.

Now, it was the more familiar sounds of restlessness and moaning, someone calling out for water, which waked her. A croak through parched lips, jumbled but enough to understand, set off her own horrors. She waited, listening for one of her co-workers to attend them, but she listened in vain.

Given the sheer numbers of casualties, it wasn't surprising.

Lying very still, she cracked one eye open toward where

Thomas and Celia was last seen. The spot was now dark and deserted.

The cry for water rose. Like ripples from a stone tossed into a still pond, agitation spread over the sickbay's occupants. Thirst, confusion, fear, disorientation, pain: one or in varying combinations rendering them restless.

Muffling a groan, Cate pushed upright, rubbed her face into something nearer to alertness and rose.

16: FLOATING HELL

T HE URGENCY OF THE BATTLE proper was past: no gashes to be bound; no broken limbs to be set; no torn bodies lying in wait.

Now, fevers and festering were the enemies of the day, and the butcher's bill threatened to mount. Death struck with the randomness of rolled dice, the old and weak often flourishing, while those, who should have been protected by the vigor of youth, succumbing.

Like that one, Cate thought looking over at Toby's swinging cot, a lad of perhaps seven or eight devoured by fever.

For Cate, the concept of day or night — today, tomorrow or yesterday — was long since irrelevant. Now, time was measured in increments of the next dosage given, binding changed, or body sponged. She vaguely recalled someone, sounding so very much like Pryce and his watch bill, reading a duty roster, explaining her scheduled times. With no notion of time, the notion of "on" or "off" duty had little relevance. So long as there was suffering, she would be there.

A watch lamp in one hand, a basket of necessaries over her arm and a bucket of potable water in the other, Cate made her rounds. In a certain sense, the work was less demanding, that was to say, less back-breaking, for a steady number of injured were taking their leave, preferring the comforts of home, family and friends. That meant fewer lying on the ground and, hence, less hunching down or groveling about on her knees. The casualties who remained, however, were the most severely injured, and therefore, required all the more diligence, the dreaded complications popping up at seemingly every turn. Among them were the doomed but still lingering; still more teetered on the pinnacle between thriving and failing. And then, there were those on-the-mend, but not out-of-the-woods.

Cate moved in mechanical, perpetual motion, like a clock's

pendulum caught in a singular arc, moving from one casualty to the next, and then back, vaguely aware of her co - workers working in roughly parallel paths. Celia had nothing on her in the way of private potions, stirring a bit of honey into every bucket of drinking water she fetched. The substance, used in a great number of ways, was readily to hand, in a seemingly infinite supply and its efficaciousness, by her personal experience, was beyond question.

It was no accident that pendulum's arc took in a large portion of the abused women. It took a special kind of courage to work among them, one born out of resolve and shame — shame for being weak, shame for faltering in the face of those in need. Being among them, however, Cate could feel their misery trying to attach to her, like shipworms seeking to invade a ship's hull. All diligence was required to maintain a shield as impervious as a ship's copperplates, her resolve augmented by the knowledge that, should she weaken in the least, she could easily join the pair clinging and sobbing in the corner.

"How does he fare?"

Startled, Cate jerked around to find Celia at the foot of the bed before her. Blinking, she looked down to find that she was standing by Toby's cot. It happened often, apparently drawn by irresistible forces which couldn't be either identified or explained.

Cate bent and laid a hand on the boy's forehead. It was a useless gesture; one look was all which was required: cheeks and lips bright as coals, against skin as pale as the cloth under him, and heat radiating off him like a cook stove.

"No better; no worse," Cate sighed, lowering onto a puncheon serving as a stool.

In the full analysis of it, "No better; No worse" wasn't necessarily a bad thing. If the fever hadn't spiked by then, there was a fair chance it had reached its apex, perhaps on the verge of running its course. Given fevers' capricious nature, however, the only thing for anyone to do was to continue what Cate had been doing: swab the torrid body, administer febrile tea — supplies now requiring that to be either sage or chamomile, with pinches of cayenne dip — and refresh the poultice.

Toby bore The Mark of Cornwall, as well.

"Any change for mother?" she asked of Celia. His mother lay in a stupor; knocked in the head, and yet to regain her senses.

"Same."

Cate nodded absently. Hope for many seemed in short supply.

She took up the sponge and swiped a body so hot one

expected steam to rise. Why he struck such a chord with her she couldn't explain? With a curly crop of white-blond hair, a profusion of freckles and eyes like emeralds, he resembled no one. His wasn't even a particularly engaging face. She vaguely recalled seeing someone like him the night before, running and laughing with his mates. Now, those bright eyes were rolled back in his head, hidden by lids as vivid as his cheeks.

Her heart was touched, however, every time she looked into that unremarkable face, her heart broken every time she looked at the stump. She had held him down while Cornwall did his vile deed. Now, with Toby wracked with fever, the stump threatening to fester, Cornwall was nowhere to be found.

Off drinking somewhere, bragging of his proficiency.

"When did you last sleep?"

Cate broke from her wool-gathering at realizing the question had been directed at her.

Sleep.

Ah, yes, Cate thought, blinking. *That thing people do from time to time.*

She whimsically remembered something about lying down and closing one's eyes.

She had caught herself doing something akin to that several times, pillowing her head on her arm whilst swinging Toby's cot. She shook her head, dismissing the notion. Better to just put such things out of one's mind; one can't miss what doesn't exist.

"You need a break," Celia announced. "You will be of no use to anyone, if you fall ill. It is light enough now; we need more salve," she went on over Cate's protests.

Cate looked outside expecting to see nighttime. Instead, she found not the pinkish hues of early morning, but the glaring brilliance of day.

When did that all happened?

The presence of day wasn't as much the significance as the light that it brought. In the haste of necessity, one of her co-workers had attempted preparations in the dark. She lay now with her arms swathed in bandages soaked in linseed oil and lime-water. Such preparations were made in the brew galley, a short distance away...

Away, with fresh air and open sky overhead and no press of people.

Cate closed her eyes for a fraction of a second — she didn't dare do so any longer — and reveled in the prospect of inhaling air not thick with sickness. When going to the hot water fires, she had paused in mid-step to draw in a few draughts of clean air and revel in the quiet. Stepping out from under the tent was like taking one's head out of an empty copper upon which someone was banging on.

Without waiting for an answer, Celia plucked the sponge from Cate with one hand and urged her to her feet with the other. "We cannot help Toby, nor anyone else without proper medicines," she insisted, guiding Cate by the arm. "Get yourself a bit of fresh air. You'll be of more use to all of us."

Celia had the velvet-lined, club-of-persuasion of Cate's mother: never raising her voice, brooking no argument, making you feel as if it was your idea while, and at the same time, rendering it a mortal sin to disobey.

"I'll watch him. I promise," Celia said.

There was no arguing with that, either.

"We need onions and garlic boiled, too," Celia called to her back.

Cate waved in acknowledgment as she trudged away.

"Double bubble, toil and trouble; fire burn, and cauldron bubble…"

Swiping the sweat streaming down the sides of her face, Cate ladled wax into the pot of melting tallow. Caution was required; dropping either into the fire could cause the whole batch to burst into flames, her included, as a less cautious one had discovered the day before.

"A shock to the soul to find you gone."

Startled—she'd thought herself to be alone—she turned to find Thomas standing there, a metal cup in hand.

"You weren't in the sickbay." His mild tone was a thin cover for the worry just under the surface.

Needlessly scaring him was both unintended and regrettable. "Celia bid me to make up some salve."

"Here! Hold fast. Allow me to do that, before you set your skirts on fire," Thomas cried, kicking her hem away from the coals. "You're getting careless," he said severely, pushing her aside and trading cup for paddle.

"Don't use that captain's voice on me. Don't stir so fast."

"I will, if it saves your bacon, or rather, saves you from going up in flames like bacon."

Thomas leaned over the pot, sniffed and jerked back, coughing.

"Hartshorn or at least it smells like it," Cate explained. "Celia's notion." Comfrey, calendula, plantain and a few things she didn't recognize sat waiting to be added.

Stretching her aching arms and back, Cate slumped atop a puncheon amid the tallow tubs, baskets and medicinal makings, and took a grateful sip. Youssef, Thomas' cook aboard the *Lovely*, must be lending a hand in the kitchens, for the coffee was unmistakably his: thick and black. During her time aboard, she had convinced him to brew something more palatable, but he seemed to have slipped back into his old ways. Still, it was hot, strong and God's milk.

Cate cast an eye skyward and wearily rubbed her brow. "What day is it?"

"Monday."

She mentally counted backwards—or rather tried—to the day when the *Brazen* had dropped anchor. It was all so jumbled. Still, a number popped forth, the one Nathan had pledged, his fingers jabbed in her face.

"He's late," she announced.

"Nathan?"

"Who else?"

"Aye, but only by a day. By the looks of the trees and the offing," Thomas added, with a nod toward the invisible bay, "there is a fair blow out there. You've been at sea long enough to know what that means. If he's beating into that, one league might as well be a hundred."

Cate made a dismissive noise. Yes, she knew all that, but conceding meant accepting Nathan not being there. She wanted him... now!

"You're as unforgiving as a bollard at times," Thomas observed. "Nathan's no saint, aye, but you might slacken the braces a mite. Go find something else to chew on other than his arse and mine." The last came with a peevish cut of his eyes.

It might have only been morning, but Thomas' shirt was already circled with sweat. Dark smudges under his eyes, several days' stubble on his cheeks: he looked as sapped as she felt. The air was filled with the screech of grinding wheels, now sharpening the edges of construction as opposed to destruction, the rap of mallets and clang of anvils rapping out nails. In seaman-like efficiency, Thomas' men swarmed about the island like troupes of over-industrious ants setting it to rights. Whatever a man's talent, there was need, and where talent failed a strong back would suffice. Thomas was everywhere, taking command of the island as he did his ship.

Cate's mind idly drifted back to the last time she had seen Thomas. She had bid him to not sleep alone that night. He had found Celia's arms or, at least so it seemed, for she had seen them together. One couldn't help but wonder—an idle, but still intriguing notion, one which her weary mind landed on and then lacked the wherewithal to move on—just how far things had gone?

Cate regarded him over the rim of her cup, steam condensing on his brow as he stirred. Nathan had claimed with one look, he knew Thomas hadn't bedded her. A little of that insufferable insight would have been so very useful just then.

A twinge struck, not of jealousy—for once—but envy. Seeing the two together that night had stirred Cate's own needs, the basest ones, the ones which couldn't be satisfied by nourishment or drink. Yes, she lusted, to the point she hadn't returned to her proper bed, because she couldn't face the notion of lying there cold and alone. For the first time since her resurrection, her body stirred. She needed Nathan with an ache which could only be sated by him filling her.

"What are you looking at? Did I grow a third eye or something?"

Thomas' inquiry caught Cate just as she was taking a drink. She coughed, swiping the spewed coffee from her chin.

"I... I was just thinking I should mend that shirt," she said lamely. In truth, the garment was so peppered with black-edged pin holes from the battles' fires, it looked like it had been struck with birdshot. When an idle moment presented itself, she should mend it...

... an idle moment...

Now there was a delicious thought, one she closed her eyes to muse upon.

"Are the onions boiled?"

Cate opened her eyes to find Polly standing there. "Yes, a batch is cooling over there." A vague wave indicated a steaming vessel on a table.

Poultices were using up the onions at an alarming rate. Cate made a mental note to peel more and start another batch on the fire. Garlic needed peeling, as well, along with setting the sage to steep and...

Thomas turned to watch Polly leave in the crab-like step of one bearing a heavy burden. "Was that civility I just heard? Has a treaty been signed?"

"A cease-fire of sorts, I suppose." Cate rubbed a knot at the back of her neck.

Marthanna had been among those who had taken leave of the sickbay. Cate hadn't seen her go; she just looked up and Marthanna was gone, Dorrie with her. In her wake, there had been a tangible shift in her co-workers' regard. She wouldn't go so far as to call it sisterly love, but they were now—

"Downright abiding," Thomas observed, finishing her thought.

"Don't let that burn. Yes, it is a wonder why?"

Thomas obediently quickened his motion. "Obviously, they came to see you aren't the monster they believed you to be. They see someone who sweats and cries along with them."

"Could hardly do else," she muttered into her cup.

"For you, aye, but many could and *do* turn a cold shoulder."

The sound of bubbling prompted Cate to rise to another pot. She added several handfuls of dried leaves — a local herb of some description — and then stirred with one hand, while sipping coffee with the other. Linseed oil and milk needed to be as near to scalding as possible, without it burning or boiling over.

"Hold fast!" Thomas called at seeing her prepare to lift the iron vessel from its hook.

His long reach allowed him to trade places with her, the paddle never missing a stroke.

"You need a man," he huffed, toting the steaming oil and milk to a bench.

I need Nathan, she thought crossly. *Damn him, where is he?*

"This is woman's work. Men have theirs," she said, eyeing a passing work party.

Thomas hailed two from that very group, Brazen's she thought. A brief order, a bit of shuffling, and the pot was handily slung on a pole between the two and bore off toward the sickbay.

Cate started to follow, but Thomas stopped her.

"Something amiss?"

She looked up to find him peering down at her.

"You look like a ghost just crossed your path," he observed, worried.

Was that what it had been? Were thoughts of Nathan simply that: a ghost walking?

She swallowed hard, shuddering. "What if he doesn't come back?"

Thomas frowned, puzzled. "You mean Nathan?"

Cate nodded. Fear that verbalizing her worry might cause it to come to pass made the words scarce. "What if he doesn't come back?"

He started to laugh, but sobered at seeing she wasn't jesting. "He'll be here," he announced, instead.

"And if he isn't?"

Thomas took her hands between his, roughened and calloused with work. "Nathan has beaten death twice. Nothing will stop him now."

Cate forced a smile, unconvinced. She appreciated Thomas'

intent, but his rationale was less than reassuring. Yes, Nathan had died twice, but would the third time be the proverbial charm or his doom? Hopefully, her doldrums were just the result of a bone-deep exhaustion and not premonition.

As he held her hand, her eye drifted to his forearm. When last seen, it had been red and angry, the skin ragged from a number of stitches being torn. Now, the stitches were gone, the wound no more than a red runnel in the pale skin. It should have been a wicked scar but, instead, it looked no worse than the numerous others which crisscrossed his body.

Surprised, and a lot curious, Cate looked up into a carefully arranged blank expression. Thomas shrugged, the answer seemingly obvious: Celia's hand, yet again.

They stepped apart at seeing that very person coming up the path. Thomas touched the brim of his hat, murmured an excuse and took his leave. Cate watched as the two met on the path, looking for some telltale hint as to her earlier ponderings. She did so in vain. Thomas only paused long enough for civility and kept going.

Celia drew up next to Cate and the two of them watched Thomas until he disappeared amid another work party.

"I enjoy his body." Celia turned, the translucent eyes fixing on Cate. "Someone else, however, holds his heart."

It took Cate a moment to catch her meaning. "I have no claim —" she bristled.

Celia's cool hand on her arm cut off any further expostulations. She smiled tolerantly. "You have every claim and to change it is beyond my power."

The healer poked among the baskets and bowls. Having found what she sought, she stopped before Cate once more.

"You will break his heart." The announcement came matter-of-factly, absent of malice or ill-will, challenge or taunt.

Cate ducked her head, wondering how far Celia's mind-reading capabilities might reach. "I don't mean to —"

"No, and that is the heartbreak, is it not?" She laid a hand on Cate's arm, light yet compelling. "When the time comes, do so gently. He has suffered so much already and deserves so much better."

With a swish of skirts, Celia set off down the path, leaving Cate to stare.

⚓

"Do you follow my meaning, Chips?"

"Aye, Cap'n. Bulkheads shifted and shelves rigged. Plain

as plain, sir." Chips' response came in the distracted way of a craftsman already deep into his task.

"And me cabin...?"

"My mates are on it, sir," Chips said, raising his voice in order to be heard over the rap of hammers overhead.

"Very well." Nathan idly thumped his fist on the cabin's bulkhead.

Every god and power, known and unknown, had worked against them these last days. The wind had been in their teeth. Now, finally winding their way through islands and channels, their destination within sight, the wind faded, threatening to die altogether.

"So long as we are beating out our brains, we might as well beat on a few—" Nathan began.

A "Mr. Pryce's compliments and duty, sir," cut him off.

Nathan turned to find Ben standing in the doorway, round-eyed as a startled goose. Being caught-by-the-lee had robbed the lad of discretion. Realizing his blunder, he composed himself and knuckled his forehead. "Mr. Pryce's compliments—"

"You said that, lad," Nathan pointed out tolerantly. The lad's agitation, however, was contagious.

"Aye, sir. He begs—" Ben gulped. "He begs you might wish to come see."

"Come see what?" Nathan had already brushed past and was three strides toward the aft companionway.

"Damnedest thing... sir," Ben said, racing to keep up.

Nathan mounted the steps two at a time, pausing in mid-stride to shout "Carry on, no matter what" down to Chips.

Before Nathan topped the steps, he knew something was amiss. The stench of death, extensive and old, hit like a fist. The frenzied shriek of gulls filled the air, the sky black with their wheeling overhead. A gesture from Ben directed him to Pryce at the lee forechains, stiffly gazing at the water. The entire company stood gaping. Drawing up next to his First Mate, Nathan mouthed an oath, for it was a curseable sight: bodies, scores of them bobbing in the swell in a long sweeping arc.

"Any living?" he heard himself ask.

"None so as can be seen," Pryce said grimly.

The popish among the crew reflexively crossed themselves. A good many more made horned signs. One didn't need to be at sea long to see sights which would haunt them to their graves. This one gave everyone, right down to the salty f'c'stlejacks, pause. The bodies—all male—were naked as Adam. Bloated, skin grey and taut as bladders, they might have been mistaken for sea hogs had it not been for the arms and legs, or rather, what was left of them. They floated toward the ship, their stumped arms were spread out as if they were a greeting committee...

Or, was in warning?

"As if the dead might tell us a damned thing!" Nathan muttered.

"Beg pardon, sir?"

"Nothing. Nothing."

All aboard had been at sea a good many years, had been through many a battle. Men flung or knocked from a vessel, aye. Slid from the decks in the midst of battle, aye. Sending the enemy to Davy Jones, aye. But, that had always been with some vessel of some sort, some apparent source. There was none here.

As disgusting as it was, no one could look away. Nathan snatched the glass from Pryce and scanned the horizon yet again, as they all did, in search of some glimpse of a spar or sail and, hence, an explanation.

"... to be turned into corruption..."

Mortification, gulls, fishes and crabs had erased much, but pigtails and tattoos marked a portion of the dead as sailors. Pirates? Company? Privateer? Pirate prisoners were often stripped and sometimes a few flung overboard, out of either ill-will or meanness. Again, the sheer numbers struck out that possibility.

Not a sinking, because they would have been clothed. Not a battle; it would have taken two ship-of-the-lines going at each other yardarm-to-yardarm to produce such numbers and, again, they would have been clothed. Not the work of natives, either. Hell, in these waters, they'd eat their victims. He'd seen Orientals and Mohammedans hang their dead out as warnings, but nothing like this.

One body floated past, a gull roosted atop it, squawking in defense of its newfound feast. It drifted near enough for one to make out, in spite of the corruption, that the belly had been slashed. A fight, then, hand-to-hand.

All at the rail straightened at that realization.

But, whose? And where?

Nostrils pinching against the stench, Nathan scanned the horizon for the dozenth time, running the charts for these waters through his mind. These waters were shallow, too treacherous for anything more than a turtling scow to navigate. There was only one anchorage for many a league...

"A-comin' from thataways." As brought-up-all-standing as the rest, Pryce was reduced to stating the obvious. "Wonder what—?"

The macabre parade pointed like the Grim Reaper's finger.

Nathan cut him a cold look. "There's but one place in that direction, and you know it well."

He swallowed down a cold lump which could have been either his heart or his stomach.

Nathan peered hard through the glass. No matter how much he willed it, the damned thing wouldn't stop jerking about. He lowered it, drew a deep steadying breath, and tried again. He studied each of the dead, looking for that telltale glimpse of a mahogany-colored head, chanting "Live, damn you, live!" under his breath, as if sheer will might resurrect her.

If Cate had been taken at sea, then the double-tongued hag-of-the-deep had gone back on her word. Still, he might could do something to reverse it. If she had been taken on land —

Nathan took a hard hold on himself. His imagination was running amok. Setting his jaw, he peered more intently at each body, once, and then again.

There was no avoiding it. The ship's path and the grisly line inevitably crossed. The stench thickened, many men coughing, the weaker-constituted gagging. They reached for poles to gaff the bodies off, but the thought of poking at the dead made them draw away empty-handed. And so, the grey-and-bloated bumped the hull. Torn by the barnacles, the rotting flesh clouded the water like chum, schools of little silvery fishes darting about feeding on it.

Nathan swiveled the glass to their destination. They were now close enough to make out the trees and the great holes torn in them.

"Gun barrages, heavy ones," Pryce observed, squinting.

"Aye, but whose?" The more significant question was were they still about, lurking somewhere? Nathan scanned again, alert for that telltale nick of a mast.

Nothing.

He glared up at the flaccid sails. Sink and burn him, the wind had died even more. He'd set the royals, if he thought it would answer. It wouldn't do, however, for haste to become their demise. No ship moved the faster with her keel buried in the sand or pinioned on a reef.

"I don't like it; I don't like any of it. Set moonrakers and kites," Nathan directed to Hodder. "Rouse out the boats. We'll pull her in, if we must. I don't care how the hell you do it, but get us moving. Clear for action!"

"God knows what is waiting for us," he muttered to himself, and then louder "Mr. MacQuarrie!"

With the wind dying, the water had gone to near glass, the floating dead now all the more stark. The kite's caught, and the

Morganse moved on, leaving the grisly welcoming committee swirling in her wake. She angled nearer the island at a gut-wrenching creep. Watching the passing shore was like sitting under a machineel tree after a rain, each drop eating at his flesh, eating at him, like those damned little fishes.

They were close, so damned close, and yet too damned far. Nathan swung his glass from side to side, taking in every detail, every hint. The only thing which stopped him from jumping over the side and swimming ashore was the fact that the fray — and a helllish one it had been, judging by the damage — was over. The charred tree stumps and dwellings showed a conflagration — 'Twas nothing short of a miracle that the whole island hadn't gone up in an inferno. Providence had smiled there, but where else? — but no smoke rose, no flame flickered. They were cold, by several days. No flames, no bodies lying about.

In point of fact, there was no one. He hadn't seen the place in years — had vowed never to step foot again — but it was familiar enough to know what he wasn't seeing: people, women and children. The place positively teemed with life. By now, they should be seen waving or going about their daily business, the youths capering about the shore.

But nothing.

A conquering army would at least be milling about, setting up camp, posting watches. But nothing, no one.

He studied harder, desperate for a face, a glimpse of that maddening tangle, something, anything!

Nathan clapped a hand onto a foremast shroud and closed his eyes. "Get me there, lass. For all that is holy, get me there."

17: RIDING GABRIEL'S WINGS

S KIRTS KIRTLED UP FROM THE slop and mud underfoot, Cate grunted with effort as she paddled the linen strips from the boiling pots and flung them onto a table.

A sickbay produced a staggering amount of soiled bandages. They sat in perpetual fly-blackened heaps waiting to be washed. Hauling water, stoking fires, dumping armloads of blood and pus-sodden cloths, skimming the pot—What boiled to the top wasn't for the faint of heart—dumping and refilling when the water became so foul everything came out dirtier than going in: it was hot, toilsome work and a task performed by few willingly.

Several others had been assigned the job. With one lame excuse after another, they had all disappeared. Celia had finally sent Cate an assistant. Straightaway, the girl mumbled something about "Bad crab, m'um" and scurried off, yet to be seen since.

The pots sat in a remote corner of the settlement, near enough for convenience, yet well away. Yes, the stink of boiling bandages was that noxious. As Cate worked, she was vaguely aware of the sounds of reconstruction around her. Rebuilding an island wasn't quiet business, especially when a vast majority of the population were sailors, some, Lovelies mostly, going so far as to hail as they passed. The island was much like the occupants of the sickbay: not fully recovered but, for the most part, on the mend.

Cate gathered up another armload from the reeking heap and tossed them in to boil. Hand on her hip, she poked an experimental finger into the pile on the table, testing to see if it was cool enough to be handled. The steaming mass would need to be untangled, and then hung on lines strung overhead like a giant spider's work, where they might dry and bake in the sun.

It was heavy work, but not unwelcomed. She still worked amid the stink of sickness, but now it was intermingled with the freshness of leaves and grass. The sea breeze sent its searching

KERRY LYNNE

fingers through the trees, bringing the smell of the saltwater. It dried the sweat – dampened tendrils of hair stuck to her face and neck. It had been bound up turban-fashion, but it still managed to wriggle free.

Pleasures could be found wherever one wished to find them. She wriggled her feet, taking girlish glee in feeling the ground squish up between her toes. It was muddy, but only with water, not the slurry of blood and all the dubious fluids the human body might produce in which she had been standing in for days.

The work was simple and straightforward which one might perform with a clear mind and heart, free of the mental toil of looking into one anguished face after the next, listening to their cries of delirium or pain. Still, the distance was only figurative. Many of the faces still hung with her, Toby most particularly. The lad might have been out-of-sight, but not out-of-mind. He still burned with fever, but was beginning to show the resilience so common to the young.

Cate threw herself into the labor for one reason. True, idleness wasn't her nature, but there was a grander, more singular motivation: hard physical toil was the only way to keep the creeping sensation of doom. She recognized it all too well, for she had lived on its precipice for many, many years, and it was back, gathering, with naught but keeping herself busy to keep it at bay.

Thomas had made excuses for Nathan's prolonged absence. But, so far as she was concerned, they had been exactly that: excuses. She felt betrayed, all his grand promises broken and, worst of all, abandoned, forgotten.

Frustration surged, and she whacked the paddle on the pot's edge. "Dammit!"

"Something amiss, missus?"

She turned to find a passing lad standing in the path, looking on with concern. She shook her head and waved him on his way. Composed once more, she seized the paddle's heel and reached up to rearrange the half-dried strips on the lines overhead to make room for the next batch. At the same time, she hummed a song overheard from some children as they skipped by, a nonsensical thing, but enough to block the more pressing inner chant of "Where is he?"

A looing sound made Cate turn into the limpid eyes of a milch cow, gazing benignly over the woodpile.

"Fancy yourself the great escape artist, eh?"

The big ears pitched forward in mild interest, and then back, twitching at a fly.

Cate winced in sympathy. The poor thing was in desperate

358

need of milking, but bandages were in more dire need than milk. Tying a couple linen strips together, she secured the cow to a tree, until someone came looking.

The steaming heap finally reached a workable temperature and Cate set to untangling the sodden mass. It was a bit like trying to sort out a basket of overturned yarns. The process was a pleasing one, giving her a sense of establishing order from chaos. She smiled faintly, chanting "The rabbit comes out of its hole, goes around the tree, goes back into its hole...," the whole thing somehow reminding her of her knot lessons, Nathan semi – patiently watching over her shoulder.

Perhaps he was with her after all.

Cate gradually became aware of the people trickling past on the path quickly becoming a stream and, like that waterway, flowing in one direction: toward shore. The clamor of voices increased, shouting and agitated, not unlike the day the island had been attacked.

Stopping in mid-stir, paddle poised, Cate canted her head and listened. Heart thumping, her mind raced. Had the Company returned?

Once fooled, twice cautious. The same mistakes would *not* be made again. The children: by everything in her power, she would protect them.

But there were no guns, no muskets firing.

The voices grew louder, the commotion more pervasive, especially nearer to shore. So broken by distance and the rattle of palm fronds, she couldn't tell if they were raised in cheer or anger. Tense and distracted, she ducked at the sudden passing of something heavy overhead. Not the whiz of a cannonball, as her fears brought her to expect, but the flapping of wings, too high to be a chicken, and too large for any of the indigenous birds. She spun around, following the projectile's path and gaped in disbelief at a hyacinth-colored parrot roosted atop a drying line.

Fixing a beady black eye on Cate, the bird ruffled and then smoothed. *"Dash me buttons."*

"Beatrice?!"

Hackles raised, the brilliant head bobbed. *"Flog the bastard."*

Beatrice's presence could only mean one thing: Nathan!

With a joyous shriek, Cate hitched her skirts and raced toward shore. Pushing and shoving, she ducked and wove her way through the crowd, the island's populace suddenly taking on all the characteristics of a herd of oxen. She swallowed down curses and coarse remarks, nearly bowling a few over, at the same time bouncing on her tiptoes, straining to see ahead. Meeting a knot of people, she dove into the bushes and blazed her own trail, using the sun's reflection off the bay as her guide. Crashing her way through, at one point, she thought she saw a ship, but then cursed at finding it was only a dangling branch.

Finally, she broke out onto shore, sweating and gasping. Looking anxiously, she found the *Lovely, Brazen* and *Revenge* still on their anchors. Holding her breath, afraid to hope, a slight pivot and there laid the *Morganse,* dark and regal like the queen that she was, her boats already plying toward shore.

The beach was now a teeming throng of people, all moving to meet the Morgansers pouring ashore. Pleading, cursing and being cursed, Cate elbowed her way through the press, using Thomas, a head above everyone else, as her guidepost. If Nathan was anywhere, he'd be there. Familiar faces flashed past — Billings, Hodder, Squidge, Hallchurch — some even hailing in her wake, but she had eyes for only one. She was afraid to breathe, afraid to see that Nathan wasn't there, in morbid fear of finding Pryce there instead, breaking the sad news to all present —

A voice rose above the rest, shrill with fury: Nathan, shouting "Goddammit, man! Where is she?"

Craning her head, Cate saw him, Thomas' shirtfront bunched in his fist.

"Nathan. Nathan!"

Mouth opened in mid-sentence, Nathan spun. Mouthing an oath, he broke and ran. Ducking and dodging through the crowd, they came together with an impact which almost sent them tumbling to the sand. They held each other, peered, and then clutched again, sobbing and shaking. Ignoring the press of well-wishers, eyes brimming, Nathan cupped her face between his hands, taking in her every feature.

A big hand came down on Nathan's shoulder and gave him an encouraging shake.

"I told you she was well," Thomas declared. "Well and whole, just as you bid."

"And *you* promised," Nathan added with a cautioning edge. He was still checking Cate over, turning her this way and that, seeking to prove the claim to himself. He jerked the cloth from her head and ruffled her hair as if suspecting some hidden horror might lurk there.

"She's alive and well, and feisty as ever, aren't you?" Thomas gave Cate a prompting nudge. Still dumbstruck with elation, a nod was all she could manage.

"I'll be the judge o' that," Nathan retorted, regarding Cate and clearly not liking what he saw.

Finally, Nathan broke away and jabbed a thumb toward the offing. "That's quite the welcoming party out there. Those bodies are enough to make Blackbeard haul his wind. It looks like a charnel house and smells worse."

"Bodies?" Thomas asked, puzzled.

"Aye, scores o' them. Your victims, I presume?"

Nathan cast an eye toward the shattered trees and charred skeletons of dwellings. "You've had a conflagration here. What the bloody hell happened?"

As answers were given; Nathan listened absently, nodding at the expected, cursing at the unexpected. His attention, however, was fixed on Cate, his hand squeezing and re – squeezing hers, as if testing that she were real.

"The Company came in no-quarter flags a-blazin', so we dealt them what they asked for." Thomas hooked his thumbs in his belts. "Not a survivor walks. We smoked a couple who sought to escape by shifting their clothes. We pitched the bodies off the point, thinking that millrace of an ebb would carry them away."

"It did," Nathan said grimly. He allowed Cate to then see the bowels-to-water fear suffered, the hours of seeing the destruction, with no notion of what awaited. The sound of the *Morganse's* ports slamming shut could be heard; she had come in guns-ready for whatever enemy awaited. The needless senselessness of all that made it all the more painful. Cate squeezed Nathan's hand, letting him know he hadn't worried alone. The separation had cost them both dearly.

Nathan bent to kiss her, but stopped short at the sound of angry voices nearing. A group of islanders shoved their way forward. One woman — one of several Marys on the island — drew up a bare stride away from him.

"You killed my Jackie!" Mary cried. A mixture of fury and anguish made her chin tremble.

Her heart still pounding in her ears, Cate thought surely she misunderstood. A glance at Nathan's suddenly grim face showed she hadn't. He shifted, putting himself between Cate and his accuser. A flick of fingers bid her behind him, a quelling look striking her silent.

"I beg your pardon—" Nathan groped for a name, finally landed on "Mother, I—"

With a grief-stricken cry, Mary charged. An arm shot out of the surrounding crowd, stopping her short. "I'm not your goddamned mother and you know it," she shouted, straining against the barrier. "I'm no one's mother now, thanks to you. You killed my Jackie, just the same as if you'd pulled the trigger."

"And my Joe!"

"And my—!" Amid the roar, names were shouted, accusing

fingers pointing like spears. "Liar!" "Murderer" and a number of less flattering words were added to the mix.

Cate sagged back at the vehemence. She had seen and heard the dislike, but in an undertone, lurking sort of way. Now, it was given full voice. The number of familiar faces in the crowd smacked of a betrayal worse than Lesauvage's: Banu, and some of the women she had labored with in the fields; Polly and others from the sickbay. She had worked and sweated next to them, swabbed their blood, struggled to save their lives and shed tears with them. And now, they were attacking. They hadn't come empty-handed, either, armed with everything from crutches, to brooms, a spoon, or whatever else to hand.

Like oil and water, the two factions separated. Emitting a low threatening rumble, the Morgansers formed up, Pryce, Hodder and Chin—currently blocking Mary—in the forefront. All bore the grim resolve of having expected this scene and were prepared to deal with it. The Lovelies and Brazens, Al-Nejem looming among them, shifted to make their allegiance apparent. The islanders moved to square off. Only a handful remained in suspension, undecided.

Deep in the crowd, Cate spotted Bella, her strawberry-grey head like a beacon. Neither yet oil nor water, she stood with her arms crossed, not displeased by the turn of events. Cate glared, willing the woman to step in and stop this. One word, one gesture from her was all it would require. The *Morganse's* approach would have been announced in plenty of time to head this off, but she hadn't. Damn the woman! this confrontation was exactly to her wishes.

Emboldened by their numbers, the crowd surged forward. The nearest, Mary, was small and armed with nothing more than a metal pot. The next was a man, old and bent, but wiry enough to wield a cob in his fist. Reflexively retreating, Cate surreptitiously glanced about for something which might serve as a weapon.

"Nathan Blackthorne!" Bella cried, as if just arriving. "I never thought to see you again."

Finally! Cate thought, testily.

Nathan stiffened at Bella's voice. With the resolve of one facing a broadside, he turned to face her. "My thoughts exactly."

Like the Red Sea, the crowd parted, and the island's matron came forward, face calm, grey eyes shrewd. "Looks like you came loaded for bear."

An extra brace of pistols at his belts, another pair hanging from a thong about his neck, two cutlasses, a hatchet, extra shot bags and powder horns: Nathan looked prepared for a boarding, rather than coming ashore. Cate rubbed her ribs where one of the pistol butts had gouged her as he hugged her.

"Burned and blasted out dwellings, bodies floating, strange ships on their moorings: I didn't know what the bloody hell to expect," Nathan shot back, unapologetic.

A glance at the surrounding Morgansers proved his point: all were armed to the teeth.

"You were told, last time you were here—" Bella began.

"And I agreed," Nathan finished, unrepentant. "Upon me word, I never meant, *nor* intended to ever step—"

"He killed my Jackie!"

Another roar went up from the crowd, filled with grievances and epithets, brandishing fists and weapons.

"Mothers, I grieve with you. I understand your—" Nathan shouted to them.

"Take your sympathy and shove it up your bloody arse!"

A brusque wave from Bella silenced them. "We asked you—"

"—Nay, you demanded—" Nathan qualified, with the resignation of resuming an old argument.

"—And yet, you persist. It is we who pay the price," Bella went on, unperturbed. The grey eyes flashed bright with frustration. "You brought the Company down on us, again and again."

"And I told you then I would not, I could not countenance that scum of a princock to walk this earth. Be damned, if I will apologize for taking my revenge!"

A corner of Cate's heart ached for Mary and the rest. The death of a child was the worst loss. The greater tragedy was that grief had a way of lashing out, like an antagonized snake, not always biting the hand which held the stick. Lesauvage and the Company were the most deserving of their wrath, but they weren't there. Nathan was, and an easy target he was.

"You wanna blame someone, blame Creswicke." Thomas pushed his way forward, imposing himself beside Nathan. "Nathan's suffered under his hand, and you all know it well."

The addition of Thomas' size and presence made a more formidable front, and took a bit of the wind out of the confronters' sails.

Thomas drew up to his full height and glared. "It's like blaming Nathan for trying to kill a rabid dog and someone got bit in the process."

A few mouths opened, but most were silent.

"He's the most open-handed man walking, and you know it. Hell, have you ever seen him deny one in need, if he had it to give?" Thomas' great frame shook with insult and restrained fury.

"He can't bring my child back," came a voice quavering with grief from the crowd.

Thomas jerked a nod. "Aye, no one can do that, but has anyone ever heard him set himself up as one who might?"

Nathan made to speak but was fell mute at Thomas' quelling glare.

"Those of you who have lain with him, you know him." Thomas made an all – encompassing swipe. "You know that's not a cold-heart in his chest, not as cold as you accuse."

Cate dropped her eyes, away from the agreeing faces, for it would be looking into the eyes of Nathan's past lovers.

"Damn your ungrateful souls! You speak of suffering to a man who has suffered as much or more?" Thomas grabbed Cate by the arm and jerked her forward. "This woman was stolen from the *Morganse*, from under his protection."

"Thomas, no!" Cate reeled back, writhing against the iron grip. "She was beaten bloody and raped –"

"Thomas –!" Cate's plea was lost in Nathan's threatening growl.

" – Raped repeatedly, by God knows how many, to the point of losing her child." Jerking back the linen wrapping at her wrist, Thomas thrust it out for all to see. "And then, Creswicke branded her and by his own damned hand!"

Mortified, Cate turned her head, unable to look. At the same time, fury rose its ugly head. Dammit, she didn't need their damned sympathy.

Shock and disgust were expressed in gasps and uncomfortable coughs. Thomas' grasp loosened, allowing Cate to shrink back against Nathan.

"Nathan avenged her, as would any man. Aye, he avenged himself, but every *one* of you," Thomas said, with an emphatic stab of his finger, "benefited from Creswicke's death."

"'Twas you what killed him," a voice challenged.

"I *finished* him," Thomas corrected. "Nathan's blade struck first. Ask any man there." A broad general wave toward his men. "They saw it; they know."

A few mouths took an ugly curl, but many more relented. They knew the truth in that; Creswicke's death had been the talk for days.

"Creswicke is dead; the Company is finished," Thomas went on, his force of voice quelling the farthest mutterings.

"He wiped the Royal Navy's eye. They will be on us next," shouted one, several more agreeing.

"Then blame me, too, because I had a hand in that."

With his blood up, Thomas' fair features flushed; poised and ready to strike, he was a sobering sight. He waited, but no challenge came.

"Creswicke might be dead, but the Company still attacked us," shouted one.

"Aye, they did," Thomas conceded. "But we also know that plan had all been lain down and set in motion long before his death."

He swung his gaze on several who had presumably been present at the questioning of the *Mirabel's* crewmen, Bella among them. An angling of her head was her consent.

"They killed my boy!"

"And mine!"

"And mine!"

"Aye, and so your answer is more blood?" Thomas countered. "This beach hasn't run red enough to suit your tastes?"

He let that sink in a moment. "Aye, there's no bringing anyone back. There's no undoing any damage," he added, casting an apologetic look toward Cate. "It's time to rebuild, knowing it will be the last."

In the ensuing silence, Nathan drew up before Bella, like a courtier before a royal. "I am come but for one thing." He gave Cate a meaningful squeeze. "Deny me else, and I'll put this place to me rudder within the glass. As always, I am at your pleasure."

The last was punctuated with a flourishing bow. An obsequious Nathan was an odd and disconcerting sight.

"Mark you, however," he said, straightening. "I've near four hundred willing hands, help of which you are in dire need, and a hold full o' stores, which will also take their leave."

Thomas squared next to him. "If he goes, I go, all my men *and* stores with me."

Nathan flashed a smile, one meant to charm; Thomas displayed a similar one of his own.

"Don't use those on me, gentleman," Bella said narrowly. She slowly shook her head in wonderment. "The disruption the pair of you have caused…"

"Between us, we might also offer a fair list o' matters what were left for the better in our wakes," Nathan countered, the smile still lurking.

Bella cocked a brow. "Life would have been so very much simpler without."

"And so much more boring," Nathan purred.

Bella might have been the island's matriarch, but she still wasn't impervious to their combined charm. "You'll behave?"

Nathan flicked a finger over his heart. "Upon me word. And I shall rely upon you to remind me, should I transgress."

Bella glanced about. Indecision was an odd condition for a woman of her decisive parts. An underlying tension of a different sort hung between her and Nathan, as if a second silent conversation was being conducted. Cate wondered if it was mere malice which caused her to leave Nathan twisting in the wind? Or, was the display for the benefit of her populace?

Finally, the stern face broke into a beaming smile. "Very well. Food and drink awaits! Come!"

It was the cue all had been waiting for. Cheers went up, and the celebration began. "Damn, you," Nathan grumbled through a frozen smile.

Thomas shrugged. "Don't kill me; I just saved your arse *again.*"

Nathan expelled a relieved burst of air. "I knew it was bound to come to a boil, but had hoped to at least touch land."

Cate raised a hand to swipe aside a lock of hair stuck in the sweat on her face. Seeing it shaking, she buried it into the folds of her skirts.

"You weren't afraid... or scared?" she asked, testily.

The men exchanged looks and shrugged.

Damn! They were smirking, the bastards.

"Darling, that wasn't the first time I've suffered the rough side of a woman's tongue.

Probably shan't be the last either," Nathan added, with a speculative eye toward her.

"My only fear was what you might do. The take-no-quarter flag was at your jack – staff, just now." How Nathan managed to make that sound so affectionate was a wonder. "My only worry was you finding your footing. We'd have had a cat fight on our hands then, and there would be blood anew. 'Tis rare soul willing to wade into one of those," he added, with a rueful roll of his eyes.

Thomas nodded in hearty agreement.

Cate's face heated. They weren't far off the mark. Scratching his accusers' eyes out was just the beginning of the destruction imagined. Her blood was still up, requiring every shred of will to keep from hunting the bitches down.

"Thank you," Nathan said earnestly to Thomas.

"Saving your arse is my life's mission," came back with a shrug.

"And a creditable job you've done, although you mightn't have painted me quite so white the martyr."

"They would have had your sorry arse had I painted it any

other color. A part of me fancied the prospect," he mused, gazing at Cate.

"Thomas!" Bella's beckoning call made both men look up.

"Go," Nathan grumbled. "Placate her, or be damned for your failures for the rest of your days."

Thomas made to object, but then hunched his shoulders and trudged away, the hearty hail of his greeting audible over the crowd.

The angry cries of a mob had quickly shifted to those of long-lost friends rejoining. The flow toward the fires and refreshment carried Nathan and Cate with it, their gazes only for each other. Nathan suddenly ducked behind a pile of stores, pulling Cate with him. There, he settled her in his arms and said "Hello" again, this time with dizzying effect.

"I need you... now!" He pressed her back, his hips wedging her against the crates. His searching hands found the hem of her skirt and skimmed up her thighs.

Stricken thoroughly breathless, Cate could only manage an inarticulate sound. She opened her mouth under his and allowed him to plunder as he wished. A remote corner of her mind observed that she was about to become one of those women seen that first night — skirts up, joining with gay abandon in plain sight — and she bloody didn't care!

"Miz Celia's compliments — "

A young face popped up beside them.

Nathan pulled back enough to say "Go away, little man," with an ominousness which had been known to send the stoutest of foredeckhands scampering.

The lad considered, but duty pressed him beyond caution. "Miz Celia's compliments and duty, m'um. She begs you to return to the sickbay. Some have took ill and some have took off, and she's busy with a birthing."

None of it came as a surprise. Weariness, demands of children and setting their personal lives into order had dragged away a good many of the sickbay's workers. The *Morganse's* arrival and the promise of some well-needed celebration would be irresistible.

With sinking spirits, Nathan saw as much on Cate's face. With a discontented growl, he straightened and released her.

Breathless at passions so abruptly denied, Cate finally found her voice. "There are so many wounded, so many who can't shift for themselves..."

"Aye, I daresay," Nathan mused drolly.

He regarded her for a moment, and then sighed, resigned. "Ah, from every pestilence comes a glory. You found your blood, and doing double-tides, watch-on-watch, if I know you," he added, with grudging admiration.

Cate ducked her head. He knew her too well.

She clamped her lower lip between her teeth and shrugged helplessly. "It's my watch."

Nathan opened his mouth to object, but then clapped it shut. "Going to use that against me, eh?"

Sighing, he rubbed the back of his neck, peering at her through one eye. "Since the day we met, four times a day, I have chosen me ship over you."

"I'm sorry." And she was, so very, very much so. It wasn't fair, to neither him nor her! She still reeled with the joy of his return—couldn't keep her hands from him. But neither was it fitting to leave so many helpless.

"Don't be, darling. I did what I had to, and you suffered through it. Now, the capstan has turned, and I must allow you the same."

He blew a long exhale. One arm rose and fell in surrender. "Very well, duty calls." "Thank you."

With a peck on his cheek, she turned to go, but stopped at hearing him follow. "You don't have to—"

"Like hell I don't!" he sputtered. "I just got you back."

Hand on her elbow, Nathan escorted Cate up to the sickbay. He slowed at seeing the size of it, halting completely at its threshold. She turned to find him staring up and down the rows of injured, the line of his jaw going white under the black swathe of several days' beard.

"All this?" he asked in a tight rasp.

Cate's response was cut short by hails and greetings of the male patients. Instantly composing a new face, Nathan turned to meet them. She smiled covertly at hearing "Cap'n! Might ye bear a hand?" hissed with an urgency which usually meant only one thing.

Slipping on an apron, Cate set to her rounds, changing bandages and packings, refreshing the boneset, preparing or giving doses or passing a hot iron to wounds threatening to fester. Meanwhile, Nathan was everywhere, taking command there as he did on his ship. Not in the way of giving orders, but an Ambassador of Good Will, inquiring of each and every man as to how they did, swapping gossip, while at the same time setting them at ease. They mightn't have all been shipmates proper, but listening to them one was brought to believe that any two sailors were never divided by more than two commonacquaintances. A few preliminary probing questions and connections were made, bona fides presented, a virtual bloodline established.

Every word of conversation couldn't be heard, but Cate caught enough to know what Nathan was at. His expression fixed, the Master of Masks alive and well, he inquired quietly, listened carefully and learned about the battle and — she could only assume — *everything* else there. She watched with a combination of relief and resentment, a part of her thinking "Yes, that is what you sent me into. Yes, I would have been far better off with you." A large part of her was glad it was someone else telling him. He couldn't berate them like he might her.

Many a time, Cate was frozen in mid-motion at seeing Nathan haul water, spoon gruel, empty pee bottles and adjust bindings as he laughed, jested and made rude remarks. The man never failed to surprise. She bent to turn a man who had soiled himself, and Nathan was there as for any heavy-lifting.

"You're a born nurse," she observed.

"One can't have been among blood and wounds all their lives without learning what's to be done," he said off-handedly through the grunt of effort at rolling the man over. "We tend for each other when there is no one else or when our cod-handedness did less harm than the rum-sotted chirrugeons."

Once the man was settled, Cate stopped Nathan as he turned to go. "You look a mite shaken," she said, concerned. He was distracted and oddly withdrawn. A gentle nudge was required to urge him over his reluctance.

"Aye, a friend, an *old* friend," he amended quickly. "I just learned of her passing. She was a friend of Mum's. She used to tan me bottom when Mum couldn't bring herself to — "

"Aggie!?" Cate blurted, sickened and shocked.

For once in all their time together, she had truly surprised him. "You knew her?"

"Briefly, all too briefly," Cate said, her throat tightening. Recalling Aggie's Dubliner twang, she reflexively crossed herself. The thought of those spring green eyes, so filled with spirit, suddenly gone dull was difficult to bear.

Good Lord, would there be no end to the losses?

Nathan moved the few steps to a pile of stores. He mouthed a curse and then drove a fist into it. He struck again, and then braced against it, head hanging between his arms. "She'd been beaten and raped... mutilated," he added with a gulp. "Both breasts sliced off."

Cate swallowed down a vile remark about vile acts. To do so would be assuming high moral ground to which she had no claim. She'd done as much to Monroe; some would think it worse.

"We saw enough and heard of more." Cate smiled unsteadily. Aggie had been a delightful old soul, one she had hoped to sit with and learn about Nathan's early years and family. Once more, the door to his past was slammed shut, never to be opened again.

Allowing Nathan his grief, Cate walked silently beside him up the aisle between the beds. The cry of "Cap'n!" from one jerked Nathan from wherever his thoughts had drifted. He went from grave to bright in the time it took to step up to the cotside.

"Mr....?"

"Mapes, sir," the man said, knuckling his forehead.

"Ah, yes, f'c'stle, larboard watch on the *Nautilus*. And, might I assume that you gave the Companymen the thrashing they deserved?"

"Aye, sir! Served one out directly, I did." Mapes had that West Country drawl so oft heard on the foredecks. "But, I took one in the side whilst celebrating."

"Well, Mr. Mapes, you have done it *again*," Cate said severely at the bright red blooming through his bandage.

"Beg pardon, m'um," he said, instantly hang-dog. "'Twas naught to be done fer it. The call o' nature was strong." A cant of his head toward the privy closet clarified his meaning.

Cate cocked a reproachful brow. This wasn't the first time for Mapes or a number of others. No more than a chair with a bit of canvas, it was a "seat of ease fit fer royalty" for those accustomed to sitting elbow-to-elbow, exposed to the elements on a ship's head. The chance to avail themselves of such luxury had brought many of the crustier salts to exert themselves to their own destruction.

"There was plenty 'to be done fer it'," she shot back tartly. "You rise once more, and I'll tie you to that bed." She raised her voice for the benefit of all within hearing.

"Fetch me a fresh bandage and lint from over there." Already undoing the bandage knot, Cate used her chin to direct Nathan to the supplies.

She was admonishing and scolding Mapes further, when an odd noise, startled, yet half-strangled — as if abruptly cut short — drew her attention to the corner to which she had sent Nathan. The recess between the stores pile was shadowy, but it was still possible to make him out, deep in the arms of a woman kissing him with startling familiarity.

The objective eye would have observed the ardor was one-sided but, just then, objectivity wasn't within Cate's grasp.

Objectivity would have also led her to see that Nathan was attempting to disengage—writhing out of the woman's clutches looked akin to wrestling with an octopus—but he didn't do so with the conviction, nor success she could have wished.

If asked, Cate wouldn't have been able to say by what route she crossed the sickbay, but she was there well before the "greeting" was complete.

"Not now; not ever!" Nathan hissed through clenched teeth. "I'm bespoke."

Crossing her arms, Cate patted her foot, waiting to be noticed. That failing, she cleared her throat.

"Ah! Cate!" Nathan announced, clearly relieved. "You'll know—?" His mouth moved, suddenly at a loss.

"Hope." The woman bobbed a curtsy while at the same time darted another lunge for Nathan, his stiff arm thwarting her efforts.

With a final look meant to turn him to stone, Cate swiveled an icy one on his companion. "Yes, we've met."

Hope had been among the group Cate had gone to the fields with just hours before the island was attacked. Hope wore the same knowing, sly smirk now, as she had that morning. Now, Cate knew what it meant and her hand moved at her side with the urge to slap it off.

Hope cut a glare at Cate and then posed a petulant pout at Nathan. "You're with her?"

"In every way imaginable, in life and in death," Nathan gasped, still breathless from her assault.

Her fair brow crumpled, Hope regarded Cate critically. "Very well, but you'll tire of her within the hour. *I* know what you like." The last came with an alluring cut of the eyes and sway of her hips.

With a jerk of her skirts, Hope turned on her heel, calling. "I'll be waiting at *our* spot" over her shoulder as she strolled away. "You know the one..."

"Old friend," Nathan explained in the ensuing silence.

"That wasn't your hand she was shaking," Cate observed coldly.

Nathan winced as he tugged at his waistband, smoothing himself back in order. "Aye, well, might as well have been, for all the effect it had."

"How many more of these reunions might I look forward to?" Cate pointedly glanced around, half-expecting to find the "old acquaintances" queuing up at the doorway.

"None, if there's any help to it." The answer carried a warning lilt: there could well be many, and no, he mightn't successfully fend them all off. "I've been here before — "

"Often. Yes, so I've heard." Cate checked the remarks which hung at the tip of her tongue. He'd just gotten back; she wished to do a number of things with him, but arguing was most certainly not one.

"It's such a shame to disappoint them all," she said, instead.

Nathan caught the tease in that, and his mouth quirked ruefully. "Even if I had gone with her, darling, disappointment was still her fate. You know I rise to only you."

The last was spoken in a throaty purr which made her recall with a sudden rush what she had been missing and, most of all, what she had been longing for.

Grabbing the lint and bandage roll, Nathan took Cate by the arm. "Come. Mape's side awaits."

The effect of that throaty purr, stirred Cate in both body and spirits, putting a positive spring in her step as she continued her watch.

Nathan was there!

"Heart singing" was cliché, but it was true, so very, *very* true! It was all she could do to keep from capering about like a girl, squealing with glee. Several times she caught herself on the verge of humming; bursts of giggling laughter couldn't be contained, earning her wry looks. There was no secret as to what had just put a fresh wind in her jib, or tops'l or whatever the hell the fitting sail was.

Duties demanded her attention, but not enough to keep her eyes off Nathan for long. At some point or another, he had shed his extra armament, allowing an easier view of the bend and twist of his body, the flash of his smile, so vivid against the black of his beard, the sound of his graveled voice making her smile, often at inopportune times.

Her gaiety was diminished at noticing a stiffness in his movement, a certain hitch in his step: he was favoring one leg, and carrying himself like one suffering with a bad back. In spite of the wry looks from her patients, she indulged herself, so that she might remind herself again and again that it was no figment of her imagination.

He was there!

Given Nathan's disdain — or better to say "disinterest" — in children, Cate had half - expected him to leave the younger patients to her. Instead, he approached them with the same willingness as he approached the men, showing them surprising tenderness, intuitively knowing which of the lads would respond to bravado and which required a kind word. His tenderness with the girls made Cate's breath catch, his charms answering even on the youngest.

The greatest surprise was when it came to the very ones she would have thought him to be at his greatest ease: the women. Whether it was fear of her jealousy, in deference to their privacy or just outright shyness—a trait she thought him entirely devoid—she had no notion, but it was an odd damned time for him to be frozen at the foot of their beds, hailing Cate and making inane small-talk until she arrived, and then scuttling away. It seemed a weakness of character, one which was more than a little dismaying and, if she were wholly honest, a lot disappointing. She wasn't so naïve to think a part of this reticence might rise from some of these women being past liaisons. Seeing no spark of recognition— for which Cate was as alert as a hound—beyond names, she was soon compelled to dismiss that notion.

So, what was it?

Cate was spooning broth to one patient when Emily, in the next bed, roused from her poppy-syrup induced sleep and whispered that she was in dire need of the convenience. Cate rose directly and fetched the pot. Another who bore the Mark of Cornwall, Emily was a large woman and too lethargic from her dose to manage on her own. Holding her up without jostling her arm, slipping the pottery under her and steadying her the while was a struggle. Seeing her plight, Nathan came up, meaning to lend a hand, but reeled back at seeing the stump. Cate glared, making it clear that his help would be greatly appreciated, but to no avail.

Finally, when all business was finished and Emily seen settled, Cate found Nathan where he had retreated outside the tent's confines. Shooting a reproachful glare back at the now sleeping Emily, he retreated even further.

"What is the problem?" Cate demanded, lowly.

Fuming silence was her answer.

"For heaven's sake, Nathan, surely you've seen a missing arm before."

"Not on a woman," he seethed over his shoulder. Thoroughly shaken, he reeled around and pointed a rigid arm. "That could have been you lying there."

"But, it wasn't—"

"But, it could have."

"But, it wasn't."

Nathan stalked back and forth, gathering steam. Finally,

he drew up before her. "Something happened. Not the battle," he added, cutting off her retort. "But something else: before, during... after... sometime."

She stared and then turned away. "It was nothing—" Some kind of inquiry regarding Monroe was expected, but not here, not now.

"Like hell!" His vehemence made her start. Grabbing her arm, he held it out on display. "You've been rough-handled." Dropping the arm, he seized her jaw. "You were struck and damned near strangled, too, by the looks of that neck. That's not from some goddamned gun barrage. Now tell me!"

"Thomas would be better—" she began, shying away. Neither was she prepared to relive the last few days.

"Pah! He's too busy chasing skirts."

"What about you?" Cate stormed back, mindful of an entire tent of listening ears. "Your shirt is full of holes. You wince every time you lift that arm, and you're limping."

"Pah! 'Tis nothing—"

"Nothing!" she cried, shoving her face into his. "You were in a battle, weren't you? You were damned near killed, weren't you?"

Days of dammed up fear, anguish and worries burst from their barricade. Tears brimmed at the thought of how close her worst fears might have come to being realized; how close she might have come to Pryce and Hodder, hat-in-hand, reporting their regrets of his death.

The notion that she might have been worried brought Nathan up all-standing. "None nearer than the hundred times before," he snorted. "We took on the *Resolute*, you know that! Hell, 'twas the whole point to this escapade."

"And Harte didn't mean to see you dead?"

"He might have wished it," Nathan said, amused by the idea. "He'd be obliged to improve his gunnery by a damned sight before that could come to pass, that's for bloody, damned sure. Hell, I saw his shining face and aimed to wipe that perpetual smirk off it," he added, with a distant smile. "We wiped his eye, I can tell you that. One can only hope his body was flung over the side with the rest of the dead."

Nathan stalked to a water butt and splashed water in his face. Hands braced on the iron-bound rim, he stood head hanging and dripping. "This was supposed to have been a place to relax, a place to have some women about and... and... chat," he finally landed on.

Chat?

It was all Cate could do to keep from laughing.

His head came up. Eyes still dark and troubled, he searched her face, gathering the nerve to say something else. A shriek from inside made Cate race back inside, Nathan close behind. She knew both who and what the issue was long before she reached Joe Brampton's cot. His grizzled head braced against the hatch which served as his bed, back arched, his knobbed hands clawing the air, fighting an invisible foe.

"Hold him!" Cate shouted to Nathan as she ran for some rag strips. "Have a care for his leg, but don't let him hurt himself."

Nathan flung himself on Brampton, holding him down by the shoulders. "Easy, man! Tell me where the bastards are! Stand down and we'll give 'em a taste of grapeshot," he shouted, loud enough to be heard over the tortured soul's cries.

Brampton might have been old bones, but terror provided him with the strength of one-and-twenty, leaving both Cate and Nathan sweating and shaking by the time they got him restrained.

"Delirium," Nathan concluded between gasps.

Cate curled her hand and lingering feel of the old man's flesh. No heat of fever. "No, just fear."

She fetched some Valerian tea. Nathan took the cup, sniffed and scowled. "Rum would have answered better."

In spite of his objections, Nathan lifted the grey head and trickled it into his mouth. Like parents dealing with a fractious infant, they stood over him, waiting and watching.

At one point, Nathan whipped out a much-used handkerchief and dabbed at Cate's cheek, frowning at the resultant blood. "He got you."

"One of many," she sighed, looking down at her scabbed and bruised arms. Not every wounded soul accepted help willingly.

"You knew what to do just then," she observed.

Nathan shrugged off the compliment. "Aye, Ol' Brampton isn't the first to go gun – happy. Sleeping before-the-mast, cheek-to-jowl, you learn how to see many a tortured soul through their terrors." He laid an assuring hand on Brampton's shoulder. "His isn't the worst, not by a long shot."

Ever so gradually, but finally, Brampton found his peace. Cate slipped over to where Toby laid. It had been a while since she had checked on him. As before, one look was all which was necessary, a hand on his forehead confirming what she already knew: still teetering on the pinnacle between prevailing and failing.

Nathan came up beside her. "Another reason why I never countenanced cabin boys," he said looking down. His hand automatically moved to set the cot swinging. "Seeing them blown apart or chopped up like a rabbit for a stew —"

Eyes going distant, his jaw worked. "I saw a ball cut one in half as neatly as a knife through an apple. I picked up the parts, one in each hand," he said, mimicking the motion, "and threw them overboard with the rest of the wreckage."

Nathan looked up at her. "It was like that here, wasn't it?" His voice was tight with hurt and accusation of hidden truths.

Cate sighed and rubbed her brow. "Yes."

She turned and moved away. The Mistress of Masks she was not. This was neither the time, nor the place for revelations, ones he might find too repulsive to accept. She couldn't bear his rejection. Not now. Not yet. It was difficult to know what to say, without knowing how much he already knew? Lesauvage's betrayal and treachery he would have learned straightaway. But, beyond that...?

The face of every man Nathan spoke with had been studied by Cate, straining to remember if they had been with Thomas, and hence might have witnessed the scene with Monroe. A part of her almost wished that at least one might have been there, that one of them might have related her atrocities, so she might be spared the ordeal of telling him herself. She wouldn't... She couldn't.

Was an untold truth necessarily a lie? She thought not; she hoped not. A part of her wondered why she should feel so guilty for withholding something from one who did the same with the regularity of breathing?

Taking her silence as consent, Nathan's eyes closed slowly and his head sank, his worst fears confirmed. He swore, too low to hear, but with a vehemence which couldn't be missed.

"You keep passing it with the reverence of an idol."

Cate looked up to find that she stood by Dorrie's cot, now empty. Her hand rested on the rope edge as lightly as it had on the child's head. She jerked her hand away and buried it out of sight.

"Am I?" she asked lamely.

"Someone special...?" Nathan asked with guarded concern. "Someone who died?"

So many died, she thought to herself.

"No, not that one." She openly smiled at that. No, at least that one had lived.

Still, Cate was aware of Nathan's expectant look. She had denied him so much, he deserved some sort of response. "It was a... a girl here. Her mother was over there. They both recovered enough to go home... together."

Together.

That was the word which rung the loudest and to which she clung like a talisman: Dorrie had a mother, and they were together and happy, as it should be. They were well and safe, and she had a hand in it. She had done her part to keep Nathan's legacy, a part of him, safe and well.

As she spoke, she had watched him carefully, keen as a hawk for any signs of recognition or awareness.

Nothing; he was innocence personified. Either that, or he had many days to prepare himself, or rather, prepare his deception.

"Cap'n? Might ye bear a hand?"

Urgent call was the welcomed break Cate prayed for. She waved Nathan on his way, a "We're not done" look cast back at her as he set off.

At long length, the bell rang—apparently now restored to its belfry—and Cate's watch was over.

Nathan found her, smiling indulgently as she pulled off her apron and hung it on a peg. "You've the glow of having found your purpose. Busted heads and busted guts: you've found your calling."

She scoffed. Grimed and exhausted, "glow" was hardly the word she would use to describe herself. Yet, there was no denying a sense of usefulness, of the fulfillment of being productive which filled her. She mastered her complacency, however. Looking too happy might give him cause to leave her there for good.

Instead, Cate moved to behind a pile of stores, taking Nathan with her, and kissed him.

"You are mistaken, m'lord," she said, softly. "My calling is right here."

He leaned back to regard her. "You looked so surprised when I arrived. Still do, for that matter," he added, narrowing one eye. "You didn't trust me word."

Cate blushed, ashamed. "I wanted to, but... you were so late."

"Only by a day or two."

More like three, she thought. Making that point seemed petulant.

Nathan lightly brushed a thumb over her forehead. "One could plant a crop in those furrows. It grieves me to think they are on my account."

Chuckling ruefully, his arms tightened about her as he pressed his head against hers. "I can see I've much to atone for."

He kissed her again, making a creditable start at that very thing.

Finding her hand, he pressed her knuckles to his lips. "Everyone on this cursed rock has had the benefit of these hands." He looked up through his lashes. "Might I be allowed a bit of that... now... if you'll have me?"

The lashes lowered as she cupped his cheek, the stubble of his beard a soft plush under her fingertips. "Why wouldn't I have you?"

Now, it was his brow in which one might plant a crop. "Because I sent you into another Hell, filled with naught but blood and suffering—"

She cut him off with a kiss. "Forgiven."

"Heal me now, oh angel-of-mercy," he murmured. He made to kiss her again, but she drew away.

"I'm filthy and I smell." She yearned to be with him, but...

Nathan made an impatient noise. "God's blood and wounds, darling, I don't care." His mouth hovered over hers, but then he drew back and sighed, resigned. "I mightn't care, but you do."

Eyeing her, he considered briefly. Head hanging, decision made, he put out his hand. "Come, I know a place."

18: LORELEI'S ALTAR

IT WAS DARK BY THEN. They stepped out of the sickbay into the light of a moon, a half-orb, yellow and waxen as a wheel of cheese.

To Cate's great relief, Nathan turned away from the sounds of high celebration and led her inland. The island was a bewildering criss-cross of trails, some barely more than a rabbit's track. Others, like the one they followed then, was a virtual turnpike, trampled wide by countless feet. Nathan struck off with a surety of step; it might have been years since his last visit, but such familiarity suggested that visit hadn't been brief, traversing here like he did the surrounding waters.

The forest closed in, and the sounds of laughter, fifes and fiddles faded. They clung to each other as they walked, stumbling now and then, gazing at each other in joyous disbelief.

Shortly, Nathan drew to a halt. Holding her hands, he pointed with his chin. "There's a common bathing hole just ahead, but there's a grand chance you might be seen."

Given the hour, the fact that they had yet to encounter a single soul along the way, the extent of the merriment suggesting the island's entire population was elsewhere, Cate considered it highly unlikely anyone would be about, and cared little if they were. Modesty was never her burden. The notion, however, obviously weighed on him.

A consenting nod on her part and Nathan turned off into the bushes. Pushing through the undergrowth, he followed what was now no more than a depression of grass. A gurgling rustle and waft of cool air were the precursors of water being near, fresh, judging by the smell of moss and wet vegetation. They stepped out of the greenery and there it was. Too wide to be called a creek, but less than a river, the moonlight cast shifting patterns of gunmetal and silver through the overhanging trees

KERRY LYNNE

and ferns on the still surface. The soft earth and moss put her in mind of the swimming holes of her youth.

Nathan ducked under a tree fern and swept an arm toward it. "The Altar of Hygeia awaits!"

"You make it sound like an unnatural fixation," she said defensively.

He smiled forbearingly. "Darling, you are the washingest woman I've ever met, and yet, the sweetest smelling. I'm not so cod-headed of a clot to not make the connection. It is your delight; the prospect of blood puts the same spark in your eyes as the prospect of bathing, as it does just now," he added softly, touching her cheek.

He glanced at the water, apologetically. "'Tis not so grand as one might dive and languish in glory, but 'tis sufficient to wash away all things noxious."

"It will do very nicely." And she meant it. She had expected to perform her ablutions in a bucket. Once again, she marveled at the catalogue in Nathan's head; he always seemed to know of such places, perfect for any occasion. It was as if he had spent his life in preparation for her arrival.

"Thomas didn't bring you here?" he asked, cocking a brow in displeasure.

"No," she said slowly. "But would you really have wished him to see me cavorting about bathing?"

Nathan's brow arched higher. "I would have liked to think he would have known enough to try. And then, I would have had to give him a round turn for having contrived to see you in your altogether."

They began to undress, flinging their clothing into a heap. Seizing his shirttail, Nathan suddenly hesitated. Then, with the resolve of one about to face his judgment, truths heretofore denied, he drew it off and turned his back to her. Her breath caught as a shaft of moonlight illuminated a massive bruise. With that same resolve, he pushed his breeches down and posed his leg. She'd seen the torn cloth, seen him favoring the leg, and now her suspicions were confirmed: a finger-wide scab ran up the outside of his thigh.

"I wish I—" She began, her finger running lightly along it. Crusty and nearly black in the waxen light, it was several days old and healing well, as were the myriad of other scrapes, contusions, and cuts now visible.

His finger to her lips silenced her. "... Could have been there," he finished for her. "Aye, luv, I know. But had you been, it could well have gone worse, far worse," he added emphatically as she

380

made to object. "For I would have been so mightily distracted, worried for you."

His eye traveled from her jaw and neck, and then her arms, taking in the bruises, scrapes and cuts, all her badges of war. Battles didn't happen in a vacuum. Someone would have seen, someone would have related the gory details: Lesauvage, Monroe... everything.

By then, he probably knew more about the battle than she.

"I fought them off," she said simply.

Swallowing hard, he smiled, one tight with regret. His eyes shimmered with wetness. "That's me girl; heart of a lion. God help any misguided, bungling cove what crosses you."

The curve of the river to one side and the bowing fern heads to the other were barricades which cut them off from the world. It was as if Nathan had somehow sensed her need to escape, not just prying eyes, but the press of people. Cate threw back her head and drank in the night air, its clean crispness cutting the lingering thickness of the sick and ailing which hung in her head and throat. She opened her eyes to find Nathan looking at her with something between a smile and a grimace.

Nathan put out his hand and led her to the water's edge. An odd thrill coursed through her at the sight of lean haunches, the length of body and limb as he stepped in. Compared to the night's tropical sultriness, the water was cool. She waded deeper, gooseflesh rippling up her stomach and limbs. The current stirring about her ankles was a gentle, living presence. Nathan moved slowly, feeling ahead with one foot. Finally, he found what he sought and stepped down into a hole, going in nearly up to his hips.

Cate reached for his outstretched hand, but then balked. The darkness, the still water, the unknowing: it looked too much like a black hole, a bottomless watery pit into which one disappeared, dragged into a Hell, not of fire and heat, but of darkness and bone – soaking cold. No bottom; no top. No up; no down. And worse, the soul-saturating loneliness...

She blinked at feeling Nathan seize her hands, his solid grasp so warm with life jerking her back to this world. "I'm here, darling. See, 'tis bottom just here." A stomp of his foot sent up little spurts of sand, diamond-like in the moonlight.

Nathan slipped an arm around her and held her, tight and secure. "'Tis no shame in it, darling." A small tremor coursed through him. "I was the same for a while. It took years before I could dive over the side with a clear heart."

He gave her a reassuring shake and said earnestly "She'll never touch you again. *Never!*"

Nathan tipped her face up, his eyes searching hers, willing her to believe. Cate solemnly nodded.

Her hand firm in his, she gingerly probed with a foot. Images of a bottomless world dissolved at finding one of sand and stone. Under his guidance, she inched around to find it was like a very large, very deep hip bath. Still, there was only room for one; Nathan stood like the watchful parent as Cate rolled and splashed, working her feet into the sand to remove the several days' accumulation of grime. At one point, he stepped in to curve her back over the crook of his arm and scrubbed her hair.

"You always love this," he said, smiling indulgently down at her.

She sighed, luxuriantly. "You know me too well."

Retreating to the submerged ledge, Cate sat idly kicking her feet, and watched Nathan dive and swirl, periodically casting a glance until she deemed him "clean enough." Eventually, a nod was his cue, and he sat on the bottom, the water swirling about his chest.

Droplets glinting on the black mat of chest hair, his gaze fixed on her. "You look like a siren sitting there. My Lorelei, my murmuring rock, calling me to me demise."

A hand rose to beckon her. "Come to me," he said, huskily.

Cate slipped from her perch and settled on his lap, her back against his chest. Limp with contentment, she floated a fraction above him, his hand stroking the slope of her breast the only anchor which kept the current from carrying her away. With their stillness, the forest's nightlife resumed their chorus. Insects flitted and skimmed the water's surface, their wings brushing them now and again.

It was so very, very peaceful.

Nathan brought Cate around to face him, her legs slipping about his hips. He kissed her, not out of desire, but out of the sheer pleasure of being able to do so. When he finished, he nestled her head in the crook of his neck, and they traced the curves and planes of each other's body.

Cate sighed blissfully. "I missed you."

"As did I."

She sat up and touched his cheek. "I reached for you, like before. I tried to find you, but—"

Nathan drew her back down against him, his arms tightening about her. "I know, darling. I was there, but I didn't wish for you to see, to know—" He stopped, his throat moving as he swallowed.

Since their resurrection, an odd void lingered between them. One unspoken question loomed, large and foreboding: when they finally joined, would it be as it had been before? Only a fool would believe that death hadn't changed them, but by what measure? For her own part, Cate didn't care; whatever might be different in Nathan, she still wanted him, still loved him.

But what of the differences in her? Could they be overcome? Overlooked? Even more significantly, would he wish to?

When they had first met, they had circled each other for weeks, nay months, both wanting the same, and yet neither able to summon the wherewithal to act. Fear of rejection had paralyzed them, then. Fear of another kind now hung between them, a barrier as invisible as the skim of water covering them, but as impenetrable as the copper sheeting on his ship.

If not now, then when?

Cate moved her hips suggestively against him. "I want you."

Since her return, a chill had existed, not of the body, but of the soul, the very essence of her being, and there was only one way to ease it: Nathan, inside her, hot and deep. She wanted nothing more than to devour him, leave him shaking and gasping, a quivering wreck. She had done it, countless time, but now...? Could she still do so? Or, had events changed them too much?

Nathan angled his head, finding her eyes. "You're sure? After... everything, you're ready?" The strain in his voice suggested every fiber of his being willed her not to say "No."

She moved against him, coming more alive by the moment. "You want me, don't you?"

Nathan's answer was to rise and carry her ashore. Laying her out on the discarded clothing, he lowered himself over her. He kissed her, a languorous exploration of the deep crevices of her mouth. The lingering film of water was slick on their skins; they slithered and slid as if dipped in sweet oil.

Nathan cupped her breast, the nipple tightening under his thumb. "You glow like an opal, with fire and spark in your depths."

She opened her legs to him and he poised over her, coiled and taut as a bowstring.

He audibly swallowed, his voice tight with effort. "I can't be gentle."

Cate slipped her hand down to cup the velvety weight between his legs. Nathan let out a bellowing gasp, like he'd been punched. He rolled away, curling into himself.

"Nathan, I'm sorry! I'm sorry!" she cried, shaking him. The low, breathless growl, the writhing, the clutching himself were the universal sign of a man having suffered a blow to his privates.

Now on her feet, Cate skirted around him, chanting "I'm sorry. I'm sorry."

She hovered over him as he moaned and cursed, thoroughly confused. Lord, she was no maid on her wedding night! She knew what to do, more importantly, what *not* to do and, even more importantly, what Nathan liked. She curled the offending hand, trying to recall what she might have done.

Finally, Nathan drew a breath, the sharp, sucking sound of air finally returning to his lungs. "I'm fine," he ground out. He forced his eyes open as proof.

"Is there something I can—?" she began, feeling thoroughly useless.

"Nay, it'll pass. It has already," he said, straightening a fraction.

He rolled shakily up onto his knees, but could manage no farther. There, he remained, head hanging between his arms.

Nathan waved a feeble hand and gasped "It's not you!" He choked a laugh and shook his head. "You've the hands of an angel. The mere mention and, God help me, imaging what they can do—" The rest was lost in an agonized groan.

"Until now!" She had visions of having gelded him, or nearly so, for he was making noises not unlike a bullock in the spring.

One hand seized her arm and gave her an admonishing shake. "It's not—" he wheezed. "It's... it's nothing... you... did."

"Then what the hell is it?" Her shriek sent several night creatures scampering.

Nathan sat back onto his haunches and threw his head back, sucking in air. Beads of sweat dotted his nose and mustache. He cut a look from the corner of his eye. "Dunno."

He drew several more breaths. "I've hurt for days, but I put it off as just aching for—"

His teeth clamped into his lower lip. "Time. We... I... just need a bit of time. We've all night, and the next and the next..." The last came in an unconvincing wheeze.

If only, she thought dubiously. Mastering her own disappointment didn't come as easily as she might have wished.

"But this isn't just some random pang," she pointed out.

Nathan resolutely shook his head, whether out of ignorance or reluctance to say she couldn't tell.

Still, he was correct: time did have its palliative qualities. His agony lessened, his breathing became something nearer to natural. Suddenly aware of her nakedness, Cate snatched up her shift. Nathan ventured a hand toward her as she donned it. She reflexively shied away, lest any contact might cause him further harm.

"You're thin as a jack-staff, again," he observed.

Stopping in mid-motion, Cate looked down at herself. In the moon's bluish glow, the shadows of her ribs made her look almost skeletal. No wonder he was put off by the sight of her.

He pushed up onto his feet and slowly straightened. "Food is what we require, to build our strength for later, eh?" he added, with what she assumed was meant as a leering wink.

Cate gaped. Nathanael Blackthorne thinking of food? Apparently, it was to be a night of several firsts.

She wasn't quite sure as to what she needed. A drink wouldn't fix everything, but it would be a bloody good place to start!

19: ESTABLISHING BOUNDARIES

THE PROSPECT OF A DRINK quickened both their steps. Even if Nathan hadn't been next to Cate, there would have been little chance of getting lost. The music, lights and voices were like a beacon back to the settlement. Finally, they broke free of the forest and out onto shore. Upshore they went, toward the pavilion, the difference an additional two hundred Morgansers made starkly evident.

Once at the pavilion, Nathan saw Cate seated. The act prompted several islanders to rise and move away. Nathan seemed neither surprised, nor displeased to see them go. In spite of whatever agreement had been made upon his arrival that day, ill-will and hard feelings still prevailed.

Nathan returned shortly with two drinks in hand. Stiff and strong was what Cate needed just then, and she drank deeply. In the meantime, he moved among the wrecked remains of the tables in search of their supper. He returned with a pottage made of fish, crab, beans, vegetables and rice, and roasted meat, pig, goat or some local beast.

With the crude wooden implement supplied, more paddle than spoon, Cate took a bite and found that Youssef's hand wasn't just in the coffee: the pottage was rich with spices. Sitting next to her, Nathan shoveled in his with unique enthusiasm. Perhaps because rice was so easily swallowed, she observed poking at hers. She shifted, the boards under her rump feeling remarkably closer to the bone. Perhaps gaining an extra stone mightn't go amiss.

As they ate, Cate became aware that alone in a crowd was, indeed, possible. They were in the unique situation of sitting among several hundred, and yet, with everyone so deep in their cups, she and Nathan were, in essence, alone. They could sit and chat, unheeded and unheard.

The scene by the river still had her thoroughly unsettled. She looked accusingly down at her hand as if it had suddenly gone traitor. Many a Highland night — and the winter ones were oh, so *very* long — had been spent learning how to please a man. She could learn again...

Providing, of course, that Nathan might survive it.

The male sensibilities were delicate things, fragile as crystal. Nathan was no exception. It was clear he didn't wish to talk about it — What man would? — but dammit, he would now!

"I'm sorry." Lord, that sounded so blessedly hollow and trite!

Narrowing one eye, Nathan lowered his spoon and said evenly "It wasn't you." "Will you stop saying that! Of course, it was me. No one else—"

"It's my cock. I should know—"

"It's mine, too," she huffed, and then quickly amended "sort of. I mean, I'm quite familiar, *more* familiar than you perhaps," she went on under his gaping stare. "It's physically impossible for you to have observed it as closely as I. I know its preferences and finer details... much like you know me," she added, softer.

It was difficult to tell in the dim light, but a deep flush seemed to have risen from Nathan's collar.

"I have a vested interest in it and its habits," Cate went on, determinedly. "And I can tell you I never touched you... it." On that point she was positive.

"You think I don't know that?" he sputtered, finally finding his voice. He leaned closer, tapping his finger on the table with each word. "I am *very* aware of what did or, of higher importance, did *not* happen."

"Then, what—?"

He opened his mouth, but then buried his nose into his cup. "Dunno. 'Tis better. No harm done."

The smile he offered wouldn't have convinced the village idiot.

"Mr. Cate!"

Starting, Cate looked up as Kirkland popped out of the crowd and scurried forth, Ben hard in his wake.

"Give you joy of... of..." The word "survival" loomed on Kirkland's lips, his captain's presence rendering it impossible to utter. "Well-being!" finally burst forth.

So caught up in his emotions, Kirkland nearly flung his arms about Cate. Recollecting himself at the last moment, he seized her hand instead. Ben, at his elbow, was mute but beaming.

"... Saw the bodies... so worried..." the *Morganse's* cook said, in inarticulate bursts, pumping her hand so vigorously, Cate was obliged to drop her spoon and grasp the edge of the bench to keep from toppling over.

At length, sensing their intrusion, the pair took their leave, and an uneasy silence fell between Cate and Nathan once more.

"It wasn't your fault."

He stared, failing to smoke her meaning.

"The battle, the Company attacking and all, wasn't your fault."

"Of course, it was my fault." He stabbed at his food. "It mightn't have been my guns, but it was all by my hand just the same. I had to look at the bodies, see the destruction and know if anything had happened to you, it would have been my fault."

Nathan threw down the spoon with a frustrated clatter. "Aye, 'twas Thomas' notion to bring you here, but I agreed. Your death would have been my doing, on my hands," he ended, spreading the very objects in display.

"But nothing happened. I'm fine."

He gazed at her for some moments before he finally said. "Aye, you're fine, but something did happen."

There was a meaningful lilt in his voice, of something more to say. He shook it off and set to eating again in a more mechanical way.

"So, pressing poor, dear Aggie about me," he said conversationally, a bit later.

It took Cate a moment to follow the sudden shift in topic. "I'm always interested to learn anything about you as a lad."

"As full o' meself as any, I expect," he demurred.

"She mentioned your fath—Beecher," she corrected, at the sharp cut of his eyes.

"I should imagine she had plenty to say about that ol' parasitic muckworm. The two of them went at it hammer 'n tongs after—" He gulped, and not to swallow food. "After Mum passed."

Cate heard the catch in Nathan's voice and felt the pang of loss. They had been roughly of the same age when their mother's had passed, far too young. But then, any age was too young to lose a parent.

"Heart-of-oak that one was," Nathan went on, after a few moments. "She would lay into me with a switch—when I had it comin'—like a hard-horse bosun."

He smiled crookedly at the memory. "At the same time, she would call ol' Beecher out like that same bosun, if he was to lay me out for no fair reason."

"Aggie spoke as if he still lived," Cate suggested delicately. Nathan rarely paused long enough in cursing the man to his grave to learn if he still lived.

Nathan shrugged as he stabbed another mouthful and said around it "Indeed? Couldn't prove it by me one way or 'tother. I've not had word of the ol' pox-ridden, belswagger this age and more, nor do I wish to." The last was punctuated by an emphatic thump of his fist.

"Well, at any rate, she bid me to do this." Cate leaned to peck him lightly on the cheek. "She desired me to tell you your mum would be proud."

Nathan meditatively rubbed the spot, a deep red definitely rising from his collar this time. "She did, eh?"

"She did."

Further elucidation was cut short by a pair of Lovelies stumbling up and giving him joy of his victory over the *Resolute* and joy of his arrival.

The door to Nathan's past was slammed shut once again.

❦

Once they had eaten their fill, Cate and Nathan refilled their drinks, and they idly wove their way through the crowd. A certain restlessness kept Nathan moving from one fire to the next.

One was compelled to wonder if there was an intrinsic element in rum which drove one to competition. The Olympians and Romans had nothing on pirates. Sport of every description had broken out, from cards, dice, draughts, chess — with carved pieces resembling fertility gods — and skittles to knife-flinging — the physical perils of which made Cate turn away — to looking through a horse collar in search of the ugliest face. Rat-racing, pig-riding — an insufficient numbers of the hapless beasts obliging the contestants to ride each other — and who had the worst scar and could come up with the most outrageous story of how they came by it, occupied a great many more. A cheering ring formed around a good-natured wrestling match. A bit further away, a friendly fisticuff threatened to become deadly. Split knuckles, flattened noses, cracked jaws and missing teeth would all be worn as badges of honor come the morrow. A more reserved, but no-less-quiet fire was surrounded by oratorios and poets, swaying in their seats or hanging onto each other as they recited before an enthusiastic audience with voices accustomed to reaching the foretop. Coupling might well have been added to the list of competitions, for it went on with equal numbers and industry.

Thomas was heard more often than seen, snatches of his deep laugh drifting amid the strains of music and voices. Bella popped in and out of the crowd on Pryce's arm, his destroyed face bearing a smile the likes of which Cate had never witnessed. On land, away from the weight of command, there was a certain charm about the man, a dash which made it easy to believe women would find appealing, in a devilish, dangerous sort of way.

Their step slowed at seeing Hermione moving among the crowd, nuzzling for handouts.

The sight of her glassy-eyed and swaying on her hooves brought a derisive snort from Nathan. "Drunk as Davey's sow."

Cate wondered if he referred to the Welshman, whose wife had been supposedly mistaken for a six-legged hog, or if Davy Jones was a swineherd? Such odd ramblings of mind made her think perhaps she'd drunk more than credited. She was still looking down into her cup, trying to sort out if it had just been refilled for the third, or was it the fourth, when they drew up at one fire where two fiddles, a pennywhistle, and a drum played a particularly catching tune.

They walked close, Cate's arm tucked tight to his side, his hand often coming to rest at her shoulder or waist.

"What are you looking at?" he asked.

"You. This," she said, indicating his arm hooked into hers. Such personal contact was a blatant violation of his rules-of-decorum, such a public display purported to reduce her status to merely that of the one warming the captain's bed.

One eye narrowed as one does when regarding the dim. "We are not aboard."

"I know, but—"

Nathan made a half-irritated noise. "I wish to make it clear to even the most ill – begotten, cross-eyed dolt of who you are with."

"And who you are with?" she asked cautiously.

Nathan snorted. "No point to be made there."

"Some still seem to live in hopes you might change your mind," she observed.

She directed his gaze toward the margins of the firelight where Hope, his "old friend" from the sickbay, lurked, moving as they moved, and yet never coming any closer.

And wisely so, Cate thought, uncharitably.

Since arriving at the pavilion, Cate had observed him closely. Tension bristled off him like spines on a hedgehog. It wasn't confrontation as in looking for a fight. This was anticipation laden with dread, the kind which came with expecting to meet someone they didn't wish to meet, and yet was anxious to have the inevitable event over and done.

Someone, but who?

Hope wasn't the cause of Nathan's dread. Cate knew him well enough to recognize his facades and none were present, just then. His surprise at seeing her was as genuine as his disinterest.

Nathan sighed and shrugged. "As I said, doomed to disappointment."

There was no overlooking several women circling, keen as half-starved barn cats. Cate smiled privately. So many had jeered at the idea Nathan was coming for her, and now she had wiped their collective eye. Still, she drew him that bit closer. Her presence so far was a deterrent. But, should she so much as step off to the privy, there was little doubt that those cats would pounce.

Still, as they walked, Cate's eye continuously roamed the crowd for one who was so very conspicuous in her absence: Marthanna.

Much was sure to change when she finally made her appearance.

As Cate and Nathan strolled, Morgansers often hailed or approached, obliging them to stop. The sight of so many familiar faces — Pryce, Scripps, Hodder, Smalley, and Towers — gave her a sense of connection, of no longer being among strangers. Who would have thought the sight of a man with an ass's jawbone and a necklace of trophy fingers about his neck, or one hairless as a newborn babe, the slitted eyes of his snake tattoo peering down from his bald crown, would bring tears to one's eyes?

Lovelies and Brazens approached as well, eager to give Nathan joy of his victory. The Morgansers had already regaled them, but the Captain's view was always of prime importance, and they begged to hear his version. Heads cocked, eyes bright, they questioned him on headings, points of wind, sail set, current, soundings, weather and weights-of-metal.

"You're fidgeting like you've ants up your skirts," Nathan observed upon departing one group. "The crab give you a rash?"

"It's not easy standing here listening over and over as to how close you came to being killed," Cate said peevishly.

There was no missing the pockmarks in the *Morganse's* sides, some of the balls still stuck in her sides. Neither could she ignore the *Morganse's* captain, bruised and limping. Nathan had flirted with Death, again. He'd walked away the victor, but she was confident the Grim Reaper didn't appreciate having his nose tweaked.

Grim Reaper, the Devil, Davy Jones, Calypso: who exactly was hot on Nathan's heels? Was it just one, or all, a grasping horde seeking him? To her judgment, spitting in the eye of one would only lead to rendering them all more determined. Neither was Cate convinced that Nathan's resurrection was a permanent state; by his own confession, he wasn't immortal. That, in and of itself, meant that there was no guarantee against losing him to spending eternity at Calypso's right hand.

"And, you fancy it's easier for me?" Nathan made a frustrated swipe. "Everyone has been more than eager to regale me with your escapades. And I have been obliged to look at even more, firsthand," he added, touching her bruised neck.

Checking himself, he smiled indulgently, the flames flickering on his profile. "Darling, sailors do three things when they come ashore: drink, fornicate and lie. I'm doing the first," holding up his mug. "Recovering from the second," tugging at his waistband, "and so, in the duration, have naught but the third to occupy me."

Cate fidgeted. Either the hard labor of the recent days, energy of passion undrained, the contagiousness of the night's gaiety, or the sound of Nathan's voice made her spirits positively buoyant.

She plucked at her skirts and sketched a jigging hop. "What about dancing? Do you sailors dance when you're ashore?"

Nathan blinked, surprised. They had only danced twice before: once around a fire on a night much like this, and once on the f'c'stle, trying to teach her a jig. Too close quarters and too many teachers, the latter hadn't gone well.

"Do you know this one?" he asked.

Cate regarded the drunken cavorting. This wasn't the dignified march-and-pirouette of a ballroom, with matrons lining the walls alert to call out the first misstep. The question seemed more in the way of if there was "a step" to know? It seemed more sport than dancing, with twos and threes — men often paired with men — jostling into each other as they spun and stomped.

"Would it matter?" she asked gaily.

"Not to me," Nathan declared with a broad grin. "And the devil take anyone who does."

Handing their drinks to a bystander, Nathan swept off his hat and made a courtly leg. He looked up with a teasing gleam. "Might you honor me with the pleasure of this dance, m' lady?"

Without waiting for an answer, Nathan hooked an arm about Cate's waist and spun her away. Lithe and feral as a cat, his eyes held hers as they spun and whirled, her skirts flaring wide. Braids arcing out, the amber firelight alternately caught one side of his face and then the other. As they danced, it became obvious that Cate's earlier suspicions were true: the step didn't matter. Any misstep on her part and Nathan merely caught her up, her feet skimming the sand. Her breath grew short, her stays digging her sides, and a girlish giggle bubbled out. Nathan's grin widened.

The music ended, and he picked her up in a flourishing whirl, hooting with glee. Setting her down, he kissed her hard, and gave her a final spin.

Fortified by another drink, the musicians struck up another tune. Nathan spun around, meaning to catch Cate up in the next reel, but a hail—no mistaking Thomas' voice—stopped them. As the very man wove his way through the crowd toward them, Cate groaned at seeing Cornwall being half-led, half-propelled toward them. Nathan glanced curiously at her; a small frustrated shake of her head was all which could be managed before the pair was upon them.

"You two know each other, I presume?" Thomas said.

Nathan squinted at Cornwall, presumably running through the vast list of names in his head. Swaying, Cornwall's one eye glowed red as the fire coals. The sour reek of drink— he had to be as pickled as a hog's face—made Cate wish to turn her head, but be damned if she would appear either retiring or demure before the bastard!

Stubborn, yes.

Did she care? Not a wit.

She had endured his insults, helped in his butchery and had been glad to be shut of him. Now he was back, like an annoying carbuncle.

"Joseph Cornwall, your shervant, shir," came in a slurred burst and a gesture which was presumably intended as a salute.

The ensuing silence made it clear that no such nicety would be forthcoming for Cate. The snub came as no surprise to Thomas; Nathan stiffened, one brow shooting up under his scarf and there remained.

Thomas gave the man a prompting shove forward. "Mr. Cornwall here seems to have an issue." The shadows reduced Thomas' eyes to black pits. His tone was genial enough, but something lurked behind it: a battle between mirth and murder.

"Issues?" Nathan echoed coldly.

Conducting an odd dance—one step forward, one sideway, two back—in the effort of holding his position, Cornwall collected himself and his thoughts.

"Don't go daft now, man. You've been making your opinions plain to all. Speak up and make your wishes heard." Thomas' jab should have broken ribs, but angels guard drunks and fools: Cornwall staggered under the force, but seemed otherwise unharmed.

He plowed a wavering finger into Nathan's chest. It landed, but then skittered off into space. "Blackthorne, you need to curb your wench!"

Cornwall leaned to fix a malignant eye over Nathan's shoulder at Cate. "She's a scold, a blasphemous, foul-mouthed slut. She's beyond her station; she doesn't know her place."

"You bloody, damned—!" Cate sputtered. A cutting look from Nathan silenced her.

"Teach your whore a lesson in manners. A cuff to the mouth and a strap to the backside I've always found answers best." Cornwall reached for his belt as if a demonstration might be called for.

Jaw flexing, Nathan pensively rubbed the prodded spot on his chest. "You must be much-caressed among the women-folk."

It was possible Cornwall's guardian angel now whispered of his blunder and advised something in the way of amends being called for. "She's comely enough." The tip of his tongue protruded from the sagging lips as the one eye raked her. "She looks to be a fair ride."

"I represented to him that you would have all the answers to his questions," Thomas put in helpfully.

"Aye, a number of them running through me head this instant," Nathan said, in a threatening rumble. "She's my woman, aye, and a sharp-tongued and willful one, at that, but still, mine." His mouth twitched with the need to smile.

Cornwall blinked dully, his guardian angel now abandoning him. Interested onlookers were quickly gathering near.

"Do I beat him senseless?" Thomas offered.

The notion broke Nathan's stare. "Nay, nay." He sighed with the resignation of a parent having to deal with a difficult child. "This awkward business is on my watch."

Nathan laughed mirthlessly. "I'd love nothing more than to see you try to lay a strap to her. God help any man, including me, who should try."

Raising his voice for the benefit of the onlookers, Nathan went on. "Surely, you've heard the talk: walks with Calypso she does. She can curse a man with those eyes, shriveling his manhood with one touch. Aye, I'd love nothing more than to turn you lose, but this is man's business, between... *gentlemen*."

Cornwall's indecision seemed catching; Cate seethed with

it. She wasn't some damsel in a parlor, whose future in society pivoted on someone's defense of her honor. Onthe other hand, a great bubble of satisfaction swelled at the notion of this foundering oaf finally getting his comeuppance.

"Come w' me, *sir*. We require space and privacy in which to speak." Nathan seized Cornwall's collar and propelled him off into the dark.

Cate stood in their wake. She half-expected, half-hoped Thomas would have gone with him, but a flick of Nathan's fingers and a roll of the eyes bid him to remain, whilst at the same time warned all others to do the same. Thomas' presence was a comfort. Left standing alone, waiting and wondering, was a torture she couldn't bear.

The distraction now over, the musicians struck up another tune.

Thomas turned to her and made a leg. "Madam, may I have the privilege of this dance?"

Without waiting for an answer, he swept her off into the crowd jigging about the fire. After Cornwall's malevolence, Thomas' protective arms were welcomed. As they dipped and whirled, Cate craned her head, first to one side, then the other in the direction in which Nathan had disappeared. A peremptory clearing of Thomas' throat called her attention back.

Thomas moved with the same graceful ease as he walked. She tended to forget how big he was, she thought, looking down at the hand engulfing hers, the other nearly encompassing her waist. They were broad and square-knuckled, the blond hair fuzzing them bleached to near white by the sun.

"It's grand to see you smile," he said, displaying one of his own. "'Tis grand to see you enjoying yourself, at long last. It's all because of him, isn't it?"

A cut of his eyes indicated Nathan, now standing at fire's margins, absent-mindedly sucking on his knuckles as they whirled past. She hated the notion of Thomas being brushed aside. He'd been her solace and protection for days, and weeks before that, and she was so very thankful. But there was no denying where her heart laid, and he knew it.

"Where's Cornwall?" she asked at seeing that Nathan was now alone.

"Contemplating the error of his ways, I should imagine," Thomas mused.

The music ended. Thomas leaned down to say "He's over there." A departing squeeze and gentle prod set Cate on her way.

Cate rose on her toes to see where Nathan stood, directly opposite. Idly chatting with someone, his eye caught hers and he stiffened. Dark and still, he gave her a look over the flames, one of those heart-stopping, womb-melting looks which always made her forget about everyone and everything. Gazes locked, they moved like two planets on converging orbits, until they met at the fire's edge.

She needed him, *now*! Absence didn't just make the heart grow fonder; it made it throb and burn. She had feared to never see him again, but now he was there. He'd come back to her and now was the time to do all the things she had wished so long to do.

Well, at least a few... she thought, flushing.

Seizing her by the hand, Nathan silently turned to lead her away. Barely into the cover of darkness, he spun her around and kissed her. The combined force of both his mouth and hips set her stumbling back, urgent and needing as she. She was put to mind of another night, another time, when the ridges of a palm tree had gouged her back as Nathan kissed her. He had restrained his urges then; Harte had been hot on their trail. But there was no Harte now, the restraint of shyness and newly-declared affections long gone. His thigh thrust between her legs, asking, demanding.

"I've a bed," she gasped, with a sudden recollection. She hadn't been there since her first night, but reports were that her shack had survived the battle, relatively unscathed.

Nathan drew back, intrigued. "Oh, aye?"

"A big, vast one," she explained, somewhat breathless. "Apparently, it's some privilege reserved for the few."

His mouth twisted in something between a wry quirk and a wince. "To say the least."

With decided effort, he stood back, releasing her. "Very well, then. 'Tis an opportunity not to be ignored, nor wasted."

Cate pushed through the foliage, leading the way to her shack. As they neared the dark dwelling, the moon reflecting on the thatched roof, a light went on inside, and the large shadow of someone moving around spilled through the door and out onto the stoop. Hand hovering over his weapon, Nathan pushed past Cate and stepped in. From over his shoulder, she saw Thomas standing at the lamp.

"Announce yourself," Nathan grumbled, his hand dropping to his side. "Since when are you playing the chambermaid?" he demanded, eyeing the still smoldering spill in Thomas' hand.

"I required a glim to see if Maram had fetched my dunnage."

"Your dunnage?"

"Oh, clap a stopper on that imagination of yourn," Thomas jibed. "Yes, I bunked here, but under your orders. You said 'watch her.'"

"T'would be the first damned time you ever listened," Nathan observed coldly.

"Aye, well, regardless, I couldn't very well bear an eye from the next hut."

Thomas moved, his shadow going with him, allowing the light to fall full on the bed.

"Dash me buttons and strike me blind!" Nathan cried, eyes rounding. "You said 'a bed', but..." He spun sharply around to Thomas. "And *you* were sleeping here?"

Thomas shrugged and grinned as he squeezed past. "Stop goggling like a damned fish. You said 'watch her.'"

Stopping at the door, Thomas leaned against the jamb and directed a conspiratorial wink in Cate's direction. "You explain; there's at least a hope in hell of him listening to you."

Rolling her eyes, Cate muttered a dread-laden "Thanks, mate."

"If this chuckle-headed lout comes to be a problem, just shout, I won't be far." Thomas touched his hat and ducked out the door.

"Living vicariously through someone else's joys? Hoping for a few pointers?" Nathan called to Thomas' departing back.

Cate stood waiting for the remonstrations to begin, but none came.

"My, my, my, my, my, my!" Nathan murmured, instead, viewing the bed with the lustiness of the miser before a pile of gold. "I have dreamed of—"

"As have I, for some days now," she heard herself say. Whatever his imaginings, they would have to run leagues to catch up with hers.

But now the wait was over.

It was odd how one was stricken dumb by the prospect of a dream actually being fulfilled. Several of those plans were dashed already, she thought regretfully. But perhaps, she thought, her eye settling on the trunks, hampers and lockers, there might be a way to salvage at least one or two.

"Give me five minutes," she said.

Nathan opened his mouth to object. Closing it, he bowed, perhaps a fraction mocking. "M'lady."

"Make that ten," she called to his back as he stepped out.

He stopped, made to reply, shook his head and strode out with even more purpose.

Flinging off her clothes with one hand, Cate rummaged through the lockers with the other. They were filled with the things too fancy for tramping about a ship or laboring over the sick. But perhaps the right occasion had just presented itself for at least a bit of it.

To the rumble of male voices at the end of the door path — Thomas and Nathan, it sounded like — she pulled out a shift and a pair of rose-colored stockings. A hand at the sole of her foot found it rough enough to pose a mortal threat to the sheer silk. A jar of cream was located, opened, sniffed — she didn't wish, in her haste, to wind up smelling like pomade — and then smoothed on every inch of her body which could possibly be reached, feeling more decadent than she had in many, many years. Rose stockings were pulled on and tied off with garters of a deeper hue. Another ribbon was fastened about her neck, the bow at her throat. She searched hopefully for a robe, but found only a powdering gown. That seeming too much topping-the-knob, she draped a cashmere shawl about her shoulders, instead. The thing was far too warm for the tropics, but — if everything went to plan — she wouldn't be wearing it for long.

Cate mouthed a thanks for Tabby's organization, the hairbrush now laying ready to hand. With two or three passes, however, she confirmed what was already known: unwavering resolve and several hours would be required to put her mop into anything which might resemble order. She snatched several pins from a cloisonne box and began pinning it up.

Barely one side of her head had been secured when she heard "Leave your hair alone, darling."

Arms still in the air, Cate turned to find Nathan standing in the doorway, eyes avidly aglow.

"Every night, I dreamed of you lying under me, with that maddening tangle all about your head," he said softly.

"It hasn't been ten minutes."

His shoulder moved in vague dismissal. "It felt like sixty."

Nathan's throaty purr struck whatever else Cate meant to say straight from her mind. Instead, she snatched the shawl about her shoulders and struck a pose. The eyes fixed on her narrowed as he came closer, heedlessly flinging his belts and weapons aside. Drawing up before her, he pulled off his shirt and breeches, and pitched them with the rest.

He cocked his head. "'Twould appear you know something of the arts of seduction. Coals to Newcastle, darling," he declared, fingers arcing the air. "You don't need any of this."

"It's the first—" She swallowed, her throat suddenly gone so

very dry. "It's the first time I've had anything with which to...
to try to—"

"The more you put on, darling, is just the more I'll be obliged
to remove." Still, the glint of appreciation showed her efforts
hadn't been wasted ones.

His fingertip followed the ribbon at her neck, gooseflesh
rippling in its track. "Perhaps this might remain. But this isn't
necessary." A flick, and the shawl slipped to the floor, leaving
her suddenly feeling exposed.

A pensive sigh. "And this is entirely in the way." A tug of
the ribbon and her shift fell away, kicked aside with the rest.

Nathan leaned back a fraction to see Cate's legs. The move
was a fortuitous one, for it allowed her to indulge in a bit of
morbid curiosity. Their first day back in this world, he had
assured that he was whole and yet, especially after the scene
at the riverside, she couldn't shake the niggling worry that
something about him was grossly wrong or different. Her breath
caught as her eye slid from the square-set shoulders, down to
the narrow hips, and then to his genitals, dusky eggs in their
black nest. The only noteworthy thing was their relaxed state, a
very uncommon one, indeed.

Her fingers twitched with the need to touch him, hold him,
bring him to her. The fact that her earlier eagerness had nearly
been their undoing stopped her.

"Hmm...?" Nathan said, still intent on the stockings. "Very
well, those shouldn't prove too much in the way for what I have
in mind."

"Have in mind?" she echoed weakly.

"Oh, aye, we've much, much to do," he said with gusto. "The
only pity is that the evening is already so old."

She stepped into his embrace and they held each other, hands
roving with aimless abandon. Slipping her arms up about his
neck, she lifted her face up in invitation. He placed his mouth
over hers and kissed her. She may have only lain with one other
man in her life, but she had kissed enough others to know that
Nathan was a master. Through that single point of connection,
he could compel, command or arouse. Just then, instead of
plundering as he well might, he was possessing, and yet gentle,
demanding, and yet almost chaste.

"Your mouth is the path of glory," he said, after a long while.

"I was just thinking the same about you," she said, a bit
breathless.

"Indeed?"

Nathan ran his fingers up her nape and into her hair, the pins
making little pinging sounds as they fell to the floor. He ruffled

it out, smiling as it tumbled about her shoulders. "There's me tousled siren, calling me to me destruction."

He leaned to brace his forehead against hers. "It's been barely a fortnight since I laid with you; why does it feel like an age? 'Tis all I can manage to keep from coming at you like a rutting boar."

"Perhaps I favor a bit of rutting," Cate said lightly, and then bit her lip at having spoken without realizing what he was at: taking it slower than earlier at the river's edge.

We have all night. We have all night, she chanted like a rosary. There would be no watch bells, no crewmen rapping on the door, no emergencies at untimely moments. They had all night, and tomorrow, and the next...

All very rational thoughts, but a part of her, the aching tightness deep in her belly, was far from rational. It only knew one thing: it wanted him.

As Nathan kissed her again, he winced and shifted, making her think she might have trod on his toes. "You're still hurting, aren't you?"

Nuzzling her neck, he shook his head. "For the last several days, I've ached for you to the point of barely able to walk. 'Tis only one answer for it."

He lifted her to the bed and laid her out before him. Lowering himself over her, he seized her wrists. His ankles pressing outwards against hers, he stretched her out, like a hide nailed to a barn door.

With a sideways cut of his eyes toward the expanse about them, Nathan chuckled with the glee of a child with a new toy. "I aim to make use of every square inch of this..." The rest was lost in a kiss.

Lifting his head, he hummed in appreciation, as he experimentally ran a shin along her leg and the stockings encasing it. "I usually prefer the feel of just you, but these do present a new... sensation." The last was punctuated with a waggle of his brows.

"I can't possibly be the first woman who—?"

"'Tis the first time with you; naught else counts." He smiled down at her with a mischievous gleam. "Besides, I love the way they match the color of these." He bent his head and nipped the tip of her breast.

He held himself a fraction above her, so near and yet so far. She writhed, seeking to reach him only to be thwarted.

"I saw you." He spoke in a low whisper, his breath blowing warm on her cheek. "You came to me each night. Every time I closed me eyes, you were there, so very close, and yet untouchable." The length of his body pressed to hers, he lightly touched his lips to her temple, jaw, and ear.

"A miscalculation, I find," he murmured upon reaching her neck and the ribbon there. Ducking his head, he seized the end in his teeth and pulled. The silk bow separated and the entire thing fell away. "Now I can attend this important bit just here."

He flicked his tongue; a shiver shot through her and she let out a small gasp. "Happens every time," he said, smiling against her skin.

"Every night I retraced you, seeking to recreate you, from the little bones at your wrists." His grasp tightened, and his mouth tracked a hot trail down her arms. "To this collarbone, which drove me mad from the first day we met."

Skimming with hands and mouth, his voice so soft, as if speaking to himself, he proceeded his inventory.

"Your ribs... your waist, where I could nearly..." His hands encircled, nearly touching. "Down over the curve of these hips and the round bottom..." The rest was lost in a rambling "So many nights... So many times..."

She urged him to her breast and then traced her own paths as he suckled. The smooth roundness of his buttocks fit so nicely in her hands. As he worked his way down, she explored and rediscovered him: the long groove of his spine, the dips, and curves of his shoulders and back. A certain part of her wished he would stop talking and just take her, now!

Her hands were curved over the dark crown, Nathan down somewhere near her navel, doing incredible things with his tongue, when his entire body twitched, like someone receiving a static shock. Shaking it off, he continued with a new determination. A few moments later, he grunted, like a knee had been driven into his gut. Grinding out an oath, he launched up and off the bed. Clutching himself, he staggered to a locker and sat heavily. Hunched over, he rocked in agony.

There was nothing more inane than to have someone asking if you were alright when it was glaringly obvious you weren't. And yet, there she was *again*, doing that very thing. She hovered, caught between retreating—He looked of a mood to smash something—or stepping in.

Should she offer to kiss it? Rub it?

Lord, he wasn't a five-year-old who just stubbed his toe. Days of working in the sickbay kicked in, thoughts of compresses and medicinal teas coming to mind, and she stood poised, ready to run and fetch whatever was necessary, if only she knew what!

"Flask," Nathan ground out between gasps. "Pocket."

Snatching his coat from the pile, Cate muttered a few

of her own curses as she fumbled. Finding the thing at last, she unscrewed the cap and delivered it to the impatiently outstretched hand. She watched wistfully as he threw his head back and took a large gulp. Rum or no, she could have done with a stiff tot herself just then.

An eye opened enough to catch the apparent worry on her face. He forced a smile. "I'll be... fine." His grimace took a wry twist, sauce for the gander, as it were.

If he meant to set her at ease, he failed miserably.

In the spirit of proving his claim, Nathan forced himself a bit more upright. Face contorted, his lips were still drawn back against the pain. One eye cracked open and then clamped shut. "Might you put on something?"

Mumbling an apology, Cate snatched up the nearest thing to hand: his shirt.

Careful not to touch him, Cate sat on the locker next to Nathan and folded her hands onto her lap. "Was this time... worse?" she asked delicately.

"Aye," came in a strained rasp. Sweat now dotted his brow and chest.

With passions—first at the riverside and now here—so abruptly interrupted, her own body was in its own state of turmoil. Cate buried her head between her hands, thinking "Not again!" Her head slowly lifted at the sudden, and so very disquieting realization that this manifestation wasn't just a whim of nature or ill-timed malady.

"I sense that malicious, bottom-sucking sea hag's hand in this," Nathan said through clenched teeth, as if reading Cate's mind.

"Calypso!?" Cate twisted around, half-expecting to see the amorphous being standing at the window. In truth, it could have been anyone or anything standing there for, even after being face-to-face with the entity—or so she was told—she had no notion of what she, it looked like.

"It... she can't be! She can't...?" She turned toward Nathan. "Can she...?"

Here on land, Cate had thought them safe, out of the goddess's realm, beyond her meddling reach. She rubbed her temple, straining to recall when Nathan had explained the whole curse thing. It had been nighttime, she just torn from a warm bed to hear what seemed to be nothing more than a rambling fable, like talking waterhorses, or seals turning into women. Nathan's vagueness as to the specifics made it even easier to dismiss it as just family folktales. But now, the whole thing was suddenly so very relevant.

"You claimed nothing was left of a man after laying with her?" she prompted.

"Shrivels his cock."

Cate leaned to peek between his legs and noted, with considerable satisfaction, that bit seemed to be proved false. What else might they hope for?

"With *everything...*" Cate began, with an all-encompassing gesture, "I had forgotten there would be... consequences." She shivered again, this time from chill of the pressing depths and darkness creeping back into her bones. She still wasn't entirely recovered, confusion and giddiness often sweeping in like a winter's blast through a door.

She shifted a fraction nearer to Nathan, seeking his warmth, and yet still not touching him.

Nathan glared down at his lap. "The moment the captain comes to attention, it hits. I can feel her claws in me, twisting—" The rest was lost as he hunched over and groaned.

"Aye, a eunuch, as limp as a sock is what I expected, was led to believe, at any rate." His breathing now returning to something nearer to normal, Nathan smiled crookedly. "When we first returned, and I was as randy as when I was one-and-twenty, aching for you as I had before, I counted me blessings, thinking those consequences just a lot of falderal. God's my life, I could think of nothing but—"

He shifted in discomfort. "When it grew worse, I dismissed it to needing you so badly—" He clamped his lip between his teeth at a stronger twinge. "But this. This!"

Nathan made a frustrated gesture at the offending appendage. "Being a eunuch would be a godsend. It's like a starving man put before a feast with his lips sewn shut."

His bare haunches clenched, Nathan pounded his fist on his leg in impotent fury. "She gave me leave and saw you alive, but the black-hearted slattern saw to it that I shan't have you any other way! The ill-begotten wench has devised a new form of hell for me, damn her fishified, wart-necked soul!"

"Sounds like a woman scorned to me," Cate observed. "Think about it," she pressed at his disbelief. "She can't have who she wants, so she fixes it so that no one else might have him either. I can't say I haven't had a few of those thoughts myself, a time or two," she added ominously.

"Always knew I crossed you at me own peril," he said admiringly.

A shrug conceded at least a portion of Cate's premise. "She is bloody jealous of you; her eyes go as green as a demon's at your mention."

Nathan took a drink and stared off, considering. "Damned odd to be loving the very one you mean to destroy."

Cate shrugged. "Perhaps it's not destruction in her eyes. The fact that she's so willing to negotiate every time you meet suggests she feels something more than just revenge." She sighed, resigned. "I should imagine the only way to know is to see if this happens with just me or with all women?"

Nathan made an impatient noise. "You *are* all women, darling. I rise to no others."

He cocked his head, realization lighting his eyes. "Although, 'tis a notion I wouldn't put past the scheming hag." He cut a questioning eye sideways. "'Tis something you wish me to put to the test?"

"No!"

"Thank the gods for small favors!" he declared, lifting the flask in salute. He took a drink, swiping his mouth on the back of his hand. "It makes no sense, but then, those gods are a corrupt and wicked lot. Mums going with sons; brothers going with sisters. Avarice; greed; conceit; ambition: not a sin squeaks by unaddressed with that crew."

"Listen to you, sounding like a preacher on the Sabbath."

"Aye, well, all the perfumes of Arabia mightn't sweeten these hands, but I know right from wrong."

He sighed, glaring down at himself again. "I could wish a shriveled cock was all. T'would be a far cry better than this feeling as if it were being twisted off." He emitted a low grunt of discomfort and shifted on his haunches. "When Mum explained it, I was naught but ten or twelve. If I started pressing on the details, I risked revealing how much I knew, and she would figure out that I had been lying with girls... and women."

"Women! At twelve?" Cate goggled.

"Men aren't the only ones with eclectic tastes. The point is, the whole thing wasn't a conversation a lad wished to have with his mum. God's my life!"

They shuddered together. No child wished to think their parents knew about sex, let alone discuss the finer details of the act. Still, she couldn't help but wish his mother was still alive.

"It doesn't matter," Cate declared. She had said time and again that all she wanted was Nathan, for him to come back. Now that he was there, to complain was being petulant and ungrateful. She had lived without a man for a good many years; the physical aspect had been only a small portion of the loneliness.

Her announcement caught Nathan just as he took a drink. He sputtered and coughed. "Darling, with all due respect, it matters more to you than any other woman I have ever met. You're shaken just now, but believe me, in time, it will matter so very, very, *very* much."

His eyes lit with another thought. "The bright side is she's caught in her own treachery. She's rendered me useless to you, which means I am also useless to her."

"Or," Cate went on, pensively chewing the inside of her mouth. "Perhaps now, you can rise only to her."

Nathan's lip curled in disgust. "Don't say that even in jest. I'd geld meself first." He took another drink as if to wash the notion away.

"Is all this because of — " Cate gulped, still trying to remember everything she had heard about the curse. "Serving her because you no longer have those?" She gestured toward his ravaged wrists. Regrettably, the bandages were gone, where the tattoos had once laid a seeping mess. The replacements bracelets were doing the scabs no favors, many places gone black with dirt and frequent bleeding. His ankles were no better, and the one at his waist made her wish to turn her head.

"Those should be salved and bandaged, or they will fester," she observed.

"Nay. The damned things won't stay put. I'll do."

Hands in her lap, Cate looked down at her bracelets. They were supposed to have been her protection. But now, in the face of Calypso's apparent power and presence, she began to wonder.

Nathan fingered his mustache and the vacancy where a bell once hung. "This was supposed to buy a life, plain and simple. The fawning, worm-ridden hulking lump went back on her word, so I had to..." He gulped and went on determinedly. "Do what I had to do. Now, come to find out, the old fry of treachery has gone back on her word, yet again."

"Fool me once..." Cate sighed under her breath.

Nathan nodded, gravely. "Upon me word, the shame will be on her. It shan't happen again."

The notion of returning to that pressing black void made Cate shiver. That place's cold was still in her bones, making her wonder if she would ever be truly warm again.

"Perhaps there's some way we can get you new ones," she suggested. Surely, in the midst of all this grimness, some shred of hope might be found.

Looking down at his arm, Nathan considered and dismissed the notion in almost the same instant. "Doubt it. Mum was in a great moil about them in the first place: special ink from special places; experts consulted..." A vague arc of his fingers finished the thought.

Cate grasped the edge of the locker beneath them. She wanted nothing more than to throw her arms about Nathan, hold him, take him to bed and show him it would all be well, at the same time finding her badly needed refuge in his arms. Instead, she plucked the flask from his hand. Finding it empty, she fetched the bottle from the stand and took a drink. The stuff was like swallowing molten lead, landing like that very thing in her stomach. Alas, it failed to set any part of her at ease. She handed the vessel to Nathan as she sat beside him once more.

"Nathan, I'm so sorry! This is all my fault. If it hadn't been for me —"

A sharp look and his hand over hers where it lay between them on the locker cut her off. "Shh! I made me choice; 'tis naught to be sorry for. I'd do far worse to see you live."

"But I —"

The grasp tightened, the dark eyes sharpened. "Hush," he said, low and hoarse. "Not another word."

They slumped in the ensuing silence. Sounds of the night and the celebrants still about the fires drifted unevenly on the breeze.

Nathan sat rocking, absently rubbing himself, staring into space like a man who had just lost his best friend. Given his appetites, that wasn't far off the mark. She was feeling a bit bereft herself just then.

"Shrivel a man's manhood with one touch,'" Cate mused, recalling the scene earlier that night with Cornwall.

Gone so far afield in thought, it took Nathan a moment to smoke her meaning. His mouth crooked at the irony. "A lamentable choice of words that. Never knew meself to be so much the mage."

"So now what?" she asked bleakly. Her shoulders sagged. At that hour, she couldn't begin to fathom how one went about out-running or out-wrangling a goddess. Every turn they made, it seemed she was there ahead of them.

Nathan found her hand again and squeezed, this time in encouragement. "We'll figure it out, luv. There's always a course; some just need a bit more plotting, but not tonight. It's been a hellish few days."

Hollow-eyed, battle-scraped and bruised, the smudges under his eyes matching the dark scruff of his beard: Nathan looked as if he had been through a couple hells. Cate felt not far behind him.

With a grunt of effort, he rose and put out his hand. "Come, lie with me. Allow a man the dream which saw him through it all."

Cate rose with him and followed. Her step slowed, however, the bed suddenly having all the appeal of Cornwall's surgery table. Gentle, yet insistent prodding urged her forth. At last, they laid down, both expelling a grateful sigh.

All things considered, Cate wouldn't have blamed Nathan for moving to the bed's farthest edge and away from her. Old habits, however, die so very hard. They automatically laid as they always did: like two spoons in a drawer, her back to his chest. The moment her buttocks touched his thighs, however, he barked in pain and jerked away. With considerable huffing and wrestling about, they finally arrived at the reverse position: her behind him, the fronts of her thighs to the backs of his, a measured space between. She wound her hair in her fist and tucked it under her head lest even a strand touch him.

A silence fell, the residual heavy breathing of their efforts filling the void.

"There was a time when I wouldn't lie like this, allow someone behind me, even in bed," Nathan said quietly into the darkness.

"I shan't murder you in your sleep," she assured.

"Nay worries, luv," he said with amused affection. "If you wished me dead, from the back wouldn't be your way. Look me in the eyes you would as you slit me gullet."

Nathan lay on his side, the starlight through the window limning his outline. He body heat saturated the space between them, shimmering on her bare thighs. The black head lay inches from hers on the bolster they shared. So near, and yet he might as well have been on the moons of Jupiter. She tucked her arms tight about herself, burrowing her hands into her armpits. Still, her fingers twitched with the desire to run through the ebony mass, to twine in the baby-soft down at the nape. She moved her head a fraction and inhaled the smell of tar and salt, and his own spiciness, a mix of orange, cinnamon and male.

Cate realized then what was missing, what made laying next to him then so very different times before: the musky smell of a man satisfied, the heaviness of his seed in her womb, the slow, preternatural throb of her blood. This was more like brother and sister lying there, all rendered all the more daunting at the prospect of it being that way forever.

She still wore his shirt. She tucked her nose down into the folds of it, seeking his scent, absorbing the last bits of body heat which might linger. Desperate, yes. But no other word described her better, just then.

Swallowing hard, she made a conscious effort to redirect her line of thought. She looked out over Nathan's side to the window and the night beyond. The sounds of merriment still came in broken drifts. A fiddle screeched in a false start, paused and then forged on to what might have been intended as a gig.

The rise and fall of his side indicated that Nathan still hung in the realm of wakefulness. A braid strayed across the bolster between them. She ventured a finger to flick the end of the colored thread which bound it, and then up along the rope-like contours. The yearning for human contact still made her twitch. On his back lay the scars of a lifetime of violence, blade, lash and splinter. All were incurred before they met, and so were all as much a part of him as the color of his hair or gold in his teeth. A sickened shudder ran through her at seeing the bruise across his shoulder, dark and ominous as a storm cloud.

Cate ventured a finger to lightly trace the discoloration. "What...?" she asked, softly.

The shoulder didn't jerk away. Instead, it pressed back, reveling in the connection. Then it moved in the slightest of shrugs. "You've seen battle; you know what it's like. One rarely knows who or what: a shiver, a block, a piece of someone's leg. I once saw a man sliced from clew to erring by a sword in the fist of an arm flying past."

The idle observer might think that a tall tale, but she had seen enough, heard enough to know such outlandish sights weren't uncommon in the flurry of battle.

"Pryce and the others represented it was a shiver what knocked me flat. I laid there, the wind knocked out of me, gaping like a beached fish. Had it hit me point first—" He stopped short, realizing to finish the thought would only add to her regret.

A metallic rustle marked his indignant jerk.

"Harte might have been aiming for me directly; I certainly was for him. I would have loved nothing more than to think my ball snuffed out that miserable excuse for a life."

Cate withdrew her hand, curling it closed against her chest to preserve the feel of his flesh.

"Thank you," she said sometime later.

"For what?" His voice was thickened with impending sleep.

"For coming to get me."

His head turned, the starlight limning the curve of his cheek. "You doubted me word?"

"Yes, and I'm sorry for that." She kissed her fingertips and pressed it against the back of his head.

His hand came back and found her leg. "No choice to it, Kittie. There's no living else."

His shoulders rose and fell several times, and then he wriggled back. She retreated in response, seeking to maintain their separation. The hand on her leg tightening stopped her.

He worked back until he was against her, the backs of his thighs now tight against the front of hers. He found her hand and brought it around, clasping it against his chest.

"Rest, darling. Naught will disturb you tonight. I'm here."

20: NO GOOD DEED GOES UNPUNISHED

A METALLIC CRASH — A EWER AGAINST A basin — jerked Cate awake.

"Who the bloody hell is that?" rumbled from amid the rumpled bedclothes behind her.

"The chambermaid." Cate whispered, although not knowing why; Nathan hadn't bothered to temper his voice.

"Tell her to haul her wind out of here, or I'll pull her innards out through her nose and strangle her with them." Mouth screwed against the pillow, voice thickened by sleep, his threat still carried a creditable sound.

A startled shriek, running feet and, judging by the ensuing silence, they were alone.

"She heard you," Cate hissed, scolding, although half-heartedly. She wasn't sorry to see the girl gone, either.

"Good!" came more as a grunt than a word.

"You'll hurt her feelings."

"Better than her arse burning from me belt."

Cate started to rise, but a cautioning, throaty rumble stopped her. She settled back down next to Nathan and lay blinking, trying to extricate herself from the deep, comatose – like sleep from which she had been so abruptly snatched. It took her a moment to realize that, in spite of all of she and Nathan's arranging before falling asleep, sometime in the night, they had resumed their habitual positions: her back to his chest.

The rustle of feathers and a squawk made Cate raise her head. Through the door she could see Beatrice's tail feathers and backside on the stoop. Pacing back and forth like a vivi – colored mastiff, the bird raised her hackles and cursed anyone who dared venture near.

A part of Cate — a very small, timid part — wrangled for her to rise—by the sound of it, the rest of the island had—while another louder and far more persuasive side wondered why? Nathan's deep, slow breathing indicated his intentions. And so she followed his example, allowing the mother-warm arms of slumber reach up and draw her back down into a wondrous doze, feeling quite decadent as she did.

Sometime later, Cate roused to Nathan's arms slipping about her waist and pulling her against him. Responding to his nuzzling and fondling, she thrust her bottom back against him. In the next instant, Nathan jerked, gasped and lurched away. She sat up to find him curled into a defensive ball, hand tucked between his legs, groaning.

"What...?"

A brown eye, hard and cold, glared over his shoulder. "It's morning, isn't it?"

"Ah, yes", she said, rubbing the sleep from her eyes. More than just the sun rose in the morning when Nathan was about.

The fog in her head cleared and the previous' night events came back.

"No better, eh?" Drowsiness robbed her of the ability to glean the disappointment from her voice. For a moment, albeit brief, she had thought, nay hoped it all had just been a bad dream.

"I always envied Millbridge and his ability to look upon a woman as most look upon a bollard," he said, distractedly rubbing. "God, don't I wish!"

He cast a wry eye back at her. "Although I defy him or any man to wake up next to you and not—" He choked off the thought.

Still rocking in pain, he fell pensive. Then the bare shoulders squared, and the eyes came back around, bright with inspiration. "I can't, but *you* can!"

"What? No... no! What makes you think I need to—?"

"Come now, darling." Already on his hands and knees, Nathan came across the bed toward her. "There's no denying the evidence. You've the look: your eyes have gone from the color of shoals to that idol in Vera Cruz and your breasts have gone pink with wanting."

Following his avid gaze down, she found the shirt she wore was pulled taut across her chest, the roseate ends of her breasts glowing like beacons through the worn fabric. He was near enough to flick his tongue over one, smiling at the effect. Flushing, she snatched at the bedclothes to cover herself. A firm arm blocked her.

Nathan leaned and inhaled, rolling his eyes in appreciation. "You've the scent of a woman—"

"You make me out like a bitch in heat," she said, scrambling away.

"None so promiscuous—" he equivocated.

"Thank you, for that small compliment!" She came up against the headboard, trapped.

" —But just as demanding."

Cate let out a startled yip when his hand made a fortuitous dive between her legs.

"Shame, shame, darling. You started without me."

"That's just... just... residue from... from—" His fingers— those blessedly adroit and nimble fingers—continued their explorations, making coherent thought so very difficult and everything she meant to say an obvious lie.

The hand withdrew and urged her back onto the pillows. "Now, lie back and get comfortable."

Surely, he didn't mean to —?

She made another futile grab for the sheets. Stopping her with one hand, Nathan tugged the shirt down from her shoulders with the other. She clamped her knees together, only to have them gently, and yet so very firmly pried apart.

Oh, yes, he meant to do exactly that!

"Nathan, no!"

He rocked back, bemused. "Why ever not?"

"Because... because...! It's not fair. It's something two people should be doing, not one. Unless you're willing for me to—"

An adroit arch of his body evaded her reach. "Nay, nay, the captain shall remain at his leisure this time." A shrug dismissed the rest as he pulled a pillow from behind her, fluffed it and stuffed it back. "*I* am willing. That's half present; majority rules."

"But it's not—"

Her continuing arguments were made over his private soliloquy of "That's it. Over there. That's me girl. Just here. A little this way..." nodding indulgently, only half-listening.

"Nathan, it's not—"

"I'm a grown man and master o' me own realm." He snorted wryly. "In cold analysis, I've done it alone more often than in company or, even when there was another, I was the only active participant." An admonishing finger wagged at her. "Nay worries, luv. This isn't about me. This is for you."

With considered deliberation, Nathan moved Cate's hand to her knee. He tweaked a pillow, and then the shirt, now down about her waist. He cocked his head, admiring his arrangements.

The position left her somewhat vulnerable, and could only offer the most feeble of attempts as he leant down, nibbling and nipping.

"But... but... no!" she hissed.

The soft "pop!" of a mouth pulling free of a nipple preceded "Why ever not?"

Cate looked wildly about the room, discovering that the reasons, so eloquently clear a few moments ago, were now gone, evaporated like water drops on a hot griddle.

"It's daylight." Desperation brought her to a severe, motherly tone.

Chuckling, Nathan resumed where he left off. "Never stopped us before," he said, somewhat muffled.

"I'm as much a master of my realm as you. I can... can... resist—" Cate said with increasing effort.

Huffing in frustration, he rose up on his elbows. "Why? Why should one go thirsty when the well is just to hand?"

Then Nathan grinned, one of those known to charm. "You know you can't refuse me."

Given any other place or time, Cate would have taken that as a challenge, but just... not... then...

"Now, lie back," he said, re-adjusting her. He smiled with alarming determination. "This is going to take a while."

Cate cast a final and desperate glance toward the door. Beatrice was still on patrol; few would have the courage to pass. Then, all consciousness spiraled down to the dark head between her legs. His hands cradled her hips, holding her captive—as if she had the will to move!—she succumbed, yielding to that oh, so knowing mouth. All too soon, she was reduced to being capable of nothing but pitiful little, mewling sounds, interspersed with the random delighted gasp.

At one point, she became self-aware enough to peer down over the rumpled shirt. "How ever are you managing?"

Nathan rose up on his elbows enough to display himself. "See look, limp as a sock!" And then he sank back.

"Imagination." The word came in a burst of damp heat against her most tender parts. "Salt-beef Peg: the most loathsome vision of womanhood to ever walk this earth." Frowning in thought, he lightly brushed his mustache against her damp curls. "As big around as her namesake and smells something akin to beef gone thrice 'round the Horn. She's been charging half-a-shilling a toss, since before I was old enough to know what she was selling. One thought of what lays between those thighs and..." A shoulder moved, leaving the rest to the aforementioned evidence.

"But—?"

"Believe me, I'm well-practiced at this," Nathan said with considerable asperity. Then he lightened. "Perhaps, there's a grand advantage in not being distracted by the prospect of me own pleasures. Now, I've a clear mind with which to concentrate on you."

The notion rendered her even more breathless. Nathan was a most attentive lover; if he had been distracted before, heaven help her now.

"But I can't be expected to forget—" she hissed.

From over the mahogany-colored curls came a malicious leer. "Oh, I'll make you forget. Quiet now, you're interrupting me concentration."

And, bless his bloody heart, she soon forgot everything. The grasp about her hips tightened, his assault growing more single-minded. Entirely on its own volition, one hand floated down and curved over the crown of his head, urging, guiding. A faint burning from his beard abrading the inside of her leg brought fleeting thoughts of the rash soon to be suffered. Creams might be obtained from Celia, or better yet, one of those cooling, soothing compresses.

The body between her legs stiffened. Howling like a scalded cat—a sound becoming all too familiar—Nathan jerked up and away, his hand clapped between his legs once more.

Cate cried out, not in completion, but in utter frustration and pounded her fist on the mattress. She swallowed down the choking lump of disappointment and a number of curses. Nathan sat in the now all too familiar position on the edge of the bed: hunched, gasping and clutching.

Clearly, Salt-beef Peg hadn't been up to the task.

She looked on with considerable sympathy. On a host of issues, Nathan could verge on histrionics, but when it came to his personal discomfort, he was always somber as a monk. Whatever he showed, rest assured he suffered a great, *great* deal more.

"This is ridiculous," Cate finally managed. "You can't keep—"

An inarticulate wheeze was his response.

"No more!" she announced. "We can't keep on like this."

Something between an inhalation and a grunt could have either been his consent or contradiction.

Nathan was most certainly taking the worst of this, but she wasn't out of the realm of suffering herself. Everyone knew it was bad for men to be abruptly interrupted in the sex act; the ache which filled her suggested women threatened possible damage as well. She lay staring at the ceiling, one fist rhythmically thumping on the bed at her side. Celibacy was far more endurable than this teasing, which was a cruel, cruel jest.

"Nathan, I'm sorry, I—" She seemed to be saying that a lot of late.

"You what? You regret following what comes as natural as breathing to you? You regret I desire you beyond food or drink, beyond me own life?"

"But if I'm causing you pain..."

"The ache here," Nathan said with an angry jab at his crotch. "Is far better than one here," his fist pounding his chest.

His vehemence struck her mute. She mightn't have the same anatomy, but the effect was the same: the physical yearning was nothing compared to that of a broken heart.

"So what are we—?" she began.

"Damned, if I know," came back sharp with frustration and discomfort.

Nathan playing the victim was disquieting, only because it was a state so rarely seen. The lack of answers seemed to point to a single inevitability, one which neither of them wished to put into words: returning to the netherworld, to Calypso's lair.

Posing a forced smile, Nathan found her hand on the mattress between them and gave it an encouraging squeeze. "We'll sort it out, darling. Troubles come in legions; we'll suffer them together."

A departing press of his lips to her knuckles, Nathan rose unsteadily to his feet, and jerked on his shirt and breeches. Suddenly uncomfortable with being naked, Cate primly pulled the bedclothes up over her.

It would have been so very easy to sink into a pit of futility, she thought, watching him pass an experimental hand over his cheek and step to the basin. Again, she reminded herself of her own vows: Nathan was there; the rest didn't matter.

But damn, now those vows rang like hollow platitudes.

In the spirit of proving her point, Cate closed her eyes and listened to Nathan going through the preparations of shaving, soaking in the joy of his voice, of having someone to talk to, of having someone to worry for, and most of all, having someone to worry for her. After years alone, those meant far more than... than anything else.

They would get through this. The pivotal word Nathan had used—several times— was "together," and she meant to hold him to it.

Opening her eyes, she gazed idly about the room, from the thatched ceiling overhead, to the window and the broken patterns of brilliant azure sky glimpsed through the surrounding bushes. Her attention drifted to the door and the stoop, now deserted. At some point or another, Beatrice had taken her leave.

"What's so special about this hut?" Cate inquired. "Last night you acted as though it was a surprise or something. You and Thomas exchanged a look." The skulking sneaks were sometimes worse than two little boys.

Nathan paused from splashing water on his face, blinking the droplets from his lashes as he looked back over his shoulder to see if she were jesting.

She wasn't.

Drawing his knife from his boot on the floor, he stropped it on the leather. Bending before the peering glass hanging from a peg, he began to shave.

"It's reserved for newlyweds celebrating their nuptials or reunions for the more favored," he added with an unsavory lilt. "And no," he added before she could ask, "I never qualified on any account."

"So, you knew it was here?"

"Oh, aye," he said offhandedly. "A point of interest, it 'tis, like one o' the sights on the Grand Tour."

"The hut's the same." His gaze traveled the room, stopping at the bed. "But, that is certainly a new addition."

Cate rolled onto her back and stretched luxuriously, her toes and ankles making little popping sounds. She considered the bed's slight musty smell—impossible to avoid in the tropics, where a folded cloth might take on the same dankness within a day—was probably a blessing, for it was sure to cover a multitude of other odors. How many had gone before them and what all which might have been done on it didn't bear dwelling. To do so seemed to be counting a gift horse's molars, and she was far from being that ungrateful.

"Bella put me here," Cate said, more defensive than intended.

"Aye, *and* Thomas," he pointed out. He chuckled dryly. "Rest assured, Bella has never made an unconsidered move in her life."

Cate stiffened at the notion of being maneuvered. "But, we made it perfectly clear I was waiting for you. Honest, Thomas and I never—"

Knife held at arm's length to the side, Nathan came over and pecked her lightly on the cheek. "Aye, I know, because I know you."

He crossed the room and back to his shaving. "But Bella didn't. I'm sure by now, however, she has an inkling." He paused to direct an admiring grin at her.

Cate sighed and stretched again. "She had to have been sorely disappointed when her little scheme failed."

"Aye, failure wasn't apparent until me arrival, but I should imagine she's wallowing in deep disappointment now." He stopped to turn and cock a warning brow. "Have a care, luv. Bella doesn't get angry; she just gets even. More is the reason to haul anchor and as soon as possible."

Cate sat up and asked tentatively "How long before you wish to go?"

"'Twas no fabrication yesterday when I represented I was prepared to haul anchor within the glass," came back evenly.

"Oh," she said faintly, looking off.

Nathan turned, blade poised in mid-motion. "What? C'mon, luv. They could hear your disappointment clear out to the *Lovely*."

She toyed with the folds of the bedclothes. "It's just..." She gulped and forged on. "Toby — the boy in the sickbay — ?"

He nodded.

"His fever is less, but he's not out of the woods, yet." Swallowing hard, she looked up. "Might we stay just for a couple days, until he's, well, better?"

"There has to be a hundred women on this island who will care for him," Nathan pointed out with a wave of the makeshift razor.

"I know, but I've spent so much time with him already. He's... He's..." Her hand rose and fell, her throat tightening at the prospect of leaving him, his fate unresolved.

Cate looked up at Nathan, hopeful and pleading.

Nathan turned back to the mirror and made several slow, pensive passes, the blade scraping. She rarely made requests, asked anything of him, and he knew it.

Finally, he exhaled, decision made.

"In common decency, we can't leave this place in a dire straits." Nathan grimaced, as one does when shaving. "Two hundred extra souls, working double-tides might go a long ways to set this place to rights."

The blade made a couple more passes.

"Tomorrow is Friday — no wise captain ever sets sail then," Nathan offered over his shoulder. "And the next day is the thirteenth. The men would dog me to the point of distraction if I were to oblige them to set sail on either."

Cate mouthed a silent thanks, vowing never to jeer at sailors and their endless superstitions again.

Suddenly, it seemed so very trivial to expect the welfare of one boy to dictate the lives of so many. "I'm sorry."

"No worries, luv," Nathan said lightly. "'Tis not just you. 'Tis been a hard last few months for the crew, with precious little in the way of bowsing up their jibs. They'll be working watch-on-watch setting this place to rights, but there's still plenty of opportunity for some well-earned play. Jerking them away today would have earned me naught but hard looks and even harder feelings."

He pivoted to smile down at her. "And, if you must, reasons to remain on the Sabbath can be found."

There was also the possibility that, with the events of this last week, Nathan was in even more need of a rest.

"Thank you," Cate said earnestly.

Nathan's smile softened, curving crookedly. "Surely, you realize by now, Kittie, I can't tell you no."

Turning back to the mirror, he tipped back his head and set to the treacherous task of shaving the gnarled skin of his neck.

"Here, allow me." Cate rose and put out her hand.

Without hesitation, he handed the knife over.

Head tipped back, Nathan stood so very still. His beard was like a bear's pelt, dense and black, and it was slow-going over the scar's twisted skin. She spared a brief glance just below where the tattoo had once laid. Now no more than a crusted strip, it was healing no better than the others.

In spite of his awkward position, she could still feel his eyes on her. "What are you looking at?" she finally asked.

He hazarded to lift one corner of his mouth. "I'm looking at the face which has seen me through hell," he said softly, eyes glowing. "It's the face which made this hollow vessel whole, filled my empty heart and gave me a life worth living."

Suddenly feeling unsteady, she lowered the knife.

"It humbles me to think you'd have me," he went on. "And yet, I feel like God himself because you will."

He shifted, wincing. "And if I say much more, I shan't be walking."

Like a man touching the slowmatch to a touchhole, he arched his body and kissed her. It was a brief, experimental brushing of the lips. The corner of his mustache twitched, and he did so again with a much more determined press of the lips. A tremble and a flinch, and he broke off.

"Like tuning a shroud, darling," he sighed softly. "We'll find the line between success and damnation."

A final flick of the blade tip and the task was done.

"But, if my mere presence is causing you pain, then—?" Cate began as he stowed the knife in his boot.

Nathan rubbed his face hard with the towel and grinned. "Then I'll suffer it and gladly."

"Does it hurt always?" she asked.

Stomping on his boots, he glared down at himself. "Benign, I'm fine, which is a rare state when you are about," he added with a tinge of resignation. "The least stirring, however, and it starts: a twisting, like a cramp from bad rum, but lower, much lower."

Cate faltered. By no expanse of the imagination did she fancy herself a temptress. Inflicting pain just by the simple act of existing was a daunting notion. And yet, he had the same effect on her, if not quite so extreme.

"C'mon, rouse out and show a leg," Nathan said, nudging her with his elbow.

"Unless you intend to lie about like a lady-of-leisure."

"I have the Watch—" she began.

"You'll break your fast first," he announced, sounding far too much like her father. "You're thin as a jackstaff. Couldn't sleep a wink what with the bones jabbing me all night."

The glint in his eye revealed he was teasing, but his tone represented he meant to brook no argument.

"Dress," he said from the threshold. "I'll wait."

21: MASTERING THE SHREWS

NATHAN STEPPED OUTSIDE. MOVING TO the end of the door path, he stood, hailing to one passersby or another, and taking in the day in between.

Cate looked around to find her shift still lay where it had been tossed the night before, but all her other clothes gone.

Tabby.

Presumably taken to be laundered, if not deemed beyond salvation and ripped into bandages.

"This having a handmaid was going to take some getting used to," Cate muttered.

Donning the shift, she set to rummaging through the lockers and hampers yet again, this time with an eye toward the practical. She quickly grew frustrated. It was evident that, while consulting with stays and mantua-makers, semptresses and a legion of other craftspeople, Thomas had taken into account her less-than-elegant lifestyle, and had avoided the fine silks and brocades, frilled, laced and beribboned. On the other hand, she wondered at his judgment as she pushed aside the delicately netted fichus, gossamer-like handkerchiefs and aprons.

Ultimately, the most serviceable skirt of the lot was selected, a striped linen of cerulean and drakesneck green. That in hand, she was still searching for stays, when something, someone outside, at the end of the doorpath, caught her eye:

Marthanna... standing with Nathan, a child in her arms, Dorrie, arm in a sling, at her side.

A bonnet shaded the child-in-arms' face, what features visible being too immature to make out if it was a boy or girl. At the sound of its mother's voice, the babe looked up, the light revealing fair-skin and pale eyes.

Not Nathan's an inner voice observed.

Of course, it isn't! Cate huffed. Still, she let out the breath she hadn't realized was being held.

Cuts, abrasions and yellow-tinged bruises still dotted Marthanna's face, but now it could be seen more fully. No one could call her a beauty, but an air and carriage made her seem so. Under the broad-brimmed straw hat was an oval face, a smooth brow over a pair of lively grey eyes. Her waistline, that which was visible around the child and its drapes, was quite slim.

Which means she couldn't have been far gone with the child she just lost, Cate observed, chewing on the inside of her mouth.

Cate critically eyed the woman, in search of some satisfying fault.

There were none, none at any rate which justified the dislike she strove to harbor.

Cate's eyes sharpened, keen for the first sign of connection or regard — dare she say, tenderness — between the Marthanna and Nathan, the product of which stood between them.

She looked in vain.

The seductress had been expected. But, given Marthanna's serene dignity and set of her mouth — a very wide and generous one — it would have been easier to imagine the Dowager Queen with her skirts up at the firesides. In point of fact, Marthanna's reserve ruled out one-night trysts of any sort. Whatever had been between her and Nathan, it had to have been of the long-lasting sort.

Marthanna shifted the child's weight, and metal flashed on her hand. A wedding ring.

Cate flinched, wondering who might have put it there?

"You have to stop this. You're making yourself crazy," she muttered, beating the heel of her hand between her brows.

Now holding a doll, presumably Dorrie's, Nathan crouched down before the girl. He said something and Dorrie smiled shyly. Cate made a small inarticulate noise at seeing the smile of one mirrored on the other. The close proximity highlighted the similarity in profiles, eye color and cock of the head as they spoke.

Surely, everyone else saw, everyone else knew!

Nathan took Dorrie's hand and then cupped her cheek. Returning the doll, he stood, his hand idly stroking the small head as he conversed further with Marthanna.

Lord, the temerity of the man! Talking flattery to one woman one moment and chatting with the mother of his child as conversationally as if over the kailyard gate the next.

Cate shifted, feeling the intruder in this tender family reunion.

More words were spoken, Marthanna's carefully arranged expression of neutrality — neither hostile, nor welcoming — unchanged.

A polite angling of her head, and Marthanna turned to take her leave. She paused and put her hand out, beckoning her daughter. Nathan dropped to one knee and said something to which Dorrie nodded and smiled again. Like a gallant—he couldn't help but charm—he took up her hand and pressed her knuckles to his lips. Dorrie leaned and pecked him on the cheek, and then she was gone. Still kneeling, Nathan turned his head to watch them go.

Rising to his feet, Nathan gazed in the pair's direction a bit longer. He turned toward the hut and stopped at seeing Cate standing just inside, nails digging into her palms. His head dropped to his chest. He drew a deep breath and, with the step of one determined to meet the inevitable, came up the path. Cate hastily dashed the wetness from the corner of her eye.

"The girl—" Nathan began quietly, inordinately so for him.

"Dorrie," Cate put in helpfully. Surely, the man could remember the child's name!

He paled a bit. "Aye, she wished to thank the nice lady who attended her arm." A smile was offered at the end, stiff and obligatory.

"Charming manners."

Nathan glanced after the pair. "Aye, she has her mother to thank for that."

Head bent, he drew breath several times, before he finally managed to utter "Her mother—"

"Marthanna."

Jaw working, he nodded. "'Tis clear she's been... rough-handled." He gulped and finally looked up. "Was she... abused... badly?" The last was uttered in a strained rasp.

The unspoken question was eloquent: had she been raped, as so many others had been?

"I can't say. I didn't attend her—her friends wouldn't let me near," Cate added under her breath, the fury and hurt of that scene making her voice shake.

"She had a miscarriage." Cate bit her lip, wondering what compelled her to blurt that out. Something in the unkind way, to be sure, and she wasn't proud of herself for it.

She watched Nathan carefully for a reaction.

His shoulders slumped in overt relief, but nothing more. "Ah, well, it would appear she's faring well for it."

There was that awkward moment of needing something nice to say, and at a total loss as to what that might be. Since the moment she saw Dorrie, Cate had prepared for this moment, had known this scene was coming, knew it meant a torturous amount of hearing what she didn't wish to hear, and had determined to face it with grace and dignity.

All those good intentions now crumbled away like a cliff's edge.

"She has her father's eyes." Cate's brow arched, with significance. Yes, she knew.

Nathan's brow arched with equal significance. "Her father's eyes are blue."

"Dammit, Nathan—!" Cate checked herself and went on more determinedly. "I'm not going to reprove you—"

A roll of his eyes showed how false that came off.

"—But you can't deny that child, any more than you could deny John."

"I'm not denying her," he declared with an angry swipe. "God's my life, I'd have to be blind not to. Every time I look at her it's like seeing Dorrie at that age."

"Dorrie?"

"Aye, me sister." He choked a bitter laugh. "Ironic name, isn't it? It's like one more knife twisting in me gut."

A brown head popped up at the door. "Does the mistress wish—?" Tabby began, bobbing a curtsy.

"No!" they shouted in unison.

"Off w' you. Shoo!" Nathan barked. "I'll bear a hand."

Abby blenched, uttered a small *eep!* and scuttled out.

Nathan fixed a stern eye on Cate. "Do you mean to wear that or are you aiming to swab floors with it?"

Cate followed his gaze to the skirt gone forgotten in her hand. As she stiffly jerked it on, he muttered something about "stays," and set to searching, with far more industry that what seemed warranted.

Hands on hips, Cate stood, waiting. He wasn't ducking out of this.

With a victorious cry, Nathan held up a set of stays. Chintz with soft leather trim, alas, they weren't the jumps like her others, flexible and meant for working, but neither were they the formal, heavy-boned variety.

Nathan scowled at the long row of small eyes. "They're new; they require lacing. Have you a needle?"

Overcoming her surprised that he would know of such a thing, let alone how to use it, Cate directed him to a trunk till. Deftly threading the needle, he set to work at Cate's back as she held her hair up out of the way.

Her expectant huff was ignored.

"There's been ill-will since the day I arrived," Cate directed behind her. "They— Marthanna and her *friends*—treated me like

I was poxed. I had the singular feeling I could have been your pet dog and they would have despised me."

Nothing other than the click of the ivory needle against the metal eyes and the clothy rasp of the laces pulling.

Lord, it was like trying to squeeze blood out of an anchor!

"Very well, so everyone knows you..." She swallowed hard. "Were with... her," was all she could manage. "You wish me to believe I've been shunned because of a tryst? That has to happen a dozen times a day, hell, an hour around here."

"Stand still. You're like trying to reef a tops'l in a gale."

Switching the hand holding her hair, Cate obediently did as she was told, or rather, tried.

She waited.

"I inquired, and all you said was 'nothing,'" she hissed.

"I didn't wish to burden you—"

"Burden me!" she cried, whirling around. A hand solidly turned her back.

"I've been *burdened* since I touched shore," she declared to the empty room. "I seemed to be the only one here that doesn't know why."

"Damn their scheming souls!" Nathan grumbled under his breath. "'Tis why I aimed to never set foot on this confounded rock again!"

"Oooff! Not so tight!" Cate wheezed. "I anticipate having to draw breath at least once or twice today. Any tighter and my cleavage will be up at my throat." If he didn't worry for her breathing, hopefully he might worry for her exposure.

A couple of yanks, and the laces loosened. Nathan resumed, although with a little more allowance for her comforts. Careful not to move anything else, Cate fixed glare over her shoulder. Finally, he looked up. His mouth quirked; he owed her an explanation, and he knew it. From all appearances, he would have preferred a flogging, but...

"Some years ago, we'd had a dust-up with a privateer near here. We prevailed, but took a mortal beating, and so limped in here to lick our wounds. I had a busted head, broken ribs and had taken a pike in the side. Marthanna's a kind soul, like you, what takes in everyone."

He glanced up with a questioning glare, in hope that bit was enough to placate.

It wasn't.

"I'd shipped with Robert, her husband." Nathan spoke in the measured rhythm of one hoping each sentence might be the last. "Hell, I was the one what got him drunk enough to propose to her. So t'was only reasonable for her to take me in and see me through the fevers."

Nathan wormed his shoulders as he laced. "It was a damned awkward business. I'd been in Tortuga just a fortnight since and had gotten word, from two different men," holding up a pair of fingers, "that Robert was dead. One represented seeing him firsthand knocked over the side; the other claimed he'd been cleaved in half by an eighteen-pounder. Either version, the outcome was the same: Robert was gone."

He blew a long sigh. "I fancied it might be better if the word came from a friend as opposed to a stone stranger."

Another questioning look, to see if his penance had been fulfilled.

He hadn't.

Nathan feel pensively quiet, his voice tight when he at last spoke. "A friend is someone you turn to when you're in need."

Cate reluctantly angled her head, conceding. Not all those many months ago, she had defined "friends" to him in much the same terms.

"And so, we turned to each other and mourned him," he said with a simple shrug.

"I'd known Robert almost as long as I'd known Thomas. Anyway," he went on, with a short wave, "she was tending me, and well, you know how long ribs take…"

Nature took its course, Cate thought. *Or at least, nature when Nathan is involved.*

She had pressed him and now sorely regretted it.

"I thought the wedding ring might have been… from… from you," Cate stammered.

Nathan gave her a sharp look and said dryly "Aye, I dare say."

The hard look softened, and he ducked his head. "Aye, well, it came damn near to being that."

Cate jerked and pivoted to stare in shock, but was firmly turned back again.

He sighed, gathering the resolve to see this through. "When I left, I knew she was in-child. She hadn't said as much — she's as evasive as you, when it comes to herself — but —" He audibly swallowed. "I knew."

Nathan fell quiet for so long Cate thought perhaps he had reached his confessional limits.

"I came back a year or so later, meaning to do the right thing. Me life was empty, I had no one. It seemed no great thing to give her and the child me name for whatever protection it might serve. Many seem to set a great store in that."

Including him, Cate thought to herself. In spite of his parents not being married, he had made the point that he was acknowledged by his father and, hence, bore his name, hence softening the burden of being a bastard to a certain degree.

"Nothing else would answer," Nathan went on, diffidently. "I thought, hoped a family might give me life purpose. Marthanna knew the sailor's way; she wouldn't set up a fuss when I set sail."

He paused again. "I came back to her belly growin' with Robert's child. He wasn't dead after all."

Cate whirled around, mouthing a silent "Oh, no...!" Checking herself, she turned her back and stood very still. "Was he... angry?"

Giving the laces a final tweak, Nathan snorted. "Angry would be one word. I've the scars to prove it," he added, touching his side. "He didn't blame her, but he and everyone else on this rotting patch o' sand blamed me. They claimed I'd set her up, filled her head with lies just to get in her bed. It was made eloquently clear I wasn't welcomed, and I haven't set foot here since."

Tying the final bow, Nathan turned Cate to face him. His approval of her attire faded upon coming up to her hair.

"When was the last time—? Oh, belay that. I've eyes." He steered her to a stool while reaching for the brush.

"Why the bloody hell do they think me so low as to lie to a woman, send her into endless tears, just to have me way?" Nathan's agitation was transmitted through every pass, applying the brush like she was a shepherd shedding its winter coat. "God's my life, there's an island full of women out there, *more* than willing to lift their skirts. Why the hell would I oblige meself to days, nay weeks of sobbing and blue-devils?"

"Ouch!"

"Sorry." Nathan stood back. Head bent, he rasped his thumb over the brush's bristles. "It would be so much easier if I were that heartless, manipulating cove they think me to be," he grumbled under his breath.

After a few moments, he set back to brushing again, calmer now, the strokes more even. Sitting with her hands in her lap, one thought screamed in Cate's head.

"If... if you had married her, then none of this would have ever—" She gulped, feeling quite ill. "We would have never—"

Nathan snorted. "I would have still boarded that ship; I would have still plucked a half-crazed woman from the water." He paused to smile down at her. "And I would have still lost me heart as she puked on me deck."

Cate swallowed, feeling perilously near doing that very thing just then. "You would have been married."

"Different when the oars are in a different boat, isn't it? Only one of us standing here enjoys that matrimonial state," he explained at her failure to follow.

"What...? Oh!"

That old saw again, she thought testily.

"Married or no, these women would have still been ready to lynch me on sight, calling me everything from an adulterer to a cad, and they would have been correct," Nathan went on. He leaned a bit closer and winked. "For I would have still wanted *you.*"

Cate flushed. Damn him, he could play her like a fiddle and he knew it. It wasn't the words so much as the virtual vow with which they were delivered. Still, there was a certain smug satisfaction at having cuckolded Marthanna, in the figurative sense at any rate.

She would have loved to have seen Nathan's face when Marthanna first appeared, first approached. As they spoke, his head had been turned slightly, blocking Cate's view. She knew him well enough, however, to be able to read his body: stiff, even wary, a large part of him wishing to be anywhere but there. Affection for Dorrie was the only emotion openly revealed, and even that had been checked. She had watched carefully as they spoke. Had the pair extended their arms, their fingertips might have touched, and yet the distance between them seemed more like leagues. If anything, he and Marthanna were nothing more than passing acquaintances having a word over that garden gate.

Robert's story, however, went a long way to explaining why Nathan had been so reluctant to believe Brian was dead. There were too many instances of the affirmed dead arising, Nathan himself, included, twice. She fell under that umbrella as well, now. Stories of her death would be greatly exaggerated.

"But everyone lays with everyone around here," Cate said peevishly.

"Aye," Nathan said wryly. "But by their choice, not in a lie. They all knew Robert, they had all mourned him and felt they had been played the fool."

Cate twisted around only to be set back. "But you didn't lie."

A slight angling of his head conceded her point. "Not this time, but perhaps Providence was settling her accounts for all the times before. I've never taken a woman unwilling in me life. She was willing, more than willing," he added, with an emphasis which made Cate's blood rise. "But, false pretenses, lying about that—" He shook his head, the bells jangling. "Hell hath no fury like a woman lied to."

Cate couldn't argue. The difficulty was that there was no villain in this. Marthanna wasn't to be blamed. If someone had made up a story of Brian's death just to gain her bed, it would have been more than their head she would have been hunting for. And yet, neither could she rebuke Nathan. He had acted in good faith.

Alas, no good deed shall go unpunished.

Nathan sighed with perhaps a bit more regret than was comfortable. "I'll have to say, I barely recognized her. She's not who she used to be; life seems to have soured and embittered her."

Now it was Cate who choked a bitter laugh. "As have we all! Are any of us who we used to be?" she went on, looking down at herself.

After so many years, with so much happening, it was a wonder if Brian or even her brothers would recognize her? For that matter, after imprisonment, transportation and heaven knows what other tribulations, would she recognize him?

As much as Nathan claimed disinterest in children, his affection for Dorrie had been so very evident. Did it spring from actual paternal stirrings, or because the child put him so much in mind of his long dead sister?

"But Marthanna can't just deny Dorrie from you—" Cate pleaded.

"Can and does," he cut in flatly. "I've tried to do what I can, but she can be as stubborn as a bollard, much like you."

"Flattery will get you nowhere m'lad."

Cate hesitated and then finally ventured to ask "So, does she, Dorrie, know... who her father is?"

"Not from Marthanna's lips," came back equally adamant. "But I'd bet me grannie's nightcap, a good number of these meddling harridans around here won't scruple to tell her. Now, stand up and turn 'round, let's have a look at you."

Nathan plucked at the neckline of her shift, a distracted furrow rumpling his brow.

"It's not all your fault," Cate said earnestly. "You weren't entirely in the wrong." Given the freedoms exhibited thereabouts, the whole thing seemed a tempest in a teapot.

He glanced up, mouth twisting. "Isn't it? Odd. They think it is; Marthanna thinks as much. And, when the child grows older, she will think the same. She'll probably come to curse me name." The last was muttered heatedly under his breath.

Standing back, he regarded Cate and frowned. "You need a bodice."

"I'm fine," she insisted as he bent to the hampers once more. "I've gone without all that before."

A series of muffled huffs and snorts conceded her point whilst a more emphatic one made his own.

"This will do!" he declared at last, holding up a scarf roughly the size of a tablecloth. Rolling her eyes—the man deserved some kind of a victory—Cate stood as it was passed about her neck amidst mutterings of "sun" and "decency."

"As it 'tis, there's naught that I can do," Nathan said, tucking the scarf ends. "The child has a loving mother and father. You can't ask for better than that."

"And lost a friend in the bargain." Cate sighed. Once, she had inquired as to the number of those he could call "friend." Two or three had been his answer after a long consideration. Thomas, to be sure, and Garrick, who had led he and Thomas into piracy. And now, finally, a third... or rather, had been.

"Perhaps I could—?" she began.

Nathan's cold look froze the words in her mouth. "What: convince Marthanna and the entire island of me good intentions?" He snorted louder yet. "Tell that one to the parrot. You've good-meaning heart, as big as the world, darling, but it's not enough to soften these iron-clad souls."

He stood back to admire the results of his labors, the appreciative glow in his eyes making her cheeks warm. "The color suits you. Thomas knows his business," he added grudgingly.

Nathan's eyes swiveled up to Cate's and held, searching, the corners pinched with uncertainty. His smile faded, and he sobered. "It is the truth."

"I know," came out automatically.

The corner of his mouth tucked up. "You don't look it."

Cate made a conscious effort to rearrange her features to something more agreeable. "Better?"

"Barely. Enough, now," he declared. "All this tacking-and-jibing isn't going to make me forget you've not yet eaten. Away, w' ye," he declared, a flutter of fingers urging her toward the door.

❧

His arm hooked into Cate's and headed up the way toward the pavilion.

Cate discovered straightaway that there was something to be said for stepping out in a new frock. It had been a long, long, long time since she had enjoyed such luxury. She'd never wholly

ascribed to the old saw about clothes making the person, she thought plucking at the skirt fabric, admiring its quality and drape. It might not make the person, but it certainly went a long way to starting the day off in a grand style.

Even grander, however, was stepping out on a man's arm, especially when it involved wiping the eye of a good many naysayers that Nathan would return, and he would return for her. A small part of her—yes, a very mean-spirited, petty and possessive part— wished they might pass within Marthanna's line-of-sight, just so she might rub in the fact just that bit more. Still, given the island's talent for gossip, there was little doubt that word would reach those ears and to the nth detail.

Her buoyancy seemed contagious, Nathan moving next to her with considerable more animation. Amid hails and greetings, he swept an elaborate bow to an intervening dog and bid a pig "G'day" as they passed.

With the island's population now larger by another two hundred, what served as the settlement's mainstreet was markedly busier. Judging by the number of bodies—scattered here, there and beyond—a good number were still sleeping off the night's merrymaking. Still, through the trees, the *Morganse* could be seen sitting on her moorings in the glittering morning sun, a-swarm with men, boats and rafts bobbing at her sides, unloading with all the enterprise of bees. On shore, the incoming stores were already piled high, where Pryce and Hodder, in full voice, oversaw the ant-like industry.

Cate gave a sigh of relief at seeing the pavilion was busy with those breaking their fast; it meant she and Nathan weren't joining the day as late as earlier represented. As Nathan saw her seated, Kirkland appeared—praise his precious and blessed soul!—with coffee and at a lava-like temperature which made holding the cup by anything other than the handle a hazard. The breakfast delivered before Nathan's return wasn't the customary porridge and cold fish. It was eggs, ham, rashers of bacon, crisp and hot, and racks of toasted soft-tack, and all the appurtenances, including—no surprise—a jar of honey. It was all served up on silver platters and eaten off china plates, with silver utensils. Cate watched Nathan serve her up, looking for any telltale sign of this extravagance being his doing. All she found, however, was his natural candor. Still, it was difficult to believe such luxury was all just the perquisites of his rank. Someone was putting on the dog for someone. Who was the question?

By no accident, the honey had been set directly before Nathan. He dipped in a finger and popped a golden glob into

his mouth. As she ate, Cate watched hopefully but, alas, honey and coffee looked to be the entirety of his meal.

Thomas plunked down on the bench across from her. If harried looks, sweat and grim were any indication, he'd already put in a full day's work. She glanced to the sky and the sun to confirm the hour wasn't later than thought. He quaffed down a cupful of the steaming brew and then finally touched his hat to her.

"Top o' the morning, Mistress Harper." This in a voice calculated to reach the pavilion's farthest corner. "Strike me blind, what a striking frock you are wearing today! Where could you have managed to find something so becoming? Upon my soul, it positively matches the color of your eyes —!"

"Very well, very well," Nathan growled. "You've proven how big of a pain-in-the – arse you can be."

Popping a piece of bacon into his mouth, Thomas swiveled a jaded eye toward Nathan. "You look like hell."

"Ah, the pot chivvying the kettle, I see."

"I would have thought someone of your... *parts* would have been in a better mood," Thomas observed, munching. "I heard the caterwauling last night —*and* this morning —but fancied it was just Cate being a bit rough on you." The last came with an impish grin.

Face heating, Cate dipped her nose into her cup. Mortification, and so early in the day!

Just once she would like to lie with Nathan, without a bunch of ears flapping. Living in an estate house with ten people, plus the flow of guests and ever-present servants, she and Brian had suffered much the same. Barns, forest glens, fields: nowhere went unexplored, untried. She cut her eye toward the surrounding forest and sighed. With the island so heavily inhabited, little refuge seemed to lie there.

"Still hanging at keyholes listening?" Nathan observed dryly.

"No, just going about my daily business. Believe it or not, the rest of us *do* have a life," Thomas replied drier yet.

"Go to bloody hell," came back only a modicum of malice.

"That would be your purview," Thomas said mildly.

"Gained your appetite, I see," Nathan observed, watching the ham, bacon and toast disappear.

Thomas shrugged, licking jam from his fingers. "Been working; some of us are obliged to pick up the slack, whilst others don't show a leg until damned near eight bells in the forenoon watch."

Throughout this banter, Thomas' gaze was steady on Cate,

brows and face working, as if seeking an answer to a question known only to him.

Cate angled her head a fraction to show her confusion.

The sandy brows knit, sterner, more demanding, more insistent, but of what she had no notion? Was she to answer? Was she to move? Do something? Say something? Acknowledge? Disavow? What?

He leaned a fraction as if looking for something. One brow angled sharply down, the other up.

"Got ticks in your britches?"

Cate jerked like a child caught with its fingers in the cream. Nathan's remark, however, was aimed at Thomas. "I can hear you thinking clear over here."

Thomas swallowed down a remark along with his eggs and reached for more toast.

Nathan picked up the pot, shook it and scowled. He cocked an eye at her and then hailed for someone. Barely giving anyone time to appear, he rose, pot in fist, muttering "I know how you can get when you're not sufficiently bumpered up."

He was barely three strides away before "Are you well?" was hissed in her ear.

The urgency in Thomas' query caused Cate to almost choke. "Shouldn't I be? Don't I look it?" She looked down at herself, thinking perhaps some key article of clothing had been overlooked.

"I heard all manner of carrying on last night," Thomas said, low and hoarse. "You two usually aren't the vocal type. I was on the verge of busting in until I realized it was Nathan doing all the yelling. Did he do something to make you hit him? If he did, then good on you!" His fist thumped the table.

"Umm... no, it wasn't anything—momentary indiscretion," she mumbled, looking down.

"You're well, then," Thomas confirmed. A hunch of his shoulders indicated Nathan's imminent return. "So help me, if he raised a hand to you—"

"No," she hissed, behind her hand, Nathan now nearly beside her.

A testy silence ensued as Nathan poured, a suspicious eye shifting from one to the other. Someone needed to say something and soon.

A scrap of conversation from some days ago popped into her consciousness, and Cate directed to Thomas "Do you truly believe what you said, that the Company is dead?"

The thought of an ardent enemy being defeated brought a certain thrill, for Nathan most particularly. It would mean the culmination of a decade-long quest. On her own part, Creswicke might be dead but, in light of the recent attack, she still felt his presence. A complete demise would be a final jewel in the crown-of victory.

Thomas dabbed at crumbs on the table with a wetted finger. "T'would be a grand thing to think it."

"Pah!" declared Nathan. "There's too many what have too much to gain for the Company to perish: stockholders, the grieving widow…"

They all smiled. The image of Prudence as the grieving widow was a difficult one to conjure.

"Someone will step up to the helm, but it won't be that ill-begotten, lump o' wasted humanity," Nathan said, with a satisfied nod. "The larger question is what the bloody hell was that moldering worm Lesauvage thinking when he threw in with them?"

"Always has been a grasping bastard, anything for the prospect of a dollar," Thomas pointed out.

Nathan made a noise. "More like shilling. He's what gives pirates a bad name. Still and all, but why in the hell attack this rock? There's precious few shillings to be had here!" He cut Thomas a severe look. "Hopefully, he met a fitting end?"

"Regrettably, not among the survivors," Thomas said, frowning and dusting his hand on his sleeve. "so have to be satisfied that he was either blown to bits, or destroyed to the point his mother mightn't recognize him, and was tossed off the point with the rest of his back-stabbing crew."

Nathan nodded, clearly preferring something more glorious, like dismemberment, or hanging would have befallen the man.

"And so, the *Revenge* is yours." Nathan leaned the bit necessary to see the vessel. "Looks like you're squaring her away."

Now Thomas was the one to make a disgusted noise. "Easier said than done. Lesauvage, and that lumpish, prig Pengelly before him didn't her any favors."

"Neither one of them knew a knighthead from a butt."

Nathan scooped another glob of honey and popped it into his mouth. "Who was that cod-handed lout what had her before?"

The two struck poses of recollection, Nathan looking up as if the answer might be found in the palm-frond roof, Thomas closing one eye.

"Hatcher!" they announced in unison, laughing.

"Lord, now there was a prime example of a wasted bit o' humanity," Nathan declared, shaking his head.

Nathan waved his cup. "Scuttle 'er. With a string of captains like that, she's an unlucky ship. Scuttle 'er, before she winds up like that other one, taking all souls with her."

"Aye, well, we're looking to clean some of the bad luck out first." Thomas spoke with the easy conviction of that very thing might be done.

Nathan gazed at the *Mirabel*, or rather the two spars sticking out of the water, a distant smile growing. "Remember when we were off Sunda Strait, surrounded by Dutch, not a friendly port for a thousand miles, and we had to rig oars for a mizzenmast? We would have given a month's grog for those spars."

The men laughed together, and then fell into a conversation regarding ships, repairs and nautical details. Buttering another piece of toast, Cate listened with half an ear.

The bell clang was Cate's salvation, and she rose. "It's my Watch. You don't have to—" she began seeing Nathan push to his feet. "Stay, have your chat."

"Pryce and Hodder have things under control," he said, wincing at a barrage of cursing drifting up from the shoreline. "I'm your man!"

Nathan clapped Thomas on the shoulder as he passed. "Take notes, m'lad. This is how you watch over a woman."

"Tell me what's to do."

Tying on an apron, Cate turned. As she had walked up the path, she had wondered what he meant to do. He had lent a hand the day before, but such labors could hardly be expected again.

"You're the captain; you don't have to—"

His eyes rounded as if she had just suggested he burn his boots. "What? Watch you grovel in everyone's blood and vomit, whilst I sit on me arse, at me leisure? It should be the other way around, but I know how quickly I'd be brought up all-standing on that one!" His point was made with an emphatic roll of his eyes.

Nathan shook his head. "Aye, I'm none so humble as to not admit I've holystoned me last deck, but I don't give meself airs to the point of not lending a hand. Mum would roll in her grave with sick-and-hurt in need, and I was standing about with me thumb up me bum."

"Very well," Cate sighed. "Lord knows, my mother would rise from hers if I refused sorely-needed help. There's broth to be spooned, water to give, bandages to change, doses to—"

Nathan's eye demonstrably roamed and stopped at the first

thing to hand: the drinking water bucket and dipper. Seizing it up, he set off up the aisle between the cots.

Cate sought out the worker she was replacing, listening intently as she was briefed on the issues and concerns of those whose welfare would be in her hands for the next several hours. Securing the corners of her skirts through the pocket slits, she set to work.

She checked on Toby straightaway. No worse, but still no better. The prolonged fever was taking its toll: hollowed cheeks, dark circles under his eyes, and a pallor roughly the color of the canvas pillow under his head. She mopped the pallid face, trickled honey - water between the parched lips and — when no one was looking — kissed him lightly on the forehead.

As Cate made her rounds — moving armloads of soiled bedding and bandages, emptying sick-basins, swabbing the fevered, holding the heads of the vomiting — she cocked an ear for any mention of Cornwall. After last night's disappearance with Nathan, she wondered for his welfare. A small, very small part of her regretted Nathan's rough - handling — a safe assumption, considering he returned alone, sucking on bloodied knuckles. It wasn't so much regret for the man being beaten — she had fought the urge to take a few swipes at the bastard herself — but that it had been on her behalf. The man wasn't in the sickbay; neither was his body among those awaiting shrouds and burial. No mention was made of finding the man dead; no mention was made in any respect. Had he been found dead, and it just wasn't deemed worth mentioning? Or, was he lying somewhere, so beaten he couldn't rise?

Or, was he just dead drunk?

Cate shook it all off. There was nothing to be gained in dwelling on those not worthy of being dwelt.

"Where the bloody hell is your help?" Nathan declared, fetching water for the third time. Hot and cold, caring for the sick required a great deal of it.

"There were several lads," Cate said, glancing about. "But the *Morganse's* arrival took care of that. Your men and their battle stories are ever so much more interesting than toting water and emptying night jars."

Grumbling darkly, Nathan ducked outside the tent and hailed someone. Terse instructions were given; two stout lads soon appeared. There was no mistaking the look of harsh words given, harsh words received, admonishments, instructions, threats. The pair then raced to where Cate stood, plucked the becket from her hand and scurried off for the water butts.

Arms crossed, Nathan struck a pose next to Cate as she

resumed preparing doses. "You don't hear that!?" he demanded of her.

Cate followed his look of loathing toward a curtained area. It took her a moment, a fervent cut of his eyes finally making his meaning clear.

"Oh, that. No, I suppose not." With so many women on the island, the sounds of childbearing were almost as routine as the bells on a ship. That day was no different. All this grief, anguish and strife would bring on early pains for even the strongest of constitutions. Why an infant would be so impatient to leave its snuggery and join all that was anyone's wonder, but the simple fact of the matter was that they were, as was the case for two just then.

Nathan shied at another scream from that direction. "I'm surprised you're not over there helping."

"It's better if I'm not," she said with a significant lilt. Under no circumstances was she willing to hazard approaching that bastion of ill-will.

His expression darkened. "You represented there had been ill-will, that they treated you like—"

Cate's choke on the extent of that understatement stopped him. Hands on his hips, he leaned closer and asked in a hoarse whisper "'Twas that bad?"

She wasn't an accomplished enough liar to deny it. "I'm not saying they wished me dead," she was quick to equivocate, "but their hands would have been deep in their pockets, if I were to drown."

A stream of expletives broke from him which didn't bear repeating. "I'll go over there and—"

A firm hand on his arm stopped him. "You'll do nothing of the sort. We've come to an understanding of sorts. They're over there, and I'm over here. There's plenty enough work to go around," she pointed out, in hopes the cords in his jaws might go a little less white.

They didn't.

"Damn this feculent hellhole!" he fumed.

"Shh! They'll hear you."

"Too bloody damned right!"

A glance revealed that her assistants had disappeared again. She took up the bucket and started toward the fires and the steaming kettles there. Nathan strode to catch her up and took it from her.

"Things have improved, since you arrived." she said, lowering her voice as they walked.

It wasn't a gross exaggeration. She had thought it imagined

at first, but gradually through the day, she had become aware of a reduction in the frostiness from both co - workers and patients, especially among the abuse victims. Lygia still gave Cate her back, refusing to take her dose directly from Cate's hand, several more still answering in monosyllables to her inquiries. But, overall, compared to her first hours there, their regard for her was much more abiding.

What or why was the question? Thomas' declaration on the beach of what Creswicke's depredations popped into mind straightaway. She had represented much the same — in a bit less graphic detail — and had been met with skepticism, to say the least, as if she were topping-the-knob. But Thomas, a man, announces it on a beach, and she is suddenly anointed with legitimacy?

Or, was it simply Nathan's, yet another man's presence, objected to by some, and yet lending a large dose of veracity and validation to her claims?

It was irksome to think that a man's word would be taken over hers. She flattered herself to think that, with sufficient time, she could have established herself on her own character and merits, but neither was she about to spit in the eye of goodwill no matter the source.

"I'll have a word with them and make damned sure — " Nathan began, glaring about.

"These women are so much putty in your hands?" she asked, knowing arch to her brow.

Nathan wanted to argue, but saw her wisdom. "Very well," came with considerable effort. "I'll back me sails, but the engagement is *not* lost."

Their path necessarily took them past the childbed. Nathan hunched his shoulders at another shriek, more prolonged and shrill than the one before.

"I am not ashamed to admit a *very* large part of me is pleased and relieved that is not you in there, going through that," he grumbled under his breath.

Cate smiled; Nathan's reaction was so typical. Men could stand strong in the face of war or violence, but a woman in labor made them cower.

"That doesn't scare you?" he demanded, incredulous.

His eye fixed on her hand now resting at her waist. Jerking it away, Cate started to say "No," but saw that wouldn't be believed. "A bit," she conceded.

Celia's confirmation of her fertility had given Cate a small grain of hope. All she needed was Nathan, and Nature would take its course...

Or so you thought, cautioned an inner voice.

Considering these latest developments of Nathan's... err... difficulties, those hopes were dashed, barrenness looming all the larger —

... And all because of one scheming, vindictive, jealous sea goddess.

Few clouds lacked silver linings, and this one was no exception. Philosophically speaking, barrenness had its benefits. A ship was no place for a woman with a swelling belly, nor an infant. Gain a child and lose Nathan, or pray for continued barrenness: if a choice was to be made, she would take him.

"I suppose it's like Eve's curse: you bear it because there is no choice," Cate explained, instead. "It's no different than an ugly task, like you having to tack for days, or going out on a yard in a storm."

"Not even close! That's just... business as business."

"And so, is that," she said, raising her voice over another querulous moan.

Bucket filled, Nathan toted it back to the bench where Cate had been working. Preparing doses was exacting work, executed precisely to Celia's instructions and repeated several times a day, nay, hourly for some.

Nathan cast a dubious look toward the childbed. "It is a wonder how a woman can spread her legs knowing the consequences which await."

"As I recall, the risks are mutual."

His head whipped around and he scowled until he finally smoked her meaning.

"Only the pox," he said, with a flick of his fingers. "Being reduced to a noseless lunatic is so far removed as to make it non-existent; odds are greater of being speared by a shiver. A woman dooms herself to a nine-month sentence, knowing hours, perhaps days of agony — damned near torture — and even death awaits," he said, rapping those same fingers on the wooden surface before her.

"If a man knows he's going to get hit every time he strays near a bosun, he makes damned sure to give the bastard a wide berth," Nathan went on, shying at another howl. "I'd rather take a caning than go through that. At least, there's hope the caning will end."

Cate smiled indulgently. "I'm trying to imagine anyone caning or starting you." The poor man needed a little distraction.

He shrugged, pleased to change the subject. "I've been set about with cob, cane and rope, often for just the sheer joy of it, but many a-time it was deserved, Thomas and I both."

"That's even more difficult to imagine someone beating him," she said, her smile broadening.

"I actually saw him snatch a start out of a bosun's — Nope, I tell a lie: it was a bosun's mate's fist and fling it over the gun'l. He nearly gave the blighter a taste of his own medicine — he was a hard-horse tartar what made everyone's life miserable — and a good many would have cheered him on. He would have been flogged for his troubles, too."

"What happened?" Cate asked, tamping a stopper into a jar.

Nathan narrowed an eye as if she were dim. "He was seized up to the grate and flogged."

"But you just said —"

"Aye, but he was only given a dozen, enough to make a show. He would have been given fifty else."

Cate shook her head. Sometimes Nathan's logic escaped her entirely.

"If I were a woman, me knees would be tied together, a chastity belt with a lock the size o' me boot, that's for bloody damned sure," he declared with a definitive jerk of his head. "What's so bloody damned humorous?"

"Nothing," Cate said, flapping a hand. "Just coming from a man who, shall we say, avails himself upon women —"

"I never took one unwilling in me life."

"And yet, you've obliged a few to 'suffer the sentence,' as you so delicately call it," she observed, entirely without malice. By his own admission, several of his wild oats had found root and flourished, one in particular appearing on her doorstep that very morning.

"Regrettable and yet, inevitable."

The muscles in his jaw flexed at another shriek. "I remember watching Mum die," he said in a hoarse rasp. "God, the agony... the blood..."

Aggie — God rest her soul, Cate thought, automatically crossing herself — had told of the grisly scene: the young boy in the corner clutching the dead babe, watching his mother die a slow and agonizing death.

She laid an assuring hand on his arm. "That's not the case for most, thank heavens, or the race would die out."

"Enough do." Nathan pulled away although not in anger. "Between war and childbed, I'd wager the butcher's bill is longer for the latter."

As much as she wished, Cate couldn't argue his point. The masses of bodies on battlefields, land or sea, made it easy to assume war was the greater hazard. But every cottage, manor, hut, tent or dwelling were private battlefields of the childbed, where the casualties were witnessed only by family or friends. One by one, the dead piled higher than any war.

"After —" He gulped, his arms crossed tight across his chest. "After I brought you back, after everything with Creswicke, I listened to you scream, watched the life pour out of you, and believed you'd never have me again, and wouldn't have blamed you for it."

He looked up at her, eyes glowing with appreciation and wonder. "And yet, you did. You took me to your bed, without reservation, without hesitation, and gave yourself, ignoring — hell, hoping I might get another one on you, knowing full well what might lay ahead."

Cate's throat tightened. She had done all that and more. It was all so simple, or so it seemed to her, for it was so reflexive, so automatic. Of course, she would have him. She smiled faintly as he had approached, so eloquent with dread, so afraid of scaring her, and yet nearly frozen with mortal fear of rejection. She could no more do that than stop breathing. And yet, there were those women who, after abuses, difficult expectancies or arduous travails, who did that very thing, who bragged of having divested themselves of a man's inconveniences, and recommending how others might do the same.

"You forget the pain," Cate said, at the end of another moan. "You remember it hurt, but —"

"Aye, but the soul remembers," he said, tapping his temple.

Alas, he was correct: the body forgot, so very quickly, but the mind remembered, as if etched in glass.

"You men do the same," she said. "You charge into battle, knowing the consequences."

Nathan snorted, even more emphatic. "If you saw your enemy suffering to that degree, you'd give them the mercy of a blade to the throat."

"Look at every woman here," he declared in wonderment. "They're smiling, for the love of all which is holy, you included!" he finished, stabbing an accusing finger.

"Because we know a new life is on its way."

A guttural noise summarized his opinion of that.

"Every person has a hell of their own making," he announced, straightening. "Mine would be listening to you, going through that. I cannot abide your suffering. If the time ever comes, if the gods are the least bit favorable, I will be so *very* far away."

If, she thought, watching him walk away. *If. I might as well be wishing for the rings of Saturn.*

Duty called them their separate ways, Cate administering the prepared doses, Nathan moving from bed to bed, proving Cate's theory yet again that he was incapable of meeting a stranger.

Her mood grew increasingly sour. Through the day, the sickbay had filled with visitors and well-wishers, to the point it was often difficult to do what needed done. One couldn't help but notice, Cate observed unkindly, that the children weren't the only ones clustered about Nathan, watching him do tricks with coins or a bit of cord from his pocket. For many — far, far too many — women visiting injured friends or relations was but a pretense. There was a good number of those who wished nothing to do with him — Good on them! — but there was also some — far too many, by her estimation — who sought him out, beaming and tittering in his presence.

And, no, Hope was not among them.

"Thank heavens for that small favor," Cate muttered, grinding the pestle into the mortar with renewed force.

It wasn't easy seeing the smile, wide and genuine, the one which always touched her heart, being flashed at someone else. There was a gaiety about him never seen before, a unique lilt to his laugh —

He'd laugh with you, if you weren't so shrewish.

She knew it would come to this and had prepared for it, promising herself that she wasn't going to do this. Stopping the sun from tracking the sky would have been easier. Leopards don't change their stripes or spots or whatever the hell they were. She was a jealous creature, ready to pounce. The philosophical might call it "being fiercely defensive of what she held dear." Too many losses, too much taken from her only made it worse. The Commandments went on and on about a vast array of human conditions, but jealousy was conspicuous in its absence. Did the Good Lord forget, or had Moses conveniently omitted it?

The forgiving soul would realize that neither could Nathan change his spots.

"And don't expect the leopard to suddenly become the lamb," she muttered, throwing another armload of soiled bandages onto the pile. She knew who and what he was. The word "Freedom" tattooed on his chest and the swallow on his arm said it all.

Nathan had made many pledges to her in the way of fealty and loyalty, but all that had come at a time when she was the only woman about. A starving man can easily claim to be fasting when there is no food to be had. It remained to be seen how binding that fidelity would be amid this banquet of plenty.

The unwholesome side of her wished they all might loathe

him. At least, then they wouldn't flock to him like snakes to St. Patrick.

Spooning broth to Sally, another with the Mark of Cornwall upon her, Cate forced herself to start humming again. The tune died in her throat, however, at hearing Nathan hail, and then step out of the sickbay to greet a group of women coming up the thoroughfare. Ah, yes, the snakes were most certainly gathering, coming out of the blessed woodwork.

It was an all-too-familiar performance: the appreciative gazes, swaying of the hips, coquettish angling of the head, laughter—just that little too loud, she judged—a squeeze of the hand, a lingering arm about the shoulders...

Lord, if they just wouldn't be so damnably obvious!

Very well, yes, she had done the same thing herself, but that had been different. Sad to say, she had executed the same performance, but only because it worked with the precision and dependability of a fine-tuned clock. That not-so-small point was exactly what made watching the current display all the more grating: knowing their efforts would not be for naught.

Damn him!

Her agitation growing by leaps and bounds, she sought to calm herself by pointing out this was just greetings, civilities, passing the time. It wasn't as if he were kissing—

Oops, strike that, she thought, looking away.

It had only been a peck on the cheek, not a replay of Hope's handy greeting of the night before, although it couldn't be ignored several appeared inclined to that very thing.

Cate renewed her attention on Sally, helping her eat, or rather trying to. More of it was being spilled than reached her mouth. Sally might have lost an arm, but she wasn't so impaired as to not ferret out the source of Cate's distraction.

"Nathan just doing what Nathan does."

"Yes, but it's not all he does, is it?" Cate said, dabbing the woman's face.

"Oh, no," Sally said, with a knowing chuckle. "The line will be forming straightaway." She slid a considering eye in Nathan's direction. "I never saw the fascination, but then I never got the full benefit of his charms, either."

The collision of anger with the urge to defend him rendered Cate mute.

Sally gave Cate a motherly pat on the arm, the laudanum rendering it heavy and misguided. "Best get in line soon, dearie, if you fancy him. He'll be like a stag in rut: tongue hanging out, too tired to walk... or anything else." The last was almost lost in a fizz of amusement.

Murmuring an inarticulate "thanks" for the well-meant advice, Cate rose just as Nathan ducked back into the sickbay. He scanned the tent, spotted her and angled in that direction. Spinning on her heel, Cate headed the opposite direction. She had nothing to say to him. He caught her up at a table.

"Old friends," he announced.

"You seem to be saying that a lot," she observed coolly.

"Aye, because, 'tis true."

"Yes, I daresay, and so *very* pleased to see you." She turned with a jerk of her skirts. "It's been years—" Nathan hissed over her shoulder, following close behind.

Aware of listening ears everywhere, both had lowered their voices.

Cate closed her eyes, striving for every shred of tolerance. "I know that. I'm not angry."

"Then stop twisting that rag like it's someone's neck, mine presumably." Glaring, she threw down the cloth and clutched the table's edge.

"You imagine I worked me way alphabetic through this place: Abbey before Annie; Beth before Betty?" he demanded.

"Having Abbey, Annie, Beth and Betty," Cate said, whirling around and ticking them off on her fingers, "regale me with their experiences doesn't help."

She pushed past to another table and took up the mortar and pestle.

Nathan came up behind her, close and pressing. "Not a belly here is my doing," he declared, pointing a rigid arm.

"Not *this* time."

Her glare sent him back a step. "I told you, darling, 'tis no secret that—"

"Yes, I know!" She threw down the mortar. It was for its own preservation, for otherwise, she would have thrown it. "All the hundreds before, as you so eloquently put it."

"You asked," he pointed out, evenly. "You would have preferred a lie?"

Yes, she had asked. In all honesty, "a few score" would have been a satisfactory response; the notion of "hundreds" had staggered her, opening a floodgate to her imagination which ran like a coursing hound.

"No... I mean, yes,... I mean—ugh!" She pushed past him to the brazier. Medicinal teas needed to be brewed.

"It could be said t'was your fault," he observed, close on her heels.

Cate glared a silent question of how the bloody hell he figured that over her shoulder.

"I knew the right one for me existed somewhere out there," he said, with a flutter of fingers. "And so, I was obliged to try each one, until I found you. Had you shown up earlier, I might have stopped at a score or even less."

"You weren't just exchanging 'Good days' with them," she shot back. "You were doing what you do: charming." The last came through a jaw far more clenched than was intended.

"And, that's a crime in your court?"

He had cornered her, literally and figuratively, and he knew it.

"Dammit, yes!"

There it was, glaring like the green-eyed monster! She had promised, nay vowed she wouldn't do this, and yet, here she was, wrangling with him like a shrewish fishwife.

She reached for the kettle handle without thinking to grab a cloth first and jerked back. "Ouch!" Swearing, Cate shoved the burned fingers into her mouth.

"I'm fine," she said, dodging Nathan's attempts to see.

He was too quick, however, and caught her hand.

"Dammit to bloody hell, sending you here was a mistake. Suffering Christ, I know that now. But it's too damned late; the damage is done," he grumbled, examining her fingers.

"Now, I'm damaged?" she huffed.

He cut her a warning glare.

"They have spewed their venom, until you're becoming like them. 'Tis nothing but a damned viper pit," he said louder, not caring who heard. "You should put oil on these."

Nathan made to kiss the burns, but Cate jerked away, burying her hand in her skirts. It stung horribly, but be damned if she would let on.

"Trust is like virginity," he said to her back. "Once it's lost, there's no regaining it; naught but ruses and facades await."

Nathan stepped around and seized Cate by the arms, forcing her to look up at him. "Do you trust me?" he asked, low and somber.

She looked away, in any direction but his. "I want to," she finally managed.

Releasing her, Nathan stood back and exhaled, resigned. "Uh-huh. And what, may I inquire, is stopping you?"

The admission didn't come easily, but dammit, he asked.

She cut her eyes sideways to a group of women milling about outside. "Them."

The corner of his eye twitched; fury lurked so very near. "They are just pleased to see men."

"This island has plenty."

"Yes," he conceded. "But all are either young enough to call them 'mum' or bent and old. They like seeing a straight one."

"Yes, I daresay," she shot back. "Some parts more so than others."

He stiffened, one eye narrowing. The entire conversation could have well been at the top of their voices and near to drawing blood. But, instead, it was low-voiced and constrained, almost conversational.

"Aye, true enough," Nathan finally said. "There are those who will raise their skirts—"

"And, you know them all."

Nathan's one foot patted the ground. "Aye, some—a few," he quickly amended. "But, the rest are just pleased, nay relieved when you don't come at them like a rutting boar. I give them a smile and a pleasantry, and perhaps a small squeeze," he added, with an equivocating gesture. "And they beam."

"We women give each other smiles and pleasantries all day," she huffed.

"You know, as well as any, that coming from a man makes a grand difference."

Grudgingly, Cate couldn't argue. Nathan had a point, and they both knew it. A "good day" from a man—especially one good-looking and a charming smile—went a great way to elevate a woman's spirits.

Nathan casually propped his hip against the table and crossed his arms. "Has it occurred to you the reverse might be the case, that I might be in need of women's company?" he asked mildly, examining his nails. "One does find himself in dire need of those who don't stink of bilges and have hair growing out of every crevice."

Cate stiffly angled her head, reluctantly conceding his point. He had made similar observations before. At the time, she had found the confession touching, his loneliness closely reflecting hers.

"And what if—?" she began and then bit her lip.

Nathan cut a cold eye. "If what?"

She turned and lifted her chin. "Sauce for the gander. What if I was to do the same: go up to a man, pass the time, give a smile, a wink?"

He shook his head at her innocence. "You forget, darling, I'm obliged to suffer *that* every day, since you came aboard."

He had her there; she'd been one woman among two hundred men for so long, she tended to forget.

"Then a friend," she amended, undaunted. "A very *particular* friend?"

Nathan's face screwed at the obvious. "I'd break his arm and then geld him, because I would know what was on his mind."

"You can't assume every man I meet wishes to —!" she began, frustrated by her entire point being missed.

"Can and do, because that is exactly the case. Hell, I suffered it meself!"

She opened her mouth to object, but wisdom clapped it shut. It wasn't the first time she had heard that observation from both he and Thomas.

Nathan cast a look toward the path and the women passing, and sighed. "I wish I could be more like Millbridge: regarding women like he regards a capstan. But I don't," he went on, swiveling back. "I was cursed with an appreciation for them all. I fancy everything in a skirt, a curve of hip, or the slope of a neck." His fingers danced, tracing those very shapes on her. "I see beauty in them all and I want them all."

His arm dropped. The walnut-colored eyes went liquid and glowing. "Or rather, I did, until I met you."

He laughed a bit self-consciously and shook his head. "Now, I admire a woman like one might admire a ship: appreciate the lines, speculate on how she might handle on a bolun and realize, whatever her merits, I already have the best."

Cate ducked her head and fiddled with the apron's edge. "All those things you said this morning —" she began tentatively.

Nathan bent, thrusting his face into her line of sight. "I meant every word." He angled his head. "Do you doubt me word?"

Cate kicked at the dirt, wanting to put every shred of faith in him, and yet fearful of being led down the proverbial path.

He thrust his face closer yet, the bell in his mustache flashing. "Tell me what I need to do for you to believe me? What pledge, oath, or vow do I need to make? What tithe, tax or penance do I need to pay?" he said, low and urgent. "Hell, if it would answer, I'd throw you down on this table and take you before all. Hell and furies!"

He wanted to hit, slam, pound, beat, bellow and fume. In impotent fury, a thought occurred, and he grabbed her by the arm and dragged her away from the tents confines and out onto the thoroughfare, obliging several to dodge out of the way.

"Attention! Attention everyone!" he shouted, with a voice geared to reach a topmast.

Nathan waited the fraction of a moment, then took Cate into his arms and kissed her. It was a most provocative, back-bending, and yes, so very, very possessive one. Arms still about her he drew back, leaving her a little stunned and a lot breathless.

"Any questions?" he directed to the onlookers.

In the confused silence, his commanding voice compelled several to bob their heads.

"Capital!"

He bore her with a look and lowered his voice to only her benefit. "Any questions?"

Stricken mute, Cate could only shake her head.

His hands moved to her shoulders and shook her in gentle supplication. "You. Only you." apart.

Struck mute, Cate gaped. The sound of footsteps racing toward them broke them apart.

Ben drew up, touching his forehead with his knuckle. "Mr. Pryce's compliments and duty, sir," he gasped, bending to brace his hands on his knees. "He begs you might join him straightaway."

"Now?"

Ben painfully swallowed several times. "He says you *really* need to hear this."

"Go," Cate urged at Nathan's indecision. "Pryce wouldn't have sent, if it wasn't important."

Nathan hesitated, and then, decision made, scanned the surrounding faces. "You, you and you!" he shouted to three Morgansers. He jabbed a thumb over his shoulder. "On your life, watch her!"

Cate watched Nathan following Ben until a combination of islanders and forest blocked her view, all the while wishing with mild vehemence Pryce to eternal and ever – lasting fires of hell.

Oh, for a little peace, for a little time unhindered, undemanded.

She returned to the sickbay, her watchdogs close behind.

Work kept her hands and body occupied, but her mind was elsewhere, half an eye slipping off in the direction Nathan had disappeared. The longer he was gone, the more her curiosity grew at what would have brought Pryce to such insistence? She mentally eliminated the possibilities, and then ran through them again, lest she overlooked some small detail. There were no gunshots, no shouts of alarm, so no attack or violence. No black smoke rolled, so nothing was on fire. No one scurried about, which meant whatever it was, the interest was confined to Nathan.

"Probably a broken futtock on the bowsprit."

She looked down into the confused face of the patient she was bent over and realized she had unwittingly spoken aloud.

"No, m'um, ain't no futtocks there," he said, looking at her as if she were devil - possessed.

Her frustration found a vent in her irritation with those who should have been watching her. Obviously Nathan should have shown greater wisdom and appointed ones not so freshly arrived. Their attentions were running in other directions, namely female company and gossip.

"Like Captain, like crew," she sighed to the basin she carried.

Time passed, Cate in perpetual motion from one patient to the next. By whatever fluke of circumstance or Nature, Nathan's absence was marked by the visitors thinning. The sickbay quieted and Cate worked against the low buzz of conversation. The laborious groans from behind the curtain reached a crescendo and then replaced by the mewling cries of an infant. Celia stepped out shortly to announce "A girl."

The bell rang; Cate's watch ended, or rather should have.

Celia stopped Cate toting yet another bucket of water, her sharp eye scanning the sickbay. "Where is Polly?"

"Not here," Cate said mildly. Relief was rarely timely in coming, Polly being one of the more infamous.

Celia plucked the bucket from Cate's hand and said "Go."

"But—"

"You have done more than you must; the others can manage until she deigns to arrive." Celia's tone made Cate glad she wasn't Polly.

"Go," Celia insisted, gently prodding. "You have a man what needs attending." A lewd wink made her meaning clear.

"Well, as to that..." Cate muttered to herself. The aforementioned "man" was nowhere to be seen and precious little in the way of "attending" could be done, even if he were.

There was also the not so small matter of dealing with her own frustrations. There was only one thing which would answer: more work, good, honest physical labor, working up a sweat, while at the same time—and much more importantly—giving her something to think about other than the "attending" of said "man," or better said, not "attending." Working in the sickbay had helped marginally, but she was still edgy and ready to fly off the handle. No one there neither deserved, nor needed her shrieking like a fish hag.

Cate signaled her pair of watch dogs, now lounging at the far side of the tent with their female companions. She signaled again and then considered making the trek across.

"No, better yet, gentlemen, you can explain to your captain as to my whereabouts," she huffed under her breath.

With one last lingering glance in the direction Nathan

had disappeared, Cate veered up the path leading to the herb gardens.

Her first day on the island — a lifetime ago, or so it seemed — she had passed the extensive plots. Like any farm or estate, the herb gardens were the island's culinary and health center, their importance indicated by the wattled borders, a solid protection against wind, predators and intruders of the trampling or munching variety. On a normal day, they would have been a bevy of activity. But in these non-normal times; they were deserted.

Cate's step slowed at the gate and she groaned aloud. Someone — probably the same ones who raided the island — had plundered it, overturning towers and trellises, snapping off stakes, bending, breaking and uprooting plants. Mouthing several of Nathan's favorite oaths, she snatched a hat from a post and set to work. She righted what she could, heeled in the uprooted, setting aside what appeared mortal, in the hopes some of it might be salvaged or preserved.

In the process of setting things to rights, she came upon the rows of garlic. The extend of the crop were a testimonial to its importance to the island, and it had been trampled to the point of near ruin. the brown-and-curled tops were indications of its readiness for harvest. It was a job more befitting for two, but wasn't impossible alone. It needed to be done.

Fetching a trug and fork, Cate began: loosening the ground with a fork, pulling the bulbs free, shaking the dirt free before tossing them in. She reveled in the smell of disturbed earth, dark from decades of amending, and drying greens, the sharp, pungency of garlic cutting through it all.

It was what she needed: a purpose, her hands in the dirt. She wasn't sorry to be alone. The solitude and peace which came with it was agreeable, allowing her to work out some of her frustrations without a lot of prying eyes. She paused, now and again, at being hailed by passing Morgansers, her spirits buoyed further by now being among friends, feeling like she actually belonged.

An increasing tumult on the path broke her thoughts, running and shouting, but dismissed it to youths running messages or playing. Her suspicions were confirmed when two appeared at the wall, called out, and then scurried off when she turned around. Probably giggling at the success of their prank, the little black-hearted villains.

She smiled faintly, recalling her and her brothers doing much the same. "And catching hell when we were caught," she told a bulb.

Only a few more bulbs had been added to the harvested pile,

when Cate became aware of a noise, annoying, like an insect buzzing about her head, growing louder at each pass.

"Damnation and seize my soul to bloody hell, there you are!"

She jerked upright and spun around to find Nathan at the gate, fists on his hips, glaring from the shadow of his hat brim.

"There you are, hiding, skulking about in the weeds!" Pushing through the gate, he churned toward her.

"I wasn't skulking. You disappeared."

"Business, a man who knew a man, who knew..." A spiraling upward motion finished the thought.

"I came to— Don't step there! That's fresh seed."

Nathan stopped in mid-step, pivoted and tiptoed toward her as one might through a cow byre. When near enough, he thrust a finger in her face, obliging her to duck to avoid an eye being poked. "*Never* alone."

"Posh! I've come here several times."

Or, I might have been, she amended to herself, *had the occasion presented itself.*

It was only a small white lie and quite innocent.

"Alone!" Nathan piped, incredulous. "Dammit to bloody hell, those men were supposed to be watching you."

"They had more important—"

"*Nothing* is more important," he intoned like the word coming down from the Mount.

"Very well, then." Cate gestured to a bench in a nearby arbor. "You can sit in the shade at your leisure, like Lord Kiss-My-Royal-Ring, if you wish, watching me sweat. *Or* you can, as you love to say, bear a hand."

At seeing his puzzlement, she demonstrated by stabbing the fork into the ground, prying with one hand, while seizing the curled top with the other.

Nathan eyed her coldly. "You're not a field hand."

Cate looked away, wondering what he might have said seeing her harvest melons a few days since.

"I'm sure the barn needs mucking out," he glowered.

"Don't tempt me," she said narrowly, shaking the bulb and tossing it in the trug. "I prefer this over laundry, or making bread, or a score of other noxious chores around here. If everyone does what they enjoy, it's none so much like labor."

Nathan cocked a brow, obviously finding grievous fault in that logic and possessing the wisdom not to say so.

"Would you have me sit about, putting on airs, now that you're here? They've reason enough to think ill of me. I shouldn't wish to give them more."

As much as he would have liked, Nathan couldn't disagree.

Cate held up the fork. "Would you prefer to dig or pull?"

"This is woman's work."

It was the first time she had ever heard him disparage or demean women — in that respect, at any rate — and she bristled.

"The garlic is for dressings and poultices. It's kept a good many of you men alive. Get on the end of this," she said, shoving the fork at him, "and I'll ask you in a bit if it still feels like 'woman's work.'"

Nathan took the implement between two fingers. Holding it as if it were a live snake, he glared at the tines. "Wood? Why not metal? T'would be easier."

"And it would also be easier to pierce or damage the bulbs. Now, hush and dig." She knelt, feeling the soil for the edges of the next bulb.

"Regular quartermaster, aren't you? They do say power corrupts."

Cate sat back on her heels and fixed an eye at him.

"Mum tried looks like that on me. Never worked," Nathan observed. In spite of that claim, he leaned more industriously into the task.

Cate half-expected Nathan to carp and lag but, much to her surprise, he leaned into the work as he did anything else: pragmatic matter-of-factness. Life at sea, like farming, was dependent upon hard labor, more so for sailors, for they had no beasts-of-burden, only their two hands. They fell readily into working as a team: Nathan loosening the soil, Cate pulling the plants, him occasionally lending a hand with the more deeply-rooted. Their conversation was reduced to the random grunt of effort or shriek of surprise at one giving way far more easily than expected, sending her stumbling backwards.

The labor had answered well, striking Cate's earlier frustrations from her mind. But now, they were back, their very source bumping her elbow, his leg brushing her skirts. Nathan was at her side, and yet still he was as unreachable, as if he were on the moons of Jupiter. In many ways, they were back to the awkwardness of her first months aboard: living as brother and sister. Except, that didn't fit either. She sought to distract herself by trying to sort out what to call this odd situation, of having everything, and yet nothing.

There was no denying that lying with him had been more than just a joining of bodies. It had brought them together in a way no other act might.

Just to prove the point, Cate sat back on her heels, closed her eyes and reached out with her mind. On the opposite side of the row, she felt — yes, not heard but felt — Nathan stop and opened her eyes to find him looking at her, the corner of his mouth crooked up. He hooked two of her fingers with two of his own and lightly kissed the grimy knuckles.

"I'm here, Kittie," he said quietly. "I'm here."

"If this is for poultices and such, isn't it more in Celia's line?" Nathan asked, a bit further down the row.

Cate shrugged. "I should imagine she oversees all this. I'm helping, so she might attend more important things."

"Like love philtres for Thomas' escapades?" he scoffed.

"Philtres would be a bit after the fact now," she said under her breath, and then asked louder "When was the last time you and Thomas were here together?"

Leaning on the fork handle, Nathan looked off, considering. "Years. T'was mebbe once or twice that we were here together a'tall."

Cate hesitated. Gossip-mongering wasn't her way, but curiosity was overpowering. "Did you know Thomas and she were... involved?"

Nathan jerked, startled. "Involved! Her?!" One lip curled, whether in shock or disgust, she couldn't tell. "By who's account?"

"Thomas."

Stabbing the tines into the ground, Nathan gave a low whistle. "Well, gut me for a preacher! Thomas always has had more ballocks than brains, but—" He chuckled in amazement. "I never had the nerve to try her. Didn't fancy anyone else was fool enough, either. One false step and she'd shrivel your cock."

Not unlike what you suffer right now, Cate mused dryly.

Nathan cut her a severe look. "You know this for a fact?"

Cate emphatically nodded. "I saw them together, when they thought no one was looking. It was very... tender." Her throat tightened at the recollection; such purity of emotion between two people was always touching.

"Tender." Nathan rolled the word in his mouth, then shrugged. "Well, I suppose 'tis possible for Thomas to have a side I've never seen."

"I have." Lugging the small trug to dump the contents into a barrow at the end of the row, she turned back into Nathan's glare and realized her mistake.

"Indeed?" he asked, one hand on his hip.

"Yes." Offhanded and forward would be her only salvation now. "After our fight— which *you* started—and I was left to believe I had no choice but to make a life with him."

She inwardly groaned. This was the last conversation she wished to be having at this point. "Thomas is sweet, very sweet, and thoughtful and understanding, in a brotherly sort of way," she was quick to qualify.

Under Nathan's fixed stare, Cate swiped the hair back from her face. She wriggled against her stays. She sorely missed her old ones, which had been softer and more suited to work. These had a chamois edging, but they still chafed her armpits and shoulder blades. The tops of her hips would be raw by the end of the day, in spite of the layers of skirt and shift.

"This garlic isn't going to dig itself," she prompted at his staring.

Nathan heeled the fork into the ground, clearly distracted.

"Mark me, darling, I'm not arguing," he began some moments later. "You women seem to have a second sense where these matters are concerned, but the face across the table from me this morning was categorically not one of a man satisfied."

"I think he has—" Cate stopped short. Speculating on what Thomas had been doing in his spare hours would be carrying tales of the worst sort. She had her suspicions, but—

"Oh, aye," Nathan said, with a casual wave, still off on his own hobby horse. "He's been bedded; that's clear enough. But he's the look of a man who knows what he wants and is *not* getting it. And I would be a fair authority on that," he added, with a rueful roll of his eyes.

"There's a fair reason for that," Cate sighed and for the next bit recounted what Thomas had told her.

"At least, that's how Thomas told it," she finished. "I've not pressed Celia." A *humph!* from Nathan conceded her wisdom on that point.

"I'd heard rumblings. I couldn't make heads, nor tails out of it. Just figured it was just Thomas doing what Thomas does. What?" he demanded at Cate's laugh.

"I've heard him say much the same about you," she said, still fizzing.

Nathan fell quiet for some while, only the rasp of his breathing and the sound of his boot driving the tines into the ground between them. The trug filled to overflowing, he lugged it to the end of the row, dumped it and returned.

"He fancies you, you know," Nathan said conversationally, as he set the basket at her feet.

He stood idly chewing a blister on his palm, but his eyes were alert on her over the edge of his hand. He was dangling bait on which she had no intention of biting. She had been through this with him, many and many a time. Whatever hole she might have stumbled into, explanation would only dig it deeper.

Attack was often the best defense and so she demanded "Then why did you send me off with him?"

Lowering his hand, Nathan regarded her as if she were dim. "Because I had no choice."

Cate opened her mouth to respond, but the ground suddenly tilted under her feet.

Nathan hooked an arm about her waist. "You're pale as a tops'l. Get over here, out of the sun and sit. Sit!"

Suddenly lacking the wherewithal to resist, Cate allowed herself to be propelled to the bench and the shade of its arbor. Nathan snatched the hat from her head, crouched before her and fanned, whilst alternately patting her cheeks and wrists. She closed her eyes, waiting for her head to clear. Finding that to be a mistake, she opened them to find two faces before her. They blurred and then became one, dark with worry.

"You there! Aye, you!" Nathan bellowed in his captain's voice to a lad on the path.

"Light along some water for the lady. Bear a hand, there. Bear a hand, I say! Mumping, villainous laggard," he rumbled under his breath as he turned back.

Still fanning and patting, Nathan peered intently at her. "Still not over it, are you?"

There was little question as to what "it" was: their resurrection, rising from the dead.

"It still hits me at the oddest moments," she said unsteadily. Given the present evidence, she, in all good consciousness, could not deny it.

Cate lifted her face into the stirring air and attempted to breathe deeply. Cursing himself for having been so thoughtless, Nathan moved behind her and jerked her laces loose, allowing her to draw in a couple reviving draughts. Kneeling before her once more, he snatched up the hat and resumed fanning.

"Aye, t'was the same for me, worse perhaps," he added as an afterthought.

She nodded feebly, recalling a story Pryce had told her, of finding Nathan during what had to have been his recovery from his first rise from the grave: a ghost of himself, drunk, ill, half-starved, barely recognizable, "a man who couldn't die who had lost all will to live." Clearly, the second time was far easier, she thought, cutting a speculative eye at him.

Cate shuddered at the thought of enduring it all again. She envied Nathan, not only for having survived this twice, but for his will and ability to prevail.

The water arrived, the bearer, red-faced, huffing and much berated for his slowness. Cate drank from the dipper, while Nathan whipped off his headscarf, wet it and swabbed her face, neck and wrists.

"I'm sorry for swooning—" She felt thoroughly foolish.

Nathan made an irritated noise. "This isn't some trifling case of the vapors! You've had a helluva shock. You can't go ramming about like a bee in a bottle. You persist at this recklessness and you risk a relapse."

Cate seized the dipper and took another drink at that disquieting thought. "You expect me to just lounge about?"

Nathan swiped the sweat from the side of his face and flicked it from his fingers. "The devil seize and burn me, I sent you here so you might sit at your ease, do a bit of sewing, chat, gossip, or whatever in the hell women do when you are together."

"You mean, besides stab each other in the back?" she asked, smiling weakly.

Nathan angled his head, conceding. "I fancied you might make some friends," he said, calmer.

Cate choked a bitter laugh. "Small chance o' that! They laughed in my face literally when I represented you were coming for me."

He nudged her leg and waggled his brows. "Proved them wrong, however, didn't I?"

Nathan took a drink from the dipper, swished it in his mouth and spat. "As we approached this godforsaken lump o' land, I could see you'd had a fight, could see the destruction, and knew what it had to have been like here."

Arms on his knees, he stared down at the ground between his legs. "I came ashore fit to vomit with fear, not knowing which was going to be worse: finding you dead, or cowering in the corner, gone mad from the chaos."

He looked up, allowing her to see once more his anguish. "Me gut was in worse knots with the fear you'd found your place and wished to stay."

"Small chance of that," she sputtered.

He swiped his mouth on the back of his hand. "But, if you had found it, then I meant to build you a fine place, up on the hill there, where you might look down over them all."

Nathan took another drink with the air of wishing it were something stronger. He wanted to look away, but forced himself to meet her gaze. He smiled, tight but determined. "I meant for you to have it all, darling. The world as your oyster, and your sword shall open it," he declared with an expansive sweep of his arm.

"Shakespeare, again?"

Fondling the dipper, Nathan shrugged. "Aye, I had a captain what was an enthusiast and obliged me to read to him many a night."

Cate stared down at the crown of his bent head.

"That is quite the... aim," she said, stricken breathless. Nathan had a flair for the grandiose, but his intentions had been presented in honesty of the purest and most sincere sort. A home: it was her single-most hope and her single-most horror, for it could only mean one thing.

Her chest tightened to the point she could barely squeeze out "Are you leaving me... here...?"

"Suffering saints on a cross!" he cried, rearing back. "Where the bloody hell did you get that notion?"

"Well, people talk, comments, looks," she offered in her own defense. "Sometimes it's what they don't say which speaks the loudest, you for one."

Nathan looked off, distant in thought. She waited, her stomach in the proximity of her throat as the moments ticked past.

"When I held you in me arms, I wondered how the bloody hell I was ever going to bring meself to do so. But I would see you happy n' safe. God help me, for that I would, if it meant tearing me own heart out in the bargain, but I'd do it." Looking down between his feet, his shoulders wormed inside his shirt. "If it was your wish, I would... somehow."

"I can't deny I would love a place to call my own, but I'd rather be with you." Cate bit her lip at how weak and desperate that sounded. She ventured a hand on his shoulder until he looked up again. "I mean that, honestly."

Nathan's hand closed over hers and briefly squeezed. "'Tis easy to say now, luv, but 'tis not so much about what you want, but who might provide it: me or someone..." He audibly swallowed. "Else?"

He pointedly fixed on the silver band she wore. She curled her fingers and buried her hand in the folds of her skirt.

"You mean Brian?" Of course, he did. The hunch of his shoulders and the significance of "else" could only mean one person, one whose name he could barely bring himself to utter.

Cate stared, wondering what path he meant to lead her down?

Nathan, the Opaque, gazed back.

"Brian is dead," she said evenly.

Nathan flung the dipper into the bucket with a clatter. "I

thought perhaps you'd had word of him," he said, ignoring her point *again*!

"Why would you think that?" Now she was the one thoroughly befuddled.

He cut a look from the corner of his eye and mumbled "Nothing" into his chest. Cate leaned to bring her face into his line of sight. "I. Have. Not."

Nathan blew out a long-held breath, one of neither relief nor hearing the answer he had hoped for. The hail of a passing group on the path drew his attention. Still crouched, he waved and called back. His brow arched disapprovingly at seeing Cate pick bits of dried garlic leaf from her skirt. His eye pointedly traveled down to the grimed hem.

"I told you I had work to do," she said, a fine silt falling as she shook it out.

"I should have had Billings and his mates rig you some purser's slops, if you intend to slave about like this."

Cate canted her head toward the sounds of industry from all around. "I'm sure the sailmaker is too busy with far more important things."

She stretched her stiff back, wondering if a chore existed which could be performed upright?

"Then, back to the sickbay, is it?" Nathan announced hopefully.

"No." The thought of that place just then, with the press of people, looking and listening, made her claustrophobic and slightly giddy once more. Over his shoulder, she could see the remaining garlic and the tools lying where they had been dropped. "There's not much more to go. Might we finish?"

Clamping his lower lip between his teeth, he slowly shook his head. "God help me, I can't tell you 'no.'"

"Better that you don't try," she said softly.

Nathan dashed some water in his face, re-secured the scarf about his head and stood, putting out his hand.

"I'm your man."

"Finished?" Nathan asked, dusting his hands on his breeches when they reached the row's end. "All squared away by the lifts and braces?"

"Digging, yes. But these need to be braided and hung before they spoil." Cate regretted dashing his hopes, but their efforts would all be wasted if they didn't press on. In the heat and humidity, mold and rot wouldn't take long to set in.

His smile fell as he tried to sort out if she were trying him on.

"Very well," he declared, seeing she wasn't. Pitching hat and weapons atop their harvest, he clapped onto the barrow handles and followed.

More opened than closed, the drying shed had a high roof against rain and sun, and latticed walls for the flow of air. Inside, the checkered light through those lattices illuminated worktables and drying racks. The air in there was dense with smells, not of earth but of greenery, as if an entire garden had been condensed into that one small space. Most of the horizontal surfaces were covered with berries, pods or flower heads spread out on cheesecloth screens. In the dim, the gay yellow and orange of pot marigold heads dotted the tables like patches of sun, the chamomile as pale as clouds scattered among them. Other baskets were filled with roots, looking like petrifying fingers curling up over the edges.

Cate found space to work and demonstrated what was to be done—gathering the bulbs in bundles of three, braiding the tops, hanging them on a rack to dry—Nathan semi - patiently observing. With the barrow between them, they worked in companionable quiet, nothing more than the rustle of garlic leaves and whir of the breeze through the lattice.

The stirring air touched the residual sweat trailing down Cate's back. After the strenuous work of the sickbay and digging, this almost seemed like languishing about. The repetition of weaving—left over right, right over left—doing the same thing until one could do it with their eyes closed, had a calming effect. Several times, Cate's attention strayed to Nathan's, the birds tattooed on his knuckles seeming to flit about the dried leaves. She admired the elegant twist of his body as he turned to hang the bunches on a rack...

Heaven help her, she wanted him.

There was a negative in working next to him, having him so near: it made the yearning all the worse. The ache wasn't confined to her womb. Her entire being was consumed with the need to touch him, to lie with him, to have him inside her, hard and deep. A private argument raged: whatever discomfort she felt, he was quite probably suffering far worse. The carnal part of her, however, didn't care. It knew what it wanted, and it kicked and screamed like a recalcitrant child for it.

At some point, she had inadvertently stopped what she was doing. As Nathan turned back to the table, his eye sharpened with worry that she might be about to swoon again. She set back to work as proof of her well-being.

"You're good at this," she said, flushing.

Nathan shrugged as he plucked three plants more from the barrow. "None so bad as picking oakum."

She smiled, remembering her first days aboard doing that very thing. At the end of the day, she'd been sticky with pitch from her nose to her toes, and so covered in hemp fibers she looked like a manged monkey. To that day, she still suspected the men of having pulled a bit of a prank: luring her into one of the dirtiest and most reviled jobs aboard.

"'Tis no different than knotting and splicing, only a bit more messy." He frowned at the pile of brown crumbles. "I've been doing that since I was old enough to know left from right. I can remember me father teaching me one or another whilst he was there... the few times," he qualified, his frown deepening.

He looked down at the bracelet on his wrist. "Mum tried to do the same, but hers were more complicated and none so practical for a lad whose only wish was to tie up his annoying sister."

"What a precocious child you must have been."

He bumped her with his shoulder. "And you were the paragon of idyllic daughterhood?" he asked, teasing.

"Well, I couldn't tie up my brothers—they were all bigger than me, even the youngest—but they tied me to everything from a post to a mule. My mother vowed I'd be the death of her. Perhaps, I was," she added, sobering.

She shook away the thought. Nothing but the blue devils awaited down that path. "Father was a right ol' Tartar. He declared girls weren't to be suffered."

"I would be obliged to call your father out on that," Nathan said, judiciously. "The world t'would be a sorry place without them, women at any rate. Nothing but hairy faces and farting."

Nathan fell pensively quiet, the dappled light curving over his head and shoulders as he worked.

"Me father didn't teach me much," he began deliberately. "But he did instill a grand appreciation for women. The species would die out, else." He turned, the light catching a smile known to charm the sweet off honey.

So many questions arose. Nathan rarely spoke of his father and rarely in a kindly way. It would seem abandonment and resentment were doomed to be bedfellows. And how could it not? Her father had committed his own version of abandonment: sending her off within months of her mother's passing. Regardless of who did the leaving, an absent father was still an absent father.

"Yours sounds like someone I would like to meet," she said, earnestly.

"So would I," he announced coldly. "I've many a bone to pick with that sodding ol' blighter, but I'd have to reach into his grave to do it."

"He's dead?" Nathan had spoken of the man so rarely, she'd lost track.

"If I've not heard of Beecher in an age, then it has been two ages since I heard of him." Jaw working, Nathan resolutely shook his head. "Odds are he's dead and rotting in the Seven Circles of Hell, if there's any justice."

Their conversation was interrupted by the sound of feet on the path running toward them. A boy skidded to a halt near the shed, emitted a cry of discovery, and shot in.

"Cap'n Blackthorne, Mistress Bella's compliments, sir," the boy gasped. Recalling himself, he made a jerking motion of ducking a bow, knuckling his forehead at the same time. "She begs me to say that she waits upon you."

Nathan waved a ladened fist toward Cate and asked mildly "Were your orders to not say as much, if the lady was present?"

Blenching, the lad's eyes rounded to approximately the size of one of the bulbs. His mouth moved, stricken speechless.

"Aye, well, t'will be our secret, lad," Nathan chuckled, clapping him on the shoulder. "I'll not feed you to the pigs on that account. My compliments to Mistress Bella. You can tell her that I am *not* at leisure, nor shall I be, for I am bespoke for the remainder of the day. She can whistle for her supper."

Under the flush of running, the boy went paler. "Anger her, sir, and we all suffer."

"Then gird your loins, lad. Batten the hatches, for thar be foul weather ahead," Nathan declared, dropping his voice to Pryce's West-Country rumble. "Now light along. Bear a hand there. There's a good lad."

A friendly shove set the boy on his way. He hesitated at the door, swallowed several retorts and then finally trudged off, stiff with dread.

Resuming to weave once more, Cate directed a questioning eye at Nathan.

He shrugged. "Nothing."

"Nathan, with all due respect, you aren't that good of a liar. No offense."

"None taken."

Her eye remained, fixed and expectant. After a time, Nathan glanced up to see if she was still looking.

She was.

"More relentless than the damned Inquisition," he sighed without malice. One shoulder moved inside his shirt. "Time has passed since I've landed, and I have not... eh, made my appearance."

A barely patient look bid him to explain.

"Surely, you've noticed by now that Bella rules this place like a cross-grained bosun, with a start in one hand and a cob in the other."

Cate nodded. That wasn't quite the words she would have used, but—typical Nathan—he wasn't far off the mark.

"Aye, she's tight-fisted with her good graces as a quartermaster with grog. One must pay homage or his life won't be worth living."

Even with the meaningful lilt in his voice, it took Cate a moment, Nathan nodding as the dawn came.

"Her bed?" she goggled.

"She's not interviewing for a chambermaid," he observed dryly.

Now Cate was the one stricken speechless. She fancied herself a fair judge of character, but that one she had missed. Thomas and, to some degree, Lesauvage's deference had been noticed, but she had chalked it up to Bella's position as island's leader. This smacked of domination.

"But how...? I mean, surely not *every* man..." she stammered. Multiplying the number of ships which had to have put in there, by the number of crew pouring ashore, the line at her door would have to stretch around the island!

"Captains," Nathan qualified. "A first mate or quartermaster, when all else fails and yes, I have, or *did*," Nathan informed a few moments later.

"I wasn't thinking—"

"Aye, but you were," came back evenly. "I could hear it from here. And no, as yon messenger proves, I have not *reported*, not this time, at any rate."

"Has Thomas...?"

"In the past, most definitely. Of recent?" His brow took a severe dip. "You tell me. One can only assume so; he's usually fairly willing to please on that score. The thought of Bella and that villainous first mate o' his—" He dramatically shuddered. "The woman has more fortitude than I ever credited."

Cate stared, trying to grasp it all. The image of Pryce being beckoned like a courtesan was difficult to conjure, Al-Nejem on bended knee impossible. It was, on the other hand, often amazing how quickly the most imposing could be reduced to hat-in-hand before a commanding woman.

"... Walking into her lair every time I came ashore," Nathan was saying. "It's not about the bedding, though I've never been one to dismiss it."

"No, never," Cate said, still dismayed.

"I'm as obliging as the next. There's always something to be gained in a performance." He smiled at that. "Only a blind man would call her a beauty but, bless her soul, she does know what a man is for!"

His emphatic gusto of that last bit jerked Cate back from her reverie. She mightn't be able to imagine the *Morganse* or *Lovely's* first mates paying tribute, but the image of Nathan doing so, lying abed, replete with copulation, came far too readily.

All the things you wished he would do now?

"Has she had a husband... ever?" she asked.

Nathan batted away a questing insect. "I believe so. She's alluded to one, at any rate. Broke her heart, he did. She's a hard woman, but not a cold one."

Cate regarded Nathan from the corner of her eye. He seemed remarkably understanding of the very person who had lead the clamor for his head just the day before.

"She's a heart o' gold—has to be, in order to run this place—but hard knocks have encased it in iron, not unlike a good many of us," Nathan added under his breath.

Cate nodded vaguely. The night before, around the fires, Al-Nejem had been nowhere to be seen, but Bella had been on Pryce's arm. Or, had it been the other way around?

"I don't fancy Pryce's attendance was entirely out of duty last night," Nathan observed, seeming to read her thoughts. "There was a spring in the old rumpot's step like he was one-and-twenty, and he was grinning like a cat what had just had its cream."

Cate nodded, distractedly. She too had observed the metamorphosis, the stern suddenly gone gay. The radical change of character seemed well beyond the powers of drink.

"But now, wait." Propping a hand on her hip, Cate closed one eye. "If all those times you came and reported like a good lad, then how did you suddenly become the pariah? When was the first time you didn't report?"

Nathan shrugged, the answer clear enough to him. "After the battle, when I was too knocked up to drag myself so far."

But not too much to find your way to Marthanna's bed, Cate thought unkindly.

"She beckoned later and even showed up at me bedside, but—" He gulped and said into his chest "It just didn't seem right then."

Cate bit her lip, fully aware of the unspoken there: going

to Bella's bed hadn't felt right because he was occupying Marthanna's by then. His conscious wouldn't allow him to do else. Once again, Nathan's strong sense of honor was both his credit and his undoing.

"And later," Cate prompted, straining to follow, "when you came back, meaning to do the right thing? Don't tell me, let me guess: you didn't report."

"Nay, I expected—" He caught himself, burying what he was going to say in a cough. "I expected a warmer reception elsewhere."

There was no mystery as to where that "elsewhere" laid: Marthanna's bed.

"That, m'lad," Cate said, shaking a finger at him, "was the nail in your coffin."

Contained fury made Cate's hands shake to the point she ripped the tops entirely off the bulbs she held. With a grunt of frustration, she flung them off into a corner.

"The scheming wench threw you to the lions," Cate seethed, clutching the edge of the table. Slamming her fist, she set to pacing in the small space between the table and rack. "She's the authority; everyone jumps at the snap of her fingers. No one dares argue with her. And, when all hell broke loose with Marthanna, one word, one nod of the head, and she could have made you being a two-faced lout go away. But she didn't."

"There might have been something, a lot to that," he said, thinking back. "There was such a grand moil, it was difficult to say who or what stoked the fires."

Somewhat calmer, Cate snatched up more bulbs, making a conscious effort to be more careful. "Believe me, if it hadn't been for Marthanna, Bella would have found something else," she fumed. "She's made you the whipping boy for everything since. Creswicke and the Company attacking, for one."

"I wasn't entirely without blame there."

"No, no she fanned those fires, too, and quite handily diverted the heat from herself," Cate said between her teeth.

It wasn't difficult for her to imagine the scene after the Company's first attack. Hell, she'd seen it after the most recent one: grieving, scared, and hurt, the islanders in dire need of someone to blame. It was the kind of anger and frustration which could easily turn the islanders on each other. Bella had provided them with a scapegoat: Nathan.

Bella, the manipulator.

Bella, the deflector.

Bella, the innocent bystander, blameless and feckless.

Ugh! And she had thought pirates to be treacherous! From all appearances, they learned it from their wives.

Cate shook her head in amazement again. It was nowhere near the Eden of her first impressions. Rarely had she been so naïve. This one caught her, snared her like the unsuspecting rabbit.

"Everyone seems happy, content. How has Bella managed to last so long?" she asked.

"Because, as any captain knows, the masses would rather dance with the devil they know than the one they don't. That simple principal, luv, is tyranny's greatest ally."

Nathan shook his head. "She might have allowed me ashore, but only so she might enjoy the results of her handiwork: putting you and Thomas in the newlywed shack," he explained. "One stab, three victims."

"What could Thomas have done to warrant that?"

The answer struck the moment she spoke: Celia.

"Must Bella have every man on the island?" Cate wondered aloud. "You should have seen her hanging on Lesauvage's arm." She couldn't help but wonder who that performance had been for?

"Not every," Nathan stipulated, "but she's not accustomed to being told 'no.' Hell hath no fury..." he sighed. "The power of a woman scorned, although why in the hell they always seem to scorn me is a wonder? What the hell did I do?"

Cate bumped him with her shoulder. "You were just being your charming self. Just don't get on my wrong side, m'lad."

"A lesson learned long, long, ago, darling," he said with a grin and a wink.

"She uses people like they were pawns." Cate threw down what she was doing and dusted her hands on her apron. "I've a mind to go—"

Nathan stopped her by the arm. "Now, now. A few days, and we can put this festering hole to our stern. We'll leave them to just stew in their own vitriolic juices."

Cate leaned away. "Since when are you the helpless lamb?"

"Since I realized there was only one way to survive this pit of vipers."

The grip on her arm didn't loosen until she yielded and set back to work.

Nathan started to do the same, but flung the bulbs down in frustration. "Aye, it galls me sore! It galls me even more to see you used," he growled through his teeth. "But I've a larger, vaster and more important goal: you!" he declared, jabbing a finger.

"And I worried that you meant to leave me here for good," Cate said. She could smile about it now... finally.

Nathan's mouth quirked. "As I said, darling, I did, briefly, so *very* briefly. My greatest fear was I'd find you happy and complacent. Or," he went on, an odd smile growing. "That you had deposed Bella and was running the place yourself."

Cate jerked at that. "Do you think she saw me as a threat?" There was no denying Bella's reception had been cool, to say the least.

Nathan chuckled wryly. "She sees everyone — man, woman or dog — as a rival."

A severe eye at the pile still awaiting urged Cate back to work. She did so, but concentration didn't come easily.

"So, if you don't — ?" she began.

"Answer her beck?" Nathan shrugged. "Given me current impairment, it is a curiosity. I'd be of little damned service."

Cate gaped, stunned yet again. "You think she knows?"

"Only a cod-headed fool would think else."

"She has spies?" Cate self-consciously glanced toward the door, half-expecting to see someone standing there.

"Everywhere. That little sniveling sneak of a charmaid — "

"Tabby?"

"Without a doubt has reported every move, every word. She's not just for m'lady's leisure," he added dryly.

Cate shook her head. It seemed all she could do of late. Several times, she had come close to reproving Nathan's treatment of the child. Thank heavens for a guardian angel stopping her!

"How much do you fancy she knows?" Cate asked, still stunned.

"How much might a chambermaid know of her lady's doings?"

For one responsible for everything from dressing to bathing to emptying pots, the answer was simple: everything.

"Bella will know tension abounds, that something is going on. As to the specifics, she'll have no notion," Nathan said with a smug complacency.

"And no explaining it, either," Cate sighed, the helplessness of the situation dragging at her once more.

"Perhaps it might work to our benefit," Nathan said, brightening. "Bella's demands mightn't be so... eh, demanding."

"Then, why did she send for you?"

"'Tis simple enough: she couldn't resist the opportunity to humble me, make me admit to what she already knows."

Cate bristled. "Will you... admit?"

Nathan's smile was a bright spot in the dim. "Not bloody

likely. Whatever the hell is going on in that treacherous mind, we'll know directly. Expulsion wouldn't be the worst, I can bloody well assure you of that."

"Will she... expel you?" Images of a rushing pack, of two hundred men making a hasty exit, flashed through her head.

Nathan considered briefly and shrugged. "I shouldn't mind being shut of this place." He stopped, his eyes settling on her. "I've got what I came for."

"I'm sorry, for... for everything, Nathan." There seemed to be no end to the misery he suffered on her account. Lord, what she wouldn't do for just a few long, peaceful hours of lying in his arms.

He jerked, round-eyed. "You apologize to me? 'Tis I who owe you the apology. 'Tis I who have cost you! I brought you into all of this, this hellish world out here. And I send you here, into this... this place! I allowed you to suffer unspeakable depredations at Creswicke's hands, and then I took you to your death, and you apologize to me?" he cried, stabbing a finger into his own chest.

"You gave me life, in so many different ways," she stammered.

Nathan seized her hand and fervently pressed it to his lips. "I've destroyed you, put you through unnameable hells, because I was too much the coward to let you be elsewhere."

He dropped her hand and paced. "I speak of seeing you safe," he choked. "But I've done nothing but drag you from one peril to the next."

Nathan turned, the light catching the wetness in his eyes. "I owe you so much, what a score of 'I'm sorry' couldn't serve."

Venturing closer, he took her hand again, this time kissing it with eloquent gentleness. He smiled, his mouth quivering, and said quietly "I'll sure as hell not hear anymore of yours."

Cate silently nodded, chastened, but by no means feeling rebuked. She darted a peck on his cheek. "Thank you, for doing this with me. It's not dignified work for a captain, but..."

Nathan stood back, his smile shifting to one of admiration. "You are in your glory, aren't you?"

"I am," she beamed. She could say that now, without reservation. "But only because you're beside me."

"Don't move. Just... stand there. Remain so very, *very* still." He drew a deep breath, like a man about to fling himself over a cliff.

Nathan inched forward, the eyes holding hers liquid with want. He stopped near enough to feel the heat of his body, his breath tickling her neck. Stiff, hands at his sides, his eyes traced her every feature with an intensity as tangible as fingers at her brow, temple and jaw. Cate stood equally still, fearful any move might cause him pain. Sweat sheened on the bridge of his nose, a bead of it collected in the hollow at the base of his throat. Her tongue moved against her teeth with the urge to flick it away, tasting his saltiness. All her will in the world couldn't stop a finger from moving, brushing his wrist. Eyes fixed on her mouth, Nathan leaned forward with infinitesimal care. Like antenna, his mustache sought her lips, guiding his mouth to hers to kiss her, tentative and chaste. Like a rope stretched taut between two poles, through those two fragile connections she felt the tremors of restraint coursing through him.

Nathan drew away with a muffled grunt. The corner of his mouth lifted in an attempted smile. "Well, it's something. Not enough for a starving man to live on, that's for bloody damned sure."

22: ATONEMENT, AND ITS UGLY SISTER, DUBIOUS

SITTING BY THE EVENING FIRE, Cate looked down at the drink in her fist. She was going to need a great deal more of that, if things didn't improve.

The day had gone well, or so she thought, she and Nathan working closely, coming closer in a number of ways.

She sat at the fires then, only because Nathan had wished it, or had represented as much, at any rate. Now, she wondered.

Nathan was drinking, heavily even by his standards. Drink usually rendered him even more abiding and genial, but not then. Still steady of step and speech, he was edgy and churlish, threatening ugly at any provocation. Those who knew him, gave him a wide berth. Those who didn't quickly learned the consequences of their ignorance and did the same.

The diminishing of his mood from in the gardens, where he had seemed relatively buoyant, hadn't been a precipitous tumble, but slow, sinking with the sun. Earlier in the day, he had been positively buoyant. Now, he sat or stood next to her, bristling like a taunted mastiff, especially whenever any male approached, growling and glaring, with looks fit to kill, when they merely walked past. Nothing said, nothing done, and yet here she sat next to a powder keg, dreading the inadvertent match.

Earlier in the evening, when Cate had been under the misguided impression they were at the fireside for enjoyment's sake, she had danced when asked by one man or another. Nathan had made no objection, but the cold reception awaiting upon her return brought her to decline any further offers. Sitting obediently at his side, however, didn't seem to placate him, either.

The bewilderment deepened when, amidst his truculence,

Nathan would seek her hand on the seat between them and squeeze it, not in affection as earlier, but more in the way of assuring himself she was there. After all his claims of caring and endearment made through the day, especially at the drying shed, it was a bewildering change. And yet, if there was anything she had learned these months of knowing Nathan, it was that around him "bewildered" was, if not a permanent state, then a regular companion.

Just ride it out, she muttered to herself.

The cause would make itself known. It always did, but only when Nathan was ready; any prodding would only cause him to batten down all the more.

She kept thinking back to earlier conversations, trying to fathom what might have been said, what might have precipitated this precipitous tumble. One name dominated all others: Bella.

So far, the island's matron had yet to make her appearance. Cate had sat at Court awaiting royalty with less trepidation.

"Have you seen her?" Cate asked, finally, looking about.

Nathan jerked from his brown study. "Eh? Who? Oh, umm... nay. Haven't seen Pryce either, for that matter," he added with significance. "The ol' tarry-breeks has always had an inordinate compulsion where orders are concerned, or anything which smacks of duty."

"Duty?"

"Duty to do exactly what he wished to do in the first place," Nathan finished with overt innocence. "I only planted a few... eh, notions. Pillow talk and all that," he added with a flutter of fingers.

Cate tried to picture Pryce in such an intimate scene.

She failed.

"Notions?" she echoed. "As in pleading your case?"

"*Our* case," Nathan qualified. "Whether you wish it or no, darling, we're in this together... aren't we?" he added with sudden caution.

Her fingers found his on the bench between them. "Of course, we are."

The briefest of pressure was returned, and he pulled away. He stood abruptly, claiming the need to relieve himself. "You'll be here when I return?"

"Why shouldn't I?" she stammered. Given his mood, she was sorely tempted to disappear. Only very frazzled guardian angels kept her in place.

Nathan's jaw worked, mulling an answer. Ultimately, he just strode away, casting frequent looks back, visually nailing her in place. Cate sighed, wondering if she should have bid him to pee on her shoes, marking her as his territory.

Perhaps it was just as well she hadn't. In his mood, he might have done it.

As if waiting for Nathan to leave, Thomas slipped in next to her. He leaned forward casually enough, elbows on his knees, and smiled, but one which seemed more for the benefit of those looking on.

"What the bloody hell is eating Nathan?" He swiveled his attention from the subject, now visible across the fire chatting, to an accusing glare at Cate. "He's scratchier than a whore when the fleet's out."

Cate buried her nose into her drink. "I wouldn't know."

"Have you seen Bella?" she asked, pointedly changing the subject.

"Nay, I spent the day aboard, mostly. On the rampage tonight, is she?" he asked warily.

Cate demonstrably shrugged. "I have no way of knowing."

Thomas stared, as if thinking she might be trying him on. A hail distracted him. A parting "Do something with him!" through clenched teeth, and he was gone.

The crowd thinned now and again, allowing her glimpses of Nathan, now in the firelight's margins. The surprise would have been if he hadn't been surrounded by women. If bewilderment was her constant companion, then women were his. St. Paddie's snakes were still coming out of the woodwork.

Rolling their eyes, laughing gaily, swaying their hips and leaning to display their cleavage were all so universal and unvarying, to watch them was almost comical... almost. The naïve might wish to give them the benefit of doubt, allowing that they were unaware of his demonstration in front of the sick bay. Experience, however, knew that gossip on the island possessed the same lightning qualities as on board.

It was spreading even then, Cate mused, seeing the heads bent together, with whispers and knowing looks. She lifted her cup in a toast, smiling into it as she drank. She had wiped all of their eyes, every doubting and skeptical one of the meddlesome Jezebels.

Nathan returned. Sitting next to Cate, he resumed his stare into the space before him, one heel tapping the ground, until a hollow formed, his fist flexing about his drink like he was wringing someone's neck.

The musicians at their fire went for a whet. Storytelling filled the lull. It was a pastime as common to sailors as grog, especially on the f'c'stle of an evening or, as just then, around the fires. As on the f'c'stle, it wasn't long before a story from Nathan was called for. Cate shifted uneasily. Given his current mood, there was no telling what might be forthcoming.

"Let Thomas tell it. He's the better liar," Nathan announced without looking up.

A cheer went up.

"Give us the sea witch," cried one in the crowd.

"No, the one about devil ghost of the *Princess Avilda*."

"No, give us Nathan!"

There was a cheer of enthusiastic agreement.

Aboard the *Constancy*, during her crossing from England, Cate had first encountered the tales of Captain Nathanael Blackthorne. Living with him in the isolation of a ship — a virtual island unto itself — she tended to forget that he was the stuff of legends.

Elbows on his knees, drink in his fist, the legend sat oblivious.

Thomas, now lounging in a high-backed chair across the fire, frowned, considering. He took a drink and swiped his mouth. "The *Morganse* was lying off Luzon. On the prowl Nathan was and neither man, woman, nor ship was safe. Finally, she came upon a fat merchant, flyin' a French flag. 'So, French we'll be,' calls Nathan, and we ran up the *fleur d' lis*. A couple o' warning shots and they struck."

Arm resting atop a bent knee, Thomas spoke loud enough to be heard over the merriment of the neighboring fires.

"The boarding planks weren't even set, when Nathan clapped onto a sheet and swung across, only to come face to face with muskets and the gun ports opening, set to blow the *Morganse* from the water. Come to find out, she was a letter of marque, sailing for the local *alcalde*. They slapped Nathan in irons and announced the *Morganse* his prize."

"Not bloody likely!" came from amid the crowd.

"As was me thinking," Nathan shouted back, his gaze still fixed on the ground at his feet.

"As he sought a parley of some sort," Thomas went on, hunching forward. "Nathan seized a boarding ax. Screaming like a banshee, those spineless Spaniards scramblin' for their lives, he cut the grappling lines. Before any of those scrubs could say 'Bob's yer uncle,' the *Morganse* hauled her wind. You all know what she's like on a bolun."

Murmurs of approval rumbled through the increasing crowd.

"By that night, Nathan was in a dungeon, set to be hung in the morning."

Cate pressed a hand to her stomach at the thought of Nathan

being caged, waiting to be hung. Obviously, he had escaped, but still the notion made her queasy.

"Nathan starts caterwauling, claiming he's Popish, and needs to make his confession, so he might avoid eternal hell and damnation. The guards, being Popish themselves, sent for a priest. The priest comes in. 'Forgive me, father, for I have sinned,' Nathan says, and starts listing all his mortal sins."

"They weren't enough o' mine; I had to resort to yours," Nathan said to the ground.

Cate felt the boards under her buttocks vibrate. She turned, thinking perhaps someone was leaning against the bench. No one was there. Feeling it again, she twisted back around. It was coming from Nathan, his heel tapping the ground faster, his knuckles white around his drink.

She cut an eye sideways, wondering why? Tension? Displeasure at Thomas' story? Fear? Bella?

Thomas waited for the laughter to die. "Aye, well, Nathan represents a confessional should be private, and the guards are sent away. Sometime later, the priest represents he's finished. The guards show concern at seein' Nathan layin' curled up in the corner in a blanket, but the priest bids them to just leave 'im lie. 'The wretched soul is exhausted.'"

"And?" asked an anxious voice.

"That weren't Nathan in the corner, and that weren't the priest strolling out the gate," Thomas shouted back.

A roar of laughter went up.

"There he was, free as a bird, when lo-and-behold, he hears someone calling 'Father! Father!' He turns to find the *alcalde* himself running after him in a red-faced passion. He claims his wife is having a spell and needs to see the priest directly. So, Nathan goes along, riding like a prince in a coach-and-four, the Governor next him. They reach the residence, and the *alcalde* himself escorts Nathan up the stairs and to his wife's chamber door. Then he excuses himself — "

"Sweating like a pig, he was — " Nathan said, dispassionately.

"Claiming his wife insisted on absolute privacy when with His Worship. Never being one to deny a lady's boudoir, Nathan goes in and finds her a-laying there naked as Eve, breathless for her amour," Thomas finished, dramatically clapping a hand over his heart.

"She's fit to scream, but then Ol' Nathan turned on his charms. She demands he either serve her, or she'll call the guards. Now, we all know that Nathan's not a man of discerning tastes, but — "

"She was the size of Salt-beef Peg and old enough to be her mother," Nathan interjected.

Under the ensuing laughter and ribald remarks, Nathan leaned to say "If a woman's so unhappy, she should speak her mind, don't you think?"

Cate started at realizing his last had been directed at her. She made to respond, but found none was expected for he had already turned his head.

"There's a frantic knock at the door: the *alcalde* himself, shouting that a scurrilous pirate has escaped and he fears for his wife's safety. He's posted guards at the door to protect her."

Shifting uneasily, Cate had to snicker, in spite of herself. Only Nathan would have such luck, if such a word could be used.

"I felt sorry for the witless lump," Nathan grumbled bitterly, so low Cate wasn't sure if it was meant for her ears. "No man deserves to be cuckolded, no matter how wretched, don't you think?" the last being directed at her, again.

"What—?"

Nathan lurching to his feet cut her off. "Need another drink." Snatching her cup from her hand, he stalked off leaving her to stare.

"Nathan starts sweet-talking," Thomas was saying. "Telling Madame Governor all those things a woman wishes to hear and about the newest rage in Paris: bondage."

The crowd hummed with approval; Cate squirmed. Living in London, she had heard of the new fad among those who could afford such things as leather straps, chains, and other specialty implements. She failed to understand the fascination. To her mind, there was nothing erotic in being bound and whipped.

"He tells her how much more titillating it would be if she were blindfolded, and her hands tied with her stockings. Being the adventuresome sort, she played along. The last stocking, however, is shoved into her mouth. He fills his pockets with her jewels and takes his leave, instructing the guards the governor's wife was deep in penitent contemplation and should be left to her prayers for the night."

Nathan returned amid the cheer that brought. He shoved Cate's drink at her, the contents sloshing out. Instead of sitting once more, however, he stood as if loathe to be next to her.

"How'd ye get back to the *Morganse*?" asked a nearby grizzled face.

Nathan jerked and replied dryly over his shoulder, "I found me loutish crew in the *cantina*, drunk as Dutchmen—"

"We'd come to pay honor at your hanging," Thomas countered, indignant.

"My honor wasn't between that whore's legs," Nathan insisted.

"Tis where we were sure to find you." Thomas shouted over the hoots and guffaws.

"I'd heard it was the mayor of Charles Town," called one from the crowd.

"I heard it was the governor of Malacca," shouted another.

"Then tell your own damn stories!" Thomas declared, with a good-natured wave of his hand.

"Is any of it true?" Cate asked, wondered if this might have been more of the pair's theatrics.

Distracted, Nathan glanced down at her and shrugged. "Some."

He started to take a drink, but then lowered it. "One has to wonder why Thomas chose that particular one to tell."

The remark dripped with significance. He was baiting her, but it was the prime opening to find out what the hell was gnawing at him. Casting aside all voices of caution, Cate drew a breath, but a lad popping up at Nathan's elbow cut her off.

"Mistress Bella's compliments, Cap'n—"

The rest of the message was lost as Cate and Nathan's heads whipped around. The island's mistress stood stern and straight near the crowd's margins, the strawberry-colored head almost golden in the fire's light.

Cate started to rise, but Nathan's hand on her shoulder kept her in place. "This next bit mightn't be fit for even your seasoned ears."

"Nathan, be—" she began in earnest worry.

"Shh!" he said quietly. He gave her shoulder an encouraging squeeze and allowed the most indulging smile of the evening. "She'll not slaughter me before all these witnesses."

Cate ruffled at being excluded, but then relented. This was between the two of them. She had nothing to offer, nothing which would be constructive, at any rate.

Putting his back to the crowd, Nathan privately winked, much to Cate's increasing bewilderment. He took a drink, more in the way of stalling than thirst, and then strolled away. She visually followed his route through the crowd, more circuitous than might have been necessary. Upon reaching Bella, he touched his hat in greeting. Cate scanned the faces in Bella's immediate company, and then broadened her search in ever-widening circles. Her heart sank at finding Pryce nowhere in sight. He would have been the equivocating voice in Bella's ear.

On the edge of her seat, in the most literal sense of the word, Cate watched, trying to read their faces, hoping to glean some notion of what was transpiring. It was difficult to make out much in the flickering light. Murder or exportation didn't seem Bella's intention. Neither did there seem to be harsh words. No butting of heads. Nathan was contrite, in an irritating sort of way: hands folded behind his back, head slightly canted, listening. His expression was carefully noncommittal, but the rigidity in his shoulders revealed much. The sight of Bella standing over him, dressing him down like a lad before a schoolmaster, made her furious. She was tired of him being used and manipulated—of both of them, and would say so!

Cate lurched to her feet, but was grabbed by the arm. She whirled around to find she was surrounded by three women: Hope, Polly and—shock of shocks—Marthanna.

"We've been watching you—" the latter hissed.

"Coveting our children—"

"Stirring against us—"

Cate whirled, first at one accusation, then the next as they were fired off.

"You've bewitched Nathan. You've sunk your claws into him and he's miserable."

"What the bloody hell do you care?" Cate shot back at Marthanna. "Yesterday, you were all wrangling for his head."

"No one deserves such misery."

"Putting on airs—" Hope sneered, her lip curled in disgust.

"Queening yourself about—"

Cate was grabbed by the shoulder, and then by the hair. She reflexively swung her fist, with a resulting meaty *smack*! A shocked shriek and they all tumbled to the ground. Kneeing, biting, and scratching, they rolled in a tangle of skirts. Cate elbowed one and drove a knee into another, fingers curled to claw the next. She'd had no sisters, but her brothers and their friends had taught her plenty. Her opponents had tied up their hair; Cate's was down and provided an easy handhold. Amid the fracas, she was dimly aware of a surrounding chaos of a gathering audience. Some called for them to stop, but most were cheering.

A deluge of water broke them apart; Cate taking it in the back, her opponents square in the face. Amid oaths and sputtering, the hand at her throat and fist in her hair fell away. An arm hooked her by the middle, and she was lifted up and away. Thomas' face blurred past as he reached into the swarm of skirts to help break up the fight.

Her temper not so readily doused, Cate bucked and kicked, shouting to be freed. A curse and "Avast. Belay that caterwauling!" Nathan growled.

Bella's face was thrust toward them, flushed with fury. Shouts and demands collided. Was someone crying?

Amid Nathan's thorough berating of both her and women in general, Cate was hauled away under one arm like a cumbersome sack of grain, being given another shake every few steps.

"Put me down! Let go of me! Damn you—!"

Another admonishing shake silenced Cate's cries but not her struggling. She wildly groped for a face, an arm, anything! She would have bitten him if a body part had come within range.

The turmoil faded and Nathan finally stopped. Cate's feet touched the ground, and she whirled around, fist balled. Nathan caught it in mid-air with infuriating.

"Damn you!" she cried. "Why did you stop me—? I was just about to—"

"Yes, I'm well aware of what you were 'about to...'" The corner of his mouth quirked.

"Did you have to throw water?" she demanded, squeezing it from her hair.

Breathing hard from exertion, Nathan laughed mirthlessly. "Me or anyone else was about to stick our hands into that fray. God's my life, you women are nasty fighters!"

"Mind, I've no complaints about you fighting. Lord knows you can hold your own!" he declared, with glowing admiration. "I only worry for you getting hurt: eyes gouged, nose bitten off, mouth torn..."

"Women don't do all that," she shot back, shaking out her skirts; she was sodden to the skin and her stays were gouging her sides.

"On that, I beg to differ! I'd rather reach into a pair of wharf curs going at it. 'Tis far less likely o' getting bitten or dragged into it yourself," he added, with a dramatic shudder.

"Saw it happen once," he said, now checking her over for the aforementioned injury. "T'was not enough o' the poor unsuspecting soul left to seize up into his hammock and send over the side."

Cate considered the story a gross exaggeration. She swiped the sweat from her face with her arm. "Why do men have such a fascination and horror of women fighting?"

He shrugged. "It's sort of like seeing an abiding lapdog suddenly tear a rat apart. It makes us realize that there, but for the grace o' the gods, we might go next!"

"Never punch a woman wearing stays," she said, sucking on her torn knuckles. "It's like hitting a board."

"I'll take that under advisement," he said, almost losing the fight not to smile.

Nathan tipped her face up into the moonlight and squinted at her.

"Ouch!" she cried, trying to dodge his probing.

"You'll not have a black eye, I don't think."

"I don't even remember being hit." Truth be told, she didn't remember a lot of it.

Once assured she wasn't seriously injured, Nathan stood back, crossing his arms. "Dare I ask how it started?"

"They started it," she said, rubbing a sore spot at the back of her head. At least, she thought as much. The whole thing happened so fast. Had he countered her conjecture, she would have been in no position to argue.

"I daresay," he said, unconvinced.

"They started firing off all these ridiculous things about... about—" Cate said around the split knuckle she was sucking on. "They wished me to leave you be. They were accusing me of coveting their children and bewitching you—"

Nathan's wry snort cut her short. "Aye, Bella was giving me an earful of approximately the same thing when all hell broke loose. Telling me to control my woman. Marthanna said, as much earlier—" He grimaced, realizing he'd just said too much.

"This morning?" Cate goggled. It had to have been. So far as she knew, he hadn't spoken to the woman the rest of the day. "That manipulating bunch of—!"

"Have a care, darling, or they'll think you're me."

"I'm not a child-eater. I'm not some spell-casting hag—" She stopped short. It wasn't the first time she'd been accused of such things. Suspicions of that nature had followed her her entire life. It was those damned odd eyes and Judas-colored of hers which made it all the more infuriating. Her blood surged again, making her wish to go back and finish what she had started. Nathan's firm grasp stopped her.

"It was three against one," he declared. "The wise would have just walked away."

"Tuck my tail and run?"

"Nay, live to get your comeuppance one-by-one."

"I fancied my odds," Cate declared boldly. Finally, she relented and conceded his point. "I didn't have time to think."

"Nor the wherewithal for wisdom to prevail."

She jerked away from his grasp, glaring. "Since when are you the equivocating sage? How many times do you tuck your tail?"

"More than you think." The end of his mustache hooked up the corner of his mouth. "Bent over a gun, with your bum being lashed, gives one plenty of time to review the error in their ways."

It was difficult to imagine that being done to him, and yet, being all too familiar with Nathan's quickness of mind, exceeded only by his quickness of tongue — neither of which would have been tempered by youth — it was very easy to imagine. He quite probably spent a great deal of time having his bum tanned. Had she been a bit quicker in the mind category, she might have saved herself a few tannings.

"The only path a temper leads you down is one of destruction," Nathan concluded.

"You're sounding like my father."

"Then he was a wise man," he said, sounding even more like that very parent.

Cate flexed her aching hand and arm. "I've never seen you so abiding," she observed, sucking on her knuckles once more.

"Because I'm not in command," he said evenly. One brow arched. "The first thing you learn when you sign on anew is how to get along."

Nathan set to pacing. "I can bull-and-bellow when it's me own ship, me own crew, but this," he said with an all-encompassing wave, "is neither. If it were just me, I'd raise all sorts o' hell. But it's not. I've a crew." He stopped and fixed an eye on her. "And, so very much more significantly, I have you in the crossfire."

"I can hold my own."

"Yes, as you so adequately proved."

"I'd rather wound up with a black eye than having to watch you skulking about, scared speechless of them all," she said, with a similar wave. "It doesn't help that you've been acting — "

She stopped short, realizing passion — the one he had just warned her of — had just led her down destruction's path.

He drew up before her, hands on his hips. "Acting? I'm acting!"

"I've sat next to a powder keg with less worry." Full ahead was her only option now. "You've been prickly as an old bear worried — "

Upon reflection, he had been predisposed since Pryce had begged Nathan to wait upon him earlier that day.

A sharp wave cut her off. He opened his mouth, but then thought better. "'Twas nothing. Someone who knew someone, who knew someone."

That was the fourth "nothing" that day, and she pointed it out, adding "You're not that good of a liar."

"That's the second time you've said that today," he said, eyeing her coldly.

Several couples stumbled out onto the beach a short distance away. Another group was ambling up the shore, laughing and calling out.

"I'd rather not have this conversation amidst a lot of listening ears and nosey noses," Nathan announced.

This was serious, whatever "this" was. Cate was still staring when he took her by the arm—kind, clearly meaning to brook no argument—and steered her away. Cate observed him from the corner of her eye, alert for some clue as to what this was all about. Stern and silent, Nathan still wasn't as opaque as intended. He was tense—His fingers sometimes digging into her arm, until she complained—and no small wonder. They were both becoming as frazzled as old ropes, or hawses, or whatever those things were.

"No sickbay?" she asked, when finally realizing his destination was their hut.

"Nay. Too far and you're not that hurt, are you?"

An assuring shake of her head was his answer.

"And I wished this conversation private. There's been enough damned intrusion for one night."

Inside their hut, Nathan saw Cate seated on a locker and struck a light. Still sucking on a split knuckle, she watched semi-patiently as he fetched a basin and cloths. The surprise came with seeing him seize the bottle from by the bed and splash a bit of rum into the water.

"I've been watching you long enough to know what's to be done," he said simply.

He pulled a stool up before her and set the basin at his feet. The end of a cloth was ripped off, wetted and pressed to her bruised cheek. "Hold this for a bit. It should help keep the swelling and bruising down. Leeches would be best, but—"

They shuddered simultaneously.

Dipping the remainder of the cloth, Nathan set to washing Cate's face. She twitched when he touched a particularly sensitive spot, but he held her in place, gentle, yet unyielding. She wasn't his prisoner, but neither was she going anywhere, not until he had seen this through, whatever "this" was. A glance at water going more grey with grim than red with blood proved her suspicions. That lack of serious damage meant Nathan's attentions were merely a guise, a preamble to whatever lurked in those troubled depths.

His demeanor set her even more on edge, if that was at all

possible. His voice was low, his motions tender, but he was still the aforementioned powderkeg. She curled her toes on the dirt floor and resolved not to be the match. Stomp and rant was usually Nathan's style; this quiet was, well... disquieting.

Still, the silence was unbearable.

She fingered a spot at the back of her neck, feeling so very much like a bite.

"What did Bella say?" Cate finally asked. "You remember? A short time ago, when you were called over...? Before 'all hell broke loose' as you so eloquently put it...?"

"Eh? Oh, uhh..." Nathan's brows drew down. Smiling faintly, he opened his mouth, reconsidered, and then shrugged. "'Control me woman' was the general gist of it. You starting a fight only helped make her point."

"I didn't start it."

"We shan't be expelled, if that's what you're worried about," he went on. "Nay, Bella might be a user, but she's a pragmatic user. She needs me men to help rebuild, and she needs me stores with which to do it."

"Coldly pragmatic."

A smile flickered under his mustache. "Ice isn't in it. Mark me, she can be as kind and open-handed as St. Teresa herself. Did you see the smile on her face?" His own smile broadened. "T'would appear Pryce didn't disappoint."

Cate scowled. No, she'd missed that, somehow. She was beginning to question her own sanity and powers of observation.

"Very well," Cate began, determined not to be dismissed. "Since we know what is or isn't pleasing Bella, then perhaps we might move on to sorting out the same with regards to you?"

Nathan's face was necessarily inches from hers. His eye moved up to hers, one brow arched, and then returned to the task.

"Are you going to tell me who he is?" he asked conversationally. "Does the mistress desire —?"

They both jerked, startled by Tabby's appearance at the door.

Nathan was the quicker to recover. "Light along to the sickbay and fetch your mistress's blood box."

"I'll do," Cate insisted, when they were again alone.

"Nay, nay, these scratches will require salving."

Cate eyed Nathan. She knew what he was thinking. My, he was in a mood! Number XXXVII was in that box, a salve she had used on him a number of times. Application usually involved oaths and exclamations, for it stung like the dickens.

"'Who he is?'" Cate echoed, his last remark finally soaking

in. She sat back, following the question, heavy with inflection, to its ultimate end.

"You think I've been with another man? You think I've been playing the tart?" she asked in an incredulous croak.

Nathan's mouth twisted wryly as he dipped the cloth and squeezed it out. "The fair denizens of this moldering rock have been more than willing to keep me apprised of your activities in me absence. Four represent you've gone with this one or that. Two more represented you've gone with every man — bent or straight — on this island. Another claimed, with his own eyes, to have seen you suck the life from a man whilst he slept, and then rise in the form of an owl and fly away. Aye, aye, I dismissed it all out of hand," he added over her oaths and sputtering.

"So that demonstration in front of the sick bay this morning was for their benefit?" Cate winced at the rum-laced water touching torn skin.

Intent on cleansing a scratch on her chest, one shoulder moved. "A bit for them; a larger part was for you." His eyes flicked up, and then away. "Mostly, however, it was for the benefit of other 'interested parties,' as *you* so eloquently put it today."

"'Interested parties,'" she repeated dully. "That was just —"

A cut of his eyes stopped her short.

"What the bloody hell...? How much have you had to drink?"

Nathan snorted. "Not nearly enough, and quite probably going to require a great deal more, before this is seen through."

Had he been Catholic, she would have thought Nathan blessed himself before he began. He drew a deep breath and said carefully "You're different. I've been watching you — out there, in the sickbay, in here, everywhere — and you're different."

"Of course, I am," she shot back testily. "I was dead. You said yourself today that I'm not over it."

"Nay, nay, nay not that." Nathan batted the air as if the notion were an annoying insect. "This is since... since I sent you off with Thomas. At first I feared something had happened, something worse than... before, with His High-Arsedness..." he ended awkwardly.

"You're the one that sent me off with Thomas." "You think I don't know that!"

Vexation could have caused them both to be shouting by then. Instead, the conversation was being conducted in a growling hiss.

Nathan blew a long breath and went on determinedly. "I couldn't be in two places at once: I couldn't protect you and at the same time, be there for you when the yearning started."

Ah, yes. The driving need for warmth and touch of another human being of which he had told her about.

"You think I'd be so desperate as to—?"

"I know how desperate I was. Believe me, I know of which I speak," he said with an emphatic rap of his fingertip on her arm.

"As I said," he went on, composing himself somewhat. "I couldn't be there for you. Me only hope was that Thomas could."

Clamping his lower lip between his teeth, he shook his head. "God knows it would kill me to see you go with another man, but I knew at least he would be kind and wouldn't beat you."

"But, Thomas and I didn't—"

"I know that, or rather knew it the moment I laid eyes on him."

Cate sat back, now at a complete loss.

"Then, I thought perhaps you'd had word of Brian," Nathan went on. "But when you said not, I could see you were representing the truth. But there was still... someone..." The last came in a half-strangled rasp.

Cate stared, mouth agape, thinking she must have been hit harder than credited. She worked her jaw experimentally. It was sore, but nothing to account for being so addled.

Nathan took her speechlessness—How could she be else!—as a refusal to respond.

"Thomas didn't bed you, I can bloody well see that," he went on, in almost a conversation with himself. "He has the look of a man who's given up on what he wants. He's the only one here more miserable than I. I know you've not gone with whoever in the hell the dogfish is, not yet, at any rate. That's not your way."

"My being with another man is that the worst you can think of?"

Nathan's ministrations slowed, and he glared. "Short of you being dead or dismembered, aye."

"You think I'm playing you false?" A stirring of air pointed out that her mouth was hanging open, yet again.

Nathan sat back to regard her, long and pensive. "I think you'd deny yourself the air you breathe, if it would avoid hurting those you didn't wish hurt."

"I'll give you credit," he went on grudgingly, fondling the bit of rag. "Both of you have been discreet, and believe me," he said with a severe eye. "I've been watching, waiting for whomever the skulking lout is to finally step up like a man and not the skulking, cravenly coward he appeared."

"And if he had?" A desperate inner voice suggested perhaps, if she made light of this whole thing, it might finally make Nathan tip his hand: that this was all some wretched, ill-conceived jest.

Nathan sobered. "I would have been caught between killing him on sight and allowing you to be happy." He smiled crookedly and shook his head. "I'm not sure which would have prevailed."

"I'm damned if I can find a single cove on this island worthy of you, but I suppose I should have a care and not speak so ill of the lick-spittle, smellsmock—" He stopped short and went on in measured determination. "Of the gentleman you have chosen to toss the handkerchief. Don't bat those eyelashes at me."

"That's not coy. That's dumbfounded." She would have laughed, had the whole thing not been so ludicrous.

"What, in all which is holy, makes you think—?" Cate checked herself. What she was about to say would be cutting and irretrievable. They were on dangerous ground here, very treacherous and dangerous ground.

Balancing the basin on his knees, Nathan took her hand and cradled it with eloquent care. He lifted it to his nose and delicately sniffed, smiling nostalgically. "Still smells of garlic and earth."

Nathan lowered her hand into the basin; Cate hissed at the rum—diluted as it was— touching the raw skin. With eloquent care, he began to wash, his fingers gently stroking the knobs and bones. He stopped, his palm pressing against hers, it reflexively closing around his. His head was bent; she couldn't see his face—probably a mask, anyway—but his jaw worked, his shoulders rigid. The same minute tremors coursed through him now, as they had when sitting at the fireside. Cate closed her eyes, reveling in the connection, wishing what else those hands might do.

"We're connected, darling, as never before," Nathan began, his palm working against hers. His tone was conversational, but there was an odd quake in his voice. "You proved it today: you closed your eyes and touched my heart. I can do the same; I feel you, here." He struck a fist on his chest.

"But now, there's a levity in you, as fresh and alive as a spring flower." His gaze swiveled up sharp with accusation. "I've eyes: I see you go about now, gay as a girl, your eyes gone bright and a color I've never seen. I couldn't help but wonder if I were seeing you as you had been with him, before... everything." His voice pinched with emotion at the end.

Cate groaned inwardly. "Him" could only be one person: Brian. Nathan rarely even so much as alluded to Brian, and now he had mentioned him two or three times just that day.

"All I can do is wonder who put all that there, all that I never could?" Nathan's hands stilled around hers. He squeezed, urgent and fierce, as he looked up, searching. "Who put the joy back in your life, Kittie? Who gave you the peace to lie so quietly?" He smiled indulgently at her seeing confusion. "You didn't cry out last night —"

"I don't —!" She tried to jerk away, but his grasp was unyielding.

"Aye, but you do. Not every night," he qualified, "but near enough. Since the day you came aboard, I've watched you sleep, always with that little frown, as if it were an unpleasant task." He ventured a finger toward her mouth. "Last night, the little ends of your mouth curled up, and you smiled, peaceful as a lamb."

Cate looked down at the dark crown as he patted her hands dry. She was caught between wanting to laugh at his innocence and cry at his heartbreak.

"Duplicity isn't in you, darling," Nathan said, flashing the briefest of smiles. "Straight-at-'em is your way, no skulking and sneaking about. You'd only have a man of the same courage, with the ballocks to step forward and make his desires known."

Fury beginning to get the best of him, he checked himself and went on determinedly. "I've been watching, holding me breath, waiting for the damned lout to show his face, make his claim, at the same time wondering how the hell I was going to keep from running him through when he did."

Nathan sat back and blew a weary sigh. "When he didn't, I worried that the codless git was trifling with you." He looked up, his expression darkening with vehemence, the hand on his knee curling into a fist. "And if that is the case, just point out the lurcher, and I'll lay his head and balls at your feet."

Cate woodenly nodded. Nathan could have flown at her, as was his usual way, but he hadn't. Upon retrospection, she had caught him several times since he'd touched shore, peering at her, studying as if she were a two-headed kitten. So fixed on her own shades of red and green, she had failed to notice his.

"I wanted nothing more than to throw you on that bed," Nathan said, with a frustrated gesture, "and make you forget whoever the hell he was, but I couldn't," he added, glaring down at himself. He shook his head in dismay. "But even then, at the same time, I couldn't bear the thought of your heart being with another, lying next to me wishing you were elsewhere."

Cate glanced toward the bed with regrets of her own. So much could have been settled there, hidden feelings made known, hurt ones appeased. Instead, they were left with words and, far too often, those had proved so very troublesome, often falling far, far too short.

Nathan found her hand where it now rested on her knee and

grasped it. The tremors now had free reign, coursing through him so hard his voice quaked. "You're my heart's joy, Kittie, but I can't bear the thought that someone else might bring out of you what I can't, it—it..." He clamped his lower lip between his teeth and mournfully shook his head.

Living alone for years, her greatest wish had been to have someone who knew if she lived or died. But more tears were shed from wishes that where answered. She had someone who cared, deeply, but that meant having to answer for herself. And that meant having to confess what she had hoped to forget.

Tabby burst in, providing Cate with a temporary respite. Sweating and breathless, the girl bobbed a curtsy and darted forward to set the blood box at Nathan's feet. Round – eyed, she retreated to the door.

"Your mistress is faint," Nathan announced. "Light along and fetch a drink for both of us. Bear a hand there!" A snap of his fingers sent Tabby off.

"I'm not faint," Cate protested in her wake.

"Then pretend, if and when the shiftless urchin ever returns. It's one way to make sure she's not snooping about."

As Nathan rummaged through the box, Cate plucked at the folds of her skirts. She had heard of places in the world where the earth would open up and swallow people. She wished fervently that it would do so just then.

With a jolt, she realized something: she *did* feel much like Nathan's flower: fresh and new, with a lightness-of-heart not experienced for a very, very long time. She glanced at her dim and blurry reflection in the bit of peering glass over the washstand. Her old self had been gone for so long, this one of late had left her wondering who was looking back? Thomas had noticed, but she just put it off to Thomas being Thomas.

It had been such a sweeping relief to have it all behind her, the dark leg of her life gone, forgotten. And now, she had to drag it all up again, risking those burdens latching onto her again.

And yet, there was no choice. She had to tell Nathan. Ignorance and his imagination were eating him alive. On the surface he was calm, but the match was hovering so very close to the touchhole.

"Did it ever occur to you that this glow of mine is because you came for me?" she said in a small voice.

Of course, it wasn't, she sighed at his dubious expression. *That would have been too* easy.

No, this went deeper, much deeper, to depths she would have preferred forgotten.

"Yes, I'm different," she reluctantly conceded. "But what

if... if... it's not what you think? What if it was something else?" She slumped at the end. Just getting that bit out was a victory.

Nathan stopped in mid-motion opening a jar. "Convince me." Number XXXVII didn't disappoint. Cate sucked in sharply.

"You're taking inordinate pleasure in my discomfort," she observed, squirming as he spread it on.

Nathan batted his lashes. "Why, m'lady, you mistake my motivations."

Finished with swathing on the ointment, he set the jar back in the box and sat back with all the appearance of intending to sit there until dawn broke, if necessary.

With visions of the eternal abyss looming before her, Cate drew a deep breath. "What if it... it was worse than you can imagine?"

One brow cocked. "*That*, darling, is impossible."

"Thomas didn't say... anything?"

Of course, he didn't, she thought moodily, rubbing her temple. *We wouldn't be having this conversation if he had.*

At times, Nathan could be as insightful as a mage. Other times — such as now, alas — he could be as blind as an eyeless bat, or as dense as one of those knightheads or kevels, or whatever in the hell those things were.

Cate launched to her feet. Nathan sat, watching her from alternating corners of his eyes as she paced.

"What if you learned I've done something horrible, something thoroughly despicable, inhuman and vile?"

He twisted around at that. "Darling, you couldn't possibly —"

"But if I had?"

Nathan pursed his lips, considering. "Out of malice?"

She stopped, staring out the door into the night. "Depends on the definition of the word."

He exhaled through his nose. "Ah, so only for the sheer joy of the doing."

"It was something that couldn't be helped. Well, no, not exactly that, either," she said, furiously rubbing her forehead in frustration.

"Then, out of circumstance," he put in, helpfully.

"Maybe —" She let out a frustrated gasp. "Dammit, except it wasn't that, either."

Nathan cocked his head, his face screwing in disbelief. "Darling, if this is about what happened out there with that damned Companyman, I've heard all that. Hell, everyone has."

Cate whirled around, horrified. "*Everyone* has?"

Now Nathan was the one fighting with the urge to laugh. "It

was battle, luv. Tho' every bone in me wishes else, you've seen it before. You know how it 'tis."

"But, it hadn't been just the battle," Cate pleaded. "He was already dead." Or nearly so, she thought. Monroe had that slack-faced look of the dead. In retrospect, in the blur of the moment, she couldn't swear to it one way or the other. "He'd not laid a hand on me and I—"

"Given time and opportunity, he would have, luv," Nathan said with cold finality.

"I don't know what happened." She paced once more, feeling like a caged cat. "One minute, I— I mean, it all happened so fast. First, they were holding me, trying to—"

"Goddammit, Thomas was supposed to have been watching you," Nathan fumed, lurching to his feet. He waved an admonishing fist. "You never should have been out there in the first place."

"He was... mostly... as much as I would allow."

Nathan eyed her narrowly. "T'would be a grand convenience if you might co – operate, at least once in your life."

"I tried, I mean, I meant to. He was being so brutish about it—"

"And justifiably so."

Seizing Cate, Nathan turned her to face him. Flushed with shame, she turned her head, but a finger to her chin forced her back.

"Darling, you think I or anyone else here cares a blessed wit about some Company shabbaroon getting his just desserts? He was the enemy! You destroy him, by whatever means or opportunity what presents itself. And, if in the process, you manage a bit o' purging the humors, then more's the better."

"You don't know," she cried, voice quaking. "You didn't see what I did."

"You mistake," he said firmly. Seeing her flinch, he softened his tone. "I didn't have to! I've seen what I've done; I've seen the aftermath of God knows how many others. I've heard enough and said 'Well done!'" The last came with glowing pride.

He turned and paced the small space between bed and locker. "How can I, hell, how can anyone on this island reproach you for something we've done countless times?" he implored to the rafters. "You fancy no one else has ever taken another swipe at the already – dead? Never skewered a liver or hacked a limb already severed? God knows how many unfortunate louts have been chopped to pieces, because all I wished was to see His High – Holiness dead."

"Everyone is talking about it." Worrying her hands in her

lap, Cate cast a horrified look toward the door. As appalling as the notion was, it went a long way to explain the looks and murmurs all these days since.

"As they should," Nathan declared proudly. "It brought you up several notches in the eyes of many, and made a good many more, if not afraid, then vastly respectful, that slab-sided mump Cornwall aside. Nothing could penetrate that drunken haze."

"They must think me a monster," she said, shying.

"Do you think me and Thomas as one?" he asked mildly.

"Of course, not!"

"Then allow yourself the same leave. 'Tis an odd court you're running there, Mistress Mackenzie."

Nathan took Cate by the shoulders and gently shook. "You're no monster, nor barbarian, nor that host of other names you seem to be calling yourself," he urged in low – voiced insistence. "You finally allowed yourself to be angry and avenged yourself. Well done, darling! Well done."

"That's what Thomas said," she said with a faltering smile.

Nathan released her, grinning. "Aye, well, he learned from me."

Few people were lightened by being proved wrong, but Nathan was positively buoyant just then, with that very thing. He wasn't being cuckolded. She could have set his shoes on fire and he would have congratulated her.

"For years, from the first, I had myself convinced nothing I did could change anything," Cate offered in her own defense.

"Aye, but with all due respect, luv—as we all tried to tell you—you were wrong, weren't you?" He shook a fatherly finger at her. "Do not underestimate the curative power of a few drops of blood."

Throat tightening, Cate bowed her head and nodded.

Nathan laid a hand lightly on her crown and said in a confessional whisper "*Ego te absolvo.*"

He shrugged at her shock of such a thing coming from him. "I've lived among sinners most of me life and a fair number were Romanish."

Stalking to the door, he glared out. "I need a drink. Where the bloody hell is that bird-witted child?"

"The bottle is still over there." An angling of Cate's head indicated the bedstand. Unsteadiness struck, and she sat on a locker.

"Ah, yes!" Nathan seized it and took a grateful drink. Swiping his hand across his mouth, he sat next to her. There they companionably shared what was left, which was surprisingly quite a bit. Tabby must have refilled it, as the dutiful chambermaid might.

Cate looked at Nathan from the corner of her eye. If there was an expert on this earth on pain and suffering, on being wronged and maltreated, Nathan would be it. Stripped of a livelihood, banished, branded and declared a slave, tortured and abused, flogged and God knew what else: much of it had all been at the hands of one man.

"Did killing Creswicke help?" she asked delicately. Since their resurrection, she had yet to see Nathan in his purest state. On Dead Goat Island, he had been staggering from the experience, preoccupied with privateers and the Royal Navy hunting him. Here, with the man-eating Mistress-of-the-Realm breathing down his neck, old liaisons at every turn, a daughter he was forbidden to acknowledge, and now the suspicion of being cuckolded eating at him, it was blessedly impossible to sort out what, if any, changes in him might exist from seeing his decade old nemesis finally dead.

Nathan pensively stared at his feet for a good while. "Aye," he said, with perhaps not quite as much conviction as she might have hoped. He glanced shyly from the corner of his eye. "I killed him for you, as much as for meself. But there is no denying the world is a better place without him. It will be positively Fiddler's Green when—" He checked himself and lifted the bottle. "I give you joy o' your victory, however."

Cate stared at his sudden change of subject. Then the name struck like a lightning bolt: Hattie, the woman who had shot him, stole his ship and left him for dead. The fact she still lived obviously overshadowed any joy he might gain from Creswicke's death.

Nathan nudged her with his shoulder. "Apologies on that other foolishness. I've always known you to be a one-man woman, but—"

"Then, why did you just accuse me of being something else?"

Nathan shied, his hands spreading on his thighs. "Old habits, darling," he finally said. "I've lived among the treacherous and wicked for so long, I've forgotten not everyone is corrupt. Hell, St. Teresa would be corrupted by this place!"

Head bent, he opened and closed his hands slowly, but seemed to be seeing something else, so far gone in thought. Finally, both rolled into fists, his knuckles going white. "I've known you to only have room in your heart for one. I was afraid to hope, it was too much to hope that one might be me."

Nathan rose and moved to the door to stare into the night, bottle in his fist. The unspoken between them was obvious, what neither of them could say: if they could have shown each

KERRY LYNNE

other, lain together, bared their souls, rending so much of this conversation unnecessary.

He turned back to her, and she found a perfect reflection of her own thoughts. Indecision pinching his eyes, he swayed toward her, jerked to a stop and swayed again.

"Oh, what the hell," he rumbled.

Throwing his head back, Nathan drained the bottle and took her into his arms. Stifling a pained grunt, he buried his fingers into her hair, turned her face up and kissed her, hard and fierce. He jerked as if from a blow; his mouth broke away, but he held her, still.

He braced his forehead against hers and gasped in agonized frustration. "Bloody Christ, this intolerable! There has to be something —"

His furor faded, and he straightened, his eyes lighting with inspiration. Tabby appeared at the door just then, a mug clutched in each fist. Cate and Nathan separated, like two youths caught in a clandestine kiss.

"There are penalties for fighting," he announced.

Cate stammered at the sudden change of topic. "I've seen fights left and right around here."

"Fisticuffs, no more."

Cate considered that what she had witnessed to have been far more than that, but then she wasn't the final judge. That elevated role was reserved for someone with a far more jaded eye and the desire to put she and — more specifically — Nathan under their thumb.

He sighed, resigned. "I'll have to settle up with Bella, somehow or another."

The mental wheels were visibly rolling, but Cate wasn't convinced the island's rules acted as the hub.

"Concessions will have to be made. It was three against one, and you were holding your own," he added with glowing affection. "So that should cast it in a whole different light."

He snatched one drink from Tabby and drained it in a single gulp.

"Attend your mistress," he directed to the girl, and then "Wait here and keep a weather eye" at Cate.

He leaned closer to Cate as he passed. "Put on that little thing you wore last night," he said with a whisper and a wink.

And then, he was gone.

⬧

Cate dismissed Tabby directly; the child's anxiousness to rejoin the festivities and her friends rendering her more annoyance than help.

She churned about the small space, from the lockers to the bed and back. Nathan had left in such a stew, but for what purpose, was the question? Had he gone looking to avenge her being attacked, make amends with Bella or something else? The mind reeled.

He had left little doubt, however, that she was to remain there. Submissive obedience didn't come readily. Twice she started for the door; recollection of the trouble she had caused already and the extents Nathan would be obliged to go in order to make amends with Bella, stopping her.

"... that little thing you wore..."

Now that was an even greater puzzle. She looked down at herself, straining to recall her hasty preparations the night before. Truth be told, she had been so distracted, she didn't recall exactly what. She still wore the shift Nathan had admired. He had also taken great notice of the rose-colored stockings, comparing them to some of her more delicate parts.

Those, however, were ruined beyond salvation, thanks to his haste to remove them. Diving into the trunks once more, a bit of searching produced a pair of petal pink, her cheeks heating at the thought of what they might be compared to.

What she had lacked the night before — time — was what she now had in plenty, and used it to her fullest advantage: washing with great care, then creaming and powdering every reachable inch. The stockings were pulled on, the garters tied off in pert bows. Another ribbon, calculated to match the color of her eyes, went about her neck. Hair brushing was saved for last, for that, of all things, would be expendable if Nathan was to return, as was expected momentarily.

After brushing for a good while, she went to the door and leaned out into the night. She stiffened at seeing several men in the shadows and then relaxed upon recognizing them: Morgansers. Guards, meant to either keep intruders out or her in. She angled her head straining to hear the first hint of Nathan's approach. Once or twice, amid the music and merriment, she thought she heard his laugh.

Damn him! If he was out there just having a jolly good time...!

Having worked herself into a thorough state, Cate retreated to the bed. Turning down the corner of the bedclothes in a particularly inviting manner, she arranged herself against the bolsters, fluffing her hair about her shoulders, tugging the hair bow into extra jauntiness, and arranging the neck ribbon streamers just so. She glanced out the window, taking half-notice of a particularly brilliant star; Nathan would have known its name.

But he wasn't there.

Hours ticked by, or so it seemed. The star dipped out of sight. Nothing.

The candles burned down. Cate slumped lower and lower, until she lay curled on her side, counting the intervals between the chirps of a frog in the beams overhead.

The tinkling of bells and someone humming, tuneless but jolly, coming toward the hut, stirred her from her torpor. She barely had time to sit up before Nathan appeared at the door. Swaying, eyes which seemed to have a mind of their own traversed the room.

"There you are!" he declared finally spotting her.

"You're drunk," Cate observed, swinging her legs over the edge of the bed.

Weaving, Nathan spread his arms. "Very!"

"You say that as if it had been a challenge."

Nathan's face went momentarily vacant and then brightened. "It was!"

She had been primed to berate him for keeping her waiting. A more abiding voice pointed out that after everything he had been through of recent, he was deserving of a little over-indulgence.

He took a few steps into the room with the determination of one unsure of where the floor might be, then stopped, bracing on a locker.

"Might I assume that Thomas had a hand in this?" she asked. It would be so very much like Thomas' convoluted sense of humor to get Nathan drunk as Davy's sow.

Nathan's eyes wandered and then snapped back. "Just so! He, Pryce and that walking-mountain-of-a-first-mate of his. They're out cold as codfish," he said, stabbing a misguided thumb over his shoulder. He aimed the same digit into his chest. "I, however, am still walking!"

"Barely," Cate murmured. "Barely."

With some difficulty, Nathan fixed his eyes on her, or rather, a spot somewhere over her shoulder. He shook an admonishing finger at her, or at least that general direction. "It took a long time... Gallons!" he said with a grand swipe. "But I did it!"

"Oh!" He fished into his waistband. Pulling out a fist-sized pouch, he pitched it so that it landed with a metallic clank at her feet. "Won in your name!" he beamed.

"I thought there was no gambling."

Nathan made an expansive wave. "Gentleman's wages between...eh, gentlemen.

Thomas was ripe for the picking."

He took several steps, raw determination the only thing

holding him up, and then struck another victorious pose. "Look! Numb as a Number One Anchor!"

Seeing her failure to comprehend, he looked down at himself. Grunting in dismay, he flung off his weapons, pitched them on the table — or at least, aimed in that direction — and began to fumble with the flaps of his breeches. Quickly seeing that helping would be the humane thing, Cate stepped in.

"Avast and belay, woman!" he declared, batting her away. "Mind your own oars. I'd have to be a Dutch-built, fiddle-handed clod not to be able to manage me own business."

The act of shoving his breeches down before they were completely undone caused him to lose the battle of standing, and he sat heavily on the locker. Cate dove to keep him from toppling off. She knelt to pull off his boots and then breeches, a task not so easily done amidst his attempts to kiss her. Nearer now, he smelled not unpleasantly of rum and, tobacco and wood smoke. More significantly was the absence of the lingering essences of the female origins.

Once free of boots and breeches, Nathan lurched to his feet. Flinging off his shirt, he propped his hands at his waist and wriggled his hips. "See! Numb as a bollard and limp as a fid!"

Still kneeling, the flaccid member was but inches from her face. Cate saw, with considerable disappointment, that things were exactly as he proclaimed.

His brows and hips waggled in an odd unison. "Come to me, darling," he purred. "Tonight, I am at your pleasure! We can finish what we started this morning... finally."

She watched his mental wheels spin in their quagmire of rum, his wandering gaze ultimately settling on the hammock. "Remember that journal, and all the uses it represented for one of those?"

She followed his line-of-sight, now suddenly as straight as a musket barrel, and nodded. The battered book, found in the swag pile, had been the handiwork of an anonymous traveler, one with a fair hand at drawing and a keen eye for detail in portraying a number of ways two people might conjoin in a hammock, a surprising number given the limitations.

"*Girando y jugando como un mono,*" Nathan said, with a dreamy roll of his eyes.

While Cate was still pondering the prospect of cavorting like two monkeys, Nathan hooked her into his arms and kissed her. His tongue was quick and intimate; the taste of rum was so strong enough to make her slightly giddy. For as impaired as he was, his hands were surprisingly adept, finding the hem of her shift, plunging between her thighs.

She let out a startled gasp, and he smiled against her lips. "Ah! Slippery as a river rock."

Cate twitched; it wasn't quite the comparison expected.

Urgency and habit made her hand move to return the favors. Realization that might be the last thing he wished, however, made her withdraw.

Nathan goaded her backwards on an uneven path toward the bed. At the last moment, he lost his balance and stumbled backward, dragging Cate with him. His legs came up against the hammock and he tumbled back into it. There, he flailed, amorously calling for her.

"I'm right here," she sighed.

Disappointment being shoved aside *again*, she stood, considering. If Nathan were to be sick—a fair likelihood, given his current state of drunkenness—the hammock would be better than the bed. Good conscience, however, wouldn't allow her to leave him sprawled half-in and half-out of the thing. The task of getting him in, however, was like managing an ox with limbs gone to jelly, one or another slithering out as another was lifted in. Finally, she gave up and left one arm dangling. Patting Nathan's chest, Cate bent to kiss him goodnight. He stirred, inhaling like a dog after a bone, and then slumped.

Cate started to turn, but stopped at the sight of his cock slowly rise, and then bob to and fro as the hammock swung.

She pensively angled her head. "*Jugando como un mono*" might have been out of the question—the act, to her judgment, being improbable, even hazardous under the best of circumstances—but "*quietud de la noche*" offered definite possibilities. The hammock in which Nathan swung wasn't one of those deep-sided, slung chest-high ones, like on board. This one was more a land version, nearly flat and more the level of her hips. It would be a small thing to straddle it and ride its occupant like a horse. She wanted nothing more than to bury her fingers into that mat of chest hair and ride him to an end.

A strident inner voice insisted that Nathan's intent was more than obvious, physical evidence the proof: if capable of answering, he would have wished her to use him. That voice, however, was spurred not by good will, but by animal lust. It would mean using him in a most egregious and degrading way, reducing him to nothing more than a male version of a whore.

Not surprisingly so, she realized that a very large part of her joy in the act came with an active partner, fondling and holding him, seeing his pleasure and response. Besides, there was the not so pleasant thought of the risk of causing him yet more pain.

She ventured a finger along the silken length, watching

it quiver in anticipation. "A pence for your thoughts," she whispered and lightly kissed the tip.

Under his mustache, Nathan's mouth drew up into a smile, and then fell slack. The sound of his throaty snore followed Cate to her bed.

23: ADAM'S CURSE

THE NEXT MORNING, CATE STOOD over the hammock and its recumbent contents, naked as Adam, the same errant arm still flung over the edge. Mouth agape, the soft rattle of Nathan's breathing assured that he wasn't dead, all other evidence to the contrary: unresponsive, limp and an odd greenish tinge. The familiar burned-sugar smell of rum had an acrid edge of sweat and tobacco which made her inclined to turn her head. His lashes marked dark crescents on his cheeks, however, make him look so angelic, so peaceful...

Until he awoke.

She looked down with a certain amount of satisfaction at knowing what awaited when those eyes opened: the worst torture and misery to be visited upon a being, augmented by the added misery of knowing it was self-inflicted.

She'd seen Nathan in drink countless times.

Drunk-as-a-lord?

Only once, as best she could recall, smiling faintly: one night, when she had taken a moonlight stroll on a beach with Thomas. Alas, the next morning Nathan had been his chipper self. This time, however, had been a new high, or better to say "low": insensible and near paralytic. Only a fool would put their faith in Providence's hands in hopes of "chipper" being the case today.

The voice of a guardian angel warned it would be better if she were far away from witnessing this awakening.

"A word to the wise," she directed to Beatrice roosted in the window. "The rooftree won't be far enough."

The bird emitted a protesting squawk. "*Flog the bastard*" and flew away in a blur of blue.

Wincing, Cate flexed her shoulder and experimentally moved her arms. She bent to inspect the damage from last night's scuffle in the peering glass. She couldn't in good conscious call it a "fight"; she'd suffered worse at the hand of her brothers. As Nathan predicted, her eye wasn't black, but there were some unsightly splotches of purple and yellow. The now-livid bites and scratches on her neck and arms made her look like she had a run in with a painter.

Tabby came in from where she had been sitting on the stoop, Nathan's half-mended shirt in hand. His breeches laid finished on a locker. "Does the mistress — ?"

"Shh!!" Cate hissed. "The Captain is *not* to be disturbed." In truth, a brace of cannons going off probably wouldn't rouse him, but it wasn't worth the risk.

Her mistress's warning, combined with Tabby's innate terror of the Captain, was enough to make her dress Cate in efficient silence. Cate stepped out, leaving the rasp of snoring behind her.

By island standards, Cate was running late, again! Its people had long since broken its fast. The thoroughfare to the pavilion was crowded, obliging Cate to dodge racing packs of children and dogs, and stop for a sow and her brood to pass. She nodded and exchanged idle greetings to familiars and strangers. At first, she thought it to be just her imagination, but soon found some individuals, those who had barely stirred hat or hem to her before, now bent and bobbed as if she were long-lost kin.

As she walked, she pondered on what might have prompted this sudden change? As Nathan had suggested, it might be the results of her violations on Monroe. That, however, seemed so much ancient history. Perhaps she was enjoying the fruits of newborn respect after last night's scuffle.

She shook her head. Whatever the cause, it was a welcomed change.

Arriving at the pavilion, Cate glanced hopefully about the hearths for Kirkland. Today was one of those rare times when breakfast waiting would have been a delight. Alas, the man was nowhere to be seen, nor found. A short time later found her at a fire, sipping coffee, a piece of soft-tack on a toasting forks over the coals.

A girl skipped up next to her. "If you please, mum." She twitched the side of her skirt, rolling her eyes straining to recall. "Miz Celia begs that you might lend a hand in the herb kitchens today. She represents we are woefully low on everything."

"I should see to Toby, first."

"Miz Celia said you'd say that!" the child beamed. "She begged me to say he's sitting up, ate a breakfast fit for a thresher and is calling out for more."

Cate smiled. It was an encouraging sign, a testimonial to the resiliency of the young.

Perhaps the crisis had passed, she thought touching wood.

"Very well, my compliments to Mistress Celia and tell her I'm at her disposal."

Shortly thereafter, still chewing her toast, Cate cast an eye back toward her hut from the pavilion's threshold. No one stirred there. Nathan had made his wishes clear enough in the way of her going about alone. The kitchens were the veritable hub of the island's activity. She would be neither remote nor alone. He couldn't possibly find fault or take exception with that!

She hitched her skirts and made her way up the path. As she walked, her earlier suspicions of a new amiability were confirmed: hats tipped, curtsies bobbed, pleasantries called out, joy-of-the-day given to the point of one man stopping to earnestly inquire how she did. It was the reception she had hoped for when first arrived, hopes which had been dashed so thoroughly, she found made gracious acceptance not an easy thing.

Her step slowed at seeing the herb kitchen was crowded with at least a half-dozen women. A-typical of the usual buzz of a group of women working, they were quiet. As she neared, she could hear one holding audience before the rest.

"... And then Nathan said 'Forgive me, Father, for I have sinned —"

The ensuing laughter came to a brief end at seeing Cate standing there. Dusting her hands on her apron, Bess, the mistress of the kitchen, stepped forward. Introductions were made, niceties exchanged, the undercurrents of dislike and distrust entirely absent. Essie was the only one roughly Cate's age; the rest were older, Livy the eldest, if wrinkles and silver hair were any gauge.

Mary, one of several on the island, was near enough to stare with motherly concern at the marks on Cate's face and neck. "Nathan is not usually one to be so rough —" A murmur from her neighbor and her mouth rounded in a comprehending "Oh!"

Plucking an apron from a peg, Cate asked brightly "What's to be done?" in the ensuing silence.

"Those roots need pounding," said Bess nodding toward a table. "Pass them on to Livy when you're done."

Livy and Essie shifted aside to make room. Cate picked up the mallet, arranged several roots — of some unfamiliar, local variety — and set to it. The recounting of Thomas' fireside story resumed. As Cate worked, she noticed the difference in reception there, too. The women didn't ooze kindness — she was never directly addressed — but neither did they seem to wish her gone.

So this is acceptance, said an internal voice.

It took them long enough, said another skeptically.

As she beat, the rhythmic "thump!" became more muffled as the stringy fiber was reduced to pulp. She soon became grateful for the apron; it was messy work, the flying bits of root spattering her face and arms, and the smell was increasingly more putrid. Eventually, a scraper was required to scoop the wet mass up and dump it into a bowl, ready for Livy's strainer. Cate directed a smile into her chest. It wasn't heavy work, not like digging or hauling, but it was unpleasant enough to have been left for someone else. Still, she didn't mind; she was being useful.

"I never believed Nathan could be so low."

It took Cate a moment to realize it was Livy who had spoken and that it was directed at her. Essie, to her other side was chatting with someone else. Even though her hair was more grey than silver and her eyes were dull instead of bright green, in many ways Livy put Cate in mind of Aggie, God rest her soul.

"That ugly business with Marthanna," Livy went on under the general conversation. "He mourned Robert as much as she; there was no counterfeit in that."

Sobering, Livy took a firm grasp of Cate's arm. "You do need to strive a bit more to keep him content, my dear," she said earnestly. "In bed."

The elder smiled primly as she pressed the pulp through the strainer. "'Tis the case with any man, but Nathan's lively appetites require special attentions, if you know what I mean."

Cate would have had to have been as dense as the mallet in her fist to miss the meaning of that.

With a tolerant smile frozen in place, Cate listened to Livy expand on her point. A few times she tried to break in, either to point out that she had been married before, or "But, Nathan prefers—" but to no avail. Livy's wisdom was offered in the most well – meaning of spirits, good intentions, however, which were to be neither declined, nor questioned.

Still, to not outright laugh was painful. Livy was of the old guard, firmly entrenched in the old ways, which meant her advice centered around a woman's duty. Never was there a thought for feminine pleasures, a point which made one wonder if Livy knew such a thing was possible? Alas, it was so very reminiscent of the well-intended lectures Cate had received from the Mackenzie matrons on her wedding night. Luckily neither she, nor Brian were easily molded by the hand-of-custom.

Cate's salvation came in the way of Bess asking if she knew Indian borage?

Cate nodded, perhaps with a bit more confidence than was warranted. She knew enough to be able to figure it out.

"It's in the back, near the arbor," Bess added. "Cut it back hard and bring the basket as you fill it, so we might get this salve making."

It would have been a task for one of the youths, but with all the Morgansers, Lovelies and Brazens about, those had suddenly gone precious thin on the ground; men fresh from the sea were ever so much more interesting. Cate grabbed a basket and crossed the path to the herb garden, hitching her skirts as she clambered over the stile. Following Bess' directions, she wove her way through the garden, noting with a sense of fulfillment the positive effects of her efforts to set things back to rights the day before. As represented, back near the arbor where Nathan had sat with her, she found the borage, its fuzzy, silver – green leaves standing out like a beacon amid the verdant green. Knife in hand, she cut the arching stems, dropping them in the basket.

The task allowed Cate's mind to wander. None of this talk about her "womanly duties" was helping with the strain of abstinence. Last night's false hopes had catapulted her yearning to near obsession. She was beginning to feel like an artifact on a museum shelf: admired and valued, and yet never to be touched.

Living the spinster wasn't new. Like hunger and destitution, for years she had dealt with it, mastering it, dismissing it like everything else regarding her former life: never to be brought to mind again. At first, it had been a monumental struggle but, like hunger, one eventually came to not notice. But now, the body had been fed and, like an over-indulged child, it wrangled for what it wanted.

It wasn't just the carnal act, however, which made her ache. It was the lying together after, her body pressed the length of his, their skins damp with exertion, their limbs entwined, he idly twirling a lock of her hair.

The scuff of boots behind her made her think Nathan had finally joined the day. She straightened, meaning to turn to greet him, but her arm was seized and twisted behind her back, the knife knocked from her hand. Her head was jerked back by the hair far enough to see her assailant from the corner of her eye. Having long relegated the man to his grave, it took Cate a moment to recognize him: Gascon Lesauvage!

"Go ahead, scream," he growled. He nudged her with his hip and gave her a shake. "Shriek like a harpy."

Had she the breath — the pain having knocked it from her — she would have cussed him. She stomped and kicked, aiming for his arches and knees, but the effort was ill-timed and ill-prepared.

Lesauvage gave her arm another wrench. "Scream."

There was a brief battle of wills. Glaring, Cate clamped her mouth shut, refusing.

"Bitch!" He twisted again. A crackling sound in her shoulder sounding like a limb being torn from a half-cooked fowl. The tearing of her scalp felt like the same creature being skinned. Another violent twist, and a throat-tearing scream broke free.

Lesauvage grinned. "Got a good set o' lungs on you."

The voices in the kitchen raised from calls and shouts to shrieks of alarm as the women scurried off, all except Livy. With the impunity of one her age, she charged across the path and drew up at the wall. "You there! You, I say! What is the meaning of this?"

"Get Blackthorne, now, you old biddy, or she suffers."

The Frenchman torqued again, the resulting cry from Cate cutting off Livy's objections. Huffing in indignation, the elder jerked her skirts and sped off. From the corner of her eye, Cate watched Livy disappear. She was alone now.

Cate's heart pounded, the blood throbbing in her temples. She fought down the panic, rising like a sour gorge. She had suffered much at the hands of men. It was the stuff of her nightmares, ones she had finally conquered. Her demons were vanquished. Be damned if she would let them be imposed upon her again!

Lesauvage had smelled like a dead boar before. Now, he had ripened, as if that swine had lain in the sun for several days. He stunk not only of sweat and old urine, but of soiling himself. At some point, someone or something had literally scared the shit out of him, she thought smugly.

"Scrappy little spitfire, aren't you? I'll bet you're a real hellcat in bed, too. Nathan always liked the lively ones."

Lesauvage thrust his nose against Cate's neck and inhaled deeply. His eyes rolled closed in pleasure. "Sweet as a spring day. I wonder what you taste like?"

He kissed her. His teeth ground against her lips, forcing them to open, his tongue plunging so deep she fancied she might vomit. Contorted, her other arm pinned, she could only writhe under the assault.

He leaned back, grinning. "A pleasure, indeed. Nathan will most certainly pay handsomely to get you back."

"He'll cut off your cock and feed it to you," Cate gasped, spitting to clear the taste of him from her mouth.

"Perhaps I'll cut off his and feed it to you."

Nathan!

Cate closed her eyes and concentrated, willing him to stay

away. At the same time, she wished for nothing more than for him to show up and serve out this bastard.

Where the bloody hell did Lesauvage come from? The answer seemed starkly obvious. He had the wild-eyed look of the hunted of having been in hiding. Given his success, it was a wonder why he suddenly chose to appear?

"Gascon!"

Lesauvage jerked around at hearing his name shouted from the garden's gate.

Cate choked a gasp of joyous relief. Thomas!

"Gascon! Where the bloody hell are you?" Thomas called. "Stop skulking about like a goddamned sneakthief and show yourself like a Christian."

Lesauvage stepped out of the arbor's shadow into the glare of daylight. Cate couldn't stop another pained cry as she was swung around on display. Thomas stood just inside the gate, arms crossed over his chest, hat low, shading his eyes.

"Where is Blackthorne?" Lesauvage demanded.

"Coming soon enough, I expect," Thomas said off-handedly. "He's... eh... indisposed."

Lesauvage gave a lewd chuckle. "Shagging a wench, eh?"

"Aye, one of his favorites."

"I thought this one was his favorite," Lesauvage said, giving Cate a shake.

Thomas shrugged. "She was, until this morning. He threw her out. 'Tis why she's out here working, I should imagine." A sandy brow was flicked, so subtle Cate wasn't sure if it had been intentional.

Thomas took a step closer, but stopped at seeing the Frenchman press a knife to Cate's throat. "What the bloody hell are you at? You're in no position to negotiate."

"I see myself in the perfect position. Now get back!"

Raising his hands in surrender, Thomas retreated. Emboldened by Thomas' presence, a gallery of onlookers gathered at the fence, peering over it like a crowd at a fair. From the corner of her eye, Cate saw a more definitive flick of Thomas' brow, emphasizing his warning for her to bide.

Bide, hell! He wasn't the one with the knife at his throat!

Moisture dripped from her captor's chin onto her chest and made a slow path downward. Hope sprang anew: if he was sweating, his hands might be damp. Cate coiled, preparing for the instant his grip might slip.

"I require a boat. Small, one which can be single-handed... and weatherly," Lesauvage added, as if heading off any notions of trickery. "And the treasure, of course."

"Treasure!" Thomas barked.

Cate rolled an eye at Lesauvage, thinking the agony in her arm and scalp had affected her hearing. Treasure?

"*Oui*! Do not deny it! With an island full of pirate wives, any fool knows there is treasure about."

Thomas started to laugh, but quelled it. Looking to the ground, he cocked his head and sighed. "Ah, so you heard about it then, eh?" He jerked off his hat and ran a hand through his hair. "Damn, I was afraid of that. I told them this would happen."

He kicked the ground in disgust and sighed. "Aye, well, you've got us on that one. You're no man's fool, are you?"

Settling his hat once more, Thomas peered up, one eye closed. "You desire all of it? Belay that. Of course, you do." His arms rose and fell in resignation. "Aye, well then, you'll need a bigger boat."

"Eh...?"

"A ship, a schooner, at the least," Thomas went on, ignoring Lesauvage's shock. "Something in the range of a three or four-hundred tons. It'll founder the *Brazen*. The *Lovely* might do... mebbe," he added, screwing his face in calculation.

The body against Cate's vibrated with anticipation.

"I'll have to gather my men," Thomas said, still deep in his estimations. "We'll need a score, at least—"

"A score!" Lesauvage was titillated nearly to the point of salivation.

Thomas nodded absently. "There's the digging in the cave—we buried it nice and deep, so the animals mightn't dig it up—and then the hauling, of course. Damnation, what I wouldn't give for a yoke of oxen just now. Hell, you know how it 'tis: each man's share would founder a brace o' mules." He chuckled, shaking his head in amazement.

Thomas swiped a hand over his face again, sobering. "Very well, you have us over a barrel, but I'll require a show of good faith on your part."

"No tricks." The knife was pressed harder at Cate's throat.

"Nay! Wouldn't dream of it," Thomas said dryly. "Just put the knife down. After all, we wouldn't wish your impatience to be her demise."

Whether by will or distraction, the knife lowered a fraction. Eyes narrowing, Thomas went motionless. The Frenchman jerked and sucked in sharply. He stilled for a moment, and then his legs buckled, taking Cate with him. Sinking to his knees, he swayed, and then pitched forward on top of her. She struggled out from under him and came up braced for a fight. The sight of a blade protruding from his kidneys stopped her. Bare of chest and foot,

Nathan stood over him. Thomas was there then, sword in his fist. Pryce miraculously appeared at his side, armed as well.

Nathan planted a foot on the Frenchman's hip and jerked the sword free. Fury blanking his face, he raised the weapon over the prone body, ready to strike. Cate looked to Thomas or Pryce for help, but found both were lost in the same blood – lust.

"Nathan, no!"

Still poised, Nathan's head lifted at the sound of her voice. "He laid hands on you," he said, mechanically. "He—"

"Nay, Cap'n, not here." Recovering himself, Pryce slid an eye toward the increasing number of onlookers at the fence. "Not here, Cap'n. It ain't fittin'."

Nathan finally blinked and lowered his arm.

Bella pushed her way through the crowd jammed at the gate and came up, red-faced with running. She looked down at the body, and then up at Nathan, accusing.

"In the back, aye," he declared, unrepentant.

"I bore witness," said Thomas boldly, squaring himself before her. "It was self – defense, plain."

Pryce stepped up beside him. "I saw the same. Anyone see different?" he directed to the crowd.

Silence was their consent.

Bella gave Pryce a sharp look. He and Thomas standing shoulder-to-shoulder made a formidable front, one which only a fool would press. Bella was a lot of things, but not that.

"You killed for her?" she demanded of Nathan.

"I did. And I'll do it again, should the need arise."

Murmurs of approval came from the crowd, a large portion of them now Morgansers, Lovelies and Brazens. The trial was over; the verdict was in. The case was closed.

Bella cast a worried eye at Cate, in the protection of Nathan's arms by then. "Is she hurt? Does she require being taken to the sickbay?"

Cate adamantly shook her head. "I just need somewhere... quiet," she whispered hoarsely into his shoulder.

"Nay, she'll do," Nathan announced.

Bella frowned, unconvinced. "Very well, take her home; I'll bid a brew be sent, something to soothe her nerves."

The excitement was over. Seeing there was naught else to be done, Bella took her leave, taking a good many of her aggregation with her. Pryce and the sailors, however, remained.

At some point, Cate had begun to shake. A shawl from an anonymous well-wisher was wrapped about her, Nathan's arm solidly holding her. He held Cate back and peered intently at her. "Do you wish your revenge?"

"And damn the livers of anyone what dare to protest," put in Pryce.

Scalp still burning, arm aching to the point of limp, Cate looked down into the lifeless eyes. As much as she wanted to, she found nothing, not even cutting that now – frozen smirk off Lesauvage's face, would erase what just happened. She mutely shook her head.

Nathan angled his head, searching her eyes. "Very well," he said at last.

"I want every hand what can put one foot afore the other to turn-to and comb this godforsaken hole. Turn over every rock and log, and find every skulking worm left," Nathan growled to Pryce.

His arm about Cate's shoulders, Nathan turned to lead her away. "What about him?" she asked, looking back at the body.

Thomas looked up at the gulls, already circling overhead. "He's exactly where he belongs."

"Nay, he'll stink the place up directly," Nathan sighed. "Pitch him with the rest of the refuse."

Pryce leaned and said in a low rumble "Rest assured, Cap'n, 'tis a fair long ways to that point yonder. His own mum won't recognize 'im a'time he gets there." A meaningful wink punctuated his meaning.

They set off in a small parade, Thomas in the lead, Nathan supporting Cate behind.

Barely through the garden's gate, she sagged. "I think I'm going to be sick."

Nathan knelt beside Cate, supporting her by the shoulders as she wretched. The toast — she'd eaten precious little, else — came up with the first heave. Her gut convulsed several times more, with a violence which seemed to originate from somewhere near her toes. A finish — far too long in coming, by her measure — finally came; a nod was all she could manage to make the men aware. They guided her, gasping and clammy, in the general direction of her hut.

"I need to sit," she said.

A small clearing under the sweeping branches of a live oak tree was conveniently to hand. Scattered seating — stumps, stools and rough benches — and trampled ground marked it as a work site of some sort. Thankfully, just then it was unoccupied. The last thing she needed was being gaped at. Seeing her seated, the men squared off: Thomas on the one side, looking like the

Colossus of Rhodes; Nathan, as intransigent as the Rock of Gibraltar, on the other. Both too choked with rage to speak, the space between them directly over her head was so charged with tension, she might have been sparked had she extended a finger.

"What the bloody hell just happened?" Cate hoped her shaky demand might head off the impending storm. "Treasure?"

Nathan jerked from his glare. "There's always been some cockamamie story going 'round about treasure buried here. T'was rumors... mostly."

"Hell, I think I recall Garrick repeating it a time or two," Thomas added.

Her ploy of a distraction answered well, Nathan calming a fraction. "Pirates' wives, ergo pirate treasure." He even managed to crack a smile, brief but a smile, nonetheless. "The whole thing makes no bloody damned sense a'tall. Death and damnation, I'm confounded to sort out why the hell would anyone worth their salt go through the trouble of taking a prize, just to haul it God knows how far inland, with a lot of sweat and toil, to bury it somewhere, with every man involved as witness? Why not just share it out and let every man carry away what's his in the first place?"

"Rum-talk, mostly," Thomas put in.

"But apparently convincing," Cate observed grimly.

She massaged her still-aching arm, feeling as if she had just been the victim of an ill - planned prank. "So, Lesauvage betrayed an entire island for a treasure which didn't exist."

"He always turned on people faster than a capstan," Nathan said, with a brusque wave.

Thomas distractedly nodded. "More importantly, it convinced his men to throw in with the Company."

"What about them, the Company, I mean?" Cate rubbed her temple, trying to follow Lesauvage's convoluted line of thought. "Did he mean to share it with them?"

Both men barked a wry laugh.

"Probably planned to betray them next, I expect," Thomas finally managed.

Nathan couldn't disagree.

"All that death and destruction — lives lost, lives ruined — all for the sake of money?" she said, staring in disbelief.

"That pretty well sums up the world in general," Thomas sighed.

"This world especially," Nathan said, rolling his eyes.

Alas, the exchange wasn't long or involved enough to dispel the rancor between the two men. Not wishing Cate to be in the middle of it, figuratively and literally, Nathan jerked his head, leading Thomas a few steps away, ostensibly out of earshot. His barely contained fury apparently clouded his judgment, for he didn't go quite far enough.

"Where the fucking hell did he come from?"

"Where the fucking hell do you suppose?" Thomas shot back.

Nose-to-nose, toes-to-toes, remonstrations and accusations were lobbed like a broadside, waving fists and jabbed fingers emphasizing every point. It was so reminiscent of her brothers, Cate had to turn her head to hide a smile. Thomas balled a massive fist; Nathan jutted out his chin, daring. Cate held her breath, waiting. Finally, Thomas proved the cooler head. With a dismissive swipe, he spun and came back to kneel before her, Nathan hovering.

"Jesus, lovely, I'm sorry!" The sandy brows knitted, his mouth moved. "I had no notion that treacherous toad was skulking about. If I'd thought for a moment— If I'd—" He looked to the ground between his knees and shook his head.

"It's not your fault," Cate said mechanically. "No one could have known."

Thomas found her hand and pressed her knuckles to his lips. "I swear I'll oversee the search myself—"

"You damned right," Nathan hissed. The back of Thomas' neck should have glowed red from his glare. "About time you did your duty—"

Thomas lurched to his feet, and the pair squared off again, fists cocked. Once again, Thomas' restraint prevailed. Swallowing down a retort, he forced his fist to open. Touching his hat to Cate, he stormed away, heels pounding the ground.

"You shouldn't be so hard on him," Cate threw into the ensuing silence. "It wasn't his fault."

Nathan spun around. "Curse and burn him, it was! He represented that scupperlout was dead."

Cate rubbed her temple and the lingering soreness from her hair being pulled. "He, *we* all thought he was. Just one more rising from the dead," she sighed, suddenly weary.

A girl racing down the path spotted them under the tree. She scurried forward, her rounded-eyes fixed on the horn cup she carried. "Mistress Bess sent this, representing it should cure what ails."

"God's my life, she makes it sound as if it's a bloody case o' the vapors!" Nathan cried.

The girl shied at Nathan's vehemence and gladly took her leave. Cate experimentally sniffed the cup's contents. Curling her nose, she set it on the bench next to her, untouched.

Cate's aimlessly roving eye finally landed on the leg of Nathan's breeches and the mending.

"Tabby does fine work," Cate observed grudgingly. The sight of his torn clothing had been like thorns jabbing, constant reminders of the near hazards he had dodged, and even more significantly, of her failure to care for him.

So far afield, it took Nathan a moment to follow her meaning. He plucked at his bare chest. "Good thing she finished me breeches, or I'd been saving you naked as the day of Creation."

"There's a fair number who wouldn't complain," she mused. There was no ignoring the eyes which winsomely followed his every move.

"It is admirable work," he conceded, fingering the patch. "None so fine as yours, but—"

He caught the questioning lift of her brow and stiffened. "We sailors have a needle put in our hands about the same day as a rope. Either a lad learns to dip a needle, or he goes about with his arse bared to the four winds."

"You! Sewing?" The image of Thomas Pryce, Hodder and Al-Nejem all hunched together stitching away just wouldn't come.

"Aye! Most vessels have make-and-mend days. I could whip out a shirt within a few watches' time."

Cate's derisive laugh was stifled at the last possible moment. The rough life of a sailor posed hazards to more than just his body. It made sense that a man would have to learn to apply a needle or, as Nathan represented, be obliged to go about as bare as Adam.

Nathan shifted on his feet. Glancing about to confirm that they were alone, he crouched before her and looked up. "So, last night, I took off me clothes and...?"

"You don't remember," she smirked. "You are looking a bit worse for wear," she observed without sympathy. The evidence of over-indulgence was still upon him.

Nathan cut a cold eye. "Being jerked out o' me slumber with word you'd been snatched starts the day out worse than a damned bosun's mate bellowing in one's ear." He touched a hand to his stomach. "Bloodshed is always the best nostrum for what ails."

Running an unsteady hand down his face, he closed one eye and returned to the subject. "I remember a bit: drinking with Thomas; making it to the shack... barely. Umm, did I...?" The eye opened to fix hopefully on her.

"Sorry, m'lad, your mission failed on all accounts."

He sat back on his heels. "Damn! Then you didn't...? I mean, you haven't...?"

"No." Her disappointment refused to be masked.

"And I would have been too damned gone in drink to remember any of it," he grumbled. "Where the bloody hell is the joy in that?"

The corner of Nathan's one eye ticked with what had to be a horrific headache. A slightly greenish tinge about his jawline suggested queasiness and little wonder. He would never set himself up the martyr, but he was very close to it just then. The misery might be self-inflicted, but it had been for her sake.

"Peppermint tea might help settle what ails," she suggested sympathetically.

"A hair o' the dog would answer better," he said, with a hopeful yet futile glance about the grove.

Suddenly unable to sit, Cate lurched to her feet. She took several steps and then stopped at realizing she had no idea where she meant to go. She began to shake, but not from cold. It came in violent waves, as if someone grasped her about the knees and shook, as one did to get apples from a tree. The crunch of dried leaves marked someone coming up behind her. She turned and fell against Nathan.

"Hold me. Please, just hold me," she said, clutching him.

She almost cried out in the blissful elation of his body against hers, so warm, so alive and giving. It was dreams answered, wishes finally fulfilled. She clung to him, her fingers digging into the hard curves of his back. There were no tears, at least she didn't think so, and yet wetness slickened his chest under her cheek. She turned her face up and kissed him. At first, his mouth was soft and yielding. But then his lips gradually stiffened, becoming almost reluctant.

She leaned back to find his brow furrowed, his lips pressed in a hard white line.

"I'm sorry," she said, retreating further. "I'm hurting you. I wasn't— I mean, I should have thought—"

"Dammit, come here. I need this as badly as you, " he said hoarsely. "Give me your mouth, your body... Anything so I might have reason to live."

Nathan gathered Cate with new determination. One hand at the back of her head, the other at the small of her back, he pressed her hard against him and kissed her. A small part of her thought he might ravage her right there; a larger part prayed he would.

The body against hers grew rigid, quivering like willpower being pushed to its absolute limit. Finally, with an agonized gasp, Nathan broke away and staggered back. He stood in the now all-too-familiar pose: half-bent, clutching himself.

"I'm sorry. I wasn't thinking. I don't know what's wrong with me. I've been through worse, far worse than what just happened back there!" Cate cried.

Tentatively straightening a fraction, Nathan freed a hand to wave her off. "You're still not in fighting trim, still fragile, still susceptible to skulking coves jumping out and putting a knife to your throat," he wheezed. "And, the devil burn me, I've been precious little help."

Nathan gingerly made his way to a bench and sat heavily. Rocking, arms on his thighs, he pounded a fist into his palm. "There has to be a way I might push through this. There has to be—"

He stopped, eyes brightening with inspiration, and then sprang to his feet. "By Christ and thunder, yes. Stay!" The last came with a rigid point at her.

In a flash and clatter of silver, he darted away, leaving Cate gaping in his wake.

Cate hesitated... briefly.

Nathan had bid her to remain, but good conscience wouldn't allow her to leave him to be alone. It wasn't a matter of him possibly doing himself harm, like self-murder or something. But, given his mood, heightened by a large dose of desperation and natural appetites, he wasn't beyond doing something daft, *very* daft.

What, was the worry?

And so, she struck off after him.

Instead of taking the path, Nathan had shot into the bushes. The undergrowth had closed in, rendering him invisible almost the instant he passed. She used the still-moving branches and blades of grass as a guide. She hadn't gone far before she heard sounds from up ahead, furtive, grunting and huffing, like a struggle of some sort. The nearer she went, the surer she was that the struggle was limited to one person. Ducking under a branch, she stepped into a small glade and stopped.

To one side, in a spot of shade, was Nathan. Kneeling, his back to her, the leaf shadows danced over his bare shoulders. His breeches sagging about his hips, his fist pumped rhythmically, low against his belly. There was little doubt as to what he was doing.

Emitting a growling hiss, his hand worked faster, his entire body reverberating with the force which now seemed to verge on self-destruction. He threw back his head. The sun now full on his face, his lips writhed back, not in anticipation of pleasure, but in agony. A cry, like that of a tortured soul, tore from his throat, startling the birds from the trees. Choking an inarticulate curse, he fell forward onto his hands, gasping.

"Nath—! My god, what—?" Cate breathed.

Panting, Nathan peeled an eye over his shoulder.

"Wouldn't it be better if...? I mean, shouldn't I be the one doing that?" she offered.

Nathan shook his head, but it was some moments before he regained the breath to answer. "You've stated the obvious, whilst entirely missing the point," he said dryly.

Back heaving, his head dropped between his arms. "Would that I could, darling. Believe me, I would much prefer your hand on me cock to my own." He choked a laugh. "Truth be told, it was that very thing I imagined just now."

"Oh." Flattery lay in there somewhere, she was sure of it. "Do you wish me to leave, so you might... finish?" There was the not-too remote chance his discomfort stemmed from being so rudely interrupted. Her hand twitched at her side with the desire to grasp him. She knew his body well: one touch and she would have known how near to completion he might have been. One look could have been just as revealing, she thought craning her head, but in vain.

"Nay." Nathan laughed again, this one hoarse with futility. "I'm not man enough to bear it."

He pushed back on his heels and aimed a glare down the slope of his belly. "Me hope was that perhaps it would be like a boil in need of bursting: were I to gut it out, somehow finish finally, all would be aye." His hand rose and fell. "I'm a failure on all counts."

Nathan threw back his head again and let out another bellow, this one guttural with frustration. Cate shifted on her feet, feeling small and useless.

Recovery came for Nathan as quickly as the outburst, and he went about setting himself back to rights. "Me lads ache and me cock has gone over to the enemy, that's for bloody sure. 'Tis a curse constructed by the mastermind of all what's evil, I'll warrant you that."

Cate couldn't disagree. The extent of Calypso's diabolical mind was becoming more apparent each day. The level of torture and retribution pointed more and more toward a woman scorned, a woman meaning to drive a wedge between Nathan and all others. So far, score one for the goddess, successful on all counts.

"Castration might be a blessing." Nathan laughed sharp and

sardonic as he buckled his breeches. "That would clap a stopper on ol' sea hag's capers, wouldn't it? I'd be entirely useless. She could take these and go hang." He jerked his head hard enough to jangle his bells.

Cate reluctantly smiled. The irony was delicious.

"That is not something to be said, even in jest," Cate said uneasily.

Nathan snorted. "Who's jesting?" His voice held just enough bleakness to make the notion seem plausible.

Seeing her growing horror, he flashed a smile, bright against the black of his beard. "No tears, luv. The lads are secure for today. I'm not ready to render meself a gelding, yet." Still, he touched his crotch, as if to assure himself all was well there.

He paused from what he was doing to look up. "Have you considered that this condition might be forever?" he asked conversationally.

"No," she said, in a small voice. It was an outright lie. Of course, she had, with approximately the same frequency as drawing breath!

"Well, I have. I'm not even half o' man. I'm no good to you."

One eye glared back at her. "Don't you see? I can't lie with you. I can't pleasure you. Hell, I have to imagine every wart-faced, oyster-hag ever met just to hold you. I'm as useless as a eunuch."

"This isn't about me!" Her voice quavered with the uneasy feeling that this conversation was about to take a drastic turn.

He twisted around. Hand on hip, he gaped, incredulous. "Who the hell else would it be?"

"You." It seemed stating the obvious, to her, at any rate.

Emitting a small groan, Nathan looked skyward, imploring the heavens for patience. "It doesn't matter. I don't care — " she began.

A barely tolerant expulsion of air cut her off.

"Darling, the bedding means more to you than any woman I've ever lain with. And if you wish to shoot me for saying that, then here's me pistol," he said, with a sharp gesture toward the weapon lying beside him. "You have my leave to put me out o' me misery."

Cate cautiously sidled near enough to lay a hand lightly on his shoulder. "You aren't that easily replaced," she said earnestly.

He laughed dryly, but squeezed her hand in appreciation, nonetheless.

Nathan finally gathered the wherewithal to stand. He

stopped short of fully upright, hand on a knee. Cate reached to help him, only to be sidestepped and batted away.

He closed his eyes, jaw working. "Could you, pray, just turn your back?" he asked with considerable effort. "That's a good lass. It eases matters a mite if I don't see your face."

Cate obliged him, but only just so far. Literally or figuratively, she wasn't about to turn her back on him. She positioned herself enough to satisfy him whilst at the same time could still see him, bearing an eye, just in case.

"You said once that you wanted me, even if all we might ever do is talk," she threw over her shoulder. Not that long ago, Thomas and Pryce had marooned them on an island, forcing she and Nathan — going at each other hammer-and-tongs, at the time — to make amends. Souls had been bared, pledges made.

"Well, I was a cuckle-headed fool to think it, and damned desperate at the time, might I add in me own defense. At that point, wrist-slashing wasn't far in the offing had you refused me."

"Perhaps if we were to try something...?" There had to be a way for two intelligent, resourceful and determined people to work out something amicable all way 'round.

"What? Less arousing?" Nathan quipped. "We tried that, remember?" He made a frustrated noise. "You women can find your pleasures any number of ways, but we men have but one. 'Tis Adam's curse."

He started to straighten further, but thought better of it.

Nathan bent his head, his fists balling on his thighs. "Don't you realize? I'm living my worst nightmare: I laid with you for the last time and had no notion. I took you for granted; I thought we had... time." The last came in a rasp, tight with regret.

The notion was sobering. A number of things came to mind of what might have been different had she known. She and Brian had the benefit of knowing it was their last night; goodbyes were said, memories — enough to last a lifetime — gathered.

Cate started to turn toward Nathan, but checked herself, determinedly planting her feet. "I don't care about the bedding." She could bear it, whatever "it" proved to be.

"Aye, but you will. You haven't been back long enough... yet. Remember, darling," he went on at her dubious cough, "it wasn't all that long ago for me. I know what it 'tis to yearn and nothing else will answer."

He stood for some moments, head hanging between his arms. "I was desperate, damned desperate with the longing. I told you, 'tis no secret: I laid with everything in a skirt."

"That was you. I'm not some bitch in heat." Yes, she yearned but, unlike that dog, she didn't lust for just any man. She lusted for one: Nathan. She was a one-man woman...

Under normal circumstances, observed an inner voice. Coming back from the dead, being trifled with by a goddess: none of that was normal, which put nothing out of the realm of possibilities.

Nathan shrugged, unfazed. "You mightn't be able to help it, darling. Desire is as much a part of you as those damned eyes. It'll be like a sot after a drink, a starving man for food: one won't satisfy you. Hell, a dozen mightn't," he added bleakly.

He lifted his head to peer at her, his eyes pinched with worry. "I knew when I was negotiating for your life what you would suffer: misery which I wouldn't wish on a cur. And yet, I bestowed it upon you as if it were a bloody crown." A swipe of his fist punctuated his frustration. "I fancied it mightn't be so bad — perhaps you'd be spared altogether being a woman — because you wouldn't be alone, as I had been. I'd be there to help you through it."

The need to hold him was becoming a compulsion. Cate wrapped her arms about her middle, holding herself in place.

"You have been a help," she pleaded to the bushes. "In countless ways. Hell, just knowing you've been through all this before, means —"

"Pah! I'm no damned good to you."

A queasy feeling, the kind brought on by dread, seized her. A desperate Nathanael Blackthorne was a scary sight. One wallowing in the blue devils was alarming. Minutes ago, she had dismissed the notion of him doing himself harm. Now, it loomed in the realm of likelihood.

"But every time I come near you, you're in pain."

"And that's the hell of it," Nathan conceded, wincing. "Me balls feel the size of bladders and fit to explode."

He blew a long resigned sigh. "The decent thing would be give you to Thomas. He's a fine figure of a man, don't you think? Ah-ah!" His bark stopped Cate in mid-turn, a twirling finger spinning her back around.

"He's vigorous and more than willing," Nathan went on over her sputtering objections. "He fancies you, you know. He could attend you, satisfy you, in all likelihood. With a bit of guidance and determination on his part, he might well give you a child."

"I'm not a brood mare being sent out to stud!" she cried, whirling around.

Nathan pointedly pivoted aside. "A child would be the answer to your dreams."

"And what am I to call the product of this answer: Blackthorne or Thomas?"

"Mackenzie," came back without hesitation. "Or Harper, if you fancy Brian might object."

Seeing Nathan flinch, Cate acquiesced and assumed a more abiding stance. "And you could watch my belly grow with another man's child?" The hurt and insult brought by that notion dissolved whatever sympathy she had harbored. This was skirting too close to another argument they had not that long ago, one fraught with violence and ending with her leaving both him and the *Morganse*.

There was a long struggle between what should be said and what begged to be. Finally, Nathan clamped his lower lip between his teeth and dolefully shook his head. "No," he said in a hoarse whisper. "I said it would be the 'decent' thing." The corner of his mouth tucked up wryly. "But decency is a claim to which I have never aspired."

With a gasping heave, Nathan finally straightened to his full height. The flush had faded, and he assumed something nearer to his natural color. He took an experimental step and then another, his shoulders relaxing incrementally. Each step brought him around until he faced her. His hand came up, reaching for her; checking himself, he tucked the offending limb to his side.

"Do not take this to mean I don't want you, darling. I burn for you as I never have. It's just every time I want you, every time I—" He made an aggravated gesture at his groin. "It will be this."

It was awkward seeing him so down. The blue devils were upon him. Or was it Calypso's hand weighing him down? If he had been on the verge of something daft before, he was perilously near diving over the edge now.

"Are we going to allow Calypso the satisfaction of knowing she's won, of letting her have her way?" Cate demanded. She was tired of being trifled with, tired of feeling like a marionette at Bartholomew Fair, tired of seeing the one she loved being so reduced.

Being caught with his cock in his fist mightn't abash Nathan, but being caught wallowing in self-pity did. He grinned, wide and earnest. "There's that go-to-the-devil attitude I've always admired. I'm the one dripping and shivering to be picked up off the deck, eh?"

Nathan squared his shoulders and declared with newfound vehemence "Suffering Christ on the cross, no! We'll knock her hand away. Hell, we'll break her damned arm, fin... whatever."

His elation of spirits was short-lived, and he sank once more. "I'm to the bitter end, luv, caught on a lee shore and there's no clawing off. But I'm still clapped on and with both hands. I — we can't go on like this, that's for bloody damned sure. God's bloody wounds, if I could find a way to stop the wanting, I could—" He stopped short, his mouth curving around the next word.

He snapped his fingers. "Dash me buttons! Why the bloody hell didn't I think of that before? Stand by!"

The last was almost lost in the rustle of him ducking into the bushes, nothing but a stirring branch to mark his passing.

He was gone... *again*!

24: NECESSARY EVILS

"**S**TAND BY? NOT BLOODY LIKELY!" Cate cried and dove into the bushes, hard on Nathan's trail.

Pushing through the thick undergrowth wasn't a quiet process. In his haste he made a lot of noise, and she aimed to follow it. Too soon, however, the branches moving with his passing merged with those stirred by the breeze, the snap and crash drowned by alarmed cries of birds and small creatures. Still, she had a sense of his general direction and followed it.

"Nathan. Dammit to bloody hell— Nathan!" she shouted upon glimpsing a flesh - colored patch amid the greenery.

She doggedly pressed on, afraid to slow lest she be too late for whatever the hell he meant to do.

"Desperate men do desperate things."

How many times had she heard those words from his lips? She had witnessed Nathan in a vast number of emotional states, but never this desperate. His threats of castration were alarming. *He couldn't... He wouldn't...!*

And yet, if not that, then there was no denying that he had been inspired to do something. As much as he denied the effects of the resurrection, neither was he in "fighting trim." If nothing else, this mood of his proved it.

Cursing under her breath, Cate pushed through the dense growth, jerking her hair and skirts free from questing twigs, unable to shake the ill-feeling that this whole thing had finally gone far beyond her capacities to deal with. Wisdom advised she should break off and send for help: Thomas, Pryce, Bella... someone, anyone!

Sweating and cross, Cate finally broke out onto one of the island's innumerable thoroughfares. Rising on her toes, she craned her head in both directions, hoping for a glimpse of Nathan, but in vain. Whatever Nathan was at, he was in a tearing hurry. Inquires of passing islanders produced nothing;

all claimed ignorance, whether in earnest or at his orders she couldn't tell.

A decision begged to be made: left or right? She closed her eyes. Something, either instincts or the hand of Providence, pulled her to the right and so she struck off. Judging by the thinning of both people and buildings, she was heading away from the settlement proper. Further along, things began to look familiar, and she realized she was on the path to Celia's shack. Her worries eased a bit. Nathan's regard for the *medsen fey* usually involved poles of the ten-foot variety; going there only put a finer point on his determination.

On that thought, Cate lengthened her stride, often breaking into a half-trot. Nathan's view of Celia might be jaded, but his seeking her out couldn't be seen as a total surprise. His thinking was running much in the same line as her own: their travails being involved with the bizarre or occult, then that shack might be where their last hope lay.

The forest closed in, obliging Cate to duck and dodge the encroaching fronds and limbs. Thoughts of the shack and its oddities, eyes peering at her from every direction brought her to approach it with wishes for Nathan's ten-foot pole. Her earlier visit with Celia hadn't gone badly, but neither had it gone well, Cate thought, looking down at the lace binding on her forearm. As forecast, the brand and a number of other things had been entirely out-of-mind since taking her leave. It all came back now, however, with startling clarity.

"There was a child, a boy, with his mother's eyes and his father's smile."

The revelation of having successfully conceived had been Cate's greatest joy. That silver cloud, however, had a very dark lining: she had lost yet another child. Her first impulse had been to tell Nathan, but discretion struck her mute. He was already flagellating himself to the point of bloody; given his current inabilities, telling him now would only rub further salt in an already raw wound. And yes, the fact that child might have been the last he might ever produce weighed like a millstone. The injustices just kept piling up and all on his back.

"Your womb will bear no fruit, until it is drained of the poison which fills it."

Cate had done as Celia bid: she had vented her spleen, taken her fury out and claimed her revenge. It had been an inadvertent and spontaneous eruption, but a cleansing of the soul, nonetheless. It had to be deemed a success. She felt a difference, a vast lightening, one which both Thomas and Nathan had seen and noted.

But had it been enough? she thought, pressing a hand to her belly. Did the vengeance Celia demanded need to be of the plotting, cold-blooded sort? Did it need to be of the eye-for-an-eye level: if a score had violated her, then a score was necessary for vindication?

Cate stumbled at the thought. She'd done what she could. It would be enough. It had to be.

"You hold his heart. Do not allow your hatred to consume it."

And what if that were still the case? It explained so much. Nathan had declared everything — affections, loyalties, fidelities, protection — and yet, from a certain point of view, he had said nothing. Pryce had once told her that "it wasn't what the Cap'n said, but what he didn't say." It was precious difficult to hang one's hat, their life's hopes on that thin hook. Had Nathan's failure been merely a matter of oversight? Or had it been as pointed as the end of his sword?

The path grew more winding. The trees closed in, enveloping Cate in the too familiar, unnatural stillness. She was beginning to think she might have gone the wrong way — This damned island and its paths were like a rabbit warren — when she smelled smoke and glimpsed the angles of a roof through the thick growth.

So cloaked in greenery, the shack still looked as if it had sprouted up from the forest floor. Flowers the garden and talismans in the windows and doorway, were the only bright spots in the otherwise dull palette of green and brown. The smoke lazing up from the chimney proved someone was there. A downdraft caught it, dragging it in ghostly wisps among the tree trunks.

Cate's step slowed. She and Celia had worked elbow-to-elbow for days. She'd witnessed the woman's compassion for the sick and injured, and enjoyed the kind of kinship which came with enduring tribulations together. Still, she wouldn't presume to go so far as to call Celia a "particular friend" or even "familiar." Now, there were none of the concerns of being cursed or turned into a toad, but she was still unsure of her reception. There were no signs, nor omens, nothing to discourage a visitor. The trodden path was proof a great number had made this same trip. The dooryard gate stood ajar, whether in welcome or the result of someone else's haste was anyone's guess.

Her hand was still on the gate when she heard voices from inside, Nathan's, low yet unmistakable, among them. Her shattered nerves eased a fraction. He was well... so far.

"Come!" Celia beckoned from inside long before she could have seen Cate.

Making her way onto the porch, dodging an amulet hanging

from the lintel, Cate stepped into the shack. The room was familiar. It still reeked of things long dead, and the gallery of onlookers, furred, finned, feathered and scaled, stared back in frozen wonderment. The pair turned at her entry, Nathan seated on a tall stool at the workbench, Celia stopped in mid-motion, a bundle of smoldering stems in her hand. The scene was nowhere near one of self-destruction and mayhem she had feared.

"Didn't you hear me calling?" Cate panted. If questioned, she couldn't have vouched having taken a full breath since Nathan had disappeared into the bushes.

"Didn't you hear me bid you to stay put? Do you ever do as you are asked?" Nathan asked mildly.

"No." Ducking under the feet of a dead creature hanging overhead, Cate dimpled and batted her lashes. "The simple thing might be to stop asking."

Cate found Nathan's hand and squeezed in a silent pledge. He might prefer she wasn't there, but he could just jolly well whistle for that! They had died together and would now figure out how to live together, whatever that entailed.

With a parting flex of his grasp, Nathan turned to Celia, calling their meeting back to order. "So, as I was saying, is there aught to be done?"

Celia slid a teasing look at Cate. "In the way of rendering her more obedient?" It would seem the herb woman wasn't beyond a little humor.

Nathan gazed at Cate. The corner of his mouth tucked up. "Woe that you could."

He shook his head and sighed. "As I was saying before the rude interruption," he began, with a mildly accusing cut of his eyes. "I need to stop the wanting."

The smoke from the smoldering bundle curling about her turbaned head, Celia arched a suspicious brow. "It is a curious request. Most run in the opposite direction: philtres and aphrodisiacs. You are usually a man of large enough appetites."

"That blessing is now me curse, thanks to that lurching, she-devil o' the deep. I supposed saltpeter to be in your perquisites," he added, with a gesture toward the cluttered shelves.

"Saltpeter!" Cate cried.

"What the bloody hell else?" Nathan declared, rounding on her.

"I thought—I mean, you said— And then, you—!I raced all the way out here, worried to death that you were about to do something drastic—"

"And you don't consider rendering meself insensible to the

point of viewing you with the same appeal as I view this table as drastic!"

"Then why—? Oh, never mind," Cate moaned, sinking onto a stool.

"Never resorted—willingly, at any rate—to such nostrums in me life," Nathan went on blithely, ignoring Cate's further remonstrations. "I've always been master o' me own domain, mostly," he added, with an equivocating wobble of his hand. "'Tis a wonder how something what makes gunpowder go off, might stop a man from desiring to do the same, but the proof lies in the pudding."

"Is this for you or her?" Celia mused.

"Her!" Nathan jerked back, struck momentarily speechless. "Such things answer for women?"

Cate knew Nathan well enough to know when he was honestly surprised, and he was then. Given his worldliness, his ignorance was both odd and endearing.

Celia flashed a broad smile, brief but genuine. "But, of course."

"Indeed," he said, unconvinced. Narrowing one eye, he considered Cate, his jaw twisted to one side. "Nay," he finally announced. "T'would be too much like breaking a spirited horse. T'will be for me and me alone."

"Very well. There are things which answer far better: monk's pepper, rue, *bois bonde*." Celia's mouth twitched with a ghost of a smile. "Or, I could just render her wholly unattractive in your eyes."

Nathan dismissed the suggestions with a curt wave. "The point of this exercise is that I might still desire to lie with her, to fulfill her needs."

Celia stepped to the brazier to deposit the smoldering bundle, dusting her hands after. "But, I do not understand why you think this is Calypso's doing. You still have the stink of her about you, but you are shielded—"

Nathan extended an arm and jerked back the grimy bandage to reveal his wrist and the scab encircling it. "Gone."

Turnabout was fair play; now Celia was the one shocked, the translucent eyes rounding. "Gone? How? Why?"

"Circumstances demanded. Suffice to say they were answering too well. And avast those regrets, darling," he said, rounding on Cate once more.

"I'm not—"

"Aye, but you are. It's written on your face as plain as this." He stabbed a thumb at the banner and "Freedom" etched on his chest. "It has been since the day we came back and I'll have no more of it," he said, gentle but firm.

He found her hand and fervently kissed the knuckles. "I did what I must, luv, and I'd do it again. No apologies. No worries."

"But, I—"

He pressed a finger to her lips. "No. Worries."

Reluctant but resigned, Cate mutely nodded.

"So, saltpeter it 'tis," Nathan declared to Celia. "Every ship carries it; surely it's somewhere in all this." He moved to one of the shelves and began picking up bottles, peering at their labels.

"Yes, Cate spoke of you doing this; I was reluctant to believe it." Celia disdainfully flicked one of the knotted bracelets on Nathans arm. "What are these?"

Nathan stopped to look down and flashed a tenuous smile. "I thought, nay hoped they might offer the protection they offered Cate."

Celia regarded him as if he had gone dim. "Cate is not of the bloodline she seeks. For you, they offer as much protection as a net in the rain. They are a bit of help, yes, but nothing like the tattoos."

Celia shook her head and sighed. "It is regrettable what your mother unleashed when she conceived at sea."

"She was young, and me father had his charms."

"Not unlike his son," Celia mused, with a knowing glance toward Cate.

"'Twas an old curse," Nathan went on. "Probably seemed no more than idle gossip to her, at the time." A bare shoulder lifted and fell. "Young passions can drive one to great extents."

A flush reddened his bare chest. No child liked to consider their parents in the sexual act, and yet his mother had done so and in a most flagrant way. Seeking privacy aboard a ship was like searching for hen's teeth; the young amorous pair had to have been quite determined to find their secluded nook. Cate's own cheeks heated, recalling similar escapades on her and Brian's part, not all being as successful as planned.

"The sins of the father and all that," Nathan declared with a gruff wave. "It boils down to the matter of what's to be done now, or better I amend that to 'what is in your powers.'"

"Mightn't we—someone just re-tattoo him? We know the pattern, don't we?" Cate ended lamely.

Celia's mouth twitched at Cate's well-meaning innocence. "The pattern is but a small part. The power lies in the ink."

"Woad," Nathan offered.

The herb woman angled her head in affirmation. "But not

any woad. It must be that which grows on the island where Morrigan is buried."

"You mean Morgan LeFaye, the witch, sorceress, I mean?" Cate bit her lip, regretting the slip of the tongue. Uttering either word was known to be a death sentence.

If Celia heard, she overlooked it. "Some say one became the other."

"Wasn't she of Merlin's making?" Cate had heard of the mystic, but always in reference to King Arthur's court.

"Or one saw a kindred spirit in the other and they combined forces," said Nathan, pragmatically. "Morrigan is the queen of it all, risen from the sea, or some such." A barely tolerant roll of his eyes summarized his opinion of it all.

"Is the *Morganse* named after her?" Cate asked.

Nathan hunched an equivocating shoulder. "In a manner o' speaking. In Celt, *mor* means sea, ergo you could call her 'Morrigan's gift.' Morgens are water spirits, mermaids."

"Black gift from the sea" had been his translation her first day aboard. The name had seemed apt then. Now, it was even more fitting.

"So, we have a Celt god, goddess, sorceress... whatever, lending a hand against a Greek one?" asked Cate, straining to follow.

"Calypso is but one name she answers," Nathan pointed out.

"And they are all connected," Celia added. "You find one appearing as another throughout the ages. Venus shows up as Aphrodite, Ishtar, Astarte or Isis. If you pray to the god of thunder, you can do so in either the name of Jupiter, Odin or Taranis."

Nothing further was offered; as the seconds passed, it became obvious that nothing would be forthcoming, either.

"Then we'll get more ink," Cate insisted, getting back to her initial point. "Where is this island?"

Celia smiled once more at Cate's innocence. "That is the great question of the ages." She cocked a curious brow at Nathan. "Your mother was a Great One; she did not tell you?"

"She was just Mum to me." Nathan shrugged, shaking his head. "I was but a babe for the first and a mere lad for the second," he added, looking down at his ravaged wrists. "There was a great moil in preparation for the latter: letters, messengers, visitors in the night..."

A time or two, he had mentioned his mother living under suspicion of being involved in the dark arts. Given that, her secretiveness would have been justified. And yet, at the same time, a little suspicion would be a small object in the face of a mother seeking to protect a child.

"Ah, well, it is a pity," Celia sighed. "The island is one of the great wonders. Many spend their lives in its quest. So much to be learned; so much to be gained."

Celia crossed her arms over her chest, the smooth brow crumpled in thought. Turning, she went to rummage among the books, not the tumbled and jumbled of the oft – used, but those almost white with dust, motes of it swirling up as she consulted with one, and then another. Nathan and Cate exchanged looks as they apprehensively watched Celia's finger track across page after page, her lips moving as she read.

"Yes," she finally announced, marking her place with a bit of string. "There are things which can be done, or tried, at any rate," she added, with a cautioning dart of the eyes. "Nothing the level of your mother's efforts, but things are possible. Luckily, we are inland; Calypso's grasp is weaker. Were you to go further inland and remain—"

"And live the rest o' me days on a mountaintop?" Nathan snorted. "T'would be a new form o' hell, only lacking the flames."

Cate's hopes soared at the notion. "Why not go farther inland, now?"

"There is no 'further,'" Nathan countered, bluntly. "This is an island; we are as far as far can be. Perhaps a few feet higher in the hills, but— 'Tis all water over the decks now. We've larger and fresher fish to fry."

His eyes lit, struck by a thought. "Would the old tattoos' ink still have... whatever need be needed?"

Celia eyed him sharply. "Possibly."

"You have them!" Cate gaped.

"I have *them*, ergo I have *it*. Well, it seemed a bloody shame to just pitch them," he went on at Cate's growing horror. "I have a bit of a connection with them, you understand. Those have been with me through thick-and-thin; they were one of the few things o' Mum remaining. I always felt her with me," he added shyly. "I wasn't about to just pitch them."

Cate cringed. It was too much like someone hanging onto a leg after it had been cut off.

"I figured, if they had protected me the while, then they would protect you all the more."

"Me!" Cate cried, reeling back on her seat.

"Then we have what we need," declared Celia.

Nathan's gaze fixed on Cate, indecision etching his features. "I gave them to you for your protection. I'll not jeopardize your safety for me own purposes."

"Nathan, take the damned things. Use them for... whatever. They were yours in the first place," Cate hissed under her breath. The more pressing question was where he had put them? They had to be somewhere among her dunnage.

She knew the look of Nathanael Blackthorne with his mind made up and looked to Celia for added support. "I'm... safe, aren't I?" The word "safe" was used with singular intent. It was Nathan's most oft used in reference to her; hopefully calling upon it now would help drive her point home.

"Cate was free of Calypso's touch before?" Celia asked.

His gaze still fixed on Cate, Nathan nodded. "Even in her lair, the hag circled around her like a witch around a cross." He smiled distantly at the recollection.

Celia nodded, as one does when hearing the expected. "Then the tattoos are like feathers to a goose."

Nathan rounded on Celia, ready to argue. Seeing her confidence in her claim, he exhaled, long and reluctant. "Very well. On to it, then."

Pulling his knife from at the small of his back, Nathan stepped around behind Cate.

"Hold this, if you please," he said, gathering her hair in his fist.

She did so, bending her head forward, out of the way. There was a brief fumbling about her nape and shoulder blades, and the ends of her necklace which hung there.

"Avast there," he grumbled. "You're gigging about like a f'c'stleman waiting for his grog."

Cate did as he bid, but only with effort. She loved Nathan to the core of her heart, but the thought of wearing bits of his dead skin made her queasy and anxious.

"Here!" he declared proudly, at last.

Cate cut her eyes sideways to see the half-dozen ends displayed. Hanging down her back as they did, she rarely heard more than saw them. Like her other adornments, bits of shell, stone and coral decorated them. The difference in these, however, was something which looked like light-colored leather knotted into beads at the very end of each.

"Calypso sure as hell didn't give a fig what I did with them, so long as they were gone. So I did the next best thing: I put them on you." Nathan smiled, proud of his adaptiveness.

Cate nodded woodenly, barely appeased.

A flick of the blade and the beads, bits of the cord protruding from their centers, were dropped into Celia's hand. Cate and Nathan both looked on with trepidation as Celia closed her eyes and experimentally rolled them in her palm.

"Yes, the power is with them!"

Nathan threw off his weapons onto a chair and clapped his hands together. "Very well, then what's to do?"

"Much depends on many things," Celia cautioned. "What do you aim to do?" Cate asked warily.

Celia cocked a brow at what seemed the obvious answer. "Replace them."

Cate gulped and looked down with mounting horror at the little balls, now lying in a shell dish. "You mean make bracelets out of them?"

"No," Celia said, patiently. "Replace, as in return to their proper place and, hopefully, recall them to their duty."

"Sit, darling, you're the color of turtle soup." It was Nathan's voice, but it had suddenly gone hollow and distant.

Numbly nodding, Cate allowed herself to be backed a bit further, until she came to a stool and sat. Suddenly, their audience before Calypso wasn't as far behind her as she had believed. The sight of Nathan peeling his own skin like one might skin a rabbit came back with startling clarity.

"I'm fine. I'm fine." Her chant proving unconvincing, she flashed a smile, but too soon. A few moments later, she managed another more successful one.

Celia pointed Nathan to the table at the center of the room. With a departing glance to Cate, he sat, legs dangling over the edge. With a few flicks of the knife, Celia removed what remained of Cate's feeble attempts at attending him. Cate braced, waiting for the remonstration sure to come for the wounds' deplorable condition.

It never came.

Instead, the *medsen fey* stood considering the scabs. Closing her eyes, she lightly pressed her fingertips to the corrugated surface of his ankle. Her lips moved ever so faintly and her head bobbed as if ending a prayer. Without warning, she dug in a fingernail and ripped off the scab. The side of Nathan's face twitched, and then stoically fixed on Cate as Celia continued to remove, the more stubborn bits being excavated with a knife tip. Celia moved to his other ankle and, with a slight flipping sensation in her stomach, Cate realized she meant to do the same to each and every one. Blood welled from the rudely-exposed flesh and tracked in small rivulets; Cate broke away long enough to fetch a basin and water and began cleaning it away.

"Plenty more o' where that came from."

Cate looked up from swabbing to find Nathan smiling at her. She numbly angled her head in assent, her mouth suddenly gone too stiff to manage a smile.

Celia moved from Nathan's ankles to his wrists, ripping the scabs off, alternately humming in approval and clucking her tongue in dismay. When it came time for his neck, Cate shuddered as she lifted the mass of hair out of the way. It was difficult to watch the tender skin being so abused, and yet it was, with the same cold calculation. His waist was next. Nathan obligingly lifted an arm up, leaving his tender middle looking exposed and vulnerable. Nathan's expression grew a bit more set, one fist working on his thigh, as the scabs were ripped away, Cate flinching in sympathy at every pull.

"If these had healed, little could be done," Celia announced, plucking out the final bit.

"Aye, well, they didn't," Nathan directed under his arm. He shot Cate a victorious "all that worry for naught" look. Damn him, his hard-headed resistance had been a fortuitous thing.

Celia moved to the shelves and began poking through the bottles and jars. She paused with a hand hovering over one and asked of Nathan "Milk of the poppy?"

Cate shifted uneasily, wondering why such a powerful pain-killer might be necessary.

"Nay," he replied out-of-hand. "I need me wits about me when the horror-o'-the – deep is involved."

"She'll know?" Cate asked in a strangled gasp. The hairs rising on her arms, she shot a nervous glance toward the door and then window, expecting to see someone, something standing there. The room's shadowy corners loomed like bottomless pits, perfect lairs for a skulking goddess to lurk, from where a tentacle might snake out, seize Nathan and drag him away.

"Oh, aye, she'll know." Nathan said heartily. He wormed where he sat. "Her claws are in me innards, like she means to gut me like a fish."

"Calypso will not be best pleased," Celia warned ominously.

"'Tis my experience precious little pleases her. She can jolly well go hang for the rest. Make it so."

Celia sketched a bow, touching her forehead and then heart. "Very well."

She hesitated, as if inclined toward saying something. Instead, knife in hand, she took Nathan by the wrist. "Sadly, there are some places—small ones—which have already closed…" With the deftness and ruthlessness of a butcher, she sliced away the pink, newly – healed skin. Nathan emitted a muffled grunt; Cate turned her head.

Celia paused, blade poised, and looked up at Nathan, silently asking if he wished her to stop.

"Lord knows I've suffered worse," he said dryly and set his jaw a little tighter.

It was no boast The lacework of scars on his body were proof that he had suffered far worse. Those, however had been through either through accident or battle. Well – intended or no, this was butchery, brutal and cold-blooded, cutting at him and tossing the severed bits into a dish like someone preparing a meat pie.

The worst was saved for last: his waist. Watching the scabs being ripped from it was one thing; seeing a blade applied there was quite another. Nathan's detachment, however, didn't include his reflexes: he twitched, his skin shuddering like a horse with a fly at every slice.

In desperate need of a distraction, Cate dabbed the blood, now streaming from every quarter of Nathan's being. As she swiped his neck, she looked up to find the coffee-brown eyes on her, soft and intent. He hooked a blood-streaked arm around her and drew her close, the chest hair tickling her nose.

"It will all be aye, darling. Celia's never led me astray before."

Cate leaned back, earnestly searching his face. "You don't have to do this."

Nathan met her gaze with one of his own. "Aye, but I do."

"Further preparations must be made," Celia announced and moved to the workbench.

"You mean to leave him like that!" Cate cried, staunching the flow from several points. Bloodied and butchered, looking like a hog half-slaughtered, to say Nathan was in pain wouldn't be a gross exaggeration, no matter how much he wished not to show it.

Celia held up the bowl containing the severed bits of his flesh. "This was necessary."

Cate was barely appeased. First, offering Nathan opium, looking to render him as insensible as a stone, and now plans for his flesh: no confidence could be found in either of those. Still, any delay would be intolerable.

With effort, Cate composed herself and asked "What's to be done?"

"Aye, I'm your man," Nathan chimed next to her.

Celia stepped away to what she referred to as her "storeroom." She returned shortly, arms loaded with bundles, jars and bottles, two thick twigs, a bit longer than her forearm, in her fist.

"This is the branch of a blackthorn," she said, holding up

the darkest. Cate reflexively backed away. "That's the Crone of Death's tree!"

The branch had been divested of its infamous thorns, but there was no mistaking the gnarled ebony bark. She wasn't one given to superstition, but in the Highlands its twisted black skeleton, stark against the snow, was enough to scare anyone from even mounting the hill where it grew. Only the most daring would venture to pick its sloes for tonics and ink. Cate looked to Nathan for confirmation—He, of all people, should be aware of the sinister elements of his namesake—but found only bland complacency.

"Its gentler sister tree, the hawthorn, will be present," Celia said, holding up a lighter-colored twig. "Together, they bring the power of healing, the sea silk," she went on, picking up another bit, "to blend and mollify."

Cate peered at the gossamer-like threads. "Sea silk?" She looked to Nathan, who looked on as if it were as common as cotton. "I don't— I mean, I've never heard—" She stopped, painfully conscious of showing her ignorance and, worse yet, encumbering the proceedings.

"Harvested at great pains and even greater peril," Celia said. "As poison as a cross to the Devil." She fondled the blackthorn with the tenderness of one stroking a pet, and said more to herself, "It would have been better if it was green and a different phase of the moon, but—"

Sobering, Celia handed the twigs to Nathan. "Strip the bark, carefully," she instructed, with a cautioning finger. "And then, shave them, as long and fine as possible."

Nathan nodded as he listened, absently testing the knife's edge with his thumb. He then set to work, the space around him soon looking like a cooper's shed, the curls of shaved wood, some bright orange, but most a light tan piling up before him.

Cate was put before a small iron pot at the hearth. Tallow and wax were dropped in. She frowned into the pot, puzzled. The proportions and absence of resin suggested a salve was on the make, not a sticking plaster. After all, how else would one go about reattaching someone's skin? She didn't press Celia, however, who was dividing her attentions between Cate, Nathan and a concoction of her own, an oil of some sort. Several massive tomes, decades deep in dust, were searched out and consulted. Apparently, ousting a goddess wasn't a common thing. At one point, while Celia was distracted by searching the remoter niches of the shelves, Cate craned her head toward one of the books in hopes of gaining a better notion of what might be to come next.

Her efforts, however, were for naught, the writing resembling chicken tracks.

A frisson shot through Cate, one of several since she stepped over the threshold, at what they were about to embark upon, and worse yet, what Nathan was about to endure.

A prompting hiss from Celia made Cate resume stirring. More ingredients, often involving incantations or ritual motions beforehand, were tossed into the pot. Smells, many of the noxious sort, rose when they hit the viscous mix. At one point, the *medsen fey* reached to swipe a finger in the blood trickling down Nathan's side and flicked it in, several hairs snatched from his head meeting the same fate.

"*Double bubble, toil and trouble,*" rose to mind again. Cate shook it off, lest Celia read her mind. Referencing witches, even if one's of Shakespeare's making, mightn't be appreciated.

Everything was knocked from Cate's mind when Celia stepped up to the pot and tossed in the bits of Nathan's flesh.

"Stir."

Cate looked down to find she had stopped yet again, the wax and tallow now beginning to smoke. Gulping down a queasy lump, she resumed, only to find her hand had suddenly gone non-cooperative, the circular pattern now more like a square. Unable to look into the pot, lest what she might see, she fixed her attention on the glassy eyes of a desiccated amphibian hanging near her head.

Shortly, the pot was swung off the fire. Stirring now became a more physical exercise, the tallow and wax thickening as it cooled.

"The name 'Blackthorne' just a coincidence... isn't it?" Cate asked.

"You mean, am I related to a tree?" Nathan asked wryly.

"It is Morrigan's spirit tree," said Celia, from her work spot.

"You'd have to ask me father on that one," Nathan said, with a perturbed crook of his mouth. "I know precious little of his ancestors. Can't recall him ever mentioning anyone, other than his mum, now and again," he added, looking off.

Cate reddened at her foolishness. One never questioned someone named Oaks or Birch; she personally knew a Maplewood and a Hawthorn, and never questioned their bloodlines. At least, that is what she kept telling herself. The coincidences — hair and eyes as black as the tree's bark and a stubbornness which often brought to mind a stump — were precious difficult to ignore. And yet, there was the strong possibility, nay, probability that it was exactly that: a fluke of fate. His father would know which meant, considering his twenty-plus years' absence, they were delivered right back to their original place: deep in the Land-of-Ignorance.

Nathan finished shaving the branch; Celia gathered up the long bits. Tidying them into a bundle with a bright bit of string, she moved to the end of the workbench, putting her back to them, effectively blocking their view. Feeling a bit like unwanted company, Cate and Nathan obligingly turned aside too, feigning interest in the pot he now stirred. Ostensibly, he did so to relieve Cate, but it struck her as more in the way of needing to be occupied. Still, from the corner of her eye, Cate could see Celia's arms moving like someone working dough. Faint conjurations came from her direction, whether asking a blessing or placing a curse, who could tell?

Once again, she was struck by her and Nathan's vulnerability. They were putting their blind faith in Celia, as one always did when consulting one of her ilk, persons who could make or break, enliven or destroy at their whim, and naught to be done for it. For Cate, blind faith didn't come naturally; Nathan, however, seemed to possess it in abundance, she observed with a cautious glance. She shifted a little closer, hoping a bit might rub off.

"You're dripping." Cate snatched up the wet cloth and pressed it to Nathan's bleeding wrist.

Nathan glanced dispassionately at it. "Probably do a lot worse, before this is over."

"You don't have to do this, not for me." She lowered her voice, not to keep from being heard, but more in the spirit of not disturbing whatever Celia was at.

The paddle in the pot stopped, and he eyed her narrowly. "And who else do you fancy this would be for?"

He shook his head, his motions resuming at Celia's prompting hiss. "You flourishing is my salvation, darling. But 'tis your choice."

"You never leave me much in that category, do you?" she said, striving for levity.

Nathan grinned, the one employed when he had been found out. "Not if aught can be done for it."

"I don't like this," Cate said, lower and more emphatic. "I have a bad feeling that this is going to be like ramming a stick in a hornet's nest."

"Often, 'tis necessary to be rid of the little blighters," Nathan said, with a wink.

Any further remarks were cut short by Celia turning back to them reverently bearing a long roll. Barely a finger's diameter, it looked like wood, and yet was as pliable as leather when laid on the table. To her displeasure, Cate noticed that it still retained the ominous blackthorn black. Like a craftsman gathering their tools, Celia collected and arranged other impedimenta. Salve, scooped from the cooling pot, was placed in a shallow dish, the one containing the balls of Nathan's knotted skin next to it.

Celia straightened, swiping her hands on her apron. "Ready?"

༺ঞ্জৎ༻

A vessel was filled with a hot liquid from the fire, clear, but too viscous to be water alone. The balls of skin were dropped in, pinches of this and that sprinkled in. The stink of rotten seaweed, mud, and things long gone foul rose on the steam, and hit Cate with staggering force. The room began to swim. Her stays were suddenly like iron bands, the air like breathing water.

She was vaguely aware of hands catching her and being guided to a chair. The acrid, burning-feather stench of hartshorn cut through the fog which enshrouded her. Snorting and gasping, her vision finally focused on Nathan kneeling before her, Celia standing next to him.

"I'm sorry. It—that," she said, with an unsteady nod toward the vessel. "It smells so much—too much... like... like... *there*."

"Excellent!" Celia cried, clapping her hands together. "We have found the door to her lair."

By the time Cate's head cleared enough to sit on her own, the balls of skin had bloomed, opening like flowers. Celia probed each with a finger, teasing them nearer to their rightful shape. Translucent and pale, the long, slim strips looked more like inscribed parchment.

"I cannot predict what—" Celia began, cautioning.

"I'll bear it," Nathan said, shortly. "*We'll* bear it." He directed the flash of a smile at Cate, the charming one which always touched her. The fear she might never see that smile again made it impossible to return it. Harnessing several more dark and dubious thoughts, she arranged her face into something nearer to confident.

Celia plucked a strip out, dredged it through the warm salve, and then stopped. "Left or right? Ankle or wrist?"

Nathan peered at the bit dangling from her fingers. "Wrist, I think. As for the other, damned if I can tell."

Lifting the strip, as if in offering, Celia briefly closed her eyes and announced "Right."

A deft swirl laid the piece on Nathan's arm. The strip settled in, as if being returned to its rightful place. Spread by Celia's fingers, the salve served as both glue and bridge between it and Nathan's living flesh. Lighter and more translucent than his arm, the piece still wasn't fully a part of him, but a sense of fulfillment instantly suffused Cate, to the point she wondered what had worried her so? Perhaps this might answer after all; Nathan seemed to think as much, smiling like one regaining an amputated limb.

A piece was severed from the blackthorn roll and worked out like pastry dough to roughly the same dimensions as the newly-returned strip.

"This is a binding," Celia said, forming it around Nathan's wrist into something akin to a black cuff. "So she cannot fling this off. As soon as Calypso realizes—"

Nathan sucked in sharply. "She realizes," he said in a strained rasp. "Unless these things have been dipped in acid, she knows." The white line of his mouth and the cords rigid in his forearms told the truth of it.

Celia had no more than moved to his other arm, when Nathan emitted a muffled growl and swore. The skin around the first turned fire-red, and then erupted in watery blisters, bubbling like a cauldron over a flame.

Setting his face, Nathan jerked a nod, bidding Celia to continue. Each tattoo returned was of little consequence. Each binding applied, however, broke out like the first, bringing a new level of agony. Nathan fixed his gaze on Cate's face, finding the strength he needed there. Cate balled her fists in her skirts, biting back the compulsion to demand Celia work faster. And yet, the faster she progressed, the more Nathan suffered.

Limbs completed—at last!—Celia hesitated. "Those of your neck and waist are older, the ink more powerful." The observation reflected a great admiration for the creator. She looked up and swallowed. "She will fight these all the harder."

The lilt in her voice held the question: Did Nathan desire her to stop? Did he wish the opiate now?

Speech no longer an easy thing, Nathan resolutely shook his head to both.

The tattoo at his neck was laid in, the blackthorn neatly molding to the curves and contours. Nathan gave a shuddering gasp and clamped his eyes shut. As predicted, the eruption was even more instant, even more violent. A viscous substance, like pus, now oozed from all points. White and stinking, the foulness had a shocking undertone of rotting fish.

Celia took the last remaining strip, the longest yet, from the bowl. "The waist next," she said apologetically.

Snorting through his nose, Nathan's lips drew back in a fixed grimace. "On to it."

Cate wormed her hand into his fist. He cleaved onto it.

Realizing he was hurting her, he flung the hand away and closed his eyes, determined to fight this alone.

Not as determined as me, cully, she thought and forced her hand back into his, clasping hard enough to make his eyes pop open, straight into hers.

Holding Nathan's gaze, Cate tightened her grip, clinging as if her life depended on it... and it did. If he was gone, taken, then she would find a way to be taken, as well. After all, there would be no life for her anywhere without him.

The task complete, Celia stepped back. Nathan shook and then swayed.

"Lie down," Cate suggested. The sickly shade he suddenly took on was alarming.

Mouthing an inarticulate oath, Nathan sank slowly, sprawling on his back like a sacrifice on an altar. He went distant, withdrawing into himself to fight an invisible battle. The white mess, dripping from his limbs and sides, pooled in the hollows of his throat and on the table under him. Cate wetted a cloth, meaning to swab it away. She barely brushed his skin and Nathan emitted an animal-like howl, twisting away.

From Nathan's other side, Celia craned her head to see the resulting mark: bright red mark, as if he had been burned.

She wasn't displeased. "Fresh water burns," she observed, under her breath. She bent to peer into his face. "He is in her world, now. Only seawater can touch him, now."

Cate flung the cloth aside and dashed her hands dry on her skirts, lest a droplet might linger. If seawater was needed, then seawater was what she would get. She could race to shore. What held her back was it meant leaving Nathan. Nothing could tear her away, now.

And so, Cate stood, the impotent bystander, her presence her only asset.

Nathan heaved and writhed like one in a profound delirium, except there was no fever. The case was quite the opposite: a chill radiated off him, like a block of ice. The translucent eyes alert and keen as a hawk, Celia was at his side, mouthing an unending, but ever-changing chant. Herbs were cast onto the corner brazier and on a smaller one at her elbow, some even placed on his skin and set afire in a smoldering flash. Cate's head began to swim again, a dull ache settling behind one eye, as the air grew thick with smoke and the alternating smells of acrid, to pungent, to sickly sweet and back.

"It's like an exorcism," Cate breathed, in horror. Nathan's words "desiring to gut me like a fish" rang in her ears. God only knew what tortures were going on inside.

A woman of passions, refusing to release her lover. A vindictive and vengeful goddess, to say the least!

Celia smiled at the notion of a religious rite. Her eyes unwavering from Nathan, she angled her head, conceding. "Driving out a demon more devilish than the Devil himself. We must help him, and yet, not interfere."

Cate stared into Nathan's tortured face, wondering where the clues to that difference might lie.

Nathan's skin bubbled and oozed, the stink reaching nauseating levels. Cate gripped the edge of the table, swallowing down the rising gorge. He slithered and writhed, his braids coiling like black snakes in the stinking mess.

"Do not let it touch you." Celia's warning held a note of strong uncertainty as to what the consequences might be.

Cate withdrew her hands, but no further.

Suddenly, Nathan went deadly still. Celia's invocations stopped. "Speak to him!"

Startled, Cate stared down and then bent. "Nathan. Nathan!"

His head jerked and his entire being twitched. His mouth took a more determined, more rebellious set, and the writhing went from agony to striving to be free. His body heaved, his heels digging into the surface.

"Call him!" Celia's voice cracked like a whip.

"Nathan."

"Louder."

"Nathan!" Cate cried in a near shriek. She grasped the table, her fingernails gouging the wood. "Dammit, Nathan, I didn't come back from the dead just to lose you now!"

With the speed and accuracy of a snake, his hand shot out and seized Cate's, clutching like one clinging to a precipice. She hung on, sending the force of her will through the connection. Nathan's grasp tightened, grinding her bones together. Swallowing down the pain, Cate clung. The sense of descending seized her, being dragged back into those black depths, the pressing cold closing around her once more. She wriggled her toes into the earthen floor, seeking an anchor in this world. She closed her eyes, concentrating, reaching for Nathan, willing him to prevail.

Limbs twitching, chest heaving, Nathan panted like a man running for his life. In the next instant, he went deadly still, his hand cold and flaccid, his face assuming the slacken pallor of the deceased. The lividness of his skin faded, and the ooze stopped. Cate looked to Celia, round-eyed and frozen. The healer imperceptibly shook her turbaned head, whether in uncertainty or bidding Cate to wait was the wonder?

A time-tick, and then another. With a galvanic heave, Nathan gasped like a drowning soul bursting to the surface. His hand, now warm with life, flexed in Cate's, acknowledging her presence.

He lay gulping in great draughts of air. Finally, his eyes cracked opened. Unfocused and roving at first, they finally found Cate and settled. His hand moved against hers again, and he smiled. He made to speak, swallowed, and then tried anew.

"No worries, luv. I'm here."

Cate was increasingly unnerved by the sound of water dripping to the floor: in the Highlands, it was said to portend a visit from Death.

Her voice having abandoned her, Cate mouthed "Is it over?" to Nathan.

Nathan's head barely stirred. "Aye," came more as a rush of air than speech.

"Can I touch you?" she asked stupidly.

He jerked and scowled. "Suffering Christ, I hope so, or this has all been for naught!"

Too weak to lift them, a twitch of Nathan's arms beckoned her. With a small joyous cry, Cate threw herself down and hugged him. He was wet as a whale, but it was only water, fresh and sweet!

While Nathan gasped, recovering, Celia busied about the room. She stepped to the small brazier and sprinkled dried leaves on the coals. The wisps of smoke rose and curled through the room, bringing the sharp smell of sage and something sweet. A branch, not unlike the one she had brandished the first day, was dipped in a bowl and employed like an aspergillum at Mass, sprinkling the liquid over and around Nathan.

Nathan made a flailing attempt to rise. "Help me up!"

"Lie still," Celia said, a hand on his chest.

"Pah! I'm fine, fit as a fiddle." Brushing both women aside, he sat up, swinging his legs over the table's edge. Contrary to his claims, he wove precariously, but dodged their attempts to assist.

Once steadied, he grabbed Cate's arm. "You're well, unharmed?" he demanded, looking her over.

Confused—he was the one who just endured the ordeal!—a mute nod was all Cate could manage.

Satisfied she was unscathed, Nathan ran a hand down his face. "I feared for your safety, that she had come for you—"

"She!" Cate blurted.

"Aye, the skulking, double-tongued jade—"

"*She* was here!" Cate stammered, taking a faltering step away.

Nathan's retort died in his mouth at finding a mirror image of Cate's disbelief on Celia's face.

"Aye, right there," he said with a jab of his thumb behind him. "Had her claws in me, she did." He thrust out an arm to show several long, bloody gouges, as if he had encountered a great cat. "I thought for sure she had come for you, meaning to use you against me."

Cate looked to Celia, questioning.

No, she hadn't seen anything, either.

He smiled at Cate. "T'was your hand, your voice, *you* which recalled me to me duty, to where I belonged."

The sight of running blood jerked Cate from her stunned gape. Grabbing up a cloth and water, she set to washing, while Celia returned to her worktable. Cate worked with one shoulder hunched, glancing now and again toward one corner or the other, the shadows there now seeming to provide perfect cover for skulking demons. Feeling Nathan's concerned gaze, she put on a brave face, but apparently not as convincing enough.

"She wouldn't have gotten you," he said, solemn and earnest. "I'd have made her take me, if there was naught else for it."

Cate choked a self-conscious laugh. "If that is supposed to assure me, it doesn't. It's just... just... knowing she was right there, and I didn't know it."

She had fancied herself recovered from the whole ordeal with Calypso, had prided herself on having put it all behind her. But now, knowing she had been within the goddess's reach without realizing had her thoroughly shaken.

"You weren't meant to, the devious harridan." Nathan touched her bracelet. "It means she can't touch you, which means those bracelets are working."

"You're wearing them. How can she touch you?" Cate pointed out, now dabbing salve from a tin.

"I should imagine the difference is your family isn't the one cursed," Nathan pointed out, pragmatically. He held out his arm, the scratches livid against his skin. "She's lost her grip, literally and figuratively. Beyond that, there is no sorting out what the bloody hell she is thinking, nor do I care."

"Avast that pottering about. I don't need your possets," he directed over his shoulder to Celia.

Oblivious to his remarks, Celia continued at whatever she was about. Shortly, she brought forth a cup and thrust it at him.

Nathan leaned away, eyeing it warily. "Unless that's rum...?"

The smell, noticeable from even where Cate stood, eliminated that possibility. Alas, she thought, for she could have used a tot herself just then.

The proffered cup didn't move.

"I don't need —" Nathan began.

"Drink anyway." She spoke with the tone of one accustomed to their orders being followed. "It is part of a final cleansing, to wash away the last vestiges of her."

A cocked brow indicated that, on that note, Nathan could hardly refuse. He took it, sniffed the contents, scowled, and then neatly downed it, making a face at the end.

Celia produced a glass vial from her pocket. Its curved, cone shape resembled a tiny cow horn, with silver fittings at each end. One might have mistaken it for perfume or a lachrymatory, had it not been for the content's oily consistency and color. If "rotten" had a color that would be it.

With a bit of ceremony, the bottle was opened. The cap dangled from a fine chain as Celia tilted it over Nathan's wrist, allowing a single drop, hanging like discolored dew, to form on the lip. "This must be applied with the three phases of the sun: rise, zenith and set."

The drop fell. For a fraction of a moment, it beaded on the cuff's surface, and then melted in. The fluid spread quickly, darkening the woody surface, eventually covering the entire cuff, the adjacent skin gleaming faintly.

Cate turned her head slightly, her nostrils pinching when the smell reached her. Rotten, indeed. It verged in the realm of eye-watering, something between asafoetia and that which might have been drained from a boil.

"Stinks like the vapors of hell," Nathan observed.

"Or that which might drive one from it," Celia countered, securing the cap. "Apply this through the next two cycles of the moon. Follow exactly or live with her hand on you forever."

"Yes, mum." He delicately plucked the bottle away and tucked it into his waistband. "A sentence of diligence, but one I'll gladly serve."

Nathan pulled his knife and set the tip under a rope bracelet. "Time to be rid of —"

"Not yet." The sharpness of Celia's voice stopped him short. "Do not remove those until you are confident of our success."

"There is a doubt?" he asked, scowling.

Celia's mouth took a wry twist. "Always, where she is concerned. I believe our efforts to be successful, but —" A shrug, palms spread, expressed the capricious nature of exorcising gods. "Their protection is slight, but still helpful in loosening her grasp."

"Would it be over-ambitious to say I feel a difference already?" Nathan asked, touching the wooden cuff.

Celia bent her head. "Then the powers were on our side today."

Like a hound catching a scent, the herbwoman's head came up and around to fix her full attention on Cate. A hand was laid on the ball of her shoulder, not in exploration, but as if confirming what was already known. "This is inflamed."

Cate jerked and shied—either the woman had hands of ice, or the joint was on fire. With everything else, she had forgotten about Lesauvage twisting it so violently.

"It's torn, but not irreparably." The grip tightened and Celia's eyes closed. In a very brief interval, the hand lifted away. It might have been Cate's imagination, but she felt a pulling sensation, like strings taking the inflammation with it.

Celia smiled at Cate's obvious relief. "Comfrey compresses and rest will answer nicely. I will have them sent on the morrow."

"Is there aught else might you do for her?" Nathan's query was directed to Celia, but his gaze didn't waver from Cate. "Name the favor and then name your price; you know me pockets always run deep."

Celia sniffed disdainfully at the notion of money. Cate shifted self-consciously under Celia's eye. It wasn't easy being regarded like a cow at a fair.

With a semi-amused curl of her mouth, Celia said "She is already beautiful."

"I know that," Nathan said, with a brusque wave. "Your talents usually run far beyond that."

Celia's consideration continued, a knowing brow arched. "Her heart has been empty, but it is now filling with another."

Cate glowed, her hopes confirmed. At the same time, she couldn't help but wonder if the woman had read her thoughts on the way there.

"Life has marked her, in more ways than one," Nathan began. "More so than 'tis fitting for anyone."

"Yes, we spoke of them, did we not?" Celia directed to Cate with a significant lilt.

Nathan looked to Cate, suspicious. A twitch of one shoulder acknowledged no, she hadn't told him everything of her first audience and no, the omission had been wholly unintentional.

"And?" Nathan prompted.

Celia's eyes closed, and she breathed slowly for several moments. Then they opened straight into Cate's and held. "The one on her arm will be no more annoyance than the color of her hair."

Cate found herself nodding, accepting the notion as her own.

The gold eyes blinked and broke away. "The other marks are too old." Celia spread her hands, apologetic. "As I have said, the life, the child, is gone too long."

"Child, eh?" Nathan mused, cutting a look toward Cate.

"Very well, yes, I know now that I—" Cate swallowed, sudden emotion tightening her throat. "That there was one. Are you satisfied?"

Nathan smiled, wide and sly. "I knew it all along. You were the one who—"

"You aren't going to be boorish or tedious about this are you?" she asked narrowly.

Oh, heaven help her, he was puffing his chest already. Next he'd be strutting around like a cock in a barnyard.

"I'll be as insufferable as 'tis required for you to say I was correct," he said with a malicious gleam. He shook her in gentle admonition. "Go ahead, say it. Say it."

A gloating Nathan wasn't a pleasing sight, and yet there he was, in his full glory. "Yes, you were correct," she finally managed.

"What was that?" he prompted, canting his head closer.

Looking to the ceiling, Cate said louder "Yes, you were correct." The admission didn't come easily, not because she hated saying it, but because of the flood of emotions which came with admitting what Creswicke had taken from her, from them.

"Ha! I told you!" Framing her face with his palms, he kissed her forehead.

Nathan straightened, still holding Cate's face. "Might you give her more?" he asked of Celia.

"No need. That was decided long ago."

Nathan's head whipped around at that. "Indeed? And how many?" he asked, eyeing Cate speculatively.

Celia opened her mouth, but then, sighing in strained patience, she thrust out a palm before Cate. "Spit."

Cate's mouth suddenly went dry. After several tries, she finally managed to produce a creditable amount. The moment the liquid touched her palm, Celia smacked a finger into it and peered at the result.

"You shall have many," Celia said, exhibiting the results to all. "Alive and well," she added, cutting off Cate's next question.

"You must go," Celia announced matter-of-factly, ushering them toward the door. "Our work here is complete."

Nathan drew up at the door, sobering. "I started the day a

bit more abruptly than I could have wished. I came unprepared in the business way o' things. Name your price and a lad with a purse shall be sent."

"The usual will do," replied Celia, off-handedly.

"The usual was not performed here today," Nathan countered.

The translucent eyes fixed on Cate. "Sometimes more than one purpose is served."

Nathan gazed pensively, noting the meaningful lilt and trying to digest it. Finally, he inclined his head, conceding, and turned to take his leave.

"Have a care. You are not dealing with who you think."

Celia's warning stopped Nathan in mid-stride. He pivoted slowly and asked "Who, then?"

Celia coughed and shied deeper into the room's shadows. "Too much has already been said."

"Duplicity is it, then?" Nathan mused. "I fancied me coin bought at least a modicum of honesty."

Celia hesitated and then said in a low hiss "The powers are not always aligned as we could wish."

They had barely stepped over the threshold when "Defeat her; send her back to the Hell from which she arose" came from vehemently from inside.

Nathan stopped and swept a bow in the direction of the invisible voice. "Your wish is but my command!"

❧

Cate and Nathan stepped off the porch, wove through the gardens, and then struck down the now-familiar path leading back to the settlement.

As they walked, Cate reeled from one emotion to the next, some striking with such intensity she didn't even know what they were. Overarching them all, however, was unmitigated joy, the words "Alive and well!" ringing like a ship's bell.

It was all she could do to keep from capering about. Years of disappointment, years of loss, years of barrenness, years of hopelessness were gone, vanished! A part of her was reluctant to believe it, but there was no denying the existence of hope, shining, gleaming, resplendent hope! She was no longer dead inside, but life-giving and alive.

A blessed future had been laid out before her, allowing for more than she ever could have hoped, nor dared to pray. Granted, it all hinged on a glob of spittle in a palm, but Celia was no crone on a street corner reading bones. Kings had ruled empires on less.

The prospect of impending child-bearing, however, brought several sobering thoughts and her step slowed. As Tiacita, her nurse, used to say, more tears were shed over prayers answered. She could conceive, but no joy came without a price: hers would be losing Nathan. She knew her time with him was limited; a growing belly would end things very quickly. She would have his child, but nothing more. It would mean being left on an island, living her nightmare.

Lord, please not here! she thought, looking around.

She pressed a hand to the flat plane of her stomach. She was getting the cart before the horse: first, and foremost, she needed to be in that delicate condition. Celia's revelations were to be believed, that was a given. But, given Nathan's current debilities, the possibility was removed to somewhere on the farthest horizon.

Looking ahead at Nathan's back, Cate found she was oddly alone in her soaring spirits. The expected strut wasn't to be seen. Nathan had been so fixated on her being with child, she would have thought him to be crowing just then. If anything, he was hang-dog, verging on dejected.

"Something fouled your holystone?" she finally asked.

"'Hawser,' darling. It's 'fouled your hawser' and yes, 'tis fouled, indeed," he added, with a jerk of his shoulders.

"Well, didn't you hear Celia? There was a child."

He cut a look back at her. "No sense in celebrating what I already knew."

Cate stopped, deflated. "I didn't know, not the first visit, at any rate. But still, didn't you hear—?"

"I did." He drew up and rounded on her. "But, I also heard what she didn't say."

"'Didn't say?'" Cate echoed dully.

"Aye, the one grand omission," he said, with an aggravated swipe. Hands on his hips, he arched a severe brow at her failure to follow. "Who?"

Cate was so far gone in the notion of the first, it took her several moments before she could grasp the second.

"'Who?'" she said, in a thin rasp.

Nathan nodded solemnly. "Aye, *who* shall get these *several* upon you."

He turned and struck off, a new heaviness in his step. "The session was called to a close before that significant bit was made clear."

In truth, Cate had heard precious little after Celia's revelation. Anything after "alive and well" had been lost on her.

"But... but... but, of course, it has to be you... isn't it?" she stammered, speeding to catch him up. Surely, they missed something: a word, a gesture... something!

"'Tis not written, or so it would seem," he huffed. "What if I prove to be useless as a eunuch?"

It was difficult to hear him through the sound of her world crashing around her.

"But after all you just went through...?" Cate sputtered, with a helpless gesture toward the cabin behind them.

"Oh, aye, one might assume all of this is going to work," Nathan said, plucking disdainfully at one of the blackthorn cuffs. "But, what if it doesn't?"

Heart sinking, Cate had the sensation of tumbling down a steep hill in a barrel.

Nathan took her by the arms and gently shook her. "I swear, I'll see you happy. I swear I will see your future fulfilled."

Cate was barely heartened, feeling more like she had just been sentenced, not promised. "But I—"

"We'll find another," he declared and struck off up the path once more.

"Oh, no, not this again," she moaned.

"T'would have to be someone fitting, someone suitable— Don't want some cross - eyed, mumbling, drooling offspring," he added, under his breath. "And willing. Thomas: he's a fine figure, don't you think?"

Nathan turned, surprised to find she wasn't next to him. Little spurts of dust shot up as he patted his foot, waiting for her to catch up.

"You never seemed to care much before about children," Cate pointed out when she finally did. "Why the fixation all of a sudden?"

Nathan made an indifferent noise. "Aye, I can't tell one blighter from the next. They're all one to me: human larvae, white and wriggling like worms in a biscuit."

"And you don't care a bit about fatherhood." On that point she was sure, as well. He had declared that at the top of his lungs when John had shown up.

"I don't care a fig for someone to call me 'father.' But I would give me last farthing to see you called 'mum.'" His finger carved the air with conviction.

Cate wanted to deny it, but a particular thrill which struck just at the thought, made it impossible.

"'Tis no secret Thomas wants you," Nathan called over his shoulder, as he strode on. "Badly, worse than ever seen."

"He's a friend —!" Cate shrieked, hurrying after him.

"Aye, but is he a good enough friend to do it? There's the crux o' the matter."

"But I'd never —"

"No, not willingly. But I also know his powers of persuasion. He can be a charming cuss when there's something in his sights."

"But I haven't —"

"I know."

Lord, if he would allow her to finish a sentence!

Cate stopped dead and shouted "I will not go with Thomas or… or anyone!"

She was keenly aware of how petulant and pouting that came off; stomping her foot wasn't far off. She looked down to find a small cloud of dust hanging about her ankles; apparently she had done that very thing. The impersonation of Prudence was complete. Dammit, she didn't care! On this, she would win, if it meant kicking and screaming all the way.

"I want —" She stopped at realizing Nathan was far ahead and deeply tangled in his own machinations. She knew the look of a preoccupied, and therefore, unhearing Blackthorne.

Nathan stopped abruptly. He stood head hanging, whether gathering thoughts or patience she couldn't tell. Suddenly, he turned and crossed the small distance between them, his gaze fixed on hers. He found her hand and fervently pressed his lips to her knuckles.

"Believe me, darling, it tears me heart out to think of you lying with anyone, but I *will* see you fulfilled. I *will* see you have *everything* what's coming to you. I'll not stand in the way of your happiness."

He spun away, leaving Cate staring, the weight of that pledge hanging like an anvil. "We'll have to catch Thomas whilst he's to hand," Nathan called back.

Cate hitched her skirts and raced to catch up. "He's leaving!?"

"Aye, represented he means to haul anchor, sooner than later, this tide or the next."

"When did he announce that?"

"Last night."

"I thought you were too drunk to remember anything."

Nathan snorted. "I'd have to be a water-hearted, twopenny dull-wit not to remember that. No doubt he's making ready as we speak."

"I thought he meant to search the island." Those had been Thomas' parting words that morning, she was sure.

"Three hundred men on that shore; t'would require no more than a hundred to beat the bushes. That leaves the rest to wood 'n water, 'n whatever the hell else need be done. The *Lovely* looked shipshape already. It shouldn't require much. We'll be doing the same and soon," he added as a cautioning reminder.

"He's in a tearing hurry," Nathan went on, lengthening his stride. "Strikes me 'tis more in the way of desiring to be away from here, as opposed to having a place to go. We'll have to show a leg, if we're to catch him and put him to mind of his duty."

Cate was both furious and affronted at learning this second hand. Even more overpowering, however, was the ill-feeling which came at the thought of Thomas leaving.

"Damn him!" With a jerk of skirts, Cate elbowed past. "Where is he?"

"Feeling fertile are we?" Nathan called in her wake.

25: BULLS 'N ROCKS

ONCE BACK IN THE SETTLEMENT, Nathan wove his way through its dwellings and people, with the determination of a man with a single purpose.

As most humans required air, pirates required rum and—when on land—contrived for it to never be far from reach. Puncheons, firkins and rundlets were set up everywhere. Where those wouldn't answer, pitchers, bottles and any other vessel designed to contain liquids were employed. At length, Nathan spotted what he sought: a rundlet, the loose gathering of men around it proof it wasn't empty. Elbowing his way through, Nathan filled a horn, threw his head back and guzzled it down.

Gasping when finished, he dashed his arm across his mouth. "Going to require a great deal of this to get through this next bit."

Cate wondered if "this next bit" was dealing with the exorcising of Calypso or his plans for Thomas?

Nathan refilled the horn and handed it to her. "You're looking like you need a bit o' this yourself."

Cate eyed it with loathing, but necessity led many a person to many a desperate thing. Noticing the liquid's surface quaking, she switched hands, only to find the effect the same. Apparently, emotions were running much higher than credited. With that thought in mind, she took a bold drink, gasping and shuddering at the end.

It turned out—damn his insufferable, all-knowing soul—that Nathan had been correct: Thomas' men were in high gear with making ready to depart. Water casks being floated out to the ships dispelled any lingering doubts. Further inquiries revealed Thomas was somewhere in the island's interior, on the hunt for fugitive Revenges or Companymen, leaving Al-Nejem to oversee preparations.

A lad popped up at Nathan's elbow, requiring and desiring his attentions elsewhere.

Momentarily torn, Nathan finally barked "You there, bear a hand!" at a pair of Morgansers. "Fetch Mr. Cate a chair."

Either the Cap'n's urgency or one look at Mr. Cate — Did she really look in such dire need to sit? — prompted them to knuckle their brows and scurry off. Sooner than one might have thought possible, they returned bearing an armed chair, more stuffing showing than blue damask covering. Nathan directed them to a spot of shade, overseeing with both sharp eye and words, until it was aligned just so.

"Sit... *sit*," he insisted at Cate's hesitance.

She did, gingerly and apprehensive. Nathan stood back, hands on his hips, admiring the arrangement. With a sudden inspiration, he grabbed a bucket, upended it, and set it before her, arranging her feet atop. He stood back to regard his handiwork, a jerk of the head marking his approval.

"There are... matters which shan't wait. Duty calling and all that. You," Nathan said, fixing Cate with a stern eye, "shall sit here and—"

"I can't just sit—!" Cate cried, making to rise.

"Can and will," Nathan insisted, firmly pushing her back down. "Celia bid you should rest that shoulder and rest you shall. Nay, nay, there's no denying it. I heard with me own two ears. Gods wounds, I should think you've had enough activity for one day." The last came with an arched lilt and a rueful roll of his eyes.

Cate looked in any direction but his. There was no denying her wayward ways of that morning — and several other times, if she were wholly honest — had precipitated unfortunate events. Not all had been bad: if Lesauvage hadn't popped up, would Nathan have ever gone to Celia, and hence, broken Calypso's grasp? Not all had been good, however, she thought flexing her fingers, working out the persistent tingling. Neither could she argue against resting her shoulder; several times, she had caught herself favoring it. Celia's touch had eased it — a laying-on-of-the-hands, in the truest sense of the word — but it still ached like a demon.

"I can't queen myself about, doing nothing," she insisted.

"Queen Catherine the First, of the Island," Nathan announced, with the grandeur of at Court. "Has a nice ring to it, don't you think? Besides," he went on, ignoring Cate's gainsaying. "You shan't be 'queening yourself about,' because you'll be sitting right here." A finger, rigid enough to nail her in place should she offer to contradict, was pointed.

Cate bent her head, reluctantly conceding. Surely, just this once, she could manage.

"I shan't be long." Nathan turned to take his leave, but within a few paces, stopped to call back "And know, the trees have eyes" with a cautionary tone only the village idiot could miss.

She sank deeper into the cushions under the weight of a good many eyes on her. Whether drawn by duty or Nathan's command, Tabby soon appeared and hung near-to - hand.

Cate suddenly found herself at odd ends, adrift in a sea of industry. The reverse flow of good and stores back to the ships was nowhere near the volume which had come ashore, but still, the bare necessities for two ships and crews was considerable. Leave-taking weighted the air, making it thick and difficult to breathe...

Or was it dread of Thomas' imminent which tightened her chest?

Every time she moved her arm—and there was no position which alleviated the ache—she was reminded of the consequences of her wandering about and resolved to be, or rather, strove to be the paragon of obedience. The inability to sit quietly, however, had been an affliction since girlhood, much to the dismay of her mother and Tiacita. She had spent many an hour under their stern eye and being lectured: "no girl of grace or good - breeding moved her feet, tapped her heel or knotted her hands." Age had barely improved her skills.

The sound of collective female laughter drew her attention to a group of women. Craning her head slightly, she could just make them out, sitting about a table under the sheltering arms of a live oak tree. Baskets of clothing piled high about them, the flash of needles and bob of darning eggs indicated they were mending. Her fingers twitching with the need for purpose, Cate made to rise, meaning to go join them. The ghost of Nathan's admonishing finger in her face, and the likelihood of a cool reception, as received so many times before, stopped her.

Still, the drive to do something was as primal as the need to breathe. She sent Tabby to fetch one of the over-flowing baskets, and then the hussif from her shack. Needle and thread in hand, she settled down to her greatest love: being useful.

Tabby was set to the same utility; a lady's maid's prime duty was the mending of her ladyship's clothes. Alas, it was a hazardous assumption. It became very apparent, very soon that the needle was not Tabby's friend—nor, even a familiar—and no amount of tutelage on Cate's part would remedy it.

"How did you ever manage to mend the Captain's breeches this morning?" Cate demanded testily.

Tabby screwed her face. "I traded Mary Morningate: she did it for a peek at him in bed."

Cate shifted uncomfortably. "Did she get it, the peek, I mean?" "No," came back simply.

"A pirate's child, to be sure," Cate muttered and ended Tabby's torture, by plucking away the needle.

Shortly—so very, very shortly—the girl was squirming and huffing at her chairside, anxious to be away. Cate looked up to learn the source of the girl's distraction. She followed the doe-eyed gaze, again as straight as a hawser to where Maram was loading stores, a short distance downshore.

Cate felt a certain compassion; she had experienced her own youthful flirtation. This one was about to come to an abrupt end. Judging by the small gaggle of girls hanging about the boy, Tabby wasn't the only one to be charmed by his flashing eyes.

"Do you have some pressing chores... somewhere?" Cate finally asked, in strained politeness. This being mistress wasn't as easy. Suddenly she held a far greater respect for her mother, who had managed an entire household of servants with seamless ease.

"Er, umm... yes, mum."

It was an obvious lie, and exactly what Cate wished to hear. "Very well, then you may—"

With a squeak of relief, Tabby sped off. Within in a few strides, duty reminded her to stop and curtsy, and then darted away.

Awareness of the activity around Cate faded, and she lost herself in the mesmerizing rhythm of the dip and rise of the needle. A peacefulness befell her, as it always did. That had been a blessing—and salvation—when sewing had been her living, with twelve to fourteen hour days the normal, and longer not a rarity. She reveled in seeing mayhem tamed into orderliness: holes vanish, tears disappear, seams return to their duty, buttons snug in their rightful places.

One ear, however, was still cocked for the first sound of Thomas. She needed to get to him before Nathan. Nipping this foolishness of Nathan's in the bud was one thing, but prime in her mind was talking Thomas into staying.

He couldn't leave! Not yet!

Loss of love, loss of marriage, loss of family and home had given her an enduring loathing for departures. For a while now, she had been able to see Thomas as himself and not Brian's surrogate. Still, his physical similarity made it too much like losing Brian all over again.

Cate's hand shook, and she dropped the needle. She sat back and took several deep breaths. From there, she could see the derelict *Mirabel,* out in the bay. She felt a kind of kinship with the wreck, not necessarily sunk, but on the verge of doing so, the least ripple on the water threatening to swamp and founder her. It had been nearly a fortnight since she had returned from the dead and she still was nowhere near "in fighting trim," as Nathan called it. What if, this proved to be her permanent state? What if, like the *Mirabel,* she proved to be beyond salvation, too damaged and battered to be of use to anyone?

Celia's forecast suggested else. And that was where Cate would hang her hat.

She shook her head, fished for the needle, and set back to mending.

It was just this business with Thomas had set her aback, or her sails or on her heels, or whatever the hell they called it. First Lesauvage popping up, and then the scene at Celia's... and now this! She just needed to plead, implore, beg, wheedle, shame... whatever it took.

She was confident that, with time, she might gather her wits, bring herself to terms, and be able to wave goodbye with composure befitting of a monk. But, just not yet, not now, not—

A cautioning voice observed that perhaps there was a benefit in Thomas taking his leave: Nathan's grand—and insufferably insane—scheme would be dead in the water. If he were to remain, Nathan would be set on making it happen.

"Not bloody likely."

She spoke unwittingly loud and vehemently enough to cause several nearby to take pause, fraught with indecision as to whether they should beckon the Cap'n? Displaying a simpleton smile set them back to their duties.

Nathan's grand scheme would require her full cooperation, and *that* would *not* be forthcoming, no matter how bullish he became.

She heard a frustrated noise and looked up into that very bullish face peering down at her.

"What the bloody hell! What are you doing?"

Cate looked down in her lap and then back up. "I'm mending a shirt."

"I'll be hanged if you'll grovel to—" Sputtering to an incensed end, he attempted to snatch it away. A kind of tug-of-war ensured: Nathan seeking to take it, Cate refusing, if for no other reason than there was a perfectly good needle in peril of being lost. Ultimately, she prevailed.

"I did it for years. A holey sock was the difference between starving and eating many a day." She realized, in instant retrospect, that was the worst thing to say. Nathan was always over-sensitive to any reference to her years of living alone.

He imposed himself over her, glaring down his nose. "Not. Any. More."

Nathan stomped back and forth, momentarily stricken speechless. "What was the last thing I said?"

Cate closed one eye, straining to recall. "Umm, 'know that the trees…'"

"Tach! I told you 'at your ease.'" Each word was uttered with the force of the Word from the Mount. "That doesn't mean slaving away —"

"Mending a shirt isn't slaving —"

"I'll not have you slaving about like a skullerymaid —"

"Scullery does pots and pans; I only —"

"Your precious husband might have left you to shift for yourself and starve, but not me," he declared, pounding a thumb into his chest. "Be damned, if I would leave you without a place to sleep, means or a friendly face."

"He did what he could," Cate muttered defensively, regretting it as soon as it was uttered.

Sometimes this competition with Brian went far beyond the average envy, or resentment, or whatever the hell which ground on Nathan so. Someday, it would be interesting to sit and learn just exactly what he imagined her previous life to have been like. It would be adventures through a fairyland, to be sure.

"I just can't sit and —" she began.

"Can and will," came through bared teeth.

Suddenly aware of a good many looking on and listening, he made a visible effort to collect himself. Once composed, he knelt at her feet and found her hand.

"You will *never* want for *any*thing again," he said, low and earnest. "It's arranged. It's given. You couldn't possibly spend it all, even if you set up your coach-and-six in a dozen places."

Cate stared, wondering as to the how, when and where all of that might have come to pass?

"Your shares alone would set you up," he explained in face of her doubt. "Arrangements have been made: letters sent, men-of-business —" He coughed, catching himself on an unwitting path.

"You'll not lack for anything," Nathan went on, now back on track. "You'll not be hungry; you'll never worry for a place to sleep; you'll be fed, clothed, housed..." he went on, ticking them off on his fingers.

His hand made an adroit dive and plucked the offending garment from her. It was delicately held aside, between two fingers, as if it were a dead varmint. "And you sure as hell won't be taking in mending."

He flung the thing aside, dusting his hands.

"Now, you've lost my needle," Cate observed coldly and rose to find it.

Nathan took her by the arms. "I'll buy you another, hell, a whole gross of needles." He pushed her back down and shook her in gentle supplication. "'At your ease.' What, in all which is holy, makes that so bloody, damned difficult to comprehend? It's the very reason you were brought to this moldering patch o' sand in the first place." His voice almost broke with desperation at the end.

"Now," he said, standing over her. "I must away. Might I count on you to be at least a bit more abiding?"

At some point, he had donned his shirt and hat. Guilt struck, again, at his day having started so abruptly. Again, the rigors of a sailor's life had served him well, years of being jerked from his rest for whatever emergency had allowed him to be jerked from it once more without the least recrimination or reproach... Well, not much at any rate. This was her penance and she would willingly serve it.

Cate folded her hands in her lap. She had studied under the master of changing subjects and she did so then. "Permission to rise, sir?" she said, assuming a prim formality, to the point of being blatantly false.

Instantly smoking what she was about, Nathan cocked a brow. "To what point or purpose?" he asked, assuming his sternest captain's voice.

"Nature calls, sir," she said, unblinking.

"Didn't it call once already today? Try me, and you'll taste the lash."

He shook her again, gentler, yet just as demanding. "I mean it... please?" He punctuated his request with a boyish grin, one even the most cold-hearted couldn't resist.

Clamping her lip between her teeth, Cate nodded. Her eyes unwavering from his, she probed with her foot in the direction the shirt had been thrown, searching.

Nathan leaned closer, narrowed his eyes and said through a fixed jaw "Don't even think it."

Her foot slid back to its rightful place. A peck on the cheek and a final shake as a none-so-subtle reminder marked his departure. He was but a few strides away, however, before he stopped, and spun around.

"Come here," he said mildly, hooking a finger.

Cate moved the few steps between them. Tipping his head, he regarded her, studying as one might if she had a smudge on her face. Suddenly, he kissed her. Restrained and stiff, it was unfamiliar, not his usual. Given the events of the past few days, how long it lasted was a surprise. Nathan seemed of the same mind, and yet pressed more firmly, becoming more like himself, as it went on.

"You're feeling better?" she gasped at the end.

Nathan reflected, for the briefest of moments, and declared "Aye, I am!"

He took several steps, and then stopped, as if struck by a notion. Over his shoulder, he waggled his brows and winked. "Oh, aye, you're going to need your rest, lots and *lots* of rest."

Before Nathan took his leave, an escort was called forward from among the surrounding crowd, an inordinate proportion of them being Morgansers, Cate observed ruefully.

She bridled at the notion of such oversight—there were, after all, some things which were better performed solo—but then, a minatory arch of Nathan's brow—unmissable, even at that distance—reminded her of her pledge to both him *and* herself.

Once the business was done, she plead and wheedled until her escorts agreed to move she and her newly-appointed throne to a more central location, one not far from where Bella conducted the island's daily business and, hence, where the first word of Thomas and his impending arrival might be heard.

Nathan's mysterious preoccupation only added to Cate's agitation. There had been a certain secretiveness of what he was about, too subtle to sort out, and yet too unmistakable to be ignored. "Duty," as he described it, seemed more a cover than a reason. In her more benevolent moments, she conceded that three ships, their accumulated crews, and an island of women, in a state of repair and reconstruction, would make endless demands on his time and attention.

Cate sat, one heel tapping. Much to her chagrin, Bella was nowhere to be seen. Either there was no island business that day, or it had called the matron elsewhere. The only idle one on the entire island seemed to be Cate.

"*...You are going to need your rest...*"

It could only mean one thing, and she needed to get to

Thomas and nip it straightaway. The whole thing was insanity. She wasn't some cow in season, one dash with the parish bull and the deed was done. Lord knew how many times she might lie with whomever until the ultimate end was achieved. Her irregular monthlies complicated matters even more, both in the begetting and then knowing. If previous experience was any guide—and on this, she had no reason to believe it wasn't—she could be months along before she actually knew.

No matter what Nathan might think, she didn't like going contrary to his wishes. Perhaps, it was why she was so determined to obey him just then: because she had every intention of disobeying should he press this, this farming her out like a broodmare, as if tall and fair were desirable traits for a new bloodline.

This could get ugly... *very* ugly.

"Bulls and rocks aren't in it."

"Beg pardon, m'um?" came from a bystander.

"Nothing, nothing," she said to her lap.

And so, she waited.

The hot ball of the sun tracked across the sky. The bonfires were lit and, if the increasing numbers of fond farewells at every quarter were any indication, leave-taking became more imminent. A few days were enough time for powerful connections to be made, resulting in the departures being as heart-felt as the arrivals, and Cate felt it. One would require a heart of stone not to. Perhaps it wasn't the farewell so much, as what always came after: loneliness, isolation, drifting... starvation. Her life had been a litany of loss and farewells. Granted, her situation now was far different. She wasn't the one leaving; none of those threatened. But that not so small difference made little odds and failed to overcome a lifetime of hard-learned lessons. The best cure was to just avoid the whole morbid scene altogether and prevail upon Thomas to remain.

Cate had a sense of time running out in more ways than one. She began to worry that perhaps Thomas might have sneaked out to his ship, in hopes of avoiding the ugly goodbyes...

... *and Nathan's demands*, said an inner voice.

She was in a thorough state by the time she heard over the general buzz of activity—several hundred sailors did nothing quietly—the commotion of a large group approaching. The search party was returning, Thomas, a head above the rest, leading the way. Even from that distance, she could see he was still flushed with exertion. He hadn't been back for long, which gave her hope that Nathan hadn't yet found him.

Thomas' step slowed as he scanned the shore. Spotting Cate, he veered in her direction. "There you are!"

He waited until he was more within conversation range before saying "What the bloody hell happened out there, at Celia's?" he clarified at her failing to follow. "Looks like Nathan is wearing a collar and shackles."

Damn, that meant Nathan had already gotten to him.

"Oh, that," Cate said, flapping a hand. "Nothing, nothing which could be readily explained."

"Now you're beginning to sound like Nathan," he said, narrowly.

She peered up at Thomas, trying not to be obvious while at the same time trying to see if any sign of his intentions or reactions might be detected. Alas, it suddenly seemed he had acquired Nathan's mastery-of-masks: he was as inscrutable as the proverbial sphinx.

"Has Nathan said...?" Her question died in her throat at seeing Thomas' puzzled look. There was the off-chance, however — very off — that he was just being his typical open self, allowing her to see everything, which was nothing, for Nathan hadn't spoken to him yet.

"You mean like 'damn your infernal eyes,' 'where the bloody hell,' or 'suffering Jesus...?'" Thomas teased, dropping his voice to a version of Nathan's gravel.

"Well, if that was all," she sighed. Perhaps her fears had been for naught. Perhaps Nathan's determination had found its limits.

Or, he had just finally come to his blessed senses.

"Just know, whatever he says, it's *not* my idea," she said, emphatically. "Nor, do I have any intention of —" She stopped short. The horns of indecision were sharp ones. To explain further meant running the risk of saying too much, spilling the proverbial beans, delving into that which needn't be delved in, if Nathan had finally returned to the land of reason.

She rubbed her temple, a headache having suddenly settled there. "Whatever it... is, just... just say 'no.'"

"Whatever are you about, woman?" Looking behind her, Thomas straightened and sobered. "Oh-oh, batten the hatches. There be a black squall in the offing," he cautioned, low and through stiff lips.

Cate turned to find Nathan churning toward them, determination sticking out from him like spines on a hedgehog. She inwardly groaned. Steering off a decided Blackthorne was like trying to steer a tumbling hogshead.

"Thomas was just leaving," Cate announced, putting herself

between the two men. "He's in a tearing hurry, time and tide, wind and all that."

"I know that!" Nathan huffed, squinting at her as if she had gone dim.

"You're not taking the *Revenge*?" Nathan directed to Thomas. Compared to the bustle about the *Lovely* and *Brazen*, the ship looked quite forlorn and ignored. "She's now a part of your fleet, *Commodore*."

"Nay, I'm leaving her and the crew to man her," Thomas said, ignoring the dig. "Now this place won't be so cut-off, and they can be their own masters, as opposed to having to depend on the whim of whomever decides to show up. It's the decent thing; one can only wonder why the hell it took so long for someone to do it."

"And besides, who the hell needs three ships?" Thomas went on, diffidently. "All that upkeep, and managing captains..."

"God forbid anyone should represent you as giving yourself airs," Nathan observed dryly. "So, then, you're aweigh?"

Thomas jerked a nod. "Directly. Morning tide, preparations..." The rest was lost in a confused jumble into Thomas' chest, all sounding more like excuses than reasons, to Cate's judgment.

Thomas took a step toward shore, as if to prove his point, but stopped in mid-stride, misinterpreting Cate's dismay. "Hark ye, I've kept my oath: the island is safe. We found a couple more stragglers and scragged 'em. Not a dormouse could have slipped through without we noticed. It's safe, now." The last was uttered more in the way of convincing himself.

"No, you can't go! Not now... not yet!" Suddenly, whoever or whatever was lurking in the island's inner regions was the last thing from Cate's mind.

Thomas looked down, with a grim smile. "Aye, 'tis time."

"The tide, darling—" Nathan began.

"The devil with the tide or time or wind, or whatever the hell!" Cate said, with an irritated swipe.

The two men rocked back at her blasphemy. Realizing her blunder, Cate charted a different course. Thinking perhaps she might be able to appeal to Thomas' better nature on a personal level—and without Nathan's ears flapping—Cate ushered Thomas away. She drew up at the edge of the firelight.

"Why now?" she pleaded. She tried to find his eyes, but he kept ducking away.

"Just seems like it's time, that's all," Thomas said into the night.

"Why? I wish you wouldn't. Please, no. It's too soon. It's

too—" There had been too much loss of late, too much turmoil and chaos. She couldn't bear it... Not yet, not... now!

"Stay, please?" she insisted, grasping his arm. "Just for a little while, just one more night? It's good for Nathan to have someone..."

Thomas whirled around with a vehemence which set Cate back a step. "Stay, so I can see you two go off together!"

With considerable effort, he checked himself. Balling his fists at his sides, he strove for a more amenable tone. "Do you have any notion of what it is to see you two together?" His voice threatened to break. "I'm not sure how much more I can control—"

"You think it might come to blows?" she asked faintly. Strife, in the day-to-day flow of life, was one thing. Two friends going at each other was quite another and more than she could bear.

"We did once; it's only a matter of time before it happens again. Maybe, if we can head that off, it mightn't take ten years before we meet up again." The only recrimination in that was aimed at himself.

"You know how Nathan is when it comes to you. Well, perhaps you don't," Thomas amended a bit more kindly. "He goes a bit maniac. Both of us run a bit on the too possessive side for our own good. Living out here does that to a man."

Cate considered that both men ran more than "a bit" in the possessive direction. It made her visions of the three of them coexisting—a Peaceable Kingdom, two lions lying with the lamb—seem insufferably naïve. She cared deeply, so very deeply for him... But she loved Nathan. She had room in her heart for both, but there wasn't enough room in her world. Perceptive as ever, Nathan had known as much from the first. And now— finally— she realized the futility as well.

"Stay, for Nathan's sake; he needs you. He's so different when you're about," Cate pleaded.

The change in Nathan had been apparent from the moment Thomas arrived. Having a friend meant having an ally and an equal, someone of the same mind, someone with whom he could reminisce, and—above all else—could trust with his back.

Thomas' mouth worked as he stared off into the night. "I can't help but wonder, if we—you n' me—had met first, before... him." He angled his head toward Nathan, now talking to a pair of Morgansers.

The notion struck Cate slightly ill. Indeed, what if it had been the *Griselle* which boarded the *Constancy;* if it had been Thomas who had plucked her from the water...? Would it all have been different? Or, would Fate assured events reached the same end?

How strong was Fate's hand? How much was "given" and how much was just happenstance? Nathan filled her so completely, it was impossible to imagine anyone else doing the same.

"But, you care for Celia, not me. You've said as much. Hell, I've seen you two together," Cate said. There was no mistaking the emotions between them at Celia's shack, and then one night, in the sick bay, when they fancied themselves alone.

"Go to her," Cate urged. Perhaps something good could come out of this. "You're leaving. No one will know the difference."

"One bite to a starving man?" Temptation etched Thomas' face as he pensively ran a finger along the scar on his chest. "Nay, 'tis better to starve. We said goodbye once, years ago. Don't wish to go through that again," he added bleakly.

He shook his head. "It's the damnedest thing, like some bloody spell or something: she never comes to mind, until I step foot on this shore, and she's there, like a damned obsession."

Thomas glanced sideways, embarrassed. "But, I know as soon as I put this place to my stern, she's out of my mind."

He looked up with a heart-stopping blue look. "You, on the other hand, are always here," he said, pounding his finger to his temple. "And here," he added, thumping his fist on his chest with a drum-like sound. "And elsewhere," he added, with a significant lilt. "I'd seize you up and take you with me this minute, if I thought you could ever come to look at me like you do him." He snorted. "But that's waiting for snowflakes in Hell."

Celia's words from days ago echoed back "I hold his body, but someone else holds his heart." Cate swayed, recalling Celia's final words in that conversation: "You'll break his heart."

Thomas sighed, shoulders slumping. "You two belong together, more than any two I've ever witnessed. One can't hold their breath without the other turning blue."

In truth, Cate had no notion... nay, had never paused to consider what Thomas might be suffering. His feelings for her had been declared straightaway, clear and eloquent, and she had dismissed them as... what? Flattery? Lip service? Deference to Nathan? How it must have hurt to have been so summarily dismissed.

And yet, there wasn't a damned thing she could do. There was no denying the mathematics: three was an odd number, one which could never extract an even number without one standing alone. She felt like some odd version of Solomon, asked to settle what couldn't be settled. Alas, even in that parable, ultimately there had been one winner and one loser.

"But that's all water over the decks, isn't it?" Thomas shook his head, his mouth twisting ruefully. "Gonna take a helluva woman to replace you."

"I'm not so different than—" Cate stammered, cheeks heating.

"Yes, you are," he said, softly. "And that's the hell of it: you have no idea."

He caught his lower lip between his teeth and shook his head. "I envy what Nathan has, what both of you have. I couldn't dare hope that Providence might provide me with the same."

Cate reached up to touch his chin and bring his gaze to hers. "She's out there." It sounded so much like a platitude, and yet it seemed so very true. "Look, I'm proof positive there's at least two for every one of us."

The corners of his eyes pinched, as if to smile but, as was the fate of every platitude, not a word was believed. "If she's about, I can't see her, because I'm too blinded by you. I need to get these blinders off, start seeing the world again, and stop teetering on the verge of becoming something I won't recognize."

"So," he said, with a decisive expulsion of air. "Away, gone, is the best place for me, and so that is what I aim to do."

"Please...?" she heard herself murmur. "Please...?" and she bit off the rest. She sank, dejected and resigned to the inevitable conclusion he had long ago reached. She hated departures, now more than ever: heart-wrenching, gut-tearing, and worst of all, the helplessness of it all. Pleading and groveling only demeaned everyone involved. All she stood to gain was his contempt.

"Do you wish to send Celia a message?" It was a struggle to keep her voice steady.

Thomas smiled down at her. "No need. She knows. Believe me, she knows!"

"Where will you go?"

His mouth worked, considering. "Colonies, maybe. I was thinking about here in the Caribbean, but it seems just a bit crowded... right now... what with Harte on a tear, and all."

He loomed over her, the fire flaring on his profile, his eyes darkened to blue flints. His hand drifted up to her neck, hesitant. Then he took her in his arms, decision made. He had kissed her before, but always with restraint, chaste. This was no polite brushing of lips or hasty farewell. He meant to take his time, and he did, with dizzying effect, a parting message which said everything he wished to say: the power of feelings, the power of desire and the power of what it took to deny it all.

Cate stood back, a bit breathless.

"I mean it, Cate." His hand was a hot weight at the small of her back. "If that fool ever hurts you, if he ever lets you go, you send for me, anytime, anywhere."

"And how am I to do that, with you on the other side of the world?"

"The sailors' world is a small world." He winked. "Just pass the word; it'll spread as fast as the wind that carries it."

It was barely a comfort. The whims and vagaries of life, in general, and life at sea made it an impossible prospect. She buried her fists into his shirt, knowing that once she let go, he would be gone. She inhaled deeply, desperate for that scent which was uniquely his, searching his face for the little details thus far overlooked: the sweep of temple and brow, the little scar on his upper lip, another tiny one angling across his chin.

The clearing of a throat made them turn to find Nathan standing there. "What's this?" He spoke mildly, but suspicion still lurked.

Thomas' arm tightened, reluctant to surrender her. The two stood squared off, ready to draw blood. Bristling with weapons, formed and scarred by violence, blood was sure to be spilled. So much, too much had been spilled already. It wasn't unthinkable that she would be the only one left standing, left to clean up the mess, the blood of both of them on her hands, literally and figuratively.

And so, in the spirit of that blood preserved, she leaned back. The shift was so very subtle and yet perceived by all involved, one move realigning three worlds.

"Nothing, Nathan," Thomas said, his eyes holding hers. "I was just telling Cate goodbye."

His mouth quirked at the irony. "Hell, any fool can see how it is between you two. 'Pears as though you were the winner this time, mate." His fingers closed around hers knotted into his shirt. Determinedly prying them free, he held her at arms' length, the space between them yawing like an ocean.

Insinuating himself between them, Nathan slipped an arm around Cate's waist and drew her closer. "She'll be fine."

Thomas' was still fixed on Cate. "Aye, I know." He swallowed, clearing the hoarseness from his voice. "That's what she said."

Breaking his stare, Thomas extended a hand to Nathan. "Well, mate, it's been good."

A mere handshake suddenly became too awkward and insufficient. The two men hugged, heartily slapping each other on the back.

"On the next horizon, eh?"

"On the next horizon."

Cate rose on her toes and threw her arms around Thomas' neck. "I'm going to miss you."

The big arm curved around her and tightened, committing to memory every detail. With the greatest reluctance, she released him, dabbing the moisture at the corner of her eyes. "Dammit, don't you dare let anything happen to you."

Thomas winked, the triangle of his eyes glinting in the fire. "Wiser words never spoken. Our courses will cross, rest assured. Keep her safe, Nathan. I'm not so sure you realize the treasure you have there."

"Not all treasure is silver and gold, mate." Nathan's lips briefly brushed Cate's temple. "I know what I've got."

With a final nod, Thomas turned and, in his long, ground-eating strides, walked toward the waiting longboat.

Nathan turned Cate to face him. "What was that all about?"

Cate rose on her toes to watch Thomas over his shoulder, feeling as if a large portion of her life was going with him. "What was what?"

Nathan took her by the chin and brought her face around. "Come, now, darling, leave the acting to the professionals. I looked over here to find you wrapped all over him. Thought there for a moment you'd taken up the offer."

"I should have, just to teach you a lesson. What made you change your mind so suddenly?"

His mouth twisted to one side. "I'm not quite so ready to declare meself the eunuch... yet."

She shrugged, unable to deny anything, especially with the feel of Thomas' kiss still on her lips. "I was just saying goodbye."

"Dammit! I hate goodbyes. I hate them!" She spun in his arms and pounded his chest. With the tears brimming, it was either that or risk making a worse spectacle of herself. "Nothing good ever comes of them, nothing but grief and loneliness and—"

Nathan narrowed an eye. "You've had your share, haven't you?"

Cate choked a self-conscious laugh. "Yes, far more than 'tis fitting." She leaned against him murmuring "Too many, too many" in a tear-thickened chant. Catching herself on the brink of an ugly breakdown, she straightened. "I just need—"

She stopped, clamping her lower lip between her teeth. What she wanted or needed didn't matter; the final outcome wasn't going to change.

Nathan touched a finger and lifted her face to his once more. "Don't you find 'hellos' ever so much more enchanting?"

"What?" she asked, half-annoyed.

"'Hellos.' You know: rejoice, reunion, back with the old, on with the new," he declared with a jocularity which made her smile, in spite of her failure to follow.

Nathan was usually more handy in veiling what he was about; this was one of the most heavy-handed attempts ever.

"Yes," she said, sniffing hugely. The man needed some kind of a bone thrown. "I do much prefer 'hellos.'"

"Capital! Then I've just the thing." He stepped back, swept off his hat and made a courtly leg. "This way, m'lady, if you please..."

26: COZY COVE

NATHAN LED CATE OFF TOWARD shore, but at a sharp angle away from Thomas' path, away from the general hubbub and lights. He steered her to a quieter stretch of beach, to where the island's small fleet of utility boats were moored. For a good many, it would have been more fitting to call them "craft," for they barely resembled any boat she knew of. Logs or casks lashed together, hollowed-out logs, or a host of other contrivances: for an island of pirates, one would have expected something a bit more in the way of seaworthy.

Without another word or warning, Nathan scooped her up in his arms and waded out to one.

"It's the driest one to be had, used to collect coconuts not turtles, so it doesn't stink. Well, not quite so much," he added, wrinkling his nose as he set her down in an ungainly, squat-looking one.

It was roughly the size of the *Morganse's* gig, but with a mast instead of oars. Hitching her skirts from the several inches of water sloshing in the bottom, Cate sat with her back against it—as instructed—loathe to move. The least shift of her weight set the thing dipping and bobbing. With his customary cat-like agility, Nathan vaulted in, stepped to the sternsheet—the damned boat barely moving, she observed—and plunked down. He clapped on to a rope, tiller in the other hand. A jerk on the first brought the sail to attention, a shove on the second swung the bow around. The breeze caught, the sail bowed into a taut curve, and the water began to make a rustling sound at the sides. Ungainly and squat the boat might have been, it proved a lively thing under sail, or at least to Cate's lubberish observations. A glance to Nathan proved uninformative. Their momentum built, the water soon gurgling against the hull.

Leaving the shore's lights and voices behind, they slipped further out into the bay. The shore's lights and voices faded, and the dark and solitude settled over the little boat like a heavy cloak. Water has an odd, random way of distorting sound, augmenting the farthest, as if through a speaking trumpet, or deadening the nearest with no apparent rhyme or reason. The effect was evident then: intermittent voices and music could be heard, sometimes with a clarity which seemed to put the conversants in the boat with them. Light suffered much the same distortion, refracting and flaring, sometimes the shore fires gilding Nathan's profile, the starlight limning him in silver.

At one point, Cate craned her head in the direction of the *Lovely* and the boats streaming toward her, in hopes of a glimpse of Thomas. Distance and darkness made it a futile effort, the ship no more than the glow of her lights on the night sky.

The boat had a considerably lower profile than any before, the water only a few inches from the gun'l. It was too easy to imagine a hand rising from the depths to seize one of them. A worrisome crystalline glimmer proved to be only the bottom, threatening shadows naught but coralheads. She started at a silvery darting, feeling quite foolish at realizing it was a school of fish. Seeing her apprehension, Nathan smiled, a flash of white under the black slash of his mustache, the gold firelight catching his eye as he winked. She chided herself for being so faint-of-heart; Nathan wouldn't have brought her if he didn't think it safe. Still, she kept her skirts close and a hand away from the gun'l.

Instead, Cate focused on Nathan. A dark outline against the starlight, he steered as reflexively as one breathed. Being on the water and under sail had a rejuvenating effect on him, a sea creature returning to its habitat. The difference was so marked it made her realize what a reduced version of him was seen on land. She reached out with her senses to that habitat, seeking to soak in every detail and sensation. The mast at her back was the most revealing: living, a direct connection with the wind and sea, what he loved most.

She had been in many a boat, but always cheek-to-jowl with the coxsun and his mates, surrounded by the grunt of hauling on oars. That had been plowing through the water, being driven against all principles of Nature. This was being borne by Nature, skimming the water, controlled by nothing more than a bit of wood at the stern, rope and a dingy scrap of canvas, Nathan at its center. The practical side of her noted that the boat was probably moving at roughly the same rate as a horse's fast walk, but it felt like they were flying. Wrapping her hair in her fist, she put her face to the breeze, feeling the same press as the sail above her, imagining what it might be to spread her wings and soar.

"It's beautiful out here," she sighed.

"Hmm..?" Nathan said, stirring from far afield. "Oh, aye."

Cate bit her lip, her own voice suddenly seeming an abomination in the sanctuary – like stillness. She wasn't a religious person, and yet there was something reverential and spiritual about being out there.

Neither spoke for the next while. The tails of his headscarf wafting about his shoulders, Nathan was a fascination to watch. He was in his element, and yet there was a certain tension about him. Not fear – thank heavens! – but something rooted more in the way of anticipation, like a boy hiding something behind his back.

Over the silken rustle of the bow wave, she heard something like humming. She canted her head, first to locate it, and then confirm her suspicions. Sound might bounce on the water, but there was no mistaking this: it was coming from him. Surely not! Nathan had his jovial side, but never to that degree.

She lent a stronger ear. Seeing it, Nathan cleared his throat and fell quiet.

It had become apparent straightaway that their course was for a small point, a dark, jagged-backed wedge between sky and water. Cate had presumed this to be just an evening excursion, Nathan's guise to distract her from the pain of Thomas' departure. As the point drew nearer, she fully expected them to come about and angle back toward from whence they came.

Just off the point, Nathan said "Ready about."

"What?"

"Make ready to duck your head," he said with the enunciation reserved for the dull – witted.

The explanation came a bare instant before he hauled on the tiller and cast loose the sheet. The boom brushed the back of her head, now between her knees, as it swept from one side to the other. Cate followed Nathan's example, shifting her weight slightly to accommodate the boat's new attitude. She looked up, expecting to see they were heading back. Instead, they were weathering the point and into a small cove on the other side.

She sat up, a bit more alert and a lot more curious. She'd been foolish to think this was just a pleasure trip. Simply going for a ride was completely out-of-character for Nathan; he never did anything out of pure recreation. The sham of pretense on the surface might vary, but underneath there was always a thick under layer of practicality.

In the lee of the point, it was more protected, the wind

rippling the water like a horse's skin twitching at a fly. Whether by plan or wind, the boat angled in. Nearer yet, she saw what she had thought to be fireflies ashore was actually lights of a camp. Alas, they weren't alone. She resented the invasion of their solitude, and yet, how could it be else on an island occupied by hundreds? Nearer still, a glimmer revealed a small waterway, like a lagoon or river mouth, next to the camp.

Cate slowly came to realize they weren't just passing by; Nathan meant to put in. For as many lights, there had to have been a goodly number of people, and yet none were to be seen. The nearer to shore they came, the more it became apparent that the site was deserted; no one moved, no one came down to shoreline to greet them, no one hailed.

At the precise moment, the sail dropped, allowing momentum to carry them in. The keel ground to a halt on the sandy bottom; a flick of the lines, and the sail dropped. Nathan swung over the gun'l into the water, plucked Cate up and waded ashore. While he secured the boat, she looked around. As suspected, not a soul was about; no sound other than the call of night creatures and the flick of the campfire's flames.

An eeriness hung over it. The lights were recently lit, the campfire recently attended. A small amount of stores, lockers, and a stack of firewood all indicated someone meant to spend more than just a few hours. And yet, no one was in sight. The lamps and dips, many fashioned out of coconut shells, had been arranged in a definite perimeter, giving the space a certain welcoming air, as if in anticipation of awaiting guests.

An uncertain glance toward Nathan; a short gesture urged her on. Still, she waited until he was behind her before she advanced, curious, yet cautious. At a newer angle, she could see more lights were arranged in an inner circle. Coming around a clump of bushes, she stopped and stared, taking a moment to fully realize what she was looking at.

She whirled to find Nathan bearing the smug grin of one having pulled off a grand surprise.

"The bed!" By some means of extravagance and energy, the bed from her shack was now there.

"What else?" he said, affecting nonchalance.

She spun back, staring. "But how...? I mean, why...? I mean...?" Her mouth moved, stricken speechless in the most literal sense of the word.

Her eyes rounded with the realization and she whirled back to him. "You intend for us to try to—?"

Nathan cut her off with a kiss, showing her just exactly what his intentions were and to dizzying effect.

"Not just 'try'," he purred. "*Do*."

"Are you sure we, *you* can...?" Her hopes had been sent soaring, only to be smashed so many times, she was reluctant to suffer disappointment again. Seeing as much, he took her in his arms and did all he could to set her mind at ease. He brought her hips against his, rod-like hardness prodding through the folds of her skirt.

"Are you sure?" she asked, now a bit breathless.

"As I have ever been of anything in me life."

She searched the cinnamon and gold, and found not the least exaggeration. Her gaze unwavering from his, she experimentally touched his arm. Nathan stood, tense with the desire to prove his point. Her hand slid up and then spread out over his chest. Alert for the least movement, she flicked his nipple with her thumb. In spite of his wishes, his breath caught slightly, and the muscle at the corner of his mouth fluttered, but nothing else. No fighting off pain. No flinching or shying or jerking as he had these days since. The opposing end of his mustache hooked up the corner of his mouth, quirking at the success of her experiment, as pleased — and perhaps even more than she — relieved.

"This is what you needed me rested for?" she asked, recalling his earlier admonishments.

"Stroke of genius, don't you think?" he said, stooping to fling another log on the fire. "Your dunnage is there, most of it at any rate. We've wood, fire, light, and most importantly, a store of the sweetest water what could be availed upon on the island, the puncheon fresh holystoned and swabbed."

With stark recollections of the water butts aboard — rank with having been filled with water from the rivers of the world since time out of mind — Cate obligingly stuck her nose over the rim and sniffed. A slight whiff of vinegar, but as delightfully fresh as represented.

She looked around, taking in the scope of all which he had achieved. They were standing on an island populated by no less than five hundred and he had managed a small nook of privacy. No ears listening, and more importantly, no prying eyes. No lights, no smoke, no voices, no sound of anyone or anything else aside from the night creatures and the lap of waves on the shore. It was barely the size of the *Morganse's* deck, but for that night, it could have been all the world.

New curtains of canvas hung from rings, shining with freshness from the forge, adorned the bed. Lanterns sat about, so they needn't grope about in the dark. A privy was set up in a corner, a piece of canvas hung for privacy. Most shores were littered with branches, leaves, and storm wrack. The sand had been swept — by palm fronds, judging by the lines in the sand — of all debris, including all the footprints of the gang necessary to achieve all this.

And all necessarily achieved — he had even shaved — in one afternoon, since their return from Celia's.

Duties, forsooth!

"Sometimes, I am positively dazzled by your ability to deceive," she said.

Nathan ducked his head. "Aye," he said, kicking the sand. "But it makes for an interesting life and some grand surprises, does it not?"

He sobered. "I can only promise the night. The morrow — "

Her finger to his lip cut him short. "I don't care about tomorrow."

He smiled against the pad of her finger. His lips moved to kiss it, then he grasped her hand and brought it to his chest. "Most women might be plied with jewels and baubles. Alas, if it were only that simple," he added ruefully under his breath.

"You," he continued, in a slightly accusing tone. "For you — " He stopped. In a combination of resignation and anticipation, he stepped aside and swept an inviting arm. "I give you this..."

She followed his point to the fire and a steaming pot hanging on a hook. "Hot water?!"

"And this." He reached into his pocket and held out the barest sliver of soap.

He moved to a makeshift washstand: a China basin atop a puncheon, a bit of cloth for a towel, and a lantern to see by. "This, too." He plucked a sponge from beside a basin. "Fresh picked and cleaned."

A whiff of sandalwood and jasmine came from the soap, one never seen before. "Where...? I mean, how...?"

His eyes rounded in overt innocence. "Ask me no questions and oblige me to spin no tales."

"You thought of everything."

"Aye, well, I tried."

Nathan stepped back and made a grand sweep with his arm. "Your shrine to cleanliness awaits!"

Nathan took the basin to the fire, ladled hot water and carried it back. Cate cautiously dipped a finger and then tempered it with a bit of the cooler water from the butt.

"Allow me," he said, pushing her hands away from her laces.

It was just as well. The husky purr in his voice had rendered her fingers useless, anyway.

They slowly peeled away each other's clothing like petals from a rosebud. Suddenly free of the confines of the stays, her breasts strained against the fabric of her shift, taut and full, eager to be taken. His arms slipped about her waist and brought her against him, his cock hard between the cleft of her rear. That he could reach that stage of readiness without writhing in pain — made her believe that his travails, their travails were truly past.

Cate dipped the sponge, passed it over the soap and began to bathe. It was a ritual performed many an evening in their cabin, often with Nathan as her audience. Then and now, guilt of playing the seductive temptress was absolved by the avid gleam in his eye. Her body was as sensitive as a cat's whisker; she could feel his gaze, intent with longing. She slowly ran the sponge up an arm and then shoulder. She reached to lift up her hair, only to have Nathan do it for her. He took the sponge and continued its advance up her nape, and then down to her back, there tracking in slow circles.

They soon came to exchange the sponge, one bathing the other, each pass of the sponge a caress. The world around them melted away, and Nathan became her world, filling her senses: the warm, wet slick of his skin, the faint rasp of his breathing, or the soft jingle of his bells as she pushed back his hair, the smell of jasmine and sandalwood mingling with the mustiness of male desire.

The soap bubbled between his fingers as he delicately swiped her face, neck, and then down along her collarbone. He drew her close in a near-embrace to wash her back, his hands riding on a film of water over the curve of her ribs and swell of her buttocks, pausing to place a kiss — some lingering, some brief but tender — just below her ear, on the slope of each breast, the swell of her abdomen, and the inside of each knee. His scarf was lifted away so that she might reach his forehead and temples, down the curve of his mustache and then line of his jaw. She passed over the throbbing pulse at his throat to his shoulders. The flat of her hand trailing behind, she went from his arms down to his sides, his skin twitching as she touched a particularly ticklish spot. From behind, she reached around to his chest, pressing her breasts to his back, small curls of steam rising between them. His back was broad and smooth against her cheek, the tattoos and scars softened by the dim light. She placed a kiss between the twin arcs of his shoulder blades, and then lower, at the small of his back, tasting faintly of soap and salt. Their eyes rarely broke from their mutual stare. He made a point of freshly warming the sponge, before slipping it between her thighs, moving it with a gentleness that made her abdomen tighten and her body rush in yearning. She knelt as she bathed his legs, muscular columns, one thigh marred with a gnarled scar, twisting up. His breath quickened, and then caught, as she gently afforded him the same luxurious benefits of the freshly warmed sponge on his genitals.

At one point, with a wet splat, Nathan dropped the sponge to scoop her up and carry her to the bed.

Spreading himself over her, his eyes glowed as he smoothed the hair back from her face. "I took you for granted before." His voice was hoarse with emotion. "But, by the powers and all which is holy, I vow it shall never happen again."

Her objection was cut off by a kiss. He smiled against her lips at the end.

"And now, I finally have all the space I could wish and all the time to spare! I mean to take you here." He rolled across the bed, taking her with him, ending on top once more. "Then I mean to take you here." He rolled again, angling toward the foot. "And then, I mean to take you here. And then, over here—"

"But, first," he declared more formally. "I recall some unfinished business." He rose on his knees and began working her back toward the bolsters. "I committed the ultimate sin: I left a lady in dire need, wanting—"

"Wanting?" she echoed, already a bit breathless.

"Oh, aye," he said lustily. "Wanting, as in dire need of proper attending."

One eye closed, like an artist preparing one for a portrait, he began arranging her amid the pillows. "Now, you were here... No, just a little over. That's it. This leg was here. Bear a hand, there. Clap onto those knees and give a man room to work."

He sat back a bit to give her a final critical look. With an approving nod, he settled comfortably between her legs. "Now, allow a master his craft." The last word came with a burst of warm air on her most tender parts.

Damn him, master, indeed. He knew every groove and rise, every crevice and nub, and attended each one with dismaying skill. The alarming, and so very disconcerting, thing was how handily he picked up exactly where he had left off, and even more so, how readily her body did the same.

He emitted an appreciative hum, producing an even more disconcerting sensation. "You're as salty as the sea!"

She succumbed to a swirl of sensations: the slither of his braids trailing over her leg, the bristle of his mustache, his razor-smooth cheek like satin against her thigh, and the hot, slick of his probing tongue. "Clap on" or no, her hand slid from holding her knee to rest on his crown, not so much as to urge or guide—he needed none of that—but as the need to hold onto something, an anchor, something solid in this tumbling chaos. She was seized by a long, rolling sequence of convulsions, like waves one building upon the other, until she fell back gasping.

Nathan rested his cheek on her thigh as she recovered.

"Are you...?" she asked.

"Shh." He planted a kiss at the crease of her groin, flicking his tongue at the end.

"I'll do. This is your time." With a menacing chuckle, he set back to his attentions.

"But—"

"Mmm??" The interrogatory hum came with an odd vibration, one which struck all further thought from her mind for the next while.

When she was once more reduced to breathless and limp, he heaved up on his elbows.

"Smug bastard," she said at seeing his grin.

Cocking a brow, the grin broadened. "You'll have me believe you didn't enjoy it?" He rolled his eyes skyward and sighed like a martyr. "I'll just have to try harder."

"No, no, not... not... yet...!" she gasped, hand flailing. Every fiber of her being screamed for her to reciprocate, to make him moan and writhe as he had her. Just then, however, lifting her head off the pillow seemed an insurmountable challenge.

"What about you?" A glance proved his distractive efforts were answering, to a degree. He wasn't limp, but neither was he at a stand. "Salt-Beef Peg?"

"Her, and her cohort, Slush-bucket Annie—poking her was said to be like poking a bucket o' moldering slush—are alive and well up here." He tapped his temple. "Only way to hang fire, rather than going off like a fountain."

His brow rumpled as he peered thoughtfully down at her midriff. "A third in there, I think."

"No, I can't."

Avoiding her floundering resistance, he settled back. His hands firm at her hips, he brushed his mustache through the damp curls, and smiled at the resulting gooseflesh. "I always fancied five. T'would be a new record."

"You're counting? Whose achievements are we measuring, here?" she asked narrowly.

With a devious chuckle, Nathan began again. Cate was struck with the disturbing vision of a new version of eternal damnation: Purgatory through pleasure, the possibility of that infinity growing more imminent as another spasm threatened. This one, however, "hung fire," promising, and yet denied.

"I need you—" she cried, scrabbling at his shoulders, seeking to pull him to her.

"No, I'll do," he said, resisting.

She struggled up, groping in desperation. "Dammit, come here! I need you, inside me, *now*."

"Very well," he sighed.

Cate's hand twitched, instinctively reaching for him, but then hesitated, still haunted by the episodes of the recent days. Nathan took it and guided it down between them, pressing himself into her grasp.

His eyes rolled blissfully closed. "Hands of an angel, I swear."

A few strokes and he was ready. He poised over her, his body eloquent with indecision and fear: fear of failure, fear of disappointment. She thrust her hips as a silent pledge: whatever happened, they would suffer it together. With a set look of determination, he sheathed himself. For a fraction of a second, they waited. Finding all was well, he drew back and plunged again. With the force increasing with every stroke, she writhed and bucked under him, her awareness diminishing to his hot breath against her neck and the single point of their joining. She dug her heels into the mattress and absorbed the battering, each stroke felt to her depths. Nathan lifted his head to look down at her in wondering awe. The masks fell away, allowing her to see his utter affection and yearning. Then he threw his head back in a silent desperate cry and spilled himself.

Nathan lowered over her, and they clung as they shook. He sighed, one of a monumental task achieved.

"Hello," he said, huskily.

Humming pleasurably at the still throbbing presence within her, Cate moved her hips in answer. "Hello."

❧

Nathan slid off next to Cate, one leg still flung over her. The throb in her ears matched the one in her womb. Gradually, the pounding faded and the sounds of the night returned.

"So, Salt-Beef Peg answered?" Cate mused when speech was finally possible.

It took a few moments, but Nathan finally emitted a rumbling chuckle. "A bit too well, there for a bit." He groped blindly between them until he found her hand and squeezed. "I had to see you under me, with that maddening tangle all about your head. After that—" A slight movement of his shoulder finished the thought.

Half-lidded with complacency, he rolled onto his back and stretched out before her. "You still like it then? Nothing's... changed?" he asked, suddenly shy.

"Why would it?"

Nathan toyed with the rumpled bedclothes. "I just worried that after... everything, something... me, might be different."

His mouth moved, searching for words. "God knows this dying thing changes you. It tears you apart, like a 24-pound ball hitting a spar. You gather it all together, as best you might, but you're never sure all the pieces are back. Inside," he said, touching his chest. "I'm not who I was after the first time and even less after the second. One can't ignore the possibility of other things being... different."

What ravages did Death wrought? Being obliged to serve a demonic goddess, curses, exorcisms: it would be a small wonder if either of them were recognizable, inside or out.

"Hmm, well..." She cocked her head, considering. She curled her fingers into the hair on his chest. "This is the same." Her hand moved to the divot in his chest. "This is the same, although your ribs stick out a bit more," she went on, tracing those. "You're horribly thin. Your hip bones are kind of pokey, too," she added, coming to rest on one.

She slipped her hand down. Closing his eyes, he obligingly spread his legs so she might cup the now soft mass there. "This is very familiar, although..." She stopped, angling her head a bit sharper.

His eyes opened to peer down. "What?"

"It's... familiar, this bit, at any rate," running along the length. "And this bit, I know intimately," she said, encircling the end. "But...?"

She bent and placed a kiss on the very tip and then sat back. She shrugged, smiling. "My mistake. I'm not accustomed to seeing it so... relaxed."

"True enough, darling," he sighed. He lifted his head to glare down the slope of his belly. "I'm rarely decent when you're about."

She bowed her head in false shame. "Such a treacherous tease, am I?"

He dropped his head back down and exhaled, long and resigned. "There was a time when I would have taken you again, right now. But, alas, with the wisdom of age comes limitations of the flesh."

"'Tis a cruel jest for we men. We're given what we long for, only to have it over in a flash. Our own bodies contrive against us: when we least wish it, there it 'tis, like a damned flagstaff. And, when we wish for it to remain with every fiber of our being, 'tis gone, burrowing like a damned shipworm."

Cate looked down at the now recumbent member. Given the description of shipworms — six or seven foot-long, corkscrew things, with munching jaws — she failed to see the resemblance, and gratefully so.

She patted his arm, encouragingly "Perhaps, it knows when I need a rest." Nathan made a disbelieving noise, but was clearly appreciative of the sentiment.

Cate stretched luxuriantly next to him. "All I wish to do is lie here for a bit. I don't wish to move, not... yet."

"Ah." He raised up and kissed the spot over her womb. "Feeling fecund are we?"

That wasn't quite what she had in mind, but now that he mentioned it, it wouldn't hurt to just lie there that bit longer.

He sat up and announced "We require sustenance, a replenishment of the energies. Linger a bit, whilst I see to our other needs of the flesh."

❧⁂❧

Cate watched Nathan rise. It required every shred of energy to move her head enough to admire the light playing on his back and limbs as he stoked the fire. He moved to a locker and a bag atop it, one she vaguely recalled seeing him carry when they came ashore. Returning with it, he drew out and spread a veritable picnic on the bed before her: cheese, folded-leaf packets of rice and vegetables, fish, cold beast, fruit and bread. From next to the bed, he brought up a couple bottles of ale and a flask of port.

Jelly-limbed, much as she would have loved to just lie there, in light of all his preparations, to do so seemed rude.

Pushing upright, she looked around at the campsite, marveling. "How did you ever manage all this?"

"Commanding nigh on to two hundred has to have some benefits," he said off – handedly.

They sat cross-legged, shoulder-to-shoulder on the bed and ate, Nathan's knife their only utensil.

"You're eating," she observed.

He looked up from slicing meat to waggle his brows. "Need me strength for the next round. Lying with you requires the strength of a legion."

With several parts of her body still tingling with their

lovemaking, her cheeks heated. She didn't consider herself all that different, not to the degree that he always claimed. But asking him to explain meant comparisons to others, which she categorically didn't wish to hear.

Breaking her fast seemed not just a matter of hours, but days since, and she was ravenous. Very soon, however, she noticed the bulk of the meal was being steered her way. Only when she was chewing did Nathan take a bite for himself, and so, she made a deliberate effort to slow down.

As Nathan reached for the fish, her eye caught the dark cuff about his wrist. Thomas' analysis had been correct: Nathan did look like he was wearing shackles, like a slave bound at limb and neck.

"Are they bothersome?" she asked.

"Can't say as I notice, except for this," he amended, touching his neck. "It feels too much like... something."

That "something" was undoubtedly the rope which had nearly hung him, a sick prank gone bad. No one could blame him for being overly sensitive about anything about his neck. She struggled to imagine him tolerating the high collar and stock as was the men's fashion. It had to have required every bit of his resolve to endure that cuff now... and for the next two months.

With a couple deft flicks of the knife, and the bones were removed from the fish, the skeleton flung aside.

"Do you think they, the cuffs, will work?" Cate asked.

"Have to," came pragmatically back.

"They smell," she said, wrinkling her nose.

"Like the vapors of hell," Nathan said agreeably, and then grinned. "Fitting, don't you think?"

He offered the bottle of ale. She took a grateful drink and handed it back. "She's still out there, isn't she?" Cate asked, dabbing her mouth.

Nathan took a drink, pensively rolling it in his mouth before swallowing. "Oh, aye, as she has for the last millennium or so, and will be for the next two or three to come."

He paused to slip his arm around her. "She can't touch you. The old bunter can scratch and claw and kick up and throw a grand fit, but she can't lay a hand on either you or I."

Cate shifted uneasily, feeling a bit haunted. "You keep saying she can't come ashore, and yet she appeared at Celia's."

"Have the scratches to prove it," he declared, extending his arm. He looked down and gave a startled grunt as he tilted it toward the light.

The long gouges were gone, the skin of his arm now smooth

and perfect. "I know they were there," Cate insisted. "I cleaned them, remember?"

"How the bloody h—?" He choked a wry laugh and shook his head. "The ill - begotten witch o' the deep was playing mind tricks on us all."

Now he was the one to stare out at the water. Finally, he demonstrably shrugged. "How she happened to be there I have no notion: proximity of the sea — we're surrounded by it — whatever the hell Celia had beckoned, or perhaps just the foothold she already had on me. Who knows, and more importantly, who the bloody hell cares?"

I do, thought Cate privately.

A great deal of security had come with knowing land was a refuge. She shivered; that safety being taken was like having a warm blanket jerked away on a frosty night.

"Are we safe anywhere, ever?" This having to worry about a goddess popping up was wearing. Just when she thought they might finally have a bit of peace-of-mind, there is another ugly turn of events.

"Yes," came back definitively. "That was a first, I'll admit, but it was exactly that: a fluke, a quirk, a happenstance, a one-time wonder." He thrust out his arm again. "All evidence has disappeared. I'll take that as tangible proof that her influence went with it."

With a final definitive jerk of his head, Nathan slipped a morsel of fish into her mouth.

"She could make our lives miserable," Cate said around it. "She doesn't strike me as one who takes rejection easily."

"None of us, not even goddesses, get everything they wish," he said, censoriously. "Just look at mythology: 'tis naught but one betrayal or disappointment after another. One more shouldn't come as any great shock."

"Shouldn't," Cate qualified, dryly.

A rise and fall of one shoulder acknowledged her point while at the same time dismissed it. "Besides, she's breeding now."

"As if we know what that means," Cate sighed to herself.

"True enough. You know how these damned gods are; for all we know she may have popped out the motley little, crossbred mongrel already."

"Fine way to speak of your child," Cate sputtered.

He cut her a cold eye. "No, it is not." A portion of his lip lifted in disgust. "The point is she has what she wants."

For now, Cate thought. *And then, what?*

The flesh and stomach might have been sated, but the soul still hungered. They sat intertwined, touching and needing to be touched. Nathan leaned against the headboard, Cate between his legs, head pillowed on his chest. Gazing at the night and the water, they made little random gestures—a flexing of a hand or arm, lips pressed to her temple or crown—so very aware of each other, waiting for that small signal—a look, a word voice, a spark of eye—which said it was time to join again.

The breeze had all but died, only little convection currents stirring the leaves. The bay had flattened, the moonlight stitching its gunmetal surface with silver at each undulating roll of a wave. They lapped the shore with a shushing sound similar to what one might utter to soothe a fretful child.

It was quiet, quiet enough to hear the fire flames lick the air and the beat of the bats' wings as they whirred past. After the furor and crash of being attacked, the din of the injured in the sickbay, the clamor of rebuilding, and press of people, Cate drank in the silence like a rejuvenating elixir. In the Highlands, such a thing was no further than a stroll across a field or up a lane away. Years of city-living, and then going to sea, where motion and sound were as ever-present as the need to breathe, had robbed her of it for so long she had forgotten how glorious it could be.

A rumbling sound made her lift her head: distant and coming from the opposite side of the island.

"Thunder?" A faint accompanying flicker of light from the same direction made her think as much. Her spirits sank: even the coming of rain seemed too much an intrusion.

"Nay, guns," Nathan said laconically.

Cate's heart tripped a beat. "Thomas?"

"More than likely." He paused at the sound again, slightly stronger and slightly longer. "He's probably encountered one of those sea-wolves sniffing about out there." He smiled at another rumble. "He's giving them a good drubbing, passing them under the harrow, to be sure."

He gave her an encouraging squeeze. "'Tis naught to be done, darling. He's out there in the offing, well beyond any helping hand we might extend."

Head canted, they both listened, Nathan perhaps a bit more intently than he wished to appear.

"There, 'tis over," he said at last, as if that would ease her worries.

It did... barely.

"Will we ever see him again?" Even though a bare whisper,

the sound of her own voice seemed an abomination to the solitude.

So far gone in thought, it took Nathan a moment to return. "Thomas? Oh, aye, I suspect as much. He pops in and out of one's life like a damned flying fish. I'm surprised he lingered this long."

"But, we've only been here a few days."

"Aye, and a tribulation to be sure. Lounging about is his torture."

"Come to think on it, I don't recall ever seeing him just sit." He had always exhibited a certain restlessness, but she had always marked it up to tensions or preoccupations of the moment.

"Wanderlust isn't in it. A gypsy is a stay-at-home compared to him."

"But, he stayed about when... when you careened the *Morganse*." That was easier said than "when I was recovering from Creswicke beating me senseless." The careening had been more of an excuse than reason, but the outcome had been the same: nearly a month of blissful quiet on shore.

"A trial-of-the-ages, suffered only on your account. He had a trench worn in the beach, with the pacing to be aweigh." Nathan angled his head a fraction to look down at her. "You'll recall, he had already gone off just before... everything."

With a faint movement of a shoulder, Cate conceded his point. Thomas had, indeed, made his adieus, claiming places to go, and yet unable to name one. By whatever coincidence, he had reappeared in Bridgetown just in time to aid in her rescue, or so she had been told, at any rate. She had no personal memory of so much of what happened.

"He's gone off in a huff before with whatever trumped up excuse to hand. 'Tis why he resists gaining another ship, like salt on a bird's tail."

"I always thought that of you," Cate mused.

"I'm the veritable cat-on-the-hearth compared to him. I, at least, have the wits to appreciate when I'm content."

Cate looked up at Nathan, the firelight dancing on his nose and cheek. "Are you... content?"

The light glinted on the gold of his smile. "As content as one could ever wish: fulfilled, satisfied and gratified; elated and exulted; blithe, blissful and blessed —"

"Oh, very well, you've made your point," she huffed, giving him a good-natured elbow to the middle. She settled her head back on his chest. "I shan't ask again."

He smoothed her hair from his face. "You press the obvious,

darling. 'Tis none so difficult state to achieve: me ship to hand and you next to me 'tis all which is required, being allowed to your bed naught but the icing on the cake."

Ducking his head, he peered through the thick lashes and asked shyly "Are you... content?"

She turned enough to gently seize the point of his beard, so he was obliged to look her in the eyes. "Eminently, ecstatically, gloriously—"

Nathan drew her against his chest to muffle the rest. He pressed his lips to her crown. "Then, the gods are smiling on us both."

Resuming her position, Nathan's hand found hers, his thumb idly stroking her knuckles. Somewhere, in the trees behind them, a tree frog set off a lonely churr.

"How did you two come to go your separate ways? Thomas told me some," she added, heading off any intention to decline answering.

"He did, eh? Figures; Thomas has always considered himself the bloody town-crier. Aye, well, 'tis a vague chance at least a part of it was the truth."

"It was over a woman: Camilla?" Her hand resting on his leg, Cate felt for a reaction—a twitch, a quick intake of air, quickening of heart—at hearing the name, some indication of any lingering regard. But nothing, the thump of his heart, like a low, distant drumbeat, unchanged.

"Aye," Nathan said cautiously, keenly aware of that alertness. "A woman in years, at any rate. She was one of those who would always be a girl and, at that point, a girl seemed all I sought." He sighed at the fallacies of youth. "That was back when I fancied the demure, doe-eyed, blushing and pure. The swish of a skirt, flip of a fan, the waving of a bit of lace-edged handkerchief, and I was putty in their hands."

He bent his head and whispered "I'd yet to learn the glories of a woman."

"I'll take that as a compliment."

"Of the highest order," he said, glowing with admiration.

Nathan looked back out at the bay. "I promised her the world; he promised her the stars. She wouldn't lift her skirts for me, but she jolly well did for him."

Cate noted that Nathan's version—surprise, surprise—wasn't quite the same as Thomas', but the essence of it was the same: a woman choosing one friend over another.

"He said she ran off with someone else," Cate offered, as if that might mollify at least a portion of the hurt.

"Ah, so the stars weren't enough for her, eh?" Nathan's

attempted indifference was barely successful. The satisfaction of a payback delivered was very near the surface.

"So then, you and Thomas parted?" Cate prompted.

"You make it sound like an old married couple divorcing."

"Friendships breaking can be almost as bad, perhaps worse," she said, suddenly feeling the sage. It was one of those axioms uttered by elders which proved to be so very, very true. The loss of a friend brought the same grief and mourning as the loss of a loved one. The worst was when you lose both all in one person, as she had with Brian.

"True," he said, reluctantly. "But not then. The truth is, in bald-faced honesty, I was already coming to breaking with her. The only thing which stopped me was that golden Romeo sniffing about. Hell, had they asked, I would have stepped aside and gladly, but they didn't."

He shifted restlessly, the leg under her hand tensing. "It wasn't the cuckolding, but the betrayal."

"There's a difference?" she asked, looking up.

"Aye, a grand one. He skulked about behind me back, allowin' me to make a fool o' meself the while."

"But, surely you trust him now."

"With me life, and all else which is precious to me," he said, his arms tightening about her.

Eyes hooded, he fell into a brooding silence. "An even larger truth is that Thomas and I were set to split like an old hawse. If it hadn't been Camilla, it would have been something else. We were beginning to squabble like that old married couple, coming to loggerheads over anything and everything. He gets his Dutch up and there's no dealing with him."

"I've never seen that," Cate said. Not exactly, at any rate. Flashes of temper and bullishness had shown their ugly heads, but rarely without provocation.

"Then you've not pressed him," Nathan said succinctly.

Nathan fell quiet for some moments. "Some months after they ran off, he reappeared, announced Camilla was dead — as if I had something to do with it — and then sailed off. I heard of him, now and again, from whalers or the odd Indiaman, sailing with a letter-of-marque from the caliphate of Malacca or some such capers. But never a direct word. Never."

His tone was dispassionate, but not enough to veil the loneliness of losing a lifetime friend. Who left who was a minor point; the result was the same: friends divided, one alone, one not.

It felt too contrary to point out that, in the ultimate analysis, Nathan was the one doing the leaving, not Thomas.

Nathan's arm tightened around Cate, this time in reassurance. "Buoy up, darling. This was none of your doing. And no," he added more sternly. "There's nothing to be gained in arguing you weren't thinking that. It's been plain on your face since you learned he was leaving. He was as bound to leave then, as he was bound to leave now."

A dozen arguments came to mind, all of which would have proved Nathan wrong, but she appreciated his intentions, just the same. A woman would have to have a heart of that same flint if refusing a man, who just laid his heart at her feet, didn't make her feel wicked.

"Aye, Thomas is miserable," Nathan said. "The best place for him is out there. Let him blow a jib on his men, not us innocent bystanders."

"That's what he said about you."

Nathan smiled without humor. "Did he now, the scheming rake?"

Going somewhat distant once more, Nathan gazed out at the water. "'Tis only one place to mend a broken heart," he said, quieter. "Out there."

"That sounds like the voice of experience." She mussed her head against his chest. "How many hearts did you mend?"

"Many, too many." His entire body curved around hers in an embrace. "But, I have discovered that it is also where you might find it."

❧

The logs on the fire collapsed, sending a spiral of sparks up into the night. The quiet returned, drawing in over them like a warm comforter. Nathan gathered Cate closer, an arm at her waist, a hand cupping her breast, not in seduction, but simply because it seemed the natural place to be. Cate closed her eyes and soaked in his nearness, basking in it like a cat before the fire.

"How fares the lad?"

"Blooming," Cate said after a moment to follow his meaning. "Toby's left the sickbay, and I caught a glimpse of him romping about with his mates."

"Ah," came back polite yet mechanical.

Something else was on Nathan's mind. Waiting, however, was the best. Pressing never answered.

A snuffling sputter, like a diver surfacing, made her open her eyes. The sound led her to something out in the water. Near the far edge of the lagoon, where the smoothness marked a deep hole: a head, dark and round, popped up. A sea hog was her first thought, but immediately eliminated that. This was larger, not near so streamlined, and far more lethargic.

"What is that?"

Even at that distance, she lowered her voice, lest the maternal scene be disturbed.

"A sea cow, grazing looks like. Pour enough grog down the hands, and they will claim it's a mermaid," he added wryly. "At least, this one is a female. See the babe at her side?"

Sure enough, a little head bobbed next to the larger. The mother nuzzled it, and then rolled on her back, a protective flipper curved over her young as it nursed. Cate could have sworn she heard little sucking sounds amid the stir of treading water.

"There is a child," Nathan began haltingly, his gaze still fixed on the creature. "Shh, easy, stand down, luv," he said, his arms tightening at feeling her tense. "Don't blow a boltrope. I'm not about to announce it's another bastard."

She quieted, in spite of his hesitancy and trepidation, which was barely reassuring. "You'll have to admit, it seems of late every time I turn around that's the case."

"Aye, well, not this one. Woe that it was, for it would make things so very much simpler."

When Nathan deemed it safe, he loosened his grasp, although still held her. He drew a deep breath and began again. "There is a child…"

Cate nodded shortly.

"The father is unknown; the mum a victim of Lesauvage's foolishness."

Cate considered that was an apt description of a number of infants on the island. "Is it a boy or a girl?"

"Umm, a girl… I think. 'Tis beside the point," he said with a short gesture.

"Not to some," she replied, tartly. Typical Nathan: paying no attention to that which didn't interest him. And yet, many a time since his arrival, she had seen him surrounded by the island's youths, telling stories or jests, doing coin or rope tricks, making them marvel and laugh.

He slid her a quelling look and pressed on. "I promised you a child." The knob of his throat bobbed as he audibly swallowed, the rest coming in halting bursts. "The uncertainty is the how and who of it. I know I spoke of Thomas, or finding someone to get one on you, but—but, sink and burn me, I'm a coward. I could not bear to see you go with another man, let alone watch your belly grow with another man's child. You can gut me, if you wish, and I'll hand you the knife, but damn my eyes, I couldn't do it." His eyes going unnaturally bright, he turned his head, blinking.

"Rest easy; I shan't murder you in your sleep," she said, patting him on the arm. She glanced at the tumbled bedclothes. "But we just — ?"

Nathan resolutely shook his head. "What we just did proves nothing beyond the fact that we can do it, praise the gods. But we both know the act and the siring are two different things." He paused, jaw working. "Your fertility is given; mine is still in question."

"And so — ?" She stopped, her mouth falling open as the realization struck. "You're suggesting I, we take that one?"

He arched his brows at the obvious answer.

"Have you seen it?" Her throat had suddenly gone tight.

"A child's a child, isn't it?"

Cate coughed, words failing her.

"It's still in drapes, not made its first year, yet." That point was offered more in the way of his own defense than information.

"As I understand it, any child is to be raised here, isn't it?" In the face of so much death and destruction, that point had been of prime concern, and she had made inquiries. It occurred to her then that perhaps those inquiries were what had precipitated Marthanna and her friends into confronting and accusing her the other night.

"There is no such thing as an orphan here," he pointed out. "They protect their young like sea hogs against a shark."

There was no arguing with that point, either. She had experienced that ferocity first - hand.

"She might live here, with a score of mothers. Or..." The coffee-colored eyes fixed affectionately on Cate. "It might live with one mother, but the most incredible one ever, and never want for anything."

The warm flush of flattery was suddenly chilled by a rising suspicion. "This child wouldn't happen to be — ?"

Nathan's eye narrowed. "As I have represented, and as testified by many, I have not been here in years." The last word uttered with the emphasis of the convicted soul seeking reprieve.

"You could have been somewhere else and — " Cate stopped, finding herself on a path she hadn't wished to take and now with no notion of how to credibly get off. "The mother could have come here after. After all, isn't that essentially the function of this place: a refuge for the wayward and homeless?"

"Do you think me so low as to foist a child on you?" The query came not so much in anger as a point of curiosity. In point of fact, the entire exchange was conducted in a near whisper, in deference to the nursing mother.

Cate sat up, toying with a braid at his shoulder. The dark eyes were intent on her, the cinnamon glints almost amber in the firelight. "I think," she began, with all sincerity, "that you would say or do anything in the spirit of giving me whatever you fancied that I fancied."

A smile flashed, relieved but brief. "You know me too well. But nay," he went on, solemnly. "I'll swear on whatever you desire, including me mum's name, that it, she is no more of my blood than Pryce."

"But, I find it highly unlikely they will just give her over." The women had snarled like she-wolves at that prospect of her just going near one they perceived as theirs.

"Then I'll take it. Pirate, remember," he said over her incredulous sputter. "Treachery unto others, before they treachery unto you."

Cate choked a laugh. "That's an odd gospel you have there, lad."

"Aye, but one to which I have learned to."

"But you can't just —?"

"Can and will," he said with cold finality. "If it, she is what you wish, then I'll take it — her and damn the consequences." His point was punctuated by a finger jabbed at her. "Hell, it'll just give this meddlesome bunch o' slatterns one more reason to blackguard and curse me to damnation. Aye, they'll be all stirred up like a beehive rammed by a stick, but they'll settle... eventually. We'd have to be prepared to make weigh straightaway, which means..."

He went off on his own train of thought while Cate went off on her own. Preparations: if all this came to pass, first and foremost a wet nurse would have to be arranged, she thought, a hand ghosting to her breast. Then there would be cloths and clothing, blankets and —

"What?" she asked, distracted. Her heart had taken to pounding so hard it was difficult to hear.

"I said, just give the word and it, she is yours."

Cate leaned back to eye him. "What makes you think I'm so desperate for a child?" Speaking of children to a man with "Freedom" emblazoned on his chest — now inches from her face — hardly seemed wise. "I never said —"

Nathan smiled indulgently. "You don't have to, luv. The need radiates off you like the halo about a Madonna. Hell, even the women noticed." His hand curved under her breast. "And just now," he went on softly, "at seeing her out there, your breast went hard in me hand, your nipple tightening with the need to suckle."

Flushing at being so transparent, Cate reflexively shielded herself.

"I made a vow to both you and meself," Nathan said. "Neither do I take lightly."

Cate vaguely nodded. She was touched, touched beyond measure, and felt an odd thrill. Her arms twitched at the prospect of holding the warm heavy weight, a little head wobbling on her shoulder. It was tempting, so very, *very* tempting, the answer to countless prayers and dreams all dangling before her like a great huge, juicy plum.

At the same time, her heart pinched. The prospect of a child made the prospect of Nathan leaving her behind all the more immediate. The possibility had always hung like a distant storm cloud. Now, it was racing toward her. He spoke of "taking" the infant, which meant he didn't mean to leave the two of them on the island, thank heavens! So, somewhere else. The house he had spoken of rose as a possibility, along with all its appurtenances.

She shook her head, dismissing it all. Yes, a home, a place to belong, with a garden and a child, but it would all come without the one thing she wished for most of all: Nathan.

Cate pressed her hand to his cheek, still smooth from shaving earlier. "It's all so very, very thoughtful, but —"

His brows drew down, nearly touching. "But what? 'Tis the perfect answer. The only wonder is why the bloody hell it took me so long to come to it."

"I tried to explain before, but you wouldn't attend," she began, careful to sound neither reproachful, nor ungrateful. "I don't wish for a child, just for a child's sake. What I wish for so desperately is your child, so that when you're gone —"

"I might be absent, darling, but I'll never be gone," he interjected, wagging a cautioning finger.

"I want a piece of you," she went determinedly on. "So I might look down and see your eyes and your smile, and —"

"Might we wish for jade instead of brown?" he asked, touching the corner of her eye. "And a smile like this, what curls at the corners on its own," touching her mouth, "and that little turn up at the end of your nose?" he said, touching that.

"Yes, of course," she said, swallowing a large lump. "I would come love any child as my own, but please don't rob me of the hope of having my own." She searched his face, pleading. With Celia's words ringing in her head, she wasn't ready to give up. "Not yet," coming out in a tight rasp.

"But, there's no knowing if —"

"Time: that's all I ask, just a little time."

He cocked a warning brow. "You might be dooming yourself to a life of barrenness."

"Let's not get the wrong oars in before the boat, or whatever your saying is. You promised me a child," she insisted, tapping him on the chest. "And now, I'm going to hold you to it."

Nathan slipped his arms about her and grasped her to him. "Ah, a woman of conviction and infinite memory." He sighed and smiled crookedly. "I shall think carefully before I ever make a blood pledge to you again."

"No blood vows, if you please," she said, shuddering. "We've had enough of that spilled of late."

He kissed her, the decision made, the matter closed.

Bracing his forehead against hers, he sighed. "Bloody woman. God help me, I can't tell you no."

Nathan sat up, like one suddenly struck by a notion.

"I have three words for you." The announcement was uttered with the huskiness of anticipation.

Cate's heart tripped a beat and then raced. There were three words she had waited so very long to hear from him.

He reached down beside the bed "I have port," he said, producing a bottle in his fist.

His smile vanished. "You looked disappointed, ready to gut me for a flashing instant."

"Only for a moment, but—I thought you were going to say something else, that's all," she stammered. A not so small part of her wished to punch him.

A silver cup was also brought forth and filled.

"This is very good," she said, duly impressed. And it was. "How did you ever come by it?"

Nathan batted his lashes. "Ask me no questions and oblige me to tell no lies."

"That again?" She closed one eye. "Does that mean you stole it?"

He straightened in indignation. "I am an honorable man, where honor might serve," he added under his breath. "When bartering doesn't answer, then one resorts to what must be resorted."

The question as to what he might be bartering was categorically shoved aside.

Instead, she resettled in his arms, and they shared the port. With so many things settled, it suddenly seemed possible to consider the future with him.

"Where to...?" She had asked before, with limited success.

"The world is yours, darling," he said with a grandiose sweep of his arm. "Anywhere you wish."

She stared for a good while, considering. This wasn't just lip-service. He truly meant it. The Seven Seas were open to them; she might close her eyes, toss a dart at a map and he would take her.

"Someplace where there is laughter," she said finally. Her heart lightened just at the prospect.

An eye cracked open to peer down the long line of his nose. "You've not had much of that of late, have you?"

She flinched at the accuracy of his observation. The accusation it came with, however, was aimed at himself not her. Arguing the point, however, threatened to dig the knife he was already twisting into himself all the deeper. A rise and fall of one shoulder conceded. These last months, dark days had seemed to prevail.

"It's precious difficult to be gay around here, with one's back prickling from all the daggers being thrown," she sighed.

"Given the opportunity, I shouldn't have been surprised if they would have thrown the real thing."

"I half-expected poison in my drink," she mused, holding up the cup.

Nathan took it and took a drink, smacking his lips. "Only if you got on Celia's bad side. Her hand would be in it, one way or another, for she would be the one they would go to."

She turned to look at him. "You say that like they've done that."

"Only a fool would think they haven't." He smiled at seeing her peer suspiciously at the cup. "Stand easy, darling. You're still among the walking, so they didn't despise you that much."

"Just the run-of-the-mill hatred," she mused unsteadily.

Cate took another drink, holding it in her mouth for a moment to allow the fragrant fumes to rise at the back of her throat, cutting away the grimness of the island.

"I'd like it to be somewhere that you can laugh, too, the open, hearty, honest kind, the sort which comes from down there," she said, prodding his midriff with her elbow. "The kind I hear when you are with Thomas. At night, when it's just you and Thomas at the fire, I hear the two of you laughing as gay as two lads. But with me never or rarely, at any rate." She twisted around toward him. "Is being with me so taxing?"

Sobering, he plucked the cup from her. "You are my joy, darling." He took a large drink, rolling it in his mouth. "Worrying, however, does have its price. Going to have to learn the ropes on this worrying."

"You've had the *Morganse* to worry for for years."

A twitch of his shoulders dismissed her point. "She's nigh on to two hundred to worry for her." He looked down the line of his nose again. "You've naught but me, and a tall order it 'tis."

"You never worried about... the others?" she finally ended lamely. Lord, could they ever get past that subject?

He cocked a brow, keenly aware of the thin ice she had led him to. "The 'others' had homes, families, friends and means," he said carefully. "You are like that sea cow out there, alone in the sea," he hastily added her sputter of being compared to such a lumpish creature. "At least, she has an offspring to keep her company," he huffed under his breath.

"Aye, I laugh with Thomas," he said, refilling their drink. "Because when we are together, we are those lads again; I see it in him, he sees it in me, along with every foolish, stupid and misguided thing we've done." He cast an awkward glance at her and added "I've not known you long enough."

Nor she known him. They might lie together, but there was still so much they didn't know about each other, a reserve which, to some degree or another, might always exist. Even as thoroughly as she knew Brian, there were still things neither would tell the other.

Nathan prodded her with his forearm. "And what of you? Gaiety doesn't seem within you," he chided.

"I'm gay... sometimes," she added at the severe arch of his brow.

He snorted. "I offer you the world, a ship laden with riches and all you wish is laughter. An estate and a coach-and-six would be easier, but..."

Jaw twisting to one side, he narrowed an eye, presumably mentally reviewing a lifetime of travels. At length, he brightened. "Aye, a place comes to mind."

As he was thinking, his hands had gone roving, growing determined with purpose. He cupped her bottom and squeezed. "'Tis been a while for you. I used to hear your laugh echoing through the ship and me heart warmed. 'Tis been a long time, too long."

Even with this reunion, there was still a part of him held back, a corner of him still reserved and distant, as it had since his return one afternoon after his supposed meeting with Pryce at the sick bay. "Someone who knew someone who knew someone," and had offered nothing more.

She hadn't pressed, because that might cause whatever he was keeping in that corner to bloom and grow, allowing her even less of himself.

He pressed his lips to her temple, and then drifted down to her neck and throat. "Hopefully, you shan't feel the urge to do that very thing this next little while."

"Oh, no," she said, gently pushing him back into the bolsters. "You always make this about me."

Nathan blinked, puzzled. "Because it 'tis, darling," he said bluntly. "A man is but a guest in a woman's bed. He must serve her well or be cast out."

Cate struck a pose, hand on her hip. "Do you imagine me casting you out?" It was a bit of a wonder, for never had she even so much as alluded to such a thing. Throwing a man out, refusing favors: many women did such things, but it always struck her as frivolous and immature, trifling with matters far too important. But then, perhaps that was the result of too many years alone in a cold bed.

"In a word, aye, were I to fail or offend," he said matter-of-factly.

"Very well, then," she said, assuming a more business-like tone. "Upon risk of offending, you *will* lie back and you *will* enjoy this."

Stretching next to him, she propped her chin on his chest, bringing her eyes but inches from his. "You have made me bare my soul, show you what no others have ever seen, made me reveal my innermost secrets, and yet you," poking a finger into his chest, "have revealed nothing. Time for atonement: time for *you* to tell me what *you* like."

His smug smile, which had incrementally grown through the early stages of that confession, faltered. "No one has ever asked me that, not outright at any rate, not without 'that'll cost sixpence extra' in the offing."

Toying with a lock of her hair, he glanced up and then away. "Your instincts have served very nicely."

"No, no, no, you're not getting off that easy," she said, wagging a finger near to his nose. "Now, lie back—that's it, just a bit over; there's a good lad—close your eyes—"

"But, I like to watch you—"

"Close your eyes."

Huffing, he did nonetheless. "I feel like a bloody—"

What he felt like was never heard. In fact, for the next while, no words were uttered. Sounds—grunts, gasps, whimpers, groans, moans—abound, but nothing in the vocal. At last, she had found the means to render Nathanael Blackthorne silent!

At one point, from the lofty position of astraddle his hips, she was able to look down at him. There was, indeed, something so very seductive about watching him. It was a first to actually watch him; before she had glimpsed him, had some awareness, but always veiled by her own preoccupations. Tattooed and scarred, tangled, dark and wild all combined to render him so very alluring, to the point she was obliged to close her own eyes and call Salt – Beef Peg to mind.

A short while later, Nathan was sweating and gasping, and staring round-eyed at the canopy overhead. Still joined, Cate draped forward over him.

"I wish we could stay like this forever," she sighed softly.

A rumbling chuckle was the precursor of "You mean, like two dogs hung up?"

She playfully slapped his leg. "That's hardly romantic." Then she tucked her arms about him in the nearest to an embrace possible given their positions. "This is what I needed, the thing which was lacking..."

"Hmm?"

"Since, since we came... back." She didn't wish to break the spell by putting a name to it. "I haven't felt right, not myself. It was like some piece of me was missing, gone, somehow was left floating out in the sea, like wreckage or driftwood."

She tightened her innermost muscles around the presence inside her. "This is what I needed: you, in me. Not next to me, but in me."

His cock twitched in answer, twice. "It's not just the lust," she insisted.

His eyes opened to look up at her. "I know, darling. It's the two halves coming together as one. Like two pieces of a clamshell: one can't exist without the other."

27: CONSPIRATORS UNITED

C ATE WOKE TO THE SOUND of sluicing water and sputtering. She cracked an eye open to find Nathan standing by the puncheon, water streaming down his bare chest and legs. He refilled the bucket and dumped the contents over his head. Setting the bucket down, he turned dripping toward shore.

It was early, very early, the light grey with impending dawn. The first rays of the rising sun touched his face, and then gilded his chest, belly and legs. He stood unmoving, transfixed on something far beyond the little cove. A hand rose and closed over a bag hanging from a leather thong about his neck. Inside were two shots, one slightly flattened and scored from being dug out of his chest.

Languid and heavy, Cate closed her eyes and dozed off, his image etched inside her lids.

How much later she had no notion, she was wakened by water pattering on her face. Rain, she thought, although there had been no thunder. She opened her eyes to Nathan's cinnamon-and-amber-flecked ones inches from hers. Humming in dreamy anticipation, she hooked an arm about his neck and pulled him down, her hips thrusting for his.

He kissed her, brief and stiff. "Tide's on the ebb; we must away."

Nathan straightened to reveal that he was fully dressed and armed, hat square on his head. The sound of voices drew her to a number of men moving to and from several boats lining the shore.

With a startled "Eep!" Cate jerked the nearest thing to hand — the bed curtain — to cover herself.

"Where did they come from?" And worse yet, how long had they been there, and her lying sprawled as exposed as Eve?

"Crew." He pitched her clothes on the bed next to her and

then circled, pulling the other curtain with him. "Dress. I'll stand by to bear a hand with the laces. C'mon, show a leg!"

Cate broke from her confused stare and began to quickly dress, or rather as quickly as one might whilst kneeling. Finally, she was presentable enough to step out. A hand at her shoulder spun her about and Nathan set about her laces. Swaying like a sapling as he tightened, she took a moment to catch her breath. Judging by the men's industry, scrambling like gypsies breaking camp, the sun wasn't meant to reach the yardarm — she thought that was the saying — before the *Morganse* hauled anchor and made weigh.

"We're not going back to the settlement?" she asked.

"Why? Your dunnage is either here, or already shipped and stowed. Is there someone you are desiring to take your leave?"

"No," she said, ignoring his mocking suspicion. "It just seems common decency to take our, *my* leave."

"I gave your thanks and I gave your adieus. There's naught more to say."

Cate wasn't quite so sanguine. Her mother and old nurse would have gone pale at such a social blunder. But then, upon closer reflection, this was a pirate island. Formalities were sure to be different.

Nathan's haste wasn't a surprise. He had been anxious to put this place in his wake since the day he had set foot there. Only at her insistence had he lingered. But now, he had fulfilled all pledges. He had proven that he was a man-of-his-word, but not one of infinite forbearance.

Nathan gave the laces a finishing tug. "All squared?"

She shifted in discomfort and whispered hoarsely "I have to go to the privy."

Nathan rolled his eyes, his patience more ruffled than rubbed raw. "Very well, then. Avast, there. Belay n' stand-by" he called to two hands in the verge of dismantling the closet.

"Err... umm... beg pardon," Cate murmured as she wedged between the pair. "I'll only be a moment."

It wasn't as if contemplation was going to be called for.

Still, the act was a bit difficult with onlookers, on-listeners so near she had to keep her elbows in. Straightening, she shook out her skirts, assuring that all was where it should before stepping out. "I'll empty the —"

"Like hell!" Nathan barked. And then, in an only slightly more temperate tone "All squared away, now?" He was already steering her toward the water's edge. "Going to miss the tide, at this rate. Should have roused you..."

Cate allowed the rest of his soliloquy to roll past.

"What about that?" she asked, looking back at the bed. With everything else gone, it looked so very out-of-place and forlorn.

Nathan sniffed, disinterested. "It'll go back the same way it came. C'mon, spread some canvas."

At the shoreline, he picked her up and splashed out to a boat. Setting her lightly on the thwart, he vaulted in over the gun'l and alighted next to her. "Give weigh" and they were off.

Cate looked back and smiled wistfully at their little haven, fading all too quickly from sight. As she turned back, she looked directly into Nathan's remote smile.

He found her hand between them and leaned to whisper "Gone, but not forgotten."

It was a wonder how water which was almost body temperature, could produce a chilling breeze. Wedged between Pattison, the coxun and Nathan, it still found her and she shivered. "I'm cold."

Nathan reached around and chafed her hands.

With each stroke of the oar, the clutches of land slipped away; the smell of earth and greenery gave way to saltwater and kelp. The bay's motion became incrementally stronger, the boat rising and falling with the long, flat swell. As they rounded the point, the sun broke free of the cloud-enshrouded horizon and, in that instant, it went from dawn to daylight.

Across the bay they went, the settlement nestled to one side. At that hour, the only signs of life were the campfires' smoke curling up through the trees and a cluster of islanders on the beach, a few farewell handkerchiefs already fluttering. Head resting on his shoulder, Cate watched Nathan to see if he were inclined to return the sentiment. Nothing. If goodbyes were called for, they were apparently complete.

Regret struck, yet again. "I wish —" Cate began, straightening.

A hand on her knee stopped her. "Do not look back, darling. Ahead, always ahead, for that we can control."

"But shouldn't we have at least said something to Bella?"

"To what point and purpose?" Nathan countered dryly. "Tearful, fond wishes and farewells? Perhaps she might knit you a comforter to remember her by?" Now he was being really sarcastic.

He looked to those in the boat for confirmation and, without exception, found it.

"Nay, darling, save your breath and your worries. Besides," Nathan added, with a smirk. "I bid Pryce to deliver our regrets and adieus. He'll have her ear —"

"And a good many other things," chuckled bow-oar, several of his mate's laughing outright.

"I don't wish to rouse her from her sleep," Nathan went on a bit louder. "And, if she's not sleeping, I wish to rouse her even less."

A chorus of fuller throated jeering laughter broke out all around.

Under the cold eye of pragmatism, it was a strain for Cate to imagine exactly who would feel slighted?

Her co-workers? Hardly.

Lygia and the others, even less.

Dorrie? The child hardly knew her face.

Bella? All penitence was swiped away by the relief of being out from under that controlling thumb.

"Do you mean to forget everyone there?" she asked.

A flick of a brow showed her meaning wasn't lost on Nathan. His mouth moved, but not as a smile. "In the spirit o' maintaining me sanity, yes."

Cate leaned to whisper "I'm not sorry for coming here."

"I am," came back, flat and final.

A cant of his head directed her attention ahead to the *Morganse,* boats and all manner of craft clustered at her sides. Their boat joined the general flow of others toward her. Sailing wasn't quiet business; even less so was the making ready. The bay's flat surface worked like a speaking trumpet, augmenting the bumps, thumps, hails, shouts and oaths.

Whatever lingering regrets Cate harbored were brushed aside by the soaring spirits of a long-awaited return. She moved her fingers, mentally trying to count back, trying to figure out just how long had it been since she had been—in every sense of the word— home? So much was so confused or just entirely lost: before recovering on that island, whose name escaped her at the moment; before Nathan sent her off with Thomas; before the rendezvous with Creswicke; before their resurrection. Lord, a lifetime... literally.

Something, a sensation more than a sound broke her thoughts: a rapid tapping, vibrating up from the boat's bottom.: Nathan's boot heel. The nearer they drew to the *Morganse,* the faster it rapped. Shielding her eyes against the sun's reflection, Cate looked at the ship now looming before them with a different eye, visions of past mutinies, and confrontations flashing through her mind. There were shouts and oaths, but just in the natural course of things—one could easily come to believe that cursing was the spawn of sweat. There was no fury, or rancor any indication of impending square-offs. A sideways glance at Nathan found not fear, but something even more perplexing: anxious anticipation, combined incongruously with a fixed smile.

"What are you smiling at?" burst from her before she could stop it. Hopefully, this condition wasn't just an extension of the previous night's "activities."

"It seems an age, a lifetime," Nathan qualified, with a significant lift of his brow. "And now you're about to be back where you belong: aboard and at me side."

Cate appreciated the sincere sentiment, but recognized it for the thin veil meant to cover something else. A survey of the boat's occupants found several faces quickly averted to hide broad, knowing grins. Amid the smells of sweat and wet wood, the essence of conspiracy was sharp in the air.

"Larboard," Nathan directed to Pattison.

A certain amount of calling, cursing and fending off, and their boat finally bumped alongside. With a combination of thrill and dread, Cate looked up to find the rail lined with faces peering down. Nathan—damn his cat-like soul—guided her over the thwarts to the gunwale and then, with an iron-like arm hooked at her bottom, hoisted her up the three feet to the bottommost step and awaiting hands. He then scampered up the side, while one Java-apelike pair of arms after another handed her up with the delicacy of a quail's egg. She was delivered on deck to find Nathan already standing there, barely breathing hard, as if he had been there the while.

Whatever chaos was at the *Morganse's* side, it paled in comparison to the frenetic scramble on her deck. The island might have been poor, but it had been rich in goodwill, which showed in the way of going-away gifts. The smells of tar and varnish were blanketed by those of sun-beaten pigs, poultry and foodstuffs. Cate hitched her skirts to pick her way through the chicken cages, baskets of fish and shellfish, piles of melons—probably the very ones she had helped harvest just a few days since—coconuts and the like. Alas, absence hadn't made her feet any surer.

She drew up short at encountering a large number of men toeing-the-line, all looking like school boys awaiting their master.

Nathan struck a stance in their midst, rocking on his toes like one more of those boys. "We've a surprise."

"We" wasn't just a figurative, a leader presuming to speak for the group. This was mass participation. As if on signal, all work on deck stopped; all heads craned in high anticipation of something. She mightn't have been with child, but they were, in every sense of the word.

There was little doubt as to the direction she was expected to go. The men parted like minions before royalty, Nathan's hand at the small of her back urging her along. Aft they went, not to the Great Cabin, as suspected, but to the companionway, and then below. The gundeck was an extension of the chaos above, rumbling and shouting indicating the condition went deep into the bowels of the ship. Hisses and whistles brought it all to a halt, with faces popping up from the hatches. The essence of scheming was strong enough there to overpower both bilges and close-packed men.

Nathan drew up before Cate, putting his back to her. "Put your hand on me shoulder and close your eyes." He patted the spot in case she mightn't find it.

Excitement was a contagious thing, but it also spawned a good deal of dread, a troupe of iron-winged moths seeming to have taken up residence in Cate's stomach. Her brothers had done this once: lead her blindly into a rollicking prank. The operative word was "once." If this turned out to be anything like—

Just act surprised, she chanted privately. *Whatever it is, just act surprised.*

Her face was beginning to ache from the frozen smile she had assumed at some point.

Aft they went, as best she could tell. Nathan moved slowly, whether to allow for the unsteadiness which came with one's eyes being closed or just to extend the suspense being anyone's guess. Like whiskers on a cat, her senses pitched ahead but only encountered the increasing sharp odors of varnish and fresh-cut wood. The scuffle of feet and nervous coughs marked a good many following close behind.

Nathan stopped. "Keep them closed."

By the shoulders he turned her and then lined her up, tweaking a bit first one way, and then another. More coughs and a collective intake of breath.

"Now!"

She opened her eyes to him standing in the middle of a room, his spread arms nearly spanning it. "*Oila!* Your own blood room."

One might have called it a closet, except there was no such thing aboard. She vaguely recalled a string of cabins along the companionway near the galley. Someone had been greatly inconvenienced or outright dispossessed in order to create the space.

"Chips and his mates worked themselves into a positive frenzy," Nathan beamed.

Usually the shy, retiring type, Chips pushed in, Hodder close behind. The pair fell off into a rapid-fire of explanations of features, problems encountered, solutions found, answers apparent. So much was lost with two, sometimes three all speaking at once, squeezing past one way or another to demonstrate one thing or another, including how the swinging bed, bowsed up against the beams overhead, might be dropped. An examining table took up one side, a worktable on the other, her blood box already sitting there like a hallowed object.

At length, Cate was pried from the corner to which she had retreated. The hand affixed to her gaping mouth was pulled down and wrapped around a cord.

"Just cast off these beckets n' cringles, n' haul on this 'ere slab-line," said Hodder.

She did, but to no effect. In a clatter of ivory rings, the bosun plucked it from her and yanked. The canvas rolled up to reveal a wall of drawers, doors, niches and shelves, the whole putting her in mind of an apothecary.

"Petrov near worked himself to a tizzy over these fittings," Nathan said, fingering the placard brackets which adorned many of the shelves and drawers. They, like the rest of the knobs and pulls, were brass polished to a gold-like gleam.

Hodder took the cord to continue his demonstration. "Drop the canvas like a mains'l, n' make it all fast n' secured. Nothin' to be struck down when we clear for action."

"Damned near every hand had a hand in it, if only to sand, varnish or rip lengths." Nathan gestured to the netting bags hanging from pegs, filled with rolls of bandages. "Have a care, it might still be wet here n' there."

"Had a scuttle put in." Nathan pointed to a window-like opening with a tube of canvas thrust through like a funnel. "And a wind sail rigged, so as to provide your precious air."

A shuffling of tightly-packed bodies and a pair of men sidled in bearing another basket. Loaded with simples, the charms and talismans hanging from the handle were indisputable calling cards: Celia.

"Kirkland's kettles are just there," Nathan pointed, the cook's round face shining from among the crowd. "You need only step across for hot water or cooking up your plasters and potions."

Nathan stood back, Chips and Hodder standing like bookends. "Well, are you surprised?"

Cate nodded idiotically.

His smile faltered a bit. "Have you something to say?"

Feeling even more imbecilic, she shook her head. She had inhaled at some point; that lingering breath came out in an explosive burst, only to be drawn in before it was entirely out, a hitch now catching her in the side.

A number of words wrangled to be heard but in no intelligent order. "All this... for me?" Her voice arced, approximating the screech of metal against metal.

Their heads bobbed like spring-loaded dolls.

"You thought of everything," she finally managed.

"We tried," came back in a baritone chorus.

Her eyes filled and then finally overflowed. "Thank you! Thank you!" She put out her arms and lunged, driven by the need to hug someone... anyone! There was a generalized scramble of retreat, leaving Nathan, as the last-man-standing, to take the brunt of her gratitude, nearly tumbling him backward with the impact.

In the ensuing vacancy, Nathan ceremoniously produced a key. "I name you official Keeper-of-the-keys, you and *you* alone. I'd advise using that against any, ahem, inquiring fingers," he added with a significant roll of his eyes toward those hanging just outside the door.

"I'm... I mean, I don't know what... I mean, it's been years, *years* since anyone ever—" Her mouth moved, words suddenly failing once more.

One of Nathan's brows shot up under the edge of his headscarf. "'Years?'" he echoed, his shock and displeasure barely veiled. "'Ever?'"

Cate's joy faltered slightly at having blundered into revealing more of her past than was wise. She braced for the inevitable tirade regarding Brian and his failings. After all, he was neither solely guilty, nor solely responsible, but that defense usually fell on deaf ears.

Instead, Nathan waved it all off. "Aye, well, 'tis a new day. You're now among those who are both willing and able. Although I've some sympathy for those before me. You're precious near with making your wishes known."

"All I ever wanted was you," she sniffed. It was so simple, and yet so very true.

"Aye, but that which is already possessed can't be given again," he said more gently. "I'd look like a lick-penny scrub trying to give the same thing twice."

Cate was literally bouncing by then. "I want to thank everyone, kiss them all."

"I shouldn't suggest that," he mused. He was hesitant to assume she spoke in the figurative. At the moment, she wasn't sure either. The magnitude of all of their thought and effort seemed to demand it.

His gaze unwavering from her face, Nathan reached behind him and jerked the curtain closed. He advanced the step or so, pressing her back against the table, and kissed her.

"You're feeling better," she observed after a long while.

Nathan cocked his head, considering. "I suppose I am," and kissed her again.

"I haven't seen you smile like that, since—" He paused, his own broadening to one so very sly. "Since last night."

"See, I told you: all I need is you, the closer the better," she said and pulled him back.

Their lips nearly touched when Pryce's "Cap'n? D'ye wish to win the anchor, sir?" from the other side of the curtain, and barely an arm's length distant, stopped them.

"Aye, trip, win, fish, thick-n-dry... whatever..." Nathan replied tersely.

Arms firmly about her he hummed consideringly. "The closer the better, eh?" He sighed and stepped back. "Aye, well then, some might claim this next bit flies in the face o' me best interest."

He slid the curtain back to reveal a waiting audience. "M'lady," he insisted at her hesitancy.

"There's more?" Surely, she was misinterpreting somehow or another.

"Oh, aye. It shan't blow your gaff quite as much, but..." Nathan shrugged diffidently.

Reluctantly—she would have loved nothing more than to linger and explore—Cate followed Nathan further aft. The ship suddenly took on the motion of being freed of land and searching for the wind. Past the galley to the aftermost companionway he took her and up, a small parade of men trailing behind. Cate's step slowed as she topped the steps and the Great Cabin opened before her: the table, the chairs, the rugs, Beatrice preening on the back of the captain's chair, the great slanted gallery and the sweeping view it afforded.

"Nothing has changed; it's exactly as you left it." Nathan's announcement was made like a goal accomplished.

He put out his hand. "Come."

The moths fluttering anew, Cate allowed herself to be led to the night cabin. Again, she was carefully aligned and then, with a bit of the dramatic, the curtain pulled aside. The surprise here was less obvious, and she looked about, worried what she would say when she failed to find it. A step further and she was once more immersed in its familiarity, so thorough she could navigate in total darkness without peril. Another step, however, and her foot met wood where it shouldn't have been. The bunk, it was larger, not by much, perhaps six inches or so, but still... Before, they had been obliged to lie like two spoons. Now, two could now almost lie side-by-side.

"We shifted the bulkhead and refitted the knees, and then..." Chips explained from the doorway.

Contrary to Nathan's claim, there had been something different about the Great Cabin and now she knew what: the foyer-like area near the doors was a bit narrower.

"Take a closer look. See," he said, lifting the quilt when she was too slow.

"And sheets?" she cried, touching them. Questions as to where he would have ever found such a thing and how much they must have cost battled to the point that neither was heard.

"And no more tow-stuffed mattress. A couple score o' geese gave their lives, so you might repose like a princess." The combined success of his surprises now had Nathan positively bubbling.

She secretly found his hand between them and worked her fingers through his. "Only if her prince is next to her."

True enough, the blood-room had been for her, but the broader importance was the welfare of his men and his ship. This had "us" emblazoned on it as if in letters as high as her head.

All caution falling aside, she threw her arms around Nathan and hugged him as closely as a full-armed man might, kissing him all over. "Thank you! Thank you! Thank you!"

Either a signal from their captain, their personal constraint, or mere fear of her attentions swiveling on them next, the men ducked out, pulling the curtain to behind them.

"Are you pleased? Truly pleased?" Nathan asked, grinning.

"I don't look it?" It was a bit disappointing to think it. She pressed her hips against his. "How much time to we have, so I might properly —?"

"None," he sighed. "Although, I suspect they fancy I'm in here serving you, as we speak. Not sure if they flatter me or you," he added under his breath.

"Then I must take advantage of opportunities as they are," she said, and kissed him again.

Footsteps passed overhead, hails and calls, Nathan shifted ever so slightly, and he was no longer hers.

"Go," she urged softly.

He cocked his head toward the salon. "Aye, well, timely: I believe I hear the clatter of breakfast being laid along and standing by."

At that same moment, the smell of toasted soft-tack, sausages and — glory, upon glory — Kirkland's coffee met her nose. Her stomach growling brought a smile from Nathan.

He led her to the door and stopped to lightly peck her on the cheek. "I'll come to you when I might."

He turned to take his leave, but she caught him by the arm and pulled him back.

"Thank you. Sincerely and honestly, from the very bottom —"

A kiss cut her off and then he left. His path veered slightly to the table where he swirled a finger in the honey jar, and then stepped out over the combing, licking like a fastidious cat.

Moving into the salon, Cate stood trying to absorb this grand reception. All of it —

Nathan's planning, efforts, forethought — all pointed to one thing: her being there, aboard, at his side, as he had said a number of times, but had been afraid to believe. And now, there was proof, no imaginings, or filling in the blanks, no straining to connect Point A to Point B through inferences and inflections. No, there had been no declaration of love, but it came close, perhaps as close as Nathan might ever venture.

Spreading her arms, she whirled, a girlish giggle bubbling into joyous laughter. "I heard that," said a graveled voice down through the skylight.

END OF PART TWO

28: DISASTER'S SWIFT HAND

NATHAN STOOD ON THE QUARTERDECK, conning his ship and looking aft.

The greatest sight in the world was that cursed island at his stern, God rot that pack of meddling harridans.

A voice drifted up, and he quickly amended that to "second-most," he thought, looking down through the skylight at Cate at-table, Kirkland feeding her like a caged goose.

And lo, that she might become as plump as one!

To call her a "woman of large appetites" wasn't just a figure of speech.

Some more than others, he thought, tugging at his waistband, bearing a smile that wasn't to be curbed.

It was, without question, his greatest joy: seeing her protected, well-fed, and cared for, all the things she had gone without for too long, far, far, far too long.

He grasped a stay and bent his head. *Just help me keep her.*

Life aboard was now nearer to normal, although perhaps a bit altered. Granted, nothing was ever exactly as it was, but there was a pervasive sense of the world settling back on an even keel. Good ship, good crew, good woman: it was Fiddler's Green!

He would have loved nothing more than to clap on all plain sail and bear away. But this Gordian knot of shoals, islands and channels demanded patience. They say it was a virtue, but he was fresh-out. The chant from the lead-line was like the tick of a case-clock, present, of mild interest, but only half-heard. He knew these waters like the back of his hand, but there was always the chance of storm or current changing the bottom. Hands were at the braces, tacks and sheets until they were out of this foundering mass of foul and even fouler realms and in clear waters.

Pryce was looking a bit apoplectic; being roused out of a warm bed and warm arms didn't settle well.

Nathan shifted, twitching his shoulders inside his shirt. Truth be told, he was suffering a bit of that himself.

There was no missing the hard looks from a good number of the people, too, irritated with the world in general for being jerked from commodious affections and good commons. Like a fish returning to the water, a few days of routine and being surrounded by their mates, and they would be back to their old, salt-to-the-bones selves.

Nathan moved to the hances and looked down. Amidships was still a-hoo, Hodder and his mates looking thoroughly harassed at the sanctity of their precious decks being so violated. Nathan considered to do the civil, and go see what a captain's presence might provide. It was often amazing the conundrums which suddenly solved themselves with one's superior standing at their elbow.

Down to the waist and forward he went. Red hell and death, it was no closer to being squared-away than when he boarded. In thanks for the *Morganse's* aid, the island had bestowed its bounty upon her. There was, however, such a thing as being too generous by half. It was like Market Day; the only thing missing were the hawkers selling oranges on a stick. Much of the green-stuffs had been cleared, but there was still the not-so-small matter of on-the-hoof.

"What the bloody—?" Nathan was cut short by a pluck at his sleeve. He turned to find a goose eyeing him, apparently considering that particular stretch of deck its private domain. A hiss was the only warning before the head snaked out. "Who's in charge here?"

Broadstreet stepped forward, thoroughly frazzled and not scrupling to show it. "Master-o'-the-hold represents—"

"Hang the master-o'-the-hold! Shall I have your hammock sent down?" Nathan directed down the hatch to the innermost depths and the environs of that very person. He waited for a response, but in vain.

No response from there brought him back around on Broadstreet. "Why hasn't Jemmy Ducks stowed these beasts?"

Broadstreet and his mate, Harrier, exchanged alarmed looks. "Ain't got no Jemmy Ducks; ain't needed one in—"

"Mr. Pryce!" The man could have been inspecting the keel and he would have heard his captain's shout.

Only abaft, however, Pryce looked up.

"A Jemmy Ducks, if you please... *now*! Have him stow these pigs whilst he's at it," Nathan directed to Broadstreet as he headed aft.

"Pigs isn't poultry. Pigs is livestock." Broadstreet seemed

astonished at being obliged to point that out, especially to a captain.

God's blood and wound! Nathan spun back on his heel. "Then fetch Butcher."

"Ain't got no—"

"Butcher, yes, I know," Nathan sighed, suddenly weary. "Well, as Captain, I declare pigs is poultry now and shall be stowed as such."

"Where, sir?" Broadstreet's barely tempered demand indicated that they had just arrived to the crux of his crisis.

Nathan dodged another anserine attempt. "Pen, coop, manger: whatever the hell you care to—"

"But, ain't got none," put in Harrier. "At least, ain't used it as such fer an age."

"What's in there now?" Nathan closed one eye, thinking. It was a bit of an embarrassment for a captain to not know, but damned if he could recall the last time he'd ventured to that part of the forepeak.

"Stores, swag, rum, shot..."

A curt swipe cut Harrier short. Fair enough. Nothing to be gained in berating the man for that. Livestock was for the long haul; in the West Indies, with food so ready to hand, they didn't ship beasts, because they were more trouble than they were worth.

More smell, too, Nathan thought, nose twitching.

Had it been a choice, he would have never shipped the meddlesome creatures now, but it had seemed the height of rudeness to refuse the offerings. A part of him considered this might be Bella's notion of a jest.

Wouldn't put it past the scheming termagant, he thought, watching the goose seize Diogo by the ear.

Still, the pragmatist in him suggested one never knew what might come in handy.

The *Morganse* was gaining weigh, the open sea wasn't far off. Hooves weren't made for decks; they would all be sliding about like loose guns, hazards to both themselves and everyone on deck.

"Well, rig something, *now*, or we'll all be knee-deep in pig shite. Swabbers!" Nathan shouted, turning away. "Gonna be worse when they start getting seasick, staggering about," he muttered half to himself.

On his way aft, Nathan encountered Hodder near the main-bitts, looking thoroughly wretched. Nathan clapped him companionably on the shoulder. "Stand easy, man. Don't blow a boltrope. Order is but a couple glasses away," he added, raising his voice to be heard over the squeal of a pig scampering past, Towers in hot pursuit.

The bosun looked neither appeased, nor heartened.

Nathan paused and lifted his face to windward. The air was freshening, open waters now so very near. He could smell it; his ship sensed it. The helm would be in need of a course, and soon. He started for the cabin and a refresher look at the charts when "On deck there! Sail ho!" came from the foretop.

"Where away?"

"Larboard, about three points. Two ships," the lookout amended.

Nathan growled an acknowledgment. His hope had been at least a few of those arse – sniffers would have hauled their wind, but apparently not. T'wasn't a grand surprise. Creswicke's coin attracted these scavengers like gulls to a carcass, he being said carcass.

To the quarterdeck for a better look he went. The move wasn't necessary: the pair of vessels would have been hull-up even from the waist. It was as represented: two, rounding the point forming one side of the passage. Not wishing to venture into this dog's breakfast of channels, reefs and islands, they had opted to just cruise the safer waters and wait, lurking like a half-starved cur at the butcher's doorway. Well over a mile n' more distant, they were too far to make out their finer details. First impressions weren't very impressive. Similar in size and rig, they were a bit small for privateers, which made them seem overly – ambitious and a bit of an insult that they fancied they might prevail. The question was how they knew to hang about that particular spot: random chance meeting or a very informed one?

He was about to inquire of the lookout, when from the maintop came "On deck, there! Sail, sail on the starboard quarter."

Nathan spun around. Indeed, rounding an island, laid another vessel, closer and much more imposing.

Pryce appeared next to him, keen as a cat. "What's to do?"

"Well, three against one does give one pause," Nathan began slowly, eyes dancing from larboard to starboard and back. Were they sailing in consort? Gut instincts said "No." No signals flying, no apparent coordination of movement: the whole thing felt more like happenstance than grand plan. Still, it was a wretched damned coincidence.

"Those two we already have the legs of," Nathan announced, dismissing the leeward pair out-of-hand. He swiveled round to windward. "That crafty, Dutch butter buss, however, has the wind."

"Dunno 'er; never laid eyes on 'er afore," Pryce said, squinting.

A look to the afterguard, and then the waist showed all were of the same opinion.

The intrigue was those gunports, Nathan thought, looking through a glass.

"She's using your old trick of painted clothes down 'er sides..." Pryce said.

"The question is," Nathan said, lowering the glass. "Are those to hide some very big teeth or toothless gums?"

They fell into an investigatory silence. With her bright checks and stripe-work, the sloop was a flashy slut; doubtless, her captain new to this line o' work and looking to make an impression. He caught the gleam of gold at her bow, or was that the brass bowchasers, polished to the point of rivaling the sun? A spit-and-polish privateer was a rare bird, usually because crews wouldn't suffer it. Only free-flowing rum or rollicking success in the way of prizes would entice them to gut it out, and no vessel could sail like that, if she were manned by a bunch of drunkards.

"She's riding high, overall," Nathan observed. "The question is whether she's running out of stores, or those are only pop-guns behind those cloths?"

"She's a-ridin' heavy at the bow, tho'. Bowchasers, to be sure."

"Those decks are elbow-to-arsehole with men." Nathan slapped the glass shut. "Light in the water, heavy at the bow and manned to the teeth: I'd bet me grannie's knickers she's no merchant."

He glanced to sky and water, and admitted grudgingly "She knows her business: she has the gauge, and has us sailing at her advantage. It's not our worst," he equivocated.

At the same time, a score of other issues were already running through his mind. Aye, the *Morganse* was certain to out-weigh the sloop in metal, broadside-to-broadside, but why unnecessarily beat oneself up? Cate's voice drifted up through the skylight. A battering was to be avoided, if for no other reason than her. She was better, but still not entirely well.

"We've naught choice but to bide until we gain a little more searoom." Nathan shot a reproachful glare to leeward, and the land and reefs looming there. "Clap on all she'll bear and let's see what that skulking cove is made of."

"Mr. Hodder, t'gallantmasts, if you please, and with all

haste. C'mon, bear a hand, bear a hand, I say!" It was regrettable that they were still stowed on the booms, swayed down during that damnable blow as they were coming in, and no reason to sway them up since. "Might as well rig preventer stays whilst you're up there. They might prove convenient so very soon," he added, cutting an eye toward the sloop.

The bosun's eyes rounded at the deck's disorder complicating an already complicated task. Better now, however, than when the ship is really pitching and yawing.

Nathan headed to the maindeck, meaning to shake things up. As he passed the cabin, however, Cate came out, looking as fresh and sprightly as a spring day.

"A ship...?" she asked.

"Sloop, one of His High-Lordliness's, no doubt, probably, with Judas-colored hair, too, no offense." Nathan was unsure of what even made him add the last bit.

"None taken," she said, smiling faintly. After all, hers was not that carrot-bright, Iscariot color.

She rose on her toes to look over the rail and aft. "Are we... worried?"

"Not in the least, not until she shows to have more than she's shown thus far. But still, an over-confident pirate is a dead pirate. You might need to — " Safety was a prime concern, which meant below, the hold the best place for her.

Cate paled and, at the same time, stiffened, a pose he recognized all too readily. "Not yet, not now, please?"

"I'll not have you in the midst of — "

"And I won't, I promise." Pure sincerity there; nothing hollow, nothing false, nothing looking to play the fool. "The minute it gets dangerous, I'll go below, to the hold, if you wish." The last came in dread-laden bursts.

Nathan made to press his point, but then chose to hang-fire. Nothing to be gained in going at loggerheads with her, not when she was still bouncing over her surprises. He didn't wish to douse her powder now.

"I'd prefer if you might do that a few moments *before* it gets dangerous," he said.

Cate readily nodded, a bit too readily by his judgment.

"Very well," he sighed, finding little joy in the small victory.

He thought for a moment she was going to hug him. She checked the impulse and feigned fiddling with her hair, instead.

"Thank you." Her sincerity made him ashamed of his skepticism, touching him all the way to his soles.

"I'll just go — " she began moving forward, presumably heading for her seat on the f'c'stle.

"I wouldn't go that way, unless you are nostalgic for barnyards." There would be no place for her anyway, not if this chase develops into anything. Whatever the case, the nearer to him the better.

"What on earth—?" The rest of her inquiry was lost in the squealing protests of a pig being toted past.

Nathan rolled his eyes skyward, hoping Divine intervention might lurk somewhere. "Don't ask. C'mon, aft w' me. We'll make a place."

∾ஐஒஐ∾

Cate was ensconced on the signal locker, a dodger rigged overhead whilst she chatted with the afterguard.

Nathan divided his attention between the swaying up, the sloop and her.

God, it felt good to hear her laugh! Just then wasn't her customary, the one he had come to love—rich and throaty, full of honesty, with none of that hen-like tittering—the one which always made him feel one-and-twenty again. It wasn't that, but it was near enough to make him smile.

Lo, that she might remain so! Lo, that the last of her misery was behind her. There was a limit as to how much any one person might bear. He had no notion as to her amounts, but surely it had been reached. Justice and just common decency demanded it be so.

The surprises had her still smiling. Her thrill had been reward enough. But, of course, one couldn't help but wonder if other rewards in other... ahem, means might be in the offing. Her gratitude for the night before had him still a bit wobbly on his pins. Today had been even grander and, hence—one might be inclined to assume—rendering her all the more grateful?

Every now and again, as he paced the deck, a dance of those eyes were spared for him. Ohhh, yes, she had something in store for him! He would need to catch a caulk sometime or another, or he'd never bear up. Alas, catching a bit o' shut-eye wasn't bloody likely with this jumper-up jack-pudding sniffing about their stern. It would be necessary to brush this noisome bit which had floated up like one of the pig turds being sluiced through the scuppers off the bottom of his boot.

With one ear toward Cate, Nathan kept both eyes on the sloop. The other two sluggards made to pursue, but the feeble attempt doomed them before they started. So far, they were running just out of gun range, the sloop hanging off that fraction necessary to allow her to yaw and rake the *Morganse's* stern. When the time came, the move could present that very opportunity. It would have to be carefully timed, with all hands looking smart and heaving hearty.

He had to admire the sloop. She had spirit, a prime crew, and a captain who knew both. No, the *Morganse* hadn't met her match, not by a long shot. The missing t'gallantmasts were the equalizers. Once they were swayed up and rigged, they could fall off a mite, bring the wind just a point or two more on her stern, and that cod buss would see nothing but her wake.

Right now, it was a breakneck chase at a screaming six knots, according to the log line, he thought wryly, at a slightly faster clip than a fast walk, a bit more when one caught a gust, an increasing occurrence with the wind growing more capricious. Not a tacking duel, but a flat out race, more a test of nerve than speed. Still, a barrage at six knots was just as lethal as one at twelve. Time, just a little of that all-precious, ever-moving, perpetual – flowing time. Sometimes, it seemed as plentiful as the boundless sea; other times it was a precious dear commodity. Which would it be today?

Nathan watched the sloop watching them, catching the flare of the sun on glass more than once. All the commotion on the *Morganse* was providing a certain amount of entertainment, hopefully a bit of perplexing thrown in.

The livestock would still have nothing to do with being sent below, nor have any truck with means of getting them there. Someone must have thought size would prevail— either that, or the promise of winning a bet—for Maori and Chin were now chasing the beasts. Size might have been on the two-footed's side, but cleverness was clearly on the four-footed's. Nathan was beginning to appreciate the sport of pig-wrestling—He recalled doing a bit of it himself as a lad, when he was younger, stronger and far more nimble—but this, however, was on the verge of turning into a game, wagering not far in the offing. He needed to clap a stopper on this, the sooner, the better.

To the backdrop of Squidge working on his necklace like a rosary, recounting to Cate the circumstances of each souvenir finger on his necklace, the cry of "Sway aloft! Launch ho!" came down from the mainmast. The fid was in; the yards next and then bend the sail. The foret'gallant was laid along, the bosun's mates and topsmen all standing by to hoist it up through the lubber's hole. Two on the capstan bars near stumbled over a pig running through their legs.

Another fracas—animal, not human, and neither pig nor fowl—came from somewhere forward. The startled howls and curses had Nathan down the steps.

"Hold fast! Avast!" to the capstan. "Hold fast and stand by" was shouted up to the foremast. It was the worst possible time, the mast dangling, swaying like a twenty-foot-long clock pendulum. Break the thing and, aye, they could rig another, but that brought them back to that ol' foil: time.

Amid animal bleats and bellows, Harrier and Woods rushed past, Hermione slung between them, eyes rolling, tongue hanging out in goatish fury.

"What the — ?" Nathan began.

"She's discovered the other goat and she's in a passion," Harrier huffed as they passed. "She tried to ram it overboard — "

"And damned near took Diogo here with 'er," Woods added.

"I think I cracked a rib," the victim groaned, holding his side as he staggered behind. "God's my life!" Nathan intoned to the sky. Further forward, laid a dead goose, its neck wrung.

Roast goose tonight... And fresh feathers for Cate's pillow! he thought, stepping over.

"Why are these pigs still loose? Clap a line on the damned things and — "

"Trying, sir," Broadstreet said, barely tempering his frustration. He made a helpless gesture toward Towers running past, marline in hand.

"Then fling a net over one, the lot... hell, fling their slops down the companionway. Whatever the hell it takes, just get this — "

Any further expostulations were cut off at feeling what he had dreaded most: the breeze dying. The sails sagged, the ship's song to drop a quarter note.

"Clap onto those tacks. Look alive, haul with a will, you dough-faced sluggards!"

He was mounting the quarterdeck when "On deck there, she's coming up" came from the tops.

A flaw in the already imperfect wind made it die for the *Morganse* and freshen for the sloop. A moment later, the freshening reached the *Morganse*, the boluns tightening, but the sloop had the momentum. It was exactly the moment the skulking sloop had been waiting for. Nathan saw the puff of smoke at her bow a fraction before the retort. The words "Get below" were forming in his mouth when he heard the ball whiz overhead, and then the wooden crack a fraction before the hail "Stand from under!" sounded from the maintop.

Nathan knew what was happening — instinctively ducked his head — but there was still a massive gap between will and reality. No amount of urgency, nor intent could have stopped the mizzentop and all its assemblage from falling, just as it couldn't get him across the deck to Cate in time. A desperate shout and a stride toward her was all reality allowed. In that odd suspension of time, he watched Squidge leap and drive Cate to the deck, flinging himself over her as the avalanche of canvas, wood and cordage came down on top of them. The signal locker upon which she had sat was smashed, its flags and banners scattering and fluttering in the wind.

Nathan almost had his hand on the wreckage when the ropes tightened, and the whole mass jerked to leeward. Some part of the sail was draped in the water, threatening to drag Cate and Squidge over the side.

Not now! He couldn't lose her, not like this!

A few danced out of the way as the mass of sails and rigging shot past. Most, however, ignoring the danger of being caught up and dragged to their deaths, strove to stop it. The wreckage came up hard up against the rail and hung, the force binding the ropes down tighter and tighter, snapping and crushing everything, everyone inside. A agonized cry came out of the mess, deep-throated, but male.

The *chunk!* of an ax, and then another, once... twice, the *twang!* of taut, wrist-thick hemp parting, and the dangling wreckage was cut away. Now free of the drag, the *Morganse* shot forward. Knife in hand, Nathan kicked aside a broken gaff and dove into the tangle. A kind of blind panic—unseen for a decade, nay, two!—seized him.

What if she'd been speared? What if she'd already been swept overboard?

His heart hung like a great wad in his throat, choking the life out of him—just like those sheets could be might choking the breath from those inside the wreckage. The rescuers slit, slashed and tore, their desperation often putting them at cross-purposes. He called her name, cursing whoever the hell was making that hoarse croaking sound that might drown out her answer, until he realized it came from him.

A shout from above and Nathan flung himself over the heap as more blocks and rigging came crashing down; another cry of someone being struck.

"Lay aloft and get that goddamnned, fucking thing secured!" he bellowed.

Damnation, there hadn't been time to rig splinter-netting or puddening chains! Add one more regret to the growing list of ever having ventured to that cursed island!

"Mind the helm!" Any waver there, and the sloop could either rake or broadside them.

More frantic searching and Nathan came upon a foot, small

and slender. Cate — or at least a part of her — was still onboard. The foot writhed and jerked at his touch; whether alive or a death jerk, he couldn't tell. Further groping found an ankle, and then a leg, but thick and hairy.

Nathan burrowed in like a frantic mole, hacking and slashing, at the same time cautioning himself to have a care, lest he gut Cate in the process of saving her.

"Here! Here! Got 'er!" Ogden called from the opposite side.

Nathan clambered over just as Odgen pulled Cate out. Swathed in canvas, face ashen, she looked prepped for burial, two round-shot already at her feet. Grabbing her up, he carried her to a clear stretch of deck and laid her out. Calling, he shook her so hard her limbs flopped like a ragdoll. Finally, her eyes opened, not the clear jade, but dull and fogged with confusion. She jerked, flailed, and then sucked in air, like she was half - drowned. With a joyous sob, he swept her up and clutched her to him.

Tumbled, wind knocked out of her, scraped and a bit addled, she was whole, gloriously and blessedly whole!

"Cap'n!?" shouted the helmsman.

A glance upward to check wind and damage, confirming what Nathan already knew. "Hard over. Run with it! Mr. Hodder!"

He could have saved his wind; Hodder and his mates were laying aloft, hard at it.

They weren't in dire straits. The mizzen tops'l was intact; his ship could sail by-the - wind and at her advantage.

Sail sweet, darling, whilst I see to her.

The helm spun, the yards swung. Regrettably, the wreckage over the side had slowed the *Morganse*, only a bit, but enough for her foe to sweep nearer, yet again. The sloop was no fool; she had seen her shot fly home, seen the damage it wrought and closed in in anticipation of inflicting the mortal blow. The shot whizzed overhead; Nathan bent to shield Cate, buttocks clenched. Hoots, jeers and arse-slapping marked the thing flew past, harmless.

Cate: she needed to be attended, somewhere relatively safe, safer than this damned deck. Picking her up, Nathan trundled down to the crowded waist with no real notion as to a destiny. A step toward his cabin and a change of mind made him to veer. Raking their stern was prime in that jackeen's mind and, hence, the cabin was the last place Cate should be.

Below, then...

And so down Nathan went. The hold: it was the safest, but...

He looked down at the quivering wreck in his arms. First,

verify she was well. Then, he'd face her acrimony at being sent there. Lord, how she despised it!

The blood-room, then.

And so aft he went, bellowing "Make a lane! Make a lane, there, I say!" as he pushed through the milling men.

Nathan drove his shoulder against the door only to find it locked. Damnation! And Cate had the key. Growling, he hit the door again, but to no avail. Shifting Cate, he stood back and kicked the thing open with a crash. Inside, he carefully laid her out on the table. Her clothing—ripped from nape to knees—guided him to where she would most likely be hurt, and so he laid her half on her side, half on her stomach.

He checked her over, heart in his throat at discovering some mortal wound. A flash of pale glimpsed on deck had led him to fear the worst but found that she wasn't skinned to the bone. In truth, by some fluke or miracle, aside from a few scuffs and scrapes about her ribs, the damage was limited to two abrasions: the back of her arm and high on her thigh just below her rump. Both approximately the size of his palm, they were pulpish and raw, but with surprisingly little bleeding. Just a pinkish seep.

Eyes clamped shut, Cate was in obvious pain. He had never thought her a polyglot, but she displayed a remarkable array of fluencies—Strike him blind, if some of it didn't sound Dutch—and familiarity with an impressive array of saints and other deities. A bit of latitude, however, was called for when it came to their attributes and habits.

"Careful, darling, you'll make me blush."

Another stream of profanity informed him of her opinion of that. "It hurts. It hurts. It feels like I'm being stabbed in a thousand places."

"More like a couple score," he said, looking closer. "In the way of things, darling, you are being stabbed: by splinters."

He pulled one sticking out of her arm like a porcupine quill and held it up in example.

Cate went slightly cross-eyed to view it. "Don't sound so bloody pleased. Just get them out."

"I'm trying. I'm trying!" he said, plucking two more. "Back yer jib a mite."

A flow of further curses expressed her observations on that, as well.

Splinters were miserable things; he would have preferred being shot or flogged. Even the thread-fine ones could feel like a dagger. None were the skewer-a-pig-size he had dreaded, but varied from the barely visible to nearly the thickness of a lead. Fiddling with a few more, it very soon became obvious that fingers alone wasn't going to answer. The next short while was going to entail a lot of misery for everyone in the room.

Spirits, whatever the hell was to hand, for both of them, and now!

The locker in which the medicinal spirits — a flask of brandy — had been hidden from snooping hands was just there. A bash with the butt of his pistol broke the lock. He thrust the flask at Cate with an encouraging nod. Drinking whilst half-lying on one's side wasn't an easy feat, especially when the mere act of breathing caused agony. She took one drink, and then a second, and then a third, at his insistence.

"What happened?" Cate gasped in between.

Nathan glanced up from his examinations to see if this confusion was accompanied by eyes rolling in her head like two round-shot loosed on a deck.

"That blackguardly hulk caught a lucky breeze." Ill hand of the Fates in that one. "Lobbed a lucky shot." Another insufferable stroke of luck. "Bounced off and hit—"

Cate bent to clutch her head between her hands. "I feel like I'm still tumbling."

"Breathe deep, darling. Give it a bit."

She did, or rather tried. "It happened so fast," came in broken bursts.

"Always does," Nathan said in grim triumph. Alas, if he could make her understand how one could be to speaking a man one moment, and he'd be gone the next: sheared in half, blown apart, slashed, speared or just swept away.

"I thought I was dead—" she wheezed.

"So did I."

He'd seen men cut in half by such things, crushed or disjointed like a roasted squab. How grand it would be if Providence's voice-of-warning was a bit louder. Truth be told, however, the warning voice had been screaming loud enough to be heard in a tops'l gale. He had ignored it, openly, willingly... foolishly. And now, he was mopping up Cate's blood.

"You said you'd go below," he said severely.

"When it got dangerous," she countered testily.

"What the bloody hell do you call what just happened?" Every fiber of his being wanted to throw her down and give her a lashing.

"I didn't have time to—"

"Exactly!" He'd seen men skewered like a roast on a spit, slab-like things protruding from arms and chests... Not her, not now, but it could have been.

Damn! Dammit to bloody hell.

"Just get them out," she insisted, squirming.

"I'm waiting for the brandy to—"

"The hell with the brandy! Just get them out." The last was squeezed out between gasps and clenched teeth. "You'll need tweezers—"

"I know what's to do," he snapped.

And that, indeed, was the problem: he knew all too well what was to do. He knew with crystal clarity what it was to lie there, while some cod-handed cove dug splinters from one's flesh, burrowing like a mole for a grub.

Loathe to move, a slide of Cate's eyes directed him to her blood box. "There should be a pair in there."

Nathan held up a pair from a drawer. "Petrov fashioned some."

Her face lit in admiration of the tool's craftsmanship. Somewhere or another in the Russian's past, he had been a silversmith and, on occasion, it showed. These weren't unlike the hands they were designed for, Nathan thought, running his thumb over the ornate scrolling, a pattern so very similar to Cate's wedding ring: delicately graceful, and yet strong and so very adept.

Blocking her view with his body, Nathan also took out a set of tiny, fine-edged lancets and laid them out, dropping a cloth over them.

Odgen and Rowett burst in, a groaning Squidge slung between them. Nathan dove to put himself between them and Cate.

"Beggin' pardon, sir, but—" they said in unison, drawing up short.

"Out!"

"But, Cap'n, we meant to—" Odgen began.

"Mr. Pryce represented Mr. Cate's blood-room—" Rowett cut in.

"The blood-room is occupied. *Ocupado!* Out!" The first command came with a rigid point, the second with a brandished fist.

In a confused grumbled, the pair shuffled out, taking the groaning Squidge with them.

"You shouldn't have been so gruff," Cate scolded once they were alone. "They only meant to—"

"Do you really wish them in here?" A meaningful cut of his eyes directed her attention to her exposure from shoulder down.

"Oh." She groped for the tattered edges of her clothing and sought to pull them to some sort of decency. The pain which came with that movement stopped her short.

"Lie still."

Cate rolled an eye up in mocking thanks for that penetrating insight. Still, for once in her life, she complied. She lay while being plucked at, giving monosyllabic responses or inflective grunts in response to any inquires.

"What happened to Squidge?" she finally asked.

"Broken leg, I think. A couple busted ribs, too, by the sound of it," Nathan added, cocking his head in the direction of the curses and moans.

"But how—?"

"He dove to—" Nathan stopped, thinking better of how to put it lest she take the entire blame. "He took a tumble—"

"Saving me," Cate said faintly. In spite of his best intentions, guilt found a home.

Regret closed her eyes, but it was determination that opened them. "I should go help," she announced, struggling to rise.

"You should be right here," Nathan countered, pushing her back down.

"But, Squidge needs—So many might need—"

A pained shriek and oaths, and Cate sank back down. If any further confirmation as to how badly she was hurting was required, there it was: the woman would rise from her death bed to attend another in need, and yet she just gave up.

"He has his mates," Nathan said, raising his voice over a pained howl from outside. There was no mistaking the sound of a man having his leg set. "Believe me, I'd trade places in a heartbeat," he muttered, with a rueful roll of his eyes. The misery out there was nearly over; the misery in here was still in its infancy.

A rap on the door frame and Ben poked his head in. Nathan whirled, shielding Cate, yet again.

"Mr. Hodder begs to report..." The part of Nathan's mind reserved for his ship now engaged: listening, inquiring, acknowledging, encouraging...

"Very well," Nathan finally said. In truth, it was the benefit of having such a capable crew: the only thing they really required from their captain was his approval. "What of that lurking blood-monger?"

Ben grinned. "She carried away a jib and looks to have sprung her jibbom."

Nathan nodded, smiling a bit. T'was fair good news, but it didn't mean they were in the clear, yet. The bastard was too much the terrier to be discouraged by that none-so-small inconvenience.

"Bear a hand there and light along some more lights. It's as dark as inside Lucifer's hat in here." An abrupt wave sent Ben off. "And brandy, two bottles! We're going to need a lot of it," Nathan added under his breath.

His eye settled on Cate and the flask, idle at her elbow. "Drink."

"I am, or rather, have. It's empty." She shook it as proof.

With a fair amount of huffing and grunting, Cate found a reasonably comfortable position, head pillowed on her forearm. She watched with a wry smirk as Nathan searched the room for necessities. "Odd that *you* should be the first one to use all this."

Nathan cocked an eye at her; he suspected an irony in there somewhere, but damned if he could find it. A part of him considered if he hadn't rigged the place, then perhaps none of this would have happened. It was an ill, ill omen.

The splinters at the back of her arm were removed with relative ease. Shifting the light, he moved down to her hip.

"Enjoying the view back there?" came in harsh rasps between clenched teeth.

He paused, taking a moment to realize his position, and then grinned. "Actually, I am."

A part of his mind reserved for such things was in its glory just then. And a spectacular view it was: the mound of her bottom, the slope of her waist, and glorious length of thigh. His hand twitched at recalling—not twenty-four hours since—the warmth of that skin, holding that firm, lively rump as she—

He coughed. "After all, I am a man. If I'm not looking, then I'm dead."

Ben reappeared, lamps in hand. His head pointedly turned away from Cate, he set them about.

"Get a winds'l rigged," Nathan said as the lad made to leave.

Ben stopped and stared as if his commander had suddenly gone blind. "There is one, sir—" he said, pointing.

"Then rig another!" His temples were pounding like he was the one who had been hit in the head.

In short order, Nathan discovered the folly of more lights was that the small space instantly achieved the approximate temperature of the galley's ovens.

"Where the bloody hell is that bottle—?"

A shuffle of feet at the door made Nathan spin, shielding Cate yet again. He relaxed a fraction at seeing it was Kirkland, the bottle in question in hand.

"Only one?"

"Another is making, sir," came back evenly.

Nathan snatched the bottle, receiving a hard, warning look from Kirkland as he took a drink.

"Need to steady me hand" elicited a dubious sniff. Nathan

glared. God's blood and wounds, the mumping lout actually thought he would get so drunk as to do her harm! A brusque wave sent the meddling scut on his way.

Nathan thrust the bottle at Cate. "Drink."

"I did."

"Not enough. Drink, again."

"I—" Her mouth opened to argue. It was a day of firsts, however, for now, for the first time in her life yet again, she realized his wisdom, briefly contemplated what was about to transpire, and did as he asked.

"One for you?" Cate offered the bottle after several swallows. "You look like you need it."

He shook the tweezers in her face. "Do you have any idea what I'm going to have to—?"

Her steady gaze up stopped him. Of course, she did. He was preaching to the ever - loving choir. In her time aboard, she'd dug more splinters than Mother Clarey had chickens. She knew exactly what was to come—

Well, not entirely, he qualified, regarding the collection. She couldn't know, for she couldn't see the extent. Perhaps there was bliss in ignorance. The easy ones had been removed; any left now were going to require a good deal of excavating.

He eyed Cate, judging. She wasn't drunk, not to the numb stage intended; given her tolerance for drink, however, it could be a fortnight before that blessed state was achieved. Decency demanded he get this over with. Waiting only prolonged her suffering, and everyone else's involved for that matter, he thought, taking another drink himself.

Nathan drew a deep breath, poised the bottle, cut Cate a warning look, allowing her to realize his intent, and then poured the brandy over her shoulder and rump. No amount determination, dignity or bravery could hold back against raw spirits on open flesh. She screamed, a high and thin, but with a volume that made his eyes vibrate.

Alarmed cries outside. Ogden poked his head in, eyes rounded.

"Mr. Cate is just taking her medicine," Nathan barked.

"But—" Rowett popped up beside Ogden. "Sounds like ye've done kilt—"

"Avast w'ye! Out, you bunch o' leering snoops!" A threatening growl highlighted their peril, and they ducked away.

Nathan looked down at the smooth, pale curve of Cate's rear, keenly aware of her vulnerability, exposed and at his will. His eye drifted to the hand holding the tweezers, quaking like a shivering jib. He swiped the sweat from his palm and re-settled his grip.

Cate lay, waiting. Finally, with an exasperated huff, she pushed up, reaching for the tweezers. "Let me try — "

"And just how do you fancy to do that?" he demanded, irritation battling mirth. Given the location, she could neither see, nor reach.

A part, a *very* large part of him wanted nothing more than to call someone else, let someone else do it. But, curse n' burn him, there was no one, no one other than a bunch of drooling lechers looking to ogle her as she laid there in all her exposed glory!

Conceding his point, she laid back down. "Just push the tip — "

"Go tell the Pope how to pray," he said, evenly. "I've been digging shivers out of either meself or me mates since I was one and ten."

"Don't warn me. Just do it." She dropped her voice to what he supposed was to be an approximation of what his. "On to it then, eh?"

Cate carefully arranged herself yet again. Her facade of calm was betrayed by the dread eloquent in her every line. Her shoulder reflexively twitched at being touched. The flesh under his hand was like ice, or was the room that damned warm? Or was he that inflamed himself?

Where the bloody hell was that foundering winds'l? A more rational part of his mind pointed out that, since they were running with the wind, a dozen winds'ls would provide no improvement.

Cracking an eye open, Cate peered up at him. An unsteady finger rose up to delicately flick a bead of sweat from the end of his nose. She had enough self-awareness to tug the edges of her stays to cover an exposed breast and then laid, ready.

She braced her forehead into the table at the first dig. Typical of most splinters, there was precious little blood until they were removed, and then they bled like a stuck pig. The repetition became mechanical: pull n' dab with a brandy-soaked cloth, pull n' dab, Cate grunting softly now and again, a small pile growing at her elbow. It was tedious work, knowing every touch, in the spirit of removing pain, delivered even more. Poking about in the already raw flesh made his skin creep.

"You don't have to keep saying that," she said at one point. The lamplight caught the beads of sweat, glistening like little pearls on her lip and temple.

Nathan jerked, tweezers poised. "What?"

"'I'm sorry. I'm sorry.'"

"Eh? Oh, was that me?" He checked the "Sorry" which hung at the tip of his tongue. "It's... It's..."

Clamping his lower lip between his teeth, he set back to it.

"The deck is so smooth," she said at one interval. "It's difficult to believe I could have gotten all of these from it."

"Mightn't have been the deck. More than just sails came down; it could have been a spar or the gaff or block..." The thought was left to find its own finish as he focused on a particularly stubborn bit.

"Done." Nathan straightened, feeling quite victorious, a miserable task behind him, behind them both, as he ceremoniously dropped the last bit on the pile.

Cate shifted in discomfort. "It still feels like I'm being stabbed."

"Splinters are like that." In truth, they often hurt worse after they were removed.

Unconvinced, Cate experimentally moved and sucked in sharply. "No, there's something still there."

"Where?"

"There." A flailing gesture was made toward her lower extremity.

Nathan regarded her. Cate had a lot of qualities, but histrionic was categorically *not* one. If anything, she was the exact opposite. No matter what might show on the surface, ten-fold lay under it.

"Where? Here...? Here...?" he asked, pressing lightly on her leg. "Here—?"

An even sharper intake verified her claim.

Adjusting the light once more, Nathan probed, secretly crossing his fingers that it would be in vain. If something was found, removal it was going to be thoroughly unpleasant. Amid the raw seep, he caught a glimpse of something approximately the size of a glass-headed pin.

"Well, you skulking little bugger." Had Cate not flexed her hip, he would have never seen it. "There is one hiding... *deep*."

The last word was offered more as warning than information.

Cate grabbed the edge of the table as two attempts were made, each confirming the thing was larger than first thought and, in consequence of his explorations, forced all the deeper.

"I'm going to have to—" Nathan began.

Cate was well ahead of him. Shoulders hunched, her fists clenched. "I know."

"I will have to use—"

"I know!" she shrieked, with a vehemence which drove him back a step. She rose up, grabbed the bottle—nearly empty, by the sound — and took a mouthful. Clinging to it, she waited, and then took another.

With stiff precision, she resumed her position and resolutely turned her head. "Just do it." Her voice had an unevenness, as if she were on the verge of crying.

Nathan picked up one of Petrov's lancets. When they had been presented, he had thought them wicked and menacing sharp, and had shied at the thought of the unwitting sod they might be used on and, worse yet, the cold-hearted, brutal cove who would use them. And now, the even more brutal irony was that he would be using them on her. Then, he put it down. This was no time for strangers. A tried-and-true friend was needed for this. Cate's sides rose and fell like bellows, her breath coming shorter and shorter. He knew the demons she fought. She had a horror of edges, and justifiably so. Her stomach was a living testimony to the horrors they could wrought. A few times, unwittingly or out of ill-thought jest, he had made to use a knife for something so simple as cutting her laces or some such nonsense. Now, he had to actually use it on her, cut her flesh, his heart's flesh, with the coldness of an inquisitor.

Nathan swallowed and said in a tight rasp "I am not the bastard that cut — "

"I know!" Her body had gone as hard as the surface under her. A sideways cut of her eye urged him on.

By his death and soul, she was correct! Enough of this backing-and-filling; it was cowardice of the highest order, torture for all involved. He also knew with even more certainty that, if those tables were turned, if it were her standing there, she would do what needed doing without compunction, with the same out-of-handedness as she had dealt with countless other dire situations.

Knife in one hand, tweezers in the other, Nathan adjusted the light, rearranged the fabric about her for a bit more decency, dried his palms, settled his grip once more.

Something fogged his eyes. Was it sweat or tears?

"One," he said, in a tight rasp. "I promise, only one. It will be short and quick... and... and done." A part of him considered that he might be promising what wasn't to be promised. But, he bloody didn't care. The hurt and betrayal in her voice and eyes cut him deeper than anything he was about to do.

A faint movement of her head was the only acknowledgment.

Nathan laid a light hand on her leg, as if in benediction for them both.

"Don't move." He winced at how inane that sounded.

He pressed the knife tip hard into the raw and seeping flesh.

He knew what it was to drive a blade into another being; he knew how hard to push—harder than one might think—without going clear to the bone. The first touch of the blade, Cate emitted a tremulous, high-pitched whimper, one so filled with accusation and betrayal his hand nearly slipped. Her grip tightened on the table edge, the cords popping out in her forearms. He braced, half-expecting her to leap up and either tear out of the room, or turn and tear at him like a tigress. The blood welled, but not before he saw his target and dove with the tweezers. Cate quivered and sucked in. He pushed deeper, searching and a cry broke, muffled into her arm. He wanted to tell her to go ahead and scream, show these whey-faced men what a woman could bear.

Remembering his pledge, he plunged a fraction deeper. A faint vibration against the tips, like something solid and then it purchased. He pulled the thing out—not quite the size of a ten-penny nail, but had to have felt like one—and flung it onto the pile as if it were poison.

Clapping the cloth over the spot, Nathan fell forward, bracing himself on Cate's hip. "It's done."

❦

In spite of the deed being done, Cate remained rigid, nails clawed into the table, still engulfed in her battle against whatever invisible demons he had unwittingly, and yet so very deliberately released. Nathan stood as close as one might and not touching, side from the brandy-soaked cloth and looked on, helpless. No stranger was welcome in this private battle.

Finally, she fell lax; the battle was done. He eyed her, wondering which side won?

Still eyes closed, Cate panted like she had just run a race. Allowing her to collect herself, Nathan doused what lamps he could reach, in hopes the temperature might lessen to something below bread-baking.

As he stood waiting, he closed his eyes and allowed a moment for his ship. As suspected, she was bearing well. Other than that hulk in her wake, naught was amiss. Her people were well, too: no racing about, no calling out. The bells rang, the rhythm of life at sea resumed.

Finally, Cate's eyes opened. He expected them to look at him like the Judas Iscariot he was. Instead, they were soft with compassion and pity, not for herself, but for him. He sank, feeling all the more the perfidious caitiff.

He stretched his arm out on the table before her, knife in his fist. "Take this knife; draw my blood, as I have drawn yours. Jab, slice, cut: do whatever you must to have your vengeance, take your pound of flesh."

It seemed to take Cate a moment to locate her limbs and then moved only enough to take his hand. Small tremors still coursing through her, she kissed the knuckles. "Your tears are enough revenge for one day."

"Tokens, to say the least," he said, dashing his eyes on his shoulder.

She pressed his palm to her cheek. "Tokens accepted."

He straightened and heaved a massive sigh. She'd forgiven him; the rest bloody didn't matter.

Nathan lifted the cloth on Cate's leg and peeked under. The bleeding seemed to be slowing, the edges already drawing together. Lowering it, he murmured a private thanks on behalf of both of them. No stitching today.

Cate's earlier anguish was now replaced by a certain dreaminess. Head now pillowed on her arm, she rocked slightly and hummed a nonsensical tune. She was even paler now, her cheeks and lips bright as summer berries against the pallor. Allowing her a few moments of undisturbed peace seemed the decent thing, and so he went about dousing all but one lamp. He was poking through the rolls of bandages, looking for something suitable, when he suddenly became aware of being watched. He turned to find her eyes on him.

"You're as pale as your shirt," she said softly. The effects of recent ordeal had roughened her voice.

Nathan snorted. "Small wonder. This wasn't quite how I had your first day aboard envisioned."

Brow crumpling, she gave a wan smile. "Lord, that seems another life ago."

"Aye, well, luckily some of us have memories of an elephant. Now, let's bind that leg."

Her gaze didn't waver from him as he slipped the linen strip about the limb. He was fumbling with the linen ends when her knee pressed into his thigh. He thought it just an idle act until the hand resting on her hip hooked a finger in invitation.

"I want you..."

"As I want you," he said smiling down.

The knee grew more insistent and—as if he mightn't have smoked her meaning— more central.

"I want you," she repeated, low and insistent.

Nathan shifted a fraction, pushing her knee away. "You are drunk." The brandy was answering admirably now.

Giggling, she spread her arms and wriggled as if the wood under her was a down - filled bed. "Yes, gloriously! Where is that bottle?"

"Ah-ah," he said, snatching it out of her reach. "You'll be drunk as a lord." Assuming, of course, she hadn't achieved that vaunted state already.

"Avast that wriggling about," he said sternly, fumbling with the binding ends. "It's like trying to stow a shivering jib."

Cate reluctantly quieted.

A distraction of some sort was called for and so he asked "Does it pain you?"

Caught far afield, Cate blinked. "Yes, of course it hurts," she said, mildly annoyed. Then she snickered as if at a secret joke. "But I don't care."

The hand resting on her hip rose. "Come here. I wish to curl my fingers into all that hair..."

"That hair?" he said, peering down at his chest.

"Well, the other too," she qualified, with a teasing leer. "But, just now —"

Drink hindered the reflexes of many, but not Cate. Her hand shot out like a viper and caught the opening of his shirt. An iron grasp pulled him with her as she sank back down. He let out a startled "Gah!" when, with that same accuracy and lightning quickness, her hand found his nipple. She had toyed with his chest before — *many* times — but this time it tickled and with peculiar effect. It was downright... titillating, a word he never used before, but there it was, fitting, so very, *very* fitting.

"'Tis an intriguing thought, darling," he said, firmly disengaging himself. "But not just —"

"Why?" She thrust out her lower lip — so plump and succulent — looking so much like a little girl, he had a sudden sympathy for her father; disciplining her had to have been the trial-of-the-ages.

An arched brow pointed out what he thought to be the obvious, but in vain. "Because only a base-souled monster would cut a woman, and then turn around and use her like a street whore." He shuddered dramatically and shook his head. "T'would be too much like some of the specialties offered in those French brothels."

With all her flailing about, her clothing had fallen open, her breasts offering like two ripe peaches begging to be taken. He tugged them back into place.

"Besides," he went on, dancing away from a questing hand,

"I'm none so desperate as to have to get a woman in drink, so as to take advantage—"

Cate stopped, her mouth rounding in disbelief. "You expect me to believe you have never...?"

"Never, not intensionally, at any rate. Very well," he went on over her incredulous sputter. "But not for a very, *very* long time." The last was offered a bit louder so it might be heard over her laughing.

"You got drunk on the island, just so I might do that very thing," she said, still fizzing.

Apparently, spirits didn't deaden her powers of recollection, either. "That was different. That was for you to—" he began.

"And so I shall... *now*," she said, coming at him with renewed determination. "You owe me."

He executed another evasive contortion. "That debt was paid, last night... or this morning... or the time..." His voice faded at the complexity of trying to sort out who was doing what, when and for whom.

"Then kiss me."

A petulant protrusion of her lower lip only added to the transparency of her intent. They both knew it was a trap, but it was nigh impossible to refuse. There was the hope it might be enough to placate her. With a precautionary barring of her hands, he bent to kiss her, thinking a brotherly peck would suffice.

"Mmmm.... I want some more o' that!" Breaking his hold, she hooked an arm about his neck and drew him back down.

She tasted strongly of brandy, enough to make him slightly giddy. Her tongue darted with disarming familiarity and effect. Damn, she knew him all too well. The woman was part sorceress, working magics to which he was nearly helpless.

"Enough!" he gasped. He firmly extracted himself from her clutches, emphatically pressing her arms down to her sides. "You're ill—"

"Injured."

"Small difference."

Nathan resolutely resumed where he left off before being so rudely interrupted. "Ehh... leg... wrap..."

For some odd reason, he'd suddenly gone cod-fisted. He paused to swipe the sweat from his face with his sleeve. It was still has hot as Hades' hearth in there. Leg finally secured, he moved to the netting bag in which the bandages were stowed. He rummaged, looking for one a bit more suitable; most being long enough to wrap a body, not an arm. Granted, he could just cut off what was needed, but that would require a knife. He'd had enough of edges for one day.

Nathan looked back over his shoulder to find Cate gazing at him, head cocked like a bird eying a worm.

She smiled approvingly. "Your breeches are tight in all the right places."

He caught the spark of that very particular hue of turquoise in those slightly unfocused eyes.

"Never mind me breeches," he said primly. Someone had to be the adult in this scenario. Granted, he thought, shifting his stance a bit, there was a certain snugness— increasing by the moment—but nothing which couldn't be ignored. After all, he was master of his own ship!

"Give me that arm and no more of your capers," he added with a warning shake of his finger.

Cate was no dullard. The deceptive wench feigned acquiescence, waited for the inevitable moment when his guard dropped and made her move, clapping onto his rear and pulling him to her with the strength of a bosun. He let out a startled and yet restrained yelp, keenly aware of listening ears just beyond the threshold. It was startling, for she'd never grabbed him in such intimate aggression, kneading and making little purring sounds.

But, they weren't the familiar hands. These were awkward and fumbling, eager and yet so very unskilled. It was like negotiating with a desperate whore in an alley.

He wanted her, aye, but not... quite... like this. His body was confused as well: Yes... No... Well, stand by... Wait... No... Yes...

Striking the delicate balance between emphatic and not hurting her, Nathan plucked Cate's hand away and pressed it back down from whence it had come. "No."

With a leering chuckle, Cate laid back and twisted her torso so that the shattered ruins of her shift and stays fell away, baring her to the waist. "Take me."

She was sloshing, rollicking in drink by then. He could have removed her teeth and she wouldn't have blinked.

Usually, Cate held her liquor like a judge; this altered state alone was a novelty... and so very, very intriguing. He'd never lain with her taken in drink. Oh, aye, after a brandy or port or two, but none so gone as this. She was already a vixen; the imagination reeled at the possibilities of what inhibitions might dissolve, what freedoms unleashed.

An emphatic rounding of his eyes and firmly pulling her back onto her side was his answer. Neither had he ever told her

"No," not in respect to this, and had no intention of making it a habit. In her current state, however, there was a high probability that she wouldn't remember, one way or the other, come the morrow.

"But, why not? I'm here; you're here...?" She undulated before him like an exotic dancer. "They'll never know." The combination of drink, pain... and yes, lust, her voice had a huskiness, rendering her yet more of an oddity.

"They'll hear you," Nathan said in a hoarse hiss. He pulled up the remnants of her shift to cover her, tucking in the edges. "They'll think I'm in here debauching you like some lechering satyr."

Snickers from out in the passageway helped proved his point. "Light along, all of you! Bear a hand, there!" he directed toward the door. He mouthed "I told you so!" under the scuffle of receding feet.

A momentary indiscretion and only a snaking twist of his shoulders one way and his hips another did he dodge another attempt at his rear.

A rap at the door and meaningful clearing of a throat. "Cap'n?"

"Aye?" Nathan replied, feeling quite beleaguered by then.

Ben hung respectfully at the door. "Mr. Hodder begs to report all squared away. T'gallants swayed up, yards crossed, and sails bent."

Nathan nodded at having confirmed what the *Morganse* had already told him. He had felt it the moment the sails were pulling. That alone was what allowed him to linger there.

A number of things ran through his mind as he looked down at Cate, eyes now closed and humming again. Decisions begged to be made.

"Where's that mumping villain of a ship?" Nathan asked, looking up. So much hinged on that.

"Hull down, sir, even from the foretop."

That was surprising. They would be, nay should be out-sailing the tub, but not by that measure.

Scowling, Nathan shook his head. "I don't like it. It's too easy." The back of his neck prickled. A trap lay somewhere, the question was where? The answer wasn't necessary just then. That distance was their cushion of time.

"Very well. Carry on, and pass the word for Mr. Cate's quilt to be fetched. Surely to blazes they can manage to find that," he grumbled under his breath. There was no need in whispering. He could have blown Hodder's pipe and Cate wouldn't have stirred.

He watched the now quiet Cate closely as he anointed the rope burns with Number XXXVIIII. Usually, it stung like the blazes, and yet not a muscle ticked.

"Out cold as a mackerel," he muttered with a certain amount of relief. No more dodging and, even more significantly, no more misery, either. The blessed state was achieved. It would take rolling a mast before she would budge.

One eye on Cate, lest she roll off the table, he jerked on the beckets and dropped the swinging cot. Yes, in that process, the voice of Providence screamed like a siren in his head. He was listening, to a degree. That voice reached crescendo pitch at the decision not to send her to the hold. His cabin wasn't safe, not with that jumped-up grobian still lurking about. Still, at the same time, the threat of hazard didn't seem that imminent.

"But the moment it is..." he warned to her slack face.

He bent and gathered her up, grunting with effort. It was like lifting a beef cask! How bloody much did brandy weigh? Head lolling at a break-neck angle, he carried her the few steps to the cot. She slid in, like a half-cooked pudding poured from a pan. A spark of life stirred, however, and her hand snaked out to, catching him square in the crotch. Her fingers worked, not quite her usual delicacy, but knowingly enough. These were the hands, the touch he knew.

His damned traitorous body saw it entirely her way. Five minutes—Nay, three—Oh, hell, two and a half, is all it would take, and he would be going off like a fountain. This was no assault, but a beckoning, and lo, that he might answer! No, he'd never told her "No," but, bleeding saints on a cross...!

Footsteps approaching out in the passageway ended all thoughts, the quilt arriving. He deftly extricated himself from her grasp, kissed the now-still knuckles and tucked her hand at her side, the quilt overall.

"Lie with me," she murmured and wriggled her bum as she did when lying next to him. "I'm cold."

Only a heartless cad could resist that.

"Aye, well, call me a heartless cad," he grumbled.

He lingered long enough to square away the room. Waking to a mess could well send her into a catalepsy.

He blew out the lamp, and left, pulling the curtain closed behind.

Nathan drew up short at finding Pryce and several others standing there. It was a wonder how much had they heard? Probably everything, in spite of the carefully blank faces. Aye, well then, they should admire him for his restraint. They would know for certain all which did *not* transpire.

"You, you and you," he said, pointing to three of Pryce's mates. "If that sloop pops up, you are to get Mr. Cate into the hold. Savvy?"

"But..."

"To. The. Hold." Each word was emphasized with a stab of his finger.

They paled, grumbled into their chests as they turned and trudged forward.

"The sure sign of a poor captain is asking his men to do what he can't or won't." Pryce muttered from the corner of his mouth.

Nathan turned slowly to eye him. "Is it that obvious?" Sink and burn him, they had him there. He was scared, not the bowels-gone-to-liquid sort, but the heart-gone-to-ice, struggle-to-breathe sort at the thought of facing her. Seeing her in harm's way, however, was even worse.

Sighing, Nathan wearily rubbed his face. "A morally chaste woman is a scary thing."

Pryce arched a severe brow. "One what can run you through on the first pass is even scarier."

⌒◌◌◌⌒

Cate and Nathan flew arm-in-arm, soaring like a pair of free-wheeling birds. The sun warm on their backs, the world stretched out before them. A tilt of their limbs and they dipped and dove, skimming the tree crowns, and then arcing up and away. The air faltered, the clouds closed and Nathan was gone. She became aware of an odd, almost flying sensation. Not side-to-side, as in a hammock, but a circular one direction, and then almost reverse, and then back.

The rush of water, humidity, creak of wood all indicated to Cate she was at sea. The general motion, confirmed that, yet it still wasn't wholly familiar. The surface under her was flat and hard—neither hammock, nor bed—stable and yet moving, reminiscent of being spun on a swing as a girl, except face down, her torso twisted.

The disorientation was worsened by cracking an eye open to find canvas inches from her nose, a wall of it, as if she were in a tent. An upward traveling—only a few inches—of her view found a bulkhead and knees, confirming that she was on a ship. Not the night cabin, however, as expected, but a strange room. She shied at a ghostly, glowing shape moving overhead. It billowed and then a waft of air revealed it to be a windsail, illuminated by moonlight. A wall of shelves and cabinets came into view, and she knew at last where she was: her blood-room.

Cate cleaved onto that point of reference. Like a stirred pot settling, her world solidified and coalesced.

Dried slobber crackled as she lifted her cheek from the canvas. Voices, night-watch voices had come down with the stirring of air.

Lord, had she been sleeping that long? The bell rang, three times: half-past whatever o'clock.

She stirred, more in the spirit of locating her limbs. The movement proved a grave mistake; she gasped and swore. The stab of pain, however, had the benefit of bringing back what happened: An accident, of some sort... Being scared more than hurt... Nathan carrying her... and, somehow, at some point, she wound up there.

A part of her wished that she might lie there forever. The pragmatic part, however, demanded that she move. She drew several deep breaths, collecting both her strength and wits, and heaved up. Extricating herself from something neither hammock nor bed proved a bit of a challenge, but finally she prevailed without falling flat on her face. Now sweating, she stood swaying. A grab for the cot proved the thing useless, and she found the edge of a table. There she stood waiting for the room to stop spinning.

Her eyes focused on a bottle squarely before her and a little more came back: brandy, lots of it. A tongue, thick and seeming to belong to someone else, passed over her lips. A tingling in her extremities and lightness of head indicated the brandy was still working its magic, and thank heavens! Taking a drink might extend this euphoric numbness, but more a stronger voice cautioned of Judgment Day looming for such intemperance.

Stooped, moving like an ancient, Cate hand-over-handed it along the table's edge. A little pile of splinters, collected like trophy souvenirs came into view. She smiled faintly at recalling Nathan's anguish of pulling them out. She poked a finger at them, ashamed by seeing how small they were; they had felt like horse nails. A careful exploratory hand drifted toward her rump, or rather, in that general direction.

A sharp inhalation and she forced herself upright, huffing through the resulting discomfort. A waft of air down the windsail made her look down to find that she was naked as Eve. A blind hand toward the cot found the quilt dangling, and she pulled it about her. Her clothes weren't to be found. Her current nakedness put her to mind of her first day aboard the *Morganse*, not so much in the way of the fear, but the muddle-headedness and "on beam ends" as Nathan would call it.

Tugging the quilt up about her, Cate checked her person for

decency and then stepped out, pausing briefly at noticing the shattered door, wondering how that came to pass. She walked stiffly, the deck not always where it was expected. Mounting the companionway one step at a time, she came up into a staggering canopy of stars visible through a pyramid of white sails. She looked over the rail, hoping for the sight of land and hence further orientation, but found only the gunmetal glimmer of a starlit sea.

Low murmur of watch voices came from both fore and aft. The latter was the direction Cate went; that was where Nathan would most likely be. She walked with as much dignity as one might whilst favoring their posterior. To say word of what had happened would have passed with the speed of lightning would have paid the speed a disservice.

"Mr. Cate copped it in the arse, the part what goes over the fence last..."

She could just hear them now, wink, wink, smirk, smirk, snicker, snicker. Everyone saw; everyone knew. They touched their hats and knuckled their obeisance as she passed, but much could be found behind those carefully blank faces.

If Nathan harbored any wryness, he had the good graces to expel it before he greeted her.

"How are we feeling?" His inquiry was posed not just out of politeness, but with the frown of honest concern.

"Sore." The hitch in her step rendered any less admission a lie.

"What time—?" She stopped at nearly showing both her ignorance and confusion. Nathan's mouth twitched with the urge to smile. "It just rang three bells, in the First Watch," he added. "Nine-thirty... at night."

"I know it's night," she huffed, hitching the quilt higher. "One hesitates to assume," came back dryly.

Idly strolling the deck, Cate found herself standing next to the shattered remains of the signal locker where she had been sitting on earlier that day. She had been chatting with Squidge, and then it seemed like the world fell in on her. Everything went dark, and she was tumbling across the deck. She jerked, Nathan bracing her up as she lurched and stumbled backwards. She looked up to the mizzen and all its appurtenances but—to her untrained eye—it looked the same as it always did, as if nothing had ever happened, which made the whole thing seem all the more disjointed. Feeling Nathan's scrutiny, she turned in search of a distraction. She found it peering over the taffrail.

"Is that a star?" It seemed not—it had an odd twinkle, and

was far too low — and yet she couldn't fathom what else it might be.

"Toplight," Nathan said, without looking.

"Are we being followed?" she asked uneasily.

"Chased, more like." Nathan finally twisted the bit necessary to look back. "Tenacious cove."

"He's keeping pace?"

"Barely. Gotta admire him for his seamanship," came with a begrudging shake of the head.

Murmurs and nods from the helm and afterguard showed their opinions ran generally the same.

"Do you know... who?" Cate asked, straining to recall. The ship's appearance was all part of that confused blur.

Nathan arched a questioning brow. "As in a name? A face? I have no notion, nor do I care. 'Tis not as if I aim to ask the infamous blighter to supper."

He tipped back his head to look up at the start-studded sky. "The moon sets shortly." The light of that very celestial element caught his malicious grin. "And *we* will disappear with it. A few less o' those would be nice," he added, with an accusing glance to the stars.

A conspiratorial snicker and knowing looks from around the deck.

"Lights doused, naught but a rag of a stays'l and jib to propel us, he'll probably pass us in the dark," Nathan added, rocking on his heels.

Cate craned her head around the sails directly overhead in order to see the highest apogee of the mainmast. "But we've a toplight, too." A quick glance found the sternlamps and decklights burning, as well. The whole deck, clear to the f'c'stle was ablaze.

"Aye, didn't wish the blundering dolt to lose us in the dark."

A fixed gazed prompted an explanation to the glaring contradiction.

"The clearer the sight, the more befuddling the disappearance," was pronounced as if it were the wisdom of the ages.

All heads nodded in grave agreement.

"We suddenly disappear and, with that scrub's tenacity, he'll circle like a hound what's lost a rabbit."

How someone could go so quickly from tenacious genius to blundering dolt and back made her head spin. "And we'll be...?"

"Gone, like a shadow in the sun."

A lee lurch — or at least, that's what it had to have been — sent Cate stumbling, Nathan's adroit seizing of her arm saving her from colliding with one of the men.

"Come, darling, before you hurt yourself or someone else."

She resisted the tug on her arm. "You think I'm drunk?" Her indignation might have been more convincing had it not coincided with a giggle.

"Nay, luv, it's just your natural ferment," Nathan said, with a wry roll of the eyes. "You're shivering; nothing to be gained in catching a chill."

She looked around to find the afterguard studiously looking in any direction but hers. Whether it was out of deference to her state-of-undress, wounded posterior or general disapprobation, she couldn't tell. To the man, she had seen every one in drink, at some point or another, and was more than a little annoyed that they might stare down their noses —

Any further contemplations or affronts broke off at being led down the steps.

Nathan handed her down, patient, without remark as she haltingly navigated them. Wrestling with the quilt was just a guise to hide her discomfort at every lurch or jolt, and he knew it. He saw her into the Great Cabin, as ablaze as the deck they left, and then the night cabin.

Nathan held the sheets as Cate attempted several positions lying down. Ultimately, she wound up roughly how she had awakened: half on her side, half on her stomach. He smiled indulgently at seeing her luxuriate on the new mattress and sheets, or at least as best one could in that position. She felt cold and heartless, but no guilt toward the geese's sacrifice for the sole benefit of her comforts. There was, of course, the probability that they hadn't died entirely for her benefit: someone, somewhere was sure to have a jar filled with fresh, new quills, and many a goose-fat home-cure brewing on the fire. She hadn't noticed before, but there was a new bolster, the old pillow gone, replaced by two plump ones.

Queenly, to say the least!

Cate briefly closed her eyes and thought a foot might be necessarily planted on the floor to keep from being flung out. The raised edge made that maneuver near impossible. Her eyes snapped open at the sudden heaving sensation in her stomach.

"I wish — " she began.

The smile dissolved and Nathan lurched back a step as if to avoid a blow. Venturing cautiously closer, he arranged the quilt over her.

"Have you any notion of where my clothes might be?" She was hesitant to inquire, for it seemed to reveal just how addled she was.

"A couple of the people were weavers in a former life. They

have been plying both their skills and their needles since you…
drifted off," he finally arrived on.

"When we're all squared-away, I'll bid your dunnage to be
roused up. It seems the master-of-the-hold can't find his arse
with either hand, let alone a few hampers and lockers."

With equal caution, as if braced for an assault, Nathan bent
and kissed her lightly. She reached to hug him, but he ducked
back, looking a bit haunted.

"Will you come to bed after everything?" she asked, in part
hopeful for own comforts, but more in the way of concern for
him.

"Nay, there shall be no rest with that double-dutchman
lurking…" He caught himself and smiled down at her. "Naught
for your to worry for. We'll run out this gambit and then see
what's to do."

Lying as she was, her cheek was the most accessible, and so
he lightly kissed her there. "I'll slip in and keep you company
when I might."

He straightened, smiling crookedly. "This is categorically
not how I planned to christen this."

At five bells in the Middle Watch, the moon did its duty and
dipped. Through Providence, guiding hands or just plain luck, a
high thin layer of clouds rolled in, veiling the starlight.

In the starlit dim, the *Morganse's* lamps doused in a single
blink and a charcoal – blackened t'gallant and jib replaced the
rest. She veered hard to leeward and there hung under bare
poles, like a black bat against a velvet cloth and watched the
sloop, lights twinkling like great fireflies, glide past.

"Not a glim. Silence, fore n' aft!" passed from the quarterdeck
in hoarse whispers.

When the sloop's lights could barely be made out from the
stars, the *Morganse* came about and hauled her wind, the sea and
night closing in behind her.

29: LUNA'S HAND

J UDGMENT DAY WAS UPON CATE, and its name was "Brandy."

She felt like the spouse of the Biblical wife who had driven a tent peg into his head. The crown of her head threatened to lift off at every move, a large part of her wishing it might, if it meant her torment might ease. The ache in her extremities paled in comparison to the one there.

Cate sat tucked into a corner of the table in the salon. Charts, logs and navigational instruments which filled the rest of the grand expanse indicated a hard night before. Her entire body ached like she had been tumbled by a herd of oxen, the mere act of dressing akin to torture. The journey from the night cabin to the table had been achieved with careful, mincing steps. She considered a hair-of-the-dog—a bottle stood well within reach, beckoning like the snake before Eve—yet resisted. It was that very indulgence which had led her down this path-of-destruction in the first place.

Head braced in her hands, she wondered how she had gone so astray? It was rare for spirits to hit her so hard. It was even rarer for Nathan to force them on her.

"Yes, it was most certainly his fault, right?" she grumbled to the honey pot.

The stern windows were open; even the breeze stirring her hair hurt. She drew a deep breath, hoping the freshness and salt might have some palliative effect. It was a bad decision; spots set to swimming before her eyes and the hammering in her head intensified.

Philosophers claimed suffering and passions to be closely intertwined, impossible to enjoy one without invoking the other. She would have suffered her penance with grace, if she could just remember which passion she had engaged. All she could remember was being in pain and Nathan pouring brandy down her like he was watering a thirsty plant.

The very man came up from below smiling like a damned Cheshire cat.

Madre de Dios, did he ever meet a day he didn't love? she thought, peering at him through her fingers. He was positively chipper... And was that a smirk?

Nathan advanced slowly, his attention fixed on the mug he bore. Finally, he set it before her with the satisfaction of a laborious task achieved. "Mother Kirkland's cure: egg, ale... and a little something..."

Cate suspiciously regarded the thing and then sniffed. The "something" smelled like a combination of vitriol and sheep's dung. She leaned away, her stomach taking a threatening lurch.

"Take the cure or pay the toll," Nathan intoned from somewhere over her.

"And if it all comes back up?" It wasn't an idle threat; there was a high probability of that very thing, she observed, pressing her hand to her midriff.

"Then we'll send another down, and then another, and then another..."

Yes, indeed, it was a smirk. Rest assured, she would remember this day. He would live to regret this!

With the pomp of presenting to royalty, Kirkland and Millbridge carried a monstrous silver urn up from below. The charts and impedimenta were slid aside, and it was set before Cate. A shaft of sun down through the skylight flaring on its mirror-like surface, she held up a shielding hand—delicately, lest she offend—as its workings were exhibited, from the gimbaled stand, to the blue flame dancing in the burner below, to the spigot from which a cup was filled. The steaming brew was ceremoniously set before her, another before their captain.

"Where did you ever—?" Upon reflection, the answer to Cate's stunned question was self-evident. In the time frame given, there was only one place something like this could have been obtained: the Island-Which-Shall-Not-Be-Named and its excesses of opulence.

"And new china, too?" she asked, inspecting the cup.

"Not everyone spends their time there dissipated and debauched," Nathan pointed out.

Cate regarded Kirkland. There was a bit of... a flushed glow about the man, and a different spring in his step, the kind which neither silver nor china might deliver.

Nathan delicately plucked the cup from Cate's hand and set it well out of reach. "None of that, until you finish this." Mother Kirkland's was slid back before her.

"You're not my mum," she glowered up.

"True enough; I'd never pass the physical," Nathan countered dryly. "'Tis to your credit that you're aware of the odds, at any rate. Now, drink up like a good'n, or shall I hail Chin and Maori?"

"You wouldn't dare." It pained her to do so—her eyes felt like hot marbles in their sockets—but she cut him a look which drove him back a step. Not only did she recognize he wasn't her mother, she also recognized Nathan, the Intractable standing there, and she too diminished to argue.

Cate leaned to take another sniff, judged the direction and distance of Nathan's boots when it came up, held her nose and took a drink. The intended sip became a singular gulp by way of Nathan's finger disallowing the vessel to lower until it was empty. She coughed, sputtered, gulped, gulped again, and sat back, gasping.

"Insensitive brute," she muttered, dabbing the sweat now prickling her temples.

"Compassionate caretaker," came back evenly.

The coffee was slid back before her as a peace-offering. She cleaved onto it with trembling hands, blew—Kirkland's coffee always the temperature of molten lead—and drank.

"Would Sir desire to break his fast?" asked Kirkland began, quickly adding "Just a sippet of soft-tack, perhaps?" when Cate went slightly green-about-the-gills.

Aware of Nathan's watchful eye, Cate grunted an affirmative.

In dire need of a diversion from her internal roilings, she asked "Is that ship—?"

"Save yourself the effort of looking, darling. It's not even a nick on the horizon from the t'gallant mast." Pleasure and relief battled in that. "Give you joy."

"I should think I should be the one to give you that. You're captain; it was your plan—"

A flip of Nathan's hand dismissed the compliment.

Mother Kirkland's answered to a degree, by way of supplying Cate's stomach with an anchor, her entire being finally finding center. The coffee, however, was the miracle draught. The steam cleared her head, the substance supplying both life and purpose. She now had reason to face the day and, even more significantly, reasonable hope that she might survive it.

Nathan intercepted as she reached for a refill. He poured another and set it before her, then pulled up a chair. Seizing hers, he drew it around, so that she faced him more squarely, their knees touching. He sat back, the hand on his leg making a fist, the other fiddling with dividers on the table.

"I'm sorry that—" His throat bobbed as he audibly swallowed.

Drawing a deep breath, he faced her fully, both hands now knotted in his lap. "I'm sorry that I had to... to take... a... a knife to you —"

She leaned to cup his cheek. He hadn't shaved, the bear-like pelt of his beard stiff against her palm. Worry pinched the corners of his eyes, making hard lines along his nose and mouth.

"Forgiven; I already told you —" Uncertainty as to whether that was a flash of memory or a fabrication of her mind stopped her.

The sable brow arched. "You're sure? Positive?"

"Positive. After all, what else might I do?"

The brow hooked higher yet. "A person of your lights might come up with a fair selection of recourse me hide playing a large part in most."

"Not this time."

He was guilt-swathed on that account, but there was something else which had him shying like a startled deer at her least twitch.

His head dropped, clearly relieved. "How does it fare?"

"Stiff and a little sore." She sat back, shifting on the pillow some thoughtful soul had left in her chair. "It was minor."

His head snapped up at that, mouth agape. "Hardly!"

"I wasn't hurt; I was just tumbled about a bit... and a few splinters," she reluctantly added, shifting yet again.

Nathan went white around the mouth. "Do you have any appreciation of what it was to stand there, helpless as you were being snatched away before me eyes?" His voice shook as he spoke.

"But I wasn't. The rail —" as best she could recall.

"Was the only thing what stopped you," he said ominously. "You were in a clinch and no knife to cut the seizing." His mouth twisted at the irony of that old saw.

"A few more seconds," he went on, tapping his finger on the table for emphasis. "And those lines could have cut you in half as neat as a knife through pudding." He sat back, stiff. "Only the roll of the ship saved you."

"And Squidge." The coffee was answering, all of it flooding back in staggeringly vivid detail.

"Yes, and Squidge. If it hadn't been for him, I don't know what —" Nathan stopped and audibly gulped, then went on determinedly. "I don't know what I would have done."

Nathan fell into a brooding silence, watching his fist as it opened and closed on his leg. "I thought for sure it was Calypso's hand, reaching up, seeking to pluck you out from under me very nose, and me standing there as helpless as a eunuch in a nunnery."

"Can she...? She could...?" Cate gulped, casting a wary look toward the windows and the sea beyond. "Could she do that?" Her stomach—momentarily forgotten—knotted and writhed. She took a drink, now wishing for something far stronger.

"She promised not. And I've made every precaution to assure that she mightn't," he added, touching her necklace. He drew back and drew a deep breath. "But we both know there's no fathoming the treachery of that double-tongued harridan."

Seeing he hadn't yet touched his, Cate offered hers. She watched with concern as he took a well-needed drink. The clutter on the table wasn't the only indication of a hard night. The red-rimmed eyes and hard lines along his nose, and mouth were even further evidence.

"Have you slept?" she asked, frowning.

"Eh? Oh, nay." He rubbed his face hard, his beard rasping. "I was afraid I'd wake and that skulking whoreson-of-a-scrub would have boarded and slit me neck."

A haunted look suggested that wasn't just a figure of speech.

He saw her worry and smiled indulgently. "I took a couple caulks, I'll take another as soon as I'm sure that—" He stopped, deciding to let whatever he had meant to say unsaid. "Later."

A hard nudge at Cate's elbow almost made her spill the precious liquid. She looked around into a pair of gold, vertically-slitted eyes, glaring at her.

"Away w' you, you flea-ridden, seed o' Satan. Mr. Kirkland! Hermione has been left wanting *again*," Nathan called.

"Aye, sir," came up from below. "'Tis on the brew."

Nathan rose and bent over the charts. Slumped in her chair, Cate watched Hermione pace around the mizzen, uttering peevish bleats. "Why is she in such a flustration?" The tea had been forgotten before, but it had never produced this level of agitation.

He rolled his eyes and shook his head. "She's been in a ferment since another of her kin boarded yesterday. Someone needs to be given a lesson on getting along with their fellow shipmates," he went on louder, directing the remark in the creature's direction. "He's apparently not to her liking, although one does wonder what is to be seen in a goat. He certainly has the—" He coughed and muttered into his chest "He appears capable of serving her to satisfaction."

"Perhaps it's not she who was the one refusing," Cate ventured.

"What man declines the attentions of—?" Nathan stopped short.

Cate had the sudden impression that they were no longer talking about goats. She observed Nathan carefully over her cup. The recollections were coming faster and clearer by the moment.

"Yesterday, in the blood room, did we...?" Cate began tentatively.

"No" came back emphatic and honest.

Her face heated, the recollections came in a flood. "Didn't I try to...?"

"No," came back, as absent of truth as the first had been filled with it.

Cate stared, waiting for something, anything further. She knew him well enough to recognize when she might as well wait for the sun to turn purple.

Very well, a direct attack isn't always the straightest path.

She looked self-consciously down and plucked at her skirt. "I thought... I mean, weren't my clothes...?"

"Torn off your back?" Nathan said, without looking up from his work. "Aye, ripped from clew to erring, they were. You don't recall me telling you about the weavers working on them?" he went on at her obvious confusion.

Flushing, she meekly shook her head. It was indeed, fine work, she thought, fingering the repair. It was precious difficult to even find.

"They plied their needles all night, finished all but the stays," Nathan added with a vague gesture toward the piece she wore instead. It was a cross between a shawl and jump – stays, with ends which wrapped and tied at her back. There was no boning, but multiple layers provided support in all the right places. She was decently covered, which was all that mattered.

"Those double-dutch, dumb-as-bollards infidels in the hold still can't find your dunnage. I'm beginning to think stopping their grog might spark either their memory or their industry," he added with the satisfaction of one in possession of power and flexing it.

Kirkland appeared, Hermione's dish in one hand, Cate's breakfast in the other. Accompanying the sippet—lightly browned and fragrant—was "a bit o' fresh custard, still warm, just to mollify the humors."

Nathan busied with pricking a chart. Cate nibbled a corner of the bread, chewed thoroughly, swallowed carefully and then waited. Encouraged by the complaisant reception, she took another bite.

Cate craned her head toward the charts, but could make out

nothing. "So, where to?" she asked over the sound of Hermione's slurping.

"Right now, just trying to figure out where the devil we are after plunging about in the dark all night."

Stabbing experimentally at the custard, testing not the substance so much as its probable reception, Cate considered Nathan's observation to be a bit of an exaggeration. Nathan knew these waters like a huntsman knew his native fields.

"Just using the wind and every sail which will answer to put as much sea possible between us, for now," he added, distracted.

Cate turned her head to watch the *Morganse's* wake, a white line sharp against the indigo blue, perpetually rising, perpetually fading without a trace. There were advantages to being on a trackless sea; all the will in the world could ever follow their path.

"And then what or, should I say, where to after that?" It was a question she had previously posed, several times, and yet still begged to be asked again.

Nathan's shoulder moved in a suggestion of a shrug. "We'll see where we are and where the wind is willing to blow us."

Cate eyed him sharply. A sizeable dose of deception lurked in there.

Someone beckoned from outside. Nathan took a parting look at the chart and then turned to take his leave. "You'll be well?"

"Of course. I should go down and—"

He stopped at that and turned back. "You'll sit is what you'll do," he said with a stab of his finger. Seeing her bristle, he added softer "The barky is skittish today. The last thing you need is to take a tumble."

She wondered if that were true—if so, it would be a relief to know at least a certain portion of her off-kilter might have been because of the ship—or if it was just another excuse.

"I already gave Squidge your good wishes and effusive due thanks."

"But I—"

"Not today." He saw her determination and softened "I mean it, darling, lie on your oars today. There's naught to be stirring about."

~~~

In the vacuum of Nathan's absence, Cate felt a certain malaise closing in. In such quiet interludes, or anytime she caught a glimpse of the water from the corner of her eye, the nearness of the disaster she barely escaped struck. Land or sea, she had always known, had been told of it, hell, had personally witnessed how quickly the hand of Fate could strike. Now, the hand had taken a direct swipe at her and it had left her not a little shaken.

It was the sort of thing which dwelling upon, however, could paralyze a soul, and there was too much to be done to wallow in self-pity. And so, she took a lesson from Nathan, and categorically, firmly, without hesitation struck it from her mind, ignoring it, in every application of the word.

In spite of Nathan's parting instructions, Cate considered that there was every reason to be "stirring about." First order of the day was to find Squidge and give her thanks. Nathan doing so was all well and greatly appreciated, but such heroics demanded hers be delivered in person.

She started for the door. Visions of the sun's glare pounding on her head and stabbing her eyes caused her to veer toward the companionway, instead. Forward past Hodder, Pryce and MacQuarrie's cabin, past the heat and clatter of the galley — Was that Kirkland humming? — she went. As she passed the blood-room, her step slowed at seeing Broadstreet, one of Chips' mates, fashioning a new door, and wondered how had that come to be broken already?

Weaving her way through the hammocks of the watch-below, she found Squidge, rum bottle in hand, ensconced like a king on a bed of thrum mats, a cushion elevating his splinted limb. A bell sat at his knee, although the odds of having to ring to gain attention seemed remote, for the gundeck was always occupied; someone would always be within hail. Two callers were with him then, several more circling. Tapping their foreheads, the pair took their leave at Cate's approach, those in wait retreating.

In her earliest days aboard, she had called him — privately, never to his face — Ass, by virtue of the jawbone which hung about his neck. The three gold teeth it bore made it impossible for the thing to have been an actual ass's jaw, teeth which compelled her to avert her eyes whenever he was about, for it was too much like a part of Nathan being worn as an adornment. Someday, she meant to inquire as to whose jaw it was? But then, there was a strong chance that ignorance might be more pleasing. From the angular bone hung a collection of wizened, leathery bits: the fingers of his past foes, not to be confused with Pickford's collection of ears.

Physically, in many respects, Squidge reminded her of the *mulatos*, *zambos*, or *castizos* of her childhood, but it was folly to believe his bloodlines were confined to the Spanish colonies.

When it came to his exact heritage, east, west, north or south and all regions in between all seemed to reside in that face.

Cate knelt next to him, inquiring as to how he did.

The hawkish face beamed. "Prime, sir, prime!"

"I came to thank you for —" The moment was a bit more awkward than hoped, for her good wishes threatened the man's embarrassment. "Thank you" would bring the grand total of words between them to something in the range of a score, perhaps less. It was difficult to tell if his reserve ran more in the way of Millbridge's general distaste of women, or if it was more just a general nature, for that would have required actual conversation.

Bottled in his fist, Squidge waved her away. "Oh, aye, the Cap'n already called, sir!" The dried bits made an odd, dull clatter against the bone when he moved.

Cate observed him closely as he spoke. His eyes were a bit unfocused, his speech a bit slurred, but she suspected the rum more than impending fever.

"The Cap'n gave his thanks, and then begged my price. I wasn't thinkin' money, at the time," he cautioned, sobering.

"No one is even suggesting that," she said earnestly.

He nodded, pleased at his point being made. "I represented as much. I told him rum was all I required, what with this aching leg and all." He shifted in search of a more comfortable position. "'You shall have a bumpkin,' he cried." Squidge angled his head toward the small cask sitting nearby.

Squidge touched his necklace. "I asked if I might have a token from his next few victims. The next score, says he. That, plus his share of the next ten prizes." The prospect of the souvenirs seemed more enticing that the monetary aspect. "It's Fiddler's Green, sir. Fiddler's Green! Naught more 'tis required nor expected." He sat back in overt complacence.

Nathan's magnanimity left Cate feeling a bit self-conscious. Her assets fell far short of his, and there was little chance of her gathering trophies from foes. Money wasn't the sole path to good-will, but it served nicely when one had nothing else to offer.

"You can demure all you wish, Mr. Squidge —"

A desisting wave of the bottle stopped her. "The Cap'n represents as you're as determined as a bowsprit."

"Then you'll know not to refuse," she said, kind but firm. His image started to shimmer as her eyes filled. He saw as much and began to squirm. She turned her head and blinked.

"I mean to double the Captain's offer out of my shares," she said, looking back when she was sufficiently dry. "And I'll give you my hand on it."

Apparently, it was the first time for a woman to offer such a thing; Squidge blinked and stared. A second, encouraging thrust called him to his senses and he took it.

"Agreed?" she declared.

"Agreed," came with a grin which lit up the deck.

Feeling the stares of a growing number awaiting visitors, Cate rose and took her leave. Echoes of her and the Captain's pledge being related to his next batch of visitors behind her.

⁓⁓⁓

The next call-of-business was saying "thank you" on a much broader scale. If, as Nathan had represented, the entire crew had been involved in constructing her blood-room, and there were two hundred aboard, then it begged to be said two hundred times. She had started with the easiest: those in Squidge's immediate company. She then spiraled out from there, first with the watch-below, the storerooms, powder-room, bosun's locker, sail-room, down into the hold, wherever they might lurk. Then out on deck she went, to the waist, f'c'stle, quarterdeck and heads, or shouting up the ratlines and to the tops.

At length, when naught else could be tracked down, Cate returned to the blood – room, with a mental list of those who would have to be found later. She paused outside, pride and pleasure filling her anew at seeing the name carved over the door. It was hers, really, really hers.

Stepping over the tools and shavings, she squeezed past the still-working Broadstreet and went in. O'Leary lurched up from further inside.

"Beg pardon, sir, but..." he began. He made an awkward gesture to a shattered locker door. A broken lock dangling from the latch indicated that, at some point, it must have contained spirits of some sort. Nothing else aboard was kept under lock-and-key.

"There's no haste on my part, Mr. O'Leary." And there wasn't. For the first time in ages, she felt like she had all the time in the world.

Now, with the room nearer to empty, she could see that it was an architectural anomaly. With the camber of the decks above and below, the curve of the hull and wedged as it was between the cabins on each side, there wasn't a square corner or angle to be had. It was only the masterful craftsmanship of the cabinetry which made the room seem plumb.

As she poked about, her appreciation of it being her own space grew, a space she could, with all confidence, refer to as "my." The rest of the ship, Kirkland's galley, the Great Cabin, everywhere were, in every sense, Nathan's and, hence, always carried the designation of "yours." At times, she might have presumed to go so far as to use "ours" in reference to the sleeping quarters. Never, nowhere could she presume to use "my", until now. Granted, its function and purpose might be in service of the men, but the physical space was hers.

Stepping over and around Broadstreet and O'Leary, Cate hummed a tune as she indulged in her guilty pleasure of arranging it to her liking, moving things about if for no other reason than that she could. She had never had a home of her own; every place she had ever lived had been under the management of someone else, including Brian's estate. His sister ran things there and there was little doubt to it. The nearest thing to her "own" had been a corner of a garret in London, wretched and mean as it was. All she needed was a satanic cat to protect it, and it would be as autonomous and inaccessible as Kirkland's galley.

As if on cue, with a snuffling and click of nails, His Lordship shuffled in. He poked inquisitively into every corner. Disappointed in his quest, he sat up, one paw braced on Cate's knee, and the shining nose twitching up at her. Hopes defeated, he lowered onto all fours and slunk out.

"Well, not quite Beelzebub." At least, she thought that was Kirkland's cat's name. Or had that been another of Nathan's attributes?

At every turn, Cate found new delights: a spirit lamp, a mortar-and-pestle, a pill – roller, a small folding scalpel and a collection of cautery irons. It was almost as if someone had been peeking over her shoulder as she worked on the island. She smelled a rat, a very large, dark-eyed, charming rat.

Periodically, she stood back to survey the results of her organizing, and then re – arranged it all again. The men had put things here and there, but a man's sense of suitable was beyond wonder. The netted bags — a wondrous bit of knotwork — hanging from pegs were an agreeable means of storing the rolls and rolls of bandages, but little else remained as it had been left.

Her anticipation heightened at the prospect of her first visitor. Who would it be and for what? A splinter? A tar burn? A marlinspike through a hand? A smashed finger? Barely a day passed without one or all. She felt a peculiar thrill at the thought, touching wood at knowing she was wishing ill upon another.

Next to Celia's basket sat a carboy of her special solution. Cate moved it to a more practicable location and then began going through the gigantic basket. Gourds, bags, jars, tins, paper parcels: one by one she took them out and lined them on the counter. A variety of implements were included: a cupping lamp, a folding medicine spoon made of horn, and a jar of leeches, dark, glistening and so very plump. She held it up to the light, wondering how often, if at all, they needed to be fed? She set it down feeling the responsibility of a receiving new pet. There was a large container of suture glue, its receipt written on the label. Just as she was wondering how or where she was to come up with dragon's blood— hopefully the plant, not the animal—she looked down to find a tin of the very thing.

Well down inside, she came upon a book, leather-bound, the ivory pages bristling with ribbon, strings, thongs and other bits as page markers. Opening it, she half-expected it to be in some foreign language, Latin at the least, but found the flowing hand was in English. It wasn't just a compilation of treatments and receipts; the notations read more like a journal, a day-to-day account of maladies and treatments. As she read, she heard Celia's honeyed-voice, felt the woman's calm presence and confidence.

Tucked under the book laid a small quill bag, beaded and bearing designs reminiscent of the Natives of her childhood. Inside was another tiny bag, light-colored and translucent, possibly a bladder of some sort. Held up against the light, a small amount of a dark powder laid at the bottom.

A note was attached, the writing in the same elegant hand: "When your time comes, blow this into the air."

Cate pressed a hand to her stomach. She had left Celia's suspecting she might be building castles of hope out of sand. In cold analysis, Celia had told her and Nathan exactly what they wished to hear, as most seers were wont to do. Only those which annoyed or peeved got to hear the real ugly truths revealed in the tea leaves or spit or whatever. But now, with this note, Celia's divination took on the air of real expectation, the kind upon which plans might be made.

The scuff of boot leather broke Cate's stare. Turning, she found Nathan standing there. Cate quickly stuffed the bag into a nook behind her back.

A meaningful clearing of Nathan's throat and a flick of the fingers sent the workmen on their way. Rising, O'Leary said "I'll bid the armorer to rig a new lock" and the newly - fashioned door closed behind them.

Nathan took a small step to the counter and idly flipped through the pages of Celia's book. "You're not resorting to incantations are you?"

"No, it's mostly just instructions." Admittedly, there were a number of drawings and diagrams in it which had a ritual look about them.

"So much like Mum and all her falderal," Nathan murmured, running his fingers along the counter. His attention came around to the pipe-like thing. "What in the world—?"

"It's called a canula or stitching quill. A gift from Celia, obviously," Cate added excited and, for some reason, flustered.

"Obviously," he said, fingering the ivory tooling and the charms dangling from the end.

"It's for stitching wounds."

He looked up curiosity and surprise vying with each other. "And you know how to use it?"

"Yes, well—" Cate said a bit unsteadily. Her hand closed at recalling the feel of it, slick with blood for hour upon hour. She saw Nathan's regret of having brought up such unpleasantness, something they both strove to forget, and offered "It's amazing how much quicker you can do it."

"Amazing," Nathan muttered, quickly dropping it and swiping his fingertips on his shirt.

He turned to her with a business-like air. "I have an ache." The announcement came in a voice loud enough for the benefit of those outside.

Ah, so her first patient.

"Indeed," she said, dusting her hands. It confirmed her earlier suspicions that something about him was off. "Where?" she asked, already inspecting him about the head and chest.

"Lower, much, much lower," he instructed as he inched closer. "One might call it an injury, for it was inflicted upon me and with grievous intent."

"How long—?" she asked, irritated by his delay. Time could often be the great difference between minor incident and disaster.

"Since yesterday, beginning in this very room." A gesture was combined with tossing his weapons aside. "Persistent, perpetual, refusing to be eased…"

He came up against her, and Cate found she had unwittingly been retreating, the table now at her back. His hips pressed against hers and she realized the nature of his problem, a very large and pressing one. Recollections of the day before—when she had been the injured party—came back, triggering some disjointed flashes, ones which, much to her dismay, confirmed his claims: she was the perpetrator-at-large.

She made a sympathetic noise. "That has to be painful." Nathan had often exhibited some remarkable stamina, but it was still highly unlikely, physically impossible—Well, at the least, improbable, that he had maintained this condition for a whole twenty-four hours.

"Oh, aye. Mortal." He cocked an admonishing brow. "Whether 'tis realized or no, vengeance has been yours."

"Vengeance?"

He moved closer, insinuating his knee between hers. "Aye, for allowing you to be injured, for putting you directly in harm's way."

Cate rolled her eyes. "I told you, I don't blame—"

"If this is me penance, then rest assured, I'm suffering, and shall suffer it, if that is your wish."

He moved deeper forcing her legs further apart, leaving her feeling stretched and exposed. "In the meantime, it's not gone beyond me comprehension that I denied you, I left you wanting."

"So, passion denied can cause suffering, as well," Cate mused under her breath.

"What?"

She turned her head to hide her amusement. "Nothing, nothing."

"I feared you might be—"

"Peevish?" she asked, looking up.

With the single bell flashing in the dim, he displayed that boyish smile, the wheedling one, the one she could never resist, and he knew it. "Not quite the word what comes to mind when you're displeased. You know I can't tell you 'no.'"

Cate cupped a hand to his cheek. "Then pray don't start now."

Nathan lifted her by the waist onto the table. His eyes settled at the edge of her bodice with the same intentness of just before boarding an enemy. A quick jerk and her stays gave way, her breasts popping out like two ripe fruit. What he did there was delightful, very delightful, and then kissed her, commanding and rough with need.

He abruptly drew back, frowning with concern. "You're well enough? Your arm? Your leg?"

"What...? What arm? What leg?" She wasn't being facetious. It was just that, at the moment, they were entirely forgotten, and in every sense of the word.

Watching her closely, he ran an experimental hand up her thigh, smiling faintly at her failure to flinch or shy.

The hand advanced further between her legs and he hummed with approval. "It would seem we both started something, which now requires finishing."

It was something of a surprise that she—much unbeknownst—

had been going about in much the same advanced state as he. The ache, low and deep, which had been put off as residual from the tumble across the deck, was from a vastly different origin.

Cate fumbled at the front of his breeches, her hands suddenly useless blocks. With well-practiced ease, a one-handed flick on his part and the flies fell open. She buried her mouth into his shoulder, muffling the half-startled, half-delighted cry at being entered. Arms and legs wrapped around him, his straining back against her calves, she clung. He thrust, hard and harder, her rear landing on the table with a rhythm anyone within earshot would recognize.

They were accustomed to the lack of privacy, of coupling with the ever-present chance of an ill-timed rap or hail at the door. But this wasn't their cabin, and it was with the entire crew—the entire watch-below, at any rate—milling just beyond. More alarming was the fact that, if anyone was to break in, there would be no stopping now. She bit into his shoulder, on the verge of laughing at the ludicrousness of the situation, dimly aware of him doing much the same.

"Shh!" hoarse whisper, his lips next to her ear. "With me… now!" Bracing a hand on the bulkhead at her back, Nathan drove harder, reaching his end.

A small, whimpering sound and drumming her heels on his rear begged him not to stop, not yet, not now! A few more strokes, and she arched back and then fell forward against him, burying her cries into his chest.

They stifled laughs into each other, at the elation of their finish and the thrill of having done so undiscovered. A cough and shuffle of feet just outside, laughter at someone making a jest, revealed just how close they had come.

His mustache bristling against her neck, Nathan chuckled, a rumbling which vibrated from deep within her. "I knew I came to the right shop."

Cate could only woodenly nod.

The bell rang—eight times, she thought—as he set himself back into order. Feeling a draft, she looked down and tugged herself back into decency.

"'Tis the zenith. I must away," Nathan said, touching the band at his neck.

He drew up at the door, hand on the knob and announced loudly "'Tis a miracle a veritable laying-on of the hands."

A final tweak at her bodice, a parting kiss—as gentle as the earlier had been commanding—and Nathan left, leaving Cate a bit dazed and a lot breathless.

"That wasn't my hands," she called after him.

The bang-and-crash of the evening's gun practice was over, its residual smoke still hanging in wisps about the Great Cabin.

Cate sat in their sleeping quarters, on a stool before the mirror. Having brushed her hair to a degree of manageability, she now wove the semi-compliant sections into the single braid.

Nathan was sure to make an appearance. He always did; the uncertainty lay in whether it was before he reported for his Watch or if it would be his Watch-below, which meant four hours of idleness, or as much as could be for a captain. In theory, the pattern was an alternating one from one day to the next but, watch-bills being what they were, that wasn't necessarily the case. Demands of the many often overcame whatever preferences of the few.

If Nathan was to report, then Cate often joined him on deck. Many a night had been spent enjoying the merriment on the f'c'stle. Or sometimes, if it was quiet as that night promised, they sat on her box seat and watched the sea flow past while Nathan regaled her with tales of the constellations.

That night, however, Cate made ready for bed. It was remarkably early—the sun had barely dipped—to be thinking of that and yet, for some odd reason, that was exactly what she was doing, whether Nathan was able to join her or not.

She heard him come into the salon, a second pair of steps indicating that he wasn't alone. Canting her head slightly, she followed his path to the table, presumably either checking a chart or making a log entry. Low words, a directive of some sort, and his accompaniment left. In the mirror, she saw him draw up at their quarters' door, weapons and shirt in hand, dripping from his customary stop-off at the scuttlebutt.

"What are you doing?" he asked in full fascination.

Cate half-turned in her seat. "Braiding my hair."

There was a momentary struggle not to laugh. "You know that won't answer."

"I know, but I just had this sudden need to assert a bit of orderliness... somehow." The act was an oddity even to herself. The routine, one deeply instilled as a child, had somehow been lost over the years, perhaps when starvation and depredation made the effort too costly.

Crossing his arms, Nathan leaned against the door jamb. Years at sea had molded him in many ways: the ability to fall asleep in an instant; the ability to wake instantly alert; an inclination toward orderliness; a strong sense of duty and chain-of-command... and the ability to find fascination in the most trivial. He did so then, watching as if the eighth wonder-of-the-world was unfolding before him. And so, she slowed her motions, prolonging the mutual entertainment.

He straightened as she tied off the end with a bit of ribbon, mildly disappointed at the show being over. Perching on the edge of the bunk, he fished out Celia's vial from a tiny pocket inside his waistband. Already with well-practiced ease, he flicked off the silver cap and dropped a single drop on the cuff at his wrist.

Cate turned her head, pressing a finger under her nose. It wasn't quite as putrid asafoetida, but it certainly called it to mind. "Does it hurt or feel any different?"

"Nay. Don't feel it a'tall, truth be told."

That was somewhat reassuring. She hated to think it might turn into some kind of long, slow torture, curbing the free-spirit that he was.

"What, in all which is holy, did you say to Squidge?" he asked conversationally as he watched the oil soak in.

Cate flushed, braced for the berating sure to come. "Nothing... much."

Nathan snorted as he applied to his ankles. "He's positively skipping on one leg—at his peril, I might add—going about claiming he aims to buy a coach-n'-four and set up as a country squire."

It was a ridiculous stretch of fantasy, but still Cate smiled at the mental picture of someone going about in the English gentry with a gold-toothed jawbone and collection of dried fingers about their neck.

"Will it really amount to all that much?" To be painfully honest, she had no true notion as to the actual extent of her pledge. The point had been whatever was hers would now be Squidge's, and she meant it, whether it meant a farthing, a crown, or a chest filled with gold.

"One could have called you Croesus before. Now, you might just pose as banker to the King."

"That much?" she said faintly. "I know you've sought to impress it upon me before, but it all smacked too much of fairy tales and pipe-dreams."

Nathan smiled up indulgently. "If it's naught but that, then it will require a pipe the size of the galley fires to conjure it."

"Well, I did make him a promise," she conceded.

"And unnecessary one, for I had already—"

"I know. But, a gesture was needed. After all, it was *I* he saved."

Nathan stilled, one brow taking a severe arch. "A point of which I am keenly aware."

Cate winced at the unintended barb. "I promised him—"

An abrupt wave cut her short. "Every man-jack aboard knows."

Cate bit her lip. Of course, they did. It was even more folly to think that Nathan wouldn't know every finite detail.

All points of his body attended, Nathan tucked the vial back into its hiding place.

"Very well," she sighed. "But I wonder if it should be written down somewhere?" She had little notion of the inner workings of pirates and their swag, aside from keeping a swag book and the more mundane aspects of deciding which is more valuable: a porcelain chocolate pot or a glass brooch. If she had learned anything about sailor—pirates in particular—with their layers of command, traditions and rules, there was most likely someone in the ship's hierarchy who should be advised of her arrangement.

"No worries there, darling. You have two hundred witnesses. They might forget their duty or the number of their mess, but they shan't forget generosity of that magnitude."

"And if I'm not about?"

Nathan stopped in mid-motion of pulling off his boots. "And just where do you fancy to be?"

"I don't know—" she said, growing somewhat peevish. "You've said yourself how quickly things can happen out here—"

"Of that point I am also keenly aware," he interjected sternly. "I just want to make sure my... my..."

"Legacy?"

"Well, not quite that, but—"

Shaking his head, Nathan chuckled. "Fear not, duchess. Your wishes are as common knowledge as the company rules. You know how fast that spreads. Lightning isn't in it."

Ah, yes, well, she had witnessed that phenomena more times than she cared to think.

Cate had the sense of having just completed her last will and testament. The oddity was of doing such a thing after one had died, she thought touching wood.

Nathan sat back, hand on his hip. "Am I the only one what finds the irony in one who doesn't give a fig for anything beyond her most immediate comforts would think to promise a man a world of riches?"

"I have everything I need," she said shyly, toying with the ribbon of her shift.

"And more's the pity," he muttered to a corner. "Alas, if only something so simple as a jewel might answer."

Something in his voice—frustration, futility—made her look

up. "You mistake, kind sir," she said softly. "I am *very* interested in jewels."

Cate rose and stepped nearer. "If you will recall, I spoke of one in particular in this very room. No, I tell a lie, it was out there." A cut of the eyes indicated the salon.

"Aye," he said cautiously.

She inched closer yet, now between his knees, and twirled her fingers in his chest hair. "I spoke of a black diamond."

The light of recognition touched the cinnamon flecks of his eyes. "Oh, aye?"

"Oh, aye," she purred. "Rough-cut and sharp-edged, and yet of the rarest quality."

Nathan leaned back, bracing on his hands, putting himself on display. The pose accentuated the square set of his shoulders and the column of his neck. With the hard angles and planes, softened only by the occasional curve, he was so much like that diamond: a product of nature, hardened by elements, its imperfections rendering it all the more valuable. The sight of him always stirred her, like someone of a more avaricious nature might view that jewel. Her fingertips followed the line of dark whorls, down the facet of his belly, to the top of his breeches.

She kissed him, perhaps a bit more aggressively than intended or expected, for he made a small, interrogatory noise to which she only pressed more ardently.

Finally, he pulled back and peered at her. "What is it?"

"Nothing."

The lie was apparent to them both. "You're not yourself. You're..."

"No, I'm fine. I just—"

Cate kissed him again, but he broke off straightaway. "Nay, something is amiss.

You're not—" He audibly gulped. "Yourself."

She sought to avoid his searching eyes. A finger at her chin made it impossible to evade him any further. "I... I don't know..." she began lamely.

There was a stranger involved here: her. She wanted, really, really, really wanted him. And yet, a larger part was detached, remote, disinterested to the point of verging on repulsion. She was going through the mechanics, but nothing stirred, nothing moved.

Cate leaned toward Nathan and surreptitiously inhaled, hoping she might find the magic trigger there, as she so often did.

Nothing.

Rising, he guided her by the shoulders to sit in his place. Hooking the stool with his foot, he sat at her knee.

Head bent, Nathan stared at the floor between his bare feet for some moments. "Is this...? Is this because of today, earlier, when I used you like a three-pence trug?"

She jerked, surprised. "Did I give the appearance of complaint?" Her recollection was that she had been far from the reluctant partner.

His lips pressed with the determination of extracting a confession. "I've kissed you in sorrow, joy, passion, jest and in fear of bodily harm. But this... you... this... isn't..."

His hand rose experimentally and — in spite of all her desires otherwise — she flinched. His mouth twisted with his point being proved. "I touched your bum and you flinched."

"It's still a bit sore from earlier," she blurted. It was no exaggeration: her fundament was still tender in certain spots.

"Hardly," he said, with a barely tolerant roll of his eyes. "Darling, I don't mean to brag, but I've been with enough... others to know repulsion when I see it."

"It's not that. It's..."

"Then what?" he demanded, testily.

"Please, believe me. It's not you. It's really, really not you, or anything you've done... or haven't done." As ineffectively as it was, she was entirely sincere. And yet, like any truth, the more it was repeated, the less convincing it became.

"Then who?" he declared, spreading his arms. "There's naught but two of us here. You're running out of options, I might point out."

Cate drew a deep breath. Such deep introspection wasn't her habit, and it didn't come readily. "You're correct: I am feeling... off."

Off. It was such an odd word, and yet it was oddly appropriate.

"It's me or something. It's just... Ugh, I don't know!" she surrendered, burying her face in her hands.

Balling her fists, she straightened. "We can try again. I'm sure I can—"

"Find the strength?" Nathan finished dryly. "Nay, darling, I used you abominably once. I shan't repeat that. Old Adam is strong, but I'm no satyr. Apology for one crime through committing another is being an offscouring scrub."

"I wouldn't call it a 'crime...'" she qualified.

"Aye, well, I would, and punishable by the law of any land you care to name."

He found her arm and squeezed it. "As I said, darling, you feel my joys, as I feel your sorrows."

They weren't "sorrows" she felt, but damn if she knew what to call it. After her resurrection, she hadn't been herself, but that had been far different. This was something... else.

Nathan leaned to brace his forehead against hers and sighed. "You would think once a day t'would be enough."

She smiled, resigned. "It's not, tho', is it?"

Nathan touched her cheek lightly and then drew away. "No, it is not." He plucked her hand from her lap and pressed the knuckles to his lips. "Come, then. Might I just lie with you, then?"

To tell him "no" would mean sending him off to walk the decks in the dark and alone, with her left in a similar solitude. Neither of them deserved that.

"Of course."

He doused the lamp and they curled up together, lying in the dark with a measured space between them, to deal with their disappointment and this new awkward state.

"Might I do this?" Nathan asked cautiously and slipped an arm about her.

"Of course." Now feeling thoroughly guilty, Cate wriggled back against him, not in invitation—as it might have been in the past—but in assurance. She basked in his nearness and warmth like a kitchen cat before a hearth, to the point of fighting the urge to purr.

He made little "pfft... pfft!" noises, blowing aside her hair, already worming free. "We've all the space in the world and here we are lying stuck together like two limpets."

"Do you wish me to—?" she said, coiling to move.

His arms tightened. "Not in life!" He sighed complacently when she resettled. "The only reason for all this was so that I mightn't beat me elbows raw, and the men snickering, knowing what I've been at."

"They know anyway, don't they?" Heaven help her, there were precious few secrets aboard.

"Aye, well, my pain shall no longer serve as their entertainment."

Seemingly on its own accord, her hand found his where it rested at her chest. Their fingers wove and re-wove as she traced the hard shapes of his knuckles. She knew those hands as she knew her own, perhaps better. What she knew them most for was the wonders they might wrought. Now, the wonder was the comfort and solace they provided, just by the simple act of being there. If she didn't need his cock, she needed him, his solidness, his support and—yes, of course—his protection, not just from whatever dangers lurked abroad, but there in the dark. That was where the true hazards awaited.

They had often lain companionably together, but for known reasons, clear to all involved, mutual agreement. This was a mystery to them both. It was worrisome that her body had suddenly gone foreign. Coming so close on the heels of Nathan's tribulations only made it worse.

Not many men could readily accept such a rejection with grace, although—if one was to believe a large number of married couples—it happened all the time. She had never been one to plead a headache or indispositions of any sort, real or imagined. She couldn't imagine what possessed her now. The greater problem was that such self-examination was exhausting, especially when there were no answers to be had.

"I can hear you thinking from here." Nathan's half-whisper broke her thoughts.

"I just—"

"Shh... Now, I'm going to take advantage of this glorious bit of neck just here," he warned. He pushed the braid aside and planted a kiss at her exposed nape, light and gentle, meant to assure as opposed to allure. "And then we shall find our well-needed and well - deserved rest, allowing our dreams to mingle."

Nathan woke with a start. A quick movement of some sort had wakened him—that much he knew—but there was no one in the room—that much he knew through a combination of illumination of the deck prism, eyes accustomed to the dark and a third sense which never failed him.

In that same instant, he also knew Cate was not next to him.

A searching hand confirmed as much, finding a warm—very warm spot, but nothing more.

He angled his head, listening for footsteps or the quarter gallery—a remote probability, for once abed she rarely rose. Nothing there either. All he heard were the sounds which occupied the larger part of his life: men, ship and sea.

That third sense still raging, he rose.

Pulling on his shirt—whatever it was, he'd not face it as naked as Adam—Nathan went out into the salon. First impressions were that no one was there either, but then his eye caught the ghostly billow of fabric at the window: Cate's shift. She was sitting on the sill, staring at the glowing wake.

He would have called out, but there was an odd solitude about her, one which begged not to be disturbed. More significantly, she was too precariously perched to risk startling. Instead, he silently padded across the room, out of habit avoiding the creaking planks and jangling his bells. He stood for several moments, near enough to feel the heat of her body, and yet not touching. Her head ticked with awareness of his presence and turned.

"I'm sorry. Did I wake you?" she asked, weak and with a strange tremor.

"No," he said, rubbing the sleep from his eyes. "I just woke, and you were gone." It was only a half-lie.

A movement, not quite a nod, acknowledged him, and Cate turned back to the view. Expelling a long sigh, she leaned her head against the frame. Nathan craned his head to look over her shoulder, in hopes of learning what might offer such a fascination at such an hour: frolicking sea hogs, a mermaid, a school of flying fish...?

Nothing.

Of course, there was the odd possibility that a lifetime at sea had jaded him, causing him to view it the same as a postilion might view his pike or a farmer his cow byre. With that thought, Nathan strove to see it through the eyes of one who came from a world of mountains and fog—so far as he could recollect, that more or less described the Highlands. He knew precious little of the country of Cate's native home; torrid summers and dust year – round, if the few times she mentioned were any guide. In any case, this vista would be in marked contrast and a possible fascination.

... If she hadn't been at sea for months already.

Cate made a small noise and tightened her arms about herself. "You're shaking." That he could see. "Are you cold?"

In lieu to the response which didn't come, a hand on her shoulder confirmed Nathan's suspicions. He shifted closer and wrapped his arms about her. She leaned back, pressing against him, cheek against cheek. His embrace tightened in hopes that he might somehow squeeze the tremors out of her. He felt a quivering hitch as she inhaled. She had been crying.

"What's amiss, darling?"

For a moment, he thought she mightn't answer. "I had a dream." He made a low encouraging, yet non-committal sound.

"After... after we first came back, they started. On the island, they went away, but now they are back."

Nathan fingered a bit of hair stuck in the tear tracks on her cheek. "What kind of dreams?" he asked, stiff with dread.

"I saw you... with me... or rather, her..." came in broken

bursts. She worked her head against his chest. "It's like before: lying in that cave..."

He nodded.

"It was cold and dark..."

No surprise there: it radiated from her, as if she had been immersed in those very depths. He shivered, the cold now penetrating him.

"... And the press of the water... and the loneliness..."

Nathan flinched. Loneliness had been his worst travail: the emptiness, the dissolution, feeling forgotten, the last soul on earth. It pained him all the more to think she was enduring the same.

"But you weren't alone, luv, were you?" he said, low and urgent. "Remember, I was there?" His arms tightened, and he pressed his cheek more firmly against hers. "Think back, see it, feel it: I was there, with you the whole time."

Her head moved in ascent, but not with the conviction he had hoped. As she had said, this wasn't this first time for these dreams. Neither was it the first time he had assured her. It was always with the same effect: like water off a whale.

"Someone, something is calling, pulling, beckoning me home. But it's not home, is it?" Cate twisted around to look at him, beseeching.

Nathan swallowed hard and attempted a smile. "No, darling, it's not that. It's..." He stopped just sort of uttering the word "nothing."

He cast a wary eye toward the luminescent wake. He'd seen the phosphorescence for a pair of decades, and yet now it took on an ominous, surreal air. He knew what lurked out there—both of them knew—but giving it a name gave it a credence which seemed tantamount to inviting it aboard.

"Come back to bed, darling. There's nothing here for us." Nathan aimed loathing glare over his shoulder as he turned away.

With coaxing, Cate rose. She leaned so heavily, Nathan was obliged to half-carry her back to their bed. He gathered her against him and held her. At length, she slept, but it was not her usual deep, sleep, with the little frown between her brows, leaving him to stare at the deckhead.

⌒⌒⌒⌒

The bell rang; it was his Watch. Nathan reluctantly slipped out from next to Cate and reported for duty.

In the general way of things, it was sweet sailing: wind

steady, flowing sheets, neither tack nor brace touched. The Watch lingered near their posts, chatting or taking a caulk. Wishing only the freshest eyes aloft, he bid the look-outs changed every other bell. His ship hummed along, pleased and content.

The Morning Watch had always been Nathan's favorite time, for it was in those small hours one found the nearest thing to privacy and solitude. Still, he paced the quarterdeck, catching himself time and again at the taffrail or hances, staring astern at the wake and eternal expanse of sea beyond. It was easy enough to understand how all the wild mariner's tales arose. Stare long enough and one's eyes obliged, seeing all manner of things. Mermaids, sirens, krakens, leviathans, jinn, hydra: the only thing which changed were the names.

"If only it were that simple, if only were just foolishness," he sighed, looking down at the cuff on his wrist.

Night terrors had plagued Cate since the day she came aboard. Those, however, had only entailed screaming, the likes of which would wake the dead. True enough, resurrection would haunt anyone—it certainly had done so to him—and now a different sort had beset her. He had held her through those on Dead Goat, had chased her up and down the strand as she wandered like some bereft soul. The tragedy of it was that the visions weren't just manifestations of an active imagination, but fact, cold, hard, unyielding fact, ones which could still fill his nights were he to let down his guard.

God help him, he'd almost told her tonight they were "nothing."

No one appreciated their dreams being dismissed out-of-hand, when every nook of their being knew they were far from "nothing." On that he could top-it the expert. If they were "nothing" then what suddenly and so abruptly jerked one from their glorious repose, sweating and shaking? How could that be if they were "nothing"? Perhaps, like so many other human conditions, only suffering it themselves would convert some to true believers. Find the most sympathetic and you've found the most haunted in the room.

The dreams had abated whilst Cate had been among the women. But now, they were back, rising from the very sea upon which they sailed, the same and yet so very different, hauntingly and disquietingly and perplexingly different. Now, she was silent, but walking the floor.

His greatest regret was voicing his concerns about that hydra-of-the-deep rising, seeking to snatch Cate from under his very nose. He had planted the notion, and now it had taken root in Cate's imagination and grown...

He should have told her, set her mind at ease. Although, in truth, neither of them would ever enjoy that, knowing the treachery which lurked in that harridan.

He had elicited what amounted to a blood vow: her blood — as if she ever had any — and his. It had been the nearest to a guarantee that Cate wouldn't, *couldn't* be taken. She could never perish at sea.

No, it wasn't immortality. He'd never saddle her with that curse. Illness, accident — like crushed by a mizzen gaff? — could still take her, but only if he wasn't about or was somehow rendered incapable of calling in his chips. Of even more prime importance, she couldn't take Cate and use her against him, not like before.

Yes, it was peace-of-mind. One which fell far short of its intended goal for, in truth, he knew to his marrow that the she-devil couldn't be trusted, would go back on her word on a whim. If anything, the best he could hope for was hesitation, the essential time which might be necessary to renegotiate. If it meant, in that mortal time of peril, having that small second chance, then a grand success it was!

He should have told Cate, and yet to do so would open up to questions, being pressed on that which he didn't wish to be pressed. God help him, he would have had to lie... And she would have known, the deception glaring back from those jade eyes-of-a-Vera Cruz-idol.

Dare he hope that was all it was?

It was the end of his Watch, the beginning of the First, when Nathan walked into the cabin, expecting to see Cate at-table, as was her habit.

She wasn't there.

The crown of Kirkland's head could be seen through the companionway posts, a pair of eyes peering over the edge. A lift of Nathan's shoulders asked the question; a resolute shake of the bald head the answer. A point toward the night cabin brought a hesitant nod. Nathan drew up at the curtain and lent an ear. Low, almost too low to be heard over the backdrop of the ship, he could hear restlessness and a muffled moan.

He pushed in to find Cate in bed. Lying curled on her side, knees drawn up, his first thought was that she had been bladed...

He soon learned a blade would have been more merciful.

"I'll be fine," she ground out, tight-lipped, fists clenched.

Bloody hell! Had the woman ever said that and actually meant it?

"Is this because... because I was too rough... today?" he asked haltingly.

Her brow furrowed deeper with trying to smoke his meaning. Finally, her mouth screwed. "Hardly." Sensing his skepticism, she reached out and found his arm. "Honest, this has nothing to do with that."

He would have been more appeased if she had managed to utter it in something more than a wheezing rasp.

"Is it...? Are you... losing...?" His mouth moved in search of the suitable expression.

By some miracle, Cate smoked that meaning straightaway. "A child?" Mussing her head against the pillow, she smiled, one tightened by pain and tolerance. "No, it's not that, either," came only slightly firmer.

He swallowed down the urge to demand how she figured that? It looked damned near the same to him. The whole thing — standing there, helpless, witnessing her agony — like another time in the not-all-that-distant past.

Dry gripes, bursted bellies, fits, strokes, palsy, wharf fever, ague: he could think of all manner of maladies which might strike so hard and without warning as render one so incapacitated, and yet none seemed fitting just then. Kirkland's concern indicated that she hadn't left the sleeping quarters, so no injury there. A glance about the room searched for some indication of fall or other incident, but in vain.

"Then what...?" Nathan stopped just short of coming off far testier than intended.

"It's just —" The rest was lost as a spasm struck. Cate's grasp tightened on his arm, grinding the bones together. She curled tighter into herself, chin hard into her chest. She shook like an over-strained shroud on the verge of parting. Finally, whatever the hell it was eased, and the grip relaxed.

"It's just my courses," Cate said with what breath she could regain. He leant forward, thinking surely he had misheard.

"You're what?"

She rolled her eyes. "My course, monthlies, although they aren't not quite so monthly in my case." A good portion of that was nearly lost in the pillow.

"This? This! This is more like dying!"

"I know. I'm sorry." The last pinched off in the high-pitched squeak of tears in the offing.

"No, no, it's not your fault," Nathan said, patting her shoulder. "It's just—" Lord deliver him, he was at a loss.

Pulling up the stool, Nathan sat, bringing his face more to her level. He brushed the hair back from her face, so that he might see it: crumpled, blotched, and swollen.

"What...? I mean, how long...?" he asked delicately.

"Just a few hours." The answer came in the breathy exhalation of bracing against another onslaught.

He swallowed down a retort. Hell and furies, how long had she endured this already?

"And then it will pass," she added.

Given her current state, Nathan doubted that, too.

He had been around women, of course, score upon score, but somehow had always, somehow avoided *this*. Certain, ahem, associations had extended beyond a month's time—a handful, no more—but those had involved nothing more than slight indispositions, being off their feed for a mite.

Cate unclenched a fist and found his hand. Hers was like a block of ice: cold and hard.

"I know what it is, and I know what to expect... and I know, in a bit, it will be over." Her eyes clamped shut, and she grunted with the effort of riding out another spasm.

"Very well," he said stiffly. Well, now, at least he knew the name of his enemy. "What's to be done?"

She shook her head and mumbled something into the sheet, something he didn't have the heart to ask her to repeat.

He ventured to kiss her temple; it seemed the least likely location to hurt her, rearranged the quilt about her and stepped away.

A weak "Nathan" stopped him at the curtain.

"Aye?" he asked, turning back.

From the dark, shapeless hump came "I'm sorry."

"Suffering saints, what the—?" He checked himself. The quiver in her voice suggested tears lurked so very, very near. Pressing might provoke a full deluge.

"S'all right, darling—" He stopped, for she had drifted off into a well-needed rest.

"And long may it last," he muttered to the room.

⁘

Millbridge and Kirkland met him at the door, hovering like two sheep-herds separated from their flock.

"She sleeps. She desires quiet. Let there be silence aft of the main. And I want *someone*," drilling them both with a look, "in attendance at all times. Do. Not. Allow her to be alone. If she calls out for anything, *anything*, I'm to be told."

Eyes rounding as if he had suggested they abandon guarding the royal jewels, the pair solemnly nodded.

"If there is any, any crisis or change, pass the word on-the-double."

"Is she in-straws?" Millbridge asked delicately.

Plague and confound him, if only it were that simple. "She represents it is the curse – of-Eve."

They uttered a sympathetic "Ah" whilst at the same time retreating, Millbridge forking his fingers, as if the curse might strike him.

Bloody hell!

Never, *never* had Nathan felt so helpless. Having had some experience with sisters, a wife and daughters, Kirkland at least knew enough to bring bricks from the ship's hearth wrapped in flannel, instructing that they be placed at Cate's womb, back and feet. They answered, at least a bit, the furrows between Cate's brows softening.

Nathan offered spirits of some sort: rum, port, wine, brandy...? "No brandy!" she cried in an almost panic.

Port, then.

It worked.

She fell back into the pillows, eyes clamped shut. Slowly, she relaxed. At one point, she stirred and reached for him. "Lie with me, Nathan. I'm cold."

He doubted it, not with bricks fore-and-aft and the room now the temperature of a roasting fowl. At first, he was afraid to touch her, as if somehow she had gone as fragile as an egg. Only when he was next to her, her back to his chest, his arms about her, did she become the one he knew. She hadn't changed. She wasn't some manifestation of an unknown creature. It was, indeed, her, and a good portion of his worry and reserve went by-the-board. All was not lost, everything he ever hoped for not gone. Her bum against his hips, a hot brick between them, it was still her, still his heart.

He stroked her cheek and temple, and rubbed her neck until she drifted off to sleep. Careful not to jostle her, he slipped out and left.

⌒≈⊙℮≈⌒

Something, something had to be done.

That thought prime in his mind, Nathan headed for the blood-room first.

A search proved Cate had filled the ship's stores and blood box with cures for every injury and malady as could be imagined for a ship full of men. Not one corner of her supply had been given to feminine complaints. He went through the provisions Celia sent. Surely, there would be something for women in all that. Alas, he stopped, realizing he wouldn't recognize it if he held it in his hand.

"Whatever, *whatever* her wishes," he said to the room.

Cate was still, for the most part, a child-of-the-land, and might yearn for it. Land was in their lee, a few hours, at most. All she need do was give the word. Even if it were a place he preferred to avoid, a hell-hole which he strained to imagine what it might provide, at least it would be action.

Nathan felt a pain and looked down to find his fist clenched to the point his joints popped. He made a singular effort to open his fist where it rested on the table.

Not in all his extensive encounters with women had he ever experienced anything like this. Oh, aye, he'd been with them, knew of their courses, but never had he seen one doubled up, as immobilized as if she were in child-bed. Men sweated and pissed themselves at the prospect of battle, at the possibility of their blood being spilled. Women faced that spilling with every cycle-of-the-moon.

Nathan glanced at the sky. It was daylight then, but his mind's eye could still see the yellow, half-orb which defined women's lives. The Lord knew what he was doing when he gave the curse to women. One couldn't help but wonder at a world where men bore Eve's curse. They would have never left the shores of Egypt; Alexander would have never left town.

He ran a hand down his face. If Cate could face this with resolve, so could he.

But something, something had to be done.

Inquiries were quietly made, seeking those among the crew who were known to have wives, sisters, or sweethearts, anyone who might offer some level of enlightenment or understanding. Overall, they were an uninformative lot, capable of only dribs and drabs, and most of that superstition—The bleeding was good for cooling a woman's emotional hysteria—or what seemed to him old wive's tales—the blood would cure leprosy. Amid a lot of eye-rolling and shaking of heads, came some delicate, well-meant suggestions were offered—Where was one to come up with burned toad ashes or sage ale? And no, under no circumstances was he going to use the blood as an aphrodisiac! The only thing consistent was the men's thankfulness that it wasn't them.

Nathan returned to the sleeping quarters a few hours later, armed with at least a few answers and a small pile of necessaries. A minute corner of his mind clung to Cate's assurances of "only a few hours" and had half-expected, nay hoped to return to find exactly that.

Perhaps it was those hopes which made the situation he found seem all the worse.

He was met at the door by a sickly, sanguine smell, one which propelled his memories — so ardently held at bay — past his defenses. It was all too much like after Bridgetown, standing helplessly by as her life's blood drained out. Her moans merged with those heard back when she had been abused and beaten.

"And we call them the weaker sex," he muttered.

Trying not to breathe too deeply, Nathan deposited his burden on a locker and moved closer to the bed, where a dispirited dullness hung like Channel fog. Cate was burrowed deep in the bedclothes, only the top of her head showing. As rumpled as the bedclothes were — serious agitation would have been required to achieve that — she still lay curled on her side.

In a bare whisper, he called her name. The low, wet rattle of someone deep in an exhausted sleep was his only answer.

And so, he left her to that well-deserved repose.

Cate lay blinking into the darkness, waiting for the surrounding elements to finally coalesce into something tangible. Darkness was the first to present itself. That, combined with a thickness-of-mind all pointed to having slept long and hard. A slight shift of her head on the pillow brought the glow of lights around the curtain into view. Someone's presence in the salon was further confirmed by the scuff of shoe leather on wood.

Nathan, probably working on his log entries.

An experimental move confirmed that her innards no longer felt as if they might drop out. That had been replaced by the overall ache of having lain abed too long. She stiffly rose, pulling the quilt about her shoulders. One hand pressed to her belly, she shuffled out.

Sitting at the table, Nathan looked up from his log and frowned as she made her way to the quarter gallery. Ill as she might have been, it wasn't severe enough as to force her into using the chamberpot, placed so conspicuously by the bed. By the time she minced to her chair, she was beginning to consider rising might have been premature. The pillow from yesterday was still there, and she arranged it at her back.

"Should you be up?" Nathan asked.

Cate raised a self-conscious hand to her hair. The braid of the night before was naught but a bit of ribbon about a snarl. Puffy, frumpish and frowzy, she must have been a fright. She didn't possess the wherewithal to do aught about it. If her appearance was too much to bear, however, he would take his leave.

But Nathan didn't leave. Instead, he lingered, thoroughly pleased to see her up.

Kirkland appeared, hovering expectantly at the top of the steps. A night cap atop his bald head, he looked as sleep-puffed as Cate felt. "Might Sir desire something...?"

She considered that there was something wholly odd about being referred to as "Sir" when they were deep in the throes of Eve's curse, but didn't have the wherewithal to point it out.

"A dish of tea, if you please," she said, instead.

The request earned her two gape-mouthed stares.

Nathan was the first to break away, muttering "Tea, forsooth!"

Kirkland recovered enough to ask "And in the way of sustenance...?"

Cate's stomach took an ill-boding lurch at the notion of another of his possets. "Just something soft," she blurted, heading off any further suggestions. "An egg, soft-boiled, and —"

The receding patter of feet cut her off. He was gone.

Nathan grinned. "You've given the man reason to continue to live."

He returned to his writing, one eye fixed on her in hopes of an explanation for this startling variance of habit. Silence was her answer, for she couldn't explain why, just then, tea seemed so much more appealing than coffee. Perhaps it was the time of day, or rather night, she amended with a glance toward the darkness.

No, tea sounded enchanting, along with something in the way of a bit solid. Not custard or soup — even sippet sounded too heavy — but something her soul might cleave onto. The faint whiff of toasting soft-tack drifted up from below and her hopes grew.

As Cate sat there, the ship pitched. She winced, bracing her hand to her lower abdomen. She hadn't been physically ill, but her stomach felt like she had been retching for hours. Nathan lurched up and went to the door. There, with the hook of a finger, he beckoned a crewman. After a low exchange — looking too much like orders being given — he returned to both his chair and his task.

"What did you just do?" Cate had her suspicions and wasn't pleased.

A flutter of fingers and a blithe shrug sought to evade her query. He finally dissolved under her insistent stare. "I bid the boluns eased a mite and the helm to fall off a point. We should ride easier."

She opened her mouth to object but, feeling the ship's motion ease, she desisted. "T'wasn't necessary," she said, instead.

"T'was entirely necessary." Pen pausing in mid-motion, Nathan looked up. "We are neither chasing, nor being chased. Hell, I'd bring everything up all-standing, rouse the boats and pull the barky, if I thought it would allow you ease."

The pen continued its path across the page with even more deliberation. "After all, there's Squidge and his broken leg to consider," he offered off-handedly.

Cate mumbled an inarticulate appreciation. Once more, a ship-load of men being inconvenienced because of her.

"It's only my monthly. Surely, after... I mean, with your vast experiences, you've experience enough to be aware of that much." She was reasonably successful at not making it come off as a reproof.

"I've been with enough to see them —" Nathan stopped, keenly aware of the hazardous territory he was navigating. He swallowed and forged on. "Most have been... discommoded," he finally landed on. "None loomed at death's door." The last came with an accusing cut of the eyes and thoroughly wretched look.

The onset came with a resigned sadness. She and Nathan knew what it meant, just as she and Brian had known: another month and no child. It only confirmed the "curse" aspect: a harsh, wrenching, bloody exhibition that her womb, once again, bore no fruit.

"Women don't die from it," she pointed out. *Although, at times, one might wish it.*

"And how the bloody hell is a man to know that?" Nathan huffed.

"The worst is over."

A severe cock of his brow revealed his opinion of that.

He stopped, pen poised. "And it happens like this...?" "Only a few times a year, thank heavens."

"Thank heavens!" he echoed, mocking.

"I explained before."

"Aye, but I was… distracted. I never credited that it meant watching you nearly die before me eyes."

Typical Nathan, what he didn't say was what screamed the loudest. Beneath the surface laid a seething whirlpool fed by worry and, above all, a suspicion of deception. Her variance of body habits being too extreme from everything he knew, he suspected her of hiding some graver condition, all evidence to the contrary.

She wearily rubbed her temple. How does one go about disproving a lie which had never been told? Sometimes it required the speed of a coursing-hound to keep up with Nathan's machinations. He should be one of those new novelists, for he certainly had the imagination of one.

"We're all a bit different," she conceded. "For me, the worst is the coming; the rest barely lasts a couple days."

His concern was touching as was his naivete.

"It would appear, Captain, that there are still a few things I might teach you about the fairer and weaker sex."

"Nothing fair, nor weak about what you just endured." He looked up incredulous. "*Every* month?"

Cate smiled faintly. "Only for some. 'Tis nothing mortal."

In the midst of Nathan's incredulous sputter, the tea came. His hand moved toward the spirits bottle, with the apparent intention of lacing it, but then withdrew and took up the pen once more. Cate poured, took a sip and sat back, the glorious restorative powers of the brew radiating through her.

Nathan's anxiety made Cate regret having not mastered herself better, for having put him through such worries, and so needlessly. Often, she had pondered as to whether the irregularity of her monthlies was a blessing or a curse. They were so far apart, she tended to forget the severity. Was she totally honest, this onset had caught her unawares. Starvation and hardship had rendered her so irregular she had to count back on her fingers to recall the last one. Before, in her younger days, when the pains had been even worse, brandy or laudanum had been dosed. Now, with age, they were endurable without such heroics. But perhaps, that stoicism wasn't the best path. She should have submitted to spirits or whatever else was offered, not so much for her sake, but to appease him. She resolved the next time—if and when it should ever come to pass and if, *if* Nathan was about—she would have to figure out how to be more circumspect.

Men were too off-put by the whole thing, let alone keep track. Although Nathan doing that very thing had brought him to leap to some unfortunate and misguided conclusions with violent results. She had explained, and they had reconciled, but apparently, as he had just pointed out, she had finally found his limits, what rattled him the most: Eve's curse.

"I put a pile of... necessaries on the locker, pins, too," Nathan said over the scratch of the pen.

"Yes, I found them. Thank you."

"I have no notion of what your—ahem—traditions might be," he went on, without looking up. "But given... everything, just, uh... just toss them out o' the quarter gallery."

A reflexive surge of economy made Cate want to say she couldn't possibly be so wasteful. Practicality's voice brought her around to the wisdom of Nathan's advice. Beyond the not-so-small matter of washing the soiled cloths was the even more— heaven help her— prospect of where they might be hung to dry.

"We've sailcloth galore," he assured through the flash of ivory.

The pen stopped once more as he looked up. "Might there be anything else?" The inquiry came with the uncertainty of his knowledge on the matter having reached a premature end.

"I'm not an invalid. I'm just—"

"Neither are you in full feddle," he announced sternly. "You are 'discommoded' and we'll leave it at that."

Of all of the things they had suffered and shared, this was the one for which she wasn't prepared, although Nathan—bless his soul—took it in the same matter-of-factness as he took on everything else.

"I suppose everyone knows." She winced. Of course, everyone knew! It was a bloody, damned ship.

Hovering over her dish, Cate slid an uneasy eye toward the door and the deck beyond, and then the skylight. Living in a small circle of family and servants, a woman's monthlies were as routine. It was the same now, except that circle now included some two hundred sun-baked, weathered and battle-scarred men. She had yearned to be amid people concerned for her welfare. Well, here it was, in all its grim glory. She passed a hand over her chest, to see it there was a big, red "E" pinned there.

She shifted at a twinge, her womb still feeling like a fortnight-old mush. "I'm sorry."

With a soft thump, Nathan closed the book and sat back. "We seem to be saying that a lot of late." Looking off, he sighed, his shoulders dropping. "So this is what being together has brought us to?"

She couldn't tell if he was reproving or jesting.

"So it would seem," she conceded. "I remember Brian and I doing it a lot." Her and Brian's "sorrys" usually entailed long evenings of softening and smoothing hard or ruffled feelings. It might be the same with Nathan, if and when the opportunity finally presented itself.

So far gone in a brown study, Nathan seemed to not notice Brian's mention, much to her surprise and relief.

"Perhaps, it's just me. So much of the time, it seems my favorite word," Cate said, self-consciously. "If you care for someone, then you care about their feelings and treading on them."

She leaned across the table, extending a hand. "Having someone *is* wonderful."

Mouth quirked he took the offering. His thumb brushed the tender skin of her wrist. "Live at sea long enough, darling, and you learn how to take the storms with the calms."

The bell ringing ended anything further. He rose and came around the table to where she sat.

"May I kiss you?" The inquiry was timid, as almost a child to a parent.

She obligingly tipped her face up. He intended something quick, but a hand at the back of his head held him, allowing her to show him that she was far from a parent. A kiss no parent would give.

A preemptive cough from the stairs broke them apart. "I thought Sir might desire another brick," Kirkland said as he made his way across the room to the night cabin and back as inconspicuously as a grown man might. Cate's first impulse was to say it wasn't necessary—she had been enough of an inconvenience—but the thought of the delicious heat was too intriguing to decline.

"You'll be... well, then?" Nathan asked once Kirkland was gone.

"Entirely." Of that she was reasonably sure. As she had already said, no one died of this.

"'Tis a bit longer to the end of me Watch." Nathan gestured toward his chair. "I'll sleep—"

A finger to his chin drew him back to her. "Don't you dare," she said, teasing and yet so very earnest. "A brick is hardly pleasant company."

30: WHICH WAY THE WIND?

A S WAS HER BODILY HABIT, the pains went as quickly as they struck, leaving Cate—and Nathan too, or so it seemed—much relieved and much drained.

There was no missing that he was inclined toward tip-toeing in the process of his search through the numerous niches where the charts were stowed. Obviously in search of one rarely used, which meant that they were headed for unfamiliar waters.

At one point, Nathan paused by her chair to ask delicately "When might the next... episode...?"

"There's no knowing." Cate idly drew a line in the crumbs on her plate. "They are random, entirely random: it might be next month, it might be three-month or even four." And that was no fabrication. Alas, if they were; regularity, predictability would have been a benefit on a number of levels.

"There's no warning, no—?"

"Like a falling barometer? Like seeing three ravens, or a halo around the sun or a cat washing behind its ears?" she mused. She shook her head. "If only it were that simple."

"Like a white squall," he sighed. "Thank the wisdom o' the powers that men don't suffer it. Odysseus would have never left the house; Troy would have never been taken."

Cate couldn't help but smile into her morning coffee. "Rest assured, I shan't be just lying about."

Nathan stopped in mid-step and turned, hand on hip. "And why not? You're clearly not in full-feddle. You're sagging like a tops'l in a doldrum."

Well, it wasn't quite the words she would have used but, typical Nathan, his perceptions had the accuracy of a marksman. Spirit was what she lacked. She felt well enough, more or less. But, like that missing breeze, she was sadly lacking.

"When was the last time you did?" he demanded.

They both knew the answer: after Bridgetown, as she recuperated from Creswicke's depredations.

A brow arched up under the edge of his headscarf urged her past that to his grander point.

The word "leisure" just wasn't in her vocabulary; it wasn't a part of the language she spoke. The whole notion was so foreign, to utter it was like being expected to speak Greek. It was one part of that bodily habit. As a girl, her father hadn't been Dutch, but he drove everyone like he was. By his notion, Sloth wasn't a vice, but the greatest of sins. The mere suggestion of its lesser cousin Lethargy was cause for harsh words and harsh looks. As a married woman, there were all the commitments which came with running an estate. And when that was gone, and she was alone, any lazing about only allowed the wolves nearer to the door.

Nathan made an irritated noise, coming to the same conclusion well before she did. "You are the lady-of-this ship and as such you can jolly well —" he declared with an expansive wave.

She sat up, dusting her fingers on her skirt. "I can't just queen about."

"Queen you shall, should you desire." His mouth twisted as he passed by. "And, just upon personal observation, it's a strain to imagine you doing any 'queening'."

"If you don't wish to queen about," he said, reaching up between the beams. "Then don't go about: lie, stay, linger, lounge. Play cards, draughts, stitch, philosophize, count birds..." He stopped to peer down at her from under his arm. "When was the last time you read a book?" Hands occupied, an elbow gestured toward the shelves along the walls, and the piles scattered about.

The retort of "And when did you last read?" bubbled up. The lingering silence indicated that they both recognized that answer as being the same one as before: her recovery on Pine Island. To repeat that performance seemed to imply that she was equally incapacitated now, and that was nowhere near the case, she thought with a soft thump of her fist on the table.

And yet, damn Nathan and his perceptive soul, neither was she in full-feddle.

Cate leaned back, resting her head against the chair back. There was a certain achiness, a lingering malaise which drained her of all ambition. If in dire need, she could have risen to whatever the call... But, there was no dire need, no reason to stir. Soft pillow, comfortable chair, everything she could possibly desire was at her beckon. Perhaps it was age, perhaps it was the first signs of the corrosion of soft-living but, in the face of no chores, no obligations or duties, no demands, lounging about, at her ease, was so very, very appealing just then.

"Your leisure is at your pleasure, as is everyone aboard." Nathan straightened, his face brightening with the occurrence of a new tack. "Consider the grand service you might do us all by making full use. You can be as bone-idle as a duchess."

Crafty Bob, he knew how to play her, and it worked, just as he knew it would.

"Very well," she sighed.

Why did she feel like she had just sold her soul to Old Nick?

For the remainder of the day, in the spirit of placating the entire ship's company, Cate didn't venture beyond the salon. For the first time since Prudence was aboard, she fetched her sewing box and indulged in embellishing the neck of her shift with intertwining of vines and roses. She was shocked, and a bit embarrassed, to discover that at some point she had fallen asleep, dozing in a chair in the sun like an old grannie, waking to a shawl having been draped over her.

The next day, a still intransigent Nathan left her sitting at the window, putting the finishing touches on her shift. It was a domestic scene with Beatrice roosted on the companionway rail and His Lordship napping in the sun on the sill. Perhaps it was that peaceable and abiding setting, the absence of preoccupation or worry, which allowed her to become aware of a shift in the ship. Not the ship proper — she was sailing along, doing what a ship did — but in her people, a tangible oddness. Cate looked up a couple times with the sense of being watched. Living in close proximity with two hundred others meant eyes were always on her. But this was different; this was more in the way of being looked in on, assuring of her location.

At one point, she heard laughter. Again, not the usual which came after a quip or the day-to-day of on-duty. This was different. Leaning a bit, she could see around the mizzen and out on deck. There a group of waisters gathered, jiggling something in their pockets, and grinning, as pleased as Pontius Pilate. There was no mistaking the look of men on pay-day.

Except there was no such thing. Nor could it be gains from gaming or wagering; both were strictly prohibited.

Odd, very, very odd.

Twice more in the next short while, Cate caught small groups of two or three straying from their stations to meet, on-the-grin and similarly animated. As she stitched, she watched for a bit longer from the corner of her eye to confirm her suspicions. At the same time, her ear was cocked toward the companionway and below, where the axis of all activity seemed to originate: footsteps coming and going, low voices and bursts of laughter, rendered unique by its abrupt end, as if being hushed.

Putting down her work, she moved to the top of the stairs to hear better.

Hackles rising, Beatrice gave a shrill whistle. *"Avast and belay, you skulking swab!"*

From below came the sound of hurried footsteps, and Kirkland scurried up, bearing a pewter cup, its smooth surface beaded with sweat. Holding it out in offering, through gestures and flourishes, he steered her back to her chair. Only when she was seated did he finally hand it over.

She took a sip. "It's cool!"

The ship's cook made a dismissive flick of his fingers, a gesture oddly reminiscent of his captain. "Oh, hang it from a twenty-fathom line and it comes up cooler than from a well."

Much like a shrub, it was lemony and tart, and yet sweet, but there was something additional. Inquiries failed, another of Mother Kirkland's secret receipts, apparently.

Cate eyed him over the rim of the cup as she sipped, dancing first one foot, then the other.

"Thank you, Mr. Kirkland," she finally said. She made a show of leaning back in her chair and settling in. "This will make a fine accompaniment as I work." She picked up her needlework once more and poised the needle.

It took a few moments of more of convincing display, but Kirkland finally took his leave. Cate watched from the corner of her eye as he cast a final look from the steps to assure she hadn't moved. She remained for a bit, stitching and sipping — Mother Kirkland's concoction was very good — with all her senses pricked. Nothing had changed; if anything the crew had grown even more animated and, as a direct result, even more restrained. Curiosity finally reaching its crescendo, she put down her work and made her way to the steps. Beatrice jerked her head from under her wing, hackles rising.

"Shh! Don't you dare!" Cate hissed.

Hackles still erect, Beatrice angled her head to fix Cate with a beady eye. Kirkland still kept a plate on the table filled with enticements for Nathan; Cate plucked an orange from it and made a show of tossing it from one hand to the other.

Cate held it out in offering, but snatched it out of reach just as Beatrice reached out a claw. "For your silence."

The hackles lowered, the fruit delivered.

Cate's foot was poised over the first step when she saw His Lordship raise his head. "As you were," she said in the nearest approximation of Nathan's voice possible.

A few steps down brought Cate's eye in line with the bird's, now industriously peeling her treasure, a small pile of rind forming on the floor. "Who told you...? Oh, never mind." The answer was so very obvious.

Cate eased down the steps, keeping her weight at the edges on those known to creak, and slipped past the galley door, holding her skirts into silence. Few of the watch – below had slung their hammocks – another oddity – and so she had a clean view. Far forward – as far from her attentions as possible, she observed – a table was slung, a line of men before it. She heard the low murmur of a name being called and saw said man stepping forward.

Ducking between the guns, Cate advanced unnoticed. Nearer, Pryce came into view, seated at the table, writing in a book. Nathan stood at his elbow, a strongbox, one never seen before, opened before him.

Towers received something from his captain and knuckled his forehead as he turned away. So intent on whatever was in his palm, he nearly collided with Cate. He stopped dead, paled, and then gaped. A chicken-thief caught with a fowl in each fist and two in a bag would have looked less guilty. Someone in line gave a significant cough and Pryce leapt to his feet, Nathan going rigid, fowls apparently in their fists as well. The extent of their guilt suggested the crime to be far greater than what seemed apparent, for she was at a loss to figure out exactly what she had caught them at.

"Payin' out shares," Nathan finally offered.

As they stood there, their overt boyish innocence made it impossible to chide them, or even utter a cross words. Pickford, with his necklace of ears; Rowett and his trophy snakeskin vest; the massive Maori stooped under the beams: they had all scared her to morbidity her first day aboard. And now, they all stood hang-dog, looking like boys who had just been caught with their fingers in the pudding.

She moved closer and looked down. "What the hell happened to my book!" With certain heartbreak – and yes, a large dose of frustration – she saw her meticulous entries had been reduced to looking like Beatrice had dipped her feet in ink and had walked across it.

"Just notations, so as to keep track o'..." What Pryce was to have kept track of never materialized.

"They… *we*… I didn't wish to press you," Nathan explained.

She rather doubted that. There was only one in this band-o'-thieves who could have masterminded this.

Cate reached to pluck the pen dangling forgotten in Pryce's hand. "Very well, show me what's to do."

Cate checked off the name, called out the amount. Nathan made a show of counting out the coins on the table, witnessed by all present. The receiver made his mark in the book and then collected his share. It was the same for every man, the tedium allayed by working with Nathan at her elbow, and seeing the men's beaming faces as they walked away.

They must have been at this clandestine activity for a bit, for there were only a score or so names, and Nathan called it finished.

Cate sat back with the satisfaction of a task completed. She was rifling through the book pages, wondering how in the world she was ever going to straighten out the mess, when a notion struck.

"If shares have been paid out, then we'll be making port somewhere or another." She was a bit slow on the pickup. Perhaps she was, whether she wished to admit it or not, more reduced than credited.

He smiled at her perceptiveness. "Aye, the crew are all squared-away, but there's still the matter of the ship's share. We'll be needing to re-fit and re-vittle."

"I thought you said the ship was… umm…"

"Well-found," Nathan finished for her. "She was, until back there," he said, with a jab toward Wife Island.

Cate nodded vaguely, recalling the endless stream of boats and barges coming ashore, and the resulting heaps of stores.

It was one of the first times she had ever heard him speak in terms of economy— given her current state of protection and ease, she had almost forgotten what it was like to worry for money—and it sent her spirits sinking a bit.

"There's not enough in the box?" The gleam of coins could be seen in the bottom as he had closed the lid.

Nathan's mouth quirked tolerantly. "Nay, not near enough."

There seemed to be a point in all this lurking somewhere.

"The swag, then." She closed one eye and, after the briefest of estimations as to the costs of both outfitting a ship and feeding two hundred hungry mouths, she sagged. "You're going to need a lot."

She rose and turned, but Nathan's stopped her.

"Back yer tops'l. Done and done." He pulled a sheaf of papers from inside his shirt and thrust it in her hand. "A list, and copied fair," came with a mixture of pride at the accomplishment and dread of her reaction.

"You've an elegant hand," she observed as she leafed through.

"The schoolmaster claimed I wrote like a cat."

Secretly, she was grateful for his efforts, for it saved her a trip to that dank version of Dante's circle.

"You knew you were going to... to..." she began, suspicions rising.

"Sint Maarten."

"Days ago," she finished. After all his talk of "together" and offering her the world for a destination, it was a bit annoying to learn plans had been made and without a word of consultation. The fact that she felt entitled to harboring such expectations was even more dismaying.

"Aye, well, as of yesterday morn, at any rate. The selections have been made, noted," he explained, pointing. "All stowed and standing-by. All you need do is square-away your accounts."

Easier said than done, she thought, scanning the tightly written pages. "And they all...? I mean, everyone has agreed on... everything?" At her last sharing-out session, the assessing of the value had entailed endless wrangling over the last ha'penny's worth.

"Done and done" was delivered with all confidence. Still, she had her doubts that all was achieved with the ease he claimed.

"Very well, then," she sighed, gathering herself up for the drudgery ahead. "There's no time like the present." She reached for the book, only to have it plucked away.

"You are to lift nothing more than this," Nathan announced handing her the quill.

Before she could object, a meaningful clearing of the throat flushed Chin and Maori from the shadows.

"Neither shall you do stairs."

"I came down them," Cate pointed out with some asperity.

A cut of the eyes indicated his opinion of that.

"I'm inconvenienced, not incapacitated," she said testily. At the same time, she recognized a lost cause. There was no reason for blood on the decks over this.

He batted his lashed, affecting to have not heard. And so, they struck aft in an odd little procession: Nathan leading, Cate behind, Maori and Chin framing her like ushers in a church. Upon reaching the steps, she was lifted by the elbows, Nathan admonishing them from a few steps further up to "Bear a hand. Handsomely, handsomely there. Keep 'er at an even keel."

At the top, Cate was carefully set down, her two bearers disappearing silently below. Nathan steered her to a chair, sweeping aside the charts. The book and list were arranged before her the quill, previously plucked from her hand, returned. Once satisfied with the arrangements, he moved around to the other side and his charts. Taking the hint, Cate set to work. All too soon, however, she found the lines blurring together, and that she was checking off things already checked. Leaning back, she glanced out the stern window at the groove of their wake and then up through the skylight and the press of sails.

"We're sailing south?"

"South with a fair amount of west in it," Nathan corrected. Still, he was clearly pleased by her acumen.

She rose and bent to look at the charts before him, and then straightened. "You said Sint Maarten? I don't see it."

"This is current waters." Another was produced from underneath and opened. "There," he said, tapping.

Sure enough, there it was in his elegant scroll. "How far?"

"'Tis two days, perhaps less, if this wind holds."

She nodded vaguely; that qualifier went without being said.

Cate closed one eye. "Can't say I've ever heard of it."

"Probably not; French and Dutch mostly. England has had it, Spain too, at some point or another."

"French and Dutch: that's an interesting combination. What's the line down the middle?" Well, not quite the middle, but a line was definitely there.

"The border. The story goes they co-existed for a while, with all the niggling falderall which comes with that. So, they decided an official border was needed. A fractious lot they are, to say the least," Nathan said with a barely tolerant roll of the eyes. "They each sent a delegation walking from their respective sides, the border to be where they finally met. If one is to believe the stories, the French carried a bottle of wine; the Dutchmen, being the way they are, took a jug of jenever." He paused to shudder. "Dutch gin, most vile contrivance ever to be made; like drinking pine pitch. The jug being heavier, and the drink more insidious..." He shrugged, as if the rest were an automatic conclusion. "You know how those Dutch are."

Umm, no she wasn't quite sure what or how the Dutch were, but he was already well off on his hobby horse.

"I'd hoped for something more Spanish, that being your native tongue—"

"I grew up speaking English."

"Yes, but you speak Spanish like a native. But the wind seems settled on blowing us this way." He aimed an accusing glance up toward the sails. "It's not English, so there's no worries as to the authorities there."

"Oh," Cate said with a self-conscious laugh. "I'd nearly forgotten about that."

"Fair enough, but I haven't. And I'd wager the perfidious lot o' them haven't either, including His Bumptiousness, Harte."

Cate reddened at his bringing up that old bone-of-contention: his suspicions of what might have gone on during her time at Lady Bart's. So far as she was concerned, Harte was long gone, out of sight out of mind.

"It has a town?" she asked instead. Two could play his game of changing the uncomfortable topic.

"Aye, two, actually. You've a choice between going among the frog-eaters or the butter-busses. Papists abound, but that should pose no tribulation either." A sideways cut of the eyes asked the question and answered it. "Neither side is exclusive; there's enough o' one lingering about to make you glad there aren't more."

His jaw screwed sideways in thought. "The Dutch run the one. You've no Dutch, have you?"

"Umm... no." Her sum total experience with that language was limited to hearing Thomas utter a few which sounded like they might have been that, ones which were surely coarse words and therefore not to be repeated.

"Aye, well, Marigot it 'tis then." A thump of his finger on the chart declared the matter decided. "You'll have to bear with those frog-eaters, but you'll speak the language."

"Barely," Cate muttered. It would require a serious brushing up before her French could be anything near conversational. Yes, she had been to France, but she had ridden on the coattails of Brian's fluency.

"You can caper about free as a spring lamb," Nathan went on with a flutter of fingers. "No one will either know nor care. 'Tis a decent-sized town with a few shops, all the comforts and amenities, and a respectable inn what serves the best chowder this side of the Line."

"Where we can laugh?" she asked, remembering her request.

He stopped, his gaze softening. "Aye, darling, where we can laugh."

"What about you?" she asked, concerned. "Might you safely go about?"

He blinked, and then dismissed the notion of with a flick of the fingers. "Oh, aye. I've not lurked those waters for a bit.

'Tis all relative to whose ox you gore or, once you've gored it, who gets the choicest bits. Slush the right palms and you're allowed any number of transgressions and shortcomings. There's a Dutchman — a merchant, he calls himself — that's more scavenger than shopkeeper. He'll take any swag you might offer and present it to his customers with the sobriety of a monk."

"At a fair profit, of course."

Nathan grinned and winked. "Now you're thinking like him."

"So, it's a stalling ken." Cate jerked, wondering where a word straight from the lower streets of London suddenly came from?

Nathan was equally puzzled. "Aye, only ours is not stolen. It's taken, earned through out-witting those who would do the same to us. The finer point is that we know each other's ways, or rather more significantly, I know his. Where the bloody hell have the parallels gotten off to?"

He rifled through everything on the table and then moved his search to the desk.

"What's a Dutchman doing on the French side?" Cate asked, having joined in the search. Anything was better than the work which awaited.

"Making money," Nathan replied, coldly. "The Dutch could give the Jews a lesson on cutting a profit. They gave up their royalty so they might worship the dollar, instead."

"Don't let Thomas hear you say that."

Nathan made a caustic noise. "He'd be the first to say if, if he were."

"And yet, you do business with him?" Cate asked, stooping to look under table and among the chair legs.

"Cutting off one's nose — and every soul with a share — face if I didn't." An arched look drove home the point that she was included in that. "He pays the best prices because he knows I'll take me goods to the competition, else, which means a huge loss for him."

Her searching hand about the table encountered something hard. Clearing her throat loudly, she held up the implement in question.

"What the blazes are they doing there?" Nathan huffed as he came back to the table.

Plucking them from her hand, he bent to work. Cate watched in awe, as she always did. Spherical geometry could baffle a schoolmaster, and yet he did it in his head.

Cate sighed, feeling a bit deflated. "So this isn't entirely a pleasure trip."

Nathan glanced up from his calculations. "Not entirely," he reluctantly admitted. "The whole thing should take an hour o' me time, probably not even that. Then, I mean to squire you about, make everyone on that miserable rock turn seven shades of green."

Cate couldn't help but smile. It was something she hadn't done in a very, very long time. In a sizeable town, clothed, fed, all the comforts and confidence which came with that, free of fear of watchful eyes, threat of arrest or prosecution...

"Sounds like Fiddler's Green," she heard herself say.

"Aye, Fiddler's Green it 'tis!"

Sobering, Nathan paused, tapping the tip of his lead. Finally, he looked up and asked delicately "Will you be... up to it?"

"By then, certainly." On that she was confident.

"But it will only have been— I mean, doesn't... this... that... last—?" He coughed and went on stronger "I'd always heard references in terms of a week."

"For others, true, but as I said earlier, I'm... different." Alas, if only she were "normal." Perhaps a number of issues might be solved. On the other hand, she counted her lucky stars, for it was a daunting notion to have to deal with all this any longer than she did.

There was a double entendre in his query, however, one she perceived, but chose to ignore: would she be up to something more in the intimate line? These few days of abstinence — one by tacit agreement — were telling on them both. At her insistence, he had come to bed at night, but as they lay together, he had held her more as a comforting parent than lover. Intercourse was, of course, possible, but it presented a discomfort and awkwardness for all involved.

But now, Nathan was looking ahead. He was planning something, but what she couldn't tell. The hooded looks and change of subject — all so very familiar — were proof pressing the issue wouldn't be in vain.

She leaned across to look him square in the eye. "Whatever comes to pass, I will be ready."

He jerked a nod, clearly pleased.

"And so, a visit to the broker means all this." Cate held up the sheaf of papers. She could, of course, hope for some well-meaning spirit-of-the-deep to pop up and do it, but as Nathan often said, "If wishes were trees..."

"I supposed I must earn my keep, eh?" she said.

Nathan's grin broadened. "Just keeping a smile on the captain's face wasn't enough to earn your salt. Granted, the cat rarely comes out of the bag when you're about. We've not gathered the company for punishment this age n' more."

He was correct. The last she could recall was that unfortunate scene with John, and Nathan having to be the one to apply the cat.

Her musings stopped at seeing his eyes settle on her. Dropping everything, he came around and kissed her.

"What are you doing?" she asked, thoroughly surprised. They were at the table, with the doors open and in full view, in full violation of all his rules-of-decorum.

He kissed her again, even more firmly than before. "Kissing you, for the simple reason that I can."

"But what about them?" A canting of her head indicated the entire ship's company. They could have been looking; they weren't just then, but they could have.

He gave a mirthless chuckle "You are the lady-of-this-ship, as every f'c'stlejack to jack-in-the-dust knows. Consider that I would be brought up with a round-turn or rigged to the grate were I to be so foundering dim-witted as to not treat you as they expect you to be. Consider that you have two hundred protective uncles, all waiting to call me out, were I to falter."

31: FACADES AND FLOURISHES

CATE STOOD ANXIOUSLY AT THE rail as Sint Maarten's harbor opened and there laid Marigot, like a little festive jewel snuggled up against a hillside of green. It was a bustling port, the harbor jammed, but even at that distance one could see its Dutch flair in the orderly, brightly-painted homes of Upper Town. Those dwellings stared down their noses at the dingy and coarse Lower Town along the wharves.

Pryce drew up beside her. "Figures the Cap'n would a-droppin' anchor here." Seeing her puzzlement, he added "See that there yellow place yonder, with the blue shutters?"

Squinting into the glare of the sun, Cate followed his point to a bright yellow house. Situated behind the warehouses jamming the wharves, it was a three-storied affair with blue-delft shutters. Even at that distance, one could see the planters tumbling with flowers at its multiple balconies. A rose clamoring up one side and across the eaves, nearly obscuring the roof, was a testimonial to the establishment's longevity.

"That's Marguerite's," Pryce announced with an unseemly gusto. "The best whorehouse in these waters." The last came with an emphatic thump of his fist on the rail.

Cate stiffened, her anxiousness fading quickly into apprehension. Nathan had said he knew of a friendly destination.

Destination, indeed!

"Cap'n's already issued shares. Every man-jack has got a full purse and balls to burst, beggin' yer pardon, sir," Pryce added quickly, his face going an unseemly puce.

Neither was there any missing the men prettying and primping in anticipation, she observed shrewdly, her suspicions now soaring to the heights of the t'gallant mast. Pryce was most remarkable of all, virtually patting his foot, pacing the hances like an expectant father as they had rounded the island.

She turned at the sound of water splashing and found Nathan was the source, standing next to the scuttlebutt, bucket in hand. She had left him instructing Hodder near the forehatch. Now, he was naked. Refilling, he poured another bucketload over his head.

He was washing. Not in the evening, after the gun practice, as was his habit, but nearly the middle of the day, the sneaking dog!

Dripping and sputtering, he took his clothes from where they hung on a bitt and headed aft. No one paid heed, for everyone already knew which way the wind was blowing. Cate followed the trail of wet footprints. Not that long ago, upon their arrival at Tortuga, she had the leisure of warning and time to attempt to divert Nathan's attention from the pleasures which awaited. The operative word there, however, was "attempt." For all her efforts, he had still gone ashore. The exact extent of his activities she had never learned, mostly because ignorance was so much more blessed than knowing.

Now, she was faced with the same threat, and no paint hot... or pitch... or whatever the hell their saying was.

Damn him! Damn all his high-words, all his declarations and admirations. They had all just been part of a grand scheme to butter her up and soften the blow of going off... *there*! she thought, with a glare toward the yellow house.

As Cate saw it, she had few weapons at hand. She dismissed guilt out-of-hand; Nathan was rarely burdened by that. So, what plea was left: the possibility of injury; a fight breaking out? By his own admission, through some fluke of that damned curse, there was no risk of the pox? Long waits at Marguerite's...?

"As if Nathan would ever be left waiting," she huffed under her breath.

Anger? Tears?

Cate mouth a coarse word. None of those struck as sufficient motivation to keep Nathan away from those bright blue doors.

You have to stop this, she thought, grinding the heel of her hand into her forehead. *It couldn't be... He can't be...*

But only a fool would ignore the evidence to hand: bright and yellow.

Sure, they hadn't lain together in a few days. But it had only been that: a few days. Apparently, an intolerable lifetime in Nathan Blackthorne's book.

By the time Cate entered the cabin, Nathan had donned his

breeches and was standing before what served as his shaving stand.

"You're shaving!" Unlike his usual habit of using cold water, steam rose from the bowl and he was lathering up with her soap. This was primping up of the highest order.

Damn him!

"I am," he said, stropping his knife. "I would have done this at first light, but I wished it to be extra close," he said around the grimace of shaving.

He was humming, and chuckling to himself, as if to a private joke.

Indecision and desperation had her pacing. It was difficult to think with every voice in her head shrieking "Stop him!"

"You're making preparations," she said stupidly.

A sideways glance. "I am."

"You're... looking to go ashore."

"I am," Nathan said more cautiously. "As we have discussed this last days."

"You're going... there, to... to..."

Lowering the blade from his throat, he said "Marigot. Marigot," with the emphasis one might allow the dull-witted.

Nathan poised back before the mirror and tipped back his head. "What are you at? You've been giddy as a girl at the prospect." He stopped in mid-motion. "Why all of a sudden are you acting as though we're going to a charnel house?"

"They... Pryce... Someone..." A bulging roll of his eyes urged her to the point. "Marguerite's!" came out in a frustrated, half-tearful burst.

Holding the razor off to the side, Nathan visually followed her rigid point toward the stern window. With the *Morganse's* anchors having caught, the town—and the infamous house yellow and bright as a damned storm beacon—were now visible through it.

"Eh? Oh, aye, she's still there, eh?" He turned back to his task. "Well, I give her joy of her success."

Cate paced while he finished. If there were going to be hard words, she would rather do it without him holding a knife to his own throat. If there was throat-slitting to be done, she would be the one holding the knife.

"Wouldn't you rather stay here?" she finally said as Nathan dried off. She side - stepped to intersect his path. "Is there anything I can do to keep you from going?"

Nathan smiled uncertainly. "Why would I desire that?" He gave his brows a conspiratorial waggle. "I've been planning this for days."

He dodged around, shaking his head. Nathan could be single-minded, but she didn't think he could be that oblique. As she saw it, she only had one bargaining chip. Catching him, she threw her arms around his neck and kissed him. Surprised, he still responded warmly, a hand coming to rest at the small of her back.

She flicked his earlobe with her tongue. "Stay."

Her hopes soared at feeling his indecision. But then he held her away.

"Temptress." A sly smile grew. "And it is tempting, so very, *very* tempting. But why should one linger here, where so much more awaits there?" he ended, with a cut of his eyes landward.

He went where his shirt draped over the back of a chair.

"Nathan, please don't go." As she saw it, there was naught else but to beg, crawl, grovel, whatever it took.

"Why ever not?" was muffled by the folds as he donned it.

Twisting her hands, unable to look him in the eye, she gulped. "I just... wish... wish..."

"Yes?" he coached, head popping free of his shirt.

Balling her fists, she forced her eyes to meet his squarely. "I just wish you wouldn't go... *there*."

Nathan's face fell honestly blank as he tucked in his shirttail. "There?"

She pointed again. "Yes, there! Marguerite's!" Feeling like a shrewish harpy, she nearly choked on the word. For the love of heaven and earth, surely the man wasn't that dense!

The dawn finally broke, and he snorted. "You think me so rammish I mightn't pass up a nunnery?"

No one appreciated their greatest fears being laughed at and, damn his black-hearted soul, he was on the verge. "Sometimes I don't know what to think."

The bells in his hair tinkled as he stepped closer. "Well then, think on this: there is a tavern—very respectable—what serves some of the best chowder and sea-pie in these parts, this whole corner of the Caribbean, for that matter. It also has rooms upstairs, with very nice beds and," he said, a finger pointing skyward. "And—attend carefully, because this most salient point comes on the authority of me own personal observations— it is clean." He purred the last word. "Believe me—and I offer this conjecture with all honesty and without fear of retribution— your needs, your every need *will* be satisfied." His lashes batted with insufferable innocence.

He seized the gaping and dumbfounded Cate by the shoulders and bodily turned her. "Now, will you spread some canvas, show a leg and start shifting your clothes?" The last came with a gentle shove.

"I'm going?" she goggled, whirling back.

Nathan rolled his eyes in dismay. "'Tis what we've been talking about this age n' more. Honestly, darling, you're going as balmy as ol' Millbridge there."

He gestured toward the ship's elder, visible through the door. Out on deck, he sat in a bit of shade, passively watching the furor of squaring the ship away.

"I do wonder about him. He's not himself," Nathan added from the corner of his mouth.

Chastened, Cate's cheeks heated. "I'm sorry, Nathan. It's just..."

"Yes. Yes. I know." He flapped her concerns away as he pushed past. "Trust and old habits do make strange bedfellows, do they not?" He stopped to regard her. "I thought there for a moment, if there had been a knife to hand, you would have gutted me."

"The thought occurred," she confessed, head hanging.

Chuckling, he waved her on. "Tog yourself to the nines, duchess, so I might squire you about and let every misfortunate dolt we pass die of envy."

With a peculiar girlish thrill, Cate was half-handed, half-lifted up from the *Morganse's* boat to Marigot's launch dock. She shook out her skirts, smoothed her hair, and squared her tucker and hat. The sights, sounds and smells reaching across the harbor as they had rowed in had prepared her as to what to expect, but only to a degree. Now, taking Nathan's waiting arm, she forged forward.

The Lower Town was wedged in between the water and the hill at its back. In the late afternoon heat, the air was thick with the sweat of men and beasts-of-burden, dried hides, barrels of salted fish, molasses, tobacco, coffee, indigo, tea, rum. It was crowded, dusty and loud, and stifling, and she loved it! Like any spot where ships gather, it was a Tower of Babel in the way of languages, but the most pervasive was French. The complaining of livestock — cows, pigs and sheep — in their holding pens added a monotonous undertone.

Her only regret was her fan, still lying in the till in the Great Cabin. Nathan handily guided her, dodging handcarts, hurdles, laden slaves, and staggering drunks. His arm strong in hers, he kept glancing at her, as if half-expecting her to faint, or fall over, or fall-out, or whatever. He was clearly in his element, however, barely advancing a few strides up the wharf before he was answering becks and hails, often being obliged to stop for brief exchanges, shouting to be heard in spite of being virtually toe-to-toe. Parallel to their path, a group of Morgansers moved when they moved, stopped when they stopped, never farther ahead, always within easy hail.

The images on the shop signs were vaguely familiar: ropeworks, sail-lofts, carpenters, coopers, smiths of this specialty or that. Like any waterfront, the rum and ale houses were as plentiful as fleas on a dog, the same customers filing in and out, and slouched on the doorsteps. The whores were the same as well, perhaps a few more, perhaps a bit less dressed due to the tropical temperatures. Broad daylight notwithstanding, they were doing a brisk business.

In her new frock, one of the finer from Thomas' trove, she felt like a bright flower. In her other clothes, she could have slogged along in the muck and mire, and blend into the general squalor and no one the wiser. But now, she was aware of a good many taking notice, touching their hat brims and smiling as she picked her way along. Walking on an uneven surface which went from wood, stone, brick, oystershell and sometimes just placed dirt within a stride or two required the greatest of concentration. Typical of the Caribbean, it had rained recently, filling every dip or crevice with oozing pools of collective filth, which made her so very grateful for her new shoes.

"Shoes!? How...? I mean, where...? I mean...?" she had cried when Nathan presented them.

He had shrugged off-handedly, but grinned like a boy. "Just have to know who to bribe on that place and who was a saddler in their former life."

Whoever the nameless soul was, their training as something other than a cobbler was starkly evident: the stitching was lovely, but the finished product was more clog than shoe. The inelegance was only heightened by the bright blue ribbons tying them off.

Still, they were shoes, something of which she was in dire need.

Nathan pulled her aside just in time to avoid a train of hogsheads rumbling by. Shortly after, she was pulled the other direction to allow a dray team to plod past, the driver perched high atop the stacks of freight. Eventually, they drew up to a door with "*MM. Simon Donker, proprietaire*" on the sign overhead. They stepped inside, closing the door on the dust and chaos.

In the cool quiet, it took Cate's sun-dazzled eyes a moment

to adjust. She had expected a craftsman of some sort, sailmaker, or tinsmith. The tall desks and clerks indicated it was an office of some sort.

One of the clerks slipped down to meet them. "*Capitaine* Blackthorne," he said in measured recognition and a semi-civil inclination of his head.

While Nathan inquired for Monsieur Donker, Cate shook out her skirts and tweaked herself into respectability.

A flick of the eyes took them both in, and then a response was murmured in a disdainful sniff.

As they were led to a waiting area, they passed a small alcove where two men stood. London might have been leagues away, but Cate recognized a hired thugs when she saw them. Nathan nodded, whether in civil acknowledgment or recognition she couldn't tell. He saw her seated in a soft chair and then stood next to her, never allowing the pair his back.

"Where did you learn French like that?" Cate asked from the corner of her mouth. It hadn't been the gutter-French heard outside, but one fit for salons.

Nathan shrugged. "Advantages of having a French tie-mate for many months" came from the corner of his mouth.

Just before conversation became a necessity to fill the awkward silence, a delicate cough from the clerk beckoned them to a door. A scratch on the wood, a response from within and they were shown into a spacious office. It was opulence at its most tasteful, with rosewood and ebony furnishings, high-backed elbow chairs, Turkey carpets, and ivory, silver or gold appointments everywhere.

"*Le Capitaine Blackthorne et son ... associé*," the clerk announced, with another sniff.

Cate and Nathan were several strides into the room before the man sitting at a vast desk finally rose. Dressed in the tasteful attire of a merchant, he was a prosperous one, and didn't scruple to show it.

"Mistress Catherine Harper, may I name my business associate, Mr. Simon Donker."

Their host hesitated slightly at Nathan making the introductions in English, but then bowed. "Your servant, m'm," was uttered in an accent more Dutch than French.

Darting Nathan a curious look at her maiden name being given, Cate bobbed a curtsy. Donker arranged a chair and then invited her to sit.

"A libation, perhaps?" He flashed an engaging smile, one which leaned a fraction toward the false. "Captain Blackthorne prefers rum, as I recall. Perhaps he mightn't be familiar with this fine Jamaican one." The last came with the expectation of an imminent compliment as he handed Nathan the glass.

Nathan took the obligatory sip and gave a noncommittal grunt of near approval.

A glass of canary was thrust at Cate. Either the only thing available deemed suitable for a woman, or a woman just wasn't worthy of being inquired of her preferences. Its delivery came with a waft of oakmoss, musk, ambergris and a heavy dose of civet, which struck like a glove to the face. It was cypress powder, a very popular adornment for men during she and Brian's time in France. Brian's attempts to wear it had been abandoned, for it had given her a sick headache.

Nothing has changed, she thought, touching her temple.

She graciously accepted the etched-and-stemmed crystal, and sipped, masking the resulting shudder from the vile, insipid sweetness. She regarded their host over her glass. Some might have called Donker handsome; he bore himself in a way that indicated he seemed to think so. His Dutch heritage was evident in his fair features. His hair was too heavily powdered to be seen, but his brows and lashes where that Germanic white-blond. His eyes had the strange quality of being both bright, sky-blue, and yet almost transparent. As he moved, the paunch of impending middle-age showed, his jowls showing a tendency toward the puffy. If the paleness of his hands were any indication, the face powder was coals-to-Newcastle: he had the complexion women spent fortunes to gain. He was, if ever, touched by the sun, an indoor creature, in every way.

The tension between the two men could be cut with a knife. Cate looked on with marked interest. Since they had stepped over the threshold, a change had come over Nathan. He was stiff, officious, formal, and a facade she didn't recognize, that was for bloody sure. A glance at Donker showed no surprise, no curiosity, which meant this transfiguration wasn't unique to that day. And then, like a lightning bolt, it struck her who this transmogrify — and it was exactly that, verging on bizarre — was, who she was looking at. Before her sat who she had contemplated and yearned to see: Nathanael Blackthorne, the younger, the rising star on the East India Trading Company's captain's list. The propriety, the deportment, the social manners: logic dictated that one racing up the ladder of success would have been accomplished in them all. Their absence leading her to believe that hard luck and hard knocks had beaten them out of him.

Again, the what-ifs loomed: what if things had been different? What if events had allowed him to remain in that role?

Alas, what if...?

"I heard Lord Creswicke is dead," Donker announced without preamble.

Nathan's one brow arched. "You have long ears."

"I've always found the length of one's ears to be a direct proportion to the extent of their success," Donker mused with a meaningful lilt and a cut of the eyes toward Cate.

"One man's bane can be another's boon," Nathan observed.

Both raised their drinks in a toast.

"The world is a far better place without him," Donker declared.

"Speaking ill of the dead, are we?" Nathan asked amiably. "These waters weren't vast enough for you to cohabitate?"

The Dutchman shrugged. "The entire world wasn't large enough for Lord Creswicke. None but him were allowed a profit," was muttered discontentedly into his glass.

Nathan raised his drink. "Then I give you joy of your good fortunes."

Donker regarded Nathan with a certain shrewdness. "I daresay his demise weren't cause for tears on your part, either."

Nathan's one eye narrowed and Cate wondered just how much the man really knew about the rivalry: the common version heard everywhere, or something deeper and more detailed.

"I daresay," Nathan echoed, dryly.

Setting down his glass, Donker leaned back in his chair. "Might I assume this visit is not strictly for my fine rum."

Ah, so the social phase of the meeting was closed already.

"No oakum over your eyes," Nathan observed.

"I heard the *Morganse* was in. One can only assume that is for but one purpose." Unlike Nathan's, Donker's smile wasn't the easy flash of charm, and yet he employed it as if it were. It had a smug, oily quality.

It took Cate a few moments, but she came to realize that Donker's arrangement of her chair had put her directly in his sight-line, and Nathan slightly off to one side. Now, during this exchange, one pale brow worked in her direction and, behind the cover of a stake of papers and his glass, gestures were made. They were too abbreviated, too restrained to make out their exact meaning, but it appeared as though they were meant to beguile her in some way. With an innocent—and carefully noncommittal—bat of her lashes, she lowered her eyes to her lap with a demureness which would have made her governess proud.

Nathan sipped his rum. Making little smacking sounds, he held it up to the light and then peered down into the dark, amber liquid. With a small clearing of his throat, he took another measured sip. Donker rapped an impatient tattoo on the desk. For a man of his stature, his hands were small. Pale and soft as the rest of him, untouched by any sort of labor other than pushing a pen, they took on the appearance of mole paws.

Finally, Nathan reached inside his coat and drew out papers Cate recognized as the swag list. With a dramatic flick, he opened them and cleared his throat. "Forty bales of jardiniere silk; a score of Garthwaite..."

Donker sat up, his ears pricking like a hound's. "Out," he directed to somewhere behind Cate, where the sound of a pen scratching had come.

The scratching stopped. The moment the door closed, Nathan continued.

"A six-foot silver epergne, silver punchbowl set, gilt-and-velvet elbow chair..." Nathan droned, tracking the page with his finger. He had the vision of a hawk, and yet just then, he read with a myopic squint.

Cate mentally read along; after pouring over the list, she knew it virtually by heart. Before, she had supposed the list to be random, perhaps as the items had been roused out of the hold or as they were packed up. Now she saw the genius at work. In typical Blackthorne cunning, the most sought after — and hence, the most valuable — were at the first. This theatric had been planned days ago.

An abrupt wave from Donker — the one Nathan was obviously anticipating — cut him off. He reached to deliver it to the impatiently outstretched hand. The pale eyes jerked from side to side as they scanned the tight script, the wheels of calculation visibly whirling behind them. His mouth rounded in an involuntary whistle as the sums arrived.

"There is everything to render any abode a palace and its mistress a queen. There are even a few things beyond the most fertile of imaginations," Nathan added, with a teasing grin. He coughed and examined his nails. "The only decision to be made is to whom this trove is to be delivered: here or down the street?"

Donker snorted. "You've always come to me."

"Then this could well prove to be the first day in a new way o' life."

The Dutchman pointedly studied the sheets. Cate sat very still, sipping her canary. This was the side of piracy of which few were aware: the converting of taken goods into cash. It struck her as wholly unseemly, and yet so very essential. Perhaps the stakes weren't as high as in the midst of a battle, but Nathan's livelihood and the welfare of his ship and his men were on the line. There might not be blood, but lives were being saved or lost just the same. If there was to be blood on the decks, then let it be Donker's. Nathan had called him a "grasping cove" and, unlike his tendency toward over-stating, his analysis had been spot-on. Greed oozed from the man like oil from a fish. Every pound of profit lost would be like drops of blood.

She had thought to be the forgotten one in the room, until Donker looked up, and she suddenly knew how a mouse felt when Artemis, the ship's owl, spotted it.

"Hmm... I don't see you listed here. Nathan doesn't usually traffic in livestock, but I like what he is offering now You look expensive, too." The oily smile grew into a leer. "My price is so very dependent upon what it includes."

Nathan's foot thumped the floor, and he sat bolt upright. "She is under my protection."

"Not done with her yet, eh?" Donker's gaze never wavered from Cate. Finally, he sighed. "Ah, well, too bad—such fine, fine skin—she'd bring a good price." He finally broke away and smiled at Nathan. "Just don't used her too hard: 'tis bad for the market prices."

As Donker returned to his list and calculations, a silent battle of wills ensued between Nathan and Cate, the former insisting that they take their leave that instant, the latter insisting they remain. Whatever the affront, it hadn't been severe enough to stop seeing this through. It ended with Cate prevailing, Nathan still seated, but stiff and glaring.

Donker grabbed his glass and took a large drink. The bargainer in him yearned to play coy, yearned to equivocate and qualify. The merchant in him could only see profits and would allow none of that.

A greedy grin broke out, but was quickly checked. "I couldn't possibly be expected to buy a pig-in-a-poke," he said, assuming the sobriety of a judge.

"No one suggests that you should," Nathan said shortly. "I know your quality, as you know mine. Rest assured, the trinkets and gewgaws have been reserved for the less discerning."

Cate wondered if the two men were familiars enough for Donker to recognize a Blackthorne on the verge of erupting. She gathered her feet under her, braced, wondering how effective she might be at pulling Nathan off the man once he set about him. At the same time, she became aware of a low buzz of voices coming from just outside the door. They were female, increasingly more strident, and ranging from demanding to wheedling.

"Me men and the swag are standing-by, at the ready," Nathan prompted. His patience was drawing to a quick end. "'Tis just a matter of who is the lucky receiver. Just as a reminder," he added, holding up a cautionary finger. "Once it lands, there will be no wearing about."

Donker's eyes slid from the list to Nathan and then to Cate. "Throw her into the bargain and I'll—"

Nathan launched to his feet, fists balled.

"Sit, sit," Donker waved. "Apologies," he offered, in a barely civil inclination of his head.

With visible effort, Nathan's hands opened, but he remained standing, rigid and fuming.

Donker rifled through the pages again and shook his head. "Tell me, Miss—"

"Mistress," Nathan corrected.

"Mistress... Henry..."

"Harper," Nathan hissed through his teeth.

Donker inclined his head, barely listening. "Tell me," he directed to her. "Is he circumcised? He had to be, for he bargains like a Jew—"

"Enough!" Nathan roared in a tone known to make a f'c'stlejack blench.

So braced for a fight, Cate was a bit taken aback when Nathan only offered to hand her from the chair and start for the door.

"Yes, of course, I'll take it," Donker huffed.

Nathan jerked a nod. "You know how to find me."

For a large man, Donker moved with amazing speed coming around the desk to seize Cate's hand and kiss it. "It has been a pleasure. My most fervent wish is that we might meet again." A little extra squeeze punctuated his point.

Cate pulled away, wiping her hand on her skirts.

The door opened to a small throng of women, a half-dozen or so, and more arriving. They weren't, however, those seen strolling the docks. These were the gentry, some in their finest, others clearly having made a hasty exit from their homes. Hair and bonnets askew, some had the wind-blown look of a speedy carriage ride.

The clerk, now looking thoroughly harried, was doing his best to herd them. The thugs sped from the corner moving to intercept the surge of women. Nathan pulled Cate into the vacated nook, and arm extended to protect her as the mass past.

"*Capitaine!*" shrieked one at spotting Nathan and powered forward.

Coin purses being waved, demands and sums being shouted one over the other.

Nathan took Cate by the arm and steered her upstream and for the door.

"*Patience, mesdames.* There is plenty for all," Nathan called from there. His hasty exit dampened by having to contort his body to avoid colliding with another seeking to enter.

Back out in the heat and glare of the docks, the scene was even more chaotic. The addition of carriages and dog-carts brought everything to a stand, the air now filled with the smell of hot horse and shouts of short-tempered drivers. Through the melee of bodies and conveyances, Ben could be seen waiting, gnawing on a meat pie. A brief nod on Nathan's part sent him scampering off back in the direction of the boats where the swag awaited.

Cate expelled a large breath she hadn't realized she had been holding.

"Phew!" Nathan declared, flapping his coat. "What the bloody hell is in that pomander of his?"

Cate shook out her skirts, attempting to do the same. "Cypress powder, I believe. It was very popular when we were in France."

A disgruntled "humph!" was his answer.

"Well, the business aspect of this venture is complete!" Nathan announced over the snort and stomp of the teams they wove between. "I'm your man."

"So soon? But don't you have to—"

He adamantly shook his head. "Pryce and the rest know the drill. The stuffs will be delivered and Lord Nicknackatory back there inform me of his price. I have a few calls to make," he equivocated. "But strictly that: just calls, to pay my respects, give me compliments and then be on me way."

"Old acquaintances," she concluded, her suspicions rising.

Nathan caught her meaning, saw the hook, but didn't rise to the bait. "I'll allow you to be the judge o' that," he said, offering his arm.

"Who were all those—?" Cate asked as they wove their way along.

Nathan drew up in a small clearing. "Eager customers," he said, grinning. He winked and leaned closer to whisper. "Me price just doubled."

"For a moment there, I thought—" Reddening, she bit her lip, for what she was about to say flattered neither of them.

"You thought what?" he asked with the caution of one who already knew the answer.

She drew a deep breath, for there was no getting out of this credibly. "Well, in my defense, there does seem to be gangs women wherever you go."

Muttering "What's a mother to do?" under his breath, he shook his head and struck off.

"They were shouting your name," she pointed out. At least, she thought as much; in all the chaos it was difficult to be sure.

"Nay, they were just shouting for the captain," he said, dodging another pair of women heading up the docks. "Hell, I could have been Hell-bound Bailey and they would have been after me. They were looking to go directly to the source and avoid the middleman."

Cate couldn't fault them there. She would go to much longer extents than that to avoid the man.

"But how did they know...?"

"They live on constant alert for a pirate ship to make port. It's the swag they desire; the men delivering it are just that," he said with a disdainful glare, twisting to avoid the skirts of another whisking past. "Most don't care what it 'tis, just so long as it's new and something what no one else has."

"So once again, you see yourself as some sort of Robin Hood?" He had more or less conceded to that title before.

Nathan bowed as best one might while walking and being jostled by the crowd. "Better to call us specialists in the way of procuring that which all others fail."

"If you believe some," he went on. "It's that and the money we spread about as we blow-our-jibs and kick up bob's-a-dyin' is the only thing between these islands and starvation."

Typical Nathan, he had found the proverbial silver lining in the cyclonic cloud which had blown him into piracy. Once more she wondered about that change-of-events and all which might have been different. Regardless, she could now relax on several counts: the old Nathanael Blackthorne was back, from the moment he stepped out back into his native realm.

"And you were stirring them up."

He laughed greedily. "The more the fair ladies of Marigot clamor at his door, the more he'll be willing to pay. Ah, *mon petit mere*...!"

Arms spread wide, Nathan forged toward a person — whether it was male or female was difficult to tell — sitting under a dodger, a small brazier at their feet. The massive body moved, and the sun caught the glint of gold. Large and ornate, many might have called the seat a throne. Closer, Cate decided it must have been a woman, for she looked to be wearing a dress of some sort. The thin fabric and the several wobbling mounds indicated that nothing else was underneath.

The turban-bound head came up at the sound of Nathan's hail and cocked like a bird listening. A strip of striped gauze covering her eyes, the creased face split in a toothless smile. "You have returned to me!" she cried in a grating rasp.

The head being roughly chest high, Nathan obligingly bent to meet her embrace.

The shapeless mass moved—it didn't seem like she actually stood, but it was difficult to tell—and bare arms came up to clutch him, flaps of loose flesh wobbling underneath. She then seized him by the cheeks and she kissed him, with a plunging assault of her tongue. It wouldn't have been a surprise if she had hitched her skirts for him right then. Judging by the spots and stains, it wouldn't have been the first, Cate observed a bit unkindly.

"*Mon petit chou noir et épicé.*" Two horny fingers tweaked his cheek.

"*Ma petit puce.*"

Cate looked off to hide her smile. She was familiar with the French way of affectations, but Nathan being addressed as "a spicy, dark little cabbage" was just too precious, especially with him standing there bristling with weapons. Although this vast hulk being called "my little flea" was just as amusing.

"My little pigeon comes home at last!" The great arm hooked Nathan in another embrace and shook him hard enough to jingle his bells. "You were like a little bee running from flower to flower," she said nostalgically. "Spreading the honey, no?" The great mass of body heaved with merriment.

Nathan slid free and brought Cate forward. "Mother Pattie Banana, may I introduce Cate. Cate, this is Mother Pattie," he announced with the formality of at Court.

Cate caught a movement behind the gauze over Mother Pattie's eyes and had the uneasy sense of being under keen scrutiny.

"You don't usually bring your own, eh... distractions," Mother Pattie observed. "Or, is this someone new for Marguerite's stable? Bartering in one in hopes of a fresher one, are we now?"

"She's more than just a distraction," Nathan was quick to say. "She's—"

The bare gums showed in another laugh, the great breasts jouncing under the loose fabric. "We shall see." Cate caught some reference to a jenny finding her donkey.

From Mother Pattie's brazier rose a most enticing smell. Cate looked down to find long slices of pineapple on skewers. Mother Pattie heaved forward to pluck two off and offer them up. Cate hesitated, but encouraged by Nathan, took one.

It was a surprise that, after such a warm reception—leading one to expect enduring an endless number of remembrances and recollections—Nathan was already taking his leave. Nathan slipped several gold coins into Pattie's palm and then made his adieus, embracing and kissing in the Gallic way.

Cate took a large bite of the pineapple, rolling her eyes in delight. The combination of sweet and tart had the added complexity of crunch and smokiness from the coals. The only other time in her life she had ever had the exotic fruit had been a bare nibble while at Court. "I would love more, but not at those prices."

Nathan snorted. "T'wasn't the pineapple I was paying for. Consider it a hostess gift, a token of her thanks. If nothing else, it's an indicator for any and all you pass that you've paid your tribute. Homage, security, passage, services rendered: call it what you wish," he said around the mouthful. He swallowed before adding "It's for her good wishes and goodwill."

"You introduced her as Mother Pattie Banana. But, she was selling pineapple." Not a single bit of other fruit was in sight.

"Nay, nay," he said with a wave of his stick. "The French word for pineapple is *anana*."

"Oh," Cate said self-consciously. After all, it wasn't as if the word commonly came up in conversation.

"Her name—or at least as I always knew it—was *Mon Petit Mere d'Ananas*. After a few thousand repetitions, it becomes Mother Pattie Banana."

As they turned up a street, away from the waterfront, Cate chanted it, but still failed to find the connection.

"How does a blind woman manage to see—?" she asked, thinking perhaps she was being played.

Nathan smiled at her naivete. "Consider her naught but the tip of a tree: the roots reach farther and deeper than what's seen. Nothing escapes her attentions."

"Is the pineapple smuggled?" Granted, in Europe, it was a vast rarity, widely sought and hugely expensive, but it was still a struggle to work out how something so inconsequential as a fruit could lead to such a domain.

"No, but she has controlled the market, makes bloody sure no one else manages to land any, and has eyes all around this island to assure that very thing. No one comes or goes without her knowing. She's had the corner on the pineapple market since the French frog's first landed on this rock."

Her extent of local history being weak, Cate had no idea how long ago that might have been, but she considered it highly possible that Pattie was old enough to have greeted the French when they arrived.

"Obviously, you've known each other—" she began.

"Long enough," came back with the finality that answer might suffice. Nathan finally relented to the expectant arch of Cate's brow. "Very well, we first met when... I mean, I first stopped to..." He coughed. "We first made our acquaintance when the walk to town was farther than one could bear."

Cate glanced the few hundred yards from where they stood to up the hill and the town proper and, more significantly, Marguerite's. The difference didn't seem that much, but...

"The eagerness of youth," she sighed.

"The goatishness of youth," Nathan corrected. "Men might have been spared the Curse of Eve, but believe me, the greater gift was the women being spared the Curse of Ol' Adam."

"Did I hear her say something about your father?" She was also sure she had heard something about "dash and stamina of a stallion" but surely she had been mistaken.

Nathan blinked, as if not having heard that, and then gave a disinterested shrug. "Probably just the confusion of old age."

Cate hitched her skirts and veered around a pile of ox dung. "Harper? I thought you said there was no risk from the Crown here."

So far afield, it took Nathan a moment to smoke her meaning. "Aye, there isn't, directly. That doesn't mean influences and connections don't exit," he conceded. "And no, I don't trust that grasping plump-in-the-pockets muckworm back there, what would pry the gold teeth out o' his own mum's mouth, nor anyone else on this foundering rock."

"But you do business with him."

The corner of his mouth tucked up grimly. "Aye, well, 'tis a very long spoon I brought to sup with that devil."

Up the low rise to the Upper Town they went. It was as Nathan had represented: a fair-sized town. Not quite to the scale of Charles Town, but large enough to possess several shops, a variety of homes and a market. It was toward the latter that he took her. It was late afternoon, and so a good many of the carts and stalls had packed up. Cate looked in fascination at the strange fruits and vegetables, Nathan offering his insights on many. The same cluster of Morgansers who had followed on the waterfront was still with them, always within sight, always within hail.

As they walked, that proper being from Donker's office made its appearance. They strolled with the formality of traversing in St. James Park. Nathan lost his elastic rolling gait of a sailor and assumed the stiff-legged one of a landsman. They walked close and yet far with enough space for propriety's sake, keenly aware of any familiar move on his part would instantly reflect on her, diminishing her status. It wasn't as if they were out to impress anyone, and yet they both desired to at least belong.

Respectability: she had forgotten how much that meant. As a girl, she had dismissed it as an annoyance imposed by one's elders. Now she appreciated its value, for it was through that that one belonged.

"What are you staring at?" he asked at one point. "See someone you know?"

"No," she said slowly, regarding him. "Actually, I'm seeing someone I didn't know, or rather, knew them and just didn't know they existed." Free of responsibility of crew and ship; no obligations, nor decisions begged to be made; no watching eyes, no expectations; no Bella or Creswicke or Harte: it was Nathanael Blackthorne at his purest, most natural state. He relaxed and chatted, genuinely laughing at a boy putting a pocket-sized dog through its tricks. He was still armed, still dangerous, still alert, but only in the way of the banal hazards of day-to-day.

"Really, darling, either you've had too much sun or Donker's canary was stronger than credited."

A combination of buildings, trees and distance blocked the sea breeze, and it grew markedly warmer. The sun beat on the crown of the shoulder-wide brimmed hat Nathan had insisted she wear.

"You're turning red as those peppers," Nathan declared and delivered her to a display of ladies' accoutrements which included a number of fans. Cate balked, insisting that she didn't need another; several were aboard.

"And that would be the grand point, would it not: they are aboard," came back tartly.

The crossing of his arms announced that he had no intention of getting involved in the selection process.

"You never scrupled to give your opinion on anything else," Cate pointed out as she surveyed the selection.

"Aye, but me mum also taught me the wisdom of never venturing to second-guess a lady's tastes, especially when it comes to fripperies."

Huffing her opinion of that, Cate set about choosing one. She hesitated at seeing the quality, befitting of the finest shops in London or Paris. It brought one to wonder how something so elegant had came to be in a street-vendor's stand. It occurred then that the answer was standing at her elbow, symbolically at any rate. It was physical proof of his claims: what came in at the docks below would eventually find its way to the fair citizens up there.

One was finally selected, in spite of Nathan insistence on one twice as large, twice as lavish and, no doubt, twice the price. Huffing in defeat, he paid, and she walked away brandishing it to its full capability. He was right, damn him, the stirring air was a welcomed relief.

As they progressed, Cate was aware of Nathan's name being whispered and the anxious points, a peculiar buzz following him. It wasn't the buzz of caution, of an outlaw in their midst; it was the buzz of impending good fortune. The *Morganse* had delivered not only a trove of vast proportions, but it had also set near two hundred ashore, their pockets jingling with coin. Those coins might only currently be crossing the palms of rum-shop owners and whores, but they were just the conduit, the funnel through which the wealth would spread.

He looked down at her from under the shade of his hat brim and grinned. "You turn every head we pass."

Cate worked her fan a little faster. "I was just thinking the same about you."

Nathan jerked, reddened and then mumbled something like "Hadn't noticed" into his chest.

"Nay, duchess," he said, glancing about. "That is envy, pure, simple, clean envy of me being with you." He took an unseemly pleasure at seeing her taken aback, her fan applied with even more industry.

Envy: it was a wholly foreign notion for her, rarely suffered and even rarer still to imagined receiving. But there it was now, she thought glancing about into several appreciative stares, and as bold as the *Morganse's* figurehead. It was an uncomfortable, but not entirely unpleasant experience.

A runner came up to hand Nathan a folded note. He took it, opened it, dramatically held it at arm's length, one brow taking a severe arch as he read. Making a disgusted noise, he ripped it in half and handed back a piece. "My compliments to your master, and tell him this is what he gets for that."

Over the next while, Donker's runner—now sweating and blenching at the prospect of having to deliver more bad news—popped up, Nathan tearing off incrementally larger portions and sending them back.

"Do you need to go back and—?" Cate offered.

"Oh, no," came back flatly. "He knows what's to be done, or better said 'offered' to gain what he desires. Better he be left alone to stew in his own soup."

As they strolled, the inevitable finally came to pass: they reached the limits of the space. A turn was made, crossing what served as the street, and Marguerite's loomed ahead. Until that point, Cate had successfully ignored it, but it was like trying to ignore a whale, a large, yellow, sprawling whale. Now, up close, the thing was even more rambling than realized, with wings running off in several directions. The house was doing a brisk business; the parlor apparently full, the overflow of waiting customers spilled out onto the porch and into a side yard, under the sweeping shade of a live oak.

Cate's grasp on Nathan's arm reflexively tightened, bracing against the green-eyed monster raging in its cage. Throughout the day, she had observed him carefully for any sign of wistfulness or temptation. She knew him well enough to recognize stilted artificiality or put-on-for-show disinterest. All she found, however, was disinterest of the most pristine variety, allowing the house the same regard as one might allow the horse trough.

Nathan did the civil, however, and acknowledged a call from a second story window as they passed the gate.

"Careful, darling, you're stiff as a preacher passing a pot-house on the Sabbath."

"I'm sorry, it's just—" Cate stammered.

"Yes, I know *just*." He knew better than to smile, but lost the battle, nonetheless.

Nathan rolled his eyes pensively skyward. "Let me see. Allow me to venture a guess as to what you are thinking..."

He closed one eye. "Have I been there?" The eye came down to fix on her like a falcon on a mouse. "Yes, more times than can be counted. Hell, me coin had to have financed that new wing and the new roof. Some lovely girls," he said, with the same dispassion as observing the weather. His arm tightened on hers, he lowered his voice to whisper "Not a one could I rise to now."

Looking up at that profile, sharp against the sky, there was a certain martyrdom about him. And, for the first time, she realized how justified it was. Never had she caught even so much as a yearning glance. She knew men well enough to know that if they weren't looking then they were dead, and yet, never, never did his eye even so much as threaten to wander. Not even when they had him by the ballocks, in the most literal sense of the word, did he waver. No hint of temptation, no contemplation of what he might be missing. Back at the island, never had there been a moment's stray, a wistful lingering, cause for concern, and it hadn't been for lack of opportunity. Now, there was a building full of whores and he gave them the same attention as he had given that pile of dung back there.

Cate found Nathan's hand in the crook of her arm and gave it a squeeze. "I believe you."

He almost missed a step. Drawing to a halt, his shoulder as a shield against the prying eyes, he fervently kissed her hand. "Thank you," he said, fervently hoarse.

As they walked along, Cate discovered, much to both her dismay and her pleasure, that the walls which had existed for so long between she and Nathan had been of her own construction. The barriers were gone now, and there Nathan stood, waiting. There were no masks, nor facades. To a large sense, there never had been. Nathanael Blackthorne claimed a lot of things, but perfection, flawlessness was never, never among them. From day one until then, he had allowed her to see him with all his warts and scars, and shortcomings and foibles.

He had never uttered the word "love" — it was entirely possible that, given what life had dealt him, the word had been stripped from him — but he had said it in an infinite number of ways. He had done for her as no other man might, performed deeds and acts many men would blench and run. But he had performed them as matter-of-factly as he did everything else life chose to pitch in his path. Reproach; recrimination, rebuke, blame: he didn't possess them, at least not where she was concerned. He was no knight in shining armor, but neither did he ever claim to be one. Absent one particular word, he had willingly and repeatedly pledged everything she had longed to hear. It would be the true shrew to demand more.

"Thank you," she said with all the sincerity possible.

Nathan frowned, puzzled. "'Twas just a fan—"

"No, not that, although I do appreciate it," she said, applying the thing a bit more industry. For so late in the day, it was warm. "I meant for all of this."

She threw her head back as best the hat would allow and closed her eyes, trusting in him that she wouldn't fall in a hole or step into some pile of filth. "I had forgotten what it was to walk about free, without worry, without wondering what eyes were on me, who might recognize or who might attack."

He looked away to hide the grin he couldn't contain.

"For a moment there—" She stopped and stammered. "Oh, it's silly."

"What?" came with an urging tug on her arm.

A curiosity-peaked Blackthorne wasn't to be denied. "Very well, just for a moment or so, it was almost—well, almost as if—"

"We were normal folk?" he finished, teasing and yet serious.

For just a few moments there, she was almost back in Charles Town, almost living what a young girl imagined what her future might be. She started to skip, but then remembered both her shoes — she was sure to break her neck, if she did — and propriety. Just then, they were the picture of that, or as near as one might achieve with a man wearing a battered leather tricorn and armed to the teeth.

"Do you miss it?" Nathan asked. "The island?"

"Hmm? No," was her first impulse. A skeptical lift of his brow made her to further consider. "I do miss the women... some women, women in general," she finally amended. "Not all, and not en masse, but..." She sighed, having nearly talked herself out of the point.

"Land under my feet was nice," she went on more definitively. She turned to look at him. "I don't think I could have been happy there, especially with you being so... so..."

"Ill at ease?"

She smiled unsteadily. That wasn't quite the word she was looking for, but it answered well enough.

"The milk-of-human-kindness certainly didn't abound."

Her step slowing, Cate emitted a delighted and covetous "Oohhh!!" at seeing a basket of ribbons on display. Fingering them, she found it was the same case as with the fans: they were of a quality common to the finest European shops, and sure to have come there by the same circuitous route. As she poked through she discovered a score or more of ivory bobbins, wound with silk thread in such luscious colors her fingers twitched at imagining what might be stitched with them.

"Anything catch your fancy?" Nathan asked. Something in his voice suggested that he knew the answer already.

"May I...?" she asked, looking hopefully up. Nathan rolled his eyes. "I said anything..."

In her halting French, Cate inquired as to price and the haggling began. Nathan shifted from one foot to the other, often interjecting when Cate's fluency fell short. The price was finally down to where Cate was to the point of trying chose between one and the other when Nathan blurted "How much for the whole bloody thing?"

The woman vendor stared; the air stirring at Cate's mouth reminded her to close it. While she was still listing all the reasons why such an extravagance was impossible, negotiations were concluded — including the basket in which they were displayed — the agreed sum handed over, and Nathan hailed a blackguard boy to deliver it away.

As they turned away, Donker's runner tugged at Nathan's

sleeve and shakily delivered yet another folded note. Going through the same dramatics, the latter opened it. "Very well, my compliments to your master, and tell him we have a deal."

An explosion of relief burst from the lad. Nathan fished into his pocket and tossed him a coin. "For the suffering of having to deal with that overblown, knight-of-the-road."

With a huge gap-toothed grin, the lad tucked away the coin, knuckled his foretop and sped off.

"All settled?" Cate asked.

"All settled, and at nearly thrice what I hoped for."

"And you called him 'a grasping muckworm,'" Cate mused.

Nathan struck an imperious pose. "I seek money for what it shall allow for my ship and men." His shoulders slumped and his mouth took a downward curl. "He seeks it strictly for what it will allow him and him alone."

"He doesn't have a wife or family?" Cate asked, mostly out of common curiosity.

"If he does, they're candidates one-and-all for martyrdom," he said with a judicious sniff.

They walked the town proper, a collection of perhaps a score of businesses which constituted the day-to-day life: draper, silversmith, apothecary, bank, solicitor, and the like. At that hour, most were closed and so they just peeked in the windows. The milliner had two of the most cunning little hats, and Cate curbed a smug smile at seeing the mercer's selection of ribbons was only a fraction of what Nathan had just purchased for her.

"I didn't catch how much, but I know you spent far more than was necessary. I didn't need all those. I could have —"

"What? Managed?" Nathan demanded, caught between a smile and a scowl.

"I just can't accustom myself to not having to —"

"Well, accustom yourself to it somehow or another, for 'tis a basic fact. 'Need' is a word to be stricken from your vocabulary."

"It's difficult to believe that —" She wasn't just being coy: it went against all basic nature. Even as a girl, her family was one of the grandest and yet, true to his Scots heritage, her father kept a very tight knot on the coin purse strings. Brian's family were lords-of-the – manor, and yet every pound and pence had to be watched.

"Well, figure out a way," Nathan said, in a tone nearing his captain's-command.

She stopped. Looking up at him, she pressed the flat of her palm over his heart. "Really?"

The coffee-colored eyes holding hers, his hand flattened over hers and pressed. "Really."

As they resumed walking, he tightened his arm about hers and gave her an admonishing shake. "You'll never want again. Say that, if you must, three times every morning wake, until you finally believe it."

The sun was dipping, the shadows growing long, when Cate finally admitted that her feet hurt. It seemed too much like complaining about a gift horse, but the discomfort was beyond being ignored.

Nathan brightened. "I know just the place."

32: TARTS N' TAUNTS

THE *LA SIRÈNE VIERGE* TAVERN's sign over the door was
remarkable in that, despite a lack of legs, the artist had
managed to depict the mystical creature-of-the-deep in a very
compromising position. As represented, the inn was one of the
nicer ones, several steps above the ones down on the waterfront.
It was far enough from the docks for a more elevated clientele,
where merchants, businessmen and ship-owners, those who
oversaw all that below, might gather away from the waterfront
rowdiness. Typical of most taverns, inside was low ceilinged,
the beams darkened by smoke and soot. It was clean, tidy, with
glass in most of the windows and no whores hanging about.
The owners were a middle – aged couple—well, perhaps a bit
beyond middle—and the serving bawd didn't appear of the
nature to spit on your drink... unless provoked. The smells from
the hearth fires weren't of old grease and burned pots, and the
thresh on the floor looked like it was changed in recent memory.

It was a surprise to find Pryce and a handful of Morgansers
there. Judging by the reception, they had been regaling all with
the adventures of the very man who now swaggered into the
room as if he owned it.

In a way, he did.

They were funneled toward a seat in the middle of the
room. By guile and guise, ostensibly to be better heard, Nathan
maneuvered them to a bench where his back would be to the
wall and her in between.

"Surprising to see them here," Cate observed under the
crowd noise as Nathan saw her seated. "One would have
thought Marguerite's would beckon stronger." Given Pryce's
anxiousness at making port, lounging about a taproom hardly
seemed likely.

"One must nourish the body before entertaining the soul."

"The food is that good?"

Nathan rolled his eyes closed and demonstrably smacked his lips.

Between the press of bodies and the lingering heat of the day, it was even warmer in there, and Cate sat fanning herself as she listened to one tale after another, as best she could decipher at any rate in the face of Nathan's rapid-fire French. It didn't help matters that he took the same liberties with that language as he did his native tongue, improvising words to meet his demands.

She watched going from amused to enthralled and back. It wasn't the first time she had seen Nathan in his full, public persona. That character had made his appearance some months ago in Charles Town. There, vitriolic with resentment, the persona had been wrapped in a heavy coat of showing away, strolling into the room amid accolades and cheers befitting a conquering hero. It had been a performance for her and her alone, with sharp edges of bitterness and rebuke. This was strictly a performance for the crowd, and what a performance.

Nathan was in his element, working the room like a thespian. It was a calculated performance. Always the stage master, for all his strutting and melodrama, he was never more than a few steps away, a barrier between her and the crowd. With each round, he grew a little more grandiose, his demeanor incrementally more drunken. With visions of a re-enactment of his drunken night on the island, Cate cautiously sniffed his tankard, under his knowing smile.

"Ale. The night's young." He winked and flashed a heart-stoppingly seductive smile.

"And I don't want to miss a minute."

Not much later, Nathan abruptly took his leave. Amid the crowd's objections, he bowed graciously and bid adieu. In a cloud of disappointment, he took Cate by the arm, and steered her to the back and a quieter space. Sitting on the bench next to her, he leaned an ear toward Pryce launching into a tale which remotely resembled their latest encounter, if one was to believe the foe had been an 80-gun, first-rate.

Nathan shook his head, quietly chuckling. "The man knows no bounds."

"Isn't that rather like the pot calling the kettle black?"

After attempting indignation, Nathan smiled, one of those easy, honest ones reserved for times of discovery. "At least I stay within in the world of credibility… at least a little more," he added defensively at her skepticism. "Most of them believed me."

Cate scanned the rapt—although with eyes drunkenly

unfocused—faces. "By the look of it, they're doing a pretty good job of believing him, too."

"A good storyteller is worth his weight in rum or gold. I've seen the cook flogged, just to keep the storyteller in subject matter. If for no other reason than for ones' own sanity, one needs to be able to tell himself a good tale."

"Talking to yourself to keep your sanity? That hardly sounds healthy."

"Then you've never seen the ravages of rampant boredom." He pushed to his feet and held out his hand. "Enough about ancient history. This night is for you."

At what served as both serving counter and desk, Nathan asked for a room. With a knowing smile, the wife-of-the-house came around to lead them upstairs. A shout of "Mr. Cate, sir!" in a quarterdeck voice stopped them.

Cate turned, almost colliding with Mr. Pryce, coming toward her as if he were on that heaving deck. The grey eyes, known to cleave a person to the bone with one look, were somewhat unfocused. With a bit of effort, they focused on her face.

"God n' Providence go w'ye!" Seizing her by both shoulders, he kissed her lightly on both cheeks. He stiffened, realized himself and spun away, nearly colliding with his companions.

"He's drunk-as-a-lord" Cate observed, watching his stiff-legged journey for the door.

"The old sot is bowsing up his jib, that's for bloody sure," Nathan muttered and guided Cate onward.

Candle on high, the proprietress led them down a narrow hall, past the common rooms—men to one side, women to the other—to a door at the end. A clatter of keys, the complaining squeak of moisture-hindered hinges, and they were bid inside. The light was set on the table and their escort turned to leave, a glimmer of a smile moving her stern mouth when Nathan discretely pressed several coins in her hand.

It was a corner room, at the back, away from the heat and noise. The grandeur was that being on the corner it had two windows, both standing open.

"More for that precious air of yours," Nathan said. The grin, which hadn't faded since they entered, did so then. "Here on land, all those do is allow in noise, dust and smell, and God only knows what the night air brings," he remarked under his breath. "But for you, it all seems to be the manna-of-life."

"And I see you're not without your water within view," she observed, leaning over the table to see out. One of the windows allowed a view of both the roofs of Lower Town and the harbor beyond.

"Aye, well, we all have our lifelines."

She carefully fingered the curtains, so worn and eaten by the sun, they threatened to crumble, but they were curtains, nonetheless. Nathan followed along with eager eyes as she took in each special touch. The day's purchases sat atop a stool in the corner. A small vase of flowers was arranged on the table and a small rag rug spread at the bedside. The mattress was lumpy, the counterpane stained and worn, but it was still a bed, a frame-and-rope instead of the boards. She pulled back the counterpane and — miracles of miracles — sheets, time worn, but freshly aired and pressed.

"Thank you, Nathan!" Bouncing like a schoolgirl, she made to throw her arms around his neck but was stopped by the restrictions of the frock. Still, she could kiss him, which she did with all the earnestness possible.

"I thought you'd like it," he said when she finally released him.

"Aye," he began at the silent question which hung in the air. "I knew it was here. And no, it was not in the company of... of... of someone of the female persuasion," he finally landed on. He braced for the jealousy which always surged at such a mention. Cate bowed her head, conceding her habit of gross and so very erroneous assumptions. "Donker keeps a room over on the other side."

"I worried that you might wish to go... over... there."

It required little for him to smoke which "there": Marguerite's.

"Oh, ye o' little faith. Why should I wish to go with some cob-handed, half-starved, fumbling stranger, when I can lie with one who has the most enchanting and skillful hands, a most enticing stretch of neck, and who knows me every like and every whim?"

His reply was made with a lustiness which almost made her forget her question, or even if she had spoken at all. If she had any further thoughts, they were rendered insignificant as he kissed her.

He was in the process of helping her off with her hat — the dress prevented her from doing that, too — when there was a scratch at the door, and a girl came in bearing a tray. A meal was laid out on the table and she left. With a bit of ceremony, Nathan uncorked the wine and filled the glasses. A tweak of the light and then the vase, and he turned, swept off his hat and ducked a bow.

"A table with a view for m'lady."

The meal consisted of bowls of chowder, thick wedges of fresh bread and butter. Cate couldn't help but smile at seeing a jar of honey laid along as well. Nathan could never be far without that.

"Oh, my....!" Cate cried at the first spoonful. "Good, isn't it?" Nathan said, clearly pleased.

Whether it was the freshness of the fish, mussels and crab, or the quality of the cream and butter, or the heady delightfulness of the sherry—of which there was a heavy, heavy dose—which made the difference, she couldn't tell. It was, of course, entirely possible that it was a combination of all of the above, but whatever the case, if there was such a thing as heaven-on-the-tongue, this was it!

She had taken only a few bites, her stomach calling out loudly for more, when Cate found herself staring, spoon poised in mid-motion over her bowl, at Nathan voraciously attacking his.

Gulping down a mouthful he said "Men have braved squall and squander for a bowl o' this."

Nathan made to take a bite, but lowered his spoon, scowling. "You're squirming about like someone who wishes they were somewhere else."

"Well, to be honest, my feet would love nothing more than to be somewhere other than these shoes. Don't get me wrong, they were grand," she was quick to point out. Considering the filth encountered on the wharf and streets, they had been a godsend. "But they really hurt."

"Then, for the love of... Take them off! Hell, I'll take mine off as well," he exclaimed, shedding his boots and flinging them into a corner.

A quick prying of one foot against the other, and she sighed "Ohh, that's so much better," and wriggled her toes inside the stockings.

As Nathan slathered butter on a piece of bread, he glanced at her and then away. "You looked prime today... the attire Thomas gave you and all."

Cate looked up at him over the candle. "That didn't come easily, did it?"

He cut a look from the corner of his eye and slowly shook his head. "Admission of me failure to provide for you doesn't come readily."

"Provide!" she cried over the clatter of her spoon dropping. "You've given me a home, a place to belong, a reason to live, and then my life to live it, several times over, by my count."

A skeptical noise made his opinion of that evident.

"Might I point out that I would appreciate a little of that leave as well?" she went on. So long as she had the floor, she meant to take advantage.

A long look from under his brows bid her to expand further.

"It would be so very much appreciated if you would allow me a hand in my own provisions," she said striking for a balance between anger and forcefulness. Her single hope was that her point mightn't fall on deaf ears, as so many times before. "I'm a sempstress by training; I'm capable of more than putting little roses on things."

A slight inclination of his head indicated that he was listening... so far.

She drew a deep breath. "For example: those stays the crew made...?"

A short nod.

"Whatever they were made out of would be very suitable for some shifts."

A brow twitched. "The sailmaker is as restless as you with staying busy. You'll rob the man of his purpose."

"I would have suggested it before, but I had no notion that you had such materiel about." The excuse wasn't as lame as it came off. She had, with all industry possible, searched the swag and wherever else she thought likely, and had come up empty-handed. The sailroom never occurred, for all she had ever seen come from there was only suitable if one wished to make a tarpaulin jacket.

The brow from under which he had been viewing her took a severe arch. "Darling, we live in a world propelled by fabric. We've a sail-locker filled to the deckhead and another brimming below."

Cate's first urge was to point out that the Number 8, or as it had been represented to her, used in constructing the stays wasn't the stuff of "propulsion" in any part of the ship she frequented.

"Haven't seen a tops'l or a skys'l unbent, eh?"

She resisted pointing out, with considerable asperity, that she wouldn't know a skys'l from a tris'l.

"Bonnets, moonrakers...?" Nathan was on the verge of mocking now, damn him. He shook his head, decision made. "The sailmaker can—"

"Ply his needle to his sails," she cut in firmly. "I know which end of a needle to clap on."

She caught Nathan's hand as he reached for the bread barge. "Allow me to be useful... please?"

There was another jousting of wills. Ultimately, it was Nathan who finally sat back.

"Very well," he sighed, spreading the butter with a force which tore the bread, causing him to butter his palm instead. Glaring, he reached for a handkerchief. "I'll pass the word to Scribbs that he has a new mate," he said, swiping his hand. "Try not to harry the poor man to the point of fearing for his position."

Pleased with her small victory, Cate picked up her spoon and resumed her meal.

"Anyway," Nathan huffed, bruised at his good intentions going unappreciated. "Me point remains: you looked very nice today."

Cate took a sip of wine—the selection a wonderful compliment to the meal—and sighed contentedly. "It was nice." And she meant it. "I'll have to say I haven't felt that grand in... in... in a long time."

Looking back to earlier that day, now she understood and appreciated all of Nathan's preparations: rummaging through her dunnage, selecting just that right frock, helping her shift into it, even going so far as to insist that she pin up her hair.

"If you must be married, then we'll use it," he had announced, eyeing her ring. At the time, she'd found it remarkably odd, for the very fact seemed to pain him. And yet, that day, he was virtually celebrating it.

True enough, she thought twiddling her ring between her fingers, the state of marriage brought certain privileges and allowances which were denied the single woman. Primary among them was respectability. The status provided that bit of caution, a warning to all that she wasn't a woman alone, she wasn't without resources or connections and, even more significantly, that she had a man willing to defend both her and her honor. She had always thought it stuff and nonsense. After all, she was the same person before the ring went on her finger as after. But the change in how she was received had been as tangible as the metal circlet about her finger.

Not to put too fine of a point on it, but she was in fact, not married, but a widow. That status carried a portion of the same protections, but she had always been hesitant to use the word mainly because of the reactions it inevitably brought: sighs, sympathies and inquiries to which there were no answers.

"You, duchess, were the envy of every man we passed. Not a one could keep their eyes from you."

She smiled in spite of herself, pleased by the simple notion of pleasing him, being a point of his pride.

"Virtually every woman we passed couldn't keep her eyes off you," she countered.

"Me?!"

"Yes, you. Don't pretend you aren't aware of your charms, and with you strutting about—"

"I don't strut!"

"Yes, you do," she went on over his indignation. "Although most of the time you can't help it. It's just the natural order of things."

"Aye, well, except for today," he qualified. "But I defy any red-blooded man to do else were he in my shoes, which not a one we passed didn't wish that very thing," he ended with a point of his spoon.

"If Donker is so important, why didn't you spruce-up a bit? At least a stock at your neck or something?" The prospect was framed in morbid curiosity. Cate had a rich imagination, but it failed miserably at conjuring the image of Nathan all decked-out.

Swiping a finger around the edge of his bowl, Nathan gave a half-shrug as he licked it. "I didn't wish him to be too impressed with himself."

He was interrupted by the arrival of the second remove: sea-pie, and a towering one it was.

"The true name is *cipâtes*," Nathan explained. "It means—"

"I know: six layers. I only see three," she said, probing with her fork.

"You count the pastry, not the layer in between."

"It still doesn't come to six," she said eying it.

"Aye, well, 'tis better the cook learnt her arts as opposed to her numbers, eh?"

Like the chowder, the pie was incredible, the crust light and flaky, deliciously oozing with juices of several meats, savory with spices, and done to a turn. It was quite the culinary accomplishment, except...

"I don't taste the fish."

"Because there is none. Well, aye," Nathan said refilling their glasses, "if you're at sea, and fish 'tis all which is to hand, then it would be naught but that, but then one imagines that we'd call it fish-pie at that point."

"But— Oh, never mind," she finally surrendered and ate.

Cate stopped, fork poised at seeing Nathan pick at his. "A bowl of chowder is all you mean to eat?"

A disinterested shrug was his answer. Cate shook her head as she dove into hers. "I'm not sure how you manage to hold body and soul together. You don't eat enough to keep Beatrice alive." In truth, his consumption of the bowl of chowder was probably the largest consumption on his part ever witnessed, but it was still a wonder sometimes as to what held body and soul together with him.

He waggled his brows over the edge of his glass. "Me body has other sources of nourishment."

Cate set down her fork and wished for her fan. The evening had suddenly become so very warm.

"I knew if Donker gets too full of himself, then he starts topping-the-knob and there's no dealing with him then. You, on the other hand," Nathan said, admiration aglow, "can top-the-knob with the best. You looked positively born to it, duchess."

"A far cry from that first day I came aboard?" she mused.

"Hardly. I knew quality the moment I saw it."

"It must have been the quality of my rear," she said, shifting on that very part, "considering that had to have been in the air as I was puking."

"Or ribs I could count from the main-royal bitts," he added with a teasing lilt. "I fancied there for a moment that the stories of a skeleton dancing on the bowsprit netting were true."

"I was a wreck," she conceded.

"Aye, the vision of that glorious rear was enough to turn me head. But there were those pink little toes..." Under the table, his foot found hers. "And this long, incredibly enchanting line of your collarbone..." reaching across the table to trace it. "And this..." tapping the end of her nose. He sat back. "Those breasts looking at me like two great pink eyes, and me heart was gone."

They smiled together at the memory, hers a bit more restrained. She had been exposed in more ways than one that day.

Nathan took a drink and smiled whimsically. "And then, you told me to go to bloody hell—"

"I said no such thing! I was too afraid to—"

"Not in so many words, but you were eloquent in your intent." He spread his hands as if in surrender. "You bit me, and I lost me heart."

For the most part, her first few hours aboard were a blur. She did recall being roughed up, her shift torn, baring her nearly to the knees. Her hand came to rest on her stomach. With the layers and layers of cloth, she could see more than actually feel the scars there. The tight cut of the bodice pressed on the one at the back of her shoulder. She rarely thought of either these days.

"And the scars didn't—?" she began.

"Those only revealed the spirit within, darling," he said, with an adamant shake of his head. "I knew you to be a fighter and a survivor."

715

He took another drink, rolling it thoughtfully before swallowing. "I did worry that perhaps you would be too much like the last one what caught me eye. Me record at that point was a mite tarnished, if you follow my meaning." He spared a half-embarrassed look.

Ah, yes, they were back to Hattie, again. Speaking of skeletons, one wondered what would be required to be rid of that old one in the closet?

"But then, I saw you attend me men." Nathan looked up, the candle's flicker in his glass matching the spark in his eyes. "And saw you had room in your heart for every one, that you had decency and caring in you."

She flushed and not entirely from his flattery. All the while, his foot had made a sinuous path up her ankle to stroke her calf. Now it slowly tracked back down, his toes doing the same at the inside of her arch.

"All that from just sewing up a leg and binding an arm?" she asked lightly.

"You did more than that," he said with an expansive wave. "You were down there for a Watch n' more, going from one to the next, until every one of those blackguards had been attended. I suspected a few of doing self-harm just so they might gain your attention."

"It wasn't admiration I was feeling with Maori following me about whacking that start at every falter." Her recollection might have been faulty, but the vision of him looming over her — massive, silent and somber — was eloquently clear.

Nathan snorted. "He wasn't whacking at you; he was fending off at any man what ventured to try you."

"Me?"

"You," Nathan declared with an emphatic point. "Granted, you were before-the-masts' dream come true: a fair lass below in naught but her shift." His expression softened to almost beatific. "I know I dreamt of it more than once, or twice, or… hell, a score o' times. T'was every man's greatest hope, Millbridge aside. In that gloom, you looked like a fair spirit flitting about."

"Is that what they told you?" She had a strong sense of being gamed just then, for the whole thing was a far cry from her recollections, however brief they were.

"Nay, 'twas seen with me own eyes," Nathan said, tapping his cheek.

Cate stopped in mid-bite. "You were there?"

Nathan ducked an emphatic nod. "Every minute, well, minus a couple here or there, perhaps."

Cate stabbed at her plate, wondering how one soul could be

so mistaken. Isolated and alone, cast-off and forgotten, thrown to the veritable lions was how she remembered it. "And I thought you'd gone off doing... doing whatever captains do."

His mouth fell open, eyes rounding in horror. "And leave you down there will all those slavering dogs? And believe me, a number were circling, Bullock and his lot, for one," he added when she meant to argue. "Shoulda just killed the skulking cur straightaway and saved everyone a grand dose of grief." The last came with a guilt-laden glance her way.

"You couldn't have known what he would—"

"Could and did," came back flatly. Nathan took a large drink as if to wash the bad taste out away. "He'd been a handful before; had to check him and his band o' snakes more than once. Every time I did, it only seemed to make him meaner."

Cate laid down her fork and leaned back, groaning. "I wish I could eat more, but with these stays so tight, I don't dare."

"Then loosen the bloody things. Hell, take 'em off!" Nathan was already up and coming around before she could decline.

The frock chosen had been something in the way of a *robes à la française* design, the bodice and skirts all of a piece. Thankfully, Thomas, through his infinite thoughtfulness in ordering the frocks, had also taken into consideration her lack of a maid to help her dress, and had the designs altered with hooks-and-eyes. Still, getting into it had been laborious, involving a lot of Cate staring at the top of Nathan's head, being admonished to stand still amid a trove of new colorful expressions.

Now, with a bit of coaching and cursing, and a victorious cry of "Ha!" the bodice fell open and was peeled off.

Cate gasped in relief. Working her arms and shoulders, she hadn't realized how restricted her movement had been until it was gone.

Nathan angled his head a bit to see her as he set about the multiple ties. "I'm obliged to admit, t'was like a different person next to me today, stiff n' straight n' all, with your hair up."

"I was thinking much the same about you," she mused.

He saw her point and ducked his head to his task. "T'would seem neither of us are built for this line o' work." A few jerks of this tie or that, through skirts, petticoats, bum roll and she was down to just her stays, which were handily dealt with.

"Oh, that's so much better!" she exclaimed. The stays had been made with only the most general of measurements— Thomas' eye, to be specific—and so didn't fit as well as they might, leaving her chafed and raw in several places.

"Now you might eat to your heart's content!" he said with a beckoning sweep of his hand.

And so she did under his benevolent smile.

"That day I came aboard, your men were injured," Cate pointed out. "Others would have done the same."

"Others?" he echoed with first a blank, then an all too knowing look.

Neither were willing to utter the name: Hattie.

Nathan made a caustic noise. "She would have thrown a rag at them and bid someone else to dirty their hands. No milk-of-human kindness in that one." The last came in a spurt of loathing.

"So seeing me up to my elbows in someone else's blood poses as an attraction to you?"

Leaning back in his chair, Nathan spread his arms. "Guilty as charged."

In the meantime under the table, now atop her foot, his had resumed its activities.

"Was I down there that long?" Cate asked, unsteadied not by that, but by the unique sensation of his toes working in a suggestive rhythm between hers in spite of the stockings.

He took another drink, softly smacking his lips. "Wouldn't quit until every man was bound, every gash stitched, every break splinted, every head bound. Sewed two ears back on, saved Joe Welby's pigtail—slapped his scalp back and stitched it, hair attached—"

"How could I have forgotten all that?" she said faintly.

Nathan shrugged. "The men saw it too. Word passed quick."

Ah, yes. She was very familiar with that phenomena.

He leaned forward so that his eyes were but inches from hers. "You won their hearts almost as quickly as you won mine."

Dessert arrived: a tart accompanied by a bottle of dessert wine. Nathan pitched what was left in their glasses out the window, mopped the inside with his handkerchief and then poured afresh.

He took a testing sip and rolled it in his mouth. "Constantia, I think. What?" he demanded at her surprise that his knowledge would run to those depths. "One doesn't live on rum alone."

"Apparently not." Not smiling was particularly painful.

She took a testing sip. The Constantia was good, a rare selection, and yet couldn't be called a surprise. After all, this was French territory, where wine and food were seen as not just necessary subsistences, but the essential pleasures of life...

Along with a few other things, she thought casting a glance toward the bed.

She took a bite of the tart. "It's pineapple!"

Nathan tipped in the tine of his fork and touched the bare morsel to the tip of his tongue. "Aye, so it would seem."

"So that's why you kept me aboard: for my kindness?" Cate prompted. For some reason, she was taking particular delight in his renditions of that day.

"That, and an aching set o' collops which would allow me no peace," he said breezily. He leaned over the table once more. "They wanted you, and you alone." His eyes were the color of burnt molasses and bright with mischief.

"And if I had left...?" she asked, now feeling the flirt.

"Doomed me to a life of monkdom you would have." The certain amount of tease in his voice was a thin cover to the desperation and fear which she now knew he had suffered. "I would have been obliged to shave me head and shuffle about in sandals and a hair-shirt, praying eight times a day. You doubt me word? Observe me now." He spread his arms in display. "I'm already a eunuch, so far as other women. Clipped, cut I am, as innocent as the babe unborn."

The outlandishness of that made Cate cough. Taking a sip to clear her throat, her eye landed on his untouched plate. "Would you mind if I finished that?"

Laughing, Nathan slid the china toward her. "As you desire! Hell, I'll order the entire kitchen, if you wish. Just don't let Kirkland see you eat like that; the poor man will be devastated."

"And if I get fat?" she asked, taking another bite.

"Then I'll give you to Pryce. He's been seeking a fat widow for years."

Her appetites in the way of her stomach now sated, appetites of another variety made their presence known. She had been aware of him all day, moving next to her, the fabric of his coat pulling across his shoulders. Just then the cloth of his breeches was taut over his thigh, defining every curve and dip. With effort she forced her attention back to her plate. As she ate, she became increasingly aware of him watching, particularly intent on the neckline of her shift.

"That's a fine bit o' fancywork there." His eyes shifted a bit lower. "The pink matches your... your... cheeks," he finally opted for.

Blushing under the heat of his gaze, Cate looked down to find that the fabric was, indeed, far more diaphanous than thought. Her breasts pressing against it left very little to the imagination. She self-consciously tugged the fabric into something a little less revealing. "With a smaller needle and finer thread, I could do even smaller ones."

"The devil seize my soul, you'd need a spy glass to see them." He sobered, scowling. "The damn thing is so damned thin. What the bloody hell was that lurker thinking—?"

Cate looked down at herself. It was, indeed, a gossamer-like thing. Light and airy, the mere brush of it against her made her nipples and belly tighten. "I'm sure Thomas didn't—"

"I know exactly what was in that double-Dutch-dealing head."

"Oh, come now. How could he have—?"

"Expected to see you in it?" Nathan cut in sharply. He tapped a finger on the table for emphasis. "Rest assured, he's never done anything without a grand plan."

Cate plucked deferentially at the neckline. "It's no worse—well, barely worse than the one you had made for me." That one had been fashioned from a lawn shirt.

"That was out of necessity," Nathan announced, emphatically stabbing the same digit at her. "This was out of malice, pure and simple."

"Malice?"

"Evil-doing," he intoned in preacher-like sanctimony. "The lecherous skulker was planning on seeing you wear it. Malice-of-forethought of the highest order."

Cate hid her smile in her glass. Jealousy was usually her demon and yet here Nathan was, wrestling with an even larger version. Now void of it herself, it was a struggle not to laugh at the futility of it all. But alas, that was the tragedy of it: so much wasted energy to so little end. Surely he knew by now that Thomas was no threat to her affections; never had he even been so much as in the running.

"Well, you fouled his horse—" she began off-handedly.

"Hawse."

"Whatever, because it is only you seeing me," she said, pleased with out - circuitousing the king-of-circuitous.

Nathan flashed one of those gold-and-ivory smiles. "And praise the heavens that his loss is at my pleasure. He always has been the sacrificing sort."

"He's been naught but a friend to me."

"Beware of Vikings bearing gifts." Nathan took a drink and shook his head. "Although, one is inclined to admit that he is doing something right—curse, spell, whatever—if he has me sitting here with you and talking about him."

"Oh, I can't take another bite," Cate announced pushing away the plate.

It seemed to be exactly what Nathan had been waiting for, for he rose directly from his chair. "Then the repast portion of the evening has drawn to a close." He touched a finger to his chin as he slinked around to her side. "Allow me to think what else we might do to bide our time? Read? Play whist? Draughts?"

Each suggestion came with an increasing lilt that they were an increasingly remote possibility.

"I know!" he exclaimed and drew her to her feet.

❦

The light was beginning to attract flying insects and so Cate blew it out as she stepped around to the window. As Nathan moved about the room, Cate stood there admiring the night. The West Indies was a world of precious metals: golden days and silvery nights. By then, the moon had risen, laminating everything in its lustrous hues. Out in the harbor, the ships' anchor lights winked like giant diamonds, the *Morganse* aglow and busy as a kicked-up anthill.

Nathan came up behind her and slipped his arms about her. Through the shift's sheerness she could feel every crease and curve of his now naked body and a distinct hardness against her rear.

Pulling her close, he nuzzled her neck. She turned in his arms. He tickled the edge of her upper lip with his mustache and then lightly kissed it. He then drew the plump of her lower lip between his. A parting kiss and he skimmed upward along her jaw.

"T'was all I could do to keep from taking you up and kissing you right there on the street before all. This bit right here," he said, taking her earlobe between his lips, "was almost my undoing."

A peculiar little thrill, like a mouse scampering, raced down her back. "What stopped you?" Cate said with some effort.

"You," he breathed simply. "I wished you to be seen as the lady you should be, not being pawed like a three-pence street whore."

"My dignity thanks you." She executed a curtsy as best one might in that position, and then tilted her face up in invitation. "There's nothing stopping you now."

Nathan ran his fingers up into her hair and shook it out, the pins making little pinging sounds as they fell to the floor. "There's me wild-haired siren, calling me to me demise. With the moonlight behind you, you look like—"

She hooked an arm about his neck and dropped her voice to an approximation of Mother Pattie's. "Come to me, my little, dark, spicy cabbage."

It was her first time for such an affectation, and it felt not a little strange. Nathan twitched, surprised as well, but said nothing more for the next while as he kissed her.

At one point, he emitted a low hum of pleasant discovery. "Now there's something I've overlooked all this while: I've not kissed you, I mean really taken the time to do it properly," he added over her objections.

Resettling her in his arms, he showed what he meant: an unhurried exploration of every surface, every crevice and dip. She had thought him skilled before. Alas, much to her dismay, she found that any meeting of the mouths these last months had been far, far too brief.

He kissed her there in the window, the breeze stirring the curtains about them. He kissed her on the edge of the bed, she curled on his lap.

And then they kissed lying down, Cate on her back, Nathan on his elbows over her, his braids falling in a curtain about both their shoulders.

"Ah-ha!" he murmured, somewhere near where her neck and shoulder met. "Here's a spot I've not kissed before."

"Yes, you have."

"Oh, no, not this one. I did this one," moving an inch or so over. "But not this one," he said, moving back. He slipped the shift down from her shoulder. "And miracles of miracles, here's another!"

"No, you got that one the first time we laid together," she quipped. She had no idea—How could she possibly?—but was seized by the inexplicable need to slow things down.

"Nay, not the first, or I'd remember a place so delicious... Tach, let's be rid of this bit o' nonsense," he grumbled, tugging at the shift's ribbon. "'Tis too much like having that blackguardly snoop watching us."

The shift was pulled off and flung aside, and his eyes lit. "Oh, look at this one...!" he said, near the crease of her breast.

He rose to plant a kiss on her shoulder. "The last time was all about me," he said against her skin. "Make that last two."

"I'm not keeping score."

He raised his head and smiled, one filled with taunt and tease. "Fair enough, but I am. By my meticulous count, 'tis your turn."

His eyes took on a malicious gleam. "I've promised a night of delights. That," with a cutting glance toward the table and the remains of their dinner, "was just the first remove."

"Oh?" she said faintly, suddenly a bit breathless.

"Aye," came in a low, beguiling growl. "Now, lie back—" "I am."

"—Relax—"

"I'm trying." Anticipation rendered that feat precious difficult.

"— And enjoy the wonders which await." The last came from somewhere near her collarbone.

Their first time abed, Nathan had bid her to guide him, to plot a course. Now, he knew her like he knew the waters that he sailed, and he navigated employing every tool at his disposal: lips, hands, tongue and — Lord help her! — even his braids. He worked with the gentle determination of coaxing a rose to bloom, and bloom she did. He moved in inexorable precision. Slow could be a glory, but it could also be a torture. His attentions soon verged on taunting; she knew exactly where he was headed and was taking his jolly time about it. An impatient push elicited a knowing chuckle as he settled comfortably between her legs, his hands warm and solid at her hips.

Arms flung up over her head, Cate closed her eyes and enjoyed the results of his attentions. There seemed no end to what Nathan could wrought from her. Just then, it wasn't the usual spasms, but a series of something like little bubbles bursting inside, unique and so very —

A mirth-laden puff on her tendermost parts brought it all to an abrupt end.

"You taste of pineapple!" Nathan exclaimed.

"What?" she shrieked, struggling to sit up. "Impossible —! But how —! I mean, what —?"

"No denying it: simple fact."

She looked around, baffled. "It has to be a leftover from supper."

"Ah, but you forget: you ate it all. I had none," he pointed out in his usual pragmatism. He raised up higher on his elbows. "You desire proof?"

"No, no!" Her attempt to scramble away was impeded by his grasp on her hips. "I quite take your word. How...?" she asked shakily.

"I should think it obvious." Angling his head, he considered between her legs with the relish of a starving man before a feast. "This opens entirely new realms!"

Cate didn't need to see the wheels turning in his head; she could bloody well hear them, a prospect which left her not a little faint.

"Lie back." Two luminous eyes peered up at her. "Allow me my dessert."

And so Cate obeyed: she laid back and drifted off once more on a cloud of pleasurable sensations. As divine as Nathan's attentions were, however, a singular, need grew, one which went far beyond what his tongue or lips could provide.

"I need you..." she said, scrabbling for him, her hands sliding uselessly off his sweat - slickened skin.

The vibration of his negating hum only served to augment her need.

"Dammit, Nathan. I need you... in me... now!" she gasped in short, urgent bursts. She snatched at him again. Failing that, she seized upon the next thing which came to hand: a fistful of his braids.

Huffing, he complied and rose over her, but only to prod and tease. She whimpered impatiently, arching under him until—glory of glories—he finally allowed her, with a few readying strokes, to guide him home. She bucked under him, spurring him on. At one point, while still joined, Nathan rolled, taking her with him, so that she came up astride him.

"Use me, Kittie. Use me, make it good for you."

The command came wrapped in velvet, and so she did, part out of obedience, a larger part out of raw need. Arching his back, he poised, allowing her to use him. Bracing her hands on his shoulders, she heard a low growl, realized it came from her. Her finish came in an incrementally more powerful series until she doubled over. Feeling her release stroking him, Nathan's restraint fell away. Fingers digging into her hips, he thrust. Mouth drawn back in a grimace, a sharp inhalation, he threw his head back and let out a long, querulous groan.

Cate fell forward. Draped over Nathan, she rose and fell as he sought to catch his breath. Through their joining, she felt the slow dull thud of his heart through her flesh and echoing in her own heart.

Nathan raised a shaky hand to swipe the moisture from the side of his face. "Someday... *someday* we are finally going to do this in our own bed."

⸎

The metronomic tick of a moth up near the ceiling was like a case-clock marking off the passage of time. The moon had marched around, its light now streamed in to make a luminescent pool on the floor. Cate lay with her head pillowed on Nathan's chest, idly tracing his shapes, enjoying the simple freedom of touching him anywhere, as he could her. Now and again, she placed a kiss here or there, just for the sheer joy of her lips on his skin, tasting of salt and sated male.

Suddenly, her head bounced up and down with Nathan silently chuckling. An interrogatory hum inquired as to what he found so humorous.

"Oh, nothing... It's just..." A coaxing nudge with her shoulder got him over the hump. "I was just wondering why is 'tis that every time I lie with you, I'm as nervous as our first time?"

She raised her head. "Nervous?"

"Apprehensive, self-doubt... dread..." he continued in his litany.

"Dread? I've never complained—"

Nathan stopped to smile at her. "As I am painfully aware. And therein lies the hell of it," he sighed to the ceiling.

He found her hand and held it up, watching as he worked his fingers between hers. "I worry of measuring up, of going the distance, not leaving you wanting." The last came with an explosion of air at having finally arrived at his ultimate point.

She raised up further to register her disbelief. It was almost too silly to even acknowledge and yet, nothing about him suggested he was jesting.

His head shifted restlessly on the pillow. "You don't realize, because it's so natural to you. It's like breathing or eating pineapple tart."

"But everyone—" Cate stopped at realizing she had little notion as to what *everyone,* or *anyone* for that matter, did or didn't do abed. As a girl, growing up on a farm and with five brothers, she had a fair notion of what two people did, in the general sense. As to the finer details, she had never dwelt.

"Nay, not everyone," he said firmly. He gulped and went on determinedly "I don't mean to brag, nor stir up waters what have finally calmed, but... but... just rest assured, darling, you are... unique."

The body under hers tensed in anticipation of the reproof sure to come after alluding to his previous experience.

Instead, Cate planted a kiss at the damp hollow of his throat. "Rest assured, sir, you have fulfilled me in every way possible."

In the moon shadows, it was difficult to be sure, but she thought he blushed.

That small assurance answered. He reclined with the air of pride in a task well-done. Heaven help her, a smug Nathan was a more abiding to deal with—was more accustomed to dealing with, at any rate—than one wallowing in a bout of the blue-devils.

He turned her hand this way and that, admiring as if seeing for the first time. Occasionally, he brought it near enough to kiss some part of it: fingertips, knuckles, back, or wrist.

"What would you have done if I didn't enjoy this?" she teased, thrusting her hips against his. "Or, what if I wasn't very good at it? Many women don't," she pointed out.

A sharp eye swiveled at her. "Don't I know it! You're preaching sermons to the saved on that one." His mouth worked. "Ah, but you do enjoy it, so—"

"No, no," she insisted, prodding him again. "You aren't wriggling out of this. Just play along for once: what would you have done?" She propped her chin in her hand, waiting.

"Well," he said slowly. Working his fingers through hers in a particular rhythm, he waggled his brows and dropped his voice to a seductive level. "I'd seek to convince you of the error of your thinking."

"And if that didn't work?" she insisted, now a bit breathless.

Intent on her hand once more, Nathan opened his mouth to argue, but then shrugged. "Then I'd be obliged to go back to me old practices of self-abuse and building some very thick callouses on me right hand."

She dipped her nose to his chest and inhaled deeply. There it was, the mingling of cinnamon and orange which always touched her in so many places.

With a slight adjustment of her head, the *Morganse* was visible through the window. On her anchors, a steady line of boats laden with the stuffs of life flowed out to her like an umbilical cord. Seeing the ship sitting there took Cate back to the first time she saw her: looming over the *Constancy* like a falcon hovering over its prey.

"I'm thinking about how lucky I am, for this," Cate sighed, splaying her hand over his chest. "And yes, this," moving her thigh against the soft mass between his legs. "But I'm also grateful for everything else you've given me." She stopped, emotion making her voice begin to break.

"I'm so grateful," she went on a bit steadier. "But the more I realize how lucky I am, the more I realize how easily it mightn't have ever come to pass. I wouldn't have all this; I wouldn't have you." She hugged him as best one might lying and one hand otherwise occupied.

"Don't you ever find yourself wondering 'what if?'" she mused. "What if... if we had met elsewhere, under different circumstances...? Had we passed on a street or met somewhere...?"

His thumb brushing her wrist, Nathan stirred from half-listening. "You mean, if you looked as you did today?" He considered all too briefly and the corner of his mouth tucked up. "I shouldn't think I would have had the nerve."

The bitter bile of panic rose at the back of her throat. "You would have passed me by?"

"Not sure I would have had the nerve to approach, with that ram-you-damn-you air." Closing one eye, he moved a shoulder in equivocation. "But then, on the other hand, I might have seen it as a challenge, were I of the mood to tarry, and given you hadn't told me to go to blazes."

A slight shift and Nathan was on his side, Cate on display before him. He took her in, viewing her like an aficionado look upon a fine painting. He leaned forward a bit, the shadows hiding his expression.

"Nay, I would have sought you out," he announced. His hand roved from her shoulder to arm, waist to hip, not in invitation or overture, but as she had done: for the simple joy. "Providence delivered you to me before; it would have found a way then. Who knows?" He directed a crooked smile at her. "Perhaps we were meant to meet on that street, in Charles Town or Baltimore or Savannah or wherever, and it didn't work out, you or I took a turn we weren't supposed to have taken. You have to admit, it would have been far easier to arrange that, than trying to make two ships converge at the same spot in the middle of the bloody ocean."

She prodded his rib with a finger. "You had to be there so you could save me."

"You make it sound like I'm some bloody guardian angel."

"Well," she said, closing one eye. "I hadn't meant it quite like that, but now that you mention..."

"Ha! I'm no bloody guardian angel," he huffed. "No halo, no purity. I struggle to imagine Creswicke or Bailey being sent for anyone's benefit. Pryce, Hodder, Maori, that mumping first mate o' Thomas' as holy messengers?"

Leaning back, he scoffed. "I've met precious few—here at sea, at any rate—who would qualify for nothing except Ol' Nick's welcoming party. Perhaps on land, the decent might be a score-a-shilling."

"You haven't been on land much of late, if you think so highly of its occupants," she countered. "No plethora or purity or kindness there." Bella's island surged forth as one prime example. Good conscious, however, prompted her to add "Although, there were those in London who were certainly kind."

"The ones that left you freezing in an attic, living on what wasn't good enough to throw to the pigs, as I recall you telling it?" He snorted in disgust. "The milk-of-human kindness was a bit soured and curdled, I'd say. You emptied pisspots and skulleried for every bloody scrap." His hand traced the curve of her ribs, gooseflesh trailing behind. "If one had to subsist solely on that milk, we'd all be as half-starved and bony as you were."

He resumed his explorations, sometimes studying, sometimes just outlining, as if confirming the familiar. He fondled her breast, not in seduction, but viewing it like it was a jewel.

"The Fates brought us where we needed to be when we needed to be there." He looked up, the moonlight catching the cinnamon-colored flecks in his eyes. "Although, t'would have been a bit more preferable if you had shown up a bit later, when me life was a bit more in order."

A whimsical smile crooked his mouth as he continued his explorations. "Oh, aye, there are times when I wish we might have met sooner, that I might have been there for you. I might have saved you from..." He swallowed hard. "From so much."

He stopped short, but it was so easy to follow his thought and finish it: the specter of the hazards and travails she might have been exposed to if she had been with him.

Cate reached up to take his face between her palms, drew him down and kissed him. "I regret nothing."

And she meant it. Whatever hell she had endured out there, it paled in comparison to those of desolation and starving.

She pushed the braids back for an unimpeded view of him, from the square-set of his shoulders, down the hard curves of his arms, to the flat slope of his belly, the angle of his hips and down to the lean columns of his thighs.

She loved Nathan. Yes, she had loved Brian, but that now seemed so very distant, and naught but the fooleries of youth. It paled in comparison to this visceral, soul-soaking sort she felt now. One couldn't help but wonder if dying together somehow made the difference, but she negated the notion out-of-hand. Her passion for him had existed *long* before that. Brian had been but a warm-up, a training ground, Providence preparing her for what was to come. As a maid of eighteen, she would have never been able to handle what Nathan brought. Her youth and inexperience would have made her bungle and botch. But then, the whole notion was a false equivalency, for a girl wasn't what Nathan sought. Neither of them would have been ready if they had met at ten and five.

"I wish I could have known you back then," she sighed.

He resolutely shook his head. "No you don't."

"Funny, Thomas said the same thing," she mused.

"Wisdom of the ages, he has," Nathan said sagely.

Cate smiled to herself at how Thomas had gone from skulking lecher to Solomon in a matter of moments.

"One has to wonder if we could have even borne each other years earlier?" Whenever she looked in a peering glass she barely recognized herself. So much had happened; so much had changed. Nathan would be no different.

A shoulder moved in a vague shrug. "Neither of us were who we are now.

Providence needed time to mold us, to sculpt us into who we are."

"Providence, Fate or guardian angels, call it what you will, but we found each other," Nathan announced. "All the rest 'tis by the board."

The soft callus of his thumb against the delicate skin of her nipple made it harden, and he smiled. "There's that little noise you make."

"I don't—"

"Aye, but you do. And then there's the one—" He ducked his head and closed his lips about her nipple. "Mmm...that's one."

Declining to argue, Cate curved her arms about his head and closed her eyes.

At the end, they rolled to fit together as they always did, snug as two spoons, her breast cradled in his upturned palm, the sheet pulled up over them.

"Lay your head, duchess," he whispered against her ear. "Sleep and dream of castles and gallant princes and all yours to command."

For most of Nathan's life, the specter of waking to the same woman for the rest of his days was a staggering concept. The mere thought of one woman forever knocked the wind from his sails and left him all-standing. In no corner of his imagination could he conceive the possibility of extracting joy from lying with the same woman night, after night, after night, after night.

Now, he couldn't imagine anything else. The mere allusion of bedding another woman made his lads tighten... with fear.

Chin propped in his hand, he watched the light play on Cate's face, admiring that angelic sweep of brow, one which could turn a man to stone with one arch. On her side, half-curled into herself, an arm was flung out over the edge. It was almost as if, even in slumber, she knew he was there and was reaching for him. He tucked his hands into his armpits against the urge to touch her, to feel that skin. His eye traveled the delicate bones to the elegance grace of her fingers... and lo what wonders those fingers could wrought! Just then, she slept in a placid, almost child-like innocence, a peacefulness he had strove to attain since the day she had come into his life, sodden and flopping on deck like a fresh – caught fish.

He had considered collecting her perspiration where it beaded on her lip and brow; surely it would be an aphrodisiac. No doubt it would have affect him more deeply than any potion purchased in a bizarre or from conjure woman. She was an addiction, a narcotic: the more he had the more he wanted...

But aye, he was hers.

Cate jerked awake at the frightening sensation of being watched. Startled, she yelped at seeing a dark figure hunched at the bedside. With a familiar metallic rustle, the figure leaned closer, Nathan bringing his face from the shadows into the pinkish-grey of impending dawn.

"Shh." A finger brushed her cheek. "S'all right, luv."

Sitting up and rubbing the sleep from her eyes, she found he was sitting on a stool, his bare back and shoulders ghostly pale in the dim.

"I didn't mean to wake you." His graveled voice was roughened by the hour.

A strange tremor in his voice made her ask "Did you have a nightmare?"

"Nay, nay, I'm awake. I was watching you sleep."

A tentative finger traced her lips. "The corners of your mouth curl up like you're smiling, and yet..." His voice tightened, and he swallowed hard as he touched the smooth space between her brows. "You used to frown, as if it was a great task." His thumb brushed her lips. "The frown is gone; now you glow."

He looked down to the floor between his feet. "I need you, Kittie."

"Then come lie —"

"Nay, not like that," he said, suddenly shy. He peered up at her through the veil of his lashes. "No, not like that. I mean, yes, God! I want you all the time. But, 'tis more than just a matter of the flesh. I need you."

Touching a finger to his chin, she lifted his gaze up to hers. "What makes you think it's any different for me? Years ago, I stopped breathing, and never drew another breath until just a few months ago."

It occurred to her, in this confessional of the darkness and hour, that perhaps she hadn't said that, voiced her feelings as often as she should, not as open and honest as might have been.

She moved her hand to cup his cheek and felt the fine tremors coursing through him. "You're shivering," she said, lifting the quilt. "Come to bed."

He started to slide in, but then stopped, kneeling between hers legs. Gathering both of her hands in his, he clutched them to his chest. He leaned forward to brace his forehead against hers.

"Say, 'I will.' I need you to say 'I will,'" he insisted at her hesitancy.

"But why...?"

"Just say it," he whispered in a hoarse rasp.

The eyes inches from hers filled, the liquid trembling as it threatened to spill. She searched them for an explanation. All she found was something between morbid fear and rampant hope. The coffee-colored orbs stared back, willing her to comply.

With a bare nod—with no idea as to what it was she was agreeing—she whispered "I will."

Throwing his head back, he let out something between a laugh and a sob. He then stretched out on the bed, bringing her down with him.

She bit back a gasp, his body was so startlingly cold against hers. They held each other, waiting for that glorious equalization sure to come. The space between them quickly warmed and she opened herself to him. As he spilled himself into her, she was filled with something greater than his seed.

At the end, he shook and half-choked a sob. She moved her head and felt a wet spot on the pillow.

Cate held him, shushing and soothing as he had done for her so many, many times, all the while staring into the night wondering what else she might offer?

The flapping of the curtains and a chill woke Cate the next morning. For the first few moments, she lay quietly, blinking away the sleep. For a fleeting moment, she puzzled to remember where she was. Compared to the blaze of daylight, the room had looked radically different.

The weight of something more than the sheet made her think it was Nathan's arm, and yet, in the same instant, she knew it wasn't. Raising her head a fraction, she found it was only his coat which they had pulled over them for additional warmth in the pre-dawn chill.

She rooted her head into the pillow, luxuriating in the feel of sheets and a real bed. She wriggled her rear, feeling for Nathan in invitation. In the absence of the demands of his ship and men, there was a fair chance he might linger. Wriggling back a bit more, she discovered she was alone. She leant an ear toward the privy closet. It was nothing more than a screen set up in the corner—another of Nathan's special arrangements, she suspected—but instantly knew he wasn't there; no one could use the convenience in complete silence.

With that, she suddenly noticed an odd stillness in the room, the kind which came with being entirely alone. A glance showed that everything of his was gone: hat, pistol, boots... everything.

Gone, then, on some errand or mission. Duty had called, no doubt.

She rose and went to the window and looked to the corner of the harbor where the *Morganse* had sat on her anchors, but found nothing but a squat, fishing boat. She craned to check the wharf, thinking the ship, contrary to all of Nathan's claims, must have warped in, but in vain. Leaning further out, she scanned the more remote corners of the harbor, but nothing.

The *Morganse* was gone.

Cate's knees buckled and she sat heavily in a chair.

"He's gone." Caught between wanting to scream and being physically ill, she swallowed hard. "He's gone."

The breeze brushing her shoulders reminded her that she was naked. As she rose to fetch her shift, her eye caught the flutter of a small piece of paper near the flower vase on the table, anchored by a leather pouch. The metallic clink of coins came from the latter as she slid out the paper. Her hand began to shake at recognizing Nathan's florid handwriting on the outside: *My Lovely Kittie* She started to open it, dropped it and then tried again, blinking as she tried to read through the tears:

My Duchess,

You'll know I've gone. I could not bear to wake you, to see your face as I took my leave. Call me a coward, but at least you'll live to do so.

Darling, I will be back. Know that! There are things, which I must do, which I cannot, if I must worry for you.

The room is paid and you've funds.

I _will_ be back. A month and I _will_ be back.

Be well. Keep me in your heart as I will keep you

N

An excerpt from *Cursed Blessings* the continuation of *The Pirate Captain, Chronicles of a Legend*

S TEPPING AFT, NATHAN CHECKED THE traversing board and then glanced to the sky, sails and seas. Moving a step, he clapped a hand around a backstay and bent his head.

Straightening, he asked of the helm "How goes it?"

"The barky's a mite skittish, sir. She's tendin' to gripe with all this sail."

"Aye, well, let's allow the Watch their rest for at least another glass." Nothing to be gained in calling all hands then just for a sail change. "By the looks o' things, I feel a change coming."

The glass said as much, too. How much and in what direction was the only question?

She was, indeed, too heavy by-the-head, and too encumbered by a top-hamper and sail. She was skittish, wallowing like a bloated whale on every swell.

Nathan clapped a hand about the stay once more. *Bide w' me for just a bit more. Just bide w' me.*

It wasn't just the stowing and the sails; she was crank about something else, something of which... a state-of-events to which there wasn't a bloody damned thing to be done. He was encumbered, clapped in irons, caught by the lee, and she knew it! Nothing more trying on one's nerves than dealing with a contrary woman. The odds were better of winning an argument with the Rock of Gibraltar.

The *Morganse* took a hard lee lurch and from the waist came a pained cry. Cursing and men moving confirmed its origins.

Descending, Nathan met the group coming aft near the companionway: Potts and Smalley half-supporting, half-carrying Towers. "What's amiss?"

"Towers laid his arm open," Potts explained.

Swaying, sweating and pale, Towers was half-suspended between his mates, uttering whimpering sounds. His bulging eyes fixed on the blood-soaked cloth around his arm, he looked fit to either vomit or swoon.

"What dundering lobcock trusted him with anything sharper than a spoon?" Nathan demanded. The man was a hazard to himself and every unsuspecting cove around him. He'd been forbidden a fid after dropping his down the hatch and spearing a fellow shipmate's hand to a cask. "How bad?"

Potts shrugged and said over Towers' high-pitched moans "Don't see bone."

"Fair enough." Minor, but the blood was running through Towers' fingers and dripping all over the deck. "Get 'im below n' patch 'im up."

The directive was needless: the three were already making their way down the steps. Nathan doubted the injury would require all three, but if it allowed them their peace, then good on them. A well-tempered "As you were" sent the gaping hands back about their duties, Hodder's "Swabbers!" spurring the slower-witted.

Broadstreet intercepted Nathan as he made to return to the quarterdeck. "Mr. Chips' compliments and duty, sir," he said, rapping his forehead. "He awaits yer leisure in yer cabin, if ye please."

"About bloody time," Nathan grumbled, brushing past. He felt more than saw the wry looks in his wake. The bloody hell with them all!

The carpenter stood by the mizzen wearing a look of mild curiosity. Not missing a stride, Nathan hooked him by the arm and ushered him toward the sleeping quarters. Shoving aside the curtain, he rigidly pointed at the point. "I want it gone, every screw, every plank, scuff in the wood… everything, as if it had never been changed."

Chips' eyes rounded, the craftsman in him already deep in imagining the task and its magnitude. "But, I'll have to—"

"I don't care what the bloody hell it takes. You managed to do all this. Now, I assume you can undo it! If not, say the word, and I'll find someone what can!"

The ship's carpenter retreated a step at the increasing vehemence. "Aye, sir, directly. Aye, sir, directly," he chanted overlapping the last of his captain's orders.

Nathan paused to give the room a final glance, in mortal fear of spotting that incremental crumb, that lingering shred of her which might remain.

"Her," only "her." He resolutely refused to even call her name to mind. Nameless she was, and nameless she would be kept, for if she was nameless, then she was non-existent. The washstand and mirror were gone, the latter skimmed out the window like he was playing ducks-n'-drakes.

Nathan did the same to the salon as he passed through, as he did every time he passed. He had suffered the blood-freezing horror of seeing a ray of sun through the skylight glint on a mahogany-colored hair wafting in the breeze from the back of her chair. The bloody thing had broken when he'd sough to free it. Too fine, too short, too elusive to be removed, he'd thrown the entire damned chair out the window and then had the bosun's mates caulk it shut, all of them shut! He'd gone so far as to have the floor holystoned and swabbed, and still crawled about on his hands and knees to assure no hair, no ravel of clothing might still.

He turned and was headed for the door when a name echoing up from below stopped him dead in his tracks. Roosted on the rail, Beatrice's head came out from behind her wing to eye him severely as he neared the head of the companionway. Hackles raised, she appeared on the verge of saying something. A cold eye brought her to think better. She'd had precious little to say these last days and fair enough. If she didn't have anything decent to say, then she could bloody well keep her own damned counsel.

Nathan cocked his head below, listening. Men bickered and squabbled all the time, and usually he left it under-hatches. Most matters were better-handled before-the-mast. It was one of the great benefits of having a prime premier and prime seconds.

But, nay, his ears hadn't deceived. He heard it again, ringing as loud as Kirkland's coppers.

"Curse and burn those cross-grained, skulking, dunder-headed louts!"

Beatrice's startled squawk fading behind him, Nathan pounded down the steps and forward, past the galley. Elbowing his way through the wad of men at the bloodroom door, he drew up. "What the bloody hell...?"

The men broke and scattered like quail for the corners, leaving Towers perched atop the table, his bleeding arm crimson in the dim.

Potts' milky eye rolled independently of its partner. "We wuz jest—"

"I know what you 'wuz jest'," Nathan sneered.

"We wuz jest seekin' to find where Mr. Cate—" The rest of Potts' point was cut short by Nathan seizing him by the shirt and driving him back up against the counter.

"Dunno where Mr. Cate might o'—" Smalley began from behind him.

Nathan whirled around and drove Smalley back, his head making a hollow *clunk!* when it hit the bulkhead.

"Never!" Nathan shook the man, his head hitting the wall with each one. "Never utter her name! She's to be struck from your mind," he said, drilling a finger against Smalley's temple. "Not a word, not an allusion, not a vague reference... Don't even breath the thought...!"

"Cap'n, stand-off! Ease off" loud and sharp in his ear, and a firm hand on his shoulder brought Nathan to his senses. He looked up to find Pryce standing there. A pluck at his hand brought him to realize at some point he had drawn his knife. "'Tisn't worth a'killin' a man over," Pryce urged, level yet not to be denied.

Blinking, Nathan eased back. He drew several ragged breaths, keenly aware of being stared at like an oddity in a fair.

"Anyone, anyone who dares to argue will be bunged up in a cask and flung over the side," he called as they collided with each other in their hasty withdrawal.

Nathan waited until they were all out of earshot before he growled "And yes, it 'tis worth killing a man over" to Pryce under his breath. He turned to look the man full on, imploring. "Surely to God you, of all people, understand that."

In the ensuing silence, Nathan looked about. Dust motes swirled in the greenish light of the deck prism. The sudden absence of humanity rendered the place all the more vacant. He swayed at the sickening impression of standing in a virtual shrine to her. Her presence, her essence saturated every nook and board. Slumping against the table, he clamped his eyes shut, trying to strike the image from his mind. It was a daily, nay hourly, painful battle, but essential.

"Close it... lock it... secure it. No one is to enter except you." He tapped a finger on Pryce's chest. "So far as I am concerned, it doesn't exist."

68336793R00445

Made in the USA
Columbia, SC
06 August 2019